T0283454

ALSO BY ADAM ROSS

Mr. Peanut

Ladies and Gentlemen

PLAYWORLD

PLAYWORLD

A NOVEL

ADAM ROSS

ALFRED A. KNOPF | NEW YORK | 2025

THIS IS A BORZOI BOOK PUBLISHED BY ALFRED A. KNOPF

Copyright © 2025 by Adam Ross
Penguin Random House values and supports copyright.
Copyright fuels creativity, encourages diverse voices, promotes free speech,
and creates a vibrant culture. Thank you for buying an authorized edition of this book
and for complying with copyright laws by not reproducing, scanning, or distributing
any part of it in any form without permission. You are supporting writers and
allowing Penguin Random House to continue to publish books for every reader.
Please note that no part of this book may be used or reproduced in any manner for
the purpose of training artificial intelligence technologies or systems.

All rights reserved. Published in the United States by Alfred A. Knopf, a division of Penguin
Random House LLC, New York, and distributed in Canada by Random House of Canada,
a division of Penguin Random House Canada Limited, Toronto.

www.aaknopf.com

Knopf, Borzoi Books, and the colophon are registered trademarks
of Penguin Random House LLC.

Grateful acknowledgment is made to Alfred Music for permission to reprint lyrics from
"How High the Moon," lyrics by Nancy Hamilton, music by Morgan Lewis. © 1940
(Renewed) Chappell & Co., Inc., lyrics from "Amsterdam," words and music by Jacques Brel,
English words by Eric Blau and Mort Shuman. © 1968 (Renewed) Pouchenel, Editions, and
Mort Shuman Songs. All rights for Pouchenel, Editions administered by Unichappell Music,
Inc. All rights for Mort Shuman songs administered by Warner-Tamerlane Publishing Corp.,
and lyrics from "If We only Have Love," English lyrics by Mort Shuman, Music by Jacques
Brel. © 1968 (Renewed) Unichappell Music, Inc., Mort Shuman Songs and Romantic Music
Corp. All rights for Mort Shuman Songs administered by Warner-Tamerlane Publishing
Corp. All rights reserved. Used by permission of Alfred Music.

Library of Congress Cataloging-in-Publication Data
Names: Ross, Adam, [date]- author.
Title: Playworld : a novel / Adam Ross.
Description: First Edition. | New York : Alfred A. Knopf, 2025.
Identifiers: LCCN 2023048923 (print) | LCCN 2023048924 (ebook) |
ISBN 9780385351294 (hardcover) | ISBN 9780385351300 (ebook)
Subjects: LCGFT: Novels.
Classification: LCC PS3618.O84515 P53 2025 (print) | LCC PS3618.O84515 (ebook) |
DDC 813/.6—dc23/eng/20231018
LC record available at https://lccn.loc.gov/2023048923
LC ebook record available at https://lccn.loc.gov/2023048924

This is a work of fiction. Names, characters, places, and incidents either are the product of
the author's imagination or are used fictitiously. Any resemblance to actual persons, living or
dead, events, or locales is entirely coincidental.

Jacket photograph by Adrian Samson/Trunk Archive
Jacket design by Oliver Munday
Griffynweld map design by David Lindroth
Frontispiece photograph by Steven Sebring

Manufactured in the United States of America
FIRST EDITION

To my mother, father, and brother

CONTENTS

PROLOGUE

ix

PART ONE: THE CARTER ADMINISTRATION

A CRISIS OF CONFIDENCE

3

VOICEOVER

17

THE OCTOBER SURPRISE

31

HALF DAY

45

THE FIFTY-MINUTE HOUR

64

THE AGONY OF DEFEAT

85

DOUBLE FANTASY

123

THE TWELVE DAYS OF CHRISTMAS

160

HOSTAGES

190

PART TWO: THE REAGAN ADMINISTRATION

THE SWIMSUIT ISSUE

215

RAWHIDE DOWN

231

TAKE TWO

260

DUNGEONS & DRAGONS

276

THERE IS NO TRY

306

VOICEOVER

340

CHARLES AND DIANA

360

UNION BUSTER

387

VIDEO KILLED THE RADIO STAR

434

MORNING IN AMERICA

466

In the fall of 1980, when I was fourteen, a friend of my parents named Naomi Shah fell in love with me. She was thirty-six, a mother of two, and married to a wealthy man. Like so many things that happened to me that year, it didn't seem strange at the time.

Two decades later, when I finally told my mother—we were on Long Island, taking a walk on the beach—she stopped, stunned, and said, "But she was such an ugly woman." The remark wasn't as petty as it sounds. If I was aware of it then, it neither repulsed me nor affected my feelings for Naomi. It was just a thing I took for granted, like the color of her hair.

Wiry and ashen, it had the shading but not the shimmer of pigeon feathers. Naomi kept it long, so that it fell past her shoulders. I knew it by touch, for my face was often buried in it. Only later did I wonder if she considered herself unattractive, because she always wore sunglasses, as if to hide her face, large gold frames with blue-tinted prescription lenses. When we were driving together, which was often that year, she'd allow these to slide down her nose and then look at me over their bridge. She might've considered this pose winning, but it was more likely to see me better. Her mouth often hung slightly open. Her lower teeth were uneven, and her tongue, which pressed against them, always tasted of coffee.

Naomi's car was a silver Mercedes sedan—300sd along with TURBO DIESEL nickel-plated on the back—that made a deep hum when she drove. The interior, enormous in my mind's eye, was tricked out with glossy wood paneling and white leather, back seat so wide and legroom so ample they made the driver appear to be far away. It was in this car that Naomi and I talked most often. We'd park, and then she'd lean across the armrest to press her cheek to mine, and I'd sometimes allow her to kiss me. Other times we'd move to the back. Lying there with Naomi, her nose nuzzled to my neck, I'd stare at the ceiling's dotted fabric until the pattern seemed to detach and drift like a starred sky. This car was her prized possession, and like many commuters, she had turned the machine into an extension of her body. Her left thumb lightly hooked the wheel at eight o'clock when traffic was moving, her fingertips sliding to eleven when it was slow. She preferred to sit slightly reclined, her free hand spread on her inner thigh, though after she lost her pinkie the following summer, and even after being fitted with a prosthesis, she kept it tucked away.

"I was worried you'd think it was disgusting," she said, the digit hidden between the seat and her hip. She'd bought herself a diamond ring to hide the seam, and for the most part the likeness was uncanny, but at certain angles you could tell—the cuticle's line was too smooth, the nail's pale crescent too creamy to match the others. Like my father's fake teeth, which he occasionally left lying around our apartment, I was fascinated by it, though my curiosity wasn't morbid. I was a child actor, you see, a student of all forms of dissembling, and had long ago found my greatest subject to be adults.

PART ONE

THE
CARTER
ADMINISTRATION

Politics is just like show business.
You have a hell of an opening, coast for a while,
and then have a hell of a close.

—Ronald Reagan

We were at the fortieth wedding anniversary celebration of Dr. Barr and his wife, Lynn. The Barrs lived in Great Neck. We'd driven from Manhattan just before the sun was beginning to set. As we crossed the Fifty-Ninth Street Bridge, Roosevelt Island's towers flashed, the shadows of Manhattan's buildings just starting to climb their faces. By the time we arrived the sky was a buffed pink, with plenty of light for my younger brother, Oren, to name the make and model of every car parked in the driveway, ending with Dr. Barr's Cadillac Seville. It was a vehicle whose cachet we associated with the bold gilt letters on the door of his Gramercy Park office, but the high esteem in which we held him did not change the fact that in our house, and on nights like these, he was known only by his first name: Elliott.

He was my father's best friend and our family's psychologist. All of us consulted with him: Mom midweek, Dad and Oren and me on Saturday mornings. My father had been Elliott's patient since before he met my mother; she, the year after they married. Oren had only recently started therapy because his grades were sliding, but I'd been seeing Elliott since I was six, after a family death I'd caused. It never struck me as odd, the thinness of the membrane between patient and friend, between husband and wife, brother and brother, perhaps because Elliott had been such a ubiquitous presence for as long as I could remember. If anything, it made Elliott seem even wiser, able, as I imagined he was, to keep so many secrets from four people without judging them.

The Barrs' home was so packed with guests it made me feel like we were standing in a closet, the men's blazers and the women's wraps and scarves muffling the music as we moved through zones of perfume, Scotch, and cigarette smoke. Oren and I made repeat trips to the buffet (the salmon soon only a head and a tail), watched some of ABC's *Wide World of Sports* in the guest room (Elliott had one of the biggest TVs I'd ever seen, but the reception was terrible), and then checked out Elliott's collection of masks mounted in the dining room's display case, whose glass Oren tried to open: arrow-headed shamans, saber-toothed Kabuki demons, and our favorites from the Chinese opera, their designs like superhero masks and as colorful as pinball machines. But having exhausted ways of relieving our boredom, we split up.

This was when Naomi and I ended up alone together for the first time. She was sitting on the living room sofa. I sat on the coffee table, facing her. I was telling her about my acting career. She had asked me about playing Roy Scheider's son in *The Talon Effect*.

"What was it like working with him?" she said.

"He was nice," I said. "Roy and I ate lunch together my first day on the set, and when I opened my soda it sprayed his face, so he angled his can's mouth toward mine, popped the tab, and got me back."

"And Joan Collins," she said. "Is she as pretty in person?"

"She *is*," I said, "though one day during makeup the hairdresser stuck a teasing comb behind her ear and lifted a wig clean off her head."

Naomi found this hysterical. She snorted when she laughed, pressing her fingernails to her chest. Between her rings and bracelets and her gold earrings shaped like cymbals, she clinked whenever she moved. She was a Great Neck Jewess. She had the classic up-Island accent, one I could mimic on command: "A *vawhdville* act, this kid is," I said, imitating her, "a regular *prawdigy*." She was wide-hipped; she wore sheer stockings beneath a wool skirt. Her blouse was a tailored silk, open at the neck, which revealed, when she leaned forward, a peek of collarbone and the lacy spray of her bra. On her cheek was a light brown birthmark, the texture and color of a burned egg white.

It was the heat of Naomi's attention that got me so excited, plus the odd way we sat hidden in plain sight—how the party, by now well into its swing, domed us in a kind of privacy—because it was at this point that I did something remarkable and fateful: I got into character. She'd asked me about the Saturday morning TV series I'd been doing for several seasons, "the one," she said, "that adults watch too." She snapped her fingers, trying to conjure the title as if from the narrow space between us, and then laid her hand on my shoulder. "*The Nuclear Family,*" she said, remembering, and then leaned back to clap once. It was more spoof than superhero show, vaguely educational, each episode organized around a different scientific concept. An exposure to radiation had altered the DNA of my character, Peter Proton, along with that of his parents, Ellen Electron and Nate Neutron. Before we fought bad guys, we'd summon our powers by yelling, "Split up!" After Three Mile Island had nearly melted down, everyone called the show prophetic. Naomi wanted to know how we did the special effects—the atomic eye blasts and flying sequences. I was explaining chroma-keying to her, how we'd hang from wires in front of a green screen, when I suddenly stopped. My expression changed. I turned away and, through my nose, forced all the breath from my chest. It was a trick I'd learned in order to make myself tear up.

"Sweetie," she asked, "are you all right?"

"I'm going to tell you a secret," I said. "But you have to swear not to tell anyone." I had a tear perfectly balanced—it was like palming a beach ball in the wind—and when I faced Naomi again, I let it fall down my cheek. "Will you swear?" I asked.

Naomi looked over her shoulder and then leaned forward and whispered, "Of course, honey."

I told her that I'd lost my virginity to Liz, the director's assistant. She was twenty-four. On set, she was everything from gofer to script girl, and because I was extra busy once school started—what with the tighter shooting schedule, I explained, and my homework on top of that—I'd struggled to memorize my lines. She and I often rehearsed together, and for several weeks straight we'd found ourselves alone in my dressing room. One night while going over a scene, it just happened. We'd been secretly dating ever since.

"She's worried she'll get in trouble," I said.

"Because of your age, you mean?"

"You're the first person I've told."

Naomi shook her head in amazement.

"Is it wrong?" I asked.

"To be having . . . relations with her?" she said.

"To like older women so much."

And while Naomi considered how to answer—struggling, through the fog of these details, to process my bald-faced lie—I leaned forward to kiss her. This was a ridiculous gesture, made more absurd by my open-mouthed, tongue-first nonchalance, plus my disregard for her status and our surroundings (the fact that she was married, for example, or that guests were standing five feet away). I briefly pressed my lips to hers. It's possible she'd never moved so fast in her life, rocking back to laugh at my ludicrous bravado while simultaneously pressing her fingertips to my shoulder.

"Griffin," she said, "you are *something*."

I shrugged, then thanked her for the talk and went to go find my brother.

Oren was always worth seeking out at these parties, because he was a fearless explorer of other people's rooms. Closed doors meant nothing to him. Closets were never off-limits. Bureaus begged to be opened, whether they belonged to strangers or to our parents, whose wall-length dresser he regularly raided with abandon. He'd found treasures there: rolls of quarters stacked like Lincoln Logs, reserved for the basement laundry machines but that we skimmed to play *Missile Command* at Stanley's Stationery Store; my father's dog tags, their gunmetal stamped with risen letters like Braille and revealing his given name, *Hertzberg*. (When Dad became an actor, he'd changed it to *Hurt*.) Buried beneath Mom's underwear, Oren had also uncovered her diaphragm, waiting until I was present to pop its plastic container. He stretched its dome with his fingers to a near-porous transparency.

"I think it's a yarmulke," he theorized.

"For what," I said, "the rain?" I sealed its ring over my lips and blew as hard as I could. "Plus," I added after it failed to inflate, "Mom isn't even Jewish."

At the Barrs' house, I found Oren in the twilit driveway with my father and Naomi's husband, Sam Shah. One gull wing of his Bentley's hood was raised so Oren could admire the engine. My father was already seated shotgun. When he spotted me, he made a hurry-up wave.

"Join us," Sam said, clicking the hood's panel back in place and walking toward the driver's-side door. "We're taking her for a spin."

Sam Shah made a powerful impression standing beside his gorgeous machine. He was dark-skinned—Pakistani on his mother's side, I'd learn later that year—with a head of luxuriant black hair that added at least an inch to his height. He was full-lipped, his fluffy mustache as dense as his brows, and his glasses had such thick lenses his eyes seemed to float in them. To use an expression from back then, his charisma was *serious.* Chin up, he watched me as I approached and then extended his arm toward the back seat. I always thought that Mr. Shah's clothes were fantastic. This evening's blazer was a buttery chestnut tweed, his silk tie brilliantly colored. His loafers' tassels looked like tiny squid dipped in expensive chocolate. Shoes to shirt, these materials seemed to gather the fading light to them, as did the Bentley's oyster-gray paint.

"Everyone buckled up?" Sam asked. He pulled on a pair of leather driving gloves, perforated above the clasp, which, when he snapped closed, I noticed my father admiring. Sam started the car and the needles jumped. He eased the Bentley out of its space, but the moment we were on the road he gave it gas, and the engine sang.

Oren was thrilled. He immediately pulled down the tray table—an act I copied—admiring the molten grain of polished walnut. Oren leaned forward, looking over Sam's shoulder to regard the dash. The white-on-black gauges had stenciled abbreviations, the car's major operations adjusted by silver knobs that looked pleasurable to touch. The only visible sign of wear surrounded the ignition switch, the key having chipped away the veneer each time it had missed the slot, but to me such scarring was a sign of use and meant only one thing: Sam drove this car *everywhere.*

"What's the make and model?" my father asked.

"This is a 1960 S2 Continental," Sam said.

"It's beautifully appointed," my father said. He often made such statements in his baritone, and the usual effect was that his words somehow attained a solemn authority that masked their obviousness. Earlier, I'd overheard him talking to some of Elliott and Lynn's guests. Of the Iran hostage crisis, he'd intoned, "It's a very, *very* complex situation," and his audience vigorously nodded their heads, as if by saying so he'd explained Middle Eastern geopolitics. But Sam had no reaction to his comment, and this made my father fidget more than usual. He ran his fingers along the door's wood grain and then checked them for dust. He turned the radio on, off, and, after adjusting the dial, left it on, as if this were *his* car.

"Where'd you get it?" my father asked.

"On the Cape," Sam said.

"It must've been expensive."

"It was sitting, uncovered, in the owner's driveway, turning into a hunk of rust."

"A bargain, then," my father observed.

Sam leaned toward him while keeping his eyes on the road. He lowered his voice conspiratorially. "The restoration was what really cost me."

We'd made our way out of the residential part of Great Neck and onto a four-lane road. Freer now, Sam stepped on it again, and the car accelerated effortlessly.

My father pointed to the speedometer. "Ever gotten it up to two hundred?" he asked.

Oren, shielding his eyes, shook his head miserably. "Those are kilometers."

Dad, who liked to hurry past mistakes, shot him a look. "Still," he said to Oren, and then to Sam, "it's close."

Over Sam's shoulder, Oren said, "So it tops out at what, Mr. Shah? One-twenty?"

"*Very* good," Sam replied. "And no," he told Dad.

"It's a V-8," Oren continued, amazing me. "The S1 was a straight six."

"I see you know your automobiles," Sam said.

Oren shrugged and then sank back into his seat, crossing his arms, wearing a pained expression as he watched the darkened trees whip by. "I know a little," he said.

I could tell Dad was uncomfortable in the presence of Sam's material success, which baffled me. He sang on Broadway, and his voice was all over TV. *Give,* he said, *to the United Negro College Fund. Because a mind is a terrible thing to waste.* He had nothing to prove to me.

"What do you think of American cars?" Dad asked Sam. We'd just bought my grandfather's Buick LeSabre for a dollar—an amount Grandpa had demanded to make the transaction, in his words, official.

"Not much," Sam said.

"Elliott certainly loves his Cadillac," my father observed.

Once again Sam leaned toward my father. "Even Dr. Barr has lapses in judgment."

While Oren and I were recovering from this heresy, my father's voice came on the radio—his commercial for Schlitz. It was suddenly obvious to me why he'd turned it on in the first place. Oren was so mortified he hid his face behind Sam's seat, while I, being the more dutiful son, exclaimed, "Dad, it's you!"

Sam raised the volume.

You only go around once in life, said my father, *so you have to grab all the gusto you can!*

Sam laughed, delighted. Dad shrugged like it was nothing. *You drive a Bentley,* he seemed to be saying. *I am the voice of malt liquor.*

A moment later, Sam asked, "How do they pay you for that?"

"What do you mean?"

"Is it a one-time thing?" Sam said. "You do the commercial, get a check, and you're done?"

"Not exactly," my father said. He sat up straight, then pinched his thumb and index finger together as if to make a fine point. "They also pay you for a thirteen-week cycle. After that, if they want to renew the commercial, they pay you again." He sat back and crossed his arms, satisfied.

Sam appeared to do a quick calculation. "So during that period, they could play the ad a million times and you wouldn't see an extra cent?"

My father opened his mouth and then closed it. "In theory, yes."

Sam smiled, blinking. "Someone's union needs to renegotiate."

Dad had had it with his unions. They'd been on strike since late July, the walkout over cable TV and videocassette revenue, which made me happy—finally, I wasn't on set shooting my show over the summer. My father hated being out of work, but he took Sam's observation as a more personal affront: he suddenly also felt underappreciated. Now it was he who faced the window to watch the world unspool past him.

"I'll talk to them," he replied, as if his SAG and AFTRA reps were just waiting for his call. He was distracted now, but when we took a sharp curve and Sam accelerated through its apex, he managed to step back into character. "The handling is just *remarkable*."

"Yes," said Sam, "but it's nothing like my Ferrari GT."

"You have a Lusso?" my brother asked. "That's the rarest car they ever made."

"It's a 365," Sam corrected, and then rolled his eyes at my father. "I'm not *that* rich."

"Is it red or black?" Oren asked.

"My dear boy," Sam said, tilting the rearview mirror so he could look my brother in the eye, "I think we both know the Ferrari only comes in one color."

Confused, Oren said, "What's that?"

"*Fast*."

Evening had descended during our drive, the pines black against the night-blue sky. Upon our return to the Barrs' house—the very moment Sam cut the engine—the front door opened, throwing on the driveway's gravel the interior's yellow light and the party's din. Though the foyer was crowded, the first person I saw was Naomi.

She kissed her husband and asked my father and brother in passing if they'd enjoyed the drive, but when we faced each other, I had the distinct impression she'd been on the lookout for me, because she gave a slight start when we made eye contact, and then her expression softened into something more than affection. I hadn't given her a thought since we'd parted. My attempt to kiss her earlier had been so spontaneous, and so impulsive, it seemed to have been perpetrated by an impostor; it had been merely an opportunity for me to flex a familiar muscle, to perform for her, for someone—anyone—and been thereafter forgotten at the end of the scene. Now, however, I suddenly felt ashamed by my behavior. This was coupled with a terrifying realization that I'd won her fondness, but for no good reason. In response, I hurried inside—I spotted Mom and called to her, as if excited to tell her about what we'd just done—

though not quickly enough that I failed to notice Naomi's head tilt ever so slightly when I passed, her expression at once plaintive and perplexed.

My subsequent efforts to avoid her were not successful. Every time I looked up, she was there, waiting to catch my eye and remind me of what had transpired between us. It didn't matter where I positioned myself. Even later, when my father sat down at the Barrs' grand piano and played, when the chords rippled out and silenced conversations one by one—a hypnotic, softening effect as the guests, having suddenly noticed something very beautiful was occurring, turned to give him their full attention—I spotted her staring at me. I feigned devotion, smiling appreciatively at the ghosts of my father's hands reflected on the piano's fallboard, which was as black as the faces of the Bentley's dials. The parallax view of his hands, at once crablike and blurred, made his virtuosity seem effortless and all the more remarkable. I knew that she knew I wasn't fooling her, or myself.

Realizing all eyes were on him, my father glanced over his shoulder, raising his brows and then jerking his head back as if startled, a gesture that elicited laughs from nearly everyone, even my mother, who listened with one palm pressed to her chest, a wineglass cradled in the other. When my father performed, her expression was always an odd combination of admiration and melancholy, as if the melody reminded her of something from long ago, or a place to which you were sure, upon leaving, you'd never return. Sam Shah stood at my mother's side. He leaned toward her in that stiff-backed way of his, bending from the hips, his hands clasped behind his back, and said something, whether flattering or witty, I couldn't be sure, because she barely acknowledged his remark, as if to underscore that my father had the stage, and the time had come for everyone in the audience to please be silent. Elliott and Lynn joined Dad by the piano, and in a moment so perfect it seemed rehearsed, my father gestured toward the couple with an outstretched arm, the guests applauded, and, returning both hands to the keys, he sang in their honor:

If we only have love
Then tomorrow will dawn
And the days of our years
Will rise on that morn

If we only have love
To embrace without fears
We will kiss with our eyes
We will sleep without tears

If we only have love
With our arms open wide
Then the young and the old
Will stand at our side

He played for another several verses and, upon concluding, stood to bow as the gathered guests applauded. Naomi began to walk in my direction but stopped when Al Moretti, tapping a spoon to his highball, seized the chance to make a toast.

"Ladies and gentlemen," he said, "you're gonna have to indulge me for a sec, 'cause I gotta speak from the heart."

A hairdresser and part-time social worker, Al liked to describe himself as a "Jew-Woppie." He was my parents' close friend and another of Elliott's patients. Tonight he was wearing an orange shirt unbuttoned to the sternum, tight white pants, a white leather belt and shoes, both with gold buckles. His complexion, always red, now appeared closer to boiled. He had that familiar Queens inflection and idiom, the direct object of his sentences occasionally preceding their verb like a caboose pulling a train.

"Elliott, Lynn, this speech I didn't carefully prepare or nothing, so please bear with. I know I'm not alone in saying that when we first met, I was a fucking *mess.*" Everyone whooped at this, including Al. "But the pair of you"—he draped his arms around their necks and pulled them in to his sides—"you picked me up and took me under your wing. Ten years ago, Elliott, we started therapy together, and what can I say? With your able hands you wrung every drop of *mishegoss* out of my mind, while Lynn, you filled me up with a mother's milk." He took a moment to blow his nose with his cocktail napkin, stuffing it in his back pocket afterward. "Just the other day, Elliott, you said something that was such genius I thought about it on the whole train back to Astoria. 'Friends,' you said, 'are the family you get to choose.' But you're the family that chose *us.* So thank you for that and for sharing this blessed day. May the Lord God see fit you enjoy many more." He raised his glass. "You're fucking gorgeous."

Everyone else's glasses went up. But before a single guest could say "mazel tov" or Naomi could make her way to me, I'd escaped into Elliott and Lynn's room, where I found Oren. He'd managed to fix the television and was watching *Charlie's Angels*.

When any evening at the Barrs' home concluded and the guests were seen off, a core group that included Al Moretti and my parents always remained behind. It made me feel like we were special. If their son, Matthew, was in attendance, as well as their daughter, Deborah, and her husband, Eli, they too could be expected to hang back—it made all of us feel like we were nearly family. Imagine my surprise, then, when Oren and I emerged from the bedroom, and I noticed Sam and Naomi had been welcomed into this cohort. The grown-ups, still talking, tarried at the front door. Elliott and Sam were arguing heatedly. "If it moves," Sam said, "they tax it. If it keeps moving, they regulate it. And if it stops moving, they subsidize it. But not Reagan, I guarantee it." In response to which Elliott shook his head and said, "The only authentic form of trickle-down economics is the president's character." And then I noticed Naomi wave my parents over to her.

"That *boy* of yours," she said, either mischievously or vindictively, I couldn't tell, and then shot me a look that promised revenge. She gathered my parents into a huddle, resting her hands on their shoulders as she whispered to them, which built toward, I was sure, the embarrassing conclusion of my attempted kiss, upon which they all burst out laughing. "I mean," Naomi said, and touched her fingernails to her chest, rolling her eyes, "I *nevah*."

After evenings such as these, during the drive home, my parents often asked me, "Well, Griffin, what did you think?" Both considered me perceptive, they regularly told me as much, and I found I could intensify this effect—could get them to exchange that knowing look—by withholding half of what I'd noticed or framing my observations as questions. The trick was to be just off point. "How come everyone checks with Elliott after they say something?" I might ask, or "Do you think Al's laugh sounded lonely?" But I dreaded this discussion now, for I was sure Naomi had exposed me, and I wanted to avoid the topic at all costs, especially in front of Oren, lest I combust with shame.

Surprisingly, it was he who broached the subject. "Why does Mr. Shah think lower taxes will save the country?"

"Because it's an election year," Mom said. "And for some people politics is only about how much you pay the government."

"He just wants to keep more of the money he makes," Dad added.

"Doesn't everybody?" Oren asked.

"Yes," Dad said, shaken by the question's obviousness, "but it's not that simple."

"Mr. Shah said," Oren continued, "that reducing top rates would incentivize investment, which would spur the economy and bring down unemployment—take the 'stag' out of 'stagflation.'"

"What's your point?" Dad asked.

"It sounds straightforward to me."

Dad, anxious to change the subject, said to Mom, "I think Sam was quite taken with you."

"*Ugh,*" she replied, "he just went on and on about his orchids and his wine cellar."

"If you'd married a man like that," Dad said, "he'd've given you the royal treatment."

"You'd definitely be going home in a nicer ride," Oren said.

"A man like *that,*" Mom countered, "treats his cars like women and his women like cars."

Oren wouldn't have it, but Dad was delighted by her turn of phrase. That her witticisms might get a rise out of anyone, let alone my father, always surprised her, and this always made me slightly sad for her.

When Oren asked what Mr. Shah did for a living, Dad said, "He's in the *schmatta* business." And then more bafflingly, added: "Rags. Seconds." He often alluded to further explanations that he never supplied. Because my brother and I had inherited his fear of not seeming in the know, Oren refused to press, although I could tell he'd filed this away for further investigation. In *my* mind, I pictured Mr. Shah as a dealer in washcloths or, somehow, time.

Dad, who'd noticed my silence, eyed me in the rearview mirror.

"Naomi said you two had quite the conversation." He glanced at Mom, barely suppressing a smile. "She said you told her all about the people you'd worked with. Several of the actors and . . . crew."

Oren, smelling blood, gave me a sharky grin.

"And?" I said.

Mom turned around. "She said you struck her as being exceptionally mature."

I glanced at Dad in the rearview mirror, then back at Mom. "That's it?" I asked.

After a shrug, she added, "That's all."

Mom never lied to us. This characteristic cut two ways: you had to be careful what you asked her. I faced out my window so that only I could see myself smile.

We were crossing the Fifty-Ninth Street Bridge on the lower roadway. Its traffic was often worse than the Midtown Tunnel, but Dad preferred this artery into Manhattan, partly because there was no toll. I did too, especially at night. After you passed Roosevelt Island and traversed the East River, you descended from many stories toward Second Avenue, so that it seemed you were a pigeon come flying between the skyscrapers' twinkling lights. Up here, I caught glimpses into corner offices and onto rooftop gardens, of the tenants in their luxurious apartments. They were each a promise of some greater future in which you might revel in height, in roominess, from a purchase wherein you might regard all you had achieved, once you'd decided where to land. Even now, when I find myself returning to New York after a long absence, I feel that same thrill, that sense of ownership that I did then, and one that particular view conferred.

And then a tram rose toward us. Within its hospital-bright interior, there stood a woman, alone, leaning on the railing and facing the bridge. Right before we flashed past each other, in that stilled clarity conferred by speed, she caught my eye and, I was certain of it, smiled at me. And in that instant, when one stranger notices another and somehow agrees they'll keep that glance to themselves, I swear it was as if Naomi had sent a telepathic message through her that said, *We're safe*. It came so loud and clear, this confidence between us and the mercy she'd showed, that

I was overwhelmed with gratitude. *So this is how adults communicate.* I pressed my temple to the window, my breath fogging the glass. When, I wondered, would I see Naomi again?

Oren nudged my arm. In the streetlights' flash, he flapped something on the seat between us: Sam Shah's driving gloves.

The death in the family I caused occurred in 1973, when I was six and Oren four, but it took decades until I learned what truly happened that night, the blast radius of that conflagration, and its attendant consequences, widening to this day.

At the time, Al Moretti and his lover, Neal, were our neighbors at Lincoln Towers, a residential complex on Manhattan's Upper West Side. Its eight buildings were an agglomeration of nondescript gray brick high-rises, each thirty stories tall, though Oren and I always subtracted the absent thirteenth. They were a bit sandier and brighter than cinder block; on certain days, if the light was right, the sunset turned them gold. The higher floors enjoyed views of the Hudson and midtown's landmarks, like the Chrysler and Empire State Buildings, but our fifth-floor view was more claustrophobic, looking onto the complex's other towers, whose windows filled ours and blocked the sight of the river or the sky, and its parking lots, circular driveways, and green spaces below. It was only at the property's northernmost edge, above Seventieth Street, that West End Avenue took on its legendary character. There the cupola-topped walkups abutted buildings with rusticated limestone facades, blackened by car exhaust but magnificent despite the grime. Their iron-work was inset with decorative lions or tritons, and their awnings, taut with the occasional gusts, snapped their canvases like expensive kites. Their marble lobbies, where a plush couch and wingback chair might be set beneath a nineteenth-century landscape, seemed more like a rich man's smoking room than a place to wait before the doorman permitted you upstairs.

Our building's modern, high-ceilinged lobby, meanwhile, had all the charm of an airport concourse, with a wall, opposite the mail room, covered with an ugly mosaic, the abstract image its tiles formed as large as a stegosaur but so nebulous in shape that it resisted any attempt to morph it into something I could categorize as animal, vegetable, or mineral. Our hallway was two bowling lanes long and similarly narrow, its floor tiles the hue of a neglected aquarium. As I passed each apartment's heavy steel door, I'd catch snippets of our neighbors' lives: the Von Wurtzels practicing their harps, the angry yap of Miss Kapner's Chihuahua. In Al and Neal's case, what could be overheard through their door was often shouting and, when things got really bad, the sound of a flung plate shattering or a piece of furniture thudding against a wall. Al always made a single-knuckled knock at our door afterward—three gentle taps—as if to apologize for the ruckus.

"Lily," he'd ask my mother before she answered, "are you there?"

I made it a point to get a look at Al during these visits. The result of one brawl: his lip, swelled until its underside was exposed. After another scuffle, his plum-colored eyelid glistened so brightly it looked shellacked. Once he showed up with a gash above his hairline, the blood spidering across his forehead. He pressed his palm's heel to his scalp to stanch it, but the wound leaked in rivulets so fast-moving it was as if he'd squeezed a soaked sponge atop his crown.

"It's not as bad as it looks," he said to my mother, then shut his eyes in shame before she took his elbow and led him to the dining table to clean him up. When she was done, she poured him a drink, and they spoke in hushed tones. Al rambled, sobbing occasionally, while my mother, who was naturally reticent, listened patiently, waiting while he once again talked himself into leaving Neal. When Mom urged him to stay the night, Al said, "I can't impose," but then stood and walked shakily toward the couch. "Maybe I'll just put my head down till I get *unfercockt*."

I liked watching Al outstretched on our living room sofa, an ice pack pressed to his cheek. All adult pain seemed gigantic to me. With one arm draped over his eyes, the other would reach for the highball's rim, its base leaving a circle of condensation on the floor whenever he lifted it and loudly sipped his vodka rocks. He was always gone when I woke the next morning, the only proof of his presence the ring his glass had left on the parquet.

In person, Neal was soft-spoken, almost demure. He had large, expressive eyes, and a mustache and beard that seemed more apparatus than facial hair, as if integral to the workings of his jaw. Once or twice a week, Mom had the couple over for martinis, Al excusing himself after the second to retrieve a bottle of wine from their apartment, leaving my mother and Neal alone for a few minutes. He always seemed so indrawn sitting there, his hands clasped on his lap or tucked beneath his bulging biceps. He was one of the rare people able to coax my mother out, to get her talking, to make her laugh, and in Al's absence, them getting along almost felt like a betrayal. But I favored Neal. Al was never reluctant to correct or reprimand Oren or me in our parents' presence, and he often failed to keep our names straight when he told us to shut up or to maybe go play outside. But Neal always greeted us with interest, actually looking at the drawings we showed him or the papier-mâché sculptures we made at school. If my mother had to step out to the store for wine or couldn't get a sitter when she was seeing the ballet's Sunday matinee, she occasionally left us with him, walking us down the hall, Oren and me admiring her pretty dress as she rang his apartment's bell and then caught the elevator as soon as he answered.

Neal was a dealer in Eastern art. He owned a gallery in midtown, but he also did a great deal of business from home. Their apartment was a menagerie of paintings, silk screens, and religious sculpture that even now I'm tempted to see primarily as a reflection of their relationship: hydra-headed Naga, the snake goddess, emerging from a dragon's mouth like a stream of Al's profanity; fanged Kali, trident and scimitar in hand, and poor Al, I imagined, pinned like Shiva beneath Neal's foot; boar-toothed Raijin, the Japanese thunder god, whose puck-sized drums orbited him as he squared off against Fujin, shouldering his bag of winds.

"Are they enemies?" I asked Neal as we regarded the two-paneled screen.

"Companions," Neal said. He shrugged sheepishly and added, "They make a lot of noise." He laughed, so I did too. To pass our time together, Neal liked to read me stories from the New English Bible. In Genesis we reread the stories about Jacob and Esau. Neal was especially fond of Exodus, while I preferred Judges—those Old Testament superheroes—but most often we returned to the adventures of David and his tussles with Saul, whose spear-throwing at his adopted son I found strangely upsetting.

"Do you trust your parents?" Neal once asked me after concluding a chapter. I was playing myself in chess—Neal had taught me the game—on an antique Indian set and moved my camel diagonally across the board to take the opposing elephant, at which point Neal apologized, adding, "Please don't tell them I asked."

Their corner apartment was the floor's only three-bedroom. Our parents were in the market for more space, and upon first getting a tour my father had remarked to Neal, with his typical unwitting bluntness, "If you ever decide to move, let us know."

But our family moved first.

That winter, my father had been touring with *The Fisher King,* the first of two Abe Fountain musicals in which he'd perform. Sunday was the only evening of the week he was home. After the matinee, he'd take a train from Philadelphia or D.C., then depart again the following evening. "The house is dark on Monday," he'd explain, which always felt to me like a strange thing to say as he unpacked his bag. That night—I remember the Christmas lights were strung around our window—my parents were in their bedroom when Oren and I snuck out of ours. On the living room's coffee table, beside a pair of empty wineglasses, were several lit candles my mother had left burning. I took the holder by its knob and, careful not to let the melted wax bleed over, led Oren into our front hall closet. "It's a cave," I told him upon entering, pushing away the jacket sleeves above us. "Watch out for the stalactites." I recall him crawling past me, while I slid the door closed. When I turned and raised the candle to illuminate the darkness between us, it *whuffed* a sheath of dry-cleaning plastic, instantly igniting the coat within it, the jacket wondrously visible amid the flames. I dropped the candle holder and, in a panic, scooted backward, Oren doing the same but deeper into the closet.

From this point forward, my recollections grow fragmented. There is first blackness, and then I hear our cat meowing, its pitch high and desperate, a mournful sound that mimicked her name, which was French for "kitty": *Minou,* she seemed to cry, *Minou, Minou.* The next thing I recall is Oren and I hiding behind my bed. "It's a fire," I said to him, "a real fire." Then the pair of us racing to my parents' bedroom to alert them to the blaze. Next I see my mother near the foyer, separated from me by a wall of flames. "Shel," she screams to my father, "get the bucket!" I was sure she meant the plastic pail that I took to the beach, orange with a white handle and my name written on it in black marker, but why did she say "the bucket" instead of "the boys"? And then I was borne aloft, my father yanking my wrist above my head and carrying me in such a fashion that I occasionally touched down. My foot stamped a patch of flame on the entryway rug but didn't burn. The lobby was filled with the evacuated tenants, all of us watching the firemen unhurriedly file in and march up the stairs. Smoke crawled along the ceiling's recessed lights. I was in my father's arms. He was wearing his bathrobe, the one with brown and black stripes, his only article of clothing to survive the blaze. All I could think while I held his neck was: *Me, I did this.*

We lost a great deal of property: clothing, furniture, jewelry. The work of several artist friends that my father never failed to remind me "might've become valuable one day." The Stickley dining room set Lauren Bacall had gifted Dad for voice-coaching her in *Applause.* Minou, who had hidden so well my mother couldn't find her, died from smoke inhalation—the death I caused. While my mother scrambled to secure us a new apartment, Al and Neal were kind enough to let our family move into their place. I'd have my first Saturday session with Elliott a few weeks later. For nearly a decade, and in spite of therapy, this was *my* version of the event. It was not that the fire was verboten in our family; more accurately, and like so many subjects in that era—think religion—it was an issue left to me to raise. As for Oren's version, there was one critical difference in our accounts, a piece of missing information he'd ultimately supply that for years he protected like a state secret.

.　.　.

My parents had a ten-thousand-dollar insurance policy and filed a claim. Enter the agent handling it: Nick Salvatore. In the ensuing years, after my father and mother had retold the story so many times I made it my own, the on-the-nose irony of the agent's name would never be lost on me. My parents met him in the lobby for the inspection, this young man memorable for many reasons but to my mother because of his heart-stopping good looks. Salvatore was a classically beautiful Italian man, from his curly, squid-ink hair to the amber-buttered hue of his skin, which made his teeth appear whiter when he smiled. He wore a camel hair coat over his black suit, a pressed white shirt with a dark tie— funereal colors, my mother thought, entirely appropriate given what had befallen them. But the beacon-bright accents of his shirt and overcoat, even his name, suggested he was more like an angel—he was here to help, after all. What made her swoon, however, were his hands, in both of which he cradled hers when she greeted him. Something about their size and squareness, the hard angles of his thumbs' metacarpals and the pronounced, indented triangles where they joined his wrists, made her desire take flight and then bloom inside her chest like fireworks. She was a deeply loyal person, incapable of infidelity, and yet it took all of her self-control not to turn to my father and say, "Why don't you go find something else to do?"

Salvatore couldn't have been older than twenty-five, and while my parents rode the elevator with him to their devastated apartment, she was transported back to Rome, to her honeymoon, the afternoons she had to herself after the movie star Anthony Quinn, who had brought them along to Europe so my father could continue as his voice coach, had decamped with Shel to play tennis—a daily ritual that always ended with the pair eating lunch so late it pushed back dinner until nearly midnight. Come midday, when boredom and exhaustion had overwhelmed her, she fled their stuffy hotel room, abandoning her typewriter and Quinn's rambling recorded dictation (she was transcribing his autobiography), to find somewhere to eat first and then window-shop a little, killing the rest of the afternoon at a café with a book and a carafe of wine. This was followed by an early-evening siesta that left her bright-eyed for the endless dinners, which she was bathed and dressed for long before Shel and

Quinn returned. During these several-hour jaunts through Trastevere or Prati, the Foro Romano or Via del Corso, she was often accosted by such similarly gorgeous men walking Rome's streets singly or in packs, their English poor but for the most obvious blandishments—"pretty lady" or "my beauty." It was at these moments that she suffered neither temptation to stray nor regret at her newly betrothed state but something far sharper and more crushing because it was an emotion entirely new to her: she felt alone in her marriage.

Standing beside my mother in the lobby, my father also had a strong reaction to Mr. Salvatore's appearance. Why, he thought, were such good looks squandered on an insurance salesman? Why couldn't *he* have been similarly proportional, more symmetrical, instead of his own enormous face, from chin to crown as long as a canoe, with a brow so tall one asshole casting agent once said, "You remind me of a Jewish Herman Munster."

To my mother, Salvatore said, "Mrs. Hurt, I'm sorry for your loss, but I promise: Nationwide is on your side. We're gonna take care of your family."

My father had noticed my mother's reaction to Salvatore, her already severe shyness so intensified by his presence that she was rendered speechless. Her attraction to him was so obvious, an obviousness so closely akin to a poor performance, that my father couldn't bear to watch. Lily grew talkative the moment they got on the elevator. By the time they arrived at the apartment door, she'd not only recounted to Salvatore the whole disaster but also confessed to a lingering sense of guilt for leaving the candles burning.

"I don't know how I could've been so thoughtless," she said.

Salvatore pressed his hand to her shoulder. He rubbed it somewhat hurriedly, like he might a homely aunt's, but so far as Shel was concerned he kept it there a little too long.

"Aw, c'mon, Mrs. Hurt," he said, "you're being too hard on yourself."

"What if one of the children had been injured?" she said. "Or worse, like our poor cat?"

Lily was crying now, and Shel was relieved. When calm, confident, her ballerina's beauty was angular and regal, as long-necked as she was; upset, however, her features collapsed like a shrunken apple.

"Thankfully neither of them was," he noted.

"I rushed the kids to bed," she continued. "I left dishes in the sink and those *stupid* candles on the table. Shel had been gone all week, and I wanted us to have some time alone."

What was she going to tell him next? my father wondered. That while they were making love and heard the kids scurrying around, he'd told her to ignore them, that sooner or later they'd go to sleep?

"Let the man do his job," my father said.

Her expression grim, my mother nodded toward the door. "I don't think I can bring myself to go in there."

"There's no need whatsoever," Salvatore said.

Gathering herself, she offered her hand to him once more. "Thank you again, Mr. Salvatore."

"Please," he said. "Call me Nick."

Lily smiled, then snapped open her purse and found some tissues, dabbing her eyes with them. She laughed, and the transformation back to her old self was miraculous: her face reconfiguring, her cheeks blooming with color. Salvatore smiled back.

"I have to go see about an apartment for us uptown," she said.

Salvatore waited until her elevator arrived. Lily stepped on, and the moment after its door closed, his face darkened.

"Let's take a look at this place already," he said to my father.

Salvatore's bad mood persisted throughout the inspection, which to my father felt perfunctory, infuriatingly quick. He seemed put out by having to breathe the several-day-old smoke's still-overpowering odor, a frustration he further underscored by pinching the tarred clothes and soot-covered bed linens and then holding up his index finger in disgust, as if his pitch-black pad were evidence of a failed white-glove inspection—a sign of messiness in our life instead of its ruin.

When they were back in the hallway, Salvatore finally spoke. "Just so I've got this straight. Your kid sets the closet on fire. Then your wife tries to put it out while you get the building's extinguisher. But it doesn't work?"

"That's right."

"Did you keep it?"

"What?"

"The fucking defective, probably-never-inspected-in-a-million-years fire extinguisher."

"No, I . . . of course not."

Salvatore shook his head miserably. "I bet you all the money I got," he continued, "that the superintendent raced up and down these stairs checking every last fire extinguisher the *second* after your kid torched the place."

"It was an accident," my father said.

Salvatore rolled his eyes. "Tell me why you're not taking these guys to court again? You're looking at a helluva lawsuit."

My father shook his head. "We have you," he managed to say. He'd never considered bringing a negligence claim. For one, he distrusted the process. The lawyers, the courtroom drama. What if it were all for naught? It was like multiple callbacks for an audition that ended with a producer's rejection: getting one's hopes up hurt more than the final refusal. This was coupled with his reluctance to cause a stir, consistent with his actor's disposition, a common flaw in that breed's character but one my father suffered from acutely, for he saw such relationships as personal, based on more than simply commerce. Sue management successfully, and by recouping his losses, he risked inviting that state of relations most anathema to him: he would be *disliked*.

"So what now?" my father asked.

Salvatore shrugged. "We got problems."

"How's that?"

Perhaps because they were standing in the hallway Salvatore lowered his voice. "Put yourself in my position," he said. "I got a client whose kid ignites some combustibles, and now he wants *me* to give him the full amount of his policy. No offense, but that's like if your dog bit me and I'm the one being asked to pay for his chipped tooth."

My father couldn't bring himself to argue.

"You don't seem like a fine-print kind of guy, Mr. Hurt. But you understand when I say this looks *bad*."

My father spoke the words he'd wanted to utter from the moment he'd first smelled smoke: "I'm sorry."

Salvatore sighed. "Look, I'm gonna pull some strings, get you and your pretty wife your check." He glanced at his watch and then brightened. "This afternoon, in fact." Then he slapped the back of his palm against my father's chest and pressed it there. "But to do *that,* there's something I need you to do for me first."

It was brutally cold outside, but especially here, where Broadway intersected Columbus Avenue. Even Lincoln Center's fountains, their jets almost furry in the January brightness, bent slightly, the spume steadily sheared off in the prevailing wind and spraying unwitting passersby. Men held the brims of their hats, staggering as stiffly as zombies against the blast. Women pulled their scarves over their mouths, the trailing fabric snapping behind them as they leaned forward or sometimes even turned to walk backward against the gale. At Columbus Circle, a few blocks down, the flurries seemed even more powerfully channeled by the GW building, swirling before the Coliseum's facade, whistling like some maritime squall. Shel would catch the downtown train there, to meet Salvatore as planned, but only after he stopped at the bank.

Get started now on your road to riches, my father had said in the commercial, *by saving regularly at the Dime. Offices in Manhattan, Brooklyn, and Long Island.* His tone was gentle, reassuring—solid as the branch's black marble facade. As the bank's TV spokesperson, he had been given complimentary checking and savings accounts, and when he'd first started doing his business there, he couldn't help offhandedly mentioning this to the tellers, just so they knew with whom they were dealing.

"Mr. Hurt," said Glenda, as he stepped to her window, "what can I do for you today?"

"I need to make a withdrawal. From my savings."

Glenda passed him the slip and then folded her hands on the counter. "How much, then?"

If he hadn't been there just the week before, he wouldn't have known his balance: just over $4,100. As a rule he preferred to ignore it, thereby going longer stretches not tormented by its shabby state, or, more recently, to be pleasantly surprised by the amount, boosted by weekly checks from *The Fisher King.*

"All of it," my father said.

At this, Glenda winced. "I'm sorry, Mr. Hurt, but we do ask you maintain at least a hundred-dollar balance. Otherwise you have to pay a penalty."

"Four thousand, then," my father said. He smiled wearily. "Keep the change."

Salvatore had demanded Shel pay him a kickback to get the insurance money, and really, my father thought, what recourse did he have? Without it he'd be wiped out, ruined. He'd agreed to meet the agent at the edge of Chinatown, on Canal and Bowery, the district's easternmost corner, to make the exchange. It was a madhouse. Aproned street vendors stood before their carts, loudly negotiating with customers. In the restaurants' windows hung rows of glazed piglets and ducks, their hooked bodies shiny and brown. From barrels, the fishmongers tonged chains of blue crabs into paper bags. Here, pedestrian traffic changed, its density fivefold that of midtown. All the micro-allowances to right-of-way were outright ignored, the lack of concessions to flow creating crowded eddies so slow-moving Shel was forced to sometimes walk turned sideways or, at the worst bottlenecks, stand completely still. Salvatore had said he'd be in his car, that he would park in front of the Citizens Savings Bank, and this seemed appropriate to my father, for in the shadow of its limestone dome it was as if a robbery were about to take place—because what else was this bribe he was about to pay?—the insurance agent playing both thief and getaway driver. And then there was his car:

It was a black Lincoln Continental Mark III, not so different in design from the model Anthony Quinn had driven in Europe. Its hood was similarly long and formidable, its front-to-rear fenders tall and pronounced. Seeing it, my father was suddenly seized by a memory: he and Lily were driving behind Quinn in a van. It had struggled to climb hills, but loaded with the movie star's painting supplies and knee-jerk rug and furniture purchases, my father wondered if it had the horsepower to make any major ascents. Would he and Lily simply roll backward? They had trailed Quinn all over Italy and France in this vehicle: from Naples to Rome to Perugia to Venice; from Milan to Biarritz and back; from Genoa along the Ligurian coast to Imperia. But now, most harrowingly, on their journey's final northward push through the Alps to Paris, they drove along the mountainous Col de Turini, its hairpins so sharp it was like a carnival ride, Quinn's Lincoln disappeared behind walls of rock rising into their path, only to reappear far ahead, almost out of view, as if he were flaunting its handling and speed. *I am not this man's voice coach,* my father realized. *I am his Sherpa.* He imagined this trip would end with them losing their brakes on one of the dangerous descents and rocketing through the guardrail to plunge into the valley, dying on this fool's errand called their honeymoon.

"What took you?" Salvatore said when Shel got in the car. The insurance agent was eating noodles from a take-out carton, exhibiting impressive facility with his chopsticks. When my father didn't answer, Salvatore tilted the box top toward him. "Want some?" he asked. "It's lo mein."

My father shook his head. Out the windshield, Shel could see the Manhattan Bridge's triumphal arch and colonnade. From where they were parked, its span wasn't visible, nor Brooklyn's low-slung buildings: just sky. In New York, a rare view. Like a gate to nowhere. The structure was reminiscent, in its pillared horseshoe design, of Saint Peter's; and overwhelmed by memory yet again, Shel recalled Quinn and his mistress, Jolanda, standing beneath the Sistine Chapel's pietà, the priest pouring holy water over their bastard child, Francesco. Lily, who stood next to Shel, had leaned toward him to whisper, "This is the most profane, ridiculous thing I've ever seen."

Salvatore put down the carton. "We gonna do this?" he said.

From his breast pocket, my father removed the bank envelope. Salvatore produced the check and held it in the air between his fingers. It was a larger slip than most, as if its additional surface area were necessary to accommodate such a figure, the amount typed in capitals: TEN THOUSAND DOLLARS AND ZERO CENTS.

"I don't understand," my father said.

"What?"

"The math."

"You lost me."

"Of *this,*" Shel continued. "This transaction."

Salvatore smiled. "You wearing a mic or something?"

"I give you four thousand so that you'll give me ten—"

"Okay," Salvatore said, "if this is how you're gonna play it—"

"You give me ten thousand, but it's really only *six.*"

"Out," said the agent, reaching across to pull the door's latch.

"If it's only six," Dad said, and knocked his arm away, "why not make it that to start?"

"Don't fucking touch me."

"It doesn't make sense," my father said.

"Get out of my car!"

"It doesn't make sense!"

The two men grabbed each other's coat collars, but the stiff-armed fashion in which they clasped made it appear closer to a pose, the pair deadlocked, like those crabs my father had seen in the barrel. Still the parting finally did come, albeit suddenly and more violently than Shel was prepared, for he was ejected from the car, tumbling backward while Salvatore peeled off in a great screech. The check was wadded in my father's palm, the slip crumpled but intact, and his money gone. For the briefest moment, it seemed the people around him paused, giving him space and time to stand and dust himself off; and then their hectic rush and crush resumed. Salvatore merged into the traffic's stream and disappeared, over the bridge, into the thin blue air.

Mom had found us a place uptown, on Eighty-Eighth and West End, the new apartment so much larger than its predecessor that Oren and I no longer needed to share a room. It was in a building that would prove so expensive we'd be forced to move back to Lincoln Towers within a couple of years—a different sort of trauma altogether. What I recall then, however, was the excitement, the sense of hope. We were meagerly packed and ready to move from Al and Neal's by the following Sunday. But when my father appeared at their door, I somehow knew he'd come for me *alone.* I ran, terrified, into the room Neal used for storage, the one where Oren and I slept, and hid beneath a bed. My father dragged me by my wrist from its safety. I vividly remember backpedaling with all the strength I had, grabbing a doorknob, a sculpture, a table's leg—I was as willing to pull my arm from its socket as a lizard is to detach from its pinned tail. But it was no use. My father gathered me into his arms and carried me down the length of the hallway to our decimated apartment. I remember my feeling of utter surrender during that seemingly endless walk. The sensation of flying—of being held aloft—with the hallway floor far below. Of dried tears staining my cheeks. The girth of my father's neck, which I clutched now. And the strangest sense that the smallest space—not even a unit of measure I could name—had opened up between my thoughts and my face; and the conviction that, so long as I hid behind this mask, I'd be safe.

Our door's lock had been punched out by the firemen. A thick tuft of pink insulation, flecked with soot, was stuffed in its bolt hole. My father touched the door, and it swung inward, easily, revealing that the floor was still covered with a layer of water. This standing slick was black, debris-flecked and dotted with ash. I was afraid that its inked surface hid falloffs, sharp objects. That he might deposit me in it and abandon me there. Instead, my father walked me through every room. Past the galley kitchen's blistered cabinets, the stovetop powdered white, as if with flour. The dining table and chairs only a piled outline. My parents' mattress nothing but springs. The room Oren and I shared, our ceiling's paint hanging in tattered flaps. My favorite book, *World Atlas of Marine Fishes,* whose charred cover now read *Atlas of Mar.* My father pointed out the charcoal streaks where flames had licked the walls, the melted fixtures, our blackened clothes. Though most terrifying by far was the stench—this cold mustiness—like the carcass of a drowned dragon. Having finally returned to the front door, my father stopped so that I might take a last look. When he was satisfied the image was indelible, he broke his silence:

"Never again," he said.

Within a year, I made my first television appearance.

THE OCTOBER SURPRISE

Several weeks after the Barrs' party, Naomi and I went for our first drive.

It was one of those fall days when the sun, rising in a clear sky, shined white and blindingly down the cross streets, while the avenues, blued and gusting with chill winds, made it seem as if New York were stitched of two weathers. I was returning home from an audition, walking west past the Juilliard School, when, to my right, I heard a persistent rapping on glass. A car's window hummed down, erasing my reflection, to reveal Naomi's face.

"Well," she said, "if it isn't the movie star."

Naomi had a newspaper draped over her steering wheel and a cup of coffee in her hand. She wore the same expression as when we'd first met: open-mouthed, expectant. I was as surprised to see her myself, and just as pleased—it was as if by thinking of our time together at the party I'd somehow summoned her. When I asked why she was parked here, she explained that her daughters, Danny and Jackie, were in the school's program, they were performing in New York City Ballet's *The Nutcracker* and rehearsed at the school. "But the Mouse King's soldiers," she said, "Mother Ginger's kids." She rolled her eyes. "Not big parts or anything." When Naomi asked where I was headed, I told her we lived just down the block, between Amsterdam and West End, in response to which she looked toward the river and said, "Huh." I'd moved closer to her window and now stood slightly bent, a thumb hooked beneath my book bag's strap, my other hand at rest on her door, waiting—for what, I wasn't sure. She seemed to be waiting as well—her eyes darted across mine— but then said, "Come sit before you freeze to death."

It wasn't especially cold, but I came around and, once seated, Naomi rolled up her window, sealing off the city's noise. We smiled at each other. Naomi sat up straight and then took her necklace's pendant in her fingers, running it up and down its chain. She watched me watch this, and when our eyes met again, she said her daughters wouldn't be finished for at least an hour. There was the distinct feeling, which would dominate our time together that year, that each was waiting for the other to make a decision. "Do you have somewhere you need to be?" she asked. I shook my head. I leaned forward to look out her window at the school's entrance, at the kids milling about, at the pedestrians passing by. "Okay," she said, and, almost gingerly, turned the key in the ignition. She listened to the Mercedes idle; she shifted into drive but kept her foot on the brake; she put her hands on the wheel, then pressed her back against the seat, locking out her arms and thinking for a moment. "Okay," she repeated, then checked her side mirror. And we left.

Of that first drive I recall a few distinct impressions. The way Naomi signaled and then calmly glanced at her side mirrors before changing lanes. How she turned the wheel one-handed and let it hiss against her palm when it spun back. Were these acts memorable because my mom did not drive? The breadth of the car itself: how it seemed less an interior and more like a room. The pretense that we were in no rush, but if we stopped moving it might alter the mood or our ease together. Yet there also hung over us a kind of anxiety, a feeling, nearly impossible to articulate, that she was looking for someplace to *get to,* one that was specific but as yet unknown, and this made her slightly distracted and me more watchful, on the lookout, as if I'd been appointed her navigator but lacked both a destination and a map.

We turned north first, up Amsterdam, toward Seventy-Second Street, where it intersected with Broadway, and when the Ansonia came into view—that famous hotel with its Caribbean-blue railings and black mansard roof, the turquoise patina on torpedo-shaped turrets and port-hole windows—I remarked that it always reminded me of a castle from Atlantis. I immediately felt stupid for saying so, thinking my comment childish. But surprisingly, Naomi agreed. She leaned toward me, as if she were telling me a secret, and said, "You know, the original owner kept cows on the roof," a fact I tried to picture. My interest prompted her to head west again, so we might pass before the building, then to Riverside Drive, where Naomi continued north once more. The Hudson, visible beyond the park, ran on our left. Naomi gestured toward the buildings on our right—"These gorgeous pre-wars," she said wistfully, remarking that she sometimes wished she could move the girls into the city and ditch the Long Island commute. "'But where would the kids play?' Sam says. 'And what about my cars?'" I shook my head, sharing in her disappointment. Naomi added, "Ridiculous, right? But what are you gonna do?" The Soldiers' and Sailors' Monument rose into view, that cylindrical structure whose columns make it look like a Gatling gun. I told her it was a favorite place to roller-skate when we'd lived this far uptown, just a couple of blocks from the apartment where we'd moved after the fire.

"What fire?" she asked.

I launched into my story with great flair, albeit a truncated version, since it would be years before Dad filled me in on the events with Salvatore, and Mom had yet to tell me her version of that night. I had long before discovered how riveting adults found this tale—Naomi was no exception—one I'd edit with each retelling. I had learned to give extra attention to certain moments for dramatic effect: The coat I'd ignited, visible beneath the combusting plastic, like the burning bush. The parade of firemen, shouldering their tanks and wearing masks as they marched into our lobby. The splash Dad's feet made as he carried me from room to room on our tour. And then his final command, like a door slamming shut. "Oh my God," Naomi said when I finished. "Why would he do that to you?" Her question shook me. I had never thought to doubt his decision. Unsettled, but putting on my best face, I suggested we head down West End Avenue, so I could show her our former building, the one we'd moved into after the fire, and see if Pete, a beloved doorman, was standing out front. "There's Pete," I said, as we proceeded south, and, passing it, I told her about the apartment's size, how much larger it was compared with the one we lived in now. I mentioned this with neither regret nor shame, since I didn't think of our circumstances in terms of fallen station. I described the apartment fondly: its enclosed dining room, around whose table Oren and I often raced our bikes, and in which Mom sometimes locked herself to type her undergraduate essays; my bedroom at the apartment's far end, off the kitchen, where I had my own TV and a bathroom with a claw-foot tub. Oren's room, where we kept our bunk beds, and which had its own shower and bath. The living room, which looked out over West End Avenue, and from whose open windows you could hear the trees rustle spring through fall.

"Sounds like a nice place," Naomi said. "How long did you live there?"

"Two years," I said.

When she asked why we'd moved back to Lincoln Towers, I explained that we'd been "priced out," parroting my father, forced to vacate because the landlord, Mr. Moses, had wanted to take it "co-op," a word I uttered with Dad's same headshaking amazement at people's greed in spite of the fact that I barely understood what it meant. Naomi considered this as she drove. She had her near hand on the wheel, her elbow propped against the window and a knuckle pressed to her lips. Now I see that she was pondering the reversals my family had suffered, although what happened next was just as consequential. We came to a stop, upon which she turned to face me and half smiled—a concerned, bittersweet expression I mimicked but did not understand. She reached out and placed her palm on my cheek. I had never been touched like this. I felt strangely stirred, a little sad, and I closed my eyes, instantly, like one of those dolls when you tip back its head, and then leaned my face's weight against her. I was so tired suddenly—my relief was so palpable—I thought I might fall asleep. I could feel Naomi take my temple's pulse, its fillips traveling along her fingertips and up her arm. She slowly exhaled; it was close to a sigh. I had to swallow but refused, lest Naomi hear it. The light changed. She removed her hand to take the wheel, gripping it in both fists. She shook her hair away from her sunglasses, and we drove back to my street without speaking. She pulled into the driveway. Before I got out of the car we said goodbye very formally, perhaps a bit hurriedly, and then I watched her drive to West End Avenue, signal left, and disappear.

Did I reflect on our talk? Was I stirred toward introspection afterward? Did I consider, for instance, that the next catastrophe might evict
my family from the city altogether? That the next success might permanently transport us to roomy luxury uptown? More likely, upon arriving home—before I reached beneath my shirt's collar and produced our
key from where it hung on a ball chain—I placed my ear to the door
and listened. Hearing nothing, I entered. To confirm that I was alone,
I called out *hello*. Probably I went straight to the kitchen, through our
living/dining area, and poured myself a bowl of cereal. Maybe I sat at
the table, in front of the floor-to-ceiling mirrors Dad had installed—an
improvement, he liked to say, that made the space "seem bigger"—and
contemplated the nutrition label. Or gazed through our windows' third-
floor view to the top of the Empire State Building's antenna. More likely,
I went to my study, a large closet off this open-floor plan, and, after
finishing my Raisin Bran, placed an LP on the turntable, put on Dad's
headphones, and, standing before the closed door, played some air guitar
and lip-synched the lyrics, pretending to be a jukebox hero to my roaring fans. Or I caught the second half of *The 4:30 Movie* on Mom and
Dad's television, lying on their bed. Or I stood on their dresser and from
Mom's track shelves above this—another improvement of Dad's—where
all her books from grad school were kept, pulled down, say, *The Magic
Mountain* or *Moby-Dick* and, having long ago discovered this was where
Dad stashed his dough, plucked a crisp five-spot from its center and
then walked up West End Avenue to Stanley's Stationery Store to play
Asteroids. Or I climbed to my top bunk and read a comic book. Or lay
with my legs climbing the wall and, tilting my head backward, over the
mattress, pretended our ceiling was a pristine floor. Or I marveled at Farrah Fawcett in her red swimsuit—her poster was above my pillows—as
she stared at me upside down. It never occurred to me to masturbate,
since no one had taught me how.

Dad usually got home before Mom; Mom, returning from teaching ballet, arrived soon after and went straight to the kitchen to make
dinner. Oren, back from cross-country practice, entered our room and
turned on the radio that sat atop his desk, or our small Sony TV atop
our dresser, or both. Later Mom called us to the table. Every night of the
week, and almost without fail, we gathered to eat. Mom served us and

then sat with her back to the mirrors, blocking my view of myself. Dad was to my left; Oren, to my right. "What'd you get into today?" Mom might ask me. Conversation, having commenced, was always lively and wide-ranging. We were, after all, a gregarious, performative bunch, and no subject was off-limits, except for the secrets we wittingly or unwittingly kept from one another—the ones, in my case, I knew not to tell, and the others I didn't know were secrets at all.

The following week, when I spotted Naomi's Mercedes in front of Juilliard again—she had her usual newspaper and coffee—I was so excited to see her I walked around to the passenger door without an invitation and got in. She, too, seemed keenly impatient and eager, as if she had a surprise for me, and immediately drove down Sixty-Sixth Street, crossing West End Avenue, descending a hill and then making a right turn to a short, four-block stretch Oren and I knew well that ran parallel to the Hudson and ended at Seventieth. It is now named Freedom Place, but then it had none, at least to my knowledge. It has since been developed by Trump into waterfront properties, mixed-use luxury apartment towers built on a brand-new avenue west of it called Riverside Boulevard. These begin at Seventy-Second Street and terminate ten blocks south, skyscrapers that stand nearly shoulder to shoulder, casting long shadows in the afternoon that block everyone else's view. But back then the street was merely a dead space. Its east side was fronted by a massive, windowless, two-story parking garage that stretched nearly its entire length, whose brick facade shivered with heat haze in the summer; and since it lacked any entrance or egress besides its giant blue louver doors, the whole area felt sealed off. Above it was one of Lincoln Towers' parks, with benches for the elderly and a playground Oren and I often visited, but from below all you could see was the ivy lining its railings and a few of its taller trees. Along the street's west side, meanwhile, there ran a concrete wall topped with a high chain-link fence Oren and I often scaled and then peered over. This secured what were then several hundred feral acres stretching north to Seventy-Second Street and south as far as the eye could see. We never risked vaulting to its other side, for the jump down was significant—too far, perhaps, for us to climb out afterward, and vagrants were thought to live there. This land was reed-covered and wild, dotted with the rusted hulks of abandoned vehicles and appliances peeking out from its high grasses. The breeze carried the loamy gray-green smell of the Hudson along with the stink of dead fish and trash. Its expanse continued to slope all the way to the waterfront but first ran beneath the West Side Highway, whose sibilant traffic we could hear like wind in a shell, interrupted by sporadic detonations, louder than gunshots, that tires made as they struck the steel road plates bolted to its lanes—permanently, it seemed. Absent pedestrians, this street was barren by day and forbidding at night, so isolated it was to be avoided entirely. But because of this there was always a place to park, which was why I'd assumed we'd come here. Only years later did it occur to me that Naomi had gone looking for it, that it was a place she'd watched for during our first drive and had dreamed of afterward, so close by it must have seemed genie-granted, and it was along this strip of two-lane road, hidden in plain sight, that she and I could be alone.

Naomi cut the engine. I watched her keys stop swinging in the ignition switch. She tucked her right foot beneath her leg and turned to face me—the car's seats were wide enough for that—her mouth close enough to mine that I could smell her breath. We talked for a while. I'd been having a terrible time and explained everything as best I could. When I finished, Naomi said something encouraging and, under cover of my brightening expression, leaned across the console and kissed me.

She gently pressed her lips to my cheek, and her hair fell across my face, but instead of breaking away she remained still. An even greater silence settled over the car. My mouth was urged toward her ear's small hillock with a soft nudge of her temple, and my indrawn breath caused her to shiver. She retreated, albeit slowly, pulling back until the moment the edges of our parted lips brushed each other's. On this verge, Naomi delicately reached out to lay her palm against my shoulder. And then she closed her eyes, which I saw because I stole a glance at her now upturned face, at her mysterious expression, which was as much like an inward search for a muscle's painful knot, for its precise locus, as it was the enjoyment of something abstract, so that she appeared to be listening to an almost too beautiful piece of music. Because I was an actor and knew the role I was inhabiting, I could perform these gestures along with her, utter the same soft sounds—mirroring her, as if it were an exercise, while remaining utterly aloof. We saw each other many times during that month, always returning to this place, carefully approaching this boundary and considering what lay beyond it, just as Oren and I stood with our fingers laced through the chain link. For a time, her hesitance was inviolate, a line she'd drawn between us that I instinctually realized was dependent upon me to cross. But because I was only a boy and inexperienced in these matters, I did not know how.

Nor would I necessarily have done so, given the chance. The truth was that I felt no physical desire for her—not then, at least. What I *did* want, what I desperately needed, was her audience. Hers was a great comfort I could find nowhere else, but securing it required I take on a specific role: one of a young man who seemed outwardly confident but was inwardly unsure, a watchful boy so lacking in adult guidance he'd been forced, in nearly all matters, to improvise. Every time I saw her that year, I did the very thing required of me whenever I stepped in front of the camera: I played myself.

On Saturday mornings, Dad, Oren, and I took the subway downtown to Elliott's Gramercy Park office. On the weekends, the trains seemed to pause longer on the platforms, leaving a quieter wake as they disappeared down the tunnels. Elliott's office was on the first floor of an apartment building, with a separate entrance that faced the gated park. You walked down a half flight of steps, then made a left at the end of a dark hallway into the small waiting room, against whose walls were arranged several chairs. The space had five offices: if you were standing in its entrance, then the one to your immediate left belonged to Elliott; the one directly across from you, on the far wall, was used by his daughter, Deborah, also a psychologist; his son-in-law, Eli, a psychiatrist and sex therapist, had the office to the right of hers; to the right of Eli's, on the adjacent wall, was the office leased to a psychologist named Brian, memorable, back then, for his size—he was six-six, easily. There was also a darkened, unoccupied office with a phone—this between Elliott's and Deborah's—of which my father often availed himself to "check in with his service" for messages, in spite of the fact that it was the weekend and local calls weren't free. When he excused himself to do this, it also required he close the door. I too closed the door, sneaking in once Dad and Elliott had started their session and pressing my ear to the wall, but I couldn't hear anything beyond a low mumble.

Nor was anything audible from the waiting room. A small noise-canceling machine emitted a wet, staticky sound that made eavesdropping impossible. Some mornings, Al Moretti was there, and he and my father immediately engaged in conversation that was impossible to ignore, since both men were incapable of whispering. Finally, Elliott appeared. There was a great whoosh at his door opening, like the breaching of an air lock, followed by an outrush, a gust, of emotion—a complicated current of condolence, gratitude, and relief buoying a patient as they made their way out the door, dreamy, happy, clearly having just wept, and sometimes all of the above.

Dad went first, he and Elliott often departing for a walk come rain or shine. To kill time, Oren and I often brought along our baseball mitts or a football and were just as often discouraged by the street's doormen, and so we reconciled ourselves to reading the magazines—*Time, Newsweek,* or the *Economist*—which in my case meant looking at the pictures and graphs. The boredom was profound. If Al Moretti deigned to talk to us (this only after Dad had left), the conversations were brief. "How's school goin'?" he'd ask, and while we muttered, "Fine," or made the effort to mention a book we were reading or subject we were studying, he'd trace a knuckle against the wall, considering the picture only he could see in the wallpaper. When we were finished, he'd say, "Well, work *hahd.*" Then he'd shake his head with disgusted remorse and, frowning viciously, add, "God knows I didn't."

Oren went second, glumly entering Elliott's office and exiting a half hour later even more abashed, slumping in his chair afterward and hiding his face behind a periodical.

I always went last.

In our household, Elliott was referred to so often it was a bit like belonging to a cult. "You know what Elliott calls *that,*" Dad said, nodding over his shoulder after a guy carrying a boom box passed us. "Ego boundaries." Or of attorneys: "Know Elliott's name for them? *The Gray People.*" (This in spite of the fact that his son, Matthew, was a lawyer.) I might tell Mom, "It bothers me when Dad gets up from the dinner table to take calls from his agency," or "How come Dad's eye twitches when he lies?" or, in a bit of real nastiness, "Who is Dad calling every time we go to see Elliott?"; and, after pausing to inwardly smile at the confirmation of her grievances, at the fact that her dissatisfactions were grounded in a shared reality, she'd respond, without fail, "You should talk to Elliott about that." In Dad's case, I might ask, "Why does Mom sometimes slur her words at night?" or "Why does Mom say none of your friends are her friends?" or "How come every time we ask Mom why she's crying she says it's private?" to which he'd shake his head, in a bid, I always thought, for kinship or allegiance, and reply, "Your mother is a complicated woman." In this way, it wasn't just my questions or concerns about my parents that were to be likewise outsourced but also their questions about each other.

Elliott waved me into his office, and indicated I should close the door, after which I sat. He too sat quietly for a while, writing several notes on a scratch pad with a silver Space Pen, which I coveted. I knew not to disturb him as he gathered his thoughts about Oren, but I still peeked unsuccessfully at his elegant microscript, wondering what he might have to scribble about me later. Elliott was roundish and short. He always wore a bespoke suit to work, its solid colors trending from navy blue to black, his shirts monogrammed on the cuff, his chin hiding his tie's fat knot behind his wattle. The room was illuminated by a single lamp on the side table. A tall, framed, Japanese painting of a frog hung on the wall between us, looming in the semidarkness, an elegant creature I thought strongly resembled Elliott himself—the pair of them squat, large-eyed, wide-mouthed, and lacking a neck.

"Well, sir," Elliott would finally say, still not entirely focused, removing his readers and carefully placing them in their case, "what have you got for me?" And this question magically erased every subject my parents suggested I discuss with him as well as any I might have brought up on my own. Most Saturdays, this led to much blathering on my part, the usual child-adult pabulum, broader in scope but as shallow in content as my brief chats with Al, and several minutes into my update, without fail, Elliott would begin to doze.

This was my favorite part of therapy. I'd continue talking as his lids got heavy—bemoaning my struggles in math, say, or expressing my excitement about the approach of wrestling season—waiting for him to nod off, his body listing sideways while I counted his catnap's seconds, beginning a new subject the moment he snapped awake, just to see if he was listening, which he was not.

"Is that right?" Elliott asked, his eyes red-rimmed and glassy, and I'd continue down this different path, enjoying myself in an animal-trainer sort of way, watching Elliott drift again, trying to beat his previous snooze's duration, counting Mississippis until his head jerked violently and he said, "How about we go for a walk?"

The air was good for us both. But my bafflement, now that we were outside, was suddenly more extreme. It was not simply that I'd forgotten what to say but seemed to have nothing to say whatsoever, my inner life rendered so utterly void I wondered if I possessed one at all. In Elliott's presence, I was like a Magic Eight Ball whose insides held only an inky darkness, and rather than dwell on these disturbing facts, I shifted my concern to more immediate matters, like whether we'd be stopping at the Second Avenue diner for an egg cream.

In response, Elliott filled the silence with a monologue. To these I made a great show of listening, which doesn't mean I was deaf to his speechifying. He was a master of the aphorism, and for years I contemplated Elliott's more brilliant and sometimes obscure epigrams, which he delivered as his anecdotes' punch lines. As we cut through the gated park—Elliott had a key—rather than walk around it, he'd say, "In all journeys, take the hypotenuse." Or at the diner, while I sipped my chocolate, "Strong swimmers often drown."

Years later, I'd find myself echoing one of these or realize I had incorporated one into a tale of mine to a friend. *One can resist anything except temptation,* I might say, or *If life is cyclical, lengthen your diameter.* But during this particular session, mere days after Naomi had kissed me for the first time, I idly asked, "Why do married people cheat on each other?"

He grabbed my arm at this and, suddenly more engaged than he'd ever been with me before, said, "Why do you ask?"

"I don't know," I responded, and concerned I might give something away, added, "I saw it on *The Love Boat.*"

Elliott resumed walking with one hand thrust in his pocket while he gestured with the other. "Some people never wanted to be married in the first place. They liked the general idea but had no idea the enterprise required they bind their lives to someone else's, to the limits they impose. Still others marry their problems rather than another person. So for them, cheating on their spouse is like a vacation from a job they hate but are too afraid to quit." Now he placed a hand on my shoulder and raised his finger to indicate I should pay close attention. "But mostly, infidelity is a case of what I like to call the practical use of other people." He began walking again. "We start to feel invisible to the person with whom we're most intimate. We desperately want to be *seen* by them. But rather than address it with our partner and, God forbid, risk them ignoring us, we instead seek to become the apple of someone else's eye, which causes us to drift further from our beloved until they finally notice our absence. Or don't. Which confirms our invisibility either way." Elliott stopped again for emphasis. "And *that* absolves us from the responsibility of owning our feelings." Pleased that I was taking this all in, he shrugged. "Of course, some people cheat just to blow up their lives."

"Why do that?" I asked.

"Because it's *exciting* to rebuild," Elliott said. "There's so much to do. Divorce is as big a commitment as marriage, and then being in love all over again leaves barely a moment for introspection. Plus, it's a chance to start over. Get your hands dirty. Flex muscles you haven't used in years. The possibilities seem limitless! I'll get it right this time! It's like that odd feeling of optimism you get when you see a town leveled by a tornado. But that's an illusion. Our history is always with us. You following?"

I wasn't, so I nodded.

"There's not a person in the world who's yet been able to entirely fulfill another's needs," Elliott continued. "For some people this is as disappointing as it is unacceptable."

"So how do you stop it from happening?" I asked.

"Infidelity, or disappointment?" Elliott said. He chuckled. He had green eyes that slit handsomely when he smiled, and I could tell he was deeply pleased that after eight years of therapy we'd finally got on to a subject worth talking about. "Well, for one thing, you lower your expectations. Nobody's perfect, most especially you. Best to perfect yourself before finding fault with your partner."

I nodded, even more confused.

"But as a precautionary measure," he said, and in preparation to stick the landing he paused for emphasis, "never put yourself in a situation where biology can take over." And then he winked.

As was common practice after my session, Dad briefly met with Elliott behind his office's half-closed door. The pair spoke urgently, their voices pitched low. Oren, wearing a bitter, knowing expression, elbowed me and nodded toward the office.

"Hear that?" he whispered.

I tried but couldn't decipher the mumbling.

"He's telling Dad everything we said."

What a relief it was, on those October afternoons, stepping off the bus at Columbus Avenue and crossing Broadway to spot Naomi's car parked outside Juilliard, to catch a glimpse of Naomi's face in the side mirror, to watch her read the *Times* while I reveled in my invisibility. I'd call to her, telepathically, until she looked up, our eyes meeting, she smiling first, only to frown in a pantomime of my troubled expression. *What's wrong, sweetie?* Now, thinking back on those entrances I made, it was as if I'd arrived wearing one of Elliott's masks, my expressions were so big. Frustrated, when I tossed my book bag to the floor once I took the seat next to her. Forlorn, my elbow propped on the door and fist mashed to my cheek as I watched Amsterdam flash by. She'd shoot me quick looks during that two-block drive, twisting the steering wheel in her hands or honking at the car ahead of us, its driver slow to notice the light had changed. Our arrival at the Dead Street, the slow cruise for a parking space, and, once Naomi had paralleled, both of us briefly exiting the Mercedes to get in back, so that there was no console separating us. One afternoon, when I was very sad, I paused for a moment to listen to the highway; and then, before opening the door, I stared up at the fence that ran along the top of the long garage facing us and thought of the park above it, the green space on whose fields Oren and I had often played. From up there we'd try to spot the baseballs we'd fouled to this street, even though we considered them as good as gone, and then gaze at that great overgrown expanse, its grasses swaying in the breeze. Why *did* I hesitate? Was it because my parents were so close by? Because things between Naomi and me were becoming dangerous? She smiled over the car's roof, but then she waited for a moment after I got in. I couldn't see her face, but she hesitated too, gripping the door handle, her other hand briefly pressed to the window so that her fingertips appeared dotted where they touched the glass. Was she looking up and down the block? Was she asking herself, *What am I doing?* before joining me in the back seat. But soon we were in each other's arms. *"Ohh,"* she'd whisper, drawing out the syllable, the submerged silence that followed. Our bathyspheric breathing. Some part of me remained aware of time, as is appropriate underwater. There was no fumbling to unbutton, to unzip or unclasp, which, due to my ignorance and Naomi's restraint, guaranteed that we'd return to that same calm I've described, that precipice on which we'd arrive and where she, with the tenderest touch—palm pressed to my shoulder—stopped us from walking off of. She gathered me to her afterward, hugging me hard. It was at these moments, waiting to commence conversation, that I was strangely disengaged. My chin pinned atop Naomi's shoulder, I might part her hair from my eyes to watch raindrops dot the pane.

Later, faces flushed, the windows slightly steamed, Naomi shrank down in her seat so that we were at eye level. She took my hand, pressed her elbow to mine, and then swung the metronome our conjoined limbs formed between us.

When would it be my turn to speak?

HALF DAY

Earlier that morning, I'd been woken by Dad's soft whistle, a several-note trill from my earliest childhood that could instantly rouse me from deepest sleep. My clock read 4:55. He waited by my top bunk while I rearranged my pillows and, once I sat up, handed me coffee, which he'd made *au lait,* with three sugars, the way I liked it.

"Here you go, boychik," he whispered, and, before returning to the kitchen, added, "I've got your breakfast going."

On my comforter there lay everything I'd left unfinished: *Romeo and Juliet,* Act III partially read; my lab report on boiling points and surface tension, incomplete; my algebra textbook open, this afternoon's quiz unstudied for. My mind cast forward, searching the next ten hours for time, discrete stretches when I might finish these tasks before each came due, one's completion paradoxically pushing me further back from the next, as if the day were somehow expanding from the middle and might never end.

"All set?" Dad asked when I took my seat at the dining table. He was holding a pan of scrambled eggs. He nodded toward the math I'd brought to review, though I knew his question wasn't referring to that.

"Ready," I lied.

"How're you getting there?"

"I thought I'd grab the bus."

Dad checked his watch, then shrugged, mildly irritated. He hated the idea of my possibly being late. "The train's faster."

This was exactly why I preferred the bus. It was still dark when I arrived at the Columbus Avenue stop, and the vehicle's illuminated interior seemed to float toward me. Through the bus's tall windshield, I noted its handrails narrowing toward its tail and resembling a whale's ribbed gullet. Upon boarding, I walked to the back and took the corner seat, and then slid open the window so that the breeze might mitigate the diesel fumes. I opened my book bag, considering all the things I could study in the meantime. I pulled out *Romeo and Juliet* and was about to commence reading, when one of my lines came to me in its entirety: *A proton is a subatomic particle with a positive electric charge and mass slightly less than that of a neutron.*

I placed the play on the empty seat next to me and took out today's shooting script. I studied it for a couple of stops and then promptly fell asleep.

We taped *The Nuclear Family* at NBC Studios, in Rockefeller Center, on the 8H soundstage, where they did *Saturday Night Live*. This was our fourth season. The show had been a hit. In a normal year, from June through August, I lived at 30 Rock from dawn till dusk, but come September, once school had started, I was on call two or three mornings a week, shooting for half days but never past lunch, until we wrapped— sometimes as late as the last week of October, when we ceded the space to the *SNL* cast. This schedule had been put in place two years ago, when I entered seventh grade, built into my contract at my mother's insistence, after I'd been accepted to Boyd Preparatory Academy, an Upper West Side private school, so as not to, in her words, "interfere with my education." The intention was laughable, especially with the current season in turmoil because of the actors' strike, which had just resolved. We'd been in rehearsal since the beginning of the month in an effort to complete the final few episodes at warp speed. These past few weeks, I'd missed more school than usual and was drowning.

On these mornings my routine never deviated. I stopped by my dressing room, dropped off my book bag, and hurried to costume. Alison,

who ran that department, greeted me in a husky voice that was neither
too friendly nor too warm—"Good morning, kid" was all she'd say. She
was seated at her sewing table reading the *Times,* drinking a cup of coffee and smoking. She glanced at me over her bifocals, nodded toward
my costume on the hanging rack, and then returned to the paper. When
not in his super suit, Peter Proton wore a short-sleeved button-down,
a pocket protector quivered with pens, and suspenders decorated with
physics equations that yanked my already too-high cuffs above my ankles
and, due to a malfunction I hadn't noticed until this season and was terribly self-conscious about, revealed the outline of my balls.

"Can we fix this?" I asked Alison. I was standing before her three-
faced mirror while she made adjustments. With my hands I indicated my
crotch's protuberant, cloven hoof.

"Tom likes it," she said, referring to the director. This was her way
of ensuring someone else always had to say no. She placed my Groucho
Marx specs on my face and then let out my pants' waist. My growth
spurt, raging since the spring—I'd shot up four inches—showed no signs
of slowing, and when Alison struggled to button the collar of my widened neck, she mumbled, around a mouthful of straight pins, "You're
absolutely killing me."

I had to hurry to hair and makeup. Nicole dealt with me first, silently
daubing my cheeks with base and then lining my eyes until they stood
out so vividly my caked face seemed to hover just above my skin. After
she handed me off, Freddie roughly affixed my wig to its cap and then
teased its blown-back curls into an even more shocked shape. He did this
with a fist to his hip, his comb tugging at my head, swiveling me by my
shoulders with pointed disregard.

Liz always managed to appear just before we finished.

She could've been Naomi's younger, prettier sister. She wore large
glasses, their lenses as round and thick as a soda bottle's base, so that
when she removed them to rub her eyes or pinch her nose's bridge—as
she often did in my presence—it made her face appear to shrink. She
wore her hair in a Dorothy Hamill bob, but her clothes were as revealing as a male skater's unitard: painted-on Jordache jeans and tight-fitting
designer tees—today's read PIZZA EATERS MAKE BETTER LOVERS.
Both she and Naomi had the same gummy smile, but Liz's teeth jutted

slightly forward. Standing before me now, she held open an enormous black binder containing the day's shooting script.

"Well?" she asked.

"I think I've got it." I didn't want her to embarrass me in front of Freddie and Nicole.

Liz fed me a line.

"Maybe if we started from the top," I said.

"That was the top," she replied.

Freddie mushed his mouth in his hand and shook his head.

"You don't know any of this, do you?" Liz said.

When I didn't answer, she snapped her binder closed. "I'll tell Tom we're going to need more time." Then she marched off to our usual spot.

This was in the middle of the soundstage, on a pair of director's chairs, these placed off camera before the set of Central High's physics classroom. The space was brightly illuminated amid a pool of darkness. 8H was hangar-sized, so vast I'd once enjoyed a memorable game of catch with Kevin Savage—he played Central High's quarterback—the pair of us threading a Nerf football beneath the lighting racks and hanging cable wires, through set windows and over their walls, each of us calling our throw's path like shots in pool, until Ken Wakanata the cameraman put a stop to our game and then cursed me out. "Hey, fuckwit. Knock down one of those Fresnels and you'll get someone killed." He spared Kevin the lashing, even when he came to my aid, but to whom would I complain about the injustice? "He should know better," Ken told him, and then stormed off.

Now I approached Liz unseen and, for a moment, I paused to relish the silence. The soundstage was as quiet as a submarine. It was muffled by the velvet curtains lining its walls, the balcony's empty seats adding to the bunkered effect. Thunderstorms might be raging outside, a hurricane making landfall, but here you'd be completely insulated from such weather. It confounded my inner clock. Hours crept by but months evaporated, from June through August the twilit sky was the same purple as the dawn's, the only evidence any time had passed the stifling heat, the sun's light now stored in the asphalt and radiating up instead of shining down, my own core temperature similarly elevated, but by rage at yet another summer lost.

Liz sat in one of the director's chairs with her arms crossed, her binder open across her lap. She popped her high-heeled shoe against her heel.

It might've helped me learn my part a bit faster if Liz supplied some emotion. Instead, she delivered her lines in a relentless monotone. Her disdain for me exceeded anyone else's in the cast or crew and had been a constant since the show's inception, so that my fantasies about her proceeded not from lust but rather a desire for her kindness. "From the top," she said each time I drew a blank. My shame was intense and my concentration shot. After I flubbed another line, Liz said, "Take a look at who's waiting on you. It's selfish and it's unprofessional."

"Hey," Andy said to her. "Ease up a bit."

Andy Axelrod, who played my dad, appeared before us, wearing his Nate Neutron costume. He was carrying his fishbowl helmet beneath his arm, his super suit silver and puffy as an astronaut's. Inset on his chest were his initials, enclosed by the overlapping Bohr model ovals.

"How about I finish up?" he offered Liz. Then he smiled at me reassuringly. "It's our scene, after all."

Liz said, "Be my guest."

When Andy sat, his suit aspirated and gave off a farty odor, like skin beneath a plaster cast. His freckled pate, hot from the lights, shined beneath his comb-over. We rehearsed for fifteen minutes, and when it was clear I had my lines down, Andy patted my knee and said, "Look, Griffin, I know you've got a lot going on. But try to keep in mind that these people get here early just for you. Get my drift?"

I did. "Thanks for sticking up for me," I said.

"That's what dads are for."

Andy was the person with whom I spent the most time on set. Elyse Baxter, who played my mom, avoided both of us. For the twenty-somethings in featured roles as high school students and archvillains, Andy was probably too close to the age and appearance of the fathers most of them had moved to the city to get away from, while I was like their annoying little brother. We were both shunned in our own ways, although Andy was invited to laugh at bloopers; if he broke character to lighten the mood or improvise when a scene was going poorly, it was appreciated. Because I had not earned such freedoms, my wandering off script was met with disapproval. And while I recognized that we'd been lumped together, I was not always ungrateful for his company. We discussed sports and movies, and, like Elliott, Andy waded into current events and politics while I pretended to listen—although after Liz reappeared to check on our progress and then shimmy off, he returned to his favorite subject.

"My God," he said, and leaned toward me, "the tits on that woman." He lowered his voice. "I'd like a slice of her pie."

It was at this moment that I noticed Jack Terry, our soundman, silently roll up behind us on the crane and, from the basket, lower his boom until it hovered just out of view. He caught my eye, tapped his headphones to indicate the mic was hot, and then winked.

"What about Noreen?" I asked. She played the captain of Central High's cheerleading squad. "She's just as pretty."

"Not if you're an ass man," Andy said.

"My dad says Elyse still has a dancer's figure."

"Only if he means a whirling dervish," Andy replied. "Nope, her gifts are strictly oral. Which reminds me of a joke. What do you call a woman who can suck a golf ball through a garden hose?"

I shrugged.

"Gifted."

Chuckling, Andy reached out to squeeze my shoulder, shaking his head. "Son, you've got your whole life ahead of you. You fuck your brains out. I mean it. Chase tail until you're fifty, *then* think of settling down. Are you still a virgin?"

I tilted my hand side to side as if to say, *More or less.*

"Let me give you a piece of advice. You want to get in a girl's pants, the next time you go on a date, you take her to a nice place—chichi, low-lit, you spare *no* expense. I'm talking appetizers, entrées, *and* dessert. The *works.* You pull out her chair when it's time to leave, give her your arm when you walk her home, and at her door you be the *perfect gentleman.* You kiss her on the cheek, a little tongue if she's interested, but that's all. Say good night, and here's the most important part: do *not* call her for two weeks. Tell her you were busy, you lost her number, it doesn't matter. But you go radio silent like that, and she'll be so frantic trying to figure out what she did wrong she will be your sex slave afterward."

I nodded as I considered his counsel, catching, out of the corner of my eye, Jack's A-OK gesture.

"Remember," Andy said. "Two kinds of men succeed with women: those who love them and those who hate them."

At this, I perked up. "Which are you?"

"I despise them. Except my wife, of course."

"I didn't know you were married."

"Twenty years. She's coming to the wrap party next week," Andy said, and then elbowed me. "Word on the street is that Tom's gonna share a prank he's played on the cast. Got any intel on that?"

Jack raised his boom, giving me the thumbs-up while the crane silently backed into the darkness. Tom's voice came over the PA. In the background, the control room was raucous with laughter.

"Gentlemen," Tom said, "places in five."

"Aye, aye, Captain," said Andy.

"Sorry for the holdup," I told Tom.

"My dear boy," he answered, "you are *completely* forgiven."

Because I was late to school, I took a cab instead of the bus. It was nearly eleven, third period was ending. If traffic kept moving, I'd make it to English—my favorite class. We took the Avenue of the Americas north. I had my window down, and when we hung the left on Central Park South, I saw several horse-drawn carriages lining the entrance. Attending them was the earthy smell of manure mixed with the smoke of almonds from the vendor's cart, a waft that seemed to name the season. I decided to skim the end of Act III of *Romeo and Juliet,* but just before I searched my book bag, we swung around Columbus Circle, and I spotted, on my right, my father, sitting on the edge of the *Maine* National Monument's pool, next to a beautiful woman, to whom he spoke very heatedly. Because of the speed and the fact that my eye followed them amid the pedestrians and traffic, they came into vivid focus: the woman, raven-haired, heavily made up, sitting with her elbows on her knees, staring into the distance and frowning while Dad lividly gestured. Were they having a fight? Before I could begin to marvel at the odds of this happenstance—of seeing him, of all people, at this moment—before I could even process what he was doing with this person and by the time we were several blocks past them, I realized I'd left my copy of the play on the bus. For the second time in a week. Miss Sullens, my teacher, would kill me. I pressed the heels of my hands to my eyes and whispered, *"Why, why, why,"* until we arrived at Boyd Prep.

I was in a rush. But Mr. Kepplemen, my wrestling coach, intercepted me the moment I was through the upper school foyer's second set of glass doors. In greeting, he pressed his hand to my cheek and pulled my temple toward his so that they lightly touched.

"When's your next free period?" he asked.

"Fifth," I replied. I was late for fourth period, but no matter. If English was my favorite class, wrestling was my life. And with the season beginning in November, I had all the time for Kepplemen in the world.

"Meet me in the lockers then," Kepplemen said. "Lineups," he added, and shook his finger at me, "to discuss."

I told him, "For sure," and, released, broke into a run that was partly to make up time, partly excitement at the prospect of a starting position on the varsity.

Any happiness I felt was obliterated the moment I entered the classroom.

The discussion stopped as if I'd been its subject—I *had,* it turned out. The act of removing my binder was attended by a mysterious suspense, which Miss Sullens dispelled by approaching my desk. She held my paper in hand and returned this facedown. She taught class in the round, and everyone watched as I registered its grade and comment, written in red capitals and visible through the loose leaf: *Fail—see me afterward.* Cliffnotes, my best friend—he was seated across from me—nodded toward Simon Pilchard, to his right, incriminatingly, which cleared up nothing. For the period's remainder I sat slumped and stunned, plunged, as I was, in silence, breaking only when the bell finally rang.

Miss Sullens directed me to her office, a series of three cubicles. She started in on me the moment she took a seat. "I'd be remiss," Miss Sullens said, her cheeks aflame, "if I didn't tell you I feel betrayed."

I was thankful my back was to the door, because even though I didn't know what I'd done, I admired Miss Sullens so much that tears filled my eyes.

"And the disappointment . . ." she said, and then paused. "The utter embarrassment was compounded by the fact that I began class by reading *your* paragraph aloud. Because it was exemplary, so far as I was concerned. A *model*. And I was about to give it the highest possible grade when someone pointed out that you'd plagiarized."

"I don't understand," I said. I had no clue what "plagiarized" meant.

Miss Sullens pinched my essay between her fingers and placed it on her desk between us. Then she opened her copy of *Romeo and Juliet* to the summary preceding Act II.

"This says"—and in the paperback she pointed to a double-underlined sentence—"'Meanwhile, Romeo has succeeded in leaping over the Capulets' garden wall and is hiding beneath Juliet's balcony.' *You* write, 'Romeo, meanwhile, is hiding beneath Juliet's balcony after leaping over the garden wall of the Capulets.'"

My eyes darted between both pieces of writing. "But I rearranged the words."

Still holding the book, Miss Sullens shook her head and considered me for a moment. "Griffin," she finally said, "you tried to pass off these thoughts as your own. People get expelled for this. There is *no more* serious offense in academics. Do you understand?"

"I didn't know," I said. This was the absolute truth. I had always done this.

Miss Sullens sighed and then sat up straight. She was a tall, broad-shouldered woman. The ends of her hair were roughly cut, as if with safety scissors. I could not meet her eyes. Instead, I looked over her shoulder, at the framed picture on her desk I'd often wondered about, of her sailing on a small outrigger, in northeastern waters the color of iron, with a woman who appeared to be her sister. Was this why her lips were so freckled? Miss Sullens lowered her voice. "I believe you," she said to me. "But that doesn't excuse it." The second bell rang. "You'll fail this assignment and rewrite it." She got up. "We'll discuss this further, but right now I have another class."

Cliffnotes was waiting for me outside. "Are you in trouble?" he asked.

We started walking down the empty hallway. I wasn't sure how to answer, "trouble" being more of an environment in which I existed than a temporary state. Even now I was late to meet Coach Kepplemen.

Cliff cupped his hand to tame his cowlick; his inner lips, permanently scabbed by his orthodontia, shined wetly. "It was Simon Pilchard," he said. "He ratted you out."

We stopped.

"When Miss Sullens read your essay, he raised his hand and told her he didn't know we could use the summary like that."

"No shit."

"You gonna fuck him up?"

"Something royal."

"Ready for math?"

"No."

"I'm free now if you want my help."

"Later," I said. "Coach Kepplemen wants to talk lineups."

"Catch you on the rebound," Cliff said.

We did our secret handshake, double slaps high low plus thumb snaps, and then I jetted.

In the locker room, Coach Kepplemen said, "Let's check your weight."

He had a carny's eye for our mass, and he liked to amaze us by accurately picking a number before the Detecto scale rendered its exact judgment. He slid the larger poise's tooth into the hundred-pound groove. Then he pushed the smaller one so that it hissed along the top beam till he tapped it, at thirty, to a stop. I stepped onto the platform. The balance rose, inexorably, bouncing once, twice, and then settling to a stop: 130 pounds. Kepplemen's eyes, wide-set and watery, were gloomy with disappointment. Before he could ask, I stepped off, dropping my drawers in the same motion, and, back on the scale, exhaled so hard my shoulders hunched.

Kepplemen shrugged, shook his head. His nose, long and broad at the bridge, dominated his face. He had covered his mouth with his hand in a sign of concern, and this made his prominent beak seem larger.

"It's just a pound," I said.

He shook his head. "Swain," he said. He meant Frank Swain, a junior. "He's sucking down from one thirty-five." I couldn't beat Frank on my best day.

I bit my fingernail, spit it out. The balance didn't move.

"What if I dropped to one twenty-one?"

Kepplemen brightened. "Can you make it?"

"Is the slot open?"

Kepplemen nodded. "It's all yours."

"Not a problem then." My confidence, my willingness to cut the weight, lightened Kepplemen's mood. Before I could bend to pull on my briefs, he collected the hair at my scruff and gave me a loving shake. He eyeballed me—we were the same height—from head to toe. "Christ, Griffin, you're so fucking big. How much have you grown since last season?"

"Four inches." I was five-ten now, though I hadn't filled out. Over Labor Day, when my father and I had gone to Brooks Brothers for my back-to-school shopping, there was no containing his frustration. "You can't keep me in clothes," I said to Kepplemen, parroting Dad when he'd complained to the tailor.

Relieved, Kepplemen said, "We're set," and I nodded, thrilled. A starting position! As if to sign the agreement, he reached out and palmed both my ears, gently knocked my forehead to his. Then he left while I got dressed.

I hurried to find my friends. In the few minutes before fifth period ended and lunch began, people congregated in the upper school's long front hallway, which was lined with pews on which we sat in our respective cliques. I spotted Simon Pilchard. Seated, he was circled by three friends. He was also a wrestler—tiny, a ninety-eight-pounder. There was no faculty present, so I walked over, broke through their ring, and cuffed Pilchard's forehead with my palm's heel, knocking his skull against the wall.

"The *hell*, Griffin?" Pilchard said.

"That's for English," I said, and then joined my friends at the pew across from them. Cliffnotes stood, check-swinging a baseball bat. He was a die-hard Yankees fan. The World Series had just ended, and although he was happy Kansas City had lost—they'd beat the Bronx Bombers in the pennant—he was mourning the season's conclusion. Tanner Potts, my other best friend, was seated before him, tossing a wadded piece of paper in the air and catching it.

"Just talked to Kepplemen," I said to them. "I'm starting."

"No way," Cliff said, and took his stance. "What weight?"

I sat next to Tanner. "One twenty-one."

Tanner said, "Have you got that to cut?"

"I'd drop to one-fifteen if I had to."

"That wasn't the question," Tanner said, and tossed the wad toward Cliff.

Cliff swung the bat and hit a line drive. Pilchard, who was walking up behind him—to apologize, I figured, or explain himself—caught the barrel right on the nose.

It sounded like a light bulb bursting. Pilchard cupped his face in both hands. Blood dribbled down his chin. He turned in a circle, taking a handful of paper towels from Cliff, who'd raced to the bathroom. Miss Sullens, who was walking by, suggested he come with her to the nurse's office. They departed soon after, Pilchard with his head tilted ceiling-ward, Miss Sullens leading him by the elbow.

Tanner, who had neither moved nor reacted during the episode, said, "That's broken."

Cliff took this as blame; his voice rose an octave. "He walked right up behind me!"

The bell rang for lunch.

"I'll meet you guys there," he said glumly. "I should probably go see how Pilchard's doing."

My mood had lightened. My sorrow over Miss Sullens spent, my starting slot secured, I felt a great load lift. I still had an algebra quiz to bomb, but I was for all intents and purposes back in sync with Boyd's rhythms, the reset button pressed. After eating, I went to the locker room to weigh myself again. Nine pounds to lose, if I didn't count what I'd just gained at lunch. I considered my naked self in the full-length mirror. Stoked, I did a couple of bicep flexes. I thought about Naomi dreamily for a moment, about seeing her this afternoon and telling her my news—that things were looking up! Then I heard the bell ring and cursed. After dressing, I raced to get my book bag and then ran to Introductory Physical Science. The second bell rang before I arrived. Miss Brodsky, who had a quicker fuse than any upper school teacher, paused her instructions to the class. Already mid-lab, she greeted me with *"Why?"* and when I began to explain she cut me off with *"Enough"* and then ordered me—*"There"*—to my station.

Cowed, I took my stool next to my lab partner, Deb Peryton. She shook her head at me and tsk-tsked. She regularly wore baggy, knitted turtlenecks that hid her figure, but she also liked to wear dusty-pink lipstick on lips I sometimes imagined kissing. She frowned at me, coyly. "Nice of you to join us," she said. Here I was, late again, and as usual failing to pull my weight. But Deb was either not immune to my charms or took a special kind of pity on me. She was also a science whiz, thank God, and because our lab grade was a shared one, she let me copy from her notebook whenever necessary, a task I hurriedly began. We were comparing the boiling points of various liquids, and our test tubes—Bunsen burners blackening their bases—bubbled merrily, the white smoke thickly rising from their tops like Newark's industrial chimneys.

At the station across from ours, Tanner was showing off for Justine Keaton. "Ready for a magic trick?" he said to her. From a wash bottle, he squeezed some burner fuel into his cupped hand. Justine pressed her shoulder to his while she stared at his palm. "Watch closely," Tanner said, as if she weren't already. He lit and then touched a match to the pool, upon which the liquid burst into a small cloud of flame that immediately disappeared. Justine jumped, covering her mouth while she laughed. "Presto," Tanner said.

For Deb's enjoyment I attempted the same stunt. "Check this out," I told her, and began to fill my palm with the fluid, a few runnels coursing down my wrist and covering the back of my hand.

Deb leaned back. "I don't think that's a very good idea," she said.

"Abracadabra," I said, and tapped a struck match to my palm.

Cuff to fingertips, my entire hand ignited. I screamed, then jumped from my stool, furiously beating the appendage against my leg until the conflagration was put out.

Miss Brodsky hurried over and was now bent double with me, looking with real concern as I examined my hand. She was holding a fire extinguisher. "Are you all right?" she asked.

The hair on my fingers was singed off, but the skin, now a brightening pink, was undamaged. I nodded.

"You're sure?" she said.

"Positive," I answered, and, taking a deep breath, stood up straight. Everyone was staring at us.

"Good," she replied, and then her expression darkened. *"Now go explain yourself to Mr. Fistly."*

I made the long walk to Mr. Fistly's office. When I arrived, I addressed myself to Miss Abbasi, the upper school secretary. "Is Mr. Fistly in?" I asked, as if we had a scheduled meeting. Miss Abbasi's ear for inflection was remarkable; she gave a dismissive nod in his door's direction, not a word more articulate than the disappointment she conveyed in that look and gesture: that I was back, that I remained on the radar, that I *never learned.*

Mr. Fistly kept his office lamp-lit, eschewing the overhead lights—it was an office for a reader. Along with his administrative duties, he taught a select British lit seminar. For those privileged students who intentionally found their way here to chat about, say, *Gulliver's Travels* (a favorite of his, I'd overheard), who were offered a seat across from his desk or perhaps on his couch, beside his wingback chair, where my parents and I had been called in to meet with him at the semester's start to discuss, in his words, "my inherently unique challenges" given my "middling middle school performance" and my "professional obligations," I imagined it was a very pleasant place to pass the time.

Upon entering, the rules of the exchange were inviolate: I was required to report exactly why I'd come and precisely what I'd done. He would tolerate no diminishment of my crime and absolutely no excuse. Film acting, my father liked to say, was all in the eyes, and while I incriminated myself, Fistly steadily gazed at me. His wavy reddish hair had the sculpted firmness of something detachable, like a barrister's wig. His large nose was pronouncedly hooked, more menacing because of the pride he took in its raptor-like prominence. He twiddled his thumbs while I talked. He studied me. He even chuckled when I got to my combustible moment—a breathy laugh that revealed his very long, straight teeth, though his brows remained frozen. Toward the end of my account, he began to flush in anticipation of his response, which, I realized, he'd been formulating ahead of my conclusion, and this high coloring, intensified by his chronic razor burn, blurred the line between fury and delight, for he was smiling when he spoke.

"In all my years in education," Fistly began, "I've found I cannot help but engage in what one might call a Darwinian specification of students.

This is not merely a categorization of certain types, like 'jock' or 'nerd,' but also an enumeration of their inherent qualities. It makes one more appreciative of Shakespeare's genius, he having comprehensively cataloged all of creation's characters, fool to king. Speaking of *fools,* I have always been fascinated by the class clown, by his desperate need to be the center of attention. The sadly *neurotic* way he shifts everyone's focus back to himself, in spite of the vital information his teacher is working so hard to impart. Now listen to me"—Fistly chuckled—"going on with my tiny observations, selfishly keeping you from learning science. Forcing you to lose *more* ground and making your already *woeful* academic standing more woeful still. Does that sort of behavior seem . . . familiar? You will serve detention this Saturday."

Math class, toward day's end, was where I took my final licks. After negotiating the first five problems with relative ease—these no different from our practice problems but for the numbers—there came that moment when I arrived at the sixth question, where I inevitably stumbled as I collected the variable terms and then dropped them so that they spilled everywhere. I could spend all day in this classroom and never realize its solution. I was also, I noticed, the only person sitting up. I gazed upon everyone's humped backs, listened to their pencil point taps, their eraser squeaks, the methodical tick of the clock, and what was clear to me, first and foremost, was that Fistly was right. I was losing more ground. My situation was unsustainable. And I prayed for a way out.

There was a knock at the door. Miss Abbasi entered, quietly apologized to the teacher for the intrusion, and then handed me a note.

CALL YOUR AGENT.

YOU HAVE AN AUDITION THIS AFTERNOON.

LOVE, DAD

Things couldn't go on like this. Not in November. Not once wrestling season started.

How to lose acting from this equation?

And then, with a cold certainty that strong math students must enjoy, it dawned on me I could subtract this term, at least for a while.

I turned in my quiz and, showing Mr. Graff the note, left the classroom and made straight for the school's pay phone in the front hall. When I called my father at his studio, I managed to contain my fury.

"It's a big deal," Dad said of my upcoming audition, "reading for a director like Paul Mazursky."

I didn't know who that was. "How long will you be at your office?" I asked.

"I have a booking at three."

While I tried to get my breathing under control, he said, "Everything okay?"

I told him I was fine. I said goodbye and then called Brent, my agent, who told me who Mazursky was, that he'd liked my work in *The Talon Effect,* and then he gave me the audition's address and time.

"Can you schedule it for earlier?" I asked.

"No can do," Brent said.

"Can you call my school and tell them I have to leave *now*?"

"What happened, Griff? Dog eat your homework again?"

"Something like that."

"Hey," Brent said, "whatever the talent needs."

I rejoined my math class already in progress and made a great show of listening. Within five minutes, Miss Abbasi reappeared and, excusing herself to Mr. Graff once more, handed me the note, which I in turn gave to my teacher.

I hopped the bus on Columbus Avenue downtown. It was almost two. I could catch my dad before he left his studio for his appointment. Traffic was light, and the vehicle, bashing over each pothole, made a great crash along its length, as if its scalloped steel siding might at any moment shake loose. This in-between time, before schools let out and the rush hour began, was stirring somehow. There were few pedestrians visible, and with the rest at work it was as if the city belonged to me. Because the bus was nearly empty, I had a clear view out all the windows, side to front, so I stood in the aisle's center and stretched out my arms to grab the straps, pretending that I was flying. The driver skipped two stops, gathering speed. We could see the streetlights change from red to green as far south as Seventy-Ninth, even below the planetarium, and we shared a private, communal giddiness—this rare break from the bus's halting progress and maybe from our own—our thoughts so perfectly aligned that he caught my eye in his giant rearview mirror and smiled. And when it was finally time to get off, I let the force transferred from the brakes carry me forward, palming the poles to slow my fall all the way to the front.

My father rented a small studio next to the Carnegie Deli. It was where he gave voice lessons, one of his side jobs, and took photographs (he'd taken the majority of his students' headshots), a skill he'd learned in the navy. On the space's far wall, he'd tacked a collection of their portraits to some pegboard so that the collage resembled an audience. Sometimes, on my bike rides home from elementary school, I made it a point to surprise my father and stop by, an interruption he rarely appreciated. Before knocking, a courtesy I also regularly neglected, I liked to listen to him teach from the hallway. The vocal exercises were sung to rising or falling scales, their tempo matched to a consonant's hardness or a syllable's length—words that taken together sounded like looping nonsense poems (*ma may me my mo moo ma*) designed to develop enunciation (*fee fi foh foo fum*), the phrases moving up each key until arriving at a register too high for the singer's bass or too low for their soprano, upon which they cracked into disharmony. There might be laughter after this—Dad's, the student's, or both—followed by some muted, technical instruction, perhaps even a demonstration by my father. These moments always made me proud, for his ability so obviously exceeded his pupils', and just before the resumption of the exercise I would enter unannounced—as I did now, since he was alone.

He greeted my appearance with bewilderment and looked at me questioningly, perhaps because he registered my anger. I had rehearsed our conversation on my ride here, steeling myself, and now pressed my advantage.

"How much longer do I have to do this?" I asked.

"I don't know what you mean."

"*The Nuclear Family*. Acting. *Everything*."

We'd had this fight before. It didn't take long for him to get his balance back. "Until your obligation is fulfilled."

"Are you talking about my contract? The season ends next week."

"We'll see if they want to renew."

"What if *I* don't want to renew?"

"It's not time to worry about that yet."

"I can't do both anymore." I said this more pleadingly than I'd have liked. "I've tried."

At this, Dad stood, although the upright piano was still between us. "You listen to me," he said. "I don't need to remind you how expensive your school is. Not to mention the fact that your grades these past two years have been unacceptable. Your mother and I expect them to improve. Or else."

"Or else what?"

"I'll pull you."

I had anticipated this move. He'd used it many times.

"Where were you this morning?" I asked. "I called you here and then at home."

Dad screwed up his expression.

"I called you around eleven," I said, bluffing.

"I was in a recording session," Dad said. "At BBD&O."

"No, you weren't. I saw you. On Columbus Circle. With a woman." I scanned his wall of faces and then pointed to the headshot. "Her," I said.

My father's eye twitched. "I don't know what you're talking about." He was a terrible liar.

"Wrestling season ends in February," I said. "No more auditions until then."

My father stuck out his lower lip and shrugged. It was an ambiguous gesture.

"Do we have a deal?" I asked.

"Deal," he said, and, like a conductor disappearing back into the pit, took his seat.

On the verge of becoming a man, there are times when I relished being a boy. Now, for instance, in the back seat of Naomi's car. Having concluded my story, I leaned into her outstretched arms, burying my wet face in her neck. "Oh, baby," she said, rocking me side to side. "You had a really bad day." Memory being what it is, I often wonder how I *actually* told her this tale. I'm sure it was more rudimentary, disorganized. That I'd hopped from one point of frustration to the next, so that it sounded like a list of complaints about a life that was unmanageable: I couldn't keep up with acting, with school; I'd disappointed Miss Sullens, I couldn't disappoint Coach; my father didn't care. What I *do* remember is this: when I'd finally calmed down, after Naomi took my cheeks in her palms and then kissed the corners of my eyes and pressed her lips to the edge of mine and I finally kissed her back—she suddenly stopped us. She made a great show of the effort this cost her as she gathered herself, although the effort was no act. And then she asked me a very simple question, one that revealed a key detail I'd left out and constituted the knot from which I could not figure out how to untangle myself.

"Why don't you just quit?" Naomi whispered. "The show, acting, all of it."

"Don't you understand?" I said, as if it were obvious. "I pay for my private school."

THE FIFTY-MINUTE HOUR

So began several weeks in which Naomi and I talked almost every day. She had questions from our previous conversation that she'd thought about the night before; I had things I realized I'd forgotten to tell her during our evening apart. It was strange how quickly the time passed when we were together. It made me hurry to meet her. I could not get from school to her car fast enough. The Columbus Avenue bus took forever and then, once I was in the Mercedes, the three-block drive from Juilliard to the Dead Street seemed endless. Fall in full swing now, the trees in Lincoln Towers' green space shed their leaves; beneath awnings, the heat lamps shined on passing pedestrians and conferred on them an orange rotisserie glow. With November's approach, there was an entirely different quality to the light that on overcast days imparted to the sky a color closer to granite, to the Hudson an even more forbidding opacity, a solidity, as if ore might be transmuted to liquid not by heat but rather cold. Naomi parked; we hurried to the back seat; we pretended we were rushing because of the frigid gusts off the water, which made my tie ripple and stiffen and Naomi's skirt snap. The doors slammed shut. Silence again. Often, we began to speak simultaneously. "You first," Naomi said. At some point, after what seemed like only minutes later, she'd glance at her watch and, with a tone close to regret, say, "I'm afraid we've run out of time," and my disappointment bordered on frustration, because it felt as if I was on the verge of something, of articulating a solution to a problem I could not name. It was *this* speechlessness at *this* moment that I found upsetting, a distress that Naomi seized on, and I allowed. She slid down in the seat; I did as well. With the back of her finger she might trace the line from my ear's lobe to my lips. She regarded me with an expression somewhere between wonder and caution, between curiosity and fear. She liked to kiss my eyes next, which I closed; she kissed her way toward the edge of my mouth, until I finally kissed her back. She sometimes took my hand nearest her hip and firmly pressed it to her knee, indicating that I was to touch her there—that I could, if I wished, lift her skirt's edge; that I was to feel her feeling my fingertips' progress along her thigh—and I confess this frightened me. Until, as a gentle means of pausing us, as both bookmark and interruption but now more in imitation of restraint, the wordless sounds she made became laughter. There was a feline growl to it, which didn't completely hide her nervousness and touched my heart. It was the only moment I thought she was acting.

Home soon and Mom had made dinner—tonight it was baked pork chops with mustard and rosemary and Rice-A-Roni, "the San Francisco treat," Dad said hungrily as he took his seat to my left, though he couldn't help shoot himself a look in the adjacent wall's mirrors, which I always faced, and subtly suck in his gut. Oren, sitting across from him, duly noted this and, rolling his eyes, shook his head in private disgust. Mom, who sat directly across from me, blocked my reflection. "How was your day?" she asked. "Anything to report?"

"Not really," I said, and—this still amazes me—I believed it.

Dad had already picked up his pork chop by its bone's tips and was chomping away.

"What are you going as for Halloween?" I asked my brother, because I hadn't given it a thought.

"Like I'm going to let you bite my style."

Of course, if disguise is your natural state, coming up with a costume is no easy matter.

"How," Naomi asked me one of these afternoons, "did you get started acting? Was it because of your father?" And I couldn't help it—I imi-

tated the long stress on the word's first syllable—*fa*-tha—which made
her laugh and then play-slap me. I told her about my first television
appearance. It took place at my elementary school, P.S. 59, when I was
in Miss Epstein's second grade class. She was an older lady, in her sixties.
Even then Miss Epstein seemed a throwback: pearled cat-eyed glasses,
schoolmarmish and severe in her wool dresses and white tights. Her
heavy shoes clopped ominously as she patrolled our aisles. It was not
unusual for her to rap my knuckles with a metal-edged ruler after I made
a wisecrack.

On this particular morning, there came a knock at our classroom
door. A young man entered, consulted a clipboard, and then called my
name. I stood slowly, unsure if I was in trouble. When I looked to Miss
Epstein for a sign, she flushed, clearly in on the game. "Well *go*," she
finally said.

The stranger led me downstairs to the library. Someone had taped
black construction paper over the door's window. The stranger knocked
three times and then entered. The room had been entirely rearranged:
its tables and chairs neatly stacked in the far corner. Thick black electri-
cal cords snaked to a soundboard and a pair of klieg lights—the latter
made the air stuffy and were aimed at a student's desk, where the stranger
ordered me to sit. Having grown up around an actor-father, I knew a set
when I saw one and kept quiet. I faced a false wall that climbed almost
to the ceiling, before which stood a director's chair. A man got up from
it to introduce himself. Over his shoulder I could see a small cutaway in
the wood, flush against which was the camera's lens, whose aperture narrowed, widened, and then went still.

The man, whom I immediately recognized, was Allen Funt, the host
of *Candid Camera*. He wore a light blue shirt with a paisley design,
cerulean paramecia swimming across the shiny fabric. His pants were as
white as his teeth and within a single shade of the band of hair above
his high forehead. He bent toward me, with his hands on his knees, and
pitched his voice low.

"We're gonna have a talk, you and me, okay?" he said. "I'm gonna sit
in that chair"—he wrapped his arm around his chest, pointing behind
him, though he never took his eyes from mine—"and you just relax.
Sound like a plan?"

I knew what was happening, just not what to expect. But I wanted to be on the show. So I nodded.

"Say whatever's on your mind," Funt added, and smiled. His teeth were fantastic, separate unto him, like furniture in his mouth. He returned to his seat. "So, Griffin, tell me something about yourself. You like baseball? Who's your favorite team?"

"The Yankees."

"What about football? Jets fan?"

"Giants."

"Follow the fights? You a Frazier or Foreman guy?"

"I like Muhammad Ali."

"Float like a butterfly . . ." Funt said, and pointed at me.

"Sting like a bee," I replied, taking his cue.

"Think you can make up rhymes like that?"

"Sure," I said.

And then Muhammad Ali appeared next to me. There'd been another student's chair off camera, and Ali reached between his legs to take the small seat in hand and scoot up close. This action should have been awkward, but he glided soundlessly across the floor, moving with the frictionless ease I've come to recognize in all superior athletes, mere exertion something they deign to do, lest it sap energy they need to call upon later. He was wearing boxing shoes and a pair of shorts that read EVERLAST at the waistband, but nothing else. I detected a hint of glee as he stared me down. Even though I'd been ready for a surprise, I was not prepared to see the champ, and my reaction, in acting parlance, was big.

"Rhyme better than me?" Ali said. "I'm the greatest poet on the planet, ain't met my peer. Got fists of thunder, a tongue like Shakespeare."

And then he leaned forward, so that the effect was of a face arriving from far away.

"We gonna have a battle of *wits,*" he said.

Ali jumped up and raised his fists, hopping soundlessly, and then waved me from my seat. I obeyed, mirroring his moves, bobbing and weaving. I feinted a few punches and, in response, Ali fired several jabs, their speed so strobic it made me slightly sick. His arms were absurdly long. Retracted, they appeared mantis-like. Ali continued to rhyme:

"Knocked out Liston in the third, stunned Foreman in Zaire. Beat Frazier so bad he cried for a . . ." He cupped a hand to his ear.

"*Year!*" I said.

"Good!" he cried. "Now *you*."

"Fake with my left, punch with my right. Ain't losing to the champ without a . . ."

"Fight!" Ali said. He dropped his guard and then shook his head in mock defeat. He held out an open palm. "Give me five."

I slapped his hand, and he pulled me into a hug. He asked me my name, and when I told him his eyes widened.

"The mythological creature," he said. "Guardian of great *treasures*. What're you protecting, boy?"

I hadn't given it a thought. But by now Funt was up, applauding, and he inserted himself between us.

"Great stuff, Muhammad," he said. "Absolutely *priceless*."

The man with the clipboard took my elbow and led me toward the door. When I looked back, Funt, who was still talking to the champ, checked over his shoulder to see whether I was within earshot. At that moment, Ali slit his eyes and shook his fist at me, this a secret sign of our allegiance. I nodded, disingenuously, and felt something akin to shame.

"You want to explore that a bit?" Naomi asked me.

I considered her question for a moment. "It was like I was on Funt's team instead of Ali's."

"Like you were *colluding*."

I told her I didn't know what that meant.

"Cooperating," she said, "but in secret."

A word can open a world. I thought of how I'd thrown Andy Axelrod under the bus on set several weeks ago. Was it because he never listened to me? Because when we talked, he made me disappear? Funt behavior, all the way. Whereas I wanted to be like the champ, someone who in person was exactly like Ali—a rare thing indeed. How to become my opposite?

"As for what you're protecting," Naomi said, "I think we both know the answer to that."

Being baffled, and safely allowed to be so, I remained silent.

"Yourself, silly."

I had questions. But by now, Naomi had pushed her sleeve's cuff back to check her watch. She leaned over to kiss my neck, close to my clavicle, and this caress sent a charge down my spine that zammed to the soles of my feet. "Maybe," she whispered, "we pick up with this tomorrow."

During those afternoons Naomi and I spent together, the order of operations was always the same: talk first, touch afterward. I had initially thought of the latter as something I owed her, like the check Dad wrote to Elliott at the end of our sessions, the one he folded and sometimes asked me to hand him when we were done, as if I were the one paying the good doctor. But this was changing.

After my *Candid Camera* segment aired, Dad made me an appointment at the Billy Kidd Talent Agency. There was no discussion about it. He simply showed up at school one afternoon—a rare occurrence, since Oren and I went to and fro on our own—explaining only that there was someone he wanted me to meet. Chronology dictates his real motivation: we'd just moved back to Lincoln Towers and were struggling. Why not enlist a little help? Brent Bixby, the company's founder and sole employee, ran the business out of a single-room office overlooking Coliseum Books on West Fifty-Seventh Street. He gave me some commercial sides. Unwilling to play along, I robotically read my lines. "Mr. Owl," I said, deadpan, "how many licks does it take to get to the Tootsie Roll center of a Tootsie Pop?" My reluctance should be no mystery. It was one thing to want to be on *Candid Camera,* quite another to risk being exposed. I would step into the open on *my* terms.

"That's fine," Brent said. He took back the script and suggested we chat. He folded his hands on his desk and refused to speak. We stared at each other for a while. Brent had a wooden impassivity and a perfect goatee. If he'd wrapped a turban around his head, he'd have been a dead ringer for Zoltar, the coin-operated swami that gave your fortune at the arcade. On his giant desk, there was a telephone on whose face several cubed buttons flashed, a sight I found profoundly distracting when it burbled: *Who had he left on hold?* The desk's corner was anchored by a Rolodex so big it required a hand crank, the only thing I was sure Brent would grab should the building ever catch fire. All four walls were crowded with kids' headshots, the subjects posed and in costume: The quarterback, in a number twelve jersey, smiling as he prepared to make a pass. The redhead with Pippi Longstocking braids sticking out beneath her straw hat, a giant swirled lollipop held close to her lips. The young tough in a leather jacket, its collar popped, leaning against a wall while he glared at the camera. I felt an overwhelming urge to scratch out their eyes, like the defaced ads I saw on the subway, and was reminded of one of Elliott's favorite aphorisms: "Those who annoy us the most remind us of ourselves."

"What's with all the stupid pictures?" I asked. My bluntness shocked me. Behind me I heard Dad laugh.

Brent mulled my question. "So that when I get a call from a casting agent for a certain type of kid, I know which horse to pick."

"I'm not a horse," I said.

Brent shrugged. "Fair enough," he said, "but this is a race."

"For what?" I asked.

"Attention."

While I squinted, considering this, a smile flickered across Brent's mouth.

"You're hired," he said.

Dad told me to wait in the hallway while he and Brent signed papers, though he intentionally left the door ajar. He was a big believer that an overheard conversation was more authentic than a direct one. "He's got the gift," he said, "he's in the moment."

But Brent, who had even less patience for the talent's parents than the kid, replied, "I'll be in touch."

My talent, if it could be called that—my gift, which Brent and my father had immediately recognized—was for naturalism. Down the road, as my list of professional credits grew, it would require almost no effort, in dramas like E. G. Marshall's *Radio Mystery Theater,* to play a child possessed by a demon—to speak, that is, through my own mouth as if I were inhabited by another being. To weep over my father's body after he was assassinated at the end of *The Talon Effect.* To deliver commercial taglines with total conviction: *Boy,* I'd say, *this is good-tasting tuna,* before I was made to spit the mouthfuls of bread and fish into a garbage can after each take. To bear witness, with growing shock in the shot's background, to the woman playing my homemaker mom toss her broom aside and then run her fingers over her lips, her hands over her dress, and make the same moaning sounds Naomi sometimes did when we kissed. *When I eat a York Peppermint Pattie,* she said, *I get the sensation that a cool breeze is blowing through my hair. And across my long white dress. Oh.* Oh. To fake faking it. To be at a twice remove. I could cry at will but feel nothing, feel everything but give nothing away. I did not connect it to the fire at the time, to that walk from Al and Neal's apartment to our destroyed home, but the transformation felt morphological, so that as I moved through the world in this near-perfect disguise, I felt as if I had just a bit of extra time to process things, could exert the slightest delay while I took stock of any situation before showing my hand.

What was odd was that the only time it happened with Naomi was when we were physical with each other.

"Touch it," she ordered. We had already moved to the back seat.

I placed my hand on her lap. If fur were on the verge of becoming liquid; if, like cotton candy, it might delicately melt in my mouth, that was what the material felt like. She'd laid her stole over her legs, so that I might run my fingers through it. "This is Russian sable," she said. "The most expensive kind there is."

She placed her palm over mine; her hand was cold and dry. Sometimes, as now, I was aware of how much my company meant to her, and the feeling was as weighty as the garment, as nearly suffocating as it was pleasant, and my discomfort, which won out today, was like the first night we met, so I felt an overwhelming urge to flee.

"Did Sam buy you this?" I asked, not completely innocently.

Naomi released my hand, cleared her throat. "He did."

"What about your necklace?"

"That too."

"What about the car?"

"That's all me, mister."

"Do you think he'd be jealous if he knew about us?" I asked. Sometimes, when we were together, I was certain he'd appear on the street and accuse us of terrible things.

"If he noticed my existence, then maybe."

She considered me for a moment. I considered Naomi, arms crossed and back pressed against her door.

"Is there anything about us to know?" she asked.

I shrugged. I was not sure I could say.

"Is this what you really want to talk about?" she asked.

I petted the sable again. "My grandfather was a furrier," I offered.

At this, Naomi visibly relaxed. Took my cue. "Whose side?"

"My dad's."

"What was he like?"

"I never met him. He and my grandma lived in California. He died when I was four."

"Do you know where he was from?"

"Hungary."

"What about your grandmother?"

"From Russia."

"Is she still alive?"

"She lives in Los Angeles. We don't see her much."

"Was your father not close with them?"

"I don't think so."

"Why do you say that?"

"I heard my parents fighting about him once."

"Tell me," Naomi said.

It happened after I applied to matriculate into Boyd's seventh grade class. I'd been acting for five years by then and treated my interview like another audition. Mom, who'd escorted me, was invited into Mr. McElmore's office at the interview's start. It was located in the Old School, like some Gothic dream out of Tolkien, giving on to the New School, the modern wing. McElmore was the head of admissions, and he chatted up Mom, obviously charmed. After Mom mentioned she was getting a master's in American literature, he told her he also taught senior English, and they nearly forgot me while discussing names from the spines crowding his office's bookshelf. Mom's brown hair was pulled back, her smart black sleeveless dress showing off her dancer's arms, her high heels accentuating her ballerina's calves, eyeliner bringing out her irises' deep blue. At times such as these, I was made aware of how beautiful she was. Mom's outfit somehow signaled the interview's seriousness—I could tell she was nervous—though she gave me no preparation beforehand or on the bus ride there, except that I should "be myself."

"It was lovely to meet you," McElmore said to her, and then escorted her to his door, touching the small of her back before indicating the couch outside. "Now, if you'll excuse us, Griffin and I will have a chat."

What was I thinking, then, when McElmore asked me about my acting career, and I slipped into obvious shtick? "I gotta tell ya," I said, outerborough-ing my accent and standing, without asking permission, to take off my blazer, unclip my tie, and then roll up my sleeves, as if the head of admissions and I were about to have a fight. "I'm not comfortable in this monkey suit. I'm used to wearing clothes that are more *relaxed*." I unbuttoned my collar and, after sitting again, made a great show of cracking my neck. "Now," I said, "what was your question?"

McElmore chuckled. "I was wondering if you ever suffered from stage fright," he said. His broad mustache was shaped like a whale's fluke; there were even whales on his bow tie. A port wine birthmark splashed across his cheek. He could barely hide a smile behind his steepled fingers, which he touched to his lips as I talked about the challenges of learning my lines and sharing a dressing room with John Belushi.

The fight between my parents happened soon after my acceptance letter arrived—one of their arguments that I could hear as I rose in the elevator, that grew louder as I stepped into our hallway, that made me slow-walk to our door and ensured, as I quietly turned my key in the lock and then snuck into my room, that I might eavesdrop on them in complete secrecy.

"All those synagogues your father sent you marching off to," Mom said. "All those weekends in Brooklyn or Queens. 'Here's a quarter, Shel, buy yourself some lunch, but only if they don't feed you there. And don't leave without getting paid.'"

"Oh please."

"What does Elliott think about you making your son another little cantor?"

"He's already signed a contract."

"Break it."

"Even if I could, I can't. Don't you understand, Lily? I'm short, all right? I haven't *got* it."

For a long time, my mother was quiet.

My father lowered his voice. "I can't do it alone," he confessed. "When are you going to get that through your head?"

It was, I realize now, their central conflict, the problem they were always talking around. Mom, hunkered down—she'd been a professional dancer and now taught children ballet at Carnegie Hall in the afternoons. It left her mornings to study, to write her papers and take classes, and "that's my contribution," I often caught her saying to Dad, "that's *my* training." "Your mother," Dad said to me after one of these fights—I'd ask him while we walked to the grocery store why she didn't get a different job—"isn't corporate material."

Mom, Dad, and I had a talk that night. This was formal business, conducted in our living room. I sat on the sofa, my parents across from me.

"Your father has something to tell you," Mom said, and gave Dad the floor.

Dad sat forward. His voice's register: very serious. His role: somber patriarch. Nothing he was about to say was anything he wanted to. "Your mother and I are thrilled about your new school. As you should be. Because it's a very big step, in your development. But it's also a major financial commitment."

"Which you should be aware of," Mom said.

"So that you're invested," Dad said.

"In your education," Mom said. "In your future."

"What we're telling you," Dad said, "is that you're going to be making a contribution. That part of the money you earn as an actor will go toward your tuition. Do you understand?"

It was difficult to tell if this was a request for my permission or an announcement.

"What if I don't?" I asked.

"Understand?" Dad asked.

"Make a contribution."

Dad looked at Mom, not without some alarm; Mom shrugged at this response, as if to say, *I told you.* Dad unclasped his hands and clapped them back together. When he made big gestures like these, he reminded me of William Shatner. *Billions,* I could imagine him saying, *billions and billions of galaxies.* "Then I guess we'll have to find other means."

"Okay," I said.

"Okay what?"

"I'll do it," I said. Because in a way I didn't understand, I felt like I'd gotten my answer.

Naomi's car was dark now. To my right the West Side Highway winked and pulsed. With the windows up, its flashes were silent, like heat lightning. We'd finished talking some time ago. Naomi sat there, thinking. She had unbuttoned several buttons of my shirt and lightly dragged her fingernails over my chest. It made me so hard my penis was sore. I'd have enjoyed it more if I wasn't so afraid she'd notice.

"Your little brother," Naomi said. "How come he goes to a different school?"

Shame banished my boner. "He didn't get in," I said.

"Really? He seems so smart."

"He is. But I'm not."

"What kind of nonsense are you talking?"

My guilt surrounding this subject was as heavy as cement shoes. "I got bad grades in middle school. Mom said they thought Oren would perform just as poorly. So they didn't admit him."

"Why would she tell you something like that?"

I turned my chest from her and buttoned my shirt. "Mom never lies."

"I'm sorry," she said.

I said, "It's not *your* fault."

"It's not yours either."

I watched out the window. The West Side Highway flashed its Morse code, and Naomi sighed.

"Do you like it?" she finally asked. When I looked at her questioningly, she said, "Acting."

I had to think about this for a moment. "Sometimes," I said.

"When?"

"When I know my lines. I'll do things, in a scene, that are smart or funny. It's hard to explain. It's like I know more than I do. Than when I'm me."

"For example?"

"How I might act," I said, "if a gun was pointed at me. Or if I could fly."

"And that's the fun part?"

I shrugged. "Sure."

"When don't you like it?"

I shrugged again. "When I can't keep up. When I don't want to. When it gets in the way of everything else, like wrestling."

"And then what do you think?"

"I think," I said, "that it's never going to change."

"Yes," Naomi said, and sat up. "*Exactly.* It's *never* going to change, Griffin. So the question you have to ask yourself is: Can you live with that?"

It was one of those moments when I was struck mute. She cleared my hair from my eyes and smiled. Then she caught sight of her watch.

"Oy," she said. "Look at me, late for the kids." She turned to exit the back seat and then paused. She leaned in and bit my lip, gently. "It means a lot to me, just FYI, you being such an open book. Most men I've known, they're the exact opposite."

At the end of October, with the fall athletic season having just come to a close, it was time for Boyd's sports award assembly. And since Kepplemen was also the varsity cross-country coach, it meant that he had to give a speech summing up the team's results in front of the entire school, after which he read the names of everyone who'd lettered. He sat onstage, his usually mussed salt-and-pepper hair slick and combed, all dressed up in a suit and tie, except for his wrestling shoes—a signal to those of us on the team that the *real* season, the one that *really* mattered, was about to start.

At its conclusion, we were each grabbing our book bags from where we'd slung them beneath the front hall pews. We were off to class even though the bell had not yet rung, and during this dispersal, Kepplemen intercepted me in the front hall and said, "I have something for you."

He was already walking ahead of me, toward the school's exit, and nodded for me to follow. I tugged at my bag's strap, readjusting it, and then slung it beneath the pew and hurried after him. He was out the front doors now, hanging a right. At the corner, he turned right again, south on Central Park West, briefly disappearing from my sight, turning east a block later, on Ninety-Fifth Street. I knew we were going to his apartment.

Several other wrestlers had been there. It was Cliffnotes who'd described it best: it was like being in a hamper, perhaps because there were clothes strewn everywhere: an odor of still-damp socks and, perhaps because of all the cross-country practices in Central Park, the loam of mud and tang of long-dried dog shit adhered to spikes. The building had several units dedicated to faculty, and Kepplemen's apartment was on the eighth floor. It was a one-bedroom with a small kitchen and dining alcove, whose outstanding feature was its north-facing view of the low-slung skyline, which I gazed on when we arrived, above which a very light cloud fled, and below, the Boyd Astroturf, on whose gleaming green the lower school kids now played: the boys in their navy-blue uniform shirts and corduroy pants; the girls in their blue-and-green cardigans and skirts, shouting their high calls. I watched their games from the pair of open windows: Nerf football, wiffle ball, tag. Eight stories below and the children sounded so far away and proximate, remote and magically near, I imagined if I'd whispered, *Nice catch,* the boy who'd just made it might shield his eyes and look up toward where I stood.

Kepplemen nudged my arm with something blunt. It was a rolled-up magazine, which I took and uncoiled: *Wrestling USA.* I perused its cover: an action photo of one wrestler executing a perfect hip toss. He had hold of his opponent's head and arm; the latter's feet were pointed toward the ceiling while the former was also airborne with the throw's force. Before I could express my appreciation, Kepplemen, already unknotting his tie, said, "A subscription's been mailed to you." And when I looked up from the cover again, Kepplemen handed me another package. It was still in its mailing envelope. I tossed the magazine onto his large bed. It was the only thing kempt in the room. Even its blanket had hospital corners. He said, "Open it," and his expression was strange. It was not exactly expectant; there was an aspect to it of apology, as if the gift's contents contained incriminating information he'd been ordered to reveal. I tore open the package, wanting to get this over with. I was already late for class. Kepplemen removed his blazer and tossed it onto the nearby chairback. It missed and fell into a heap on the floor. I was through the clear plastic now; Kepplemen removed his tie. I pulled a pair of neoprene kneepads from the wrapping; Kepplemen had by now pulled his shirttails from his pants. They were in Boyd's colors, gold at the knees and blue at the thigh; he was toeing off his shoes. "A starter needs proper equipment," he said. When I thanked him, he said, "Try them on." He'd removed his trousers but not his briefs. He was changing into his athletic clothes, I hoped. When I told him I would, he shrugged. "Try them now," he said, unbuttoning his collar, "in case I have to send them back."

I did not tell Naomi about this. Nor did I tell anyone how after I'd removed my pants and slid on the kneepads, how after executing, at Kepplemen's urging, a couple of practice shots to test their fit, after a tap of his knuckle to my chin and a playful slap and then some hand fighting, I found myself holding Kepplemen in a headlock on his bed, staring at the magazine's cover as he groaned beneath me. I torqued his neck, pressing his arm over his nose so that he labored to breathe. His ankle had hooked mine. His body spooned my hip and thigh, affixed. There followed a feeling of tremendous suction, of all space between us removed. I noticed that both wrestlers in the photo wore red shoes, that these matched their singlets' color, the Illinois wrestler had an *I* on his chest, the other an *OU*. At which point Kepplemen jerked once, twice, violently, against my length, groaning, and then he went rigid. During these several hundred heartbeats we lay tensed, and the only sound, before he went limp, were his teeth chattering.

Later, as I hurried out, Kepplemen said he would see me soon. He was pulling on his sweatpants behind me. I did not turn to face him. The morning's light from his windows made the hallway seem dimmer when his door closed. At the elevator bank and then on the short walk around the block, I flipped through the magazine. I did not take my eyes off it until I arrived back at school, where I threw it into the garbage before entering Miss Sullens's class.

"You're late," she said.

That afternoon, instead of heading straight home, I tarried. I got off the bus at Eighty-Sixth Street to kill time at West Side Comics. I walked two blocks downtown to Tom's Pizzeria and bought a slice. I got change and then played *Asteroids* for a solid hour. I caught the bus again but got off at the stop before mine, walking west on Sixty-Seventh Street, circumventing Juilliard. I spotted Naomi's car up the block, after I'd safely crossed Amsterdam Avenue. I could neither bear the expectation on Naomi's face when I took my seat nor her expression of joy. When I returned to the apartment and no one was home, I climbed into my top bunk and reveled in the silence, pretending, with some guilt, that everyone in my family had died and I, unbeknownst to anyone, not even the doorman, lived here all alone, and it made me feel strangely at peace.

But later that week, my discomfort inexplicably banished, I was thrilled to spot her car. I hopped in the passenger seat, and she hugged me, hard. "Where have you got off to?" she asked. "I was getting so worried I almost called your mother." We raced to the Dead Street, as if we were late for an appointment. She cut the engine and held up her finger; she reached in back and produced a gift-wrapped box, which she placed on my lap. "Open it," Naomi said.

I lifted the top and peeled aside the tissue paper. It was three neckties in patterns that were Willy Wonka colorful—of lighthouses, of tiny fish, of hundreds of little *H*'s.

"Those are Hermès," she said. "It's a French brand. Do you like them?" When I said yes, she asked if I would put one on. "Do you know how to tie a Windsor knot?" she asked. When I said I didn't she put one around her neck and told me to copy her. "I used to tie my father's," she said, and pulled down the visor to regard herself, chin up, in its tiny mirror. I did the same. "Sometimes I tie Sam's," she said, as if to assure me she loved him. When we were finished, we sat in the back seat together, each with a tie around our neck. "I like the idea of you wearing something I gave you." When I told her I did too, she said, "But maybe keep those at school."

Which I did. In my locker. Next to the kneepads.

I didn't see Naomi the next evening. It was the wrap party for *The Nuclear Family*'s fourth season, and I had asked my lab partner, Deb Peryton, to go with me.

The party was held at an event space next to the Rockefeller Rink.

The oval, recently iced, and shining whitely through the windows, wasn't open to skaters yet. The gilded statue of Prometheus presided over this. There was a buffet, and, after dinner, a projection screen was set up, and they rolled Tom's outtake reel and set of pranks, which Deb thought were hilarious, and I thanked God they didn't include my duping of Andy, since his wife was not only in attendance but sat at the table with us. As a congratulatory gift for a fourth season, I was given a brass Tiffany table clock, as bright as the statue outside, whose face cover swiveled into a stand and was engraved with the NBC peacock. Deb and I didn't have much to say to each other. It was strange how much easier it was talking to Naomi than to her. Was I unlearning how to talk to girls my own age? I was relieved when Kevin Savage, who was the show's heartthrob and could tell my date was going poorly, asked her to disco dance. Dad had given me money for cab fare home, and because Deb lived on the Upper East Side, I told the driver—also according to Dad's advice—to drop her off first.

"I really liked the DJ," Deb said when we arrived at her building. "And the outtakes of you were funny." Before she got out, she added, "Thanks for taking me. I've never gone out on a school night before."

"Me neither," I said.

"Well," she said, "this is where I get out."

Then she leaned forward and kissed me. It was a long kiss, a surprisingly sweet kiss, far less probing, less hungry, than Naomi's. With the utmost delicacy, she touched her tongue to mine. Her lips tasted like the strawberry lip balm she'd applied when we first got in the cab.

"See you in lab tomorrow," she said, and then exited.

In the rearview mirror, the cabdriver caught my eye and winked.

The next day, for no reason I understood, I felt compelled to tell Naomi about the date the moment we parked.

"Well," Naomi asked, "is she your girlfriend now?" She said this with just a hint of pettiness. I was not prepared for how much it hurt her.

When I said she wasn't, Naomi added, "I think I'm jealous. Which is crazy, I know."

When I said she shouldn't be, she asked, "Why's that?"

I considered her question. When I spoke, I did not recognize my voice. "I don't talk to her like you."

"No?"

"I don't talk to anyone like this," I added. Which was true.

In response, her face went through a moon phase: first, a sort of frown, her lower lip pressed forward, as if she might cry; followed by a smile that was warm and blooming; and finally, an expression that was slit-eyed and wicked.

"Kiss me like you did her," she ordered.

This I knew how to do. We kissed for a long time in the dark.

"Oh," she said, finally pressing herself away from me, "it's so nice to feel desire."

When I did not respond, she said, "What's on your mind? Got somewhere else you need to be?"

No, I said, but I had something to tell her. I had been keeping the news like a secret. Tonight, I explained, would probably be the last time we'd see each other for a while. "Oh?" she said, and in a tone of concern asked, "Why is that?"

"Because Friday night is Halloween," I continued, "and on Monday, wrestling season begins." Practice ran until six, I said, and she and her girls would be headed home by then.

"Huh," Naomi said.

She was watching me, I could feel it, but I refused to look at her, lest she see my relief.

"Have you decided what you're gonna dress as?" she asked, too brightly, to change the subject. "It's probably your last year to trick-or-treat, I'm guessing."

"I'm going as Peter Proton," I said. The symbolism was not lost on me. Nor, I knew, on her. "I should get home."

"I'll drop you off," she said, and hurried to adjust in her seat to face the wheel.

"That's okay," I said before she turned the key, "I'll walk."

"Well," she said, "good luck with your season."

"Thank you," I said, which felt like not enough somehow, and I exited the car.

When Naomi turned east at the end of the block, she was going fast enough that her tires squealed.

· · ·

Flash-forward several weeks. It is a Thursday in mid-November. On one hand, I can count every meal I've eaten since Monday. The rest of Boyd Prep's varsity and I are standing in our locker room with the Riverdale wrestling team. It is our season's first dual meet. We have formed two lines for weigh-ins. We are arranged from lightest to heaviest before the scale. Some of us are in our underwear; some are naked. We do not speak. There's a reverence that attends moments like this one. Even Kepplemen, who is formally dressed—blazer, tie, black loafers—pitches his voice so low it barely overtakes the hum of the fluorescents. We study one another's bodies. Some boys have acne on their chests. Some have sprouted chest hair. Some are hairy as fathers. Some are studies in disproportion, with outsized forearms or hypertrophic calves. Others are as ribbed as the Christ. The opposing coach says his competitor's name and weight class, which Kepplemen writes on a sheet, and then the boy steps onto the scale. He does this as we all do, delicately, respectfully, carefully, as if the Detecto's platform were an altar.

The boy I'm to wrestle is so big compared with me, his back so wide and shoulders so broad and musculature so comparatively developed, it seems impossible we are the same weight. And then there is his name. "James Polk," says his coach. "One hundred and twenty-one pounds." Kepplemen, who sets the scale, nods at him with great respect; it is almost a bow, as if he actually *were* the president. Polk steps on. He tucks his chin into his neck and stares at the balance with such concentration it appears as if he's trying to control it with telekinesis. In spite of his size, it does not budge.

The wrestling gym is a space just off the cafeteria, low-ceilinged and half its size. As the home team, we make our entrance second. We race through the room's double doors and then circle the mat's ring several times. Next we do our warm-ups, led by our captains. We count out our stretches and calisthenics, so loudly they are like war cries. Ten rows of foldout chairs are full, and there is standing room only at the back. Parents are in attendance. Girls from every grade. Teachers as well: Miss Sullens, Mr. Damiano, Mr. McElmore, Mr. McQuarrie, even Mr. Fistly. At 121 pounds, I am fifth up. Two matches ahead of mine, I retreat to the practice mat and shoot single-leg takedowns, fire stand-up escapes, and execute sprawls, hoping my heart, which seems made of tissue paper, might settle into a more even rhythm.

Something thunderous and final occurs behind me, at which point Kepplemen calls out my name and waves me over. I snap my headgear's chin strap and run to face him. The crowd is going apeshit. Coach screams something about "moving, always be moving," and smacks each ear guard and then slaps my face. My spit is as pasty as Elmer's glue. I feel a nearly uncontrollable urge to pee. Before I step onto the mat, the three captains—Pat Santoro, Roy Adler, and Brian Dolph—huddle around me to bark advice, which I do not hear, and then push me toward the ref. I give a final look over my shoulder. I am loosed and untouchable. Kepplemen suddenly seems tiny. Naomi is not in the audience. The gym is raucous; the cacophony is a kind of silence. The ref gives me a green anklet that I fasten. Polk stands at the mat's center and I am directed to shake his hand. Then the ref blows his whistle.

Polk takes me down. It occurs with blinding suddenness, like having a trapdoor open beneath you. As quickly, I pull a switch, a move that reverses our positions. It is half instinct, half desperation. It is perfect. From a great distance, I hear the crowd roar. With my arm wrapped around his waist, I chop at Polk's elbow. It is as stiff as a parking meter's pole. I pull at him with all my strength. He feels as big as a sofa. I cannot say what happens next, but he rolls, *we* roll, and it feels as if I have been launched in the air. I find myself on my back. How soft and pliant I suddenly am. How *relaxed*. I have never taken the time to stare at our gym's overhead lights, which, I now notice, are housed in metal cages. Riverdale's team, out of their chairs now and on their hands and knees, pound the mat, chanting "pin, pin, pin" in unison, until the ref, on his belly perpendicular to me, with great finality, slaps the mat too. He takes our wrists as soon as I stand and then raises Polk's arm in victory.

The captains are huddled around me again. In the row of chairs, I see Miss Sullens, who sits next to McElmore. She nods at me and then gets up to leave. Kepplemen is already giving Tanner a pep talk before he takes the mat.

"You did great," the captains say, "that switch you pulled was amazing, he was a two-time state champion, you never had a chance."

I sit through the meet's conclusion, blind to the proceedings, crushed
but utterly elated. I replay the match with perfect recall. Was this what
my father meant about being in the moment?

Nothing in my life ever felt so real.

THE AGONY OF DEFEAT

Of course, it was an election year. In the run-up to November, I didn't give the candidates much thought. During my sessions with Elliott, we often stopped at the Second Avenue diner. We took our seats at the counter, the waiter winked at Elliott while taking another order, and I realized that he probably saw the good doctor eight times a day. The cook kept the radio above the griddle tuned to the news. *Ten-Ten WINS,* I was sure to hear my father's voice say at least once before we left, *You give us twenty-two minutes, we'll give you the world.*

The anchor led with the presidential race, the tightening October poll numbers. Elliott slapped the Formica with his open palm, a bit of performance he played self-consciously when the waiter arrived, ordering a cup of black coffee for himself and a chocolate egg cream for me. Elliott's hands were laced around his cup. "Maybe we should've gone with Ted Kennedy," he said. "A lot of enthusiasm swirling around him. Nostalgic, to be sure. All that Camelot crap. Kennedy was no Lancelot, let me tell you. The guy didn't agonize about cozying up to the nearest Guinevere either. But there's a lesson in that. In politics, as in art, put your money where your inspiration is." The hostage crisis, Elliott observed, was like an endless stretch of bad weather for our president, "as if he needed stronger headwinds besides this economy." Elliott shook his head. "Am I right, or what?"

I shook mine too. An egg cream, I reflected, didn't have an egg in it.

"Of course, Teddy screwed up with Chappaquiddick," Elliott continued. "That was probably disqualifying."

"I can't disagree," I said, because I'd found the more I agreed, the more camouflaged I was by his monologue, the less we discussed my terrible grades.

As for my own politics, my sense of Carter was acquired by pure osmosis and was bound up in a whole other series of images from the nightly news, *Time,* and *Newsweek,* a collage soundtracked by the complaints of grown-ups—which I picked up at our get-togethers, particularly Al Moretti's and my father's, and could imitate pitch-perfectly—of endless gas lines and a small group of Saudis I figured was OPEC. "He's a fucking *disastah,*" said Al, "a hick and a scold with his bullshit red *sweatah* and his crisis of confidence crap. Don't tell me *I'm* the problem. Don't tell me *I've* got the malaise. You can lead a horse to water, but if you're the leader of the free world, you *make* the fucker drink." Failure, as I look back on it now, swirled around our president like the sands that choked those helicopters' rotors during the botched Operation Eagle Claw hostage rescue; was like the black water that flooded Kennedy's car and filled Mary Jo Kopechne's lungs after they went sailing over the bridge in Chappaquiddick.

"But this Reagan character," Elliott said to me now, "this former GE spokesperson," he added with disdain. "Don't even get me started on him as governor. At least the American people aren't that stupid to elect him to the highest office. We're not that stupid, are we, Aldo?"

Aldo, the short-order cook, visible in the service window, leaned down to look at us beneath the pennants of order tickets. "I could use a raise," he said.

"Speaking of," Elliott said to the waiter. He pulled a five from his fat black wallet, its fold stuffed with so many bills it looked like a slim book of poems. "Keep the change."

As for Reagan, Elliott, Al, and my father wrote him off as a lightweight or worse—this again entirely according to their chatter—as hawkish, racist, repressive, and dangerously unqualified, not to mention fiscally irresponsible. And here too my assessment was Polly-want-a-cracker parroted from bits and pieces I could glean from conversations at the dinner table and during the Sunday morning news shows. Play the part of the bright, underachieving kid who kept up with current affairs, and according to Elliott—which Dad reported to Mom—I was "full of potential."

"Look at his record in California," Elliott said. "Mr. Maximum Freedom until the college kids start protesting at People's Park and he sends in the National Guard."

"Bloody Thursday," I said, and shook my head in disgust.

"It's fascist, is what it is," Elliott said. Pleased by my input, he stopped and reached out to shake my hand. "You've had a bumpy start to high school. But you're righting the ship. You're turning it around."

"The wind's at my back," I said.

"Onward," Elliott said.

"Ándale," I said. "Arriba, arriba."

But as an actor, it was difficult not to recognize, even at times appreciate, Reagan's actor slickness, his stealth-comic timing made more obvious and suspect to me by his pomaded hair, the sometimes just barely perceptible tremor that he used to amplify his sense of disbelief, as if the stupidity or obvious hypocrisy of a comment set his head a-bobble. Just four days before the election, for homework in American government class, we had to watch Carter and Reagan's first and only debate and write three paragraphs about three issues discussed. "There you go again," Reagan kept saying to Carter, as if it were off the cuff, although I knew a canned line when I heard one. I called Cliffnotes to get his thoughts and maybe tweak mine based on his, but even before we could start, Cliff said, "Did I tell you about Pilchard?"

Simon Pilchard had spent the past several weeks with a taped splint holding his nose in place, his eyes fading from a raccoon-like black to blue and green after the severe break Cliff had accidentally inflicted upon him. We hadn't spoken to him since the accident, but we'd occasionally seen him trudging to the basement with Kepplemen, carrying his headgear now affixed with a face guard that resembled a hockey goalie's.

"His father's suing us," Cliff continued. Pilchard's father was a well-known judge and shouldn't have needed the money.

"For what?"

"Pain and suffering and the denial of his son's love."

"How much?"

"Fifty thousand."

"Oh, snap!"

"I'm going to kill that piece of shit," Cliffnotes said with uncharacteristic venom. "He's fucking with my family."

On election night, my parents took Oren and me with them to vote. Their voting station was at P.S. 87, on Seventy-Eighth Street. Dad let me pull the lever that drew the curtain. He showed me how to flip the smaller levers that punched his ballot, saying the names aloud as if he were narrating a documentary. I worried that other voters might hear, since his voice carried, and when I paused to ask him about one of the candidates—"Is he good?"—he said only, "He's a Democrat." A great smash of gears, as if we were on a service elevator, when he pulled the lever once more to open the curtain.

It was dark by now, and we walked down Broadway. Dad was walking ahead of us, which drove Mom crazy. "Go get your father," she ordered me.

There was an enormous crash. From our side of the street a storefront's glass exploded, and for a moment on the sidewalk there lay a man covered in frost. His jacket and pants, even his face, were powdered white. Shattered glass piled around him like rock salt. He was quickly up and running at full stride, across the avenue, headed east. Three butchers—heavyset, wearing yarmulkes and bloodstained aprons—were in pursuit. The carving knives they carried glinted in the headlights. Here Oren showed his age and huddled with Mom. We heard sirens in the distance, and within moments, a squad car's flashers strobed across Broadway. Dad was never shy about asking police or bystanders questions. His bravery in such moments was unmatched, part of his actor's chutzpah. He treated any official like his personal 411 and, after consulting with the cops, rejoined us with the official report. Mom was angry at him for abandoning us; Oren and I were angry for Mom. "Do you want to know what happened or not?" Dad asked her. It turned out that earlier in the day, along with a partner, the man had attempted to rob the store, a crime the butchers had foiled. When the two perps made their getaway, one ran out the front door, the other toward the back, accidentally locking himself in the freezer. He'd spent the day hiding out, but rather than die of hypothermia, he finally made a break for it.

Dad, chastened, made it a great show of letting Mom take his arm for the remainder of our walk.

When we arrived home and turned on the television to see the returns, nearly half the country was blue. No states west of Texas had posted their returns, but John Chancellor was already calling the race for Reagan, *a sports announcer, a film actor, a governor of California, is our projected winner at eight fifteen Eastern Standard Time.*

"Holy shit," Mom said. Oren and I laughed because she never cursed.

Dad sat down on the bed. As Oren and I were leaving, Mom, who'd draped her arm over his shoulders, asked us, over her own, to close the door.

The Saturday after Thanksgiving, the usual crowd gathered at The Saloon, a restaurant across the street from Lincoln Center. Elliott and Lynn. His daughter, Deborah, and her husband, Eli. Al Moretti, my parents. And lo and behold, the Shahs.

Their two daughters, Danny and Jackie, had performed in *The Nutcracker* matinee and were still in stage makeup, their hair bunned and cheeks rouged, their lipstick so bright they looked like pageant contestants. I hadn't seen Naomi since our last meeting, and when the Shahs arrived at our long table, I whispered to my mother, whom I was sitting next to, "You didn't tell me the Shahs were coming." "Was I supposed to?" Mom asked. Naomi brought Danny and Jackie over to greet her. She stood with a hand on each of her daughters' shoulders. The pair spoke to Mom with something close to reverence. My mother gave the two girls her complete attention, asking them about their performance that afternoon.

Naomi took the opportunity to look at me and smile weakly, almost apologetically and imploringly—for all the guests, for this encroachment upon our time together. For some sign from me that I too had missed her and wished that we could be somewhere else, alone. And beneath her daughters' conversation she said, "Hey, Griffin," and then, almost accusatorially, "It's been a while."

When I could not summon a response, Mom said, "Griffin, an adult is talking to you." She turned back to Naomi's girls, which seemed to create a zone of silence where Naomi could ask more intimately, in a tone that was almost taciturn, "How are you?"

"I'm okay."

"School going good? Now that your show's over."

"Better," I said.

"I'm glad," she said, with real feeling.

I caught Oren's eye. I sent him my telepathic red alert. He was standing next to Elliott and Sam while they talked. He noticed my alarm and then nodded that I meet him midpoint at the long table. "Oren and I are going to go play *Space Invaders,*" I said to Naomi, and left to join him.

We had some money of our own but decided to see how much we could grift from each one of the adults. We started with Al, who was talking with Dad. "Shel," he was telling my father, "what can I say? My heart's shattered. I mean"—he stretched his arm out in front of his crotch—"my cock was out to here for this kid. I was like the man of fucking steel."

Oren tapped his shoulder and blinked his eyes sweetly while I made the ask.

"Al," I said, "don't be sad, you're a good guy."

"That's sweet of you, Oren."

"Griffin."

"Whichever. Now what the fuck do you want?"

"A dollar."

"For?"

"*Space Invaders.*"

"Who?"

"It's a video game."

"Maybe for a Shirley Temple I might."

"Okay then," Oren cut in, "how about for two Shirley Temples?"

"It'll rot your teeth."

"How about to go away?" Oren said.

"Let me see what I got in change," and he put his cigarette in his mouth and stuffed his hands in his jeans' pocket.

Mom never carried cash, so we didn't bother asking and moved on to hit up Deborah's husband, Eli. He always wore a suit but on Sundays was casual and lost the tie. After pulling a dollar bill from his wallet, Eli, in a moment of earnestness, held it up and said, "Only if you teach me how to play later," to which we agreed, knowing full well it was a contract we'd never have to honor.

Deborah was next. She was smoking a Virginia Slim. She liked to make a big deal about connecting with us, about having a conversation, and turned her chair to face me. The drawer of her lower jaw slid forward to suck on her thin cigarette, so that it pointed up slightly. She palmed my elbows and properly oriented me; she finger-combed the curls from my eyes. She said, "Let me get a look at you, Mr. Handsome," so I took the moment to get a look at her—her bobbed hair and heavily freckled face, her barracuda bone structure. "Now tell me, what's going on? How's school? What's your favorite subject? What's the last interesting thing you read?"

"*Romeo and Juliet,*" I said.

"Very good, very good, I like your taste, Shakespeare's still relevant, who's your favorite character?"

"Probably Mercutio. I had to memorize one of his speeches."

"Our teacher showed us the movie in class," Oren said. "There was a nude scene and we saw Romeo's butt."

Deborah, ignoring Oren, nodded seriously at me and, after tipping her cigarette's cherry over the ashtray, took a long pull at it and blew the smoke from her nostrils. "So you like English then," she said. "The communication arts. *Very important.* You could be a corporate speechwriter or go into advertising with those skills."

"If you think about it," Oren said, "Griffin's already in advertising."

"You know," Deborah said, ignoring him again and winding things up with the same story about me that she always recounted, "I'll never forget a conversation you and I had when you were seven. You'd been watching all these horror movies, and I asked you what you liked about them so much, and you know what you told me?"

"Wait," I said, "let me think," and took my chin in hand, pretending to recall the moment I had no recollection of whatsoever. "I said," brightening, "they made me appreciate how good my life was!"

"And I thought that was a pretty profound answer."

Deborah snapped open her purse and gave us a two-dollar bill, which

Oren plucked from her. "We're keeping this as a collector's item," he said as we swung back around to Dad, who seemed to have anticipated us.

Dad said, "Can you break a twenty?" which killed Al.

"Actually," Oren said, and produced a wad from which he began thumbing change, "I can."

"Go ask your mother," Dad said.

Next to Al sat Elliott, who was the easiest to grift because of the tacit rules about speaking with him at these gatherings. He affected a sort of cloudy indifference, a happy disinterest, that I took to be a buffer. He had no desire to talk about anything personal whatsoever since all he ever did was talk to us about personal things, but especially tonight, when everyone was determined to ignore the election results or process the stunning outcome. Consequently, he did not greet us head-on but always seemed, at least at first, to notice us after a moment, like someone calling across to him at a loud and crowded party.

"Elliott," Oren said, "I had the craziest dream."

Elliott signaled the waiter and, after rattling his highball, pointed to his Scotch.

"It had episodes and cliffhangers like *Batman,* but it started with me in my bunk bed, and Mom and Dad were in there too—"

"Yeah?" Elliott said. "Both of them?"

"And Mom was naked, and both Dad and I were in our underwear."

"Let's talk about this next week."

"Okay, but Griffin and I were wondering if we could have some money for video games."

Elliott stuffed a ten in Oren's palm. Oren said, "I'll bring you change," to which Elliott replied, "Keep it, play till your heart's content," and then we steeled ourselves before approaching Elliott's wife, Lynn.

She presented a massive challenge. A hulking presence at the far end of the table, dew-eyed and manatee-quiet among so many jabberers, she sat, as she always did, directly across from Elliott, their respective seats saved before their arrival as if every event they attended were one they were hosting. She was taller than her husband and hunched forward with her elbows resting on the table, her arms folded over each, these cradling her enormous breasts. This motionlessness, coupled with her short sandy hair and her expression of permanent disappointment and intolerance, plus the fact that she'd been a high school math teacher, added to her intimidating countenance. She was the sort of person who, upon greeting you at her door on Halloween, responded to the question "Trick or treat?" with "Trick."

"And what can I do you gentlemen for?" she asked.

"A dollar," Oren said.

"I already gave to the March of Dimes."

"We're playing *Space Invaders*."

"How much is a game?" she asked.

"A quarter."

"You know," Lynn said, "when you think about it, a quarter is a lot of money." Like magic she produced a quarter between her thumb and index finger and held it toward us. When I reached to grab it, she quickly withdrew her hand. "Let me ask you this. If you saved a quarter once a week for a year instead of wasting it on a pinball game, how much would you have by next November?"

"Thirteen dollars," said Oren, who sensed a trap but remained riveted.

"Correct," Lynn said. "So you put that money in the bank at twelve percent interest, and then how much have you got?"

Oren, mumbling, tapped his thumb to the tips of his remaining fingers. "Almost fifteen bucks!" he said.

"Fourteen dollars and fifty-six cents, to be exact. Imagine what you could buy at Hanukkah with that kind of money. A *special* present," she said, slowly nodding, "that gives lasting joy instead of *bing boop bleep* over there." She dismissed the game with a flick of her wrist, and Oren shook his head. Hanukkah. Eight days of gifts we were missing out on because of our diluted blood. *"Roses are red,"* Mom liked to say, *"violets are bluish. If it wasn't for me, we'd all be Jewish."*

"I'm going to give you this quarter," Lynn said sadly, and handed it to Oren, folding his fingers over it and then laying her palm on his fist, as if she had gifted him an heirloom. "I want you to go now and have your fun, but I also want you to remember this little lesson."

Oren asked me if we should approach Naomi and I said no. When I asked him if we should approach Sam, he said, "That's embarrassing."

It was while we were sitting at the tabletop video game and sipping our Shirley Temples that Naomi appeared.

I felt her hip at my side, her elbow touching my shoulder, and then I caught her face's reflection in the black glass while the screen flashed. She bent farther forward so that we were nearly temple to temple. She tucked her hair behind her ear, her scent and the tick-tock of her necklace's pendants fogging me in embarrassment.

"What's the object here?" Naomi asked.

"Clear the board," Oren said. It was his turn and he was transfixed. "Before the aliens land."

"I like the squid one," Naomi said.

"I like the crab," Oren said.

"Which one do *you* like?" Naomi asked me.

The aliens' march was to the beat of a snare drum, and I felt like Oren's laser cannon: nowhere to hide while his bunkers disintegrated.

"You look skinny," Naomi said, still watching the screen. "You should come to the table and order something to eat."

"I've got another turn," I said, and then Oren's avatar was destroyed.

"Suit yourself," she said. "But don't leave without catching up."

We stared at the screen until she left. When I glanced up Oren was looking at me.

"Grody," he said.

Naomi did not approach me again that night, although back at the table she took the seat next to my father and, for the rest of the evening, seemed to be in competition with Al as to who could laugh loudest at his jokes. She knocked her shoulder against Dad's whenever he said something witty, or she pushed herself away from him while blurting out, "Shel, you're terrible."

Sam took the seat next to Mom and gave her his blinking, smug attention. He was quick to laugh at his own jokes. His laugh was horrible; it was like something you'd write in a speech bubble; it ended with a hideous gurgle. Throughout the rest of the evening, he would lean across Mom's person, as if to hear her better, in the rare instances when he would listen. Oren and I had been seated next to her, at the table's far corner with Danny and Jackie, who huddled in our presence or peeked toward us warily, like rabbits in a nest. What exactly were they afraid of? At one point, Mom, who sat with her elbow at rest on her crossed legs and chin propped on her palm, turned to face me. Sam was finishing up a sentence: "Don't you worry, Lily, this administration's going to unshackle this economy from so many restrictions and red tape, the energy it unleashes will be orgiastic," upon which he put his arm over her shoulders to give her a loving squeeze; and my mother, now that she held my gaze, crossed her eyes. At moments such as these, she was the only person in the room I trusted.

As for Naomi, I managed not to say goodbye.

My family walked home through Lincoln Center. We headed west past the plaza's fountains, past Moore's *Reclining Figure* sculpture, doubled in its reflection pool, past the theater and along the upper walkway that ran parallel to Sixty-Fifth Street far below. The gusts off the river assailed us here, elevated as we were. It was a lightless stretch, and the towering limestone beams to our left were perfect places for muggers to hide. Dad and Mom walked ahead of Oren and me, a little unsteadily, arm in arm, the sight of which calmed my tingling spider sense. The pavement beneath our feet was dotted with bird shit, and when I looked up, I could see the huddled pigeons, sheltered from the wind in the overhang's ledges, puffed and fat and armored against the growing cold.

Against Poly Prep and Storm King I was pinned. Against Dwight-Englewood and Hackley, pinned. Against Dalton and Trinity, pinned yet again. I toggled between 121 and 129 pounds, sucking down to the former in the run-up to our dual meets, half starved in the days beforehand. I took long trips on buses to other schools in other boroughs and states, weighed in, warmed up, and then was, in the sport's parlance, stacked, dropped, stuck, caught, decked—the outcome so certain the moment I stepped on the mat it was a challenge not to make the result seem rehearsed.

A sure victory for the opposition, I became known, in the lingo, as a *fish.*

This being insufferable to me, I ran Central Park's reservoir on the weekends and, weather and workload permitting, biked to school during the week. During free periods, it was not uncommon for Tanner, Cliffnotes, and me to abscond to the darkened gym and wrestle. The mats were hard and cold, the rubber as yet unsoftened by our bodies' heat. We shed our blazers, ties, shoes, and socks, and we rolled. Tanner, at

135 pounds, and by far the most talented of our triumvirate, was already a match for most of the juniors. He nearly touched six feet in height and had possessed, since seventh grade, the plaited physique of a superhero. Diminutive Cliffnotes, a second stringer at 115, made up for his lack of power with quickness and ambidexterity, shooting a fireman's carry on both sides with abandon. When we returned to class, our collars were sweat-dampened, hair wild, and faces still red from our exertions.

After my loss at Dalton, I lay on my top bunk, staring at the ceiling, and on its blank screen I replayed my defeat beginning to bitter end. My escapes were strong, but I had no offense, and this made me passive, especially at a match's outset.

What I needed was a bigger vocabulary.

In the upper school's library, a bright, modern space with tall windows overlooking the rooftop tennis courts, I asked Miss Adler, the head librarian, for guidance. "Well," she said, slapping both palms on her desk and then popping up from her chair, "exactly what sort of wrestling are we talking about? Is this for a research paper? Wrestling as it appears in ancient art?" A Brit, her white hair was close-cropped; her teeth, yellowed and warped as an old picket fence. She walked toward the card catalog. Deb Peryton sat at one of the long tables, her textbook open. She looked up and gave me a small wave. Miss Adler said, "It's quite the sport in India, you know. If memory serves, the first wrestling match that appears in Western literature is Menelaus grappling with the Old Man of the Sea, book four of the *Odyssey,* I believe. Have you read Chinua Achebe's *Things Fall Apart*? No? Well the protagonist, Okonkwo, is quite the champion. What about John Irving's *The World According to Garp*?" She cupped her hand by her mouth and whispered, "A bit smutty, if you ask me."

By now Miss Adler had pulled out a long wooden drawer from the catalog and was flicking through the cards.

"I just mean the sport," I said. "The moves."

"Ah," she replied, "now *that* narrows our search. Come along then."

Call number in hand, she led me to the stacks. The volume Miss Adler pulled from the shelf was exactly what I was looking for: an encyclopedia of takedowns, counters, and pinning combinations. There were step-by-step photographs, progressive sequences that, if I passed my eyes over them quickly enough, gave the illusion of movement.

"Thanks," I said to her.

Miss Adler smiled, her eyes warmly crinkling. "Happy to help," she said, before marching back to her desk.

The Ankle Pick, the Spladle, and the Peterson Roll. The Duck Under, Super Duck, and Chicken Wing. The Submarine, the Spread Eagle, and the Crossbody Ride. Every day I arrived to practice with a particular move in mind, determined to hit it on my partner at least once, no matter how badly I screwed it up or in what position it put me. At home, after a shower and a too-light dinner, after blasting through my remaining homework, Oren and I closed our door and sparred. Ferren Prep, where he attended school, was a wrestling powerhouse and allowed eighth graders to practice with the high school team. Oren, big for his age, was also competing at the 121-pound class, and during these sessions he occasionally overcame my seniority and greater power with an arsenal of techniques entirely alien to me, and I was so happy for him that he was winning—my surprise was so complete—it made me laugh. Afterward, he and I swapped new moves we'd learned that day in practice, abrading our knees and elbows on the bedroom's thin carpet until they were pink and dotted with blood.

"What was that?" I asked. I'd somehow found myself on my back after Oren, just a second ago safely secured beneath me, had somersaulted us both through the air and ended on top.

"The Flying Granby," he said.

"Teach me," I said. And then I added: "Please."

At least three times a week, Coach Kepplemen wanted to roll.

Why did I do this? I often wonder now. Why did I not simply say no? Was it because our ritual, established since seventh grade, was so prescribed in its motions—was, from its start, the norm—that I was too fixed in its repetitions to resist? He might catch me before school started, explaining he wanted to discuss my match, go over a few things, although I knew what he really wanted. We agreed to meet in the front hall at my next free period. He spotted me as I came around the corner and, before turning to walk, nodded his head, an indication that I was to follow. We made our way toward the lower school, though not exactly together. A long, carpeted corridor joined Boyd Prep's modern wing to the Old School's ancient edifice, and here Coach Kepplemen walked ahead of me by a good ten paces, past the basketball court, the cafeteria, and the wrestling gym, so that it would not be obvious to any passersby that we were headed somewhere together. Oh, how dutifully I played along, certain that he was listening to my footfalls, sure that if I were to stop in my tracks the slack between us would go taut. Not that I ever stopped.

Today he wore navy-blue sweatpants, a BOYD WRESTLING shirt, and Tiger wrestling shoes. Kepplemen had a distinctive gait. He walked turned out, as my mother might say, his feet set in second position, and this made his shoulders, which sloped left to right, seesaw, their metronomic tilt accentuated by the position of his arms, which he held out from his sides as if tracing the outline of a fat man's body. We briefly entered the Old School's high-ceilinged main hall, its marble floors and brownstone walls cool as a cathedral's. Picture its vaulting main hall, hear the vibration of accumulated sounds: the scuff of boys' loafers and girls' Mary Jane heels, an almost articulate spurt of vivid laughter. We hung a sharp left, ducking down a stairwell, also ancient, its stone banister palmed smooth by several hundred years of contact—Boyd was one of the oldest schools in New York—our descent lowering this melody's volume. It terminated at the school's weight room, a dim, nondescript space which consisted only of a multistation Universal machine.

It also housed the building's boilers. Here the heat was dry and oppressive. The far walls, shrouded in darkness, were marked by several arched entryways, as in catacombs. Their apex was maybe four feet high, all of which were bricked off except the one in the room's farthest corner, which was provisionally barricaded with a wooden pallet, its solid top painted black, which Kepplemen approached and then slid aside. Bending down, he entered, disappearing into the darkness, me following. A single dusty bulb came on, Kepplemen releasing its pull chain, and then he turned and slid the pallet closed behind us.

In this nether, not even used for storage, the low ceiling was cupped. Still bent, Kepplemen proceeded deeper into the gloom. He ordered me to turn off the light, and I obeyed. Being his height, I too walked bent; like a blind person operating by memory, I proceeded in pitch-blackness until another bulb came on. We arrived in what felt like a corridor or chamber. Its size was indeterminate; it was impossible to tell much beyond the bulb's weak illumination and directly beneath which was a section of wrestling mat. Its rubber was desiccated, puckered and cracked. Kepplemen, I was sure, had dragged this down here. He, too, had gone looking for this place—I did not make the connection then—as Naomi had the Dead Street. I knew the drill from years of practice. I stepped out of my loafers, pulled off my socks. Removed my tie, shirt, and belt while Kepplemen, who was already kneeling, watched. I too kneeled, across from him, fists to thighs. In this moment, I could always feel just how deep beneath the ground we were, the entombing silence of the building's ancient weight. Kepplemen said, "Okay," and at this we tipped toward each other and then locked up: ear pressed to ear, palms clamped to each other's necks, hands pinching triceps, our bodies forming another arch in that low-slung space, a headless creature rising on four legs.

Kepplemen was chronically unkempt. His cheeks were always rough with stubble, his wispy salt-and-paper hair mussed. He did not start the day thus. When he joined us at our lockers, when he sat on the floor with us in the hallway before the first-period bell rang, listening to our banter, relaxed enough to occasionally join in the conversation or pumping his foot while we joked, his hair was neatly parted, perhaps still shiny from his morning's shower. But by now he had rolled with at least one of us and by day's end several more. He smelled of deodorant and cheap detergent, and beneath that, an odor that was enfolded and in transformation, like the yogurt that hardened at its container's rim. Even at fourteen, after two years of wrestling under his tutelage, I felt myself to be his physical equal. I experienced no fear of being overmatched or overwhelmed, but I suffered instead the vague, humiliating sense of being *subjected*. The ceiling's height forced us to spar from our knees. The mat's dimensions, no bigger than his king-sized bed, limited the moves we might attempt—a Snap Down, a Russian Tie, an Arm Drag. Kepplemen initiated these with a great grunt. Each of these I easily countered, and then I'd reverse our position, which I knew he wanted, and assumed control, crouching behind him, my palm to his belly, hand to his elbow, chin buried in his shoulder, pelvis to his ass. At this he went still and would let me execute a sequence of pinning combinations—a Half Nelson, an Arm Bar—giving one quick tap to my hip, leg, or the small of my back to indicate that we should reset. The dust we'd kicked up hazed the bulb above, its glow haloed by this fogged nimbus. I was content to think of nothing, especially time, but Kepplemen had a keen internal clock. He ended each session similarly.

"Get me," Kepplemen said, and then caught his breath. "Get me in a headlock." Then he rolled onto his back, an act of accession, as if it were *I* who'd given the command. Lying beneath me, he reached both arms up and then waved me in, that great beaked nose of his half hiding his open mouth, upon which I scooped his neck in my arm, cradling his head beneath my biceps, and then clasped my hands, ramming my knee to his ear to reinforce my grip. My torso—my whole body's weight—draped perpendicularly across his. He bucked below me, bridging his neck, once, twice, as if to wriggle out while I held on, but this was not his intention. Soon his leg found mine; soon he used this hook to plaster himself against me. I was always surprised, as he thrusted, at how furious I was, how determined to hold him there, to make it cost him. And soon, like some creature whose bones had gone soft, he melted in my arms.

We dressed afterward. Or I did. Usually with my back to him. Although on occasion, as today, I'd glance over my shoulder to see Kepplemen facing the corner, neck bent, chin tucked, waistband stretched from his hips as he wiped his crotch with great care and then deposited the towel on the floor. And my great shame was strangely somehow for him. Of which I could not speak. To anyone. To my parents. To Elliott. Certainly not to my friends. Even later, when I joined Cliff and Tanner in the front hall and they asked, "Where were you?" I need only reply, "Kepplemen." Not even so much as a nod from them. Which was the trick, or the spell. Which was the only power we had. Because he was the only word for it we knew.

On Tuesday night, Mom made roast chicken with steamed artichokes and sweet potatoes. I was just on weight, so when she served me, I asked for a wing, and that was it.

"Are we going to do this again this year?" Mom asked.

"I have a match tomorrow," I said.

Dad, who'd made fast work of a whole leg, was attacking the drumstick's bone, biting off the knuckle's cartilage. I was so hungry I wanted to cry. "That reminds me," he said, "I got you guys a present." He pushed back from the table, disappeared to his room, and when he returned, he was holding a pair of cowboy hats. "They're Stetsons," he said after handing them to us. "Those are eagle feathers in the brim, by the way."

"Is that legal?" Oren asked.

"Maybe they're ostrich," Dad said.

Oren, donning his, considered himself in the wall mirror approvingly.

"I did some spots for Billy Martin's Western Wear," Dad said. "The reps gave them as a gift."

"So you didn't really *get* us these," Oren said.

"What difference does it make?" Dad said.

"That," Oren said like Yoda, "is why you fail."

Because of the hat, it was easy to spot Oren among the spectators before my match the next day. He gave me the thumbs-up just before I stepped on the mat. About a minute later, when I was on my back, I also noticed upside-down Mr. Fistly, seated in the second row, legs crossed, watching. It was a strangely intimate moment, like we were having a conversation with another person lying on top of me. He shook his head, disappointed and unsurprised, right before the referee slapped the mat.

"Buy you some ice cream," Oren said when he met me in the front hall.

We stopped at Baskin-Robbins and then entered Lincoln Towers at Seventieth Street, cutting through the block-long parking lot that ran between the rear of several apartment buildings and the storefronts on Amsterdam. I'd finished my double scoop—Oren was still working on his cone—when I spotted a figure on my right, racing crouched and sneaking toward us alongside several cars, and before I knew it, one kid had grabbed Oren while the other sprinted between a pair of cars and tackled me. He sat me on the cold concrete, his arm laced over my throat.

"Give us your fucking money," he said. The one next to Oren patted him down and then took the wad from his pocket. "Take whatever you want," I said, because I was practiced at this, "and then leave us alone."

Oren was crying. The second guy frisked me and, finding my wallet empty, tossed it to the ground and then smacked my mouth before they trotted off. I propped myself on my elbow and spit blood. Oren knelt beside me.

"Security!" he screamed. "Security!"

After I got up, I tried to calm him down, but he was inconsolable. "Just let them go," I said, and put my arm over his shoulders. We proceeded like that to the security guard's booth on our block. I was giving the guard the lowdown when we saw Mom, Dad, and Al Moretti walking toward us from our building.

"What happened?" Mom asked, with real concern.

"We got mugged," I said.

"Muthafuckers," Al said. "Were they Black? How old were they? Did you give the policeman a description?"

"They got all my money," Oren said. He was still crying. "And one of them punched Griffin."

"They should've taken that hat and done you a favor," Al muttered.

"It's a Stetson," Dad said.

"Stetson, schmetson," Al said. "What's he trying out for, the Village People?"

Mom hugged Oren while he wept. Dad, taking my head in his hands, turned my face side to side and then folded back my lip, tilting his chin up like a doctor. The performance was for Al, who was laughing, and infuriated me. "You'll live," he said.

The security guard pressed his walkie-talkie to his chest and said to Mom, "I'm filing a report."

"Under control, then," Dad said. To Mom he tapped his watch face and said, "We have a reservation." Then he started up the street with Al.

"There's pizza upstairs," Mom said to us, walking backward, slowly, to indicate she was sorry, her hands in her long coat's pockets. "Dad made a Caesar salad."

The pizza was cold, the romaine soggy, and Oren, still blubbering, wrapped four pieces in tinfoil and then heated them in the oven. He served us and sat down and covered his eyes and started crying again. "I'm sorry I couldn't help you," he said, and was so distraught he excused himself and went to our room. There were times, as now, when Oren acted as if he'd failed me in some far more essential manner than the circumstance, when half the time I felt like I'd failed him, and this mystery made the gulf between us seem even more unbridgeable than the fact that we no longer spent our days at school together.

At the next afternoon's practice, I was sparring with Tanner, on bottom, so I hopped into the Flying Granby position and rolled over my shoulders, but he caught my trail leg and stuck me on my back. I was in such a tightly inverted pin that I gagged.

Kepplemen blew his whistle and everyone froze.

"Hurt!" he screamed. "Don't you ever let me see you do that move again! Do you understand?"

When, I wondered, would I stop tearing up whenever an adult yelled at me?

"Because I will throw you out of this fucking gym if I catch you trying that bullshit. Are we clear?"

In response, I shot Kepplemen my death ray. It was his Kryptonite, making him think we didn't like him, although I sometimes suspected he knew that I mostly didn't. Instead of waiting for my concession, which he could tell wasn't coming, Kepplemen blew his whistle again, and practice resumed.

Perhaps I was still upset that Kepplemen had humiliated me, or that I sucked ass at wrestling, but when I spotted Naomi's car on my way home, I felt as if I'd summoned her from some secret part of my soul.

"I'm getting my butt kicked," I explained to her. We'd been parked on the Dead Street for maybe five minutes, and I'd already spilled my guts about everything. "In middle school we were all mostly the same size, but now everyone's so big and good."

"Better, stronger, faster, huh?" Naomi said.

"If I could just win once," I said.

"You will," she said.

Naomi was thrilled to see me. When a car passed in the opposite direction, the headlights revealed her giddy expression. She giggled once the darkness cloaked us again and then leaned forward to muss my hair, which she gathered in her fist and pulled me toward her to inhale my scalp, to kiss my temple, my cheek. I was still scurfy with sweat. "You taste like you've been swimming in the ocean," she said hungrily. When I did not reciprocate, she sat back against her door and smiled, and as if by some trick of the dimness her features were separate unto her, floating like a lily pad. That she had missed me so much made me both glad and uncomfortable.

"My first tournament's this Saturday," I said.

"Oh yeah? Where's that?"

"Friends Academy."

"The Quaker School? On Long Island?"

"I guess."

"Huh," she said, and considered this for a moment. "Your parents ever come watch you?"

"Dad's not much into sports."

"What about your mother?"

"She doesn't like it. Both times she saw me last year the kid I was wrestling got hurt."

"You mean like bad?"

"One broke his wrist. The other guy some ribs."

"Mr. Ferocious over here," Naomi said. She gave my shoulder a gentle push and then, resting her hand there, shook me. I went rag-doll limp and smiled, which encouraged her enough to embrace me. She did this with a great bustle at first. She bunched me to her, so that it all seemed nearly innocent. It bothered me, this attempt to disguise her intention, and she may have felt me withdraw, because when she pressed her lips to mine, she said, almost petulantly, "Kiss me back." And I remember thinking I had violated the rules between us, because I did one of the only decidedly cruel things to her I would do that year and which I still regret, since I already knew the answer to the question I asked.

"Where are your daughters?"

Naomi tensed. She sat back, slowly, and then looked down at her manicure. "They're performing tonight," she said softly. She glanced at her watch, even though they wouldn't be done for another couple of hours. "I should probably get back," she said, and then slid the key into the switch and started the car.

On Saturday, just before six a.m., our team boarded the bus and departed from school. Kepplemen was driving. The sky was still black, the bus warm. Pilchard sat at the front, behind Coach. Atop his lap there lay a large baking tin; it was an apple crisp his mother had made, tightly covered in Saran wrap and foil, to be eaten after weigh-ins, and its just-out-of-the-oven aroma drove us mad.

We woke in a parking lot on school grounds, outside a complex of buildings. The sky, rimmed by dawn, was blue-whale blue. Kepplemen led us inside the nearest structure, past the cavernous gymnasium, downstairs into an even darker locker room—a vast space. Other teams had gathered here. There was a crush of competitors. We heard the showers running and a skipping rope's wet whip. A long line had formed, leading toward a carpeted office, its interior lit. The queue snaked toward a tall scale with an oval face, where a pair of coaches stood holding clipboards. The moment we entered, we disrobed again. The host team's coach took our name and school and weight class as we stepped on the scale.

Back in the parking lot, the sky was shot through with sunlight now. It was so bright on the horizon we covered our eyes. The wind was fierce, the day freezing. The Ferren bus had just arrived. Oren, first to exit, upnodded to me; I signaled surreptitiously back as we headed in opposite directions. We boarded our bus and went straight to McDonald's. The gassiness of the egg and bread in that first bite, all of it gone before I could say *McMuffin*. The hash browns' crunch and then the salty oil seeping from the mashed mouthful. Soon we were shambling back to the bus. Our stomachs stretched our warm-ups' waistbands. Pilchard, first on board, was again seated behind Kepplemen. He had resisted breaking into his apple crisp. If you tried to touch the tin he'd have snapped at your hand. When we returned to the campus we took our gear this time. In the gym, a block of bleachers had a sign above it that read BOYD PREP, and we piled our bags here. Pilchard, seated dead center, finally removed the foil to his food and was greeted by a puff of steam. He'd brought a box of plastic forks. We passed these around while we let him have the first few bites and then set upon the food from every side and angle. Pilchard looked like Dr. Octopus, with so many arms bristling from his shoulders and back and each acting independently. But now it all was too much, *now* we'd done it. We were landed fish, worm-bellied and air-engorged. We were in so much pain the only solution was sleep.

We smushed our gear bags into pillows, some of the seniors having known to *bring* pillows. Kepplemen said, "I have to go to the seeding meeting." Still, he couldn't help it: he paused to smile at us before departing. His love for us was palpable. He looked like he wanted to kiss us each good night. We buttoned or zipped up our jackets to the tops of our collars; we covered our heads with our hoodies or pulled our stocking hats over our eyes. And we slept the sleep of the shipwrecked, safely ashore.

We woke. We sat up. We blinked at the brightness.

The gymnasium was larger in size than the one at Boyd, with high windows running its length on both sides. Our eyes were visored from the sunshine filling these by the multiple state championship pennants in every sport hanging from the ceiling wires. What gave the space its grandeur was, first, the mats, four of them arrayed atop the hardwood, with walking lanes in between each, a pair of foldout chairs for coaches and assistant coaches on points north and south of their circumference—a gladiatorial pit, then, given our bleacher's elevation, with giant Roman numerals fashioned of athletic tape, denoting each and adding to the effect. In front of these, the scoring tables, atop which sat timers and air horns and scoring charts in red and green and flipped to zero, the rolled towels taped at both ends to throw at the ref to signal each period's conclusion. The PA came on with a deafening buzz; it was as if lightning were attempting speech. A voice said, "Matches will begin at nine a.m." We were a half hour from start time, and just now, as if having been introduced, as a sort of preamble, the referees were arriving in their official outfits but still wearing jackets over their striped tops. The event's scale was now apparent, eight teams in attendance, their managers wandering the floor, talking to officials, to coaches. These were girls predominantly, although Cliffnotes was acting as ours today since he wasn't starting. I spotted Oren, also managing, who spotted me. I waved him over, and he broke away so we could steal a moment to chat, although he did this furtively, guiltily; he kept checking over his shoulder as he approached. So far as his teammates were concerned, he explained, I was a rival instead of a brother and was to be treated with extreme prejudice. "They don't think we should be talking," he said, sadly, before he departed. And then pointing to the gym's far end, as if to provide guidance: "Seeding charts are up."

Here, one of the managers was taping the posters of each weight class's brackets to the wall, a mass of wrestlers forming a crescent before her. Kepplemen appeared, along with the other coaches, at the far entrance. He looked anxious as he joined us, as we surveyed our first-round opponents.

I'd drawn the top seed, Vince Voelker, a senior from Dalton. I'd seen him wrestle in the weight class above mine in our dual meet a few weeks ago. He was fearsome enough at 129—he'd destroyed my teammate Frank Swain, pinning him in the first period—but had sucked down to 121 for today's tournament. He would go on to win league and state later that year. Still, looking back, what I first recall was sensing Kepplemen behind me. He already knew my opponent but seemed to be suffering its grim reality with me.

"Can I beat him?" I asked.

Something about the question made Kepplemen smile, made his eyes twinkle. "We'll see," he said.

From that point until our match, I remember being aware of exactly where Voelker was in the gym. I had to maintain the maximum distance possible between us while keeping him in sight. Because I hadn't yet learned the rhythm to these tournaments, I conflated the still-reigning quiet that pervaded the space with my dread, how it shrank the gymnasium as we ran through team stretches and warm-ups. How we counted out our reps as if we were performing them in a library. Over the PA, the announcer said, "Matches will begin in five minutes . . ." and then assigned the competitors to their respective mats. I was on highest alert, and what is so clear to me now is how diametrically opposite these anticipatory minutes were to when I was acting. They electrified me, because the outcome was not predetermined. In spite of how outclassed I knew I was, I sensed there was also some measure of control in the result that, unbeknownst to me, hearkened back to that dreadful moment days after the fire, hiding beneath Neal's bed, when my father's face appeared on the floor, when he turned away and his hand reached for me, when I kicked and fought him off until he took hold of my collar and dragged me forth. I was overmatched then; since winning against Voelker was just as improbable, it would mean something bigger than I could comprehend to win *now*. Every second the contest was forestalled was a suffering. I knew victory would require a remarkable performance.

Those of us in the lighter classes were out of our seats, we were pacing and hopping. We found our way to the warm-up areas behind the basketball hoops where we stretched and shadow wrestled. By now the matches had begun, and to deflect my nervousness, I invested all my attention in them. I eavesdropped on the upperclassmen lying on the mats' edges discussing the competitors' technique. Santoro joined Kepplemen as assistant coach; Captains Adler and Dolph manned the other mats when they were occupied. They were all top seeds and in heavier weight classes. In comparison to us, they seemed like titans. Soon enough, when my name was called over the PA, Kepplemen found me as I walked the lane to Mat III. From there he led me by the elbow. He whispered some last-minute coaching advice I did not hear. I kept my eye on Voelker as we approached, already awaiting me at the mat's center, hopping from foot to foot and shaking the tension from his massive arms. I noticed certain uncanny morphological similarities we shared. We were wild-haired, square-bodied, large-handed boys. Two years hence, when I filled out, I'd share Voelker's solid base, a fullback's quads that stretched my singlet's elastic enough it left an imprint on my legs. I too would become an attacking wrestler, offensive-minded and emulating his relentlessness, albeit with important differences, but no matter now. It is one of the unique aspects of the sport: You can not only absorb another wrestler's style by physical contact but also feel the competitor you wish to become. You are changed by how he moves you.

We fastened our anklets, shook hands, and then the ref blew his whistle.

Broadly speaking, there are two types of wrestlers. The first might best be described as multilingual—fluent, that is, in a wide range of attacks, counters, and escapes. Wrestlers such as these are kinesthetically creative and tend to be great athletes. They roll like the best jazz musicians play: inventively, improvisationally. Quicksilver runs through their veins. They appear to eschew strategy, flow with the go, but there is method in their fluidity: they are chasing beauty, something close to a dance, the purpose of which is to create a chain of movements so ironclad for their opponents it is a form of inevitability. They are often late bloomers but more formidable in their maturity. They bristle with weapons; they are expert in all. I aspired to this style but didn't know it at the time. The second type builds his entire strategy around an unstoppable move. These wrestlers are blitzkriegers, tsunamists. Their modus operandi is avalanche, overwhelm. Like tornadoes, they elicit the desire to take shelter or run. There is a seeming simplicity to their games, but this is a mistake: an incredibly complex set of operations is required to direct you into their wheelhouse. They are most dangerous at a match's outset. Their efficiency is nasty, brutish, and often produces contests that are short. To immovable objects they bring unstoppable force. Given the choice, they'd finish off their opponent in ten seconds and happily call it a day. This was how Voelker wrestled.

He took you down with a brutal ankle pick or foot sweep, flattened you out, and then chased what's called a double arm-bar series. You should picture it thus: Imagine you're lying facedown on a mat. Place your wrists against your lower back, like you're about to be cuffed. Next retract your shoulders, so that your arms stick up to form what look like dorsal fins. Now imagine someone lying perpendicularly atop *your* back with *his* arms threaded through the two triangles yours have formed. With *his* interlocked hands, he is driving this single fist into your spine. Properly applied, a double arm bar touches your elbows together, so that your shoulders stretch until you think they might be torn from your torso. Pinning you from here is a simple matter of leverage and torque. Your opponent walks in a circle around your head. This action flips you onto your back. If he meets resistance going in one direction, he spins counterclockwise and walks around your head in the other. The pivot point is your face.

The only counter to this is to not let your opponent collect both your arms. I spent the next three periods trying to post my free hand and far leg to stop the orbit Voelker tried to walk around my head with a single arm bar. This required an enormous amount of energy, redlining my aerobic capacity from go. Less than a minute into the match, I was gassed. This effort also abraded the skin from my cheek and, when Voelker reversed course, buffed it from the other. Picture a drill bit boring into wood, the curlicue shavings worming from the deepening hole: on a microdermic level, this was what was happening to my face. Intertwined thus, Voelker and I sidewinded out of bounds, after which the ref broke his clinch and directed us back to the mat's center. I took the down position on my hands and knees, Voelker placing one hand on my elbow, the other on my belly. The ref blew his whistle to restart us. And once again I was flattened out, my near arm immediately resecured in his bar, the fight ensuing for my free wrist, me doing everything I could to resist his rotation while he tried to secure it. I felt regressed to some desperate, pre-upright state, my entire will directed toward the effort *to stand,* tripoding, like some determined and evolving creature, against Voelker's pressure, to briefly achieve footing—which I did—only to be slammed to the mat again. My face broke my fall.

And yet I refused to succumb. Whether this was born out of a sense of injustice at my seeding or a newfound determination to wage a losing battle—to draw out this experience so early in what I'd hoped would be a much longer, more successful day—I mustered the entirety of my resoluteness and resisted. Whatever fury I'd accessed tapped adrenal reserves, and like the boy who lifts the burning car from his unconscious brother's body, I fought off the attack; and if I found myself on my back, I bridged using my neck and feet to keep at least one scapula off the mat with Hulk-like strength. This may still be the single most concentrated effort I have ever expended to prevent something from happening in my entire life. At the start of the second period, there was a coin toss, which I won. I chose the top position, and the ref indicated Voelker take bottom; I placed my palm to Voelker's elbow, my other to his iron stomach, which expanded and contracted with his breathing. There was the uncanny sense that, in spite of the fact we were the same weight, he seemed double my size. The ref blew his whistle, and for several seconds I experienced what it must be like to be dragged by a bull or a horse, or, more accurately, I suffered that first blind panic as you make your maiden attempt at waterskiing, which for nearly everyone ends with a mouthful of lake and the tow rope being ripped from your hands. And then Voelker was on my back again.

He pinned me at the very end of the third period, with three seconds left in the match.

I remember when Voelker rolled away from me. Before getting up, before joining the ref at the mat's center to have his arm raised, he remained there, on one knee, his other hand pressed to his bent leg and shoulders heaving, waiting until I sat up and faced him. When I did, he considered me with an expression at once exasperated and appreciative, narrowing his eyes with a guarded affection. Then, to acknowledge the effort I'd cost him, he shook his head in annoyance, and honored me with a quick laugh. Which was the first time all season I felt something like victory.

Then I went to find somewhere private to cry.

By the time I got myself together, the tournament's first round had concluded.

"Competition will resume at ten thirty," the PA said.

In the lull between rounds, wrestlers from different schools drifted and then intermingled and socialized on the four mats. It was a sort of reprieve, a pause in the battle; it was like the soccer games I'd read were played in no-man's-land during World War I. It was also a chance to ask other wrestlers to walk you through a technique or to discuss counters against the combinations they had thwarted you with earlier. To try out new moves. To get close to some of the league's ascendant gods. To study, without fear, the cables of their neck tendons and the size of their hands; to inventory their birthmarks and pimples and scars, which was a way of making them seem mortal. Some consciously cultivated distance; some were friendlier than others. Some shared key details that unlocked mysteries. But there were a few who distinguished themselves, in spite of their approachability, by something they could not communicate, that went beyond their physical vocabulary, the moves they so perfectly executed themselves. It was contained within them, held in abeyance during this break, secreted away in some area of their brains, a kinesthesia dormant but instantly accessible, emerging only when they competed and approaching the ineffable. It was in the way that Poly Prep's Carmelo, a 148-pounder, stood facing his opponent, bent at his hips, his palms to his knees, not merely waiting but almost inviting an attack as he calculated his combinations of counters in the milliseconds before reacting. It was revealed in Voelker's juggernaut determination, from any position, to secure his opponent's arms. It was evident when James Polk, mid-

entanglement, would almost professorially pause to consider the pret-
zeled state in which he and his opponent found themselves deadlocked,
to spy a new opening and release them from their Gordian knot, but to
his advantage. It was, in short, their *style,* fully realized, expressed as control of the moment, of their *lives,* which I, forced to play parts I did not
seek, emulated. This seemed an utterly daunting enterprise and also one
entirely worthy of aspiring to. It would take years of sacrifice to achieve;
it might never be expressed; it guaranteed failures; and I might finally
emerge victorious if I succeeded at it—might finally break free. But like
Voelker's laugh at our match's conclusion—the tiny recognition that he
too had once mustered all his power to stave off defeat—it waved to me,
secretly, intimately, fraternally, as Oren did occasionally, across the gym's
span. Upon my arrival at such proficiency, it promised what I wanted
most, which was to dictate my own destiny, no matter who the opponent
standing before me was, and amid all the tumult, it felt like an assurance
from the future, a half whisper that said, *Keep going.*

Later that afternoon, I won my first wrestling match.

Because of my first-round loss, I participated in the consolation
rounds—a mini-tournament that was essentially a battle for third place.
These matches were contested in the lull before dinner and the tournament finals that evening.

Before my opponent—he was from Horace Mann—even stepped
onto the mat, his coach spoke into his charge's ear insistently, almost
grimly. He registered these instructions without expression, nodding
occasionally but not facing his coach, sizing me up, perhaps, although he
did this with the same impassivity he considered the last-minute input.
Our ref, whom I recognized from several of our dual meets, was tall,
broad-bellied. His thick hair was combed in a pompadour; his glasses
were square-framed and secured behind his ear by a band of black elastic. He'd signaled I'd been pinned at least three times this month. My
opponent approached me, but his coach took his elbow again and, as if
he'd forgotten something crucial, spoke some more. The ref waved him
on with such firm impatience it was clear that further delay would lead
to disqualification. My opponent walked on the mat as if it were made
of the thinnest ice; the ref handed him his anklet, and as he secured its
Velcro, I took my last opportunity to study him, searching for any clue

as to what sort of combatant he might be, how strong he was—some hint, some key, that would unlock his secret weakness. We shook hands, took our ready positions. His grip was light, his palms moist. He fixed his gaze up and over my shoulder; his eyes caught the sunset's light, as if he were awaiting a revelation. The ref blew his whistle. And then, before we even began to hand fight, my opponent fell to his back and seized up, snapping taut in what appeared to be a full-body cramp. His coach, who was now on his knees by his charge's ear, confirmed that my opponent was unable to continue, and after helping him to sit up; after his assistant coach secured a banana and some Gatorade, fed him a bite of the former and made him drink a few sips of the latter; after he helped him limp off the mat, I was declared the winner by default, my arm raised in victory. With the exception of Kepplemen and Santoro, who was assistant coaching, no one in the entire gymnasium—not even Oren—noticed the result.

The consolation round finals wouldn't take place for another half hour. My match's brevity, however, made it possible to scout my possible opponents, since they were competing on the adjacent mat. It became obvious that third place and its medal ran through Peter Goldburn.

He was a senior at Ferren, Oren's school, and he was overwhelming his opponent, just now bringing the match to a conclusion with a violent throw that he followed up with a quick pin. I spotted Oren in the bleachers. He caught my eye, and his expression was dire. What struck me about Goldburn was not his physique, which was as Apollonian an expression of anatomy as any of the athletes in the tournament possessed, but rather the force and command of his moves, his blazing transitions through these combinations, which made me feel both slow and small. Shaken, I consulted the bracket sheets taped to the gymnasium's wall and saw he'd lost to Voelker 4–2 in the semis, the pair of points separating them like the span between subway platforms: a leap that was possible to contemplate but unlikely to be completed. Still, I wanted to win—to win would be to medal—and in the half hour before the match I consulted the experts.

Our team captains were seated in the bleachers, watching these contests as a triumvirate while automatically eating the remainder of Pilchard's apple crisp. There remained in the giant, flimsy pan only a third of the food left, its aluminum buckling and deformed. It was positioned on the bench so that each captain had equal access to it: Pat Santoro seated to its left, Roy Adler to its right, and Brian Dolph above.

"He goes for throws from standing," Santoro said, anticipating my question. "He's going to tie you up at the start, you're going to have to fight off his underhooks, or else he'll try to hip toss you or hit a Pancake from a Whizzer."

"He also likes a Super Duck to take you down," said Adler. "Then if you stand-up escape, he'll Suplex you."

"Ferren guys love that Greco-Roman shit," said Dolph.

"I thought a Suplex was illegal," I said.

"It is if you take the guy straight over your head," said Santoro. "Not if you take him over your shoulder."

"They're assholes like that," said Dolph, "it's all about scoring amplitude and showing off. But here's the thing. He gasses easily. Make him work."

Santoro nodded. "His wind is shit."

"Make him earn every fucking inch he takes," said Adler.

"Like you did against Voelker."

"You watched my match against Voelker?"

"Don't play to his strength."

"Put him on the defensive. Initiate, don't defend."

"Shoot your double or single leg."

"Because he'll kill you if you go upper body."

"And only hit that switch of yours from the down position."

"Because if you try a stand-up escape—"

"He'll Suplex you."

There was a long silence during which all three chewed ruminatively. The last matches before the consolation finals were going on. These were the heavier weights, the future offensive linemen and rugby players, the Little Johns and Ajaxes, the Men among Boys. Their contact generated shockwaves; their bodies hit the mats like fluke slaps. Our three captains watched them as a unit. Their eyes were all drawn to the same sequences. When one of the competitors pulled an exceptional move they said "Nice" or "Slick" or whistled in appreciation. Or they made mid-match predictions with the disinterestedness of oracles: "He's going to sell a

Snap Down and then hit an ankle pick," or "He's going to crab ride this guy into a Stack." And then, just seconds later, he would.

Nobody really cared about the consolation finals.

These matches were on the order of undercard. The main event—the finals—were a couple of hours off. Still, the bleachers were more than half full now. What had felt more like intermission, really, as if those who'd hung back didn't have the confidence or determination to leave their seats, had now built into an anticipatory energy. The gym's high windows were shading from purple to black. The change in brightness was theatrical, a luminosity less diffuse, with several of the ceiling's tube lights cut and the pendant high bays turned on so that the mats shined like billiard tables.

My name was called over the PA; it was a lonely, empty, ringing sound. Applause from the Boyd bleacher. From the Ferren bleacher when Goldburn was announced. Kepplemen, who'd just finished coaching a match, signaled to me to stay where I was. I could tell by his very pace, by the slowness of his tilted gait and the additional time he took to join me, that he too was nervous. He palmed my cheek and pressed his temple to mine, waiting to find his words.

"You can't be passive," Kepplemen said. His palm slid up my elbow to curl around my biceps as we walked. "Do you understand?"

He escorted me toward the mat, carrying enough of my weight that my shoulders were uneven. Goldburn awaited me, explosively jumping, bringing his knees to his chest. My mouth was cottony, but Kepplemen's was worse. Each time his tongue detached from the roof of his mouth, it made a click. It was at these moments that I was aware of how much he cared for me.

"If you're reacting, you're conceding initiative. If he's got the initiative, you're not dictating."

"Yes."

"To dictate you've got to move."

"I understand."

"Move out there," he said. He took me by the shoulders and turned me so that I faced him. Then he slapped me once. *"Move,"* he shouted. And then he slapped me a second time, so hard my eyes watered. It made me livid, and when I ran onto the mat and faced Goldburn, when I shook his hand and took my ready position, he noticed that I was vibrating with fury. He glanced at his coach in what was something like confusion, and in that second, I believed I could win.

Goldburn was not as strong as he looked. One of wrestling's physiological mysteries is that sometimes those with the most statuesque physiques, who from pure optics looked like they emerged from the inked corners of a comic book's panels, in fact lack fight and determination. They have a capacity to collapse, to tank; like Thanksgiving floats, their bodies, in spite of their size, feel air-filled, light. And conversely (at times) the most powerful just as often appeared otherwise: their thin arms hide bones fashioned of rebar, the soles of their feet are tethered to the earth's core, and the force they generate, exponent to your base, seems to come from a place that is spiritual rather than physical, elemental as opposed to gym-built—ocean deep or jungle dark.

That Goldburn wasn't as ferocious or overwhelming as he appeared bolstered and emboldened me. It increased my resolve and resistance, which translated in turn to desperation on his part and immediately caused him to expend even greater effort to try to bring our match to a quick conclusion. Which he couldn't.

This didn't mean I wasn't losing. Like Voelker, Goldburn tried early on to steamroll me, building an advantage in the first period before fading. The score was 6–3 in his favor, it was the third and final period, and there was a little over a minute left. He was on top but so gassed I took the risk of playing to his strength. Against the advice of Santoro, who was assistant coaching me now, and to the horror of Kepplemen, who shouted, *"No!"* I attempted a stand-up escape. Hopping to my feet, pressing the belt that Goldburn's arms formed at my waist toward my hip bone, I tried to use its point and my own pressure to unclasp his grip. In response to this, Goldburn lifted me off the mat—what crowd there was gasped—and flung me over his shoulder. When I landed head-first, when I heard my neck crunch, I saw a sudden spray of light, a fountain of sparklers that briefly dotted my vision. Fortunately, Goldburn had thrown me out of bounds; he'd neither scored points nor gained a positional advantage; we were back to neutral. But the blow was tremendous; my inner gyroscope had cracked. I could not get my equilibrium.

I began, in my confusion, to walk off the mat. I was concussed, I now know, but the ref mistook my injury for dizziness; he figured the throw had merely disoriented me and guided me back to the mat's center. And at this moment I saw, sitting on the lowest seat of the nearest bleacher, my parents. Beside them: Sam Shah. Beside him: Naomi.

My father was so wrapped up in his conversation with Sam that my match seemed incidental—that is, the pair of them paid next to no attention to the proceedings. But out of fear Mom now took Dad's wrist, and when Naomi lowered her hand from her mouth I knew that something was seriously amiss. She was gripping the bleacher's riser so fiercely her knuckles were visibly blanched. And in that short and vivid walk from the mat's outer ring to its inner one, I not only registered her fear but also realized that she had begun making plans for this visit the moment I told her the tournament's location. She had wanted to see me, to be here, if for nothing else than to let me know she'd tried. And for those several stretched-out seconds, I felt the full force of her care, and was grateful.

The ref indicated that I should take the down position; once I was on my hands and knees, he directed Goldburn to take the top. Somehow it was as if the entire match had reset; I was suddenly, utterly awake. From the scorer's table Cliff shouted, "Twenty-eight seconds!" Goldburn's grip touched my elbow and his other hand palmed my stomach. The instant the ref blew his whistle, I faked the Granby, Goldburn dropped his weight, and then I stood. Goldburn, having nearly exhausted himself with the previous throw, countered by letting me up in order to attempt the same throw again. And in that lag I'd created, that half second I'd anticipated before he secured his grip on my waist and shifted his own hips beneath mine; in that loose, interstitial pause in which there was space and contested leverage between us; with nearly the same force Goldburn had previously thrown me, I hit a standing switch. I clasped his right elbow with my left hand, cat-pawed the inside of his right leg, and then spun behind him, so that he was slung toward the ground. The mat must have seemed like a wave rising toward him. His face hit the foam with a great, wet slap.

The score was now 5–6. I scurried to Goldburn's side, perpendicular to him, and secured a cradle—a pinning combination—one arm laced over his neck and the other threaded between his legs; as I gripped my hands by his belly, I drove my head into his ribs and bowbent his body to further collapse it. I confess I was surprised by where I'd found myself. Kepplemen, in astonishment, leaped to his feet and threw his arms out, grabbing Santoro, who had also stood as if to steady himself. "There it is!" Kepplemen screamed. All I had to do to win was tip Goldburn toward his back to get the points. Again I drove the top of my head into his ribs and he began to tilt; he mustered everything he had left to resist. The match had garnered the entire gym's attention. Shouting erupted stereophonically, from the Ferren side, from the Boyd side, from everywhere. I heard my mother scream, *"You can do it, Griff!"* I heard Oren cry, *"Go!"* I needed only to tip Goldburn's shoulders only one degree past ninety and hold him there. The ref slid to the floor near my face to better observe the angle. *I have him,* I thought. I smiled to myself. I gathered all my remaining strength for a final effort, but next made a terrible miscalculation. Because when I shoved him, I pushed us out of bounds.

And then the horn sounded and the ref blew his whistle.

I had run out of time.

It was decided that I would leave the tournament with my parents. I'd skip dinner with the team and miss the finals. But there is an aftermath to a closely contested match. It occurs in the period when neither participant has yet composed himself, the shaking of the opposing coaches' hands is discombobulated, and with face buried in the crook of an elbow the loser stumbles off somewhere private while the victor breathes a sigh of relief. I shambled to the nearest doors marked EXIT. I found myself in a darkened school hallway, posters on the dim walls, signs on the windows of classrooms, and, drenched in sweat, I slid down the lockers to the floor and covered my eyes. I'd yet to catch my wind. I heard another crash of the doors. It was Oren. It was my brother. He slid to his knees and, the moment we collided, threw his arms around me; *he* was the one who was sobbing. "I'm sorry," he said, "they said I couldn't cheer for you, they said if I rooted for you I'd be betraying the team," and the pain this had caused him eclipsed mine. I hugged him while he shook, his tears mixed with my sweat, and then he staggered off.

Before I departed, Kepplemen pulled me aside. He led me to a set of far bleachers and indicated I sit; the gym was emptying out ahead of the day's last chapter—the teams off to dinner ahead of the finals. I still held my headgear in my hands.

"This," Kepplemen said. Then he gestured toward the entire gym. "Today. You really showed me something out there. You competed. You compete, and you learn where you are. Learn where you are," he continued, "and you know where you have to go." He was considering me, contemplating me, with an entirely different level of seriousness. And whereas he often used our losses as an opportunity for consolation, to touch us, now he neither palmed my neck nor pulled my forehead to his. "You won't forget it."

I took the back seat in Naomi's car. She rode shotgun so that Dad could drive. Mom was in the Bentley with Sam, since she hadn't had the chance at Elliott and Lynn's anniversary to test it out. I sat low in my seat. The streetlights rose and fell in long arcs, shining along the highway and among the trees, as if keeping time with my heartbeat. The night was black and starless. The car was warm and the seat comfortable. I thought I might fall asleep. My father was talking; Naomi, pretending to listen, occasionally glanced at me between the seats. Unaware that she'd interrupted my father, she said to me, "I thought we'd order some Chinese." It traversed the distance between us like a question and ignored my father's monologue, which I appreciated.

"That would be okay," I said, at once forlorn and dreamy and open to Naomi's imploring expression. I marked the asphalt's one-two rhythm thudding against the tires. I was thinking about my match. I was pressing my head into Goldburn's ribs. I'd taken a moment to laugh and then drove him out of bounds. Seconds I couldn't get back. My failure to recognize our position. Oh, that arena, where there was nowhere to hide, where all your weaknesses were exposed. I thought: *Know where you are on the mat.*

Acting never gifted me with such language.

The Shahs had a three-car garage. Sam's Ferrari, I noted for Oren, was gunmetal gray. The wine Sam served my parents was red; its label's letters were fashioned of a calligraphy ornate and ancient. My mother, who sat by the fireplace with Sam, said it was the best wine she'd ever had. Tonight, my parents seemed to be playing a game: they were swapping partners to get each other's attention. Mom hung on Sam's every word, sitting in that coiled way of hers, legs crossed, elbow on her knee, her other elbow clasped in her hand, her chin at rest atop her palm. His enthusiasm was nearly uncontrollable as he leaned toward her; he took his eyes off her only to toss a log into the blaze. Naomi was seated between my father and me on the couch. He was making a Very Important Point, but Naomi remained inert and quiet, her hip pressed to mine, and if she was listening to anything it seemed it was the sound of our breathing.

Danny and Jackie made an appearance; Danny and Jackie presented themselves to my mother; Danny and Jackie disappeared. We were sitting in the Shahs' living room. Ceiling-high windows faced onto their backyard, black but for the water feature outside, a koi pond that reflected the light from the interior. The white sofas were as plush as the leather in Naomi's Mercedes. Before opening the next bottle of wine, Sam held it away from his body, with his arms fully extended, as if he were farsighted. He handed it to my father, who mimicked the gesture, and spoke the vintage in a French accent so heavy it verged on parody. The Chinese food cartons were arrayed atop the coffee table like tents in an army camp. The smell was heady. I was hungry but could not bring myself to eat; I had a plate in my lap and chopsticks I could not manage. My knee pressed lightly and secretly against Naomi's. At one point, amid all the hubbub—the record Sam was playing and the music my father commented on and my mother's crying laugh—during a second or two when I felt most decoupled and disengaged and seemed so disembodied it was as if I were watching myself slump quietly within this bustling scene, Naomi, sensing my need, leaned toward me and, as if we were alone in her car, touched her shoulder to mine and said, "You doing all right?" to which I replied, "Would it be okay if I took a shower?"

I hadn't bathed, after all, hadn't tended to the mat burn above my eyes and cheeks, hadn't rinsed the soreness from my shoulders or the dullness across both my forearms that weakened my grip. To the adults Naomi announced, "Griffin says he wants to bathe," and after this was barely acknowledged, she got up from the sofa and bid me follow her. The moment we were out of sight she directed me by touching the small of my back. I was certain she might put her arm around me. I followed her up a wide set of stairs. I paused midflight, out of wooziness. I held the banister until the dizziness stopped, and then she joined me and took

my elbow with the lightest pressure, directing me to the top of the landing and down a long hallway whose light she didn't bother to turn on.
"You must be so beat up," she said. "A shower will do you good." We
padded through the master bedroom; I could feel how plush the carpet
was even through my wrestling shoes. Naomi did not bother to turn on
the light here either. "Almost there," she said. A huge bed faced another
set of windows. She snapped on the light in the master bath, and I shut
my eyes, wincing from the brightness. She leaned me against the wall as
if to acknowledge I was unsteady. She rubbed my shoulders and said,
"Don't fall over." And after sliding open the shower door, she seated herself on the tub's edge, reaching behind her to turn on the faucets, mixing the hot and cold and letting the water run over her fingers, until she
turned to me and smiled and said, "Just right." She pulled the diverter.
There was a pause in the pressure, the shower began to run, and then she
got up and walked past me to the bathroom door, which she closed and
locked.

The room was filling with steam. I was taken by the hiss, by the
water's great torrent, and stood facing Naomi, who leaned, now, against
the sink, her palms pressed to the countertop, her elbows locked, and
one leg extended so that she pressed her foot to the wall between the exit
and me. I could appreciate what she was wearing now: the long skirt and
high-heeled boots, which made her my height; a silk blouse with a metallic sheen to it. She removed her glasses; the lenses had begun to fog, as
had the mirror, which she sat before and reflected her back, which soon
reflected nothing. I knew what she was waiting for me to do.

I unzipped the top of my warm-ups and pulled my arms from its
sleeves with some effort, with some pain. I bent to unlace my wrestling
shoes, toeing off each at the heel. I removed my socks and stepped out
of my pants, and then thumbed my singlet's shoulder straps, pushing it
down at the waist along with the elastic band of my jock. By now the
room was so fogged that the sink's mirror was completely clouded in
mist, the opaque vapor floating between us and blotting the background.
I stood before her, freed from my clothing's compression that had somehow isolated each pain point's radiation and, like unpinioned wings,
spread across my entire back. Naomi pushed away from the countertop and reached out to embrace me. She ran her hands along my dewy

shoulders, down my arms to my wrists, and up again to my scapulae, her fingernails tracing these contours to my lower back, and then she gently palmed my ass. She pressed her cheek to mine. Our skin was softened by the steam, the space between where we touched slick. She remained there and then said, "My boy, my sweet, sweet boy. It was hard to watch you out there tonight." I pressed my forehead to her shoulder and leaned against her. She gently rocked us side to side. She pressed her mouth to my ear. "It's terrible not to talk to you sometimes," she whispered, her words blending with the shower's hiss. "To be so close, to be right there." Did she want a reply? I had none. Not that it would have mattered. Before I could answer, before I could summon a response, she let go, disappearing even before she disappeared from the room, a void left in her wake, the steam furled and serpentine and quickly filling the space, as if it had been conjured to finally give me some privacy.

DOUBLE FANTASY

Friday night was Taco Night at Tanner's house.

Mr. Potts cooked the meal. An investment banker at Morgan Stanley, he arrived to the apartment in his suit and overcoat. We saw him appear at the front door, shopping bag in hand, from where we sat watching TV off the kitchen. He placed this on the countertop, disappeared down the hallway to his bedroom, and, absent the tie and jacket when he returned, donned an apron, took his place behind the range— from where he cooked, he had a perfect view of the screen—aimed the remote, and then changed the channel to the news, which I knew not to protest but which Tanner always forgot. "It's my TV," said Mr. Potts, "so I get to watch what I want."

It was day 398 of the Iran hostage crisis.

At the kitchen counter, Mr. Potts began by preparing the stew beef, and while it browned, he chopped the onions, garlic, and peppers; as these sautéed, he opened a beer and took a sip, and he grated a block of cheddar and Monterey Jack cheese. He added canned tomatoes to the pan, poured the remainder of his beer into it, and, while all this simmered, he cooked each tortilla individually in vegetable oil, the hot liquid shining and then foaming at the circumference, out of which he tonged and then flipped them, arraying the finished stack on a baking sheet where, after popping them into the oven, they took on their final clamshell form.

The Pottses' Upper East Side apartment was as big as the one we'd lived in before moving back to Lincoln Towers, maybe even bigger, certainly longer, the lengthy hallway running down its center, branching off of which were, in order and to the left, if you walked it as Mr. Potts just had, Tanner's elder sister Gwyneth's room, followed by his younger sister Melissa's room; to the left again, as you made your way back, was the Pottses' master, Tanner's bedroom, the dining room, and, once again, the sitting room off the kitchen—this where nearly the majority of our time was spent and a fact that I found ironic, given all the space it enjoyed. This hallway was the apartment's spine and terminated in a living room, which I'd never once seen anyone sit in, though it was decorated with their most expensive furniture and was the only room with west- and south-facing windows—by far the brightest in the entire place.

By now the chili's smells had lured Tanner's sisters from their rooms. Gwyneth, who was a senior at Spence and the most beautiful girl I'd ever seen, sat between Tanner and me on the couch, Melissa—an eighth grader—on the rug at our feet. Mrs. Potts had just arrived home, also in her overcoat and business suit (all three of the women were blond). She too reappeared, having lost her jacket, having unbuttoned her collar to reveal a string of pearls. Her contribution to the meal was to make the margaritas, and while she concentrated on squeezing the limes, I stole a glance at her. She was, my father liked to say, "a very handsome woman," a phrase I tried to decode, something he remarked upon after the annual parents' nights at Boyd. (A banker like her husband, she called on my father once a year, over the phone, to invest money with her, and he responded to her pitch with several "uh-huhs" as if he were in a rush to be somewhere else. "Sharon," he said, and his eye twitched, "I'm working with someone else right now, but if I make a change, I'll be in touch.") Mrs. Potts, balancing her margarita, joined us on the couch, seating herself to my left, and now, with a Potts woman to either side of me and Melissa at my feet, I was in a sort of heaven.

To Tanner, Mrs. Potts said, "What happened to you?" and gently took his injured hand. He explained he had dislocated his middle finger in practice today; it was buddy-taped to his ring finger and the size of a hot dog. "I'm going to splint that," she said, and, after asking Tanner to hold her margarita, excused herself, upon which Tanner took a sip and then offered me some. She had been a nurse before she became an investment banker. True, she couldn't keep anything sports-related straight in her head: she called a home run a touchdown, a touchdown a goal. When we watched games and she joyfully screamed these aloud, her family heaped upon her endless derision, but I admired her for having multiple careers. If my mom became a nurse, I figured she and Dad might not fight about money so much.

Tanner took another sip of his mother's margarita. "How psyched are you we don't have a wrestling tournament this weekend?" He offered the glass to me again. "No making weight. No Kepplemen. We can just pig out and sleep in."

"Cheers," I said, and took my sip.

Soon we were called to the dinner table, which everyone helped set. The Pottses had a custom dining nook off their kitchen. It felt like eating in a restaurant, enclosed and intimate.

"... but preferences," Mr. Potts was saying to me, "preferences are measurable, quantifiable, and therefore somewhat predictable, at least in terms of market behavior," and I, who very much enjoyed listening to the ticker of Tanner's dad's talk, said that was true, that some people preferred *The Brady Bunch* to *The Partridge Family,* McDonald's to Burger King, Marvel to DC Comics, the Osmonds to the Jackson Five. Then I asked for another taco. "Exactly, Griffin," he said, and passed the platter, "you are absolutely right, and among other things, it is the job of investment bankers to identify the companies that have cornered the market on these preferences or that know the consumer's preference before he or she even knows what that preference is." Gwyneth said, "I thought the job of an investment banker was to determine a company's value," and Mr. Potts replied, "It is, but I'm trying to make a finer point to Griffin. Why is it," he continued to me, "that we remember certain slogans? *Crazy Eddie, his prices are insane.* Or certain taglines. *The American Express Card, don't leave home without it.*"

"*Sometimes you feel like a nut,*" I said, and asked him to pass the guacamole.

"*Sometimes you don't,*" said Mr. Potts, and handed me the bowl. "It sticks in the *mind*. Stickiness is the advertiser's modus operandi. His holy grail. What's your dad's line in that commercial? *Treat your dog to Liv-a-Snaps.* We don't even have a dog, but I pass one on the street and I want to blurt it out to its owner." To which Tanner said, "This is boring," since he thought any grown-up talk I engaged in was bullshit ass-kissing. "Well then, you're an idiot," his father said, "and your friend here clearly has what we call 'business acumen.'" Which, I realized, Oren also had, and also that Tanner wasn't completely wrong. I was only half interested in the discussion. I felt I owed the man something for eating ten tacos, a fact that Mrs. Potts *clearly* did not approve of ("Clearly," she said, echoing my father, "someone is growing") but one that Melissa marveled at and Gwyneth welcomed, if only to prevent a scolding about her refusal to eat. "The onions give me bad breath," she announced, then directed her gaze at her father, "and I plan on getting kissed tonight." Gwyneth tried to shock her father whenever possible, but Mr. Potts, usually quick with a retort, merely sipped his drink in response.

With some scorn, Tanner asked Gwyneth, "Going to *Stu*dio tonight?" and she replied, "Going to Dorrian's first." (We had heard vaguely of both but were yet to visit either.) Melissa invariably launched into a long story that had no clear point—it was something we suffered, Melissa's tortuously digressive stories, which usually began with "You'll never believe what happened in math today" but somehow managed to wend through each and every one of her classes before arriving at her stated subject. During which Mrs. Potts often did strange things, like brush something invisible from her chest while balancing her margarita in her free hand or lifting her plate in the air to look beneath it. "Did you lose something?" Tanner asked her. In response to which, Mr. Potts said, "Don't talk to your mother like that!" and then "For God's sake, Sharon, listen to your daughter." In response to which, Mrs. Potts said, "What did you say?" At which point Gwyneth, who had been examining a strand of her long blond hair as if she had a piece of gum stuck in it, caught my eye across the table and said, *"Huis clos,"* which was the title of a book I'd noticed sitting on her desk as I walked by her room, which I stared into any chance I got.

Gwyneth's walls were painted an artic blue, and of all her room's artifacts—a pennant from Yale, where her boyfriend was a freshman (she called him a "frosh"); her golfing trophies and regatta medals; her burbling aquarium, bejeweled with tropical fish—the one I admired most was her collage. Hers was enormous and themed; it used, like so many other girls' collages I'd seen, magazine ads and images, but instead of a random mash-up or agglomeration of interests, Gwyneth selected and organized her snippets by color, these the various shaded blues of Tiffany boxes, of Jordache jeans and JAG clothing, the REAGAN FOR PRESIDENT campaign poster, the *American Gigolo* poster (*He leaves women feeling more alive than they've ever felt before,* went Dad's line in the promo), the Rive Gauche perfume glossy, the blue velvet background of the Crown Royal whiskey ad, and the cover of Billy Joel's *Glass Houses,* all of which she cut into rectangular pixels to form a set of waves, from one of which, rising up, was the shark from the cover of Peter Bench-ley's *Jaws,* the Club Med Neptune trident, and the blue whale from the Museum of Natural History catalog—a work of art atop which she'd titled in bright, foamy white letters made of cotton balls: IF LIFE IS A SEA OF LOVE, DIVE IN! If I fashioned my own, what would I include in it? And what would its mantra be? I had ideas, but just the fact that it had *occurred* to Gwyneth to make such a thing was what I most envied. Or that I would never dream of such a clear announcement of self—*that* was what I lacked.

"What are you doing?" Tanner said. And I hurried from Gwyneth's door to join him in his room.

After dinner, Tanner and I did the usual. To manage our food babies, we took off our shirts, put on the Stones' *Emotional Rescue,* and then had a push-up contest—first to a hundred wins—followed by multiple sets of curls in front of his mirror. Tanner had two beds in his room. We played wall ball using lacrosse sticks, and whoever failed to make the catch on the rebound had to accept a dead arm. Melissa appeared at our door and said she was headed downstairs to sleep at Buffy Biggs's house, a classmate who lived on the second floor. Tanner said, "Who cares?" and she left. Mr. Potts, on the way to his bedroom, paused at our door, considered our toplessness, and said, "Kiss-kiss, ladies, nighty night," because on Saturdays he and Mrs. Potts ran the Central Park loop first thing in the morning and made it a point to go to bed early. He pulled the door closed and then reopened it: "You're making too much noise," he said, so we dropped our sticks. As soon as the latch clicked Tanner shot a double-leg takedown on me and we wrestled for the next hour. When we rolled, Tanner would occasionally bury his mouth in my neck when he took my back and growl, "Try to get out of it, cocksucker, you know you fucking like it," but it only made me madder and I'd Granby out of his hooks and stuff his face in his rug to let him know I was displeased. From the hallway, we heard Gwyneth say, "Bye," and later, while we both lay on the floor, spent and sweaty and staring at the ceiling, we heard the buzzer ring and hurried to the kitchen to answer it.

It was Sean, the doorman. He was maybe in his thirties. He was a giant with a thick Irish brogue, and in something close to a panic he said, "Pick you boyos up in the service elevator, I need your help right feckin now."

The door to the rear stairwell and service elevator was off the Pottses' kitchen, and we waited until Sean rose into view. His doorman's coat was laughably short at the sleeves. When he pulled open the accordion gate and waved us aboard, it wasn't clear how we'd fit on the car. "Mr. McAllister's in a mess on eleven, so no gawking."

Through the McAllisters' differently furnished kitchen with the same layout as the Pottses', down their hallway with different paintings but the same hallway as upstairs, into the master bedroom with floral wallpaper and sconces but the same bedroom, there lay elderly Mrs. McAllister in her bed, in her nightgown, her white hair perfectly coiffed, her back perfectly straight against the headboard, watching us walk by as if we were pedestrians passing her on a street bench. Sean said, "Cavalry's arrived, Mrs. McAllister, don't you worry," and led us into the master bathroom. Bald Mr. McAllister, in broadcloth pajamas, sat stuck between the toilet and the sink, having obviously slipped, a bright pool of piss spread in a circle beneath him. He appeared dejected, disoriented. "Well, lift him up for Chrissakes," said Sean, filling the doorway, and then watched as Tanner and I lifted Mr. McAllister, his darkened pants making a sucking sound as we raised him up, the small room heady with the puddled stink. We walked him into his bedroom, his arms draped over our shoulders, his cuffs leaving a trail of drippings and wet footprints behind us that marked a path to the bed, whose covers Sean folded back as Tanner and I guided the old man into position ("It's okay, Mr. McAllister, you got this, you're all right," Tanner said) and then sat him down. Following this, Tanner made a great show of tucking him in ("There you go, Mr. McAllister, nice and comfy"), and now that Mr. McAllister was safely in place but still soiled, he too sat ramrod straight next to his wife, neither of them speaking, the pair at once wide-eyed and frozen-faced, as if we were burglars plundering their home, their expressions neither embarrassed nor grateful but closer to stunned. "Okay, Mrs. McAllister," said Sean to her, "we've got your fella back where he belongs, we'll be going now."

After Sean dropped us off on our floor and thanked us and then ashamedly slammed the gate, Tanner and I stood in his kitchen, staring at nothing in the quiet apartment.

Tanner perked up. "A good deed like that calls for a drink," he said, and from the cabinet he produced a bottle of rum and a pair of shot glasses, the pair of which he filled to the brim. "Through the lips and past the gums, watch out stomach, here it comes."

We drank.

"Time for bed," Tanner announced.

He killed the lights and was soon out cold. He slept on his stomach, hugging the pillow to his smushed face and occasionally mumbling puckered nonsense. As I lay awake, I could not shake the thought of Naomi and me, standing in her bathroom together. Of her nails slowly sliding down my back. From my briefs' waistband, my cock emerged, hard as a policeman's baton, and to banish the thought of her, I imagined Gwyneth and me, doing the Hustle at Studio 54, which I pictured as the dance floor in *Saturday Night Fever.* "You sorta look like John Travolta," Gwyneth said, but in Naomi's voice, since she often whispered this to me. Was there not some way to make the perfect girl? I wondered. She'd kiss like Deb Peryton, have Gwyneth's face, but be easy to talk to, like Naomi. Did such a person already exist, and if we met, would I recognize her? If I recognized her, and we started dating, I was certain I'd be happy. Without meaning to, I next replayed the scene at the McAllisters' apartment. Of the couple's expectant muteness as they watched us march in and out of their bedroom. Were they lying there now, I wondered, just as we'd left them? Was there really no one else they could call for help? I had no answers to these questions and found myself weeping a bit, but my erection had receded, thank God, and before I drifted off to sleep, I was strangely certain of this: for as long as I lived, I would neither forget those two poor people nor their sad tableau.

Morning, and I was up with the sun. I heard Mr. and Mrs. Potts pad down the hallway and out the door, off on their jog. Tanner's clock radio read 6:57, and I forced myself back to sleep.

I woke again at 7:43, hoping I'd overslept, but it was useless. I had no excuse to miss my appointment. I got up and went to get some breakfast.

I found Gwyneth in the dining nook. She was wearing a black cocktail dress and her mascara was smeared—from sweat or tears, it wasn't clear, though she seemed upbeat, in spite of the hour. She smelled of cigarette smoke and limes. She was reading the financial section of the *New York Times,* the Saturday listings of all the stock prices, several of which she'd underlined with a pen, writing out their arcane abbreviations and symbols on a small notepad. On the table was also a plate with a half-eaten taco and a stubbed-out Marlboro Light, the pack with a Studio 54 matchbook atop it by her side as well. She had cracked the window in front of the sink; its breeze was cold. She blew her nose into a napkin that was lightly dotted with blood. "You're up early," she said, and returned to scanning the broadsheet.

I helped myself to a bowl of graham crackers and then poured whole milk over it—a Tanner Potts specialty. I ate, staring at Gwyneth intently. Her concentration was total; occasionally, she sniffled. After a few more minutes of reading, she took her plate to the window, raised farther the sash, and smoked one more cigarette. The view was an east-facing alley, a back-of-the-building, streetless one, and into this void she ashed. Afterward, she scraped her plate into the trash, then rinsed it under the faucet and placed it on the dish rack.

"Good night," she said, and excused herself to her room.

The clock above the rear entrance read 8:26.

If I didn't leave now, I'd be late.

At Fifth Avenue and Seventy-Third Street I looked downtown and then dejectedly headed north. I entered Central Park just above the Seventy-Ninth Street transverse, past the Met, the Temple of Dendur visible through its wall of glass and silent in the morning light. I merged onto the bridle path running alongside the reservoir. A beautiful woman on horseback cantered past me, prettier even than Gwyneth. It was gray and windy, the air damp and promising either rain or sun, it was not yet clear. Exiting the park, I rode uptown again, on Central Park West, to school.

When I entered the building, there was Coach Kepplemen, waiting for me on the pews.

He had been sitting as he had at the sports award assembly, his ankle, which he held in his hand, at rest atop his knee and his foot flapping. At the sight of me he smiled with unguarded fondness, an expression that, I realize now, signaled a surprised happiness, a relief or amazement that I had showed up—that any of us did—in the first place, which elicited, of all things, sympathy from me. Then he got up without further acknowledgment and walked the long hallway, ahead of me, as always, toward the wrestling gym, his preferred place for us to practice on Saturdays— though on these weekends he never turned on the room's overhead lights, choosing also to roll on the practice mats, which lay against the same wall as the double doors, so that we were hidden from view. Even if you'd gotten on your toes to peek through one of the small porthole windows, you couldn't have seen us. He was already dressed for our session, in wrestling shoes and a T-shirt, but also, I noticed, wearing shorts. I *hated* when Kepplemen wore shorts; he had neither a jockstrap nor underwear beneath these, ever. When we drilled, I could feel everything. And even though it was only the beginning of December, with three full months left in the season, I suffered the tiniest itch for wrestling to be over.

Later, at home, Dad still hadn't put away the challah French toast and Canadian bacon. I wasn't hungry but upon arrival ate a second breakfast, which Dad insisted on reheating, even the syrup. I had seconds of *that* too. I didn't understand why I did this to myself. It would make cutting weight this week hellish. The sweat from my workout was overlaid with the sweat from my ride home, and my wind-dried neck was salty with the perspiration and the smell of Kepplemen's cologne. Dad and Mom were seated on the couch, dividing the *New York Times* between them, their faces hidden behind Arts & Leisure and the *Book Review*. I'd taken the seat facing the window and was staring at the sky . . .

Dad said, "Your mother asked you a question."

I turned to him and then Mom, confused.

"I said," Mom said, "what are you up to tonight?"

"There's a party," I told her. "But I'm eating at Cliff's first."

It was a rare treat to be invited to Cliff's home for dinner, but especially tonight, which was the fifth evening of Hanukkah. The Bauers' menorah sat atop a chest in their living/dining area, and it was Cliff's night to light the candle and recite the blessings. We had stuffed breast of veal for dinner with ratatouille and latkes that Mr. Bauer had cooked. Mrs. Bauer did all the driving, the exact opposite from our family, but he did *all* the cooking, usually even the desserts—though tonight, instead of his usual cheesecake, he'd brought home a mess of chocolate and cherry rugelach. I ate so many I was like a goldfish. I could barely concentrate on the dreidel and had to lie down on the couch. We soon moved to Scrabble, which was an exercise in humiliation at Cliff's house. Shira, his sister, a senior and a dark-haired version of Gwyneth, was the only one of us who could keep up with Mrs. Bauer, an editor at the *New York Times,* at least until the inevitable inflection point when Cliff's mom considered the clotted board and her letters and in her gentle, singsong voice—it was the only time I ever caught her acting—said, "Oh, look what I have," and with a single tile plopped on DOUBLE LETTER SCORE activated so many branches of words it reminded me of lighting a Christmas tree.

The Bauers lived on Eighty-Seventh between Columbus and Central Park West, and though it lacked the grandeur our former apartment possessed, I recognized in Cliff's home some of the same rot and charm: exposed steam pipes in the bathroom dusted with soot, and the parquet floors that popped when you walked across them. Like Tanner's place, the kitchen and dining room windows faced west, onto one of the city's streetless spaces, where all the block's buildings stood bunched together and, in their varying heights, formed a set of rising and falling tar-topped roofs. These were populated with prickly television aerials and rotating air vents, with water towers and the steepled glass that crowned elevator shafts—it was easy to forget that a building is a machine. I often imagined that if I could find the right door or hop from the right window, I could walk the entirety of Manhattan by this staircase, or at least travel between my friends' apartments unseen and, like some urban superhero, permanently live the fleeting feeling of freedom I now enjoyed, deep, as I was, into the weekend.

"We were in Bayonne," Mr. Bauer was saying, now that the game had concluded, although we had still not put away the board, "in an internment camp the SS had set up there. I was ten, I think—"

"You were in Luxembourg for three years after fleeing Hamburg, so you were twelve," said Mrs. Bauer.

"And I see an SS officer berating this decrepit old Orthodox Jew. He is accusing him of stealing food. We were all starving, so I say to him, 'Leave the poor guy alone, can't you see he has nothing?' And the officer bends down to me and says, 'And you are?' I say my name, and he goes, 'And what do you do, Alex Bauer?' And I say, 'I'm a Lebenskünstler.' And he says, 'What is a Lebenskünstler?' And I say, 'Maybe someday I will tell you.' And he says, 'Maybe you will, and maybe you won't.' And he kicks me in the head, here."

Mr. Bauer lifted his eyelid to reveal the jagged scar.

"Flash-forward," he continues, "it is March 1945, we are about to cross the Rhine . . ."

Cliff kneed me under the table to say, *This is the best part.*

"I'm on patrol with my friend Mark. We're in the forest, just outside Cologne, and we realize we've wandered behind enemy lines. And as we're trying to make it back to our side, who do we capture? The very same German officer from Bayonne. We tie him to a tree. I say to him, 'You gave me this scar when I was a boy. You put your boot in my face, do you remember that?' He says, 'I do'—which I thought was brave. I say to him, 'Did you ever learn what a Lebenskünstler is?' He doesn't remember that part. He says, 'I don't know what you're talking about.' 'A Lebenskünstler,' I explain, 'is a life artist. You have to be a life artist to survive in this world.' And he says, 'Why are you telling me this?' And I say, 'Because you are *not* a life artist.'"

Mr. Bauer sat back, his expression a vengeful cousin to pleased.

I looked at Cliff and then back at Mr. Bauer. "So, but—what happened to him?" I asked.

Cliff bunched his hair in his fists and shook his head. "Oy," he said, which made Mr. Bauer chuckle.

The kitchen phone rang. Shira had her own line, so Mrs. Bauer got up to answer it. When she returned to the table, she said, "That was Tanner. He wants you to know he's leaving his apartment right now."

Like Oren, I too could be a fearless explorer of other people's rooms—or in the case of our wrestling captain Roy Adler's town house, where tonight's party was being held, other people's floors. It was one of a con-joined trio of four-story homes on Eighty-Fifth and Central Park West, distinguished, primarily, by their colors of brick (Adler's was red, the other pair a shade of off-white) and also for their comparatively dwarfish size, standing uncowed beneath their much taller neighboring apartment buildings, so that with the city grown up around them, they reminded me of Virginia Lee Burton's *The Little House*. Adler's place was on the corner, and it had what I would come to learn were the classic archi-tectural details of the Romanesque revival (oriel windows separated by acanthus friezes, decorative pediment arches above these and the doors, elaborate ironwork everywhere); however, what made it more magi-cal than the others was its cone-shaped roof. I meant to see the room beneath it with my own eyes.

Hindsight reveals several important things about our social lives as city children in a city that, for all intents and purposes, no longer exists. Monied parents like the Adlers left town on the weekends for second homes in Litchfield or the Hamptons, but in their mildly dissociative and benignly neglectful fashion they neither insisted their children join them nor cared much what they did in their absence. Their kids might, as they not entirely untruthfully warned their parents, have "a few peo-ple over"; these gatherings might, as was the case of Roy's party, swell to a number closer to a hundred. However, the fact that these parties were tacitly condoned often gave them a distinctly adult feel. They were sedate, intimate: music played but wasn't blasting; several pizzas had been ordered and sat atop the vast kitchen's island, but with paper plates and napkins provided. "Beer," as Roy indicated to Cliff, Tanner, and me when we entered this vast space, "is in the fridge and the cooler"—the former double-doored and restaurant-sized, the latter an ice-filled gal-vanized steel tub. No one was hell-bent on property destruction or put their shoes on the furniture. There was a fire going in the *Masterpiece*

Theatre living room. It was all more Apollonian than Dionysian, and it exemplified the distinctly Neverland quality to how we partied. As was the case with Gwyneth, spending all night out at Studio 54, we were impersonating the adults it seemed we knew only from afar.

Which didn't mean I didn't have an agenda. I snooped, but not inappropriately. I was determined to see the top floor. I was hung up on this, I cannot say why, perhaps because the building was as famous to me as any Upper West Side landmark: the Beresford, for instance, with its three octagonal towers overlooking Central Park, where Oren was now, at the apartment of his new best friend, Matt; or the Dakota, with its decorative iron railing surrounding it, of the bearded Wise Man framed by two dragons, the figures repeating at intervals like sentries. But given the fact that Roy was a senior and our wrestling team's captain, I asked for his permission, to which he replied, after clinking beer cans with me, "I think there are already people up there." So as not to appear overeager, I took my time. Juniors and seniors were gathered in the wood-paneled living room, grouped in loose cliques around the fire, standing by the mantel, seated on the couch and accent chairs. I spotted the members of the lacrosse team, also the preppy swimmers. Wrestling captain Santoro, who sat with Lisa Mullins on his lap, raised his beer in greeting, and I raised mine in response. Seated around the dining room table, as if they were having a work meeting, were the techies, a group of computer lab regulars and math geeks and drama stagehands: Marc Mason, Todd Wexworth, and Hogi Hyun, plus middle schoolers Chip Colson and Jason Taylor. The walnut staircase I ascended was magnificent, its decorative newel an eagle, its banisters and railings as brown as braised beef, its thick runner a deep green, as soft beneath my feet as the treads were solid. Worthy of note and attributable to a combination of my dimness and youth: I did not associate such palatial digs with wealth any greater than what the Pottses possessed, I being no Oren and entirely incurious about how the world worked. I just thought such domiciles— with their abstract paintings of three colorful lines or sculptures of men so long-legged and long-torsoed they looked like upside-down Ys—were a lot bigger than my own. The second floor's hallways were dark, though light shined from a room with pocket doors, revealing a dedicated TV room as well as a second fireplace (this even more magical than the existence of a first one) in which a fire was also roaring. Roaring on the floor, a lion skin rug. Rob Dolinski, one of Boyd's most popular seniors, was seated on the couch. If he'd had even a scintilla of interest in acting he'd have been a star, his wattage was that powerful. He wore a blazer and a sharp pair of corduroys. His hair was slicked back with sculpting gel and caught the firelight. On his left and right were the pair of gorgeous senior girls from whom he was inseparable: Andrea Oppenheimer and Sophie Evans. The trio passed a joint among themselves. "Are you lost?" Dolinski asked, and pointing to myself, I replied, "Just taking the tour." "You want a hit?" he offered, and held out the roach. "No thank you," I said. "Well," he said, "if you change your mind," and then, with the spliff, indicated the pair of ladies, as if he were offering them instead of the dope: "There's plenty to go around." In response, I continued my tour, pretending to admire the photographs on the mantel, the painting of black-and-white squiggles, sprays, and splashes above the fireplace, excusing myself immediately afterward for fear of getting contact high. "Be seeing you," Dolinski said, with a confidence approaching certitude.

Roy's room was on the third floor.

It was no bigger than the one I shared with Oren, but it did have its own bathroom and a view of Central Park. From this height, and through the leafless trees, the reservoir—dotted by the light poles palely illuminating its cinder track—was its own bluey emptiness on this almost moonless night, while the park's winding walkways and roadways, lit by the same white lights, appeared streaked with incandescent bands that resembled snow. Beyond it, as brilliantly orange as the fireplace's embers, glowed the great wall of Fifth Avenue's facades. Still, it was not the vantage that impressed me so much as the decor—the incontrovertible Royness of the space that I studied. Atop his dresser, he had repurposed a shopping crate to stand his multiple wrestling trophies and hang his many medals, and like Gwyneth's collage, I coveted the *idea* for the case—that someone so young might commemorate himself thus—as much as the hardware. Above his desk, framed posters for *Apocalypse Now* and *The Warriors,* which I also associated with Roy, he being possessed of a cool toughness to which I aspired. Like Mom, Roy also had an impressive bookshelf; however, his was tall and narrow and organized, so far as I could tell, by genre, blocks of science fiction and fantasy, none of which I had read (*The Man in the High Castle, A Canticle for Leibowitz,* a ton of Carlos Castaneda). Included among these was a cluster of Stephen King, Tolkien, the *Dune* trilogy, these giving on to *Slaughterhouse-Five, Catch-22, The Crying of Lot 49,* plus *Franny and Zooey, Nine Stories,* and *The Catcher in the Rye.* Such a library shamed me. These books were like tickets for entry to a club to which it seemed I was somehow not intelligent enough to be admitted, that demanded concentration I did not seem to have at my disposal. My mother looked up at me from such books and then back to the page. I felt this lack. This failure. (Last summer, Cliff had tackled the Lord of the Rings trilogy and *The Hobbit, by choice.*) I wanted to be someone like Roy, for whom these books seemed like bricks on which his self was built; whose identity was fashioned of the same stone as his home's cantilevered corbels, of the same brass of his wrestling medals; refined in the same fires whose smoke filled these chimneys and that forged the silver and gold of his picture frames. In one such photograph, I picked out Roy, on a dock somewhere, during a recent late-summer idyll, behind which a stately country house sat, Roy standing amid his enormous family—cousins and aunts and uncles and grandparents—who seemed, in spite of their sprawling Deuteronomy, to be straight out of central casting. Put another way, they appeared the opposite of actors, enjoying, in their unposed and unselfconscious cohesion, a closeness I feared that my family did not.

I heard girls' voices in the hallway.

From the base of the stairs, I could see the room I'd sought to visit. But several girls from my class were congregated in a bedroom adjacent to where I now stood, most notably my lab partner, Deb Peryton, who smiled at me, invitingly, so I smiled back and then joined her. They had the forty-five of The Police's "Don't Stand So Close to Me" playing and were chatting over the music.

"We were talking about the scariest movie we've ever seen," she said to me. "Mine was *Jaws.*"

Deb was wearing a black turtleneck and the same lip gloss as the night we'd kissed.

"My dad took my brother and me to see *Dressed to Kill.*"

"I thought that had an X rating."

"It was R," I said. "My brother and I were holding hands by the end of it."

"If you take me to see *The Shining,*" Deb said, "I'll hold your hand."

"I'll hold your hand now if you come upstairs and see the top floor."

"Oh my gosh," Deb said. "It's like an aerie up there—"

But now Cliffnotes, who appeared out of nowhere, grabbed my wrist and yanked me into the hallway.

"Pilchard is here," he said, and pulled me after him. On the first floor, Cliff banged on the closet door beneath the stairs and to the occupants inside said, "Pilchard is here," and Tanner emerged with flush-faced Justine Keaton, who smoothed out her sweater and hurried past us.

"What are we doing?" I asked.

"Pilchard's in the kitchen," Cliff said to Tanner, as if that also answered my question.

Tanner rubbed his hands together like he was about to eat a meal.

In the kitchen, Cliff made a beeline for the fridge while Tanner, who had spotted Pilchard by the island, grabbed him by the back of the neck, pushed him into the corner of the dining nook, and took the seat next to him. Cliff placed a six-pack on the table and shouldered up next to Pilchard on the other side. He nodded that I join him, and I hesitated. He smacked the bench and I sat. When Tanner and Cliff snowballed like this, there was no stopping them. At which point Roy Adler appeared with two rocks glasses: one brimmed with Scotch, another contained a single quarter. He had a cigar in his mouth. "It's my understanding," he said, "you boys have a matter to resolve."

"We do?" Pilchard asked.

"Oh yes," Tanner said, as if Pilchard's father had sued his family too. He was a big believer in blind loyalty, especially if it ended in violence.

Roy placed the empty glass with the quarter in the middle of the table. Seated higher than all of us on a barstool, he ashed from this purchase into a golden tray, tapping the cigar so forcefully it sounded like a doctor percussing a chest. He took on, I thought, a princely sort of appearance, wetly sucking at the head till the tip glowed and then sending out three perfect white rings, which I watched widen until, with what smoke was left in his lungs, he blew a tight stream through their tornadic outline so that they disappeared.

"You start," Cliff said to Pilchard. He had already cracked a beer and was filling the glass.

Tiny Pilchard, mackerel-eyed and full-lipped, tried to gamely play along. "Nah, you go first," he said. It was both an obvious stalling tactic and, somewhat sadly, an expression of gratitude for being included in our game.

"No," Cliff said, and pushed both the glass and the coin closer, "*you* go."

Pilchard took the quarter, placed it on the bridge of his nose, and released. It rolled and bounced on the table, *tink*ing against the highball's rim, then spinning until Cliffnotes stopped it with his finger. Taking the coin between his thumb and index finger, Cliffnotes bounced it on its flat side. We watched it arc and then clatter into the glass. He pointed his elbow at Pilchard. "Drink," Cliff said. Pilchard chugged his beer until the quarter slid into his mouth, and before he'd even finished the suds, Cliff took it and refilled it. Cliff missed, then passed the quarter to Tanner, who, with a no-look bounce, sank the quarter again and pointed his elbow at Pilchard. "Drink," he said. When he missed, he passed the glass to me, and I missed, intentionally, and passed the glass to Roy, who balanced the cigar on the table's edge and, after he sank the coin, picked up the stogie and pointed it at Cliff. "Drink," he commanded. Cliff drank, Roy missed, Pilchard sank, hit Tanner, missed, and then Cliff landed two in a row, firing an elbow at Pilchard each time. Pilchard burped loudly between each glass. When Cliff's streak ended, he slid the quarter to Tanner, who once again tagged Pilchard. He was pausing between swallows now, contemplating the glass's level, raising it above his head to consider it from underneath. "Hurry up already," Cliff said.

There were three more rounds of this. Pilchard was laughing now. "Come on, guys," he said. But he didn't have the courage to quit. Had he found it, Cliff wouldn't have allowed him to leave anyway. Within thirty minutes Pilchard was red-eyed and semiconscious, his chin drooping to his chest and lids heavy, at which point Tanner said, "He's crocked."

Pilchard said, "I don't feel so good."

Roy said, "No hurling on the premises, please."

Cliff, satisfied but not satiated, said to all of us, "Pick him up and follow me."

I looked at Roy for a lifeline, but he bit the cigar in his teeth and, before excusing himself, said, "You kids don't stay out too late."

The moment the cold air hit us on Central Park West, Pilchard jack-knifed at the waist and vomited profusely. Bent double, palms to knees, he moaned after expunging and said, "Sorry about that." He wiped his mouth with the heel of his hand and then spit a couple of times. He was so wrecked he then tipped forward, but Tanner caught his underarm and Cliff lifted him by the other so that he didn't fall into his own sick, upon which Pilchard seized and barfed several more times.

"Can someone get me home, please?" Pilchard asked.

Cliffnotes leaned down and, after bunching Simon's bangs in his fist to lift his head, looked into his swimming eyes. "Hey, buddy," he said, "don't you worry, we'll get you where you need to be."

I said, "Enough, man, he's toast."

"Are you gonna puss out on me?" Cliff said.

"Typical," Tanner said.

"Can you just tell me what we're doing?"

Allegiances had shifted. Tanner and Cliff were a duo now. They had a plan and loyalty dictated I go along with it, and this made me angry and glum. Cliff hailed a cab. Tanner grabbed the door's handle before the vehicle had even stopped. Like a cop, he palmed Pilchard's head and pushed him in first, slid next to him, and then rolled down the window. He shoved Pilchard's chin on top of the glass. I slid next to Tanner. Cliff, after closing the door, said to the cabbie, "Columbus Circle, please."

The driver hesitated to pull his flag. "That's not even a fare," he said, and craned his neck around. He considered Pilchard through the plastic partition.

Cliff stuffed a five in the money slot and smacked it closed. "Just drive," he said.

"He better not puke in my cab," the driver said.

Pilchard did barf the moment we exited the taxi, spraying the street's subway grates with tomato and cheese and then falling face-first, the odor from his guts wafting on the updraft. Tanner dipped into a fire-man's carry and, with Pilchard on his shoulder, followed Cliff, who marched up the Paramount movie theater's steps. RAGING BULL silently coursed its circumference via hundreds of bulbs, a magical marquee that made the title appear to travel its shape like a ticker.

"Where are we going?" I asked Cliff.

Tanner said, "Just keep up."

"If you don't tell me, I'm leaving."

"Then fucking go home," Cliff said.

From this elevated landing, all of Columbus Circle came into view. The wind, barreling down Broadway, seemed churned by the roundabout's traffic, as if funneled by the GW building, and then whipped past the Coliseum—RINGLING BROS. AND BARNUM & BAILEY CIRCUS read its marquee. Cliff skipped down the black steps and then down the subway's stairwell, its nautilus curve leading to the Fifty-Ninth Street station.

"Four, please," Cliff told the tollbooth operator and again pressed money through the slot. He took his tokens and put one in the plunger for Tanner, then sent him with Pilchard through the turnstile, holding the other coin aloft for the operator behind the glass to see and depositing it and spinning the bars, lest he think we were fare-jumping our sick friend. He flipped me my token and followed after Tanner. The platform was nearly empty. A homeless man lay against the wall, in a nest of collapsed cardboard. Two women leaned against the girders, watching us. They wore platform shoes covered in glitter, fishnet stockings, and bootie shorts. Their varsity jackets were as puffy-armed as ours, but satin and shiny, the only part of their outfits weather appropriate.

"Will someone *please* tell me what we're doing?" I asked.

Tanner said, "You'll see."

The twin headlights of the northbound train sparked the rails. It came bombing into the station, accompanied by its electrically charged gusts that were warm and humid—dragon-blown. It was impossible to tell the cars' original color, they were so completely covered in graffiti. The train's brakes whined and, when it stopped, made a sound like a giant round chambered into a breech. The doors opened. Tanner boarded, still carrying Pilchard on his shoulder, and laid the limp boy almost gently on the bench. Then he stepped back and blocked the door from closing with his foot. The two women who'd boarded at the other end of our car hugged the pole, eyeing us suspiciously. I remained on the platform, as if by distance I was somehow exonerated. Cliffnotes bent to face Pilchard and took his chin in his hand. He lightly shook him. "Hey," he said. "Hey, Simon." And then as hard as Kepplemen slapped us, he slapped him awake. Pilchard's head bobbled a bit; his eyelids peeled open. "Do you know where you are?" Cliff asked.

Pilchard considered Cliff for a moment and smiled. He said, "We're at a party."

Cliff said, "Do you know who I am?"

Pilchard reached out and tousled Cliff's hair, then shook his head.

Cliff said, "You tried to hurt my family."

Pilchard replied, "I didn't hurt anybody."

"Do you want to know where I'm sending you?"

And as if on cue, the conductor said, *"This is the A train express. Next stop, One Hundred Twenty-Fifth Street."* By which time he'd backed off the car.

"Uptown, motherfucker."

Years later, after I'd graduated college and returned to Manhattan—this was 1989—I got a job working for an Israeli named Uri Yaviv, who was CEO of a tiny startup called Trident. My title, computer consultant, had next to nothing to do with my responsibilities, which were primarily to oversee the editing of a several-hundred-page proposal full of data flow diagrams and technical descriptions in the coldest, most abstruse language for an antiballistic weapons manufacturing system that tested my capacity for mind-numbing work. None of this is particularly important, except for the fact that Uri ran the business out of his large apartment in Hudson Heights, just a few blocks north of Little Dominican Republic and the George Washington Bridge—neighborhoods farther north in the city than I'd ever ventured as a boy and so unknown to me in my youth that they might as well have been an entirely different state. I was living on the Upper East Side at the time. I was so busy, my hours were so long, that, weather permitting, I made the nearly nine-mile ride on my bicycle to ensure I got exercise, crossing the park and then making the remainder of the trek up Broadway, through Morningside Heights, past Columbia University, through Manhattanville, West Harlem, Hamilton Heights, Sugar Hill, and Washington Heights. When I was a boy this was considered the DMZ, the forbidden zone. And there were still stretches of urban decay on my ride but far more beauty and a vibrancy to the street life no different from any other part of town. This didn't surprise me, because I was older, because I was smarter and wiser, as I think I am now, but I did not know, then, that this northernmost province of Manhattan was the land, for instance, of so many Orthodox Jews, the Hasidim who owned much of the area's real estate. On my trip I spied Hispanic girls in Catholic-school plaid whose parents owned the bodegas and clothing shops and beauty salons, storefronts decorated in multi-colored pennants that rippled in the gusts off the Hudson. I ate my meals at the Bolivian and Mexican and Dominican and soul food restaurants that were plentiful there, at the Chinese buffets and the kosher butchers, and a McDonald's whose fries always tasted fresh out of the oil. I felt as at home and as safe in such density as anywhere in New York, and when I took the A train it was no different from any subway line but for the racial composition of its passengers, I being almost completely outnumbered from Fifty-Ninth Street north and 181st Street south. On that ride, I occasionally thought about what we did to Pilchard. My guilt had far more to do with our intent, which was to weaponize our city like a gun. It was also that I simply went along with things. As to my shame, that was retroactive, it was in hindsight. For what could we know, then, really, living in our tiny world on that infinite little island? And how lucky we were, as we grew older, to begin to unlearn such things—but not yet, not then. I am *no* apologist—"We were boys"—I grant no pardons. Our education was spatial. Racial. Tribal. Urban. *American.* But mostly—and this is the most important thing—it was dominated by Kepplemen, over whom we were each failing to gain leverage. And who wore the costume of love. And who was, day in and day out, teaching us fury, aggression, complicity, desperation, exploitation, and, most of all, silence.

Which is to say that all the way back to my apartment from the train station we neither spoke nor gave a thought to what we had done.

When we entered, I could hear the television on in my parents' bedroom. They were asleep, and before I went to turn off their TV, Dad's voice came over the speaker: *It's ten p.m.,* went the PSA, *do you know where your children are?*

Tanner and Cliff were in the kitchen. Tanner was making a quesa-dilla. After the three of us ate, we took a carton of eggs with us to the terrace and lay flat on the ground, waiting for unwitting pedestrians.

Oren appeared. He considered the three of us. "What are you losers doing?"

When we told him, he said, "Gee, guys, maybe when I'm in high school, you'll let me join you."

Tanner said, "What do you suggest, dickweed?"

To Cliffnotes, Oren said, "Let's get the map."

"Great idea," Cliff said, and jumped to his feet.

Oren and Cliffnotes had a subway map along whose arterial lines they had listed the numbers collected from the city's nearby pay phones. On slow nights like these, we picked a location and made prank calls.

We huddled in my closet and closed the door, so as not to wake my parents.

Tanner, still buzzed from the party, asked to go first. Receiver in hand and finger pressed to the cradle's prongs, he took several deep breaths to nerve himself and then called a pay phone in Times Square. He tilted the earpiece away from his ear so we could all hear.

A woman said, "Hello?"

"Hello?"

"Who's this?"

"Peter."

"Peter who?"

"Peter Piper suck my pecker!" Then he slammed the receiver into the cradle and bent double, cackling.

All of us shook our heads in disappointment.

Oren, who had a special dislike for Tanner, who thought he was the prototypical Boyd Prep prick, said, "Lame."

"Fuck you, Oren," Tanner said, "you go then," and handed him the phone.

Because I did not rise to his defense, Oren shot me a disappointed look and then consulted the map. He dialed and glanced between us while he waited for someone to pick up. When the man answered, he raised his voice an octave and whispered, "Dad? Dad, is that you?"

"Sorry, kid, this isn't your dad."

"You have to help me, mister, please, I finally got out of the closet—"

"Is this some kind of joke?"

Oren began to cry, tears and everything. "Mister, please, he only gives me a bucket to pee in."

"Look, kid, calm down, okay?"

"Please don't hang up, I have to get out of this place."

"I said calm down—"

"He hurts me. He hurts me real bad."

"Who does?"

"The man. Who keeps me locked up. All the time, whenever he's here."

"Kid, listen, what's your name?"

"Etan."

"Ethan?"

"Will you please call my dad and tell him to come get me please?"

"Holy shit. Is this . . . Etan Patz?"

"Please, mister, I've been here forever."

"*The* Etan Patz."

"Please hurry—"

"Holy fucking shit."

"He never goes away for long."

"Where are you? I can come get you."

"I don't know, it's dark in this place."

"Are you in an apartment?"

"Yes."

"Can you get to a door?"

"He locks it from outside."

"What about a window?"

"There's a window, but there's bars on it."

"Look out and tell me what you see."

"I see . . . an intersection. I see a subway."

"Are there letters on them?"

"It's hard to make them out."

"What about the street sign?"

"It says . . . Fourteenth Street."

Silence.

"And I see a phone booth. With someone in it."

Silence.

"Mister, are you there?"

"Jesus Christ."

"Mister, is that bad?"

"Holy Jesus Lord."

"Please, mister, you're really scaring me."

"You're—you're right here."

"Where?"

"Here. Where I am. I'm on your block. I'm waving now. Can you see me waving?"

"Is that you, mister? In the phone booth?"

"It's me. Which way are you?"

"The other way."

"What do you mean?"

"Your back is to me."

"Am I facing you now?"

"Yes."

"I see your building."

"You do?"

"I'm going to point toward you, okay? I'm going to raise my arm toward you, and when I'm pointing right at you say stop, okay?"

"Okay."

"Stop now?"

"Keep going."

"Stop now?"

"Stop."

"You're on the third floor. I got you, Etan. Don't worry. I'm gonna call the police and we're gonna come get you."

"Can't you stay on the phone with me?"

"Kid, I have to hang up just for a second and call the police."

"Okay, but, mister, before you do, I should probably tell you—"

"Tell me anything, Etan, it's going to be okay."

"It's that, it's that—"

"It's what? Tell me."

"It's that you're the most gullible asshole I've ever talked to in my life."

Very gently, Oren hung up the phone. He looked at me, then at Cliff, and finally at Tanner, with a that's-how-it's-done expression.

Even Tanner joined us in our reverential applause.

"My turn," I said.

I called the pay phone on Sixty-Third and Central Park West. Someone answered on the first ring.

"Who's this?" I said.

"Who's this?"

"Griffin."

"Well, Griffin, I think you have the wrong number," the man said.

"Is this 787-3858?" I asked.

"It is."

"Is this the pay phone next to the YMCA?" I said.

"It is. You know what that means?"

"What?"

"That it's fate I picked up. Swear to God, I've been waiting for your call."

"You have?"

"When the student is ready the mentor appears."

"Help me, Obi-Wan, you're my only hope."

"I'm dead serious."

"So am I."

"Then meet me in fifteen minutes by the rocks in Sheep Meadow, and I'll tell you the meaning of life."

And he hung up.

At the Sixty-Seventh Street entrance to the park, we could hear the faint clop of hooves and the jingle of carriages making the late-night loop. Through the restaurant windows, waiters reset tables at Tavern on the Green, snapping open white tablecloths that billowed before settling over the round tops. In the nearing distance stood the great black pool that was Sheep Meadow, bottomless. There was a cessation of street noise once we crossed onto its grass, this stiffened by the iron air, so that the lawn, made vaster by the darkness, crunched beneath our feet. I felt brave. I was certain we all did. We were beside ourselves, whispering and laughing, rousing ourselves, shushing each other, bashing into each other, not believing there would be a rendezvous, believing we were going to learn something. That we had decided to accept this invitation was in and of itself some sort of triumph, since good sense dictated this was the last place we should've been at such an hour.

The ambient light was bright enough to illuminate a smudged outline of the man. He was standing on the exposed rock, near the meadow's tree line, a small outcropping atop this lake bed of grass that looked comparatively bleached. He wore an overcoat that rounded his shoulders and had his hands stuffed in his pockets. Atop his head, a hunting cap, brim folded up, that made his round face seem rounder. His large glasses were tinted. He was double-chinned, closer to tubby—thick, that is, but not hulking. At the sight of us, he flapped the coat's panels a couple of times—in greeting? He seemed utterly unruffled by the fact that he was outnumbered, a confidence that we could only attribute to his adulthood and was somehow unsettling. It suggested an as yet unrevealed power— that he might, at any moment, spread his coat's wings and take flight.

"You showed up," he said.

Tanner, Cliff, and I stood in a loose crescent beneath the rocks, which made the man seem taller. Oren squatted behind us, his elbows on his knees.

"Let's hear it, man," Cliff said.

"The meaning of life," Tanner said.

"Do I get your names?" he asked.

"You do not," Tanner said.

"Fair enough," he said.

"The floor is yours," Cliff said.

"Here's the thing," he said. "You know more about your feelings now than you will know ever. Swear to God. Something happens to you, say something good or bad, it doesn't matter, and you let yourself feel it, and because it's practically the first time, you don't rationalize it or analyze it or overinterpret it, it's just the thing itself. You don't build a shell around it, it pierces you, it enters you, and, swear to God, if I could go back in time, you know what I would eliminate? What I'd lobotomize from my brain? The future. I'd let myself experience everything as it happened like you do now instead of wondering like I always did. Why isn't this some other way instead of that? When will things be different? Better? Will they get worse? Do you understand?"

"No," Tanner said.

"But keep going," said Cliffnotes.

"It's complicated, what I'm trying to explain," he continued. "It's inside-out thinking, but if I could communicate it, you'd realize that right now you are the most honest that you will ever be, and if you could somehow stay that way, then you would triumph over life, swear to God, because at some point soon, and maybe it's already happened, you're going to get hurt badly and repeatedly, small hurts over and over, things you don't feel right now, like tick bites or leeches attaching to your skin. You're going to stop listening and feeling and instead start making arguments, every day of your life asking yourself *what isn't* instead of *what is,* and then it's all over already. You'll think you've bitten the apple, but really the apple's bitten you. Your argument for what isn't becomes the world and you become the argument and then it's already happened: the beginning of adulthood."

"I don't follow any of this," I said to Tanner.

"I think I understand," Tanner said.

"This guy's cuckoo for Cocoa Puffs," Cliff whispered.

"Because phonies think they know," the man continued. "But phonies don't know what they don't know."

"Like my dad," Oren said.

"You're saying something bad is going to happen to us?" Cliff asked.

"Something bad happens to everyone," he said. "Except it's not bad. It's just *something.* That's the trick. Recognizing it's just something. That's the difference between pain and suffering. Suffering's the former and pain's the latter."

"I'm confused," I said.

"So what happened to you?" Cliff asked. "When did you stop feeling?"

"I have never stopped feeling."

"When did you stop making an argument?"

"I have not stopped feeling or making an argument. I fight against not feeling and making an argument."

"But when did you know," Tanner asked, "that you weren't . . . not?"

"Excellent," he said. "I know exactly when I knew I wasn't not. I know exactly when it happened."

"Okay," Tanner said, and rubbed his hands together, "here we go."

"It was in Hawaii. Have you ever been there?"

None of us had.

"This was when I lived on Oahu," he said.

He lived there in a way he had never been able to repeat in his life. He had a job, it was true, but his salary could only afford him an efficiency room with a warming plate, a mattress, a corner for his guitar, a bathroom with only a toilet. To bathe, he used his kitchen sink, splashed his face and, with a dampened rag, cleaned his armpits and balls, or he went to the Y to shower. On his days off, he put on the only good clothes that he had, the blue button-down shirt and white shorts and penny loafers that, after he combed his hair nicely and parted it to the side, made him look enough like a tourist that he could approach the front desk of luxurious hotels to ask what time check-in was and then join the sunburned families on the elevators. He pushed the buttons for the floors none of the other passengers pressed, nodding at the couples during the quiet ascent, and then, getting off at his floor, he wandered the hallways, looking for the maid carts from which he helped himself to pillow mints and bars of soap and a roll or two of toilet paper, which he placed in his book bag. He raised the polished lids on room service trays and feasted on the uneaten slices of mango and pineapple, the clusters of red grapes, the bitten strips of bacon, the toast points hardened with egg yolk, or, God bless, the untouched Danish or pastry, which he washed down with the miniature pitchers of heavy cream or a slug of coffee. If it were lunchtime, he'd next wander to the open-air restaurants and, like one of the small birds that landed beneath the wrought-iron legs of chairs or, bravely, on the tables themselves, help himself to what remained on unbused tables: the half-eaten Monte Cristos or tails of coconut shrimp, the curled ribbons of carrot, the split rose-hearts of radishes; even, sometimes, the parsley garnish, because the bright green bite of it was enormously refreshing. Picking up a newspaper someone hadn't bothered to properly throw away, he might even take a seat, push the tip tray toward the somewhat baffled waiter, and say, "I'm not quite done here," and then dip a soiled knife into the water glass and wipe it on his pants leg before cutting away the uneaten parts of burgers and omelets. Or, in a moment of inspiration, he'd drop a piece of cutlery so that it tinkled on the concrete loudly enough to bring the waiter over. "Could I get another fork?" he'd ask, and, upon the server's return, wrap what was left in the new napkin, thanking him, and convincing even himself that he belonged.

These days spent among the tourists were vastly different from his shifts at a factory on the outskirts of Wahiawā, near the Schofield Barracks. It was a vast, high-ceilinged space with clerestory windows that, no matter the weather, seemed to pale the light to a fossil gray. The factory was an interconnected and intestinal array of machines, laid out lengthwise, of belts and sluices and sorters that transformed one thing into another. In this case, potatoes arrived in semitrucks, whose payloads tumbled onto conveyer belts that bore the tonnage of unwashed spuds, passing them first beneath high-pressure jets that unzipped their skins, which were funneled off to be ground into animal feed, while the peeled were sorted into handfuls and washed again and then fed to the slicer, where they were multiplied into tens of thousands of discs before being spread flat and, rinsed once more, tipped into oil vats in which they were fried. To then be variously seasoned and funneled into mylar bags, crimped and sealed and boxed, and loaded once again onto another fleet of trucks. He could not help but imagine, standing among the industrial clatter, an arterial clogging—not just the bodies whose insides were spackled with this mix of starch and salt once consumed but of the roads filled with wheezing trucks, of high-density feedlots ankle-deep in excrement, of once-clear streams clotted with the starchy silt of the runoff, of the islands' winds seasoning the ozone layer with the factory's poisonous sediment—the mess and noise of it all making its ineluctable way down to the water table and seeping quietly into tributaries and then into the sea.

Behind the factory and atop a slab of concrete were several picnic tables, these adjacent a scummed pond fed by one of the factory's main drains, the water's edge fluffed with food waste, pulverized potato processed to a bubbly powder. Pigeons flocked and fed on these soapy dregs, and watching them while he ate his PB&J and free bag of chips, he often wondered about these birds that populated the island. Did they come over on ships, accidental stowaways on tankers and freighters? Or were they blown here by opportunistic storms? And when was it, he wondered, that a pigeon, with its built-in homing instinct, sensed that it was too far from land to return and sought, in exhaustion, the oil tanker's radar mast? Whenever he observed them here, victims of their own failed peregrinations, he wondered if such sights—the bejeweled throat of a dead bird floating on the wine-dark sea—had given rise to some minor myth, since most myths were answers to the question *How?*

Because how, he later wondered, had one managed to enter the plant, searching, he supposed, for food or a place to nest, perhaps just after the shift change when the first of the day's trucks made their deposit. When the noise of the engines, the clattering rumble of potatoes, the explosive hiss and bang of the hydraulic lift sending pulses outward, should have spooked it but instead somehow herded the pigeon deeper into the factory. Here, where he spotted it. Here, where the processing machines were at their most vertical and entangled, and above which, now, it thumped its walnut-sized head several times against the high windows, confused by their promise of open sky. Finding no exit or relief, the pigeon buzzed the line workers. They had nothing to fear, of course, it wasn't an owl or hawk, but they raised their arms over their faces when it swooped. Several men on the line had stopped to watch, most of them laughing as the bird tumbled and dove. Still others paused to consider its plight and to be, perhaps in some small way, impressed by it. Until one of them took a rejected potato from the belt and flung it at the bird.

He could see the idea take hold among the men. A few picked up potatoes and gave them a short toss, palming their heft. Others cocked their arms, raising the improvised missile to their ears and then either failing to nerve themselves or throwing it only half-heartedly. But then several of them took more careful aim, and when one of the men nearly bull's-eyed the creature the others, encouraged, summoned a rage—he could see it on their faces—as the bird became interloper and prize and also, in its very capacity to fly, an insult to them. By now everyone had stopped their work. No one was inspecting the belts, and this further fueled their anger, since this abandonment of their jobs, the going off-task, revealed how unnecessary to the process they were, that the system, the factory itself, would no more stop its production without their presence than it was made more efficient by it. And what they were doing now, by mandatory neglect, was daring the foreman to notice their insignificance.

Soon the air above the factory floor was flurried with potatoes, cross-hatched by their vectors, the pigeon somehow dodging and tumbling between their parabolic trajectories. The potatoes smashed with a tinny report against the walls' corrugated tin; they splatted on the concrete floor. This madness had infected all the men except him, who had realized the bird's only chance of escape was the windows. So now *he* took aim, cursing his weak arm with each toss but elated when a desperate heave finally shattered one of the panes. He fired again, knocking out another. Several of his coworkers had noticed his ploy and their faces registered something like appreciation: how he had iterated on the game, adding to it the satisfaction of breaking what did not belong but was owed to them, while introducing a new challenge—put a clock on the field, so to speak; gave the game a limit, a terminus. The pigeon seemed to sense the opening, the fresh air they could all smell. Darting, it homed toward sky. And as it climbed now, toward its escape, beelining toward safety and purpose beyond the empty window frame, it took a shot square in the chest. A great cheer went up as the bird fell. It landed on the floor, one gray wing flapping fishlike on the concrete. The man nearest where it landed turned and, with a quick and forceful step, crushed its skull with his heel. At this another cheer went up. Then he bent and pinched the prize by one of its wings, the torso appearing headless, and nodded in victory as he pivoted, stretching, for all to see, the creature's entire and surprisingly broad wingspan to receive everyone's applause. And, after taking a bow, after raising the bird above his head to what had become an ovation, he tossed it onto the conveyer belt. Which everyone silently watched as the creature slipped into the sorting machine's innards, the dark in which it would be transformed and eventually consumed by some unlucky customer, thoughtlessly biting into what was once feather, some salted piece of claw, a metacarpus bone, some brittle sliver of beak, as much a part of the food as any other ingredient.

"That's it?" Tanner said, since the man had gone silent. "That's the story?"

"I don't get it," Cliff said.

"Me neither," I said.

"I do," said Oren.

I couldn't sleep that night, my mind was racing so much. I thought about the story Mr. Bauer had told at dinner and imagined it first from his perspective, his having stumbled onto the very last person he'd have ever dreamed of seeing again, let alone capturing, and whom, it was obvious to me now, he had killed. He must have thought that God Himself had gifted him with such perfect revenge—for serving up this soldier, out of the millions, upon whom to inflict retribution, to balance the scales. And yet what sort of God arranged fate thus? Was God on the side of Mr. Bauer, I wondered, or was that only Mr. Bauer's god? Because then I thought of it from the Nazi's perspective. Tied up before these American servicemen, one of whom spoke perfect German, whom he recalled he'd once beaten, and who was now raising a rifle at his head. Was God punishing him? he must have asked himself. If this was his fate, whom in this great struggle did the Lord favor? And what of the other soldier, the one standing by Mr. Bauer's side? Did he have misgivings, or egg Mr. Bauer on? Did he watch everything as I had, silently, when we put Pilchard on the train? Was it not better, at such a moment, to be Mr. Bauer? To act instead of stand idly by? At least there was some *conviction* in acting. Oh, those moments during that year when I stood paralyzed before that of which I could not speak, that which rendered me silent! Oh, my *fury* that previous morning, at Boyd, staring at the ceiling lights and torquing Kepplemen's neck as he lay clutched to me in turn. *"You've got to move,"* Kepplemen would scream at me during practice. *"You've got to move."* Yet there we lay, strangely embraced and still. Yet here I lay, in the dark, thinking about all these things—about the story, finally, the man at Sheep Meadow had told us. Was that the meaning of life: that some people tried to kill things while others tried to save them? Was that what Oren understood? Were you always on one side, or did you daily pick sides anew? Did Oren feel like I'd abandoned him somehow? Was that why I felt so guilty? And if that pigeon had managed to soar free, would it soon forget this brush with death? Or would the sky forever be a greater joy?

It was the thing I hadn't realized I'd hoped for—my relief was so immense—to see Pilchard enter Boyd's front hall Monday morning, safe and alive. He walked past the pews, the circles beneath his eyes darker than usual, but he was otherwise unscathed. He caught me looking at him, looking *for* him, although neither of us did more than acknowledge the other with a glance. Tanner, seated to my left, sat watching the front doors, oblivious to our exchange. Like me, Cliff also gave Pilchard the stare down, but before Pilchard registered his presence, Kepplemen appeared and intercepted him, and after cupping Pilchard's cheek in his palm and touching his temple to his in greeting, he walked him the rest of the way down the hall and out of our sight, speaking to him with a hand clamped to his neck.

I didn't see Pilchard again until that afternoon, in the locker room, ahead of practice, while everyone changed, and Kepplemen, who was checking my weight—I was six pounds over and we had a dual meet on Thursday—let me have it. "How the fuck are you gonna lose this, Griffin?" Before I could answer, he said, "Put on a rubber suit and don't leave practice till you cut half." There was an extra dose of wrath in his voice. It carried over to practice, where he singled me out during drills. "Don't you quit," he shouted at me as we did stand-up escapes, "don't you dare wimp out." To conclude practice we ran stairs, twenty-five flights in sets of five, and as further punishment he made me lead the team. After the third set, I was so gassed I had to drop to the back of the line. As punishment for this, he ordered I do two more sets on my own.

Later, in the locker room, I sat trying to pull the tape off my rubber suit's wrists, but my hands were shaking so much I had to use my teeth. By now the place was emptying out, the last to shower were leaving, and having disrobed, I weighed myself. I had lost nearly three pounds, but Coach was nowhere to be seen to deliver the report. I returned to the bench and sat disconsolately, listening to the showers hiss, watching the steam crawl along the ceiling, nursing my disappointment and mourning the dinner I'd have to skip. Then Pilchard appeared at his locker. He must've just weighed himself because he too was naked—he could not have been more than a hundred pounds in clothes, his ribs were so pronounced he looked like he'd swallowed a claw clip, and his cock, which amazed us all, hung thickly between his quads like a bell clapper from a nautical rope. From his locker he tossed me a towel and said, "Here," forlornly. Before I could decline the gift, he retrieved another, wrapping it around his waist and entering the showers. "Thanks," I called to him. Then I shouldered the towel and followed. I was of a mind to say something to him; I felt so guilty for what had happened over the weekend I wanted to apologize.

There were nine showerheads evenly spaced on three of the room's four walls, and Pilchard stood under the jet directly across from the entrance with his back to me, his palms pressed to the tiles, as far as possible from Kepplemen, who was showering too. He stood in the near corner, to my right, but outside the spray, so entirely lathered with suds that he looked like a statue dusted in snow. The dark room was densely fogged. The water parted Pilchard's hair and sluiced down his back and tiny buttocks. And then he looked over his shoulder at me. He appeared almost surprised to see me there. He blinked, his lashes wet, and then glanced at Coach and back at me again—I could not read his expression. For a moment I thought he wanted to tell me something. Kepplemen stepped beneath the head, the water peeling suds from his body that splatted against the floor tiles. His eyes were closed; they'd been closed, I thought, since I'd entered. He kept them closed when he said, "We'll check your weight in the morning." And though I was versed in his subtext, though I knew this meant I was dismissed, I said to Pilchard, "You ready to split?" To which he, taking my hint, said, "Sure." We dressed quickly after drying ourselves.

On the bus later, just before he got off to catch the crosstown east, I told him I'd wash the towel he'd lent me and bring it back tomorrow. He said not to worry about it and rang the bell. He exited, and I felt relief that neither Cliff nor Tanner was here to see any of this, which did not eclipse my satisfaction that Pilchard and I were now officially square.

The next morning Dad appeared in our room to wake us. He turned on our television and, with something like excitement, said, "John Lennon was murdered last night!" In his hand he held a spatula covered with scrambled eggs. He gestured with it toward the screen. "Tragic," he said. Then he sucked some eggs off the blade. "Shot right outside his apartment," he noted while he chewed. "At the Dakota." Even through my fogginess, I could tell that he wanted to be the first to deliver this news, that by hearing it from him he believed he was somehow attached to the event. That it touched him with just a bit of its dark glamour. It was, I was coming to realize, one of his character flaws: aping pathos, he flipped it to bathos. Not that I'd have been so articulate about it back then.

Thursday's match was against Saint Paul's School, in Garden City. It was, by reputation, a shitty program with a bunch of fishes, but because I was so depleted after making weight—I'd sucked my final three pounds in a single day—I could neither bring myself to warm up with any intensity nor summon the ferocity necessary to win. With an additional week of preparation, I might have matched my opponent's velocity, but I was instead subject to his hummingbird speed. His fireman's carry I saw coming but could not stop. His Half Nelson series was executed with a relentlessness I could not counter. A lesson. *This was a lesson,* I thought, after he did a stand-up escape, turned, and shot a double leg, and took me down. And then the most shameful resignation came over me as he rammed his head into my ribs to secure a cradle. I could've kicked open his grip and freed myself. I could have prolonged the contest rather than allow myself to be muscled over. But instead I bucked on my back with just enough power to appear as if I were actually fighting. Until finally the ref smacked the foam rubber and it was over—which was all I wanted.

In short, I tanked.

I walked off the mat to the shoulder pats of my teammates, with the exception of Kepplemen, whose disgust with me manifested in total disregard and was as hot as mine was for him. There was a confrontation coming. I was certain of it from the end of the match until the ride back to Boyd—*Fuck you,* I thought, *and fuck this season*—but it did not materialize.

I hopped off the bus before my stop and got two slices at Pizza Joint. I dusted these with garlic, Parmesan, and red pepper flakes and allowed myself to taste *everything.* I drank a large Coke to wash it down, and I was sugar-flooded, carbo-loaded. I didn't give a shit if I lost, and if I wanted to pig out now, what of it?

So that to see Naomi parked there before Juilliard was like dessert. The dome light of the Mercedes illuminated its interior. Beneath it, contained within it, Naomi seemed to float, suspended above the street. She was reading the *Daily News,* the paper covering the steering wheel.

I hadn't seen her since the tournament at Friends Academy, since that night I'd showered at her house. When I knocked on her window, her face revealed more than pleasant surprise, and it filled me with anticipation. The moment I took my seat, she pulled me into her arms. Coffee, perfume, her bangles' clink, how her hair, in its light caress, seemed almost prehensile. "It's been forever," Naomi said as she smushed me to her. She started the car. "Tell me everything, tell me how you've been, how was your day?"

This was the first time I recall ever wanting to kiss her. She drove and, when she found a parking space and cut the engine, the evening's privacy settled on us. There shined through the windshield that sea-cave light of far-off streetlamps, projected onto the long garage's bare brick wall that lined one side of our secret place. That lake of blackness to our right rimmed by the West Side Highway also enclosed us. I had so much to tell her, but she wanted to kiss me too, and when we did it seemed that we might somehow burrow into each other, the force with which she pressed herself to me was so great and which I returned in kind. "Do you want to go in back?" she whispered, and although I didn't know exactly what she meant, didn't completely understand what it implied, I knew it meant more and I said yes. Naomi nodded at this, assenting, at once resigned and joyful, and I felt older somehow. She was about to open her door but then giggled and turned to kiss me again. And then a police car's lights flashed red, white, and blue, its siren sounding a single note. The interior was suddenly floodlit, and I froze.

Over the PA, the officer said, "Step out of the car, please," and Naomi, at first frozen herself, exited but left the door open. The squad car's passenger window rolled down; its spotlight blinded me. "You're parked illegally," the officer said to Naomi, and having raised my hand to cover my eyes and turn away, I noticed the hydrant outside my window. Naomi's back was to me. After she said something to the officer, he replied, "Can I see your license, please?"

The other officer came around to my side. He too shined a light in my face, then tapped the window with the butt of his baton. "Step out of the car, please," he said. When I did, he asked, "Where do you live, young man?"

And in a moment, which I now look back on as fateful, I said, with something like surprise because the answer was so obvious, "In Great Neck." And then: "Did my mom do something wrong?"

The cop holding her license glanced at his partner and nodded.

After the officers left, we found another parking spot farther up the street. But the mood had altered. For a long time, Naomi sat with her hands on the steering wheel, her arms stuck straight out, as if she were bracing for a crash. "I should go," she said, and started the car, but she instead resumed this pose and did not drive. Lips puckered, she slowly exhaled. "My heart's still not beating normal," she said. She had the heat going and she sunk into her seat. "Let me just calm down in a bit." I picked up the newspaper and pressed it flat across my lap. It was that famous picture of Lennon, the one that would become iconic, of the rock star in profile, about to enter his limousine and stopping to sign his new album for Mark David Chapman, who stood, head down, staring through his tinted lenses, his eyes visible because of the angle. He looked vaguely familiar. He appeared as if he was about to say something to Lennon—words of appreciation? Admiration? What utterance, I wondered, could be more fraudulent than any of these, if later that night you were going to shoot that person in the back, playing at destiny when you were really nothing but a coward.

"Makes you think about the future," Naomi said. "Makes you think about the signs you don't see. Makes you think about love."

The car was stuffy. I'd cracked my window, and from the river a great horn sounded, it must've been a mighty ship, like a tanker. Dad, who'd been in the navy, once told me that such a long blast alerted the crew that a journey was now under way, or it was what he called a "blind bend" signal—an alert to other vessels that might not see your approach.

"What do you mean?" I asked.

"I saw that man on the front page," Naomi said, indicating Chapman, "and I thought about those times I watched *The Nuclear Family* with Danny and Jackie. And all those billboards I saw for *The Talon Effect*. And then seeing that movie with Sam and seeing you on screen. And how before I met you, there you were, you were right there. You know how Elliott says we have our backs to the future? I had no idea you were going to come into my life. And now," she concluded, with something like resignation, "I don't know what to do about it."

THE TWELVE DAYS OF CHRISTMAS

It was tradition, on the final day before winter break, to conclude the semester with the all-school Christmas assembly. The auditorium, in its dual function as our chapel, was festively decorated. Reverend Holstein wore his cassock, surplice, and purple stole. Fistly sat immaculately dressed, wearing a dark suit and bow tie polka-dotted in bright green. He was joined by the head of middle school, Dr. Grandoff, who wore a clerical collar and black shirt beneath his jacket that made him look more severe than usual. Every seat was filled, the central block of pews reserved for the kindergartners through fourth graders, while the fifth and sixth graders occupied the balcony. The service's big finale was the singing of "The Twelve Days of Christmas." There was a mimeograph sheet containing the lyrics folded in between the exhaustive program, which included both the prayers and traditional hymns, the latter functioning, at least in my mind, as a toll ticket marking our progress through the service but also high school. Each grade, with kindergarten being the only exception, would stand to sing its verse and then sit, and so on. It being a cumulative song, there was a tidal effect to the performance, one that slowly gathered energy, building speed as it rose toward the seniors' verse, which each year they were allowed to make up themselves. Once *they* sang, once this wave had reached its highest

height, it would break, we'd race through all the verses as they crashed
to shore, and then vacation began! On the level of sheer volume there
was a grade-to-grade effort at one-upmanship, though most beautiful,
by far, and hitting the highest notes, for sure, was *"Five golden rings!"*
its concord pealing, as it were, from the heavens, since the fifth graders
were seated on the balcony, and followed by the shouts "Boom, boom,
boom!" which, in tandem with the students' stomping, sounded like
thunder. And when the juniors sung *their* verse and then the first graders
concluded this round, the applause was its loudest so far, we sustained
our cheering just a bit longer, and then the entire audience wheeled to
face the back of the auditorium. The seniors stood to sing their verse.
They were excited, edgy, fidgety, and it was only now, when there was no
turning back, that they realized their idea, like a rip current, had dragged
them out to sea:

> *On the twelfth day of Christmas, my true love gave to me*
> *Twelve Fistlies fisting!*

"What's fisting?" I shouted at Tanner before we sang our verse.

Tanner smiled, shaking his head at my ignorance, and did not explain.

Something monumentally inappropriate had been sung, and everyone, still singing, was by now focused on our principal. Fistly's happy
expression had transformed into a gorgon's. *Perhaps they might be on
detention for the entire break,* we wondered. *Perhaps they might not even
graduate.* The song concluded, the applause was confused and muted,
and Reverend Holstein stepped to the podium and embarrassedly dismissed us. We were, for more than two weeks, free.

Well, not all of us.

"The senior class," Fistly said, having strode to the podium and taken
the microphone, "shall remain behind."

And Kepplemen had also called a team meeting. It was a chafe. It
was unnecessary and we knew it. This was his last chance to see us off
before the break, to have us line up before him, which we did, slumped
on the wrestling mats, our shoes removed, some already in their winter
coats and carrying their stuffed-to-the-gills, locker-emptied book bags.
Kepplemen began to speak. He held a clipboard and consulted it as he

walked us through the entire dual meet schedule in the weeks following our return.

"Please note," Kepplemen said, "that the Wednesday we start back, we have a match against Collegiate. So watch your weight over vacation."

Kepplemen dismissed us, and it was possible that even *he* was relieved for the break, although I was not surprised that he held me back.

"A word," he whispered, "please."

Here it came, I thought. The fight we'd been meaning to have for over a week now. Kepplemen watched the last kids exit, the door banged shut behind them, and now we were alone.

"I had," he said, "high hopes for you this season." He began quietly and blinked a great deal. "But even you'll admit it's been a disappointment so far."

"It has," I conceded.

"It wasn't a question."

"I don't *want* to lose," I said.

"The *fuck*," he roared, "was that stunt against Saint Paul's then? *That* was a question." Because I remained silent, he continued yelling. "I could've subbed a lightweight like Cliff in your place. And he'd have probably lost too, but he'd have at least put some effort into it. While you . . . you threw that match."

Here was the thing: I knew Kepplemen wasn't wrong. But his anger was disproportionate. It was closer to fear. Whether it was a Granby roll or whisking Pilchard from the showers, he was no longer sure what I might do.

"Act like a starter," Kepplemen said, "from here on out. Are we clear?"

"It won't happen again," I said.

He pressed the clipboard's edge to my chest. "If it does," he said, "you're off the team."

I stood there after he left, pleased with myself. Because I did not cry. Which was something.

Boyd, being a mostly windowless space, shielded us from any sense of the day's weather. Between chapel's end and Kepplemen's meeting, it had begun to snow. I caught a glimpse of it as I passed the front hallway, headed toward my locker—it was one of those heavy snows slowly falling on a windless day, good packing snow, gentling to the ground in the afternoon's peculiar silence, the flakes laying hands on each other and padding the already-evacuated school's stillness, as if it were an extra layer of insulation. A few straggler students and teachers were leaving now, a locker or two banging down the hallway. For a moment, I stood at mine and considered its contents.

Sneakers peeked out beneath dirty sweatpants on the bottom. On the top shelf, *The Catcher in the Rye, Romeo and Juliet.* The ties Naomi had given me, still in their Hermès box. The kneepads. My algebra textbook's cover was coming apart at the corner. This scene looked like one of the staged lockers the set designer for *The Nuclear Family* would have populated. *I could take these home,* I thought, *spend the break learning all the things I missed.* We had exams upon our return from break, after all. I could pack my recipe box of index cards and memorize Spanish vocabulary and conjugations. Redo every math equation from our first lesson forward. Get a chapter or two ahead in *Darkness at Noon,* whatever that novel was about. I could come back in the new year a different person.

And I left.

For as long as I could remember, we had gone to my grandparents' house for Christmas. Ever since my grandfather had retired from the military—he was a rear admiral in the Coast Guard—they had lived in the same general vicinity: in Crystal City, near D.C., when we were very young; in Alexandria for several years after that; and now on a golf course in Manassas. We visited them nearly every Thanksgiving as well—we'd skipped this year to celebrate with the Barrs. During the summers, while I was shooting *The Nuclear Family,* Oren and Mom spent several weeks down here without Dad and me. But Christmas with my grandparents was unvarying. Aunt Maine, my mother's younger sister by two years, had followed her parents wherever they relocated, a requirement my uncle Marco, who owned an accounting firm, never seemed to balk at. He even tolerated their houses being on adjacent lots in Alexandria, the back gate that fenced my grandparents' yard opening onto their own backyard, and an arrangement that was ideal for Oren and me, since it meant easy access to our three cousins: Leo, Anthony, and Lucy.

Unlike my mother, I could not read during the ride because it made me carsick, and Oren wouldn't share his Walkman, so like Dad I watched the landscape, joining in his sense of injustice, since Mom could not help with the drive. The blue signs let us know we had crossed into another state. WELCOME TO NEW JERSEY, which was nothing, it seemed, but a highway spanning marshes full of poisonous brown water and coursed by the occasional egret, its wilderness punctured by chemical plants that belched white smoke, the smell at once sulfurous and sickening and almost magical in its opacity, in its refusal to dissipate. Pennsylvania was a long stretch of moist green fields rank with manure, the roadside absent skyline and dotted with billboards for HOMEMADE CUSTARD, which Oren and I begged Dad to stop for, to no avail. The Baltimore shipyards' towering cranes put me in mind of Imperial walkers and meant that we were closer.

To pass the time, I dreamed. My reverie was such a vivid pastiche I sometimes struggled to distinguish between memory and fantasy. A victory over Goldburn, my team, Oren—the entire gym!—going wild. Miss Sullens, first to applaud, after I recited the Queen Mab speech from *Romeo and Juliet*. Deb Peryton, taking my hand at Roy Adler's party and leading me upstairs, into that wondrous top floor. Kepplemen's eyes as he glanced at me in the bus's rearview mirror, certain he knew, as I peeked back, that I was pretending to be asleep. The expectant silence, almost like a jinx, between Naomi and me as we drove from Juilliard to the Dead Street.

We had left New York in the late morning and by now it was dark, which meant we'd traveled a great distance, and the release I felt, having left the whole confusing roil of Manhattan far behind, was so tremendous that I slept all the way to Virginia. When we merged from 495 onto 66, the roadway turned from four lanes to two, and we saw signs for the Manassas National Battlefield Park, which meant Oren and I could find our way to the Evergreen Country Club on our own. My grandparents' house was a half mile from there, its rear windows facing the third hole's fairway. So many of the trees had been cleared from the surrounding properties the landscape looked like one great hilly lawn dotted with houses. None of us golfed back then, but Grandma and Grandpa were passionate about the sport and always played together. Sometimes we would catch sight of them from their back patio. The acoustics were such that from a chaise you could hear Grandma, after Grandpa's shot and leaning over the cart's steering wheel to watch its arc, say, "That one has eyes, Butcher." She didn't play much anymore now that she struggled to catch her breath, but she continued to smoke two packs of Marlboro Reds a day, no matter how hard Mom tried to get her to quit.

"We're here!" Oren said to no one in particular. It was possible he loved coming to visit our grandparents even more than I did.

We bolted from the car without our bags.

Mexican food was the first night's meal, and we could smell it from the garage as we raced up the stairs that led to Grandpa's study. Gramps, greeting us, looked smart in his insulated overalls and watch cap. Grandma stood down the hall from him, in the kitchen, arms akimbo, a wooden mixing spoon in her hand, feigning shock at the sight of us. "Look at you two giants," she said. When she hugged us, her lungs whistled.

By the time we'd unpacked, our cousins, the Locatellos, arrived.

Lucy, being the youngest, shouted her greeting as she pounded up the garage steps. Anthony and Leo appeared wearing matching Redskins jackets. Leo, being standoffish and cool now that he was sixteen, shook our hands. Anthony, who was Oren's age, copied his reserve—a pose both borrowed from their father, my uncle Marco, who never hugged us. Unlike Auntie Maine, who said to us, "Come here!" and, roughly gathering us into her arms, kissed us unabashedly. "Jeepers," she said, "you're both huge!" Anthony's hair had gone curly. Leo, whose hair was straight and blond and whose features were fine, had grown lean, and seemed older in a way that was mysterious. Grandma rang the dinner bell.

"Are we gonna play flashlight tag after this?" Oren asked Leo.

Anthony glanced at his older brother. You could tell he was dying to play too.

Leo said, "I'll see how I feel after eating," and touched his belly like the exercise might give him indigestion.

My burps were the red, green, and yellow of the La Preferida can; for dessert I'd have eaten only one slice of pecan pie, but Leo spent an extra-long time at the adult table, so I helped myself to seconds. When no one was looking, I stood in front of the fridge and drank the eggnog straight from the carton to wash it down. After Leo agreed to play, Oren and I went to our room and put on our darkest clothes. He had filched the cork from Mom's wine bottle and burned it at one end to make eye black. We bundled up and then gathered outside.

There was an unspoken zone in which the game was conducted, a ring of perhaps fifty feet, with the house at its bull's-eye, beyond which you could not wander. The property was only marginally landscaped. There were several boxwoods and prickly hollies surrounding the house that were difficult to hide behind, so the goal was to keep as much space as possible between yourself and the person who was it. On moonless nights, the house was black against the lawn's blue and the sky's pail-flung constellations, which made it easier to go undetected, to lie down next to the lattice that bordered Grandma's garden or flatten yourself against a gutter's downspout as Anthony huffed past, the flashlight's beam shaking as he ran, its circle of light elongating ahead of him while you watched, unseen, belly down on the grass.

We'd been playing for a solid hour, and whatever reservations Leo felt about participating had dissipated. He was it now, and Oren, Anthony, Lucy, and I, crouched by the house's far corner, were lined up each behind the other, our hands hanging on to each other's waists, our fingers through each other's belt loops, cracking the whip and jockeying for position, howling and shushing each other while we waited for some sign of Leo.

Then a car came down the hill behind us, slowed at the mailbox, signaled, and pulled into the driveway.

At which point we let go of each other and stood up straight to watch.

Two people got out. In the dark, we couldn't recognize them. Leo appeared from behind the boxwood right next to us—"Time out," he said—then turned on the flashlight and shined it at the pair. "Over here," he called, and they walked up the rise. Leo met them halfway and they spoke out of earshot. Then he turned to join us with them in tow. He introduced Oren and me. He said, "These are my cousins, Oren and Griffin. From New York. Griffin, Oren, this is Bridget and her younger brother, Patrick."

Bridget wore a dark down jacket and mittens. She held a stocking hat in her hand but would not put it on, I guessed, because the attention she'd given to her hair, which was red and carefully feathered. She was slightly taller than Leo and absolutely beautiful.

"New York," she said to me. "I've always wanted to go there."

Oren, after a moment, smacked my down jacket.

"You should," I said to her, and then felt my face flush.

Patrick, who was Anthony's age, said to me, "Got any more camo?" which did not entirely relieve me of my embarrassment. He was dressed for the game in jeans and a black Oakland Raiders hoodie and a stocking hat. He was the tallest of everyone, gangly and thick-lipped. His eyes bulged slightly. He too was a ginger, and his 'fro was so big it Jiffy Popped his beanie. Nine years from this night, after serving his first tour as a Navy SEAL, he would fall asleep at the wheel driving home for the holiday and, just a few miles from where we stood, hit a tree head-on and be killed instantly. Leo explained the rules to them in a tone that oscillated between amusement and embarrassment. He chuckled, for instance, at the idea of boundaries, that there were places you couldn't go, as if this were all new to him, and we hated him for the mockery. Lucy, he said, would be it—

"I'm not it," she said.

Leo said, "Time in," shined the light on her, then placed the flashlight on the ground and bolted. "You are now."

She said, "Dang it, Leo," because the Locatellos weren't allowed to cuss. Then she started counting Mississippis, and we ran.

The game changed after that.

Usually, the four of us would cluster. But having Patrick and Bridget there splintered us. Anthony and Patrick paired off. Oren, who, to my consternation, abandoned me for Anthony the moment the cousins arrived, joined their triumvirate. So too did Bridget and Leo, who were often missing at each round's conclusion. If we called out to them, they would not answer, at least not initially. They appeared from the dark, out of bounds, to which we voiced our disapproval. And when we did search for them, we would find them sitting together against the central air unit, say, with their knees together, or lying on their stomachs at the very edge of the boundary, as if they were at the beach, their shoulders touching. Their status as a couple was not mysterious; it was their familiarity and

comfort, as if they'd known each other for a lifetime; they seemed somehow more adult and a world unto themselves, and this impressed me
deeply and filled me with a longing I could not name, one that exceeded
my fantasies swirling around Deb Peryton or Gwyneth or even Naomi.
When we accused Leo of *not* playing, he shrugged as if unjustly accused
and then said that we just weren't looking carefully enough. (The two
times Bridget was it, she managed to find Leo with nearly inhuman
speed.) He was being magnanimous toward us for Bridget while protecting her at the same time, and it was exasperating. "You just ran right past
us," he said to Oren, and then to Bridget, "Didn't he?" She did not agree
but, keen to the tension, smiled at him, warmly, and then at Oren, who
was, for the first time in his life, mute.

Strangely, it was as if Bridget were permanently it, even if she wasn't.
I was aware of her location at all times; simply being in the zone of her
person commanded the totality of my attention. She put all my senses on
highest alert: her scent was part Prell shampoo, part Cherry Smash lip
gloss; the sound of her laugh was like a muffled bell. I did not dare run
faster than her when we ran because it was an excuse to stay close. There
was a strange luminescence about her person that shined from beneath
her skin like a hand cupped over a flashlight. Even in the dark I could
make out her features distinctly. I talked so loudly Oren told me to keep
it down. Oren and my cousins had spent time together without me that
I couldn't make up; Anthony and Lucy and now, by proxy, Patrick were
his allies and in on the joke, and they snickered. It was at these moments
I realized they perceived the summers I spent on set as a sort of desertion,
not only an abandonment but a choice that revealed a crippling and selfish aspect of my character of which I was not aware.

Which was also why I think Bridget's presence affected me—now,
especially, when I was it—because she was new to our group. This made
her even more alluring, and it prompted me to violate the rules. Instead
of remaining near the house, I backed up far beyond its gravitational
pull. I clicked off the flashlight, listening for a while to the others booing,
spooking each other, trying to lure me out—"I hear you, Griffin," Lucy
shouted from a good hundred yards away. My absence only ratcheted up
the group's terror. I watched their furtive figures orbiting the house. And
I could keep track of where Bridget was. She was slightly knock-kneed,

and this made her gait slow and effortful and easy to identify, especially when she ran up the hill toward the high side of the house. It pleased me to watch her so unreservedly.

Later, she and Leo unlatched from a shadow and began walking in my direction, toward her car, which was parked behind ours. They made their way around to crouch by the driver's-side door, so that they were hidden from everyone's view except mine. The pair of them, also out of bounds, listened for the rest of us and then, at a barrage of screams, covered their mouths to laugh at our silliness. When they were satisfied that they were safe, Bridget, in her down coat, crossed her arms behind Leo's neck while Leo placed his hands on her hips. When they kissed both their spines straightened, their bodies braiding, and when one of the others came close, they'd stop and shrink against the car's bumper, resting forehead to forehead, waiting for Anthony and Patrick to go running past, for Lucy and Oren to go chugging by. Leo said something to her, and they opened the passenger door and snuck into her car, into the back seat, and then sank beneath the windows, out of view. Strangely, this did not remind me of my evenings with Naomi. And I was not a bit jealous. If anything, I felt warmed by the sight of them instead of alone and cold.

Their extended absence soon disbanded the game. I heard Oren and Lucy complaining, and, disgruntled, they retreated inside. The car's windows were by now fogged, the garage door closed, and I rolled onto my back and stared at the stars. I Morse-coded the flashlight's beam toward the heavens, because I'd heard that these pulses traveled infinitely and might somewhere be seen, and I imagined telling an imaginary someone this fact, as she lay next to me while I held her hand.

Grandma's scrambled eggs were firmer and drier than my father's. From her pan they took on the color of the link sausage. To our orange juice she added brewer's yeast, whose chalkiness we had to drink in its entirety or else not be excused. I still had room for a bowl of muesli afterward and another slice of pie. Then Oren and I departed for our cousins' house. Anthony got permission to take Oren and me shooting. We took the three .22 rifles hanging on the rack in the living room, then walked to a dilapidated, two-story house on their property, and blasted bottles till we ran out of ammo. For lunch, Auntie Maine made us sloppy joes,

French fries, and broccoli with Cheez Whiz. They got their milk from a neighbor's cow, a skin of cream coated the top of the pitcher. It tasted like a shake, and for dessert I poured this over a bowl of Cap'n Crunch, because we drank skim at home and Mom never let us buy sweet cereal.

My father's discontent during this holiday was an enormous, complicated matter. We often stayed through New Year's, and since he had no skill at throwing a football or any interest in playing cribbage with my grandmother, and since he read only the *Times,* which he couldn't get in suburban Virginia, my father had no way to occupy himself. Three days in and he was going out of his mind. So far as I could tell, his discontent was a function of his simply being out of New York. Robbed of its noise and bustle, he responded with an ever-increasing antsiness. As if by leaving Manhattan, Manhattan, in his absence, threatened to disappear, and he must get back to it in order to preserve its existence. Because of this, Dad always seemed to be passing through, especially around midday, lingering long enough to ponder Grandma and me playing gin in the living room, or Grandpa in his study, practicing Spanish on his reel-to-reel while I watched TV, and then stomping away in a huff. His consternation grew worse with each passing day. Christmas Eve morning, after breakfast, he stopped in the doorframe of the living room, where we were all gathered. Mom was on the couch, reading with a throw blanket over her legs. He waited for her to put down her book. "Why don't you go for a walk on the golf course?" she said. At this, Dad stared through the large bay window, at the number three fairway, its grass as brown and forbidding as tundra.

"Maybe I'll go to Woody's and do some last-minute Christmas shopping," he said.

"In D.C.?" Mom said.

He shrugged, and she looked at her watch.

"Take the boys with you," Mom suggested.

"I'm helping with the dinner," Oren said. He was playing hearts with Grandma and Grandpa. We couldn't go see the cousins. They'd gone off to see Uncle Marco's side of the family—they were doubling up on presents, and the fact that we weren't getting any gifts from Dad's side, not even for Hanukkah, still made him furious.

"Griffin," Mom said, "why don't you go with your father."

I looked up from Grandma's *Encyclopedia of Fish* and pointed at myself.

"Come on," Dad said, and winked. "I'll make it worth your while."

Dad asked for permission to borrow Grandpa's Peugeot. The keys hung on a hook above the kitchen's desk.

"Fantastic car," Dad said once we were inside. He pulled the shoulder belt across his chest.

"What model is this?" I asked.

Dad shrugged. "It's French." He pushed the stick left to right and then turned the keys in the ignition. The engine sounded more like a piece of farm equipment than a sedan. A thrum came up through the seats and made the gearshift vibrate. The black fumes transported me back to New York, and I rolled up my slightly cracked window. We made a left out the driveway and headed toward the country club. We stopped at the four-way intersection at the top of the hill.

"Do you like driving a stick more than an automatic?" I asked.

"Absolutely," Dad said. As if to elaborate, he let the car roll backward ever so slightly, giving it gas just as gently so that we advanced the same distance back to the stop line in a pleasant pull-me/push-you alternation. "More control."

"Is it hard to learn?"

"Here," he said. He crossed the intersection and, after entering the club's stone gates, swung around back to its large, empty parking lot. "You try."

It was not a long lesson. It might have been one of the only practical lessons my father ever taught me. I couldn't sing, after all, and I wasn't interested in opera or photography; I was already a more successful film and television actor, and Dad was no athlete. His magnanimity was as surprising as his patience. Perhaps he was relieved to have something to do. Perhaps he was also gladdened to be instructive and relished the real authority it conferred. Most likely it was both. There was no showmanship in the session. His method was very effective. Once I was installed in the driver's seat, he assured me, "Don't worry about stopping. We have plenty of open space, and if need be"—he touched the hand brake between us—"I've got it." He had me keep my foot on the clutch and then give as little gas as possible but "steady pressure on the pedal," he said, "the whole time. There. Just like that. Now just ease off the clutch." We began to inch forward. "Don't worry that we're moving," he continued as we advanced. I stalled and we started over. "I want you to feel the point of engagement. The moment the car drops into gear. Gently let the pressure off the clutch . . . *now.*" I was comfortably in first. We were moving. "Go around the parking lot at this speed," Dad said. We drove the lot's length and I turned. "Now comes the tricky part," he said, as we turned again and onto this straightaway of sorts. "Give it a little more gas. You see the RPMs revving high on the dash? Depress the clutch." I did and it felt like gliding. "Now drop it into second gear." Later, we did some downshifting. Of course I stalled several times. When I apologized, Dad told me not to worry about it, and we went through all the stages of starting the car before moving again.

Maybe the lesson lasted a half hour. I don't recall exactly, but by the end I was comfortably dropping the stick into neutral and braking before coming to a full stop and then, accelerating once more, getting it as high as third gear. We must've made at least twenty laps around the parking lot, because after several revolutions, Dad forgot himself, forgot I was driving. He seemed terrifically relaxed in the passenger seat, and he stared out the window at the surrounding landscape, as if he could finally appreciate the view, as if Manassas wasn't so bad after all, and maybe for a while he considered how nice it would be if someone shared the family's driving with him.

"If it snows tomorrow," Dad said, "maybe I'll take you back out here and teach you how to do a three-sixty."

Even without traffic, it took us almost two hours to get to D.C. and find parking near Woodward & Lothrop. Still, Dad's mood remained upbeat, and this cheered me. I felt as if I were being of assistance to the entire family. The department store was magnificent and vast, an eight-story building taking up almost the entire block. It was high-ceilinged and decorated for Christmas, with giant snowflake lights the size of chandeliers and the chandeliers covered in pine branches, pine cones, and ornaments. The tall, rectangular columns with their decorative capitals were hung with green and red velvet. And yet it retained a luxe, living room ambience. Dad was excited. He was well dressed—I only now noticed this—as if we were going out to a fine restaurant. Beneath his overcoat, he looked dashing in his brown wool blazer and turtleneck, his suede slacks and black boots. He strode down the aisle with the haughty, chin-up indifference of a star walking a red carpet, and people noticed him, and I noticed him subtly noticing this, and when he spoke to me, he raised his voice a bit. "We'll meet back here," Dad said before the elevator bank, "in exactly an hour. Oh," he added, and he handed me a ten-spot. "Some walking-around money." And then he stepped on the giant car with the gold handrails and all the other fabulously dressed shoppers. "My son," he said to the woman he boarded with, and she smiled at me and waved and, just as the doors closed, began talking to him.

Left to my own devices, I made a beeline to the television department on the fifth floor; common sense dictated it would have Atari systems set up for demonstration, and, lo and behold, it also had Intellivision. I played *Sea Battle* for a while and some *NFL Football* until my neck was sweating. I checked the time. I had plenty to burn before Dad and I reunited, so I decided to wander. Woodward & Lothrop seemed somehow grander than Bloomingdale's. This was due, I thought, to the dark wood of its display cases, which gave them an antique weightiness, their glass as thick as the frozen Potomac, the colors of their enclosed wares tropically varied, their categories less obviously discernible: shelves of Teuscher and Godiva chocolates giving on to tins of British teas and fancy infusers, stainless steel lighters and tabletop cigar cutters giving on to cedar boxes, whose burned-on, cocoa-colored labels I could taste at the back of my throat. A store, I thought, to set me dreaming—my very own costume department!—what with the arrayed driving gloves in their fancy rectangular boxes, these fanned beneath the Barbour wax caps on tree stands, and I pictured myself in a convertible in just such headgear, the Jaguar's top down, my suede jacket Italian, my cuff links glinting, my ascot paisley, my Paul Stuart collar popped, and my cashmere scarf sticking out straight behind me like a meteor's contrail. The girl at my side would be as pretty as the mothers walking these same aisles with their daughters, the latter who paid me no mind, and I cursed Dad for the lack of warning, for at least a heads-up that I too should have dressed nicely for this outing, and I wondered what gifts I would be receiving tomorrow. I no longer desired toys, in spite of how wondrous the Lionel model train passing above me was, its tracks visible through the Plexiglas beneath a replica Alpine village, its whistle echoing through the tunnel into which it disappeared. I hoped for some nattier haberdashery, since in a terrific failure of imagination, instead of asking for something specific this year besides the video game, I'd managed to only request clothes.

By chance, I found Dad in menswear, trying on suits. I had never seen my father shop for himself. At the school year's start, he'd drag me to Brooks Brothers (Oren didn't have a dress code at Ferren, although he was jealous of the spree) to buy two pairs of khakis, two button-down shirts, a new blue blazer, and penny loafers. I dressed each year as a slightly larger version of last year's blank-faced mannequins, the pair that warned me from the section of the store like sentinels. I was embarrassed and miffed at this arrangement. Was it because of the hours it took away from what remained of my paltry summer? Was it because summer for Dad couldn't end soon enough, as hot as it was in the city and business so slow, especially in the run-up to Labor Day? For the fact that I had no choice in the clothes Dad picked? That he inflicted upon me pleats? From somewhere far off, in the cold and evacuated quiet of young menswear, there appeared a salesman, pocket square matching his fatly knotted tie, who moved sleekly and quietly between the circular racks toward my father and me. I braced myself, because Dad was furious about spending money and the salesman's job was to relieve him of it. And it was at this moment that I did the closest thing I knew to praying: I hoped my father might be blessed with my career, or at least the one he'd seemed to have been chasing, with all the calm and magnanimity it promised and the recognition to boot, ever since the fire.

I spotted Dad toward the back of Paul Stuart with a tailor, standing on the three-way mirror's riser. He did not see me, at least not at first. He considered the blazer he was trying on, pulling at his lapels and then spreading them to pose with both hands in his pockets or with one arm crossed and his chin in hand. The tailor stared at him, slouched and dew-eyed as a tortoise—he had the same broadly beaked countenance as Kepplemen—the measuring tape draped around his thin neck.

"It's a wonderful fit," my father said. "Although I'm torn between this one and the camel hair."

The tailor, impassive, laid his palms on both my father's shoulders and then brushed outward, pinching the sleeves where they joined the coat. "You could always get both," he said hopelessly.

Dad did another side to side. "How long can you hold them for?"

The tailor did the calculation as if he were taking stock of the long line of men waiting to purchase these very items. "Until Friday. Then there's a sale."

My father made a great show of contemplating this before removing the jacket. "I'll be in touch," he said.

He departed. Next, an amazing thing happened. He walked straight toward me; I waited for him to recognize me; and then he kept walking past as if I were invisible. I hustled after him and tapped his shoulder.

"There you are," he said. His mood had darkened. He carried no bags.

"Do you have more shopping?" I asked.

He rolled his eyes in disgust. "I've bought plenty," he said.

"They have a restaurant upstairs. Could we get a hot chocolate?"

"Enough already."

And then someone called out his name.

It was Abe Fountain, the great lyricist and librettist, in whose show my father had previously performed. He looked noticeably older since *The Fisher King*. His wiry hair was distinctly grayer. His dark suit and thin tie made his face look gaunt. His Swifty Lazar frames had thicker lenses than I recalled, and they magnified his eyes—the left was larger and set slightly lower than the right—which gave him a wizardly appearance. On his arm was a woman so heavily made up she appeared as if she'd just walked offstage. Curly red hair. Red lips to match. She wore a silver fur coat, so thick it gave her a dandelion shape. Her long legs were sheathed in fishnet tights, and her tall black heels made her almost comically taller than Fountain. Her name—could it have been more perfect?—was Roxy.

After introductions and pleasantries, Fountain said to Dad, "It's kismet that I ran into you. You've been on my mind."

"You don't say."

It was one of the vertiginous aspects of my father's character that his bad mood in our presence could be immediately eradicated by the appearance of someone he worked with. Whether his mood sank again upon their departure was always a possibility.

"Let's have a drink at the bar around the corner. What's the name of that place, hon?"

"The Blind Beggar," Roxy said.

"We're celebrating," Fountain said. "I'm writing a part for you in my next musical. A major role. Griffin can come too." He turned his attention toward me. "You like eggnog? They have the real thing. With some amaretto. You like amaretto, kid?"

"I'm more of a whiskey guy," I said.

Fountain chuckled, then mussed my hair. "What do you say?"

At this, Dad, beaming, thrilled at Fountain's news, turned to me and, producing from his wallet ten *more* dollars, gave me the slightest nod of the head, which I knew meant scram.

"Go get yourself that hot chocolate," Dad said. "I'll find you at the restaurant upstairs."

I did not do as I was told because I knew I'd have some extra time to kill. Instead, I wandered the store some more. I even walked outside to check out the display windows. In my favorite was a city couple sitting on a bench in an arctic snowscape, each holding fishing rods, their lines sunk in a hole in the ice, the woman wearing a mink like Fountain's girlfriend, the man wearing a Members Only jacket among other fineries. In the adjacent window, the glacial motif continued with four live penguins. They swam in and out of a pool you could see into through the glass, just like at the Central Park Zoo. The best part was when their keeper appeared from the diorama wall and fed them a bucket of squid.

Later, when Dad found me at the restaurant's counter, he was as full of good spirits as I of hot chocolate and a pair of cheese Danishes. Were he not carrying several bags in each hand—they reminded me of a balloon's ballast—his happiness was such that I was sure he might float away.

"Your mother," he said, and I was not sure if he meant the bowed gifts he held up or the news, "is going to be *thrilled*."

On Christmas morning, we woke to snowfall.

It was several inches, it covered everything, and there wafted from the kitchen a smell not only of sausage cooking and the scent of tarragon but also apple and pumpkin pie. Mom and Grandma had dressed the turkey and were about to put it in the oven. Dad sat on the couch, facing the fire, which Grandpa tended. Like Mom, Grandma was still in her nightgown. She said, "Merry Christmas," to Oren and me when we greeted her, and the explosiveness of the last two syllables—we could hear this when we hugged her—caused her to bite at her breath, like a landed fish.

By now Oren had visited the tree and climbed into the La-Z-Boy, his presents neatly stacked around him. The night before there wasn't a single gift beneath it, but now the trove covered the base. Oren had methodically begun to open his presents. With each he gave a low *"Yes,"* not so much ticking off a box but addressing himself to items on a bill of lading, assurances of an agreement kept, and at this moment more than almost any other, his sense of metaphysical satisfaction seemed profound, as if, for him, our family was finally properly functioning.

"What did you get?" I asked, and he held up his Simon memory game.

"Can I play?"

"If you give me your R2-D2 Pez dispenser," he said. He had a shoebox full of unopened *Star Wars* figurines.

I got clothes.

I was not unexcited about them, but I wasn't excited either. In one box: L.L.Bean corduroys. "We'll have those fitted," Dad said. In another, a pair of L.L.Bean turtlenecks. A black sweater with a zipper on its V-neck. "That's cashmere," Dad said. Mom said, "I picked them out for you. I thought they were very handsome." In a small box, a pair of black leather gloves.

"This one," Dad said, and handed me a present, "is special."

It was too big to be Intellivision. It was too heavy to be a toy. Beneath the wrapping paper, the box read BARNEY'S. I removed a navy overcoat.

"Put it on," Mom said. It was heavier than Peter Proton's cape.

"Go get a load of yourself," Dad said.

"I will," I said, and sat on the couch, flapping the flaps over my legs and torso like a sleeping bat.

By now, Oren was opening his final present. "Thank you," he said to Grandma and Grandpa, and held up the giant book for everyone to see: *Ferrari: A History in Pictures.*

It was now Mom and Dad's turn to give Grandma and Grandpa presents. Grandpa was given his by my father. It was grown-up, it seemed to me, to do as Grandpa did: to demonstrate restraint and take one's time to consider the wrapped present's size and shape, which in this case was small, perhaps that of two matchboxes. Grandpa considered it from every angle. "Open it, Pa," Mom said, and Oren said, "I helped pick it out," and Grandpa opened the small box and gave a gravelly "Ha!" The box read BUCK, and at the sight of this word, Dad said, "I'm told it's the best knife there is," to which Grandpa, having already folded open the blade, pressed his thumb with a milligram of pressure to test its sharpness. "Lo-ver-ly," he said. He folded the blade, slid it in his pocket, and patted it there as if for later use.

Grandma was also opening her presents. The first contained slippers. "Those are real lambskin and lamb's wool," Dad said. "They're supposed to be the warmest slippers made."

"Well, I'll be," Grandpa said, showing everyone his Black & Decker drill.

Dad said, *"Quality, dependability, and innovation."* Which was the tagline.

"Calgon," Oren said, *"take me away."*

"Oh, Lily," Grandma said, nearly exasperated, and held up not one but two different nightgowns. "What were you thinking?"

My father said, "It's time for that special someone to open her presents."

My mother was surprised by this. She said, "I thought we agreed we weren't going to exchange gifts this year."

"I thought so too," Dad said, "but Santa got inspired yesterday." He got up and kneeled behind the Christmas tree to produce not one but five white boxes that read WOODWARD & LOTHROP. Mom, momentarily gobsmacked, said, "Take this please," as she handed Dad her mug and then sat on the floor. Even Oren was impressed by the sheer mass of the purchase. Mom lifted the top half of the first box and then peeled back the white crepe. She looked over her shoulder at my father and snorted, everyone waiting to see what he'd bought. Pinching the gift delicately between her fingers, she produced the piece of lingerie. It was made of black lace and there was a rose between the breast cups. Dad said, "I noticed your supply was low," and then, "Open the next one."

"Is Mom even allowed to wear those?" Oren asked.

She opened the next one and laughed even harder this time. It was another piece of lingerie, this one pink with a yellow flower, which she tossed atop the previous one. Mom might as well have been alone in the room with Dad. It was, I thought, an amazing trick, a perfect bit of acting that was, of course, not acting because it was my mother. The next box contained another negligee, and Mom, clutching it to her chest, slowly shook her head at Dad as if to say, *You are so bad.* The thick silk piled on the floor in many-colored disarray. Mom was, by now, embarrassed, but her embarrassment carried no retribution with it, as if it were my father's privilege to embarrass her, each new box making her laugh harder, its contents a rich, soft heap mounting higher, until she was nearly crying, and this generosity of spirit made all of us seem not just in on the joke but ancillary to their joy and partaking of it. "Shel," Mom said finally, "they're beautiful." She took his neck in her arm to pull him toward her and kissed him, once, on the mouth. Oren was also smiling. And it suddenly filled me with optimism for this new show, for my father's career, and it made me think, for the first time in a long time, that something good was coming. I even said it to myself in my mind: *Something good is coming.* And after watching the fire roar with wrapping paper, a sight we all took the time to enjoy before Grandma excused herself to finish preparing breakfast, I decided I would put on all my clothes and, after the meal, go for a walk in the snow.

In our room I tried on my new corduroys, tight at the waist. I pulled my new sweater over the white turtleneck with blue stripes, donned the overcoat, and then considered myself in the mirror. I'd have never chosen such an outfit for myself and I liked what I saw in the reflection, but I felt a terrific need to be seen. When I returned to the living room, Mom, in passing, said, "Don't you look sharp." Dad said, "*Very* grown-up." Oren, who was reading his new book with his Walkman on, eyed me with pity, shook his head in disappointment, and said nothing. When I tapped his shoulder and asked him if he wanted to go for a walk after breakfast, he removed his headphones and said he would but he didn't have a tuxedo. When I asked him if he wanted to play a game together before we ate, he said, "I'm reading right now." At the table later, after he finished solving his Rubik's Cube, he handed it to me and said, "Merry Christmas," and returned to the La-Z-Boy.

I drank my brewer's yeast so that I might be dismissed from breakfast. The pumpkin pie from last night's meal remained on the buffet, and I snarfed a slice to fuel my walk after I was excused. I slipped on my boots and rolled up my corduroys' cuffs and exited via the garage. I crossed onto the number three fairway. With each passing minute the snow came down harder. I rounded the water hazard before the green and walked up the hill toward the fourth hole. One of Grandpa's watch caps would've been a good idea, but it didn't go with the outfit. I felt like I'd been beamed by a transporter from Madison Avenue to the golf course. I *wished* I were on Madison Avenue looking so natty. The bare trees lining the fairway appeared black while the evergreens' branches shook off some of the accumulation in the gusts. A good five inches had already covered the golf course, and the tee box markers were topped with cone-shaped caps of powder. It was lovely to be outside, but I wanted to be holding a girl's hand. I felt dressed for such an occasion, and I once again tried to imagine the perfect girl. I'd screen-tested with Brooke Shields once; I was playing her younger brother in the scene, and she was so tall, I was practically looking up at her chin. But in my fantasy I ignored this fact. I pretended she had relatives in Manassas, she called to me from one of the fairway-facing houses like we sometimes did to Grandma and Grandpa when they were playing golf, she came running out to join me, and then she and I walked the course's entirety together, her mitten in my leather glove, our understanding of each other's souls so perfect we need not utter a word. Surprisingly, I felt a tad winded, perhaps because of all my layers and the heavy boots and the accumulation that made progress a slog. As I ascended the fifth fairway, it occurred to me that I hadn't exercised since we'd been here and that perhaps walking for as long as I could was a good idea, if for nothing else than to make room for dinner. I passed the fifth hole, then the sixth. I had never been this far on the golf course before. The snow came down more heavily now. Although the sun was still visible through the cloud cover, it was a white eye, as on certain overcast days at the beach, and from the seventh green I looked back to note my discrete footprints, the only blemishes on this perfect world. For all our freedom in New York, our lives, I realized, were unwittingly circumscribed by familiarity, by paths so narrow it would be like turning around right now and walking back to Grandma's atop my own tracks. Here, this great white way was like the financial district or the East Village or Alphabet City back home—it was right there, and I had never been, and it was entirely new, and I vowed to explore Greenwich Village as soon as I returned to New York, maybe finally figure out how the street names worked in SoHo. The ninth hole was the steepest uphill of the front nine, a par five, and I noticed a figure in the distance. Whether it was a man or woman, grown-up or child, was impossible to tell. The snow was a blinding ticker tape. The person walked directly toward me, he or she wearing a white down coat and white hat. The wind blew into my face. I lifted my hand to shield my eyes and I saw that it was Bridget.

She walked straight up to me and said, "I thought that was you."

Now that I wasn't moving, I noticed how quiet it was. "What are you doing here?" I asked.

"Looking for my golf ball."

I laughed. She laughed too. Our breaths made a single cloud. Her curly red hair framing her face from beneath her stocking hat was snow-dusted, her cheeks were flushed, and her eyes were very blue. I could now appreciate how large they were.

"Are you still doing that show?" she asked. "The Saturday one."

I was surprised she'd watched it. "Yes," I said. "We just finished our fourth season."

"Did you always want to be an actor?"

"Not really. I kind of fell into it."

"It must be so interesting to live in New York and do movies and television."

"I've sort of always done it, but yeah, sure."

"What's the best part?"

I considered this for a moment. "I like seeing the difference between rushes and the final cut. Of movies." If Leo were here, I would never have considered talking to Bridget like this. I was talking to Bridget like this, I thought, because she was Bridget.

"Rushes?" she asked.

"Dailies. After we wrap, they put together all the day's shots for the director to see, in case they need to reshoot. But it's all broken up, in bits and pieces. And then you see it straight through months later, after the editor's put it together, and you realize how good everyone has to be at their job for a movie to get made."

"Everyone?"

"The cast. The crew. Gaffer, key grip. Best boy . . ."

She chuckled at my list.

"Dolly grip. AD. Prop master. Production designer—"

"Wow," she said. "You know a lot."

Maybe it wasn't so bad, being an actor. "It takes a lot of people to make a movie, let me tell you."

"You are *so* lucky," she said. "I'm gonna live in New York when I grow up."

That she wanted such a thing made her seem grown up already.

We stood very close to each other, breathing in the falling snow. "Are you . . . headed somewhere?" I asked.

"I walk the golf course every Christmas Day. I've been doing it since I was seven. It's my tradition. I try to leave at the same time every year and think about how my life is different."

"Huh," I said, fascinated. "How'd you decide to do that?"

"I don't remember," Bridget said.

"That's really cool."

"Well, if you leave at ten in the morning next Christmas, I'll see you at the ninth hole, and we can tell each other what's different in our lives between now and then."

"Deal," I said.

And we parted.

I did not run into Bridget on the back nine. Stomping my boots in the garage, I wondered if I was simply going faster and had arrived at my grandparents' well ahead of her pace. In his study, Grandpa was practicing Spanish. He had his reel-to-reel going. The woman's voice asked, "Donde han ido los niños?" A tone sounded, and my grandfather repeated the question with almost comically perfect enunciation. The woman's voice said, "Los niños estan jugando en la playa," and the tone sounded again. In the kitchen, Oren, Mom, and Grandma were making the Christmas meal; I spied the turkey, golden in the oven, and dreamed of my favorite part: the wings. In the living room, Dad was asleep in front of the midday news. In my room, I hung up my overcoat, lay on my bed, and thought about Bridget's invitation to meet the following year. How would my life be different then? It was, I quickly concluded, impossible to know. Or was it? I could become a better wrestler. I could ignore Coach, do the moves I wanted. I could go to wrestling camp this summer and learn more new ones if I didn't do *The Nuclear Family*. But whether I did the show was not in my control. So I was back to square one. I could hear the television in the living room, the anchor's drone. It was day 418 of the hostage crisis. What if it never ended? I thought. What if those fifty-two people never came home? What choices did the hostages make, day in and day out? Whether to talk? To eat? Could those even be considered a course of action? By any metric, they were such tiny decisions, they barely made for a story at all.

The next morning, Dad announced that we'd leave for New York the following day. Saying so seemed to lift his spirits even further. He had been more upbeat after we'd run into Fountain, and it also spurred him to get home, as if being back in Manhattan might somehow stoke Fountain's creative process, make him write the musical with a major role for him faster. My father's suitcase lay on the bed, open and nearly packed. He made the long-distance call to check his service, to which Mom said, "No one is working over Christmas," and to which Dad replied, "It isn't Christmas anymore."

The snow had paused overnight, but that morning it began to snow again. I worried, watching it come down, because Dad might make us leave today. Which meant we wouldn't be able to spend the night at the Locatellos' house, which we always did the night before we went home. Which, I thought, since the conversation with Bridget was still on my mind, was one of our traditions. The houses across the fairway were mere smudges; the trees lining it were ghosts of bone. Mom sat before the fireplace, cross-stitching, Oren by her side, reading. When Dad thumped through the room, we all eyed him warily as he passed.

Once Oren and I got clearance, we headed straight to Auntie Maine's. I put on the same outfit as yesterday but wore a hat this time. The Locatellos had a barn, but there was nothing to see in the fenced yard: the rabbits were in their hutch, the chickens sheltered in their coop. Dusty, Lucy's horse, invisible in her stall, neighed a hello, as if the structure itself had offered a greeting. When we arrived in the front room, the TV was tuned to *Wheel of Fortune,* the volume high but no one watching. We heard our cousins playing music in the basement. Auntie Maine was in the kitchen but came rushing toward us and pointed at the screen.

"All's well that ends well!" she said, beating the contestant to the right guess, and then returned to the kitchen to make our lunch.

There was a lot to pack in in a short period of time. Bridget and Patrick were already here, and she and I acted like it was a secret we'd run into each other on the golf course. After some jamming (Leo on drums, Anthony on bass, me on rhythm guitar, Oren on tambourine, the girls singing backup, and Patrick, surprising us with his booming voice, singing lead), we set up the poker table beneath the living room's gun rack and cycled through dealer's choice. Oren won handily, and we moved on to Monopoly, which was interrupted by dinner, which on our last night was always lasagna: Auntie Maine's recipe was at least ten layers, and we dipped our artichoke leaves in mayonnaise and Oren let me eat his heart. In the dining room, through the sliding door, we noticed the snow had stopped falling. We were stuffed silly, but I still hit the Count Chocula with fresh cow's milk and ate a slice of the leftover pecan pie.

It was Oren who suggested we take Dusty for a ride.

Oren loved the idea of a horse. He had once gotten Dad to take him to Claremont Riding Academy for a set of lessons, which was the only thing I could ever recall the two of them doing alone together. He'd have kept a horse on our terrace if he'd been allowed.

Dusty was black and short-legged and ornery. She was named Dusty because no amount of brushing removed the dirt that seemed permanently settled on her—pat her neck or side and you could see the outline in her coat like a handprint on a cave wall. In spite of her lack of height, she was intimidating to face, so broad-bellied and scoop-backed that head-on her aspect was closer to a hippo's. Her obedience to Lucy barely verged on tolerance, and when we entered the barn and Anthony snapped on the light, she appeared from the stall's inky darkness and considered the group of us from within her stable as if she held a particular grudge from a long-standing wrong. Her eyes were black and pitiless.

She reminded me of every adult who didn't like me but revealed it only in private.

It was not clear who had the authority in this situation. Leo, who rocked back on his heels with his hands stuffed in his Redskins jacket, chuckled respectfully and then said, "I'm not getting near her." Bridget, clearly frightened, and in a gesture that none of us was prepared for, took Leo's arm in both of hers. Anthony said, "Last time I was in here with her, she kicked me in the stomach," and then he pointed at a pair of knocked-in boards, "all the way to there." Dusty seemed to follow the conversation, eyeing first Leo and then Anthony, and, uncannily, I thought—perhaps because we could not see her legs—seemed to glide along the stall's half door to where Lucy stood and then nose her, but in a fashion that bordered on unfriendly, closer to a head butt. Lucy said to Oren, "Well, you wanted to ride her." My brother took a step forward and then dug into his jeans pocket. He offered Dusty a fistful of sugar cubes. It was an odd moment, full of tenderness and almost mercenary foresight—further evidence that my brother had a life apart from me and the family about which I knew next to nothing. When had it started? Perhaps with the fire, since that was the last time I could recall Oren willingly following me anywhere.

Dusty pressed her mouth to his palm, and I marveled at the prehensile elegance with which she sampled the individual cubes, her lips as malleable and as delicate as the end of an elephant's trunk. She allowed Oren to remove her halter from her. He asked Lucy where the bridle and saddle were, and when she indicated the back of the barn he disappeared into its darkness and returned with the jingling equipment. He opened the stall door and stepped inside; he cupped Dusty's head in his arm, and when she gave him next to no resistance, he said, "That's my girl," and Bridget knocked her shoulder to Leo's in a confirmation of something mysterious. Oren slid the bridle over Dusty's face, and, more amazingly, when she resisted taking the bit, he stuck his thumb in her mouth and she opened it. His movements were so practiced, and so alien to me, that he might just as well have folded and then paneled a parachute. Again he disappeared and returned with the saddle and pad; while he laid the cotton fleece over her back he asked Lucy, "Is she a Shetland cross?" to which Lucy replied, "Old Welsh pony." With the arm of his hoodie, he wiped down the saddle and then placed it on her back. There was an elaborate bit of business with a strap beneath her belly, which he secured. Then he put his foot in the stirrup and lifted himself into the saddle. When Lucy reached beneath the horse he said, "Don't tighten the girth too fast." He took the reins in hand and then sucked at his cheek, a loud double click, in a perfect impersonation of the Central Park carriage drivers. Then Oren led Dusty out of the stable and the barn, and we followed him like a retinue into the snowy night.

The stars in the now-clear sky were diamonds scattered atop blue velvet. The waxing gibbous moon like a fat belly. Our bodies were the same near-black as the trees. The snow beneath our feet was crunchy and aglow. Lucy walked alongside Dusty and Oren. Anthony and Patrick were behind them, their fists stuffed in their jackets. I brought up the rear behind Leo and Bridget, who were holding hands. I felt everyone's admiration of my brother as well as my distance from them all. Bridget must've sensed this, for she briefly looked over her shoulder at me and, shrugging once, smiled. I shrugged and smiled in return, because I didn't know what was going to happen either and her corroboration made me feel like I wasn't alone.

"Let's take her on the golf course," Oren said, and he and Dusty waited on the dirt road while we negotiated the fence break and walked out from under the tree cover into the open. We stopped in the middle of the fairway and turned, and because we could not see either Oren or the horse through the black space in the fence, we pricked our ears. We heard Oren click his cheek again and say, *"Giddup,"* and then with a rumble Dusty burst through the break. This explosion shook the adjacent branches so forcefully snow tumbled from the evergreens' tops to form a falling curtain their bodies parted. Oren trotted Dusty toward us and then pulled on the reins and stopped. They made quite a sight: Oren's legs stretched wide around her belly and his feet in the stirrups as if he were balancing on a big round bomb. We all took another step back from the pair, and again Oren clicked his cheek and snapped the reins; in response Dusty lowered her head, shaking it once, and then snuffled the snow. Lucy said, "Maybe I should walk her a bit," and when she reached out, Dusty pinned her ears back, rose on her hind legs, and, turning around, bolted.

She ran uphill, in a great sweeping loop, away from us, toward the green, banking again, and then, by some control Oren exerted, began to circle downhill, back in our direction. I had never seen a horse gallop except in movies. Just the thunderous timpani of it, her body's action charging full tilt with my brother bent and attached to her—Oren's command being the even more amazing part. The speed seemed impossible given how round she was, how short-legged and low to the ground. She slowed as she approached us, shaking her head low and angrily, her forelegs and haunches moving in opposite directions in an action close to juking, the bridle and reins jingling, and Oren fighting for control. And then she stopped, suddenly, forelegs locked and haunches raised, so that she skidded to a halt. Oren was thrown forward, toward her neck, which he briefly clasped, for backstop and balance, and then he managed to right himself. He spoke calmingly to her and sat up straight. He patted her neck and pulled the reins so that her head turned left, and he clicked his cheek again and kicked his heels into her sides. Again she took off, this time at Oren's behest. He led her along the same path. Her hooves, when she banked toward the green, cleaved the snow-covered sod into small black divots that caught the moonlight. Oren was leaning with her; she was all action and movement in contrast to his balanced stillness above. They banked, at an impossible angle this time, hurtling downhill toward us again. We stood transfixed by her coursing. The beauty of it made us forget the punishment we might suffer when the snow melted to reveal the chewed-up turf below, and when they barreled past our loose gauntlet, I could feel Dusty's hoofbeats shake my teeth. This time we all whooped in support and shouted Oren's name. Maybe I did the loudest, because while I was a bit jealous, it was a joy to be amazed by my brother. I could tell that, like me, he too was desperate to master something, and I was suddenly certain he would exceed me in life, in all endeavors; that since we were little he had been waiting to demonstrate such prowess, and now that he was doing something so unimaginable and impossible to me—to all of us—I was thrilled for him and wished only my parents were here to see it as well. The pair made another near-perfect overlay of this darkened track, and then Dusty, headed uphill, abruptly changed direction—she snapped off the circle, she broke left, seesawing, bucking, and then turned downhill, toward us again, faster, it seemed, than even before. Oren was shouting, *Whoa, WHOA!*—it was more an exclamation than a command—and it distracted us from the danger he was in, that we were in. She gathered speed and we froze. We were pins to her bowling ball and just as still, and maybe ten feet before impact, Oren yanked her reins as if he were heaving an anvil over his shoulders. At this, Dusty slammed her hooves into the ground and ducked her head, so that Oren, launched from her back, was flung toward us, his arms and legs outstretched—he did one full revolution—to land on his back, with a great heaped thud, at our feet. Dusty, relieved of him, stood instantly becalmed and inert. She snorted, happily.

We all bent over him.

"Don't move," Leo said.

Oren, eyeing each of us, wiggled his fingers and knocked his toes together. "Was that wicked," he said, "or what?"

Did I wake up before any of the cousins the next morning to make the morning last longer? I'd slept in Leo's room, Oren in Anthony's. There was the dual sense, as I rose from sleep, that it was very early and that there was activity downstairs. It was a tradition, on our final morning with the cousins, that Uncle Marco made cream chipped beef. When I appeared in the kitchen, I found him and Auntie Maine already up, preparing the meal. The oven's clock read 6:47. The lights in here were bright. I could see our reflections in the picture window because it was still dark outside. The open oven, along with the steaming pot, which Uncle Marco stood over, warmed the room. The linoleum was the same off-white as the cream chipped beef. The food smelled peppery. In spite of the kitchen's temperature, Uncle Marco still seemed underdressed in his crewneck T-shirt and pajama pants. From the oven rack, Auntie Maine tonged toasted Wonder Bread onto a plate and disappeared into the dining room. I stood by Uncle Marco as he stirred the mixture with the wooden spoon. His belly nearly touched the range's knobs. I could hear him breathe. He did not smoke but still wheezed like Grandma. Beads of perspiration dotted his upper lip.

By now the cousins had come downstairs. We were all still in our pajamas. We took our seats at the dining room table, Uncle Marco at the head and Auntie Maine at the other. Bridget and Patrick were gone; we had our family to ourselves again. Lucy was asked to say grace and we all joined hands. The entire breakfast was cream chipped beef and toast. It had the consistency of papier-mâché. It was salty from the shredded bits of corned beef. It was best practice, after ladling some onto your toast, to let it stand for a minute so that the bread's scorched pores could absorb the steaming liquid. The previous Christmas, I had consumed seven pieces—a record among the cousins, and one I now intended to break. Because something was ending, I was sure of it ever since I'd arrived, and like a salmon before swimming upstream, I had to stuff myself with everything from this place while I could.

By the time the plate of toast made it back around to Uncle Marco, I had finished the first slice. "I'll have seconds, please," I said, my fork aimed at the next serving. Uncle Marco held the plate out toward me, and when I speared my second piece, he grinned at Leo and Anthony.

"That's two," Lucy said, meaning, *Game on.*

By my third slice, Aunt Maine said, "I'm going to have to toast another loaf," and got up from the table. Anthony, in appearance a Russian nesting doll of his father, pushed back after his sixth slice. Leo followed suit. He said, "I am going to lie down on the floor now," an act he knew his father would not tolerate. Sweat had also beaded on Uncle Marco's forehead, and his shirtfront was dotted with sauce. He had kept pace but tapped out after our eighth slice. Lucy said, "Can he do nine, ladies and gentlemen?" and when I blew past that number, everyone grew quiet and watched, since now something extraordinary seemed within reach, not simply a new record but a new power, a mutant ability: I was possessed of a superheroic capacity for consumption. I was the fish who ate the fish who ate the fish. I was a boy with ten stomachs. I was a carny creature with a camel hump growing on my back.

I was going for twelve. Twelve was an entire loaf, was drummers drumming. Thirteen was unlucky, so I needed to eat one more slice. Fourteen was the Partridge Family plus the Brady Bunch, minus Alice. Uncle Marco was mildly amazed and slightly disgusted and not displeased. "Well, go ahead and eat it, son," he said. I cut my last piece into nine *Hollywood Squares,* which I stacked on my fork into three mini club sandwiches, and after I swallowed the last bite, I said, in my best Porky Pig impression, "That's all, folks."

Because it was time for my family to leave.

Asshole," Coach Kepplemen yelled, and smacked me in the back of the head.

We were in the locker room. I was naked and standing on the scale. He'd cuffed me hard enough that I shrugged my shoulders and raised my hands to block another blow. He set the Detecto's poises back to zero. He was blinking and stiff-mouthed and now spoke quietly, which was terrifying. "Step off, please," he nearly whispered, and I did.

He slid the poises to my weight class's limit, 121, and then, after indicating I step on the scale again, fingered the square forward, to 125, to 129, and then just over 133, when the balance finally floated.

"Two days from now we have a match," he said. "You *knew* this over break."

He rubbed his eyes with one hand, then ran his palm over his mouth, down to his neck, which he held as if he were about to choke himself. "What are we going to do about this? I got no one to replace you."

"I can make it."

"I'm going to have to forfeit your class."

"I'll make it."

"It's twelve fucking pounds."

He pinched the pudge at my waist and then pushed me off the scale. He punched the wall near my head and got in my face. "You put on a rubber suit. You practice in it. You sleep in it. You bathe in it. You piss in it. You don't take it off until you make weight. And if you don't make weight, you're gone. For the rest of the season."

Kepplemen kicked a locker as he left the room. Santoro, the team captain, was sitting on the bench. He'd been late to practice and witnessed the whole exchange. "Here," he said, removing a rubber suit from his locker along with a roll of athletic tape. After I put on my jock and singlet, I pulled its first piece over my head. For a moment, everything was lightless. I smelled a stink so personal to Santoro it was as if I were inhaling his very guts. I put the pants on and then let him tape my ankles, then my waist, and then my wrists. "You can cut the weight," he said softly. "Just no liquids. For the next two days."

I was in something like shock during warm-ups. This gave on to panic. I redlined everything as practice proceeded, drills to rolls, as if I might outrace gravity's pull on my increased weight. Twice I thought I might puke and welcomed it. What had I done to myself? At the end of practice, we did ten sets of sprints on the long straightaway between the upper and lower school. Afterward, Kepplemen made me run five sets of stairs. By the time I'd finished, nearly half the team had left the locker room; the rest were finishing their showers. Kepplemen handed me a jump rope and said, "Stay in there until I tell you otherwise, and don't stop jumping until I say you can." My teammates knew to leave the showers running. The room was filled with steam. I skipped rope for what seemed like an hour. My throat and mouth felt stiff as a dried rag. Kepplemen appeared and, one by one, turned off the showers until there was only the sound of the wet rope slapping the floor.

"Enough," he said. Gently, almost lovingly, he added, "Arms up, please," and when I raised them, he stepped so close our foreheads nearly touched. He peeled the athletic tape from my waist, wrapping his arms around me so that he might pinch the end piece behind my back. When he was done, I stretched the top's tight elastic hem away from my belly, and so much sweat poured forth it was as if I'd slung a pail full of water from a window. Kepplemen removed the tape from my wrists. Liquid coursed in rivulets between my fingers.

I stepped onto the scale. Kepplemen slid the poises into place. I had lost over four pounds during practice. "See," I said, "no problem."

Kepplemen remained stoic. He closed his eyes and shook his head. "Jog home," he ordered.

It was snowing. I had on my wrestling jacket and sweatpants. I was warm enough at first, but the perspiration between the layers only grew colder. My wrestling shoes, already soaked from practice, were no defense against the slush-filled curbs, and my toes were soon numb. I had no hat, and my hair was still wet from the shower and stayed thus because my scalp melted the flakes that settled there. I cut west to Columbus Avenue; a bus gargled past. The snow fell so densely that the buildings' higher floors appeared shrouded, the illuminated apartments visible as if through gauze. By the time I reached Eighty-Sixth Street, I had so little energy that twenty more blocks even of walking seemed unimaginable. I was shivering and miserable, and yet, at the same time, I distracted myself from the discomfort calculating the energy my body was putting out to warm itself, all the BTUs and effort of respiration, imagining the arrival on my scale at home and all its progress.

Two blocks later, I caved and hopped on the bus.

I sat in the very back and had a view out all the windows. The snow was a cherished painting I had torn to pieces; it was all white yet somehow formed an image; it was the thing I most cared about, and I had dumped its torn bits in great heaps over the entire city and was now ordered to reassemble it on penalty of my life.

Mom had made meat loaf. I could smell it as soon as the elevator dinged open on our floor. I was famished, and I pictured the ground beef singed a darker brown beneath its layer of ketchup, the onions in each slice translucent and glossy as shrimp shells, the clear grease spreading on the plate toward the mashed potatoes. I hung up my coat, went to my room, greeted Oren, who was working at his desk, and then went straight to the bathroom to shower again. I hung up the rubber suit on the shower rod to dry and, with nothing but a towel around my waist, hurried to our bedroom closet and stepped on the scale, tapping the poises to the weight I was at when I'd left school.

I hadn't even lost a half pound.

Now before me lay temptation. Dinner was a crossroads. Eat now, and the next two months organized themselves around this choice, every day issuing inevitably forward from it. As Oren helped himself to a full plate, I pictured the ref calling the opposing wrestler to the mat's center and turning to Kepplemen, who would shake his head and, along with the rest of the team, not even look at me when our opponent's arm was raised, amid sporadic applause, to accept the forfeit. Six points awarded to their team, the same as a pin but without a fight.

At the table, Dad said, "Eat already," and Oren, glancing at me with an expression of apology—he could tell something was wrong—dug in. I cut myself a small square of meat loaf and speared it. I took a bite. The juice flooded my mouth's cracked Mojave; the ketchup's sugars coated my tongue. I closed my eyes while I chewed, wine-pressing the ground beef with my tongue so its grease flooded my palate. If I was going to do this, I thought, if I was going to fail, then best to enjoy every bite. The phone rang.

"That's probably the agency," Dad said, and pushed back from the table.

I made a decision and took the opportunity to wipe my mouth with my napkin and deposit the bolus into its paper. And in this fashion, I was able to make it appear as if I ate something close to a meal.

Later, lying on the top bunk, I did corporeal calculus, a metabolic math. I weighed just under 129 pounds. If I lost my usual one pound overnight and then four again at practice, that put me at 124. If I neither ate nor drank until Wednesday morning, and assuming I dropped at least another pound overnight, that would put me within a couple of pounds the day of the match. I'd have until the afternoon to cut the rest.

From the bunk beneath me, Oren said, "How much do you have to drop?"

"Eight pounds."

"By when?"

"Wednesday."

While Oren contemplated my predicament, I was recalling when we filmed the intro and outro sequences for *The Nuclear Family*, on location in Van Cortlandt Park, shots of us running in slow motion, leaping from what appeared to be great heights, throwing fake boulders, standing on cranes with their baskets just out of the frame to give the illusion we were flying. And then breaking for lunch, two foldout tables covered with a smorgasbord of crudités and bagels and breads and every kind of cold cut and condiment imaginable, pasta and potato salad, broccoli salad and fruit salad, and, for dessert, doughnuts and Danishes to be washed down with hot coffee. Was that, I wondered, really all so bad?

"Let me help," Oren said.

I woke to a blue-gray morning. In our sliver of a view, I watched the ice floes on the Hudson nose south. The entire river looked the color of slush. It appeared as if it might freeze over at any moment. What I felt was not soreness, although there was that in my neck and arms, but rather an overwhelming fatigue. It was a cousin to sadness, closer, in feeling, to guilt. Gingerly, I climbed down my ladder and hopped on the scale.

I had lost nearly two pounds overnight. This might've filled me with hope, but my mouth was so parched that my spit, what little I had, was the consistency of caulk. Oren entered the closet, had a look at my weight, and, without derision, said, "It's going to be close." The hunger pangs had already started. They were signal flares, slowly arcing from some barge floating in my deepest gut toward my diaphragm, with the acidic hiss that sputtered into my esophagus. I welcomed them, but each one also seemed to leave a contrail that hollowed out my limbs and emptied my mind, so that I did not so much long for sleep as for stillness.

Dad had WQXR softly playing on the stereo. He stood in the living room wearing a turtleneck, briefs, and black dress socks. He said, "Your breakfast is on the table." The central air unit that was half the window's length rattled. Snow had painted our terrace's railing, the building's ledges, the trees' branches, and the fire hydrants' caps. Cold radiated from the glass. Overnight, the temperature had fallen even further. The drier air had spun the snow to sugar, pedestrians shielding their eyes against the stinging gusts. My father had poached an egg atop my mound of corned beef hash, and with my knife I punctured its yolk and watched it slowly run down the ridges of cubed potatoes. He'd added green and red peppers, which gave the food a more delectable palette. My mouth watered and then absorbed the moisture. Oren sat and glanced at our father's back and then took my plate and forked half my serving onto his. I allowed myself one sip of café au lait. It was the sweetest thing I'd ever tasted, and the milk, which had formed a skin across part of the top, had, in my mouth, the consistency of food. Dad, who finished washing the pan, said, "I'm headed to the Y," and left us. Oren, who watched me drink with no small worry, said, "You better get going before you set yourself back." I licked the froth from my lips and departed.

At Boyd, I lay with my eyes closed on one of the pews in the front hallway before the first bell rang. Cliffnotes was there along with Tanner, and they framed my outstretched body so that we formed an H.

"Kepplemen's looking for you," Tanner said.

"What does he want?"

"To amputate your leg," said Cliffnotes.

"Where you at?" Tanner asked. His tone was serious, solicitous.

"One two-seven . . . ish."

Tanner wagged his foot. "That's tough," he said.

The bell rang. I swigged a mouthful of water from the hallway's fountain, which I swished around my tacky mouth, allowing my tongue, dry as a dandelion's corona, to be mercifully submerged. Then I spit in a dribbling stream.

I could rely on my colon's clockwork, and at the end of first period, right at the 9:15 bell, its Pavlovian ring shunted my morning shit into place. I had a free period before me, and I hurried to my favorite bathroom on the upper school's second floor. I had high hopes for the turd's heft—for one of those transcendent, evacuative experiences. But mine was a pebbled bit of business, not enough to fill even the bowl's throat. I didn't shy from marching back to the locker room to weigh myself. I had lost almost a half pound since breakfast. I decided to capitalize on my progress and work out, even though my bones seemed sucked of marrow and, down the hallway, the cafeteria's scents—canned ravioli and broccoli steamed so soft it was nearly white—withered my resolve.

In the weight room I removed my tie, untucked my shirt, and lay on the bench; the space was sauna hot and dimly lit, so I closed my eyes for a minute. The dark made it easier to ignore my stomach's burbling, my tongue's sand-dipped stickiness. I opened my eyes and placed the key in the slot; after just a few reps, I had to contort myself beneath the bar, twisting, bridging at the neck, and then I let the plates slam home. I laced my fingers together over my chest and promptly fell asleep.

It was a deep doze, anchor to seafloor, fluke sunk well beneath the sand, and I felt the entire nautical calm of this nap: the space between boat and bill, palm and prow, floating and submerged, the broiler's thrum creating a submarine silence. There was a boy's voice just a flight above me, like a gull's sharp and becalming call, and then nothing again except the ambient noise. I might have slept there for several hours had Kepplemen not shaken me awake.

"Let's go," he said.

It was a fact that anger didn't come naturally to him. Frustration, as now, and anxiety could stoke his temper. But true anger, the rage he might direct our way to elicit fear, this was always something of a put-on, a state into which he had to work himself. What he wielded most powerfully was approval, our desire for his approbation. He ambled ahead of me, swinging his arms more forcefully than was usual, as if he were disgusted, when really all he wanted, I was sure, was relief—he wanted to stop worrying about me. In its way, the experience was no different from when we rolled: it was about satisfying him, and I suffered the same inversion. I was ashamed I'd once again made Kepplemen feel so bad.

Back in the locker room, I stood naked and shivering as he weighed me. Kepplemen, once the balance finally fell, cupped his great beak in his hands so that his face was only his two large eyes. When he finally spoke, his mouth sounded as dry as mine. "Layer up," he said. "We're going outside."

For the rest of the period, I jogged around the snow-covered turf. I was tempted to dive, mouth open and tongue first, onto its accumulation. The field's length was oriented north-south; the chain-link fence surrounding it was perhaps thirty feet high and lacked only a guard tower. Along its northern perimeter, facing Boyd on Ninety-Seventh Street, was an apartment building fashioned of red brick that in design was a near copy of Lincoln Towers. Twenty stories tall, its balconies bisected the center of its unadorned facade; the thin white railings fronting them put me in mind of birdcages. I swung around, past the lower school, the old building, its brownstone closer in color to coal. Children watched me through the dormer windows; their teachers had called them away by the next lap. Kepplemen, standing out of sight by the entrance's steps, his only added layer an absurdly long red-and-yellow scarf, encouragingly clapped his gloved hands as I passed him. Their muffled thumps were like a coxswain's drum. I was miserable and freezing at first, but then something shifted, some invisible, inner spigot was turned, and working up a sweat, I felt flooded, briefly, with fluid and its attendant energy, so that my thirst was miraculously quenched. Soon Kepplemen waved me inside and, my torture ended, I enjoyed a relief that lasted until afternoon.

At practice, any mercy Coach felt for me disappeared. We started with wheelbarrows, taking our training partner's ankles while he walked on his hands two lengths of the gym, and Coach paired me with Angel Rincodon, our 180-pounder. When we did piggybacks, he made me carry Max Ceto, who clocked in at 195. I was assigned to Ben Bonaci, our heavyweight, for sit-out drills. And when it came time to roll, I was fed first to the team's lions—to Santoro and Freeman and Adler, who seemed to be determined to toy with me by securing positions I had to fight my way out of with maximum effort, body rides that forced me to carry their entire weight for the whole period, as if they were a carapace that I had not yet grown strong enough to support. Next I was offered to Kokra and Vrock, birds of prey who hooded me such that I was pinned over and over again. At practice's end, sprawl drills. Belly empty, I thought I might puke. When we returned to the lockers, when I peeled the tape from the rubber suit this time, the fluid issuing from it seemed more vital. When I went to piss, urine sputtered into the bowl. Its color had darkened from rusty green to an ocher dust.

My teammates showered, dressed, and weighed themselves. Because I could not see them behind the bank of lockers, they left soft ghosts of their laughter there with me when they departed. I sat on the bench in my underwear, steadying myself until the dizziness I was experiencing stopped.

Pilchard was perched at the end of the bench, watching my expression with concern. He was naked but for a towel around his waist. His hair hung just above his eyes, which like mine were sunken and—I'd noticed in the bathroom's mirror earlier—rimmed with purple. Coach, who was almost always last to leave, appeared from around the corner, strode between us, in a towel as well, and entered the showers.

"How close are you?" Pilchard asked.

It was difficult to lift my head to answer him. "Three pounds. More like four."

Pilchard was sitting up very straight. He clutched his towel's knot. The shower's jet turned on and we could hear the water crashing around Kepplemen.

"You should suit up," Pilchard said. "Skip rope in there."

I shook my head. "I'm too tired."

Steamed crawled along the ceiling. Kepplemen hawked and then spit, and the sound made both Pilchard and me tense up.

"Stay," Pilchard said.

For an instant, he reminded me of Oren.

"I need to go," I said.

I was grateful for the Mercedes's warmth. For the heat blowing through its vents, to whose grilles I raised my iron palms. For the darkness, after I shut the passenger door; for the silence, as if the car's thick steel not only sealed off all the city's noise but that in my mind as well—the subway clatter of my thoughts, the cabs' horns and buses' roars, the relentless and ceaseless hurry of it all, and to where? Naomi sat back, ever so slightly, as if startled by my appearance. She asked, "What happened to you?"

I shrugged. I was furious but wanted to laugh. "I'm sucking weight."

She didn't know what I meant. She pressed her hand to the side of my face; she covered my ear, cheek, and temple with a firm pressure and then collected my hair between her fingers and, with her thumb, rubbed my forehead. I followed her arm's path to her shoulder and rested my head there. "No fever," she said, and kissed my scalp.

"Do you have anything to drink?" I asked. It was difficult to pry the question out of my mouth. My tongue seemed adhered to my jaw's floor. She handed me her can of Tab, started the car, and drove while I contemplated it. I took a dangerously large swig, which I did not swallow but held and then swished over my teeth. I could feel, I was sure, every bubble of carbonation, and the lubrication was bliss. I lowered the window and spit it out.

Naomi found a parking space. She cut the engine. The West Side Highway's traffic flickered through the barriers. New Jersey's skyline silently considered Manhattan: there was a mile of river between us, and I believed I could drink the Hudson to its bottom.

"You gonna tell me what's going on?" she asked.

"Nothing," I said.

She considered this. "Something," she said.

I stared at the river.

She said, "I'll wait."

We waited, I did not look at her, and then I said, "It's hard to explain."

"Maybe just talk then," she said.

I told her about everything I'd ignored. How over Christmas, with every second helping of every meal, I'd heard a voice that said, *Don't*. How I did that *all the time*. All those hours I could have spent reading and catching up over break and I didn't. The scale I never stepped on before or after New Year's. The milk I drank, straight from a cow, and the cream chipped beef.

"I don't understand," Naomi said.

My words came like a torrent that I didn't exactly understand either. I told her I was always behind, I was always late. I told her that I didn't say what I saw when I saw it. When I saw it and knew what it was, I ignored it. That I didn't listen to myself when I spoke.

"So speak," she said.

I said, "Coach Kepplemen—"

She said, "The one who slaps you."

I said, "He slaps everyone."

"That doesn't make it okay."

I told her how the moment I stepped on the scale yesterday and was overweight, the leverage he'd wanted was his, he was applying it, and he would not let up until I'd done his bidding or failed.

"Done what?" Naomi asked.

"Made weight," I said.

"Okay," she said. "Failed at what, then?"

"Making weight."

She shook her head. "Like this person's controlling you?"

I told her how sometimes in the school hallways, Coach might ask what our schedules were, what periods we had free to practice, though

I knew he already knew, having once seen on his basement office desk, in his open binder, on his own schedule's master grid, Monday through Friday, our initials penciled in—*GH, TP, CB, SP*—so he would know where we were at all times.

"I know he knows, but I just pretend I don't."

Naomi placed her hands over mine, threaded her fingers through my fingers. She pinched this skin gently and then pulled at it, as if it were a glove I wore. It stretched but did not retract. It held its form, remaining bunched, as if it were a cheap costume, and she stared at this deformity, shocked.

"It happens whenever I'm dehydrated," I said.

Naomi took me in her arms. Until it was time to go, she rubbed my back, to warm me through my coat.

"You're not making this easy," she said.

Later that night, she called our apartment.

When I answered the phone, her voice had the same formality it did when we saw each other in restaurants or at parties: an act, as if we hadn't just seen each other. "Hey, Griffin, how you doing? May I talk with your mother, please?"

I waited for a moment, then opened my study's door; it let in a bit of cooler air. "Mom," I said, "Naomi Shah is on the phone."

Naomi and I waited silently on the line until my mother picked up. She said, "Hey, Naomi, what's going on?" and I replaced the receiver.

That night, before bed, while I was sucking on an ice cube, Mom appeared in our room. I could hear the television on in hers. Ted Koppel began, *It is day four hundred thirty of the hostage crisis.* She was wearing her nightgown. When she opened our door, the light from the hallway reflected against our window, and her silhouette was visible in it. She stood by my bed and let her eyes wander over my face. She placed her palm against my cheek. "Naomi said she ran into you earlier."

When I told her that was true, Mom said, "Are you feeling okay? She said you didn't look so hot."

When I told her I felt fine, she said, "Griffin, is there something you want to tell me?"

I shook my head with her hand still on my face and said, "No."

"Nothing at school?"

"Uh-uh."

She said, "Because if there is, you know you can, yes?"

There was nothing she could do to help me, so I said, "All right."

"All right, or you know?"

"I know."

"All right," she said.

She left and closed the door. In the dark, I heard her close hers, which lowered the TV's volume. My ice cube was the size of a coin, and in my mind's eye I watched it disappear.

"That was close," Oren said.

At five, when my alarm sounded, I climbed down my bunk, walked across the cold parquet, and shut the window, which whistled in protest. I went to the closet, yanked the light's chain, and dropped my pajama pants. I slid the poises along the beam until it balanced: 124.

Morning of the match, and I was still three pounds overweight.

Oren stood at my side, rubbing his eyes. His breath was bad and his hair insane. After considering my predicament, he said, "We're going for a run."

It was still dark as night. We bundled in our warmest clothes. Oren rode his bike alongside me. There were more runners in the park at this hour than I expected. I felt as if I were running uphill and downhill at the same time. It was more like a slow-motion impression of running, robotic and powerless. Sometimes I slowed to barely a jog. Because of my pace, Oren rode as if we were on a crowded boardwalk; he barely pedaled, one hand on the handlebars and an elbow resting on his knee. Occasionally he got ahead of me and then circled back. We hugged Central Park South and then bore north along the east drive, past the carousel. We took the Seventy-Second Street hill, past the boathouse and up the hill past the obelisk and then behind the Met. I ran parallel to Fifth Avenue, past the Guggenheim on my right, past the reservoir on my left, the sky just purpling above the trees. We wound down the snaking descent to 110th Street, and on the west drive Oren had to stand on his pedals to pump up Heartbreak Hill. The tennis courts came into view. The nets were down. We passed the reservoir again and then the lake was visible on our left. Oren waited at the top of the hill as I walked the slow incline toward Sheep Meadow. Now the skyscrapers' background had blued. Bearing west, I resumed my shuffle past the Tavern on the Green, and soon we were home.

Mom and Dad had still not woken. I disrobed as if I'd fallen through ice and my wet clothes might freeze me to death. Oren watched me step on the scale.

I had lost just under two pounds.

Oren breathed a deep sigh I could not read and consulted his calculator watch. "You've got eight hours to lose a pound and a half," he said.

Kepplemen was waiting for me in Boyd's front hallway. He was the rock around which the morning's river of students streamed. He looked as disheveled and as stressed as I felt. He said, "Follow me, please."

In the locker room, after weighing me, Kepplemen, furious, showed me the lineup on his clipboard. He'd left my weight class blank.

"You're on your own," he said, and left.

In science class, I was the blackened base of a test tube. My mouth felt like the dusty plains of Tatooine. In English, Miss Sullens read aloud from *Darkness at Noon*: " 'History has taught us that often lies serve her better than the truth; for man is sluggish and has to be led through the desert for forty years before each step in his development.' Do we agree or disagree with that?" I raised my hand and, when she called on me, asked if I could go to the bathroom. In the stall I sat on the lid and thought of nothing. In Spanish, Miss Daniel asked, "¿Qué les gustaría ordenar?" to which I replied, "Un helado y dos cervezas." Math may as well have been taught in Spanish. In American government, it occurred to me that I forgot to thank Oren for his help, and when I wept I could not shed a tear.

In the locker room, right before the team was to depart for our match, I weighed myself. I was still a half pound over.

Kepplemen had parked the team bus at the upper school's entrance. Our dual meet was a little over a mile away, at Collegiate, so it seemed odd to drive there. He was formally dressed, in a blue blazer, blue button-down, and navy-blue tie with the Boyd Bruin dotting it. I was the last to board. Kepplemen appeared on the black treads of the steps. Tanner and Cliffnotes lowered their windows; so did the team captains. "Well?"

Cliffnotes asked. Beneath my jacket, I was wearing my warm-ups, with my singlet underneath. My gloves and stocking hat.

Kepplemen said, "Don't get on this bus if you haven't made weight."

"I'll see you there," I said, and ran.

To add distance and to try to peel off the last half pound, I jogged down Ninety-Sixth Street, a rolling hill that terminated at Riverside Drive. I could spot the Hudson from here, the highway overpass, the cars blurring at speed. The wind, further chilled by the water, blew into my face with great force. As soon as I turned left on West End Avenue, the gusts' noises were nullified, I was shielded from them by the buildings. I felt strangely liberated; I considered not going to the meet at all. I would run to an entirely new city, in a new state, and live my life. At which point I spotted our former building's awning, FIVE SEVENTY-FIVE emblazoned across it, and Pete, our doorman, standing outside—I hadn't talked to him since we'd moved. I crossed the street to greet him. He'd just hailed a cab for a tenant.

"Pete!" I shouted and, remarkably, he recognized me. He said, "Mr. Griffin!" and took his fighting stance. He had loved my *Candid Camera* appearance with Ali all those years ago. He said, "The boy who boxed the champ!" As was our ritual back then, I put up my guard, and we bobbed and weaved and feinted and jabbed, just as we had done every day when I came home from school. He said, "Look at you, all grown up. Come get out of the cold," and then opened the entrance's iron-grated doors, and I stepped into the building's lobby. It was radiator warm, was the same bright, vaulted space, the east wall dominated by the gilt-framed mirror tall enough to reflect every bulb of the chandelier and the curling marble staircase that led to the second floor. Pete still had the burst blood vessel, as brown as a burned steak, in his brown eye. He said, "How's Oren? That boy was so sweet, I worried about him." He said, "How's your mom and dad?" He said, "Your momma was so pretty." He said, "Your dad—he still sing?"

I recalled Sunday mornings as we talked, late spring or early summer, when my mother would raise the two large windows in the living room that faced West End Avenue. There was next to no traffic. I could look north or south and lean onto the ledge and listen to the trees, whose tops reached our third-floor apartment and whose leaves indicated the wind's prevailing direction. And I could call down to Pete, who'd stepped out from under the awning and was standing watch below.

"He doesn't sing as much but sometimes," I said.

"He has a beautiful voice," Pete said.

"I'm sad we moved away," I said.

"Sooner or later," Pete said, "everybody moves away."

"But not you, Pete."

"Pete's right here."

"I have to go now. But I'll come back and say hi soon."

"You do that," Pete said, and opened the door.

Standing in the lobby's heat, I had worked up a good lather, but now, as I ran, my sweat turned terribly cold, and a few blocks later, I suffered a full-body cramp. I seized at every extremity. My fingers clawed, my calves balled up, my quads locked. The bands of my hamstrings retracted like raised venetian blinds. Like a cowboy shot on a canyon ledge, I stiffened before falling to the pavement. On my hands' heels, I managed to sit myself with my back to the nearest building. Pedestrians walked by, indifferent and unfazed. To uncoil the knot I'd become, I flexed my toes and then reached my fingers to grab the balls of my feet and stretch out everything. I sat for a while longer, breathing tentatively, on high alert, should I contract again.

And I had the most vivid recollection of the first time I'd met Coach. I was in seventh grade. It was my first week at Boyd. I'd come to school very early. I knew no one, I had no friends, and was seated in the front hall, alone. Kepplemen appeared. He spotted me and stopped. I saw him see me. It was as if he recognized me, although I had never seen him before. He looked toward the entrance and back in my direction. He seemed to hover there for a moment, and then he drew closer, gliding forward to join me on the pew, though it felt as if I were the one being pulled in. For maybe a minute we watched the front entrance together, but no one arrived. That he'd sat so close in spite of the fact that we were completely alone shut me down. If the front hall had been crowded to its gills I'd have been unable to speak, I was so unnerved. He'd placed both palms on the bench. His long pinkie nearest mine was spread so wide ours nearly touched. He spoke, but softly. "I saw you playing football the other day. You look like you're an exceptional athlete. Have you ever considered wrestling?" That was it; that was all it took. From that point forward I was in his grip. And seated on the cold pavement, I had the first adult thought of my life. Something so simple and revelatory the calm it imparted was wondrous: *This will end.* I had no idea if I'd made weight, but, oddly, I recognized the wait was over. This state of being I suffered wasn't permanent, no matter what happened. It was mine to declare concluded, should I so choose, and that broke the spell. I got up, gingerly, and was able to stilt-walk, with almost no bend at the knees, for the remaining blocks. I was laugh-cursing the whole distance, and both feelings were real. Pedestrians gave me a wide berth, as if I were a madman.

The teams were at weigh-in when I arrived in the locker room, standing lightest to heaviest. Coach Kepplemen did not even acknowledge my presence when I entered. He stood with his clipboard, filling in the rosters, and gave me only his profile while Collegiate's coach clacked the scale's poises into place, spoke his wrestler's name aloud, checked the pair of wrestlers' weights, and then waved the next boy forward. I removed my damp hat and gloves and unbuttoned my team jacket. I stepped out of my warm-ups, my singlet, my socks and shoes. I dropped my drawers. I considered the delicate, almost deerlike diffidence of these two rows of boys as they stood, cross-armed or slouched, arms loose or hands folded over their genitals. I took my place in line, though I'd have just as soon cut straight to the front, I was so furious. When it was our turn, the Collegiate coach adjusted the scale to 121 and said his wrestler's name aloud, which Kepplemen penciled into the lineup sheet, nodding to him warmly, respectfully. To me, Kepplemen said, "Step on, please," although he still would not look at me. I waited until he did. I could tell he was scared. He was certain he was about to be humiliated, some way, somehow, not because I would let him down but simply because I was here. "Step on, please," he repeated, and I did not move until we made eye contact. When Kepplemen finally did look up from the clipboard to meet my gaze, I held it as he often did when we were in private, but until *he* averted his eyes. Until *I* could take in the entirety of his person, unabashed and uncontested. His fingers were trembling, but so were mine. Because I realized that I hated him. I always had, all these years.

Not for who he was or what he wanted. I hated him because he'd showed me who he was without knowing he had. Because I knew him better than he knew himself, and this seemed the very condition of his being an adult.

"Name," the opposing coach asked me when the balance fell.

"Griffin Hurt." And then to Kepplemen, I said, "Write it down."

At school the next day, Cliffnotes asked me, "Are you in trouble?"

When I asked why, he said, "Because I just saw your mother coming out of Mr. Fistly's office."

Practice that afternoon was canceled. No explanation was offered. At dinner that night, I was too scared to broach the subject with my mother, but she surprised me by bringing it up herself. "I met with your principal today," she said, and glared, adding, "Now eat." She'd made spaghetti Bolognese. I recognized her ferocity, that it carried repercussions if I disobeyed, so I forced down every bite though this did not appease her. The following day passed without event, although Kepplemen was still absent. Through our captains came the news practice was canceled, and I remember the feeling that something tectonic had shifted. Cliffnotes, Tanner, and I shot looks at one another in the hallway as if we were hiding something, were keeping this secret, even though we did not know what it was—if it somehow implicated us and promised some undreamed-of reward.

On the following Monday afternoon, after suiting up for practice, we were greeted in the gym by Mr. Tyrell. He had a chipped front tooth and a scraggly mustache. His brown hair, threatening a mullet, was thin and parted down the middle. He had us sit against the wall and informed us that an announcement was going to be made. His West Coast drawl was raspy; it sounded like he always had a smoker's loogie lodged deep in his lungs, which he occasionally paused to bring up, fist to mouth, and swallow again. When Tanner asked, "What's this all about?" he said, "Patience, my bros, all questions will soon be answered by the man himself."

And then Fistly appeared, his heels clacking against the waxed floor. He strode to the edge of the mats and did something remarkable: he removed his loafers. He padded to the mats' center and stood on the

Bruin insignia. Beneath his socks we noticed him flex his toes. If he'd removed these garments to reveal feet as downy and taloned as a snow owl's, I wouldn't have been surprised. He considered us one end to the other. It was difficult to tell whether it was with pity or disapproval, though he let his eyes rest on me just long enough to communicate I was somehow the catalyst. He carried several papers with him, which he'd rolled into a tube. He smacked it against his leg several times. When he did speak, his tone was somber, apologetic. Could it be that he was the one who was actually embarrassed?

"I have some rather unfortunate news," Mr. Fistly began. "Mr. Kepplemen has abruptly decided to take a position at the Fessenden School in Massachusetts. His explanation is that he was made an offer he could not refuse. I am, of course, deeply troubled by the fact that he is leaving both this team and the middle school program without a coach, not to mention our physical education program short-staffed. I consider his behavior appallingly unprofessional, and I have told him as much. But to no avail. We bid him adieu and shall think of him no more. I can assure you that we have begun conducting a search in the hope of replacing him, but this late in your season I'm afraid you must lower your expectations regarding its success. In the meantime, Mr. Tyrell has generously offered to step in as head coach pro tempore. As some of you may know, Mr. Tyrell was the assistant varsity wrestling coach before Mr. Kepplemen began his tenure here. You will join me in welcoming him into this role, and I am confident you will be patient with Mr. Tyrell as he gets his bearings during this transitional period. We have high expectations of our students at Boyd. We have even *higher* expectations of our faculty. In this case we have been sorely disappointed, and for that you have my sincerest apologies."

Fistly, eyes downcast, gingerly walked to the mats' edge, slipped into his shoes, noisily marched toward the exit, and departed.

All of us shot looks at each other. Some shrugged, confused. Others covered their mouths, dismayed. I, like a boy whose pockets were stuffed with candy, awaited the shout from the storekeeper that I'd been caught. And like an unwilling accomplice, wanted someone to blame.

Tyrell turned back to us. "Everyone, this is heavy, for sure. I know you're feeling some uncertainty at the moment, but as we used to say back home, there's no one way to ride a wave. So let's get back up and have a wicked hard practice."

As the team began warm-ups, Tyrell pulled me aside. "Mr. Hurt."

"Coach."

"I'm bumping you up to one twenty-nine. For the rest of the season."

"But Swain starts at that weight."

"You want to wrestle off for the honor, you get the opportunity once a week."

"But—"

"No more buts. This comes from on high."

"Meaning what?"

"Meaning your mother."

Now, of course, I realize what had happened. It was the same thing that was happening at schools like Horace Mann and Saint George's and Choate. The offending teachers and coaches were simply handed off to other institutions, out of sight and out of mind, while we—the school's charges—were abandoned to silence. Maybe this was the shift I had felt, the continent on which my friends and I had been cast away. Maybe that isn't the right figure. Because Kepplemen's departure left a hole. Strangely, at the time, his leaving us felt like a betrayal. As for my mother, she thought I was just starving to death.

Walking home from the bus that evening, I spotted Naomi's car. The interior light was on. It shined brightly, almost unforgivingly, on Naomi's head. It made her hair's part resemble a field's furrow, revealing the white of her scalp, which disgusted me. She was reading the paper, glancing up to track, I noticed, pedestrians across the street and then checking her side mirror. I banged my fist on the window. I pulled the door closed with all my strength and stared straight forward, bear-hugging my book bag. I felt her staring at me, and then she sighed. "I guess I better put on my seat belt," she said, and then started the car.

After she'd parked, she cut the ignition so slowly and gently it was as if she were trying to silently unlock a door. She let go of the wheel with her palms out and eased back into her seat, whose leather creaked. Then she turned to face me.

"Why did you do that?" I asked.

"I didn't think I had a choice."

"My season is over. I'm done, understand? Because of you." And then I was crying, which I hated myself for.

"He was hurting you," Naomi said. Now she was crying too.

"No, he wasn't."

"You were hurting yourself. You were in danger."

"I was *handling* it."

"You're right. I'm sorry. I'm so sorry. But I can't—I can't not protect you."

Naomi took off her glasses to wipe her eyes. It occurred to me that I'd almost never seen her face without them, that their gold frames and blue lenses hid her features' plainness.

"I don't know," she said. "Sometimes I think that you need a friend. Other times I think that *I* do. That I'm lonely, and that listening—" She shook her head now and grimaced. "That listening to you and being with you is my way of ignoring that."

"Why are you talking about this?"

In response, she cried more freely. She closed her eyes and began to nod.

I couldn't stop myself. I put my book bag down and took Naomi's hand in mine and kissed her palm. I pressed her palm to my cheek, so that with it I wiped my tears until she wiped them, and I clutched her and said, "Please don't cry."

She gripped me very hard. We sat in the car like that for a time. She whispered, "Every day I look forward to seeing you. Every day I wake up and wonder if you'll come walking by. I dress for you in the morning. I look forward to hearing about your day. I think about how we're alike. That you might be the loneliest person I know. But this," she said, and then sat back against the door, "this is ending."

I waited.

"My daughters are done for the season. There are no more performances. And they've decided to leave the program. I don't know when I'll be seeing you again." She paused to cry more freely and wiped her eyes. "Which is probably for the best."

She said this almost like a question.

"I did what I did because you needed help. It's what grown-ups have to do sometimes for kids, even if they don't understand. So maybe one day you will. Maybe one day I will. Understand all of this, I mean."

Then she smiled, weakly, and started the car. As we approached West End Avenue, she indicated my building and asked, "Do you want to get out here?"

I shook my head. "I'd like to drive for a while," I said.

She was pleased by this, and when I said, "Uptown," she turned left, north. When she passed the familiar facade of my former building, she tapped the window with her nail and said, "There's where you used to live." I asked her to turn west, to Riverside Drive, and she did. "There's the Soldiers' and Sailors' Monument," she said at the light, "where you and your brother would roller-skate." She asked, "Where to next?" and I said, "Go right." We continued north for several blocks. We continued to Ninety-Sixth Street, which I suggested we take east. We rose up the steep hill. "Keep going?" she asked, as we crossed Broadway. I nodded. We were approaching Central Park West now, and when Boyd Prep came into view, I thought about our first drive together, how I was in command this time.

"Crosstown?" she asked.

"Right," I said.

We caught a streak of green lights, as far as I could see, although Naomi did not accelerate. "There's the Museum of Natural History," Naomi said. And at Seventy-Second Street she nodded toward the Dakota. "Over there's where John Lennon got shot." She read my mind and made a right, so we could drive past the entrance. People still laid flowers around the NYPD's newly installed booth and along the building's black railings.

"And this," said Naomi, stopping a few moments later, "is where you get out."

Oh, that gigantic X, as on a treasure map, where Columbus Avenue and Broadway intersected, where cars and pedestrians streamed in every direction, where people rose from and descended to the subway stations or shopped their wares on the nearby crossing island, knickknacks and foodstuffs, honey-roasted nuts and hot dogs, steam rising from their carts and the orange-and-white tubes like colorful chimneys releasing the service lines' condensation.

"Goodbye," I said to Naomi.

"Goodbye," she said.

The strangeness of saying goodbye, how I'd never thought of us or life in terms of goodbyes, how I'd never thought things ended. I opened the passenger door, exited the car; outside, I tapped the roof twice. I walked several steps facing backward, smiling at Naomi warmly, unabashedly; she returned this expression in kind, and, skipping now, stretching whatever hold she had on me until I passed Juilliard, I broke into a run, down the hill toward home. A blue sea wave swelled under my heart and, buoyed, I lengthened my stride. I believed that I had gotten away with something. That I'd been forgiven a debt, that this break was clean, my parting with Naomi final. A fact about which I was entirely wrong, and a lesson I'd already unlearned. Because very soon afterward, I fell in love.

PART TWO

THE
REAGAN
ADMINISTRATION

We are at a turning point in our history. There are two paths to choose. One is a path I've warned about tonight, the path that leads to fragmentation and self-interest. Down that road lies a mistaken idea of freedom, the right to grasp for ourselves some advantage over others. That path would be one of constant conflict between narrow interests ending in chaos and immobility. It is a certain route to failure.

—Jimmy Carter, "Crisis of Confidence" speech, 1979

THE SWIMSUIT ISSUE

At the beginning of February, only a few weeks after Reagan's inauguration and just as my one-win wrestling season was winding down—the new academic term, with all of its clean-slate hopefulness, under way—Dad, at dinner, said that he had an announcement. "I've been offered a major part in Abe Fountain's new musical." He took Mom's hand and squeezed it. "It's practically the role of a lifetime." Mom squeezed his hand back. "Rehearsals start in April, and then we go on the road in the summer. Which means I expect the both of you to help your mother hold down the fort while I'm gone."

Oren and I had entirely different reactions to this news, though looking back, I am surprised I managed any sort of response at all, as agitated and astir as I was, as distracted and dreamy. I swear I sometimes wonder if it was simply because I was eating normally—that is, voraciously—again. All that nutrition snaking through my veins to fuel my final growth spurt, a burst that, rather than bulk my shoulders and chest, widen my thighs, or inflate my arms, instead initially made my extremities outsized, bestowing me with size thirteen feet and enlarging my hands to a breadth as paw-like as my father's. What an odd-looking bird I was, mid-molt. Given my profession, plenty of pictures of me were taken. Given my age—I turned fifteen that month—my self-consciousness was acute. It wasn't lost on me how closely Dad and I resembled each other, although my aquiline nose was subtly hooked at its tip, like Mom's, and my hair, curly as Dad's, was a tawny brown to his jet black, which I, desperately seeking contrast, grew nearly to my shoulders.

True, my body's transformation was nowhere near as dramatic as what was taking place in my heart and mind, but these were still a trio of accelerants and each intensified the others. Longing, expectancy, waiting for ... what? Oh, all the energy such a process produces, all the by-products! In my case, a tear or two shed at songs like "Yesterday," "I'm Not in Love," "You Light Up My Life," or—this is the most embarrassing— Kenny Rogers's "Lady," which I often belted out in my study closet, head-phones on (*"And yes, oh yes, I'll always want you near me / I've waited for you for so long!"*). I wanted to be in love, I was in love with the idea of love, *O Romeo, Romeo, be careful what you wish for, Romeo* . . .

Another side effect of this was constant and unmanageable erections. Often in public places, notably classrooms, they demanding cross-legged techniques of concealment a magician would appreciate. I chanted mantras only a mad monk might (*dead kittens, dead kittens, dead kittens*), my tumescence so aggressively out of control, it required I, like some street fighter, play dirty and throw elbows at it, knocking it up toward the waistband of my briefs (I sometimes wore two pair to contain it), to peek out, from above my belt, at my shirt's inner plackets; or down into the leg opening of my Fruit of the Looms, so rigid I walked out of class with a pronounced limp. It was all so unrelenting—I having had no one teach me how to even temporarily relieve this pressure and jerk off—I sometimes worried I had a disease. Not to mention confusing, especially since my verb had no object. It wasn't Deb Peryton, though she and I were in English and American government together and those classes also bequeathed unto me wood. Nor was it Bridget, whose person was strictly aspirational, who lived in Virginia, after all, and whose last name I never caught. And it certainly wasn't Naomi, out of sight and out of mind, not to mention any categories beyond what I was equipped to contemplate, let alone fantasize about.

Perhaps my dream girl helped to distract me from the reality of my grades, which were all, with the exception of English, gentlemen's C's, math nearer to a D, although it was my comments that were the most deflating. Two in particular stand out:

After a rough start to the year, Griffin rallied, turning in assignments on time and promptly completing labs. Lacks command of all basic scientific concepts. Always willing to answer questions, even if he has the wrong answer. Average: 77

Griffin wants to speak Spanish and is always willing to speak Spanish in spite of the fact that he can barely speak Spanish. He has only a tenuous understanding of grammar, but his accent is perfecto! Average: 76

I was keenly aware of my superficial, surface-level grasp of all my subjects. Elliott was quick to remind me of my potential, which Dad parroted. And I wanted immersion, depth, command! But I no more knew how to study than to beat my meat. Is it any surprise my thoughts drifted toward romance?

My dreams' subject was, of course, veiled in mystery, was not yet an individuated she, though we had, in that future I so longed for, fallen deeply enamored with each other, and the romantic movie in which we starred was shot on several recognizable locations (a long stretch of beach, in the shadow of cliffs, atop which a bell tower tolled, its roof circled by martins; or the Metropolitan Museum of Art, where we'd found ourselves accidentally locked in, and through whose various kingly and queenly antique rooms my girl and I wandered before stepping over the velvet rope to finally bed down), all of which ended happily ever after.

Speaking of, Mom seemed so happy at Dad's news it was a joy to behold, but Dad was even more thrilled, and his excitement briefly lifted a pall of anxiety I didn't realize had long hung over our family. Was that another of the fire's lingering scars? I, being in the same profession as Dad, knew what this opportunity meant for him. He had toiled for so long, and for a son to behold this is a suffering. All of which is to say, I was filled with hope. First for my future, since Dad's and mine were so entangled that his success meant I could finally decide, for myself, how to spend my time; second, for our family, and all the attendant prosperity it would bequeath. Because if Dad was going to make it big, it would have to be on Broadway.

My father's job title—actor—was a broad one, best defined negatively. He was not a television star, although he'd appeared, once, as a surgeon on the soap opera *General Hospital.* This was a bit part, a walk-on in which he wore scrubs and a mask, the latter dangling around his neck, his character having just come from the operating theater to deliver news to the bereaved. In order to fully appreciate his line, you must imagine it spoken in his bass baritone—a rich, mellifluous instrument, almost British in its articulateness but lacking any highborn lilt. It was a decidedly masculine sound, tonally cleansed of his outer-borough idiom (Queens), as well as his mother's Russian and father's Hungarian accents—the pair squeezed, syllable by syllable, from his throat. It was only amplified by his diaphragmatic control, acquired at Juilliard, where he was classically trained in opera and enjoyed a full scholarship until quitting, mysteriously, after two years. His voice had a disembodied, disproportionate sound, which on first hearing could cause the listener a discordant shock, as when a demonically possessed girl speaks in the devil's basso profundo. "We've stopped the *blee*ding," he told the victim's wife, "but we won't know anything for certain until the *mor*ning." He was not a ham, but I would come to think he revered acting too much, with a love too big for small screens, so that his portrayal—even one as insignificant as this—was self-parodying, unwittingly genius, like a great actor brilliantly impersonating a bad one. It was not the first time a performance of his made me uncomfortable.

Never once did he appear in a motion picture. But his voice did, as background noise in famous scenes. Acting was involved, of course, but off camera, in a recording studio, dubbed in postproduction, the lines improvised with other actors so as to create that familiar, indistinct din you might hear in a crowded restaurant—"room tone" being the term of art. Or, as I came to think of it, trying to single out his voice from the others as we sat in the darkened theater—watching, say, *Day of the Dolphin* or *Logan's Run,* or any number of the age-inappropriate films he took Oren and me to attend—*Dad somewhere in the room.* Not that my father didn't enjoy the occasional star turn. Some of his lines became iconic. He's the first man heard screaming from a window in *Network:* "I'm mad as hell, and I'm not going to take this anymore!" "Look," you hear him say in *Superman,* "up in the sky." Or perhaps most famously in *Star Wars:* "These aren't the droids we're looking for." After that movie's meteoric success, it was not beyond him to tell a stranger who was curious about his profession that he'd had the pleasure of working with Sir Alec Guinness, that he was *that* stormtrooper in *that* scene, even though he'd done the dubbing months later, in the U.S., and principal photography had been shot in Tunisia—a long time ago, in what might as well have been a galaxy far, far away.

That he'd never made it in movies was a source of pain for him, one he didn't need to express for me to infer. I noticed the joy he took in my credits on film and television—the one-sheets from *The Talon Effect* he kept rolled in a packing tube in my study closet, or how he insisted that NBC send him Betamax tapes of every episode of *The Nuclear Family.* It was nearly impossible to get him to come to a wrestling match, but he showed up on set now and then, and I occasionally caught him studying these tapes in his bedroom and, later, when we gathered at dinner, he might mention how I'd played a particular scene—an offhand gesture I'd made in response to a line, adding how "in character" I'd been. Given how little thought went into these performances—they were, on levels I didn't fully comprehend then, involuntary—he might as well have remarked, mid-meal, that I was doing a fantastic job of swallowing.

Once, when the praise became too much, Oren chimed in: "He's a Saturday morning superhero, not Laurence Olivier."

"That doesn't mean he doesn't treat his work with professionalism," Dad shot back.

To which Mom said to me, as if I were both confidant and conspirator, "One girl, that's all I wanted."

Watching Dad do voiceovers was impressive. Picture a recording studio and my father in the live room or an isolation booth, on the other side of the control room's soundproof glass. He's wearing headphones. On a stand rests the sheets with the ad copy. There's a digital clock atop the mixing console that counts down the time sequences. "Shel," says the engineer, "I need you to shave two seconds off that last take." And uncannily, expertly, exactly, my father would. It wasn't just his efficiency, which was welcome, given the cost of studio time, but his prodigious command of tone, the humor or pathos he could inject into commercial copy, that added to his value. He'd knock out as many as three to ten spots in an hour, sometimes even more, and make enough to cover a month's expenses in that compressed span. But then he might not do another commercial for weeks, sometimes longer.

During these dry spells, when I was in elementary school and auditioning, I might meet him at his midtown studio, across from Carnegie Hall, or run into him at one of the ad agencies where we'd both been to go-sees, and we'd walk home together. I equated his distraction with suffering and considered it my job to comfort him. Were these efforts of mine to be sweet what made him at once magnanimous and miserable as we walked home? Did I, his dependent, so eager to cheer him up, remind him of his failings as a father? Crossing from the East Side to the West, Dad was regularly indrawn, eyes to asphalt. This angst made it easy to convince him to stop for a snack, since it comforted him to feed me and gave him an excuse to stress eat: he'd get me a slice of cheesecake at Wolf's Delicatessen ("Just to make sure it isn't poison," he'd say, and, with his knife, neatly scalp the dessert's graham cracker crust), or, if no crosstown bus was in sight by the time we'd reached Seventh Avenue, we'd stop at the counter of Chock Full o' Nuts, so Dad could peacefully brood and occasionally graze while I pigged out.

"How come you never did movies?" I once asked him.

Dad helped himself to one of my doughnuts. He talked while he chewed. "Quinn was supposed to get me into pictures," Dad said, "but he didn't come through." When your father is a large and intimidating man and you are a comparatively tiny and successful pro, one who knows something of how the business works, it is uncommon, at best, to call such a person on his bullshit. Dad shook his head and swigged his coffee; it was probably his tenth cup of the day. Thank God he wasn't a drinker. With my napkin, I wiped the powdered sugar from the corner of his mouth.

"Thanks," he said, "I needed that."

That was both Aqua Velva aftershave's tagline and a tic of my father's as he moved through the city. He'd eye a movie poster lining a construction site or one posted on a billboard and read its copy aloud. *"In space,"*

Dad said—to me, to himself, to the air—*"no one can hear you scream."* Or walking by a liquor store: *"We will sell no wine before its time."* Or through a sanitation truck's pungent cone of odor: *"People start pollution. People can stop it."* I had a far higher tolerance for these impromptu performances than Oren because I was rooting for him to not only land one of those multiyear, national network accounts with its game-changing residuals but also one day be the famous personality with whom a product was associated—like Ricardo Montalbán for Chrysler or Bill Cosby for Jell-O. Perhaps *then* his anxiety would finally be alleviated. Land a fish like that, and it would be game over. The old man could finally retire from the sea.

Thus, some sort of career-defining role was to be desired, for professional reasons and financial purposes. There were riches in recognition, in becoming a brand name, but he could see no path toward it, could *make* no path toward it, since he was, in the end, waiting to be the chosen and at the mercy of others, no matter how hard he kept at it. "The problem with my business," Dad once said to me on one of these walks, and here I sniffed out an Elliott aphorism, "is that there's no graduation system." If he could enjoy just one great stretch—if he could have, as he sometimes liked to say, a bucket when it rained—I might not discover him, as I did sometimes, in the living room in the middle of the night, sitting on the couch with the light on, his brown-and-black-striped robe, the one that had survived the fire, hanging open as he sat staring at the wall, sawing at his lip with his index finger as if it were a violin's bow, entirely unaware of me as I walked past him to get a late-night snack. "Dad," I said, briefly interrupting his ruminating, "are you okay?"

"I'm fine, boychik," he'd say, "why don't you go get some rest?"

He'd make Oren and me breakfast the next morning, looking even more haggard and unkempt, and was soon off to the YMCA, where he had a membership at the Businessman's Club and where he went every morning for a light workout, followed by a steam and a shower and a shave, "to get myself together," he liked to say. It was more often at night, when he returned home, that we got a look at the person he was out in the world during the day.

My father could be vain, but only in public. For his own reflection he had a sixth sense, and he was incapable of passing a mirror or storefront window without checking his profile, subtly sucking in his cheeks. But at home he suffered far less self-regard: in the mornings, he often paraded around our small apartment in only a shirt, socks, and briefs—his stork-ish, hairless legs pale as his underwear's cotton—even when Oren and I had friends sleep over. After bathing, he sat on the living room's sofa, enrobed and reading the *Times*. He might allow his gown's flap to fall open, revealing his enormous nakedness underneath, upon which he'd scratch his scrotum as innocently as a zoo ape. Nor was he ashamed of his fake teeth. A pair of bridges spanned the cuspids on both his upper and lower jaw. So it was that, when Oren and I were little, if we came upon him scraping these with his dentist's excavator or surprised him preparing the gray paste that secured these fakes to his gums, he'd turn on us and broadly smile, spooking us by this glimpse into his mouth's inner workings; or he'd make a bogeyman howl, as if we'd discovered his true, monstrous identity, then stick out his tongue through the enor-mous gap until we covered our eyes and fled screaming. Throughout my childhood, the story he always told was that his originals were too small and thus gave him a smile unfit for stage or screen, so he'd had "some light cosmetic work done" to address the problem. This sounded like a perfectly reasonable answer, and I accepted it, though when I discovered in his dresser pictures of him as a teenager and, later, as a navy seaman, I thought they looked absolutely proportional—which, I'd learn later that year, they had been.

During my dad's dry spells, he still made it a point to work. He gave his days something like a nine-to-five by teaching singing and commer-cial voice at the studio he rented on Seventh Avenue. He had an upright piano here as well as recording equipment. He also did the headshots of some of his students. He'd been a photographer in the navy, had been drafted during the Korean War but saw no action, tooling around the Mediterranean instead on a heavy cruiser, another chapter in his life I knew next to nothing about. He took my headshots as well, and I *hated* these sessions. They were usually conducted in Central Park, and were some of the more painful exercises in false spontaneity of my young life. To mitigate embarrassment and be as far from the weekend sunbath-ers as possible, I demanded we conduct the shoot by the exposed rocks at the field's southernmost end. Dad posed me in ways I hated: With my hands to my sides. With my body turned sideways. With my arms crossed.

"Look down," Dad said. "Now up."

"Stop squinting," he ordered. *"And open your eyes."*

"How about a smile?" Dad asked, holding his Nikon at his belt. "You call that a smile?"

Determined to be miserable, I had fixed my face in a frown, which Dad considered for a moment, his cheeks inflating, until he exploded in laughter. It made my misery more complete because it threatened to decouple my expression from my feelings. Sensing I was close to breaking character, he lifted the viewfinder to his eye. In the lens, I caught sight of my face, my mouth clownishly downturned, and, made suddenly aware of how proximate strong passion is to its opposite, began to laugh myself, furious. (Mom, it's worth mentioning, was a far more willing model than I. Dad might ask to shoot her, of a regular Saturday, and these pictures, which I also found in my study closet, had an intimacy, a frankness, a seductiveness, that even then I recognized as reserved for Dad only.)

My mother taught children at Neubert Ballet in the afternoons, a job—though Dad could barely bring himself to call it one—that left her days open to get her BA at Columbia and, for the past several years, her MA in literature at NYU, the latter pursuit one that occasionally drove him nuts. They often fought about this, sometimes openly, at the dinner table.

"What do you do with a degree like that?" my father might ask. "Do you teach? Like maybe at Griffin's school?"

"You mean English?" she said.

"You could get us a break on tuition," Dad said. "Even health insurance."

"I do it for myself," Mom said.

"What about becoming a secretary, then?" Dad asked. "For an executive. Or maybe writing a novel."

"What are you even talking about?"

"You could be a speechwriter. For a corporation. I see those ads in the paper all the time."

"Why don't you mind your own business?" Mom said.

"Your business *is* my business," Dad said, "because it's our business. The family business."

"Why don't you do jingles then?" Mom asked. "Georgette Fox makes all kinds of money doing that."

"You know my rule about jingles."

"What about copyediting?" Oren asked Mom.

Mom, stunned, glared at my brother. "Excuse me, young man, since when do you give me professional advice?"

"You like to read so much," Oren pressed, "why don't you go into publishing?"

"Shut your trap," Mom said to him. "And you too," she said to Dad. "And you," she said to me, "don't look at me like that!" When I said nothing, she flung her wadded napkin onto her plate, knocked over her chair when she stood.

Oren waited until he heard her lock our bathroom door and the faucets squeak, the running water canceling our noise. "My friend Betsy's mom works at Random House," he whispered. "She has an office with a secretary and gets any book they publish for *free.*"

"Mrs. Potts," I said to Dad, "works at Smith Barney."

Dad glumly shook his head, imitating the British actor John Houseman: "They make money the old-fashioned way," he said. "They *earn* it."

He glanced at Oren and then at me, and he couldn't help himself: he started to laugh. Which gave us permission to laugh too. After we fell silent, Oren, with some hesitance, said to Dad, "Why *don't* you do jingles?"

Now it was Dad who pushed away from the table.

"Because," he yelled, "you have to say *no* to *something*!" Then he marched to the front closet, thrust his arms through his coat sleeves, and, upon leaving, slammed the door.

Perhaps, I have often reflected, singing was for Dad somehow even more sacrosanct than acting and was not to be soiled by commercialism. In point of fact, Dad did perform one jingle for a local toy store. In it, a couple of kids were featured playing with a racecar set, their smiles followed by its bargain-basement price, and then comes the song. The bouncing ball, which in the commercial was a globe with a striped hat and smiley face, compressed as it hopped atop each word's syllable. To this day, I occasionally catch myself happily humming the melody and then have to suppress the urge to burst out singing it the same way the chorus of kids perform it—jubilantly:

Playworld!
A world of toys.
Great for girls.
And great for boys.
Playworld!
Where prices go . . .

And then Dad sings the descending notes down to the deepest C:

So low,
low,
low,
low,
llllllllooooooooooow . . .

Oren and I identified his voice the first time we saw the commercial. It ran during afternoon cartoons, and when we told Dad we'd heard him, he'd said offhandedly, "They give me a fifty percent discount on all their merch," a fact which, true or not, immediately slivered into Oren's mind.

"Can you take us shopping there?" he asked.

"It's all the way in Paramus."

"What about the one in Hackensack?"

"That's far too."

"There's also a store in Syosset."

"That's past Queens."

"So's Hackensack," Oren said, "depending on which direction you're going."

"What's the rush already?"

"I want a skateboard. At that rate, I can buy some Peralta wheels and still have money left over."

"Maybe next weekend."

"You mean tomorrow?"

"I mean the weekend after."

Oren crossed his arms and shook his head. "There is no discount, is there?"

Dad's eye twitched. "I don't like your attitude, young man."

"You and your endless bs," Oren said.

Dad slapped him in the mouth. When Oren covered up, Dad grabbed his shirt collar, turned him around, and mushed his cheek against the wall, giving his ass a good whupping. Then Dad dragged him to our room and flung him in the corner, where Oren sat facing him.

"No allowance for a week!" Dad said.

"Fuck your cheap allowance!" Oren cried.

"Make it a month then!"

"I've got a year saved up!"

"Two years and nothing for you!"

"Make it till I move out!" Oren screamed.

Dad stormed off. I closed our door and quietly locked it. Then I slid down next to my brother. Oren reverted to his boyishness when he cried. He whimpered and mumbled and let his nose run. There were lots of consonants in his burbling. I took a mental snapshot, in case I needed the face down the road. "You okay?" I asked.

"Cut the caring crap. It's the same load of horseshit as his."

"That's not true," I said.

"See!" Oren said, and pointed at my face. "You're about to laugh."

"I'm sorry," I said, and then climbed into my top bunk, covered my face with my pillow, and giggled into it.

"Fucking assholes," Oren said of us. "Only out for yourselves. The both of you."

I stared into the muffled dark, listening to my breathing. It wasn't the first time Oren had leveled this accusation. Even though its origin was a mystery, I knew it to be true, and didn't ask.

What my father's talents perfectly suited him for was the stage—for musicals in particular. Some of my earliest memories were of seeing and hearing him sing. But it was the attendant emotional and physical response to his voice, paired with music, that registered, in my bones, as something close to joy. I recall, for example, seeing Dad perform Beethoven's *Fidelio* on television—this at our first apartment, before the fire—playing Rocco, the old jailkeeper, in Leonard Bernstein's Young People's Concerts. It was a recital with no costumes. My father and the soprano with whom he sang wore black turtlenecks and slacks. Elliott, who was, along with Lynn, watching at our apartment with us, translated the German as Dad sang:

Nur hurtig fort, nur frisch gegraben.
Es währt nicht lang, er kommt herein.

—making the *ein* in *herein* ring with such immediacy I felt my neck tingle. *"Hurry and dig the grave,"* Elliott translated, *"it won't be long, it won't be long, and he'll arrive."* And then Dad thundered:

Es währt nicht lang,
Es währt nicht lang,
er kommt herein.

I also saw countless performances of my father in *Jacques Brel Is Alive and Well and Living in Paris* at the Village Gate. Certain songs he sang thrilled me and stay with me, so that I find myself humming them, or singing to this day:

In the port of Amsterdam
There's a sailor who sings
Of the dreams that he brings
From the wide-open sea

And I still wonder at how its lines seemed to contain both the horizon's vastness and the ocean's breadth, the pair shot through with desire. I didn't analyze it then, didn't think of it at all, much less articulate it. I merely felt it. It was like a wound, as if I'd stepped on coral and it grew in my foot.

In 1977, the famous director Joshua Logan had him appear in his revue *Musical Moments* at the Rainbow Room. Logan had seen my father perform in *The Fisher King* and went on to direct the movie, in which, to my father's consternation, he was not cast. I never once saw the man in anything but a tuxedo. At the performances he always had me sit between him and his wife, Nedda. "And now," Logan whispered to me as Dad took the stage, as he took the mic in hand and gently cracked the cord's whip to give it slack, "your father will sing one of my all-time favorite songs. He sings it as well as Ella Fitzgerald, and he *electrifies* it with desperation."

Somewhere there's music
How faint the tune
Somewhere there's heaven
How high the moon
There is no moon above
When love is far away too
Till it comes true
That you love me as I love you

And when Dad sang the last verse—when with his free hand he reached out toward the audience, as if begging them to pull him to safety; when he held the note on the word "high" for so long there followed a shocked silence at the song's conclusion—even I, at ten years old, recognized it as a howl of pain:

The darkest night would shine
If you would come to me soon
Until you will, how still my heart
How high the moon.

After the show's final performance, Logan invited our family to his town house for a nightcap. Mom declined; Oren was too tired. Dad and I rode with Logan and Nedda in his stretch limousine. Logan's tux hung on him loosely, as if he'd recently lost a great deal of weight. He was jowly and had a thick mustache; he grew his remaining hair long and combed it back. When he addressed me, it was clear that the person to whom he was really speaking was Dad.

"Would you like to know why your father is a great singer?" Logan said to me. "Because he possesses the three most important qualities a singer can have. First, articulation. He makes you hear every word in the lyric, which allows for emphasis and a wider range of interpretation. Second, magnitude. The very *bigness* of his sound, its unquestionable authority, demands you listen. And finally"—he pressed his pinkie to his thumb and held up three fingers, "storytelling. Your father makes every song answer the following question: Why is this night different from all other nights?"

My father, so guileless in his admiration of Logan, appeared childlike. He was so thrilled to be here, so close to this god, that he seemed to have forgotten I was present. Our roles—son and father—were reversed, and at such times, observing his wonder at having made it, at least this far, seated, as he was, across from such a legend, I felt happiest for him, and completely invisible.

January 1981 had been freezing. From my room's window, I watched the barges of ice on the Hudson bear south. They looked long and wide enough that I was sure I could frogger them to Union City, whose scalloped cliffs were dusted with snow. Snow drifts, piled in the parking lot beneath our terrace, were caved with footprints and dotted with soot. Dogs, their raised legs visibly shaking, hurriedly pissed through the powder's crust, flecking it emerald and saffron. Fire hydrants were snow-capped, water towers white-topped, roofs wool-blanketed: nothing, it seemed, could break the deep freeze; there was no escaping our tiny apartment. February was more of the same until that evening when Dad broke the news about the Abe Fountain musical, with its assurance of a promising spring, a summer warmed by stardom, and a bountiful fall.

"Where are you on the playbill?" Oren asked.

"Right below the two leads," Dad said.

Oren said, "So this is big money we're talking about?"

"I can't complain."

"Then maybe," Oren said, "we could actually go on a vacation this spring? Like everyone else at my school."

Our parents glanced at each other.

"I was thinking Captiva," Oren continued, and then from his back pocket produced a rolled-up *Sports Illustrated* with Christie Brinkley on the cover, which he opened for them to see. "It's an island off Fort Myers. In Florida. In the Gulf of Mexico. They have beautiful seashells you can collect, Mom, see? And if you don't want to pay airfare," Oren said to Dad, "we could even drive."

February gave on to March. Now that wrestling season had concluded, and the terms of my agreement with Dad had been met, I was auditioning again. That month, I booked a Pop Rocks radio spot (*There's bang to the bite* was my line), which was followed by an on-camera Lipton Cup-a-Soup commercial. The shoot required I miss a full day of school. It had five actors in it: me and two older guys, Ricky Febliss and Jeff Riddell. Also Rusty Feinberg, a kid I'd been seeing at auditions since I was ten. When we boarded the van at five a.m. and headed to the shoot, the actress playing our mother, Diane, was already seated in back, smelling fresh and lovely but entirely absent makeup. "Diane," said Ricky in greeting; "Diane," echoed Jeff, mocking Ricky.

"Oh," she said, "*you* two palookas."

They talked and laughed during the entire hour-long ride, heckling one another about their recent evening out at Studio 54.

"It's nothing but a bunch of private school kids," said Ricky.

"Which is just how I like it," said Jeff.

"You are both so *bad*," Diane kept saying to them.

Because of the way they talked—their level of snark and jaded know-how—Ricky and Jeff seemed like grown-ups. But once we were in costume—Diane donning her wig and her mom sweater and slacks, with her lashes added and makeup done, and Ricky in his football jersey and Jeff with the sweatbands on his head and wrists—it was as if Diane had aged ten years and Jeff and Ricky were suddenly younger than Rusty and me. This happened regularly on jobs like this. It got to the point where it seemed as if more than lighting or makeup or costuming, age itself was something you inhabited long enough to get the take, until you took it off and put an adult face back on.

We shot the commercial on location, at a house in Ramsey, New Jersey. The four of us were instructed to play basketball—there was a hoop and backboard above the garage—while Rusty's mom made lunch. We could only be seen through the kitchen window in the shot, and we were off mic, so Jeff and Ricky seized the opportunity to say the nastiest things they could to Rusty and me, trying to crack us up during takes. "I'm gonna fuck you in the ass, Griffin," Jeff hissed while I drove to the basket, smashing his crotch into my butt as he guarded me. During the next take, he said, "I'm gonna give Rusty a Dirty Sanchez." Rusty pulled up and drained another shot. He passed to Ricky, who checked back to him.

"What's a Dirty Sanchez?" he asked as he dribbled.

Ricky feigned surprise, staggering backward and clutching his chest. He said to Jeff, "Let's get Mikey to try it."

"Yeah," Jeff said. "He won't eat it. He hates everything."

From the kitchen window, Diane called us in. "Boys, lunch is ready!"

Jeff waved to her. "We'll eat your pussy in a second, Mrs. Bancroft." Then, leaning in conspiratorially to Rusty, said, "Your mom gives the best blow jobs."

In the commercial's main scene, the three of us burst into the kitchen, our cheeks rosy with the cold. Rusty is already seated at the table. Jeff's line was "I'm starving." Then Ricky said, "What smells so good?" And Rusty's mom replied, "Lipton Cup-a-Soup." And I looked at Rusty in amazement, since he was already drinking the last drops from his mug. "Hey," I said, "Harley's already finished!" I must've said the line a hundred times. After each take, the director removed his headphones to consult with the four suits seated in the row of canvas chairs behind him. Then he'd turn to us and correct our delivery: "Up more" or "Not so bright"; "Heavy on the 'good'" or "Easy on the 'so'"; or "It's *star*ving, not *stah*vin.'" When they shot close-ups of the soup, which were in four coffee mugs and semicircled by all the boxes of flavors, the set designer used a dropper to add some chemicals to the broth that smelled like ammonia and made the soup produce a wisp of steam. It was all very boring and isolating, to be somewhere for an entire day taking orders but never really talking to anyone, and at the shoot's conclusion I remember catching a glimpse of Diane, seated before the makeup artist's mirror. After they'd removed her wig and the clips from her hair, her lashes and rouge, her face possessed the unique tabula rasa quality certain women are either gifted with or cursed by—they are so entirely transfigured by eyeshadow and eyeliner, by lipstick and blush, they could rob a bank in one face and disappear into obscurity in the other. She sat there blankly and buffed clean, drinking a cup of coffee, and perused the newspaper, her tired eyes enlarged by a set of reading glasses, and my thoughts turned to Naomi, since it was by now the afternoon, when we'd normally meet, and I wondered if she was driving home from work right now. And I remember being strangely certain she was, and I thought that if I were to see her, I would tell her about how, amid so much chatter, my overwhelming feeling was one of remoteness, and she would have a better word for the sentiment. Or at least help me find one. Which is to say that I missed her.

Dad liked to check in with me after these workdays. "How'd it go?" he asked at dinner. When I said fine, he said, "Well, tell me about it." I said there was nothing to tell. "What was your line?" he asked, and I repeated it like I'd been hypnotized. "Is that how you said it?" he said, a bit ticked. "I said it," I said, "times a million." My lack of enthusiasm annoyed him. "That goes national and you'll be singing another tune." When I told him, "It's not like I see a dime of it," he bristled. "You do every day you walk into that fancy school of yours." When I told him I wanted to go to wrestling camp over the summer, he said, "It depends on your shooting schedule." When I stared him down and then asked what he was talking about, he said, "They're renewing your contract for *The Nuclear Family*." When I said I hadn't signed anything yet he said, "That's correct." When I asked if I had to sign the contract, he said, "We'll talk about it." When I asked, "When?" the phone rang, as if on cue. "That's probably the agency," Dad said, bunching his napkin and tossing it on the table, and even though he was only half finished with his food, he hurried to his bedroom to answer the call. And once again I had no leverage.

Oren, eyeing his departure, turned to Mom and said, "I have a question."

She eyeballed him back but did not speak.

"Does Griffin pay my tuition?"

"No," she said. "Your father does."

Oren was visibly relieved at this. "Does Griffin pay *your* tuition?"

"I pay for mine with the money I make. And for the record, Griffin only pays a *portion* of his tuition."

"Like a fixed percentage?"

"It depends."

"On what?"

"Circumstances."

"So basically what sort of year Dad is having."

"Plus how much we put away for Griffin's college."

"What about my college?"

Mom took a sip of wine, nodded, and then placed her glass back on the table and refilled it. "We have extra time to save for yours because you're younger."

"But nothing's in the kitty yet."

"We're doing the best we can," Mom said.

Oren whistled.

"And what's that supposed to mean?" Mom asked.

"That I'm definitely getting a job this summer," Oren said.

"Maybe you should start acting," I said. I was half needling. I also thought it would be fun if we went on go-sees together.

"Maybe I'd like to have some dignity," Oren said.

"Money can't buy you that," Mom said to him.

"It can help."

"I'm not getting into this with you."

"We can't even afford to go on a vacation," Oren said.

"What is this new obsession of yours with a vacation?" Mom asked.

"I want to come back from break with a tan. Like the other kids. I want to go on a trip, for Chrissakes."

"*I'll* pay for vacation," I said. "And wrestling camp too."

Oren brightened. "Yes," he said to me. To Mom: "Yes, let's live a little."

"You're not old enough to make that decision," Mom said to me.

"But he's old enough to work!" Oren replied.

"He's still a minor, and we decide how the money is spent."

"What sort of slave-labor shit is this?" my brother said.

"Oren, your language."

"When do I get to decide what to do with my money?" I asked.

"When you're eighteen."

"What if it's gone by then?" Oren said.

"It won't be," she said to him; then to me, since I was looking at her with alarm: "Just like there'll be money saved for your college. And since you're looking for a job," she added, turning back to Oren and getting up from the table, "you can do the dishes."

After Mom left, Oren shook his head and sat brooding for a time. "You're going about this wrong," he said finally.

"How's that?"

"You want to get out of show business, you need to go all in."

"I don't understand."

"Get rich, retard. Then *buy* your way out."

Did I really miss Naomi? I wondered. Later that evening, I kept thinking about how I'd describe to her other random things I'd noticed during the shoot. That afternoon, in between takes, one of the executives had said to Diane, so that the entire cast and crew could hear, "I think we made a mistake casting a woman as beautiful as you." To which Diane—her back was to him and she was facing me—said, "Is that right, Gerald?" To which Gerald replied, "I think you're hotter than the soup." Diane raised an eyebrow at me and said, "Better not take a sip then, you might burn your lips." To which Gerald replied, "Not if I blow on it first." And while the crew and the other execs chuckled, Diane looked at me with an expression of such slit-eyed exhaustion and embarrassment, I swore I'd never speak to a woman like that in my life. And now, when I recall her tiny privacy with me, her bid for corroboration, an effort at a sort of education—woman to young man—I am reminded that someone is always eyeing someone eyeing someone who isn't eyeing them.

And what about love? One night, when I emerged from my room, I spied Dad just back from rehearsal—they'd just started doing read-throughs of the musical's book—his coat still on but unbuttoned at the throat. He seemed electrically happy, enlarged somehow, and he greeted my mother at the dining table with an expression that was decidedly hungry. She sat facing the mirrored wall, and he reached around her chairback to cup one of her breasts, which froze me, and then bent to kiss her full on the mouth—another thing I'd never seen in my life. She raised both her arms and looped them around his neck. When their lips parted, she grabbed his scruff in her fist and pulled his cheek to hers and held it there. She looked at him in the mirror's reflection, and he looked at her, and then Mom spotted me, reflected too, and her expression did not change. I felt that she'd rent some sort of veil to reveal her true face. It was suddenly clear to me that I knew her as my mother but not as a woman, a distinction I'd never previously thought to make; and that in our family's food chain, Dad was her apex and Oren and I were at the bottom.

My inability to tell Elliott about this, or any of these things—he was dozing now as I sat across from him in his office—was, I suddenly felt acutely, the very failure of mine that put him to sleep.

"It's like I'm a mute!" I said, which startled him awake.

"Whoosis?" Elliott said, and grabbed his chair's arms.

"Like I see but I can't say."

He pressed the heels of his hands to his eyes. He shook his head so hard his lips flapped. "Let's take a walk," he said, and, donning our heavy coats, we left his office.

As we crossed the street toward Gramercy Park, he swung his arms in front of him and clapped his gloved hands several times. We walked up to the park's gate, and Elliott rummaged in his overcoat's pocket. "The most coveted key in New York," he said, holding it up for me to behold, and then opened the lock. He pulled the gate shut behind him, and we entered the tiny one-block-by-one-block rectangular space. Snow crunched under our feet as we cut through its path. Pigeons snapped their wings and rose like ash. On the fence's perimeter, the bundled pedestrians were smokestacks, were steam engines.

"You know who that is?" Elliott said, and thumbed at the statue to his right. I didn't answer. "Edwin Booth." When I shrugged, he explained: "The actor. He founded the Players club. Right there"—Elliott pointed at the mansion across the street: wrought-iron guarding the balconies, gas lanterns flickering, a purple flag limp in the cold. "Older brother of John Wilkes Booth, who . . ." he said, and waited.

"Assassinated Abraham Lincoln?"

"Correct. Now, Edwin Booth, like his father before him and both his brothers, was an actor. I read an article about the family a few days ago. They *hated* each other, by the way."

"Who?"

"The brothers did. Well, John Wilkes hated Edwin. Their father died when John was thirteen but he was clearly haunted by him. Wanted their dead dad's love so bad he tore himself up fighting for it—Junius Brutus Booth was the father's name. They don't make names like that anymore! If your father had a name like that, it would give you an inferiority complex too. Anyway, he desperately wants Pop's approval, so what does he do?"

"Assassinates Abraham Lincoln?"

Elliott shook his head. "He goes into the family business. Brother Edwin's already made a reputation for himself as Hamlet, by the way. Becomes the ne plus ultra of the Prince of Denmark. You know what that means?"

"The best?"

"Better than that. The ultimate."

"Like Brando in *Streetcar.*"

"*Exactly.* Now, John, he's considered the handsomest man in America. But he isn't getting anywhere *near* the cachet as his big brother. You know what *cachet* is?"

"Is it French for money?"

"It's *prestige.* As in admiration. So what's his solution to this dilemma, you think?"

"He assassinates Abraham Lincoln?"

"He defines himself *over against* his brother. Edwin's a great Shakespearean actor, John Wilkes becomes a naturalist. Brother won't take sides in the war, John Wilkes allies himself with the Confederates. Brother wants to abolish slavery, John Wilkes goes all in for antimiscegenation."

"What's antimiscegenation?"

Elliott stopped and smiled. He placed one hand on my shoulder and, with the other, patted my chest in approval. Then he took my elbow and we continued to walk. "It means he was against interracial marriage."

"Do you agree with that?"

Elliott shrugged. "If my daughter were to bring home a Black guy, I'd prefer it were Sidney Poitier, but to each his own. My point: John Wilkes is entangled, understand? He sees one path to love blocked and does the opposite. But there's no freedom in doing the opposite, okay, because always doing the opposite is automatic. It *binds* you to the person you're trying to break away from. It *intertwines* you with the very thing you profess you don't want to be. And John Wilkes knows this. On some precognitive level, he realizes he'll never out-fame his brother and win his father's approval, that his path to eros is obstructed."

"What's eros?"

"Love," Elliott said. "The life force. The engine of our best actions." He smiled because I was smiling as he waxed poetic, and this encouraged him to be hammy. "The flower opening its petals to the sun."

"Ah," I said.

"So what's John Wilkes's solution to this predicament?"

"He assassinates Abraham Lincoln!"

Elliott gravely shook his head. "That's just the means. He does what his brother couldn't. He enters history."

Elliott had a bit of the actor in him too. Most times, I didn't mind.

"Who had the better life?" Elliott asked me. We had exited the park by now and began looping around its fence back to the office. "Edwin plays Hamlet all over the world. Manages the Winter Garden Theatre. Has a daughter by his first wife. Names her Edwina, by the way. How's that for narcissism?"

"So who had the better life?" I asked.

Elliott shrugged. "It's pretty obvious, but here's my point. Back in the office you said you felt like you were speechless. That you had things you saw but struggled to communicate. Those are the two most heartfelt things you've ever shared with me. So maybe that's what you've been put on the earth for. To come up with a language for your life."

Admittedly, I had no idea what Elliott meant. Was finding a language for my life like a job? So far as I could tell, I had three of those. Fall through spring, I was a student, which I figured was just a way for me to do my real job, wrestling. But since I was spending the summer playing Peter Proton, and this funded the other two, maybe all of them were under the umbrella of "actor." I did have hobbies. Since third grade I'd drawn superheroes. I'd collected comics for as long as I could remember, and I'd been working on my own comic book for nearly three years that was more than a hundred paneled pages long, contained in a binder that sat on my desk, one I sometimes caught Oren leafing through with an expression between envy and amazement. Mom called it my "magnum opus." That Sunday, at a party at Elliott and Lynn's house, standing before the buffet with Al Moretti and his new boyfriend, Tony, he asked me, while he loaded his plate with smoked fish and bagels and cold cuts, "So, Griffin, what do you want to be when you grow up? You gonna become a famous actor and make millions?"

"I want to be an artist for Marvel Comics," I said.

Al frowned. "You'll get over that," he said.

Oren came up to me, miffed. "Sam Shah said he'd bring his Ferrari, but it doesn't look like he's coming."

"When'd you talk to Sam Shah?"

"I call him for advice sometimes about my career."

"What career?"

"Precisely," Oren said. He had made himself the most beautiful bagel: the lox draped over vegetable cream cheese with a tomato and red onion, these topped with capers and layered with sprigs of dill. "That guy is super smart," Oren continued, and took a bite. "He was telling me that the greatest inventors and entrepreneurs, like Thomas Edison and Michelangelo, they recognize a thing before it exists and then make what people didn't know they wanted."

"Like what?" I asked.

"Walkmans," Oren said, and then shrugged. "Parachutes."

"Who invented the parachute?"

"Michelangelo, idiot."

"That sounds like something Elliott would say."

"Actually, I ran that by Elliott last week. He told me the American Indians have a name for this: a 'vision quest.' And he said that imagination is the true form of time travel. Which makes sense, when you think about it. That you dream up something in the present and it lives in the future until you build it. Which was also the first time Elliott and I ever really talked about anything worth a shit."

"I'm glad Elliott has more of your *cachet*."

"What the hell does that mean?"

"Approval, idiot."

"Yeah, well, Elliott also said that if I didn't bring up my grades, the only job I'd be qualified for would be one replaced by androids."

"Do androids actually exist?"

"Not yet, but according to Sam Shah, the future's in automation. Also free trade."

"What's free trade?"

Oren held up his bagel. "Cheaper Nova."

I felt a twinge of disappointment that I wouldn't be seeing Naomi, but it was eclipsed by a feeling of relief that she wasn't coming, which was replaced by the same feeling I'd felt during the commercial, being around all those people and invisible at the same time. It was so intense I wanted to hug Oren when he checked his watch and said, "Let's go to Elliott's bedroom and watch *In Search Of*." Because he was my brother, he was always there; ever since the fire, he was my once-upon-a-timer, and I loved him maybe more than anyone else in my life.

We were going to Captiva.

Our parents' announcement about our spring break travel plans was unexpected, which only created that much more excitement between my brother and me. Oren said he knew a couple of "fly chicas" from his school who went every year and that we had to get buff for these ladies, so before bed we moved the dining table toward the windows and did push-ups in front of the mirrors and some Jack LaLanne calisthenics and also dug out the dumbbells Dad had stored in the back of his closet— "curls for girls," Oren called our sets. "You know what washboard abs are?" Oren said, doing his best flex. "Male cleavage." The week before we left, Oren and I went to Brooks Brothers to buy new bathing suits with the fifty dollars Dad gave me to spend from my commercial money. "The red Speedo," Oren said to me, "no question." And then, in what I wasn't sure was an imitation of Dad, added, "*Very* European." That night, from his bunk below me, Oren fantasized about all the activities he'd do when we were at the resort.

"I want to jet-ski and go snorkeling and play tennis," he said. "Or maybe sailing. I'm gonna get a Saint-Tropez tan. And I want to collect seashells and make a whole *necklace* of them, like puka beads but bigger. Do you want me to make you a necklace? Because I will."

And on certain evenings when Oren was done with it, he lent me his copy of the Swimsuit Issue. "It really gives you a feel for the place," Oren said. The articles were boring, but there was an ad that caught my eye. It read like a public service announcement and reminded me of the sorts of conversations I overheard the adults having at Elliott and Lynn's get-togethers:

THE REUNITED STATES OF AMERICA

At Time Incorporated, we happen to believe that Americans *united* can solve any problems America faces.

That's why, in late February, our seven magazines will speak to their 68 million readers on a common theme—"American Renewal."

Today most people see nothing but crisis around them. Inflation. Energy. Declining productivity. Weakness abroad and a breakdown of the political machinery at home.

There is a spreading sense of powerlessness . . . a feeling that, as individuals, we can't make a difference anymore.

Time Incorporated disagrees.

But I mostly looked at the pictures. And while Oren preferred Christie Brinkley to all the other models; while he could not help draping page fifty-two over his face, what with her nipple discreetly poking against her red suit's fabric, or pressing the two-page spread of her against the bottom of my mattress slats, as if he were benching the entire top bunk (Christie sat with her nearly naked back to the camera, on the shell-covered sand, at sunset, while terns wheeled and swooped over the Gulf), I crushed on Carol Alt, that slender, angular, wolf-eyed brunette, whose wavy hair for some reason the editors chose to corral in a bathing cap for most of her pictures, but who, in my favorite photo, let it be blown freely in the prevailing breeze as she lay supine among the sea oats, propped on her elbows in a brown-and-white snakeskin bathing suit. Clenched in her teeth was a single reed, its firm stalk slightly indenting her glossy lower lip. There were captions to all these shots, partly advertorial, that I pored over as if they contained secret information:

> On the beach on Shell Island, a boat to match one's suit is noth-ing to skiff at, and lucky Carol's handsomely harmonized ensemble includes a maillot by Moi ($60).

"It's not *mail-lot*," Oren said when he heard me practicing the word. "It's pronounced *may-yo*. And it just means one-piece."

Our suite at the 'Tween Waters Inn was on the second floor of the Gumbo Limbo building—a long, blue-roofed stucco building with two floors—and it had a view of Manatee Cove, Roosevelt Channel, and Pine Island Sound. "I figured it would be like this," Oren said with amazement, "but I didn't know it would be better!" We stood in the walkway's shade and leaned on the railing, feeling the wet-warm breezes. We each had a map of the resort the concierge had given us, and pointing to our left, Oren shouted back into the room, "Dad! I can see Adventure Sea Kayak Rental. Can we rent kayaks today?" To which Dad said, "We just got here, cool your jets!" And then Oren said, "I can see Captiva Water-sports too! Can we rent Jet Skis today?" To which Mom said, "First you can unpack your clothes and put on your bathing suit." But now Oren was pointing out past the sailboat slips at the humped backs and dorsal fins of a pod of dolphins wheeling far off on the water. "Look," he said, "there really are dolphins at Dolphin Lookout!" And then he raced off— "I'm going to go swim with them," he shouted. When I shouted back, "Wait for me," he said, "Look who's talking," and disappeared. Left to my own devices, I put on my swimsuit and slathered myself in tanning oil, since Tanner, who spent every spring break in Barbados, said the worst thing you could do on the first day of a tropical vacation was get badly sunburned. I grabbed a towel from the bathroom, took my map, told my parents I was going to have a look around, and then left our room.

Tweenie's Pass looped through the resort, and I walked it past the dock at Manatee Cove, down among sailboats' masts that gonged and pinged in the marina, and eyed the price lists at Captiva Watersports, which offered waterskiing instruction and catamaran rentals, and since Dad had been in the navy, I figured that he could maybe take us all sailing to save some money. I peeked in at the Pelican Roost Boutique and Snack Center, which had diamond-encrusted seashells and dolphins in jewelry cases, sunsets airbrushed on coral, Kadima paddles, and baseball caps and sunhats that read CAPTIVA IS FOR LOVERS or MY PARENTS WENT TO CAPTIVA AND ALL I GOT WAS THIS LOUSY T-SHIRT. I spotted the Gulf twinkling in the distance. I crossed Captiva Drive, a busy two-lane road whose noise, I realized, I'd mistaken for the surf. I admired the palms that lined the beach, their leaves clacking in the wind. The umbrellas set up by the shore were a darker turquoise than the water, the water an opal I had never beheld in person. The waves were more wavelets when I got to where they broke, and after taking off my flip-flops, I let them lap and purl at my feet. The only ocean I'd ever been in was the Atlantic, which, even in late summer, held beneath its waves a threat of cold. But the Gulf's waters were the temperature of a warm bath. And considering this contrast, one I'd liked to have shared with Oren, with Mom or Dad, with anyone—a pair of twin boys built a sandcastle to my left—I thought, *There it is again.* That feeling I'd had at the commercial shoot. I decided to go find my brother.

On my way back to the resort, I ran into my parents on their way to the beach. My father, who hated to take off his shirt because of his chubby breasts, was wearing his khakis rolled up well above his ankles and a shell-pink polo. He was also carrying his leather satchel, as if he'd just been teleported from an audition in Manhattan. Mom wore a bikini with a floral wrap around her waist, her bug-eye sunglasses, and a big, floppy sun hat, which she clutched to keep on her head; in her free arm she carried a pair of novels and a yellow legal pad with notes for her master's thesis. "Where're you going?" she asked me, to which Dad, with some annoyance, said, "Let him go." I crossed Captiva Drive again and then took the path toward the Crow's Nest Bar & Grille. I wondered, as I always did, if the *e* in "grille" was pronounced; I figured that Oren would know. As I walked toward the tennis courts, I thought I heard my brother's voice, and when I spotted two boys playing, I was sure one of them was Oren. But when I walked up to the windscreen that surrounded it, I saw this girl instead.

She was a brunette like Carol Alt, but her hair was straight and slicked back in a wet ponytail. She was tan, like she'd already been here several weeks, and was wearing a white tank top, which revealed two pink circles on each of her shoulders where she'd been sunburned and had already peeled, but looked like scars where wings had been torn off. Her long legs were lustrous and brown down to her ankles, which were delicate and pretty, cupped by her blue pom-pom socks. She was playing with a woman I guessed was her mother because they so strongly resembled each other. What was even more impressive about both of them, the whole time I hung on the chain-link fence, which I soon realized was probably long enough to be creepy, was that during their cross-court rally, they not only managed to keep a single ball in play but, even after I'd left them to go find Oren—someone, anyone—to tell of what I'd just seen, I could still hear the ball tocking regularly behind me on the Har-Tru like the beating of my heart.

"Griffin!" Oren shouted as I walked by the pool.

He was sitting at the bar with another boy. Two years younger than me, and he had no problem getting served. Oren wore a bucket hat with a palm tree insignia stitched into it. On his face: a pair of Ray-Ban Aviators that he'd bought for the trip. His friend was a hulking kid with long hair almost down to his shoulders that half covered his eyes and who was wearing a T-shirt with cut-off sleeves and basketball shorts. When I got a little closer, I noticed that his diminutive right hand was curled violently at the wrist, and his fingers stuck out stiff and pinched together at the tips, so that elbow to digits the appendage resembled the inverted neck and head of the Loch Ness Monster. Both of them were drinking piña coladas.

"Cocktail?" Oren said.

"Sure," I said.

"Virgin or regular?"

"What's the difference?"

Oren looked at his friend. "A cherry," he said. And they laughed.

"My brother, Griffin," Oren said to his friend. "He goes to the best private school in New York City. How he got in and I didn't is a complete mystery. Although Mom says his grades were so bad, they probably didn't think I could cut the mustard."

"Frazier," Frazier said to me, and stuck out his Plesiosaur hand, which I, stung by Oren's jab, pulled at twice in greeting.

"Frazier's from Dallas," Oren said. "His family comes here every year." Then Oren said to the bartender, "Hey, Kessler," who looked up from the glass he was cleaning. "A Bacardi colada for my brother, please."

"I just saw the most excellent girl," I said.

"Where?" Oren said.

"Tennis courts."

Oren squinted like he knew something. "What was she wearing?" he asked.

I told him.

"What color hair did she have?" he asked.

I described it.

"She could really play, right?"

"Like Chris Evert, but if she looked like Brooke Shields."

Oren glanced at Frazier, then nodded seriously. "I saw her too. That's Regina Goodman," Oren said, "she goes to my school."

I got my drink, took a long suck on the straw.

"Go slow," Oren said, "those are one-fifty-one proof."

I waved him off and said, "Tell me everything."

To Kessler the bartender, Oren said, "Gumbo Limbo 225, please," and then slid him a five-spot. "Take care of me this week," he added, to which Kessler winked back; and then we three went to sit by the pool under the blazing sun and cloudless sky and the log-drumming of the palm leaves, and Oren, who was covering himself in Coppertone, told me all about Regina Goodman, with whom I was falling utterly and completely in love. I took off my shirt as he spoke, squirted some more Hawaiian Tropic on myself, which pooled in my belly button and made my pasty skin look like it had been rubbed in chicken grease. "You missed a spot," said Frazier, pointing at my shoulder. I hung on my brother's every word.

Regina was a sophomore at Ferren and a tennis star. She was from a really rich family. "You know Bergdorf Goodman?" Oren said.

"You mean across from FAO Schwarz?" I said.

"She's *that* one," Oren said.

"What grade is she?"

"Sophomore. But here's the thing about her," he continued. "This is top secret, okay?"

"All right," I said.

"I mean if you're looking to get with her," he said.

"I'm listening," I said.

"She likes younger guys." She'd even dated his best friend Matt this year.

"But he's in eighth grade," I said.

"No shit, Sherlock," Oren said. "And she *always* makes the first move." In fact, he explained, she *only* made the first move. "Don't even bother asking her out if she doesn't ask you. Maybe it's a rich-girl thing," Oren figured, "who knows? But if *she* approaches *you*, you're in like Flynn. She wrote Matt a letter. He found it in his locker. 'Maybe sometime we could get milkshakes,' she said, 'and by *sometime* I mean tonight.'" They met up at Baskin-Robbins that day, Oren said. Matt got a cookies and cream shake, Regina got cherry vanilla, they walked straight back to her apartment in the Dakota, and then bingo: "Matt lost his virginity to her that night."

"Cherry vanilla." Frazier chuckled and shook his head.

"This is unbelievable," I said.

We each drank two more Bacardi coladas, during which time I thought about how Bridget had that funny run but was fun to talk to, while Deb Peryton and I could barely carry on a conversation but she was a good kisser, whereas Regina was clearly a great athlete and I was a John McEnroe fan, so probably we had plenty to talk about between wrestling and tennis while we held hands and walked along the Gulf, once I got her to notice me. This was the last thing I remember thinking before I woke up to discover Oren and Frazier were gone, the pool's surface was littered with palm leaves, and my skin, pink as uncooked pork, felt like the heating element under a stovetop's glass.

. . .

The next few days were miserable. My sunburn was so bad that by the first evening my nose, chest, and shoulders had blistered. That night, Mom made me take a cold shower and then slathered me in Solarcaine. *"Stops sunburn pain,"* Dad said, peeking in my bedroom, *"when someone you love is hurting."* The next day, Mom insisted that if I wanted to go to the beach or pool, I had to don a long-sleeved shirt and a hat and apply zinc oxide to my nose and lips. The tops of my feet were so badly burned they hurt too much to wear flip-flops. "Maybe he should wear socks," Oren suggested, a little cruelly. I couldn't do any of the things the rest of the family was doing.

Or, in the case of my father, wasn't doing. He could not bring himself to sit still on the beach. When he joined Mom and me—I had to remain in the cabana's shade—he did not read like her or even swim with his shirt on, like I had to, because he never took his shirt off. "The sand gets stuck between my toes," he said to Mom. His black bathing trunks showed off his pelican legs. He nodded at the water. "Beautiful view," he said, rattling the ice cubes in his plastic 'Tween Waters Inn cup. "What are you reading?" he asked Mom.

"The Portrait of a Lady," she said.

He said, "Hemingway loved Captiva, didn't he?"

"That was Key West," Mom said, "and this is Henry James."

He sang a few notes from his new musical.

Mom said, "Why don't you go get your tape recorder and flash cards. You can put on your headphones and learn your songs."

Dad said, "Think I'll go for a walk instead." To which Mom, resting her open book on her belly and folding her hands over it, said, "Why don't I join you?" To which Dad said, "You stay. *Relax.*"

Then he marched down the beach until he was inches tall, until he disappeared. He stayed gone for a while. Then I saw him returning, his mite-sized silhouette growing like Ant-Man. When he got back, he said, "Fabulous shells," and then fell asleep on a chaise with a towel over his face. When he woke, he said, "Think I'll go back to the room and check my service."

"What are you going to do if you get a booking," Mom said, "fly home?"

My father shrugged. "Think I'll go for a drive then," he said.

"Why don't I come with you?" Mom said.

"Get some reading done. Enjoy yourself."

"Why don't you take a ride with your father?" Mom said to me.

"I'm gonna find Oren," I said, and hurried after Dad, who was trudging across the sand to the resort's parking lot. He didn't notice me until he was in the driver's seat of our rental car.

"Sure you don't want to come?" he asked.

I told him no thanks and went exploring.

It was midday and the tennis courts were being watered.

Our room, whose terrace curtains ballooned in the warm breeze, was chillier because of my sunburn.

The fishing boats had long ago abandoned their slips for their day trips.

Neither Oren nor Frazier nor Regina were anywhere to be found.

Over those several days, when I wasn't dreaming of Regina (as we sailed on a catamaran, when we caught a sailfish, when we went to a clam bake, when I bought her a necklace with a diamond-studded dolphin pendant), I stalked her all over the resort. I followed her if I saw her headed somewhere. I sometimes ran around buildings so that I might walk directly toward her and catch her eye. When I did, I'd nod. If she nodded back, which she did, occasionally, and giggled, I figured maybe it was because there was an attraction, but it also could've been my zinc-slathered face. Either way, I was encouraged. I spied her once leaving her room, which was, to my surprise, in the Sea Grape, which had a view of the Gulf but was also right on the road. Once I saw her and her mother exiting the spa—a typical rich-girl thing to do. It was on this occasion that she looked at me and really smiled, and when I told Oren about it that night he said, "I don't believe you."

"Why?"

"You're not her type."

"What's her type?" I asked.

"Not sunburned," he said.

And on these recon missions I often found Oren and Frazier doing everything Oren had hoped to on vacation. From the room's walkway, I spotted them jet-skiing on Roosevelt Sound. I could hear Oren scream, "Woooohooooo!" as the machine *punt punt punt*ed atop the water. How did he get so good so fast? And it was amazing to watch Frazier balance on the machine, his hand like a trained pet riding alongside him, while he used the other to clutch the handlebars. In my broad-brimmed hat and sunglasses, my long-sleeved shirt and sweatpants, my socks and laceless sneakers, my nose and lips zinced, I might stop by the courts to watch Oren and Frazier play tennis. Frazier's forehand was a cannon. His one-handed backhand was a thing of beauty too, finishing his swing with both arms outflung. When he served, he pinched both the ball and racquet handle in his good hand and, with the wrist of his bad one, brushed his bangs from his eyes. He tossed the ball in the air, and as it hung above him at its arc's zenith, he readjusted his grip, twisted with all his big-bodied torque, and sent a kicking serve into Oren's court. Somewhere, somehow, and without my knowledge, Oren had managed to learn to hit very respectable strokes in return. He and Frazier could not kayak, but they did take out a catamaran, which Dad had said he knew how to sail but maybe next year. And on the second-to-last day, just when my burn had healed enough that I could wear shorts and short sleeves and hang with my brother, Frazier and Oren departed at the crack of dawn for an all-day deep-sea fishing trip with Frazier's father.

That was when I got the note from Regina.

I was applying sunblock in the bathroom. Mom was out collecting seashells. Dad, who was listening to the music for his show's songs and singing the verses, stopped and said, "This came for you." It was a pink 'Tween Waters Inn envelope with my named double underlined, and inside, on 'Tween Waters Inn stationery—also pink—in a bubbly, girly-girl script of fat *g*'s and *b*'s and hearts dotting the *i*'s, read:

Dear Griffin,

 Your brother and I go to the same school and he suggested I write. I have a tennis lesson at ten this morning but was thinking you could meet me when it's finished and we could take a walk down the beach? Maybe go for a swim? Explore Manatee Cove? I'll wear my bathing suit underneath my skirt. Maybe you could bring the towels and the tanning oil?

 OXOXOX,

Regina

"Oh my God!" I said to my reflection, to the air.

"What is it?" Dad said. "Did you get a part in a movie?"

"I have to take another shower," I said, and closed the door on him.

I bathed again in order to remove the zinc from my face. After I toweled the steam from the mirror, I noticed there was a bright pink stripe from my nose's bridge to its tip. But the peeling wasn't *so* bad, especially on my shoulders and across my chest after I used Mom's Oil of Olay. From the kitchenette, Dad sang a song from his show, *"You're the birdsong, you're my morning, you're the sun on the leaves . . ."* Then he rewound the tape, consulted his flash cards, and sang the same three lines again while adding another. I brushed my teeth twice to get rid of my coffee breath. From my father's Dopp kit I borrowed his dental excavator, scraped some plaque from between my bottom teeth, and then, after rinsing the tip carefully, used it to pop an unripe zit on my chin. I spent the next fifteen minutes dealing with this crisis, since a perfect globule of blood kept forming atop the puncture no matter how much pressure I applied to its crater. Dad sang, *"You're the flowers, you're the pollen, you're the buzzing of the bees . . ."* and then rewound the tape. I put on my Jensen's Marina & Cottages T-shirt that Dad had bought me on one of his jaunts, which had a giant tarpon on its front. I pulled my cutoff jeans over my Speedo and slid into my flip-flops, despite the lingering pain. I tucked two 'Tween Waters Inn towels under my arm and, sandwiched between them, my bottle of Hawaiian Tropic dark tanning oil.

What did I think would happen? What did I imagine Regina and I would do? What would she and I talk about? I flip-flopped toward the tennis court, wondering. Like the pelicans gliding effortlessly toward the Gulf, I felt so light and hopeful. I heard the ringing sound of Regina's strings as they contacted the ball. I spotted her lovely form divided into diamonds behind the chain link fence, and I watched her shadow play against the windscreen. She was finishing up her lesson with a volleying drill. The pro, whose face was as tan as Naugahyde, said, with each ball he fed her, "Step on the bug," and every time she stamped her foot, she kicked up a small cloud of dust. To conclude he said, "Finish on a good one." Which Regina did—a sharp crosscourt stab, which the pro watched and then nodded at approvingly.

Afterward, Regina sat on the court's bench, facing me for a while, drinking her water and toweling off. I waited, towels in hand; I waved to her once. Indicated: *No rush.* A couple entered the court. The pro said, "David, Alice, I was just finishing up." Regina waved goodbye to the pro and, racquet pinched under her arm and a towel wrapped around her neck, walked toward me. She opened the gate, smiled, and then, as she closed it, said, "Hello."

"Hello," I said.

As she turned and began to walk toward the beach, I said, "I brought some towels."

She smiled. "I have one, but thanks."

When I said, "Okay," she started to walk toward Captiva Drive. The Gulf sparkled in the distance. My mouth was so dry I couldn't swallow. I was about to speak, but at the Sea Grape suites, Regina turned and began to walk up the steps leading to the building's second floor.

"Should I come with you or wait down here?" I asked.

She turned to face me and smiled. "Do I know you?" she said.

"I'm Griffin, Oren's brother."

Silence.

"You wrote me a note," I said. "To meet you after your lesson and go to the beach together."

"I think you have me confused with someone else."

"You're not Regina?"

"I'm Meredith," she said. "And I have no idea what you're talking about."

Then she hurried upstairs, her sneaker soles scuffing each slightly sandy step with the sound of a struck match.

I found Oren and Frazier at the bar later that afternoon. They were celebrating their last day together and their fishing trip. Oren was wearing a shell necklace he'd made on the ride back; his aviator sunglasses hung at the bottom of his collar's V. He and Frazier were drinking daiquiris. When I joined them, Oren said, "I caught a sand shark! It's almost four feet long. It's in a cooler by the dock if you want to see it."

"Congratulations," I said.

"I'm gonna release it later if you want to come." When I didn't answer, he said, "I could use your help. Because it's so big."

"I'll bet it's a whopper," I said.

Frazier took a long pull at his drink. "How was your date?" he asked.

"Ha-ha," I said. "Very funny."

"Admit it," Frazier said, "your brother got you hook, line, and sinker."

Were it not for his hand, I'd have punched him square in the mouth.

Oren could tell I was crushed. "We have to meet my parents at the Crow's Nest Grille for dinner," he told his friend. *So,* I thought, *no e.*

Frazier got up. "See you next year," he said.

"Yeah," Oren said, and poured his daiquiri's remainder down his throat, "don't count on it." Then he knuckle-bumped Frazier, and they parted. Oren watched him go and then said to me, "Want to see the shark?"

We settled up and left. To my dismay we walked past Meredith and her mother on the way toward the docks. "Hi, Griffin," she said. "Hi, Oren."

As we passed the sailboats, Oren couldn't stand the silence any longer. "It was Frazier's idea. At least the part about the note."

"Whatever," I said.

"You've got to admit the handwriting was convincing."

I was so mad my eyes were welling up. "Who'd have thought Frazier was such a good forger," I said.

"His sister did it," Oren said, as if this were a consolation.

The sailboats' masts clanged when a gust kicked up. Kerosene rainbows slicked around the fishing boats. A stray cat crossed our path. An osprey flew low over the bay. I looked around. So far as I could tell, we were alone. Oren noticed this too. At the end of the dock, beneath a winch for weighing fish, with a huge hook attached to a rope, was a large cooler.

Oren opened it.

The sand shark lay half submerged in the water. It was big enough that it could not completely straighten out but was curled uncomfortably, like a cramped muscle. When the sunlight hit it, as if sensing the bay beyond its confines, the fish thwapped and thumped its tail against the cooler's walls, swung its head, and sent its saving element splashing. We stood looking at the fish as it struggled, and then it stopped.

Oren said, "I'm really sorry."

I said nothing in response.

"Please," he whispered.

I grabbed him by the collar and foot swept him. I followed him down to the deck, so that his head slammed against the dock. I pinned his biceps beneath my shin so he couldn't cover up, and I grabbed his throat. I pulled his necklace's fishing line till it snapped; when it did, the shells skittered. I punched his aviators on his chest once, twice, until both lenses shattered. I grabbed his hat and chucked it into the bay. I grabbed a fist of my brother's hair, right at the forelock, lifting him until he stood. Then I pushed him off the dock, into the water. There was a splash. And when he surfaced—he was coughing—I lifted the cooler over my head and flung it at him, the shark, midair, flung from its confines, landing with a great smack, the cooler's base donking Oren directly on the head. And then the creature disappeared into the depths while Oren treaded water and stared at me, red-eyed, but did not cry.

It was pouring on the day we returned. The cab from LaGuardia Airport smelled like wet wool and cigarettes, and the sky was gray as soot. The windows were opaque with droplets of rain, reflecting everyone's terrible mood. So little had been said on the flight home. Oren had sat with Mom, I with Dad. We both had window seats, and the entire flight Oren was either staring out his or had his face in his book on cars. He refused to acknowledge me. It had been thus since I'd beaten him, and I wanted to get on my knees and beg his forgiveness, I felt so much shame at my eruption. Because it *was* a good prank, I thought, credit where credit is due, I wanted to tell him that. Even now, in the cab, as Dad chatted up the driver, a behavior of his that drove us both crazy, Oren sat staring at the wet mess that was Grand Central Parkway.

Back home, Oren immediately left for Matt's, and Mom and Dad went to their room and shut the door. When I called Cliffnotes to tell him I was back, he said that he was taking his Intellivision console to Tanner's house. Mr. Potts had just gotten a forty-five-inch TV, and they were going to play *Sea Battle* on it. Did I want to come?

On the bus ride across town, we watched the rain. It was one of those downpours that seemed to have caught people unawares. Pedestrians ran down the streets with newspapers over their heads. Others, hatless, walked soaked, disconsolately. Lightning flashed, strobe-like, a rare event in March. Thunder clapped.

When we ran into Tanner's building, Sean the doorman said to us, "Someone shot the president!" He had a small closet off his desk and, on a shelf inside, a tiny black-and-white TV.

"Shot him as in killed him?" Cliff asked.

"Shot as in shot at," Sean said.

Tanner's elevator opened onto two apartments, and his parents always left their front door unlocked. In spite of this, Cliff and I made a point to ring the bell before entering. Tanner greeted us topless and in a bathing suit, like he'd just gone swimming. He was as dark as a mug of Ovaltine but his hair, normally brownish blond, was as white as his puka-shell necklace.

"You bleached your hair," Cliff said.

"Fuck you," Tanner said. "It was the sun."

Cliff was laughing. "What'd you use, hydrogen peroxide?"

"Lemon juice and beer."

"And chemicals," Cliff said.

"Strictly speaking, citric acid and alcohol are chemicals." Wanting to change the subject, he took in my pink-streaked nose and shook his head. "I warned you," he said.

On the Pottses' new television, Frank Reynolds was reporting live from the ABC newsroom. He was stiff-backed and wooden in his delivery. He had a deep voice like my dad's, but it was absent human feeling and toneless, though he was clearly shaken: . . . *and shots were fired apparently at President Reagan as he was coming out of the Washington Hilton this afternoon. The president was* not *hit. He was pushed into his limousine and immediately taken away to safety. However, three persons were* hit. *We believe they are two Secret Service agents and the president's press secretary, James Brady.*

Tanner said, "How many presidents were assassinated?"

"Kennedy, Lincoln," I said, "probably more."

"Yes, probably more, brainiac, but how many?"

"Garfield and McKinley also," Cliffnotes said.

"How do you remember so much?" Tanner said.

"I don't shampoo with antiseptic."

Tanner dead-armed him. Cliff, pissed, rubbed his shoulder. "Let's set up the Intellivision," Tanner said.

The TV was easily the size of a dresser, the giant screen set in a walnut housing with the speakers hidden behind a black cloth grille at its base. It had a remote control, really futuristic, even smaller than a Walkman, which Tanner let me hold while he began to slide the TV back from the built-in cabinets.

Cliff asked, "What are the specs on this thing?"

It was the difference between Cliff and Tanner and me that they could talk this sort of tech.

"It's got a three-tube, three-lens system for super high definition. You can only see the dots up close. Check it," Tanner said.

Cliff and Tanner put their faces right next to the screen. The static electricity made their hair stand up and adhere to the glass. "Whoa," Cliff said. "Look at all those pixels."

"Plus four two-way speakers," Tanner said.

"Crank it up, man."

Tanner aimed the remote at the screen until the sound blasted.

We now have the videotape.

Reagan is walking out of the Hilton.

Here you see the president coming out now. We just have to watch.

Reagan waves to his right, smiling. A Secret Service agent is right behind him and there are police all over.

I don't know if I can hear this or not.

Reagan turns to his left and, facing the camera, waves again. Shots are fired.

There, there! Shots . . . God!

Clap clap clap clap clap clap, and the camera dives to the right, to a pileup, a scrum of Secret Service agents and police against the building's brick.

Tanner said, "That guy said 'motherfucker.' Did you hear him? He said it on *TV.*"

The Black Secret Service agent screamed, "Get him out! Get him out!" which I figured meant Reagan.

"Dang!" Cliffnotes said. "That guy is like G.I. Joe!"

"Check out that Uzi!" Tanner said. "Do you see the Uzi that guy's got?"

There was a bald man, facedown, blood pooling at his head. Behind him, a pair of other men were being tended to. Then, with much shouting, the scrum hustled the assailant into a squad car.

Then they replayed it from the beginning.

Reagan comes out. He waves. This time, I watched one of the Secret Service agents turn, stick out his arms, take a bullet, and then spin to the ground.

We all sat down on Tanner's couch.

Then they replayed the shooting.

"That one Secret Service guy took a bullet for the president," Tanner said.

"He just spread his arms and *blam*," Cliff said.

"That's what I'd do," Tanner said. He stood to the side of the screen, spread his arms, winced from the bullet, and then leaped into the air, doubled over, and fell.

"People start shooting and most people freeze," Cliff said. "Others start crying. And others start shitting, literally. But only a few take a bullet."

"What makes you such an expert?" Tanner said from where he now lay on the floor.

"That's what my father said," Cliff said.

Then they replayed the shooting.

Reynolds said, *Mr. Reagan was* not *hit, he was bounced around as the Secret Service agents maneuvered or flung I think is probably the right word—flung him into the car. To get him out of there. The president then went to George Washington University Hospital, where those who were hit were taken. They include Jim Brady, who is the president's press secretary; a Secret Service agent; and a policeman. We don't know their condition, but quite obviously as soon as we find out anything . . .*

Tanner's father walked into the apartment. He was just back from grocery shopping, still in vacation mode but wearing a blazer beneath his raincoat, the latter dotted with droplets.

"Dad!" Tanner said. "Someone—"

"Put a shirt on, you little faggot."

"Someone tried to shoot the president!"

"Hey, Mr. Potts," we said.

"Griffin," said Mr. Potts. "Cliff."

"He hit—"

"Turn down the volume, you're going to destroy my new speakers."

"He hit three other people," Tanner said.

"Go put a shirt on right now or you can kiss your friends goodbye."

Tanner left the room to put on a shirt.

"You should've seen it," I said to Mr. Potts. "One of the Secret Service agents had an Uzi."

"He said 'motherfucker' on TV," Cliff said.

Mr. Potts got a big kick out of this.

Tanner came back in wearing a T-shirt. "One of the Secret Service said 'motherfucker.'"

"Watch your language," Mr. Potts said, and winked at me.

I said, "The new TV is really awesome, Mr. Potts."

"Thank you, Griffin," Mr. Potts said. "How about that picture? Tanner, what the hell are you doing?"

Tanner had gone back to sliding the giant unit out from the cabinets. "I'm setting up Cliff's Intellivision."

"You'll do no such thing."

"What's the point of having a nice TV if we can't play video games on it?"

"Keep it on the news, this is important."

Mrs. Potts walked in. She was wearing pearls and black heels; her tan raincoat was also beaded and her cheeks were flushed.

"I heard someone shot the president," she said.

"No one shot the president, Sharon. He missed."

"I said they shot him," she said, "not *hit* him." The Pottses had sudden spats like this all the time, though now Mrs. Potts doubted herself. "At least that was what Sean said downstairs."

Sam Donaldson had joined Frank Reynolds. He had a phone next to him, and all the cubed lights on it were flashing. He picked up the receiver, placed it to his ear, hung it up.

I said, "Sam Donaldson sort of looks like Martin Landau from *Space: 1999*."

Mr. Potts chuckled at this. "He does, doesn't he?"

"Hey, Mrs. Potts," I said, "you kind of look like Barbara Bain."

"I don't know who that is."

"He's right," Mr. Potts said, "but you're prettier."

"Is that an apology or a compliment?"

"It's both," said Mr. Potts.

Lyn Nofziger has told reporters at the hospital that the president was not wounded . . .

Mr. Potts said, "Griffin, is your dad the voice on that Schlitz commercial? With the guy from *Get Smart*?"

"No one does it like the bull," I said.

"Bet he made a lot of shekels on that."

"Ay caramba," Cliff muttered.

Off camera, another reporter spoke to Frank Reynolds, after which Reynolds's shoulders slumped.

He was wounded!

"Turn it up, please," Mr. Potts said.

My God . . . he was . . . the president was *hit . . . he is in stable condition. All this information—* The pages Reynolds was holding in his hands shook. *The president* was *hit. He was hit in the left chest. According to this . . .*

"Can you hear that?" Mrs. Potts said.

"Hear what?" Tanner said.

"Exactly," she said, and nodded at the screen. "All the typing in the newsroom has stopped."

She was right. Off camera and off mic, someone in the newsroom said to Donaldson and Reynolds, *One shot. Stable condition.*

Reynolds, furious, pointed at the reporter off camera. *Speak up!*

The reporter repeated himself.

Reynolds said, *The president* was *hit . . . One . . . My God . . . The president* was *hit . . . All this that we've been telling you is incorrect.* He took a long beat to gather himself. *We now must . . . redraw this entire tragedy in different terms.*

Softly, Mrs. Potts said to her husband, "Drink?"

"Thank you," he said, his voiced lowered too. "Martini, please."

"Good idea," Mrs. Potts said.

Before she could walk away, Mr. Potts gently took her elbow, pulled her to him, and, keeping his eyes on the television, kissed her half on the mouth. She half-kissed him back.

Now we have been told—ABC News has been told by a doctor at the hospital—that one lung of the president has partially collapsed.

Over Reynolds speaking, the image crosscut to the shooting, but this time in slow motion. Now that I'd seen it so many times, there were several things I noticed that I hadn't before. An old man, a bystander, in a red cardigan, leaned into the scrum as they subdued the shooter, helping the Secret Service agents pin him against the hotel's decorative stone wall. The blood around James Brady's head was diffused at its edges by the rain. In slow motion you could see the agent who took the bullet raise his eyebrow in the millisecond before impact, the muscle twitching first at the shot's sound, and who did, upon being struck, something like a scissor kick as he leaped in the air, as if the momentary separation from the planet allowed the bullet's force to pass through him. The cop in front of him, who, even with bullets flying, pinched the brim of his hat with both hands so that it would not fall off. And there was a roughhouse quality that approximated care as the agents formed a testudo around the shooter and hustled to a nearby police car. Which was to say that every time they showed the event, I realized that in several seconds so many things occurred you could spend a lifetime trying to understand just how everything converges on the now. And I reflected that men like John Wilkes Booth, Mark David Chapman, and this unnamed shooter were entirely committed to the role they'd decided to play. It was the unspoken aspect of what Elliott had observed in Gramercy Park.

I'm going to give you the name of this, uh, man that has been reported to us as the assailant, simply because everyone else has been reporting his name. He is John W. Hinckley Jr. That is the report we have. John W. Hinckley Jr. And it is understood that he is from Evergreen, Colorado . . .

Without a shred of self-consciousness, with no space between the mask and your face, you enter history.

TAKE TWO

By early April, a warmer sun shone through thin scudding clouds, the wind still stung with some of winter's lingering sharpness, but opening day at Yankee Stadium touched the low seventies. *Eyewitness News* weatherman Storm Field said the unseasonable temperatures would continue, and when it did rain, dead earthworms appeared in the concrete's cracks and the flowers planted on the crossing islands bloomed. It was a Friday, and my audition that afternoon was at a movie set, on location, at an East Side town house, on Ninety-Second Street between Fifth and Madison—a reading, Brent had explained, for the director himself, "for Alan Hornbeam," he said to me over the phone, after Miss Abbasi brought me the note in American government to call my agent. My parents went to see all his movies as soon as they came out. Mom was an especially big fan. "He specifically asked for you," Brent said. I'd never heard him sound so excited. He explained that Hornbeam had a stable of actors he worked with in movie after movie. "You could grow up with him, Griff. You would be *made.*" Apparently, at the very beginning of production, the teen actor in the featured role had a family emergency that forced him to suddenly quit the production. There was a scramble to replace him. It was a tremendous opportunity, Brent said. "It's a two-week shoot," he added. "Maybe three. Knock his socks off." Normally,

I'd have given this opportunity little thought, but ever since Oren had mentioned that my best way out of show business was through success, I thought I might bring just a tad more intentionality to this audition than usual. Plus I'd just seen Jodie Foster interviewed at Yale about her relationship with John Hinckley Jr., about the love letters he'd written her, especially the one before going to shoot Reagan: "I am doing all of this for your sake! By sacrificing my freedom and possibly my life, I hope to change your mind about me." She had no idea who he was, but I was struck that she had a normal life now, that she was a regular college freshman. Ignoring the fact, of course, that her stalker had tried to kill the president to impress her.

There was a pair of trailers outside the town house where they were shooting the film, the windows of which were covered with blue density gels. Pedestrians slowed or joined the onlookers at the shoot's blocked-off perimeter, straining behind the sawhorses that read POLICE LINE DO NOT CROSS. The location crew behind these stood with the indifference of zoo animals, accustomed as they were to being watched. I made my way through the crowd to the gofer, who greeted me and checked my name off a clipboard. People eyed me like I was someone important, and it took all my self-control not to turn to look at them like my father might and nod as I was welcomed into the empyrean. The gofer pulled a walkie-talkie from his belt and said, "I've got Griffin Hurt here to see Alan." He got clearance and bid me to follow him. A pair of thick black cables ran up the building's steps, into the entryway, and through the foyer, whose diamond-checkered black-and-white marble floor was covered with plastic, up the stairs to a second-story living room. As on every movie set, this room was suffused with the same combination of bustle and idleness as an operating theater; a muffled quiet, library-like but hectic; the stuffiness of bodies and equipment and tech crammed into the space: the low hum of power draw and the heat coming off the sound-board and the monitors, and the klieg lights, whose glare was unforgiving, set up for a shot framing the sofa and love seat. The two cables ran toward this tableau and behind a wingback chair, in which Hornbeam was seated, so that by an accidental trick of perspective, and because of his diminutive size, it was as if they were the impossibly long feeding tentacles of a giant squid.

Hornbeam stood to greet me, although when he did, he was still shorter than I was. There were people all around us, camera crew and soundmen, the gaffer and the boom operator, and while they were not entirely unaware of our presence, they were at the same time quietly busy and preoccupied. They spoke in low tones, and their inattention conferred upon Hornbeam and me a sort of invisibility that helped tamp down any self-consciousness I might feel or nerves I might otherwise suffered. Only the makeup gave away the fact that Hornbeam was in costume: he wore a pair of worn-out sneakers, khaki pants, and a patterned button-down shirt with the sleeves rolled up. His tortoiseshell glasses were so large they seemed more prop than corrective. He bid me sit, and when he sat, he placed his elbows on the armrests and folded his hands together. Hornbeam's nose was steeply humped at its bridge, his thinning hair was hippieish in length but wisped at the temples and had mostly fallen out up top. His wrists and forearms were slight; his palm, when I shook it, was slightly damp. He was an actor too, known for his antic persona; he starred in most of his pictures, but in what seemed to me an intentional contrast to this—as if Hornbeam the comedian were impersonating Hornbeam the director. He spoke so softly and seriously, even after we moved past formalities, that I had to lean forward to hear him.

"I very much liked your work in *The Talon Effect*," Hornbeam said. "Especially that scene at the dinner table, with the entire family, where your father is telling you and your older sister how the Senate will be in session through most of the spring and he'll be stuck up in Washington for a long time. Do you remember this?"

I said I did.

"And your sister just blows up at him," Hornbeam continued. "She lays into him about how he never comes to anything of hers—not her performances or sports, that he's never around. And your mother tries to referee. To explain to your sister how busy he is. And to your father how much you both miss him. Though it's clear when she's saying all this that she misses him and resents him too. And you watch all of this just"— Hornbeam raised his hand and made a C with his fingers—"clutching your glass of milk. It's making you that upset. And then your sister storms off, and you and your mother and father watch her go. And when your parents' eyes are on you, you're framed in close-up and you take this big drink of milk. You chug the whole thing and then put down your glass. And your line is something throwaway, like 'May I be excused?' But the milk's left this thick mustache on your lips. Because you're still just a boy. You don't understand all this pain. You *love* these people. And I was wondering: Were you given direction to do that?"

I had never analyzed the scene so carefully, had never thought about it this way, though I did recall attending the premiere with my family and how Dad leaned toward me after the scene concluded to whisper, "Now that, my son, is *acting*." In response to Hornbeam's question, I told the truth. "It felt right to give myself the mustache on the first take. After that, Mr. Schatzberg told me to do it every time."

A smile flickered across Hornbeam's mouth, and then he indicated the several pages we'd be reading on the coffee table. "I'll give you some background for this scene," he said. "The film's about an actor-director named Konig. Your father. Me. You're Bernie, his only child. Your mother has recently divorced Konig after discovering he had an affair with the star of his previous picture. We're talking big New York scandal here, Page Six, the works. Meanwhile, you and your father have never really gotten to know each other. He does a film almost every year and as often as not only sees you on a set like this. In fact, this scene you're about to read takes place in this living room, which isn't your family's living room but a living room on one of Konig's movie sets. Capisce?"

"Capisce."

After I scanned the pages a couple of times, Hornbeam asked, "Ready?" I nodded, and speaking his lines from memory, he became his famous, high-strung self.

```
                    KONIG
      It's not that I feel like I should
      apologize to you about how I treated
      your mother. Although she's the only
      woman in human history who after asking
      me to—I don't know—pass her the salt,
      made me want to say I was sorry for
      withholding affection.
```

                    BERNIE
Dad—

                    KONIG
Even the night I impregnated her with
you I apologized. Which if you're
wondering how I know the date of your
conception, it's because that was the
only time we'd made whoopee all year.
Which is another thing I probably
shouldn't be sharing.

                    BERNIE
Mom doesn't—

                    KONIG
You know my therapist says that if I
shared less with the people I loved,
my relationships with them would be
healthier. Which is a paradox, when you
think about it.

                    BERNIE
She doesn't blame you for what you did.
She says you're a serial monogamist who
suffers from a Madonna-whore complex and
the signs were in your films even before
you met. She just ignored them because
she loved you.

                    KONIG
Well, tell her I'm sorry for that too.

   I paused before saying my last line and reached out to squeeze Hornbeam's shoulder, I don't know why, I just did things like this sometimes
during scenes—gestures that came out of nowhere.

BERNIE
Maybe tell her that yourself.

Hornbeam tensed ever so slightly when I touched him, but then, with
something between suspicion and surprise, he looked at my hand and
then at me. And then he uncoiled, his expression melted into deep affection, into something between gratitude and pride, as if I *were* his son. We
took a long beat, and then he broke character and, satisfied, sank back in
his chair. The script supervisor, who'd been watching, stood clutching
her binder to her chest and smiled. The cinematographer sat on the jib's
seat, chin in hand behind the camera, and approvingly nodded. And I
had that feeling—one I'd experienced during casting readings before—
that was practically telepathic. There had occurred between Hornbeam
and me that conjuring of a connection, that making of a true moment—
one in which the lie is like life—which is a performance's own sort of
magic. In short, I knew I had nailed it. I have come to trust this gut reaction, and while it never guaranteed I got a part, it was a thing between
the other person and me that could neither be taken away nor forgotten.
After a beat, Hornbeam said, "Excellent." Then he stood and reached out
to shake my hand once more and held it for an extra beat. "We're about
to shoot a scene if you'd like to stay and watch."

Hornbeam's grip was firmer this time. I took this pressure less as an
invitation and more as a bid. I realized, I mean, that to say no would be
to neglect a necessary demonstration of interest. I was also, I confess,
strangely intrigued; I'd been moved by our exchange. I thought of all the
onlookers at the barricades, and here I was, inside. It was a privilege to
stay, after all. And what else did I have to do? I thanked him and went
to stand by the windows facing Ninety-Second Street, next to one of the
grips while he adjusted a diffusion panel. There was a bit of a delay waiting for Jill Clayburgh to take her place along with Shelley Duvall. The
makeup lady appeared and touched up both women's faces. Like nearly
all film actors I'd ever met, there was something outsized about the features of each woman. Clayburgh's mouth was disproportionately wide.
While Duvall, thin as a needlefish, was as tall-necked as Alice after eating
the caterpillar's mushroom.

"Quiet on the set, please."

"Quiet on the set."

"Roll sound."

"Speed."

The AD held the clapboard in front of the lens. "Seventy-two Apple, take one."

After the clack, Hornbeam said, "And . . . *action.*"

But there came a great commotion outside.

The audio engineer, irritated, shucked his earphones. "I've got pickup," he said, and nodded in my direction. Hornbeam checked his watch, muttered, "Cut," and, along with the entire crew, turned toward the windows. The grip I stood next to was already watching outside. "This," he said to me, and pointed, "is just the best part of my day."

Across the street, the Nightingale-Bamford School was letting out. Because it was so bright and balmy, all its students were congregating out front. More girls gathered in one place than I'd ever seen in my life, filling the block, their blue kilts and white blouses adding to this thronged effect: girls talking to girls, girls milling about, girls calling out to one another. A girl, here and there, standing alone. The noise they made was something louder than recess, a sound between laughter and slaughter, as if the school itself were shouting. I stared at them and, before I knew what I was doing, before I made the conscious decision to leave, I walked out of the room, down the stairs, out of the town house, and then onto the sidewalk. I crossed the street toward the school. Six stories tall, Nightingale's brick facade blazed orange in the afternoon sun, while still more girls poured from the entrance's bright blue doors to mass below the second floor's giant bay windows. These faced out from what appeared to be a theater or an assembly hall, high-ceilinged as it was, and were raised to welcome these breezes, carrying on them the park's scent of mud and grass and stiffening Nightingale's two flags: America's and the school's blue pennant. The auditorium's tall windows opened onto a wrought-iron balcony running their length. Girls sat along this too, tightly bunched, their backs pressed to the short railing, chatting shoulder to shoulder with their neighbors. Others called between the grate on which they sat to classmates on the street below. There was some strict rule against standing on it, I gathered, for they awkwardly peered over their shoulders or between its diamond-shaped pickets and ornamental

fittings but would not lean out. I was in the midst of them now, surrounded at both eye level and above; I turned a full circle once and then
gazed up at this terrace, marveling at being so swarmed, until the girl
sitting on the balcony's corner turned to look at me.

She had blond hair, thick and curly, that she'd pinned back almost
brutally, and a very high forehead. Thin lips. A lightly blued darkness
beneath her eyes. Through the thin pickets' iron, she smiled at me. And
a great silence fell, followed by a blurring of everything beyond her distinct figure: a deep focus that was closer to calm. She sat clasping her
knees and resting her cheek upon them, and she held my gaze tranquilly,
contemplatively, as a cat might, stretched in a store window, confident
and undisturbed behind the glass. It was her vividness, coupled with this
quieting of all background, that was so unique and novel I was afraid to
move. Twice in my life, perhaps, would I subsequently recall being so
captivated by the sight of someone, would time itself feel so arrested. But
this was the first. Its effect was at once clarifying and total. Any feelings
I'd had for Deb or Bridget or even Naomi paled and were then erased.
And then she glanced at something behind me. This released me from
whatever eddy in which I'd drifted, in which we'd been stuck; the whole
hubbub suddenly resumed, and, shaken, I turned to see a trio of boys
shambling up the block.

They were from another private school—Dwight or Collegiate, I
could not say. Their shirttails had sprung from their belts; like mine,
their collars were unbuttoned. They carried their blazers over their
shoulders and shouldered their backpacks. Wading into this crowd,
they seemed unfazed by Nightingale's horde. They said hi to several girls
who in turn said hi back, then made straight for the school's entrance.
At the blue door, they were greeted by a student with a clipboard, who
checked off their names and ushered them inside. When I turned again
to look toward the terrace, the girl had disappeared. I hurried toward the
entrance after the trio, certain, somehow, that they'd lead me straight to
her.

The greeter dragged a finger down her list, unable to find my name.
She asked me to repeat it and then squinted at me as if I were lying.
"Follow me," she said, and led me inside. Girls were still racing past us
and out of the school. Girls came running down the stairs we climbed,

elementary-age girls in pairs and trios jumping the final steps. A couple
of times the greeter looked over her shoulder at me, dubiously, as if I
were playing some sort of joke on her. After passing through another
set of double doors, we arrived at a stage's wing. "Shhhh," she said to me
before I could speak. The three boys were waiting here, along with several others milling about. It reminded me of weigh-ins before a wrestling
match. They were watching a boy onstage as he performed his monologue. When he finished, he cupped his hand to his ear and then spoke
to someone I couldn't see. He said thank you and exited the stage toward
us. Before directing the next boy to take the stage, the greeter took his
picture with a Polaroid camera and wrote his name on its white border.
I waited, watched, listened. The breezes gusting through the windows
mostly drowned out his voice when he began to speak, and then the boy
after him. How much time passed? Everything seemed to take forever
and happen in a blink. Until finally the third boy took the stage, leaving
the greeter and me alone, and she leaned toward my ear. She was taller
than I was, broad-faced and big-boned. She wore mascara and heavy
makeup, like a mom.

"*You're* Peter Proton," she whispered. "My little brother was you for
Halloween."

The boy's monologue had just concluded.

"He's your biggest fan," she said.

"I saw this girl," I said to her.

"I'd ask for your autograph, but he wouldn't believe me—"

"She was sitting on the terrace," I said. "Blond hair." And I pulled
mine back so hard it made my eyes slant. "Like this."

The greeter frowned and crossed her arms. "Oh," she said. "I know
exactly who you're talking about." She held out a clenched hand to
inspect her fingernails. "I can introduce you if you'd like."

"Really?"

"Maybe if I took your Polaroid and you signed it," she said.

I nodded, and she aimed the camera at me and took the picture. She
handed me a Sharpie and, after I signed the photo, said, "Follow me,"
and led me to the edge of the wing and then stepped aside and pushed
me onstage.

Beneath me, standing in the center aisle, was the teacher holding tryouts. She apologized for running so long. She had draped a sweater over her shoulders and bowed its arms across her chest. She introduced herself, and her name was obliterated from my mind, because the girl from the balcony was seated on the floor behind her, with her palms pressed to the floor and her legs outstretched, one crossed over the other. She had a friend with her, just as pretty, who had a shock of strawberry-blond hair. The friend scrunched her nose at my appearance, but the girl recognized me from earlier. She seemed pleased I'd found my way here, and her readiness to be entertained I took as both an invitation and a challenge.

"Do you have something prepared?" the teacher asked. "Or would you prefer to read from the play?"

"Yes," I said.

The girls giggled. The teacher turned to shush them.

"I have something prepared," I said.

"Whenever you're ready then," the woman said, and sat.

I began my Shakespeare monologue from Miss Sullens's class last semester. I had needed to memorize only ten lines for the assignment, but for extra credit, and to impress Miss Sullens, I'd learned it all. I spoke the lines of both characters to set the scene, shuffling to the left for one and to the right for the other. " 'I dreamt a dream tonight,' " I said. " 'And so did I.' 'Well, what was yours?' 'That dreamers often lie.' 'In bed asleep, while they do dream things true.' 'O, then, I see Queen Mab hath been with you.

" 'She is the fairies' midwife,' " I continued, and to indicate Queen Mab's size, "no bigger than an agate-stone / On the forefinger of an alderman," I stuck out mine and then closed one eye to consider its pad, which allowed me to stare at the girl's face down my sight line and consider her for a moment unabashed. As I painted the picture of Mab's carriage, "drawn with a team of little atomies," I made my hand gallop from the top of my head and then "over men's noses as they lie asleep." I closed my eyes and snored; my snoring startled me awake. I described Mab's wondrous vehicle, its "waggon-spokes made of long spinners' legs, / The cover of the wings of grasshoppers, / Her traces of the smallest spider's web, / The collars of the moonshine's watery beams." And while I lashed this team with my cricket's bone whip, which I pinched as if it were a toothpick, I turned to Mab's wagoner, "a small grey-coated gnat," who was suddenly bounced from the car. I watched him buzz about my head and land on my cheek. And bitten there, I slapped myself, so hard that the crack, which knocked me sideways, caused my audience to cover their mouths and laugh while I regained my balance. "'Her chariot,'" I continued, "'is an empty hazel-nut,'" and I held out its shell in my open palm toward the girl, so that she might look at it more closely. "'And in this state she gallops night by night / Through lovers' brains, and then they dream of love.'"

Applause followed. The teacher stood and clapped vigorously. As with my Hornbeam audition, I knew I'd killed it. She mentioned the character I'd be playing, which, like her name, was instantly erased from my memory. She also handed me the rehearsal schedule, said we'd be starting next week, and asked if I had any conflicts. "No conflicts," I said, distracted, trying to hurry things along, since the girl and her friend had gotten up and left the auditorium. The teacher confirmed the school I attended, and then took my phone number. I thanked her and jumped off the stage, straight into the auditorium, and then bashed through the doors. I looked in both directions and ran through the now deserted hallways and then down the stairs and out of the building.

I spotted the girls on Fifth Avenue, walking uptown. Once I'd caught up, I kept a good half block between us. I was in a state of high alert. It was unclear what I should do next, although the girl occasionally turned around to walk backward, just a couple of steps, thumbs tucked beneath her pack's straps, to confirm that I was still there and, with a slight nod, indicated I follow, until her friend grabbed her elbow and turned her around. They stopped at the Ninety-Seventh Street corner and waited for the crosstown bus. I joined them but remained at the edge of the crowd of passengers gathered there. I checked my watch. How had it gotten so late? I occasionally looked in the girl's direction, and each time I did it seemed she'd just glanced in mine. Her friend cleared the heaped mass of hair from her eyes and glared at me. Her disgust blew my chin east, like a weathervane. But here was the bus, finally, which stopped and growled, its engine giving off a hot diesel stink, its doors' pistons popping and hissing when they opened. The girl kissed her friend goodbye; her friend frowned at me as I boarded. I resisted the temptation to wave to her, *ta-ta*. The tokens, as the driver pressed the plunger, jangled like maracas filled with pirates' gold. The doors folded closed and the light changed, we entered the Central Park transverse, and soon we were at speed.

The bus was crowded, but somehow the girl had managed to secure a seat in the rear corner. I swung gently back and forth on the straps, catching glimpses of her as we raced crosstown: she was watching out the window, which she'd slid open; she was staring directly at me; she'd closed her eyes and was smelling the early-evening air. The setting sun's light and the trees' lengthened shadows streaked across her face. The park's high stone walls ripped by. We stopped at Central Park West, then at Columbus. She did not get off at Amsterdam but stood as we approached Broadway and pulled the bell's wire. The bus creaked to a stop, and she followed the passengers off, past me, and made her way down the rear exit's steps. Before the doors closed, I pushed them open and followed her again. She walked halfway up the block; I walked behind her half as slow. Then she turned around, waiting until I stood before her. She adjusted her book bag on her shoulder before she spoke.

"That whole ride you could've talked to me," she said.

I realized I was smiling.

"Do you have a name?"

When I told her, she said, "I'm Amanda West."

"Amanda West," I repeated back to her.

"You're not much of a conversationalist," she finally said. As if to confirm her observation, I offered no reply. "I liked your performance," she said. She had gray eyes—a color I'd never seen before. "I couldn't have done that," she continued. "Get up onstage and just . . . be someone else." I decided not to disagree. "Okay," she said, "since the cat's got your tongue . . ." Then she reached out, took my wrist, and turned my hand palm up. From her jacket pocket, she produced a ballpoint pen and bit off the sea-blue cap. Its end, I noticed, had been chewed off. She wrote her phone number on my skin and, when she finished, closed my fingers over the digits.

"When you get up the nerve to speak, why don't you give me a call?"

It was the diorama hour, when evening is just beginning to descend and everything is brilliant and discrete. When the city seems scrimshawed on a lit bulb. The lights in stores have just begun to shine through their windows, their interiors part of the exterior. The spring air, now that the sun had fallen behind New Jersey's towers, had a touch of coastal chilliness. Beneath us, the 1 Train rumbled into the station and groaned to a stop. Amanda looked over my shoulder and then let go of my hand. From the south, just cresting the hill, a bus appeared. Its roof lights were as bright as ladybugs; its corrugated siding seemed made from a thimble's steel. In its emerald interior, a shade as vibrant as a horsefly's eye, the passengers swayed. And in that cicada quiet, since the city is always in a state of ambient noise, Amanda waved goodbye and then boarded. The doors closed, and I watched her ease toward the back, the vehicle gargling as it departed, which conferred the illusion of her standing still before me, for just a moment longer, before being ripped from my sight.

Headed above Ninety-Sixth Street.

That borderland.

Where no one else I knew lived.

I got the part in the Hornbeam film.

I was still in a daze when my parents greeted me at the apartment with the news. They met me at the door as if they'd thrown me a surprise birthday party. I had committed Amanda's number to memory on my walk home; I'd walked the entire distance in a state that felt much bigger than happiness. Borne aloft and weighed down, the way swimming underwater can feel like flying. Dad said, "I'm proud of you, boychik," and cupped my cheek in one palm and kissed the other. Mom said, "Way to go, kiddo!" and when she hugged me, she slapped my back several times. Oren, standing behind them, tapped his index finger to his temple as if to congratulate me for taking his advice. All of them mistook my bemused expression for a sense of accomplishment, although I cannot say I was displeased.

"They're messengering over the script," Dad said. "Brent's coming by in a few minutes with your contract."

Oren said, "Do you want me to help you with your lines?"

To everyone, Dad said, "My son, landing a starring role, just like his father."

Mom said, "I'll call your teachers Monday and get your homework together for the rest of the week."

Dad said, "Maybe drink some coffee tonight and read the script through."

When the fact that we were all crowded in the foyer finally dawned on us, Mom said, "Let's eat dinner and properly celebrate."

The script arrived later that evening. One of the gofers brought it over along with my call sheet. My shoot lasted just over two weeks and began on Monday. Sprinkled throughout were several days when I'd be free to attend school. The script had a blue cover, its pages held fast with gold binder clips. In embossed letters were the movie's title, *Take Two,* and below that, WRITTEN BY ALAN HORNBEAM.

"I'm gonna take a bath," I said. I deposited the script on my bed, then went to the bathroom and locked the door. I undressed, lit two of Mom's candles, and turned off the overhead light. I made the water as hot as I could handle. I gingerly sank into the tub while it filled and let my body acclimate. It was the first time I ever recalled being grateful for acting. Oren was right. It was my all-access pass across police lines. It was my secret password through those blue doors. It had introduced me to Amanda. In the tub, I pinched my nose and then slowly submerged my head. I did this a few times, trying to recall the entire experience of meeting Amanda. Her delight when I took the stage, which was partly surprise, I was certain, that I'd found my way to her audience. How I could feel my pulse's small fillips when she took my wrist in her hand. And that moment, perhaps above all, on Broadway, just before her northbound bus appeared, when the place on my palm where she'd written on it was still wet and to be gently clasped, as if I held a guppy. These images bobbed before me and then disappeared, like the Hudson's wavelets. I bobbed along with them. I blew a long stream of bubbles until I'd emptied my lungs; I believed that if I drowned now, I'd die happy. I'd absorbed most of the water's heat, so I got out of the tub and turned on the light. In the mirror's reflection I saw my skin was bright pink.

Mom had written my call schedule on the inside cover of the script and marked each of my scenes with their corresponding shoot date on Post-it notes. I filmed two this upcoming Monday, both with Hornbeam. Only in the first did I have any lines ("She's my math tutor" and "I don't know. Fifteen? Why?"). There, memorized. I lay on my bunk with my fingers laced behind my head. The only sound in our room was the hiss from Oren's headphones and the distant murmur of the television coming from my parents' room. At some point Oren turned off the light and said, "Good night." At some point I climbed down from my bed to look at him. He lay facing the wall and I said his name.

"What?" he replied.

"I met a girl," I said.

"When?" he asked.

"Today," I answered.

He asked, "Can I retake the test tomorrow?"

I sighed and then wandered into my parents' room. In the television's blue light, which was lambent and flickered, I stared at them sleeping. Dad, facing me, had a fist bunched at his temple; Mom, lying on her back, had her forearm draped over her eyes. They both slept with their mouths open. They reminded me of the plaster casts of the victims of Pompeii, held fast in the moment just as they'd cried out. I turned the TV's knob, and the screen dissolved from Johnny Carson wearing his Carnac the Magnificent costume into a single dot.

I put on my sneakers and left the apartment. At the elevator bank I pressed UP. While I waited, the three shafts howled with the drafts. The car arrived. I stepped on and pressed thirty. The smell of curry, as I rose past eight, coming from the Sinais' apartment. Arrived, I entered the stairwell and walked up the single flight. At its landing the steel door had a metal stile that read PUSH TO EXIT—ALARM WILL SOUND, but the door was already ajar. I shouldered it open and walked onto the roof's great yawning space. Against the black sky, the nightscape glowed all around me; like a crossword, the buildings' faces were gridded with diagonals of lights and shaded squares. The Empire State Building's antenna shined white in the distance. High-altitude gusts, frosty as an opened freezer, mingled with the warmer updrafts. The roof offered a compass-rose view of the city: south toward the harbor, east toward Lincoln Center, north toward the George Washington Bridge, and, from its Jersey-facing side, where I took a seat on the ledge, the Hudson, black as tar. The occasional car horn rose up to sound near my ear. There'd been an accident on the West Side Highway; the north- and southbound lanes slowed. The traffic's red-and-white counterflow lengthened and contracted like an earthworm. Was it safe to say that on the entire island of Manhattan I was the only person seated this high outside? What I was certain of was that for the first time in my life, I wanted to get to know someone. Just the fact that I knew nothing about Amanda seemed a terrible deficit—one that I had to remedy as soon as possible. That I might address this lack organized my horizon, oriented me in every direction, like this view, and comforted me. Because I could now name this feeling I'd been suffering, one that had dogged me of late, during our vacation and afterward, but that I recognized from all the way back to the fire. It had been so omnipresent it was more like an atmosphere—one that, having been made aware of it, I could neither unsee nor unfeel, and its name was loneliness.

DUNGEONS & DRAGONS

The following Monday morning, Dad escorted me to the shoot. I could tell how happy he was about my role because he flagged a cab instead of us walking up to Amsterdam to catch the northbound bus.

Dad said almost nothing while we rode. When he did break the silence, he spoke only to the driver: "Take Eighty-Sixth across, please." When I asked him if we could go by our old apartment, even though it would be farther uptown and cost more, he said, "Actually, driver, take Ninety-Sixth." My desire was only partly nostalgic. While we waited for the light to change on Broadway, I scanned all four corners of the intersection for Amanda. I had an overwhelming urge to tell my father about meeting her but wasn't sure how to begin. Mostly I wanted his advice about how many days I should wait to call her. Dad had rolled down his window. His curly hair was damp and drying in the breeze.

"Are you rehearsing today?" I asked, because he was particularly well dressed.

He nodded. "There's a run-through this Friday at the St. James," he said. "I'm hoping you'll all come see."

With so little traffic, we raced down the street at highway speed. We passed Boyd Prep on our right, and I smiled at the thought of missing school, at this jailbreak freedom, and Dad, noticing where we were as well, turned to me and mirrored my expression, and it felt like it was *our* city, the one its nine-to-fivers rarely got to see, the one we, not caged by such hours, sped through, unimpeded, and enjoyed. I thought about Oren's advice, and it occurred to me that, were I to become famous, I'd never have to go to school again. Was that something I wanted? The park's smells as we entered the transverse were pungent and fresh. The birdsong was still audible when we stopped at the Fifth Avenue light.

"I met this girl," I said. "She gave me her number."

But Dad had become preoccupied. We were headed down Fifth, and the moment we turned east onto Ninety-Second Street, he said to the cabbie, "It's the movie set up there on the left." And I forgave him this bit of showing off because I was desperate for his answer.

"But I didn't want to call right away," I said.

"Wait two or three days," he said as he paid, hurriedly, and checked his watch. "That way you don't seem overanxious."

The gofer greeted us at the police barrier. When Dad tried to enter with me, he said, "I'm sorry, Mr. Hornbeam doesn't allow guests on set."

Dad's eye twitched. "But I'm his father."

"It's a strict policy."

Dad glanced at me, as if for help, then said to the gofer, "I'm an actor as well."

"You could be President Reagan and it wouldn't make a difference."

Dad blinked several times. I could tell he was disappointed. He'd skipped the Y this morning and shaved at home. He was wearing a nice shirt, slacks, and his tan Paul Stuart coat. And it dawned on me that he'd dressed for Hornbeam, he'd assumed he was going to meet him, and that the introduction might be consequential. That he'd considered this an audition of sorts.

"All right, son," he said, perhaps a bit loudly, maybe a smidge pissed, "have a good day at work." He pulled me toward him by the shoulder, kissed my forehead, and watched me leave. But when from the top of the town house's steps I turned to wave goodbye, he was talking to a pretty lady carrying a toy poodle. She pointed at me and he nodded—"My son," he said—then scratched the dog's ears.

After makeup, I positioned myself before the same living room window to watch the Nightingale entrance for a sign of Amanda. I eyed the girls strolling up the block, most with friends and a few of the younger ones holding their parents' hands as they were dropped off at school, but did not see her. Soon the street was empty of students, the blue doors had closed, and, disappointed, I settled in to work. Which meant a lot of waiting for setup, and for Diane Lane, who played my math tutor, to get done with makeup as well. Jill Clayburgh and I chatted. She too had just come out of makeup and stood with the odd stiffness of being fully in costume. She told me she admired how relaxed I seemed, given how challenging it was to arrive on set like this, midstream, as it were, no table reads to go by, no preproduction direction from Hornbeam, and that I should feel free to ask her any questions.

Diane Lane, who'd just joined us, said the same. When Clayburgh asked me what I thought of our characters' relationship, I, entirely unprepared to answer—I still hadn't bothered to finish the script—told her I was going to ask her the very same thing. She said she thought I was understandably protective of my mother, a dynamic reinforced by the fact that I was more like a father to my father, since he was as impulsive as a child and his absence in my life had made me the man of the house. Which, when you thought about it, Clayburgh continued, also made me the surrogate husband to my mother. "In short," she said, and bumped her elbow to mine, "you're a psychoanalyst's dream."

The living room where we were shooting had been transformed, swapped out with new furniture. When I asked Lane why everything was different, she said, "Last week they finished all the scenes that take place on Konig's movie set. Now we're shooting the ones that take place in his actual town house. They even swapped out the chandelier." She winked. "Don't worry, I won't tell Mr. Hornbeam you haven't done your homework." Then she put a finer point on it. "Not that I'll have to."

Several run-throughs later and we were ready to shoot. In the scene, Lane and I have just finished our tutoring session. I am walking her out, through the living room, and when she stops to briefly check in with Clayburgh, Konig, introduced to her for the first time, can't help but make chitchat. His interest is obvious; he is gobsmacked by her beauty; he is like a father talking too long to a gorgeous babysitter he's already paid for the night. In the midst of our third take, Hornbeam broke character and said, "Cut, please." He pulled me aside.

"When Diane and I are talking," he said, "I want everything here"—he aimed two fingers at his eyes—"like a tennis match: Diane, me, Diane, me. Until we're finished. And then give a quick glance at your mother. To gauge her reaction. And then react to *that*." He added, "You were with us on the last take, but then Jill read her line and your attention went kablooey. Are we clear?"

"Yes, sir."

"Just maestro will do," he said.

Hornbeam, amid all of this—between directing and acting and everything else going on—had noticed exactly where I was and where I wasn't.

Lane raised an eyebrow as if to say, *Told you.*

That afternoon, when Nightingale dismissal paused the shoot, I looked up from my script and scanned the auditorium's terrace for Amanda, and each time the blue doors opened, I watched hoping she would be the next one through. It had been three days since we'd met, and based on Dad's advice, I decided to phone her that evening. And later, when I took the same bus home that we'd ridden crosstown, I gave our first encounter an imaginary do-over, mustering my courage and taking the seat next to her, where I sat now, in reality, in order that we might chat during the entire ride. And being in the mood for pretend, having not bothered to get my makeup removed, in the hope that I'd run into her again, and noticing several straphangers notice my too-vivid features on my already too-large head—an oversight, it was not lost on me, that was not only meant to call attention to myself but was straight out of Dad's playbook—I took another imaginative mulligan and, in this version, did the even bolder thing: I hopped aboard the northbound Broadway bus with Amanda, saying something clever as we took our seats and began our journey uptown, something Hornbeam would say, or Konig, a line straight out of a movie, like "Take two."

I made the call to Amanda that night from my closet study, since it was here that I had the most privacy. I took a break from reading through the script and, finally mustering my courage, dialed Amanda's number. But the line was busy. I tried again a few minutes later. Same. I passed the time looking at Dad's photographs, which he stored in boxes stacked beneath my floating desk. There were hundreds of eight-by-ten and five-by-seven prints, along with contact sheets from when he was in the navy. There was a smaller box that contained pictures from my parents' honeymoon: of Anthony Quinn, his arms draped over my mother's shoulders; on the deck of the SS *Cristoforo Colombo,* which they'd sailed to Europe. Of Mom on a chaise longue on the ship's deck, bundled in a coat and blanket and reading. Of Mom, beaming, as she stood beneath the Eiffel Tower. It was not lost on me that their happiness of late—that is, since Dad had secured this role—most closely resembled these photographs from their earliest years. And smitten as I was, I too believed I understood the desire to sail off into the future with someone. I would tuck in Amanda's topside blanket so that she was comfortably cocooned and later we'd dance the night away after loads of champagne. Except I would leave the movie star stateside. Unless *I* was the movie star. Which, it occurred to me, was entirely possible and would not, when I thought about it, be the worst thing that could happen to me.

I dialed Amanda's number again and this time it rang, just as my father opened the door to the closet and gave me a slip of paper. WHILE YOU WERE OUT, it read.

"This woman left a message for you," he said, and handed me the note. FOR: *Griffin,* it read. *Urgent. Mrs. Metcalf. Please call.* I didn't recognize the name or number.

I cupped the speaker. "I'm on the phone."

"She said it was important."

I held up the movie script, which had warding-off powers over Dad like a cross does a vampire. "I'm *busy,*" I said.

He winced an apology and softly pulled the door closed.

I crumpled up the note and threw it away.

Then a woman answered.

When I asked to speak to Amanda, she said, *"Wer ist das?"*

When I told her I didn't understand, she said, *"Qui est-ce?"*

When I asked if this was the West residence, she replied, *"West-san no otaku deshouka?"*

When I apologized for having the wrong number, she said, "Listen, kid, Amanda's babysitting. She'll be home around seven."

Then she hung up.

When I called back at the appointed time, Amanda answered. "Oh," she said when I asked, and lowered her voice. "That was my mom."

"She speaks a lot of languages," I said.

"She mostly just knows phrases. But her accents are good."

"My dad's good at accents too," I said. "Or I guess dialects."

"What's the difference?" Amanda asked.

"He says it's how you pronounce things."

"I think that's accents. Dialects have to do with the region."

Someone on my line picked up and began dialing. Long notes on the touch tone, as if they were playing an organ.

"I'm on the *phone*!" I said.

"I need to call Matt for my homework," Oren said.

"I'm talking right now."

"Well, make it snappy," he said, and hung up with a clatter.

Amanda said, "Who was that?"

"My brother."

"Is he younger or older?"

"Younger," I said. This was followed by the sound of our breathing on the line. "Do you have any brothers or sisters?"

"A brother," Amanda said. "He's older, but he mostly lives with my father."

Dad picked up and started dialing.

"Hel*lo*?" I said.

From his bedroom, Dad shouted, "Oren, hang up the phone!"

Oren yelled, "Griffin's on the phone!" but I could also hear him clearly through Dad's receiver.

Mom said, "Would you two please stop screaming at each other?"

Dad said, "Griffin, I need to call my service." Then he hung up.

There was another long silence.

"Your father?" she said.

"Yes."

"He has a nice voice."

"It's a bass baritone," I offered.

Not unkindly, Amanda said, "Do you want to call me back and start over?"

"No," I said, "but thanks."

"*De nada,*" she said.

"Good accent," I said.

"Good answer," Amanda said.

"Do you take Spanish?" I asked.

"French."

"Can you speak it?"

"*Un petit peu,*" she said. "You?"

"*Un poco,*" I said.

"Are you going to do the play?" Amanda asked.

"I can't."

"Why?"

"You know the movie they're doing across the street from your school?"

"Yes."

"I'm in it."

"Really?" she said. "Like a part?"

"Do you want to see us film on Friday?"

"Absolutely," she said.

"We're shooting outside so just come by when you get out."

Someone spoke to Amanda in the background. "My mom needs me to run an errand now, but I'll see you at the end of the week."

After she hung up, I replaced the receiver in its cradle. Then I pulled the chain to the bulb in the ceiling. In the dark, I slid down in my chair, resting my feet against the door. I laced my fingers behind my head and rocked onto the chair's back legs. I could feel the entire outline of my body, toes to fingers, soles to shoulders. The exact width of my smile.

By now, everyone in my family had read the script of *Take Two*. On its facing pages, in her perfect cursive, Mom had taken notes that read *Motif of performance, Movie within the movie, Triangles,* or *Motif of adult injury.* Oren had put hearts on the call sheet when Diane Lane was shooting. Two years ago, after seeing *A Little Romance,* he had taped her cover photo from *Time* magazine—its headline read "Hollywood's Whiz Kids"—to the wall by his bed. Dad, who'd been rehearsing late, so that he often missed dinner, had highlighted the lines in all my scenes.

The plot of *Take Two* was hard for me to follow because it was out of sequence. It cut between Konig's past and present, between the movie that he was making as well as what was happening in his life, which was a mess because the people he'd hurt or ignored while making movies—his ex-wife, his son, his sister, and his fiancée—were all making demands on him for different reasons. His older sister, Blair (played by Cloris Leachman), who was dying of cancer, had been estranged from Konig for years because she felt that the sisters in his movies were, she said, "gross misrepresentations" of her. She wanted Konig to admit to this and apologize before she died. "I never browbeat you like Claudia in *Hershkowitz*," she said from her hospital bed, "and I certainly didn't tell your wife about your affair, like Mira in *Mishegoss*!" At the same time, Konig's ex-wife and my mom wanted to clear the air between them. Not only because she was sad and angry that their marriage had ended, but because she felt his impending marriage was a distraction from all the problems between him and me, which she believed he was running out of time to repair. "Just like you're running out of time to patch things up with your sister," she told Konig during a fight at the Russian Tea Room. Meanwhile, Shelley Duvall, playing Konig's fiancée and the star of his new movie, was having terrible panic attacks on set because she was certain he was disappointed in her performance. Plus, she was paranoid that he was obsessed with my math tutor—which was true—whom I had a crush on as well. All these factors were interfering with the completion of Konig's new film, "not least of which," he complained to his psychologist, played by Elliott Gould, "is that I keep rewriting the final act."

On set the following day, while we were mid-scene, Hornbeam called, "Cut." I could tell he was slightly annoyed. Once again, he pulled me aside. "Griffin," he said, "I need you to remember what's going on here please. Earlier that morning, you had your Saturday session with Dr. Gould. So the talk you two had about your father is very much on your mind." I recalled the scene to which he was referring but didn't quite have it at hand, which Hornbeam must've sensed, because he added, "Take the pile of manure you dumped about your father in therapy and hand it off to me first chance you get." We did at least ten takes. When Hornbeam finally said, "Print that," he was not emphatic.

And when we wrapped for the day, Hornbeam called me over to join him by the window seat. There was a view from here of Nightingale's blue doors, which I made every effort not to look at, girding myself, as I was, to be dressed down. To my surprise, Hornbeam held up a sheet of paper and from behind his ear produced a Sharpie. He laid the former between us. "You know what Freytag's Pyramid is?" he asked. When I shook my head, he said, "It describes the shape of most stories. I find making one of these always helps me to know where I am when I'm acting in one of my pictures. Kind of like a map. Especially when we're shooting scenes out of order." On the blank page, he drew a flat line that rose to a summit, dipped, and then, halfway down, extended straight out from its midpoint:

"See this flat line here? That's the exposition. The 'once upon a time there was' part. You take Latin? We begin *in medias res,* in the middle of a thing. Like in dreams. Next, we've got our inciting incident. Here. At the pyramid's base. That's the event that spins everything in a different direction. I like to call this the 'interruption of quiescence' but only because it makes me sound smart. 'Quiescence'? It means 'quiet.' You see *The Empire Strikes Back*? Of course you did. Even the Ayatollah saw it. At a private screening with Brezhnev. According to my sources, they thought it was better than the first one. Anyway, you know when Luke escapes the snow monster and Obi-Wan Kenobi tells him he's got to go to the Dagobah system and train under Yoda? Inciting incident. If we're splitting hairs, it's when they destroy the rebel base, but you get my drift. And everything intensifies from there, this rising action going up, up, up, the pyramid like a pot of water coming to a boil, there are all sorts of fights and chases, our heroes face all kinds of obstacles all way to here"—he pointed to the summit—"the climax. The point of maximum tension: the battle between Vader and Luke. No quarter asked and none given, the fight ending when Darth chops off Skywalker's hand. *'Luke,'*

Vader says, '*I am your father.*' After which there's the denouement, which is French for basically *phew,* which is falling action, is aftermath and mop-up. Luke escapes, gets his robot hand. He's permanently scarred, he is forever partly his father. The rebels live to fight another day.

"Now, me, before *I* start a picture, I make notes on this pyramid, all along these lines, about the important things that happen in the story. Here"—he made a dot on the base of the pyramid—"is where Konig reads the terrible reviews of his latest picture." Another dot. "Here: where Blair learns she's got three months to live." Another dot. "Here: the scene where Elliott and Bernie have their breakthrough therapy session and afterward Bernie confronts Konig about being a shitty father. And here: where Konig figures out the end of his movie. This sheet, I label *P,* for 'plot.'" He made a *P* in the upper left-hand corner, then laid another sheet of paper over it and traced the exact same lines. "This sheet, you label *B,* for 'Bernie.' So . . ." And he made dots along the graph. "Here's where Bernie's dad meets Diane. Here's where Bernie and his father have a catch in Central Park. Here's where Bernie finally lets his father have it for being so out to lunch his whole life." Then Hornbeam laid the B over the P. Then the P over the B. I could see the tracery beneath each. "This way," he said, "you can chart your character's movement, from alpha to omega. Because that's what every story's about, young Skywalker, it's about moving off a starting point or resisting change with everything you got. Protagonist versus antagonist until death do they part. Use this method"—he held the sheets and Sharpie toward me—"and you always know where you are when we're shooting." He retracted them when I reached out. "But it doesn't work," he warned, "if you don't make your own. *Comprendo?*"

I spent the entirety of Tuesday night doing this, to the exclusion of my school assignments. On Wednesday, after a particularly long day of shooting, and only three takes to nail my therapy scene with Elliott—we used the third-floor study as his office—Hornbeam placed both his hands on my shoulders and said, "Would that every adult I worked with took direction so well." And this filled me with pride.

But that night, I found myself so far behind in my homework, I was miserable. I had school the next day, plus a big scene to prepare for Friday's shoot, and especially with Amanda coming, I wanted to be at my best. It felt like *The Nuclear Family* all over again, plus Dad was home early.

Before dinner, Mom knocked on my door and then opened it. "I'm making pork chops," she said. "You and your dad's favorite." She surveyed the scene. "You want some tea or something?"

"I'm fine."

She cupped her hand to her mouth and whispered, "It would mean a lot to your father if you rehearsed with him."

My glare did not mean *no*, so she smiled like we'd made an agreement and went back to cooking.

If I'd had a stopwatch, I could've set it to the exact time it took Dad to knock.

"Mom said you wanted my help."

I opened the door and glumly handed him the script. He visibly brightened, and I followed after him as he took a seat on the couch. I sat across from him, on the rocking chair, and rocked as if I were generating electricity.

"Maybe you want to stand," he said.

"Why?"

"To work on appearing relaxed."

"Can we start?"

"Suit yourself," he said.

We ran through the scene once. A few lines through the second, Dad said, "Maybe a little more oomph on that one. With a dramatic pause first."

"Where?"

" 'The girl I like,' " he said, " 'she . . . she doesn't know I *exist*.' "

"There's no 'she' in the line," I said. "It's: 'The girl I like doesn't know I exist.' "

"Ad-lib it," Dad said. "For effect."

"Hornbeam hates that."

"You'll never know till you try."

"Jill Clayburgh tried today. Hornbeam told her to read the line as written. And I'm no Jill Clayburgh."

"Fair enough," Dad said, but he was crestfallen.

We proceeded.

"The girl I like doesn't know I exist," I said.

Dad held out his hand, which he bunched into a fist. *"Exist,"* he intoned.

"You sound like a depressed giant," I said.

"Fine," he said, and threw down the script. He stood. "What could *I* possibly know"—he gestured toward our third-story view of Manhattan—"about *acting*?" Upon which he thumped out of the room.

Dad was still grumpy when we sat down to eat. I was explaining Freytag's Pyramid to Oren when Dad asked, offhandedly, "How does the movie end, by the way?"

Mom snapped, "I thought you said you read it." She was pissed off at him for reasons unknown, but which had transpired sometime between our rehearsal and dinner.

"I read enough to get the gist," Dad said to her.

"Maybe if you finished," Mom said, "you could talk to your son about character motivation. Like satyriasis."

"What's that?" I said.

Mom glared at Dad as he hunched over his plate, biting the last bits of pork from the rib.

"*I* read it," Oren said. "I thought it was talky. Like our family, but on amphetamines."

"Since when do you know anything about amphetamines?" Mom said.

"Okay, then," Oren said, "cocaine."

"*I* thought it was brilliant," Mom said to him. "*I* think it's a dead-on description of the price an artist pays for his *narcissism*. Look up *that* word," she went on, turning to me, "if you don't know what it means. And I also thought"—here she glared at Dad—"the tragedy of Konig's character is that he needs certain things from certain people at certain times. And when his needs change, he discards them like old toys. As for *your* opinion," she said to Oren, "keep your half-baked ideas to yourself."

There was suddenly a terrible *crack*.

"Fuck," Dad said, and cupped his mouth. *"Fuck!"*

He hurried to the bathroom. Mom slowly shook her head as she watched him go.

"You busted a crown, didn't you?" she called after him. Then she raised an eyebrow at us in sick glee. *"Knick-knack paddywhack,"* she said, *"give a dog a bone."*

On Thursday, I was back in school and hurrying to the library, when I spotted Mr. Fistly walking toward me. He was strolling, deliberately, down the hallway toward his office, reading a sheet of paper, but just as we passed each other he paused without looking up and, having seen me through the eyeball in his ear, said, "Mr. Hurt, join me in private, please." From her desk, Miss Abbasi glanced at me as I passed. She let me register her disappointment and then returned to her typewriter's keys. I had no idea what I'd done wrong and checked off the list: I'd turned in my excuse to Mr. McQuarrie for missing school all week; miraculously, my assignments were in on time; my grades had improved since wrestling season had ended; I was wearing loafers; I even checked my zipper. Mr. Fistly took his seat, placed his elbows on his desk, pressed his fingertips together so they formed a steeple, and began to speak.

"I have just received a rather disturbing call from Mrs. Metcalf. Does that name ring a bell?"

"No, sir, it does not."

"Exactly," he said. "You are unaware of her identity because you have set eyes on her once. At the Nightingale-Bamford School. After not only auditioning for her play but apparently accepting a lead role in it. Upon which you did her the discourtesy of neither returning her calls nor attending rehearsal this week, inconveniencing her terrifically while embarrassing me as well, since she is a respected colleague. I would have you inform her yourself that you did not intend to participate in her production and apologize, but I think so little of your character I find that sort of object lesson would be lost on you. Not to mention that I trust your follow-through even less. So please reserve this Saturday for detention. I did *not* excuse you, Mr. Hurt."

I turned around at the doorway to face him.

"Make a point of seeing Mr. Damiano before this afternoon is out. In fact"—Fistly shot a cuff and checked his watch—"he is at the moment in his downstairs office. He will inform you as to how we are going to proceed with the matter."

The office to which Fistly referred was the basement theater. It was below Boyd's modern wing. The flight down was like descending through an aquifer, since Boyd's swimming pool was also located here. With each step the stairwell turned warmer and more humid, the smell of chlorine grew more powerful, and the metal handrail became slicker with condensation. The basement theater was to the left, at the end of a long hallway, past Boyd's school store and the cavernous book storage room next to it, presided over by Mr. McQuarrie. He sat at his desk now—the space's only light a small lamp—licking his finger to flip through a stack of pink receipts, like a monk over an illuminated manuscript. When he caught my eye, he flashed a naughty smile—"G'day, Mr. Hurt"—and I hurried past, suppressing a shiver.

The theater was a low-ceilinged room, long and rectangular, black-walled and dimly lit but for the tiny square of stage at its far end. Mr. Damiano, who presided here, taught honors English and drama. He was bearded and bearish in build, and his facial hair, grown to his cheekbones, hid what I'd once noticed were terrible acne scars. He was a teacher who did not have students so much as acolytes and was a fan, in all months of the year, of patterned scarves knotted at their ends. In short, he reminded me of the worst of my father's students—lovers of costume but actors in name only. He stood by the entrance, leaning against the lighting booth, and briefly acknowledged me as I entered. He was smoking a cigarette contemplatively. Everything Damiano did—but especially now, aware, as he was, of me watching him watch Robert Lord and Kingsley Saladin, his two favorite seniors, rehearse a scene—was adverbial. He beheld them *lovingly, devotedly, considerately, obviously*. Italics his. I took a seat on a foldout chair and it squeaked. Damiano raised a finger to his lips and nodded toward the pair of students. Lord launched into a monologue, and Damiano, sensing my eyes on him, began to mouth the words in tandem, as if he were so stirred by the language he had to simultaneously perform it himself. "All the world's a stage," he and Lord began:

And all the men and women merely players;
They have their exits and their entrances;
And one man in his time plays many parts,
His acts being seven ages. At first the infant,

Mewling and puking in the nurse's arms;
And then the whining school-boy, with his satchel
And shining morning face, creeping like snail
Unwillingly to school. And then the lover,
Sighing like furnace, with a woeful ballad
Made to his mistress' eyebrow . . .

When they finished the scene, Damiano placed the cigarette in his mouth so that he could clap slowly, emphatically, and then said to me, confidentially, "Not bad, huh?"

"Huh," I replied. "Not *bad.*"

"Give me a sec," Damiano said gruffly, having taken the bait, and went to have words with his charges.

Once the pair had left, Damiano flipped one of the chairs around and straddled the seat. He had a Styrofoam cup in one hand; he took a final pull at his cigarette and then dropped the butt in his coffee. "I hear you're in the new Hornbeam picture." When I nodded, he said, "I'm not crazy about his work," as if he'd recently had to turn down a starring role with him due to other commitments. "What's he like on set?"

I considered playing dumb, to confirm that I took such experiences for granted. But I recalled an exchange between Diane Lane and me during my first day of shooting, in which she shows me a shortcut to factoring and I steal a glance at her profile as she writes out the solution. "Look at her," Hornbeam said after the first take, "like you're cheating off her test but want to get caught."

"He's precise," I said, my precision surprising me. "He points you exactly where to go."

The answer drew a jealous smirk. "Lucky you," he said.

I let that one hang.

"Speaking of luck," Damiano continued, "I need a role filled in our spring production of *As You Like It.* Plan to be here from nine to five every Saturday for the next month."

It took a second to process this horror. "What if I don't want to?"

"You don't have a choice," Damiano said.

"What if I have detention this weekend?"

"Come afterward," he said. "We'll roll out the red carpet."

From his back pocket, Damiano produced a paperback copy and flapped it at me, which to my disgust was warm to the touch.

"Don't worry," he said, "it's a small part. A couple of scenes in the first act. Important role, though. Charles. The wrestler." When he registered my displeasure, he smiled and added, tauntingly, "A little typecasting."

That afternoon, I had ninth period free. I was sitting on one of the front hall pews and feeling sorry for myself about my lost Saturdays. Rob Dolinski, a senior, sat across from me. He had his arms stretched out on the pew's back crest, over the shoulders of his usual sidekicks, or girl-friends, Andrea Oppenheimer and Sophie Evans. Sophie was freckled and broad-mouthed, and she almost always wore pants—she so rarely donned a skirt with her blazer it was practically an event. Andrea, a beauty in a black turtleneck, wore her chestnut hair parted down the middle, half veiling her large eyes, the ends cut so that they appeared sharp and nearly pinched together, like a staple remover's teeth. Earlier, they'd come in from the sublevel carport across the street, "under the stairs" where everyone went to smoke cigarettes.

Mr. McElmore, who ran marathons, came into their line of sight. Runners in general, and their outfits in particular, were outlandish back then, especially since they were on the continuum of nearly naked. McElmore wore super-short shorts, shiny as silk, and a nylon tank top. He had on what looked like a cycling cap, with its tiny brim turned back-ward, beneath which he'd stuffed his curls. His skinny, shaved legs were as taut and muscular as a Thoroughbred's, and above his ankle socks each cord in his calf caught the hallway's light. He stopped to talk to a passing student.

Dolinski whispered something to Andrea, who bent double. She laughed so hard, but also silently, having blown all the air from her lungs. When Andrea, leaning over Rob's lap, cupped her hand to Sophie's ear and shared, Sophie said to Rob, flatly, "I dare you." At which point he stood and, tiptoeing right up behind McElmore, delicately pincered his shorts at the hems and then yanked them to his ankles.

For a moment, McElmore didn't react, just stood like the vase on a tablecloth the magician rips away. Because his shorts had built-in lining and he was now butt naked. The stubby shaft of McElmore's penis rested atop his nuts; it was so squat and fat it pointed straight forward. It looked like a cannon from the Revolutionary War—the barrel dwarfed by its wheels. I had never seen one like it. Clearly Dolinski hadn't either—or had expected briefs and not the head of admissions' bare ass and strange dick—since he stepped back, covering his mouth. Andrea and Sophie had also covered their mouths. McElmore bent to pull up his shorts, and when he finally did speak, it was without anger, although his port-wine birthmark had flushed a deep purple.

"Dolinski," he said, "you *ass*hole. Report to Saturday detention until you graduate."

Which meant that I'd at least have some company this weekend.

As if God were also punishing me, it rained all the next morning. The weather put the film crew in a bad mood, since it threatened to scotch the schedule and slowed setup for our exterior shots. It sank me into despair, because today was when Amanda was supposed to visit. At the town house, after makeup, and in between bouts of woe, I passed the time studying my lines—not for my upcoming scene, since I had those down, but rather from *As You Like It*.

> OLIVER: Good Monsieur Charles, what's the new news at the new court?
>
> CHARLES: There's no news at the court, sir, but the old news; that is, the old duke is banished by his younger brother the new duke; and three or four loving lords have put themselves into voluntary exile with him, whose lands and revenues enrich the new duke; therefore he gives them good leave to wander.

This was why Damiano said I was an important character: I filled in crucial backstory. On Freytag's Pyramid I was Mr. Exposition. In this scene, I was preparing to wrestle Oliver's brother Orlando. My line in the next scene, right before the wrestling match, was a great one: "Come, where is this young gallant that is so desirous to lie with his mother earth!" But apparently Orlando wins ("Shout," the stage directions read, "CHARLES is thrown"). Which meant, I learned as I read on, that I was also the Inciting Incident. It wasn't too much to memorize, although once again the thought of a month of Saturdays spent at Boyd made me want to bash in my skull. Worse, there was no telling when I might see Amanda next. Until the sun, blued by the window gels, kissed my paperback's page, and I looked up to see that the sky had cleared.

It was one of those April days in New York when the warmer breezes carried on them the estuarial tang of the city's surrounding rivers. Parked cars sparkled with beads of rainwater, and the puddles, like mirror shards, reflected pieces of skyline before being splashed to bits by traffic. Outside now, waiting on my mark as the crew tweaked the reflectors and spots and held up a light meter to my face, I watched the asphalt dry and then brighten. At the end of the block, like a Seurat in progress, Central Park was dotted with greens and browns and stony grays. A crowd had already formed at the police barrier. The camera crane rose high above the street, its four outrigger floats like a plesiosaur's flippers shuddering under its weight, and with the cinemaphotographer, Willis, and Hornbeam both in the basket, and the long lens protuberant between them, the machine looked like a three-headed monster from *The 4:30 Movie*.

After being deposited back on earth, Hornbeam said, "Run through, please," and, taking his mark beside me, called out, *"Action."* We began to stroll down the block, the cued extras walking past us. In the scene, Konig and I had just come back from having a catch in Central Park. I was still wearing my mitt and throwing the ball into its web, while Konig, in cords and a blazer, had his tucked under his arm. I was heartsick over Diane Lane and doing my subtle best to get some guidance from the one person least equipped to offer it:

```
                    BERNIE
        How'd you know you'd fallen in love with
        Mom?


                    KONIG
        Because after we met, she was all I
        thought about. Kind of like a cancer
        diagnosis.


                    BERNIE
        Did she feel the same way about you?
```

                    KONIG
          She said that as long as she was acting
          in my movie, she wouldn't date me. So I
          fired her on the spot.

     BERNIE glares at **KONIG,** shocked.

                    BERNIE
          Then what?

                    KONIG
          I took her out to dinner that night and
          hired her back after dessert.

                    BERNIE
          The girl I like doesn't know I exist.

     KONIG shrugs at this insurmountable problem.

                    BERNIE
          How do you fix it?

                    KONIG
          The same way you treat male pattern
          baldness. Look, Bernie. In matters of
          love . . .

     A BEAUTIFUL WOMAN walks past father and son.
     KONIG, SLOWING DOWN, turns to WATCH her progress.

                    KONIG
          . . . maybe let the game come to you.

    I looked up to see Amanda standing at the barricade and leaning her
elbows on its beam. She waved at me excitedly, and because the scene had
ended, I went to join her.

"This is *amazing*," Amanda said. "Aren't you nervous with all these people watching?"

I scanned the crowd. "I don't really think about it," I said.

"You never get stage fright?"

"Only when I talk to you." Which was, I could not help but notice, the most forthcoming thing I'd said to her since we'd met.

"And who is this young lady," Hornbeam said, "consorting with such a poorly mannered host?" He was standing behind me, waiting for an introduction. After I made this, Hornbeam lightly took her elbow. "Why don't you stand over here with the crew?" he said, and touched her crown as she ducked under the barrier. "Or better still, how would you like to be in the shot?"

Amanda looked over her shoulder at me and widened her eyes in disbelief. I shrugged, as if to say, *Good luck.* Hornbeam, as if he'd been planning this for some time, led her to where the beautiful extra stood. I watched as Hornbeam sawed his hands, giving them direction. As Amanda listened, a shyness left her features that made her appear older. When Hornbeam returned to my side, he explained how the scene was going to change. When we rolled, Amanda and the extra walked side by side, playing mother and daughter, chatting as they passed us, and this time Hornbeam and I both turned to regard them. During one of the final takes, Amanda smiled at me as we passed each other—this being the shot Hornbeam ultimately used—alluding, I thought, to something that hadn't happened between us yet, as well as to these unanticipated circumstances that put us where we were: on set, in this scene, and, when I thought about it during the film's premiere, forever.

Later, we took the crosstown bus together. Amanda remained quietly elated. We were seated in the back, Amanda by the window, which she'd slid open. "Not in a million years," she said, "would I have thought I'd be in a movie today." We entered the transverse, and the park's leaves flashed past like a green wind. She watched this blur for a minute and then turned to face me. "You are full of surprises," she said. She scanned my eyes after she spoke, as if to confirm a suspicion, and I experienced the dual feeling I would so often suffer in her presence: that she was waiting for me to do something and that to do so would be a complete mistake.

Which is to say that my ear's blood beat was as loud as the bus's gargle. "Why *do* you get stage fright when you talk to me?" she asked.

I shrugged.

"Am I so horrible?"

I shook my head. "I worry . . ." I said.

"That?"

"I'll say something wrong."

When I didn't elaborate, she said, "And?"

"You won't like me anymore."

Amanda raised an eyebrow. "What makes you think I like you?" To my horrified expression, Amanda said, "I'm *kidding*," and knocked her shoulder to mine. She turned chatty. Here was the difference between Amanda and every other girl I'd known so far. She noticed things I hadn't realized I had until she spoke them aloud. That on the city's East Side, for instance, the crossing islands are more beautifully manicured, but nobody sits on them. That at night its avenues are deserted, but Broadway always seems crowded. That the East River, she observed, is half as narrow as the Hudson but more menacing. "Do you know what I mean?"

I did. "I do," I said.

"This is our stop," she said, and pulled the bell string.

We got off and waited together again for her northbound bus, which appeared on the hill's crest far too soon. I was gathering the courage to ask her out when she beat me to the punch.

"Want to come babysit with me next week?"

I held out my open palm, which delighted her. "Write down the address."

That evening, Oren, Mom, and I went to see Dad rehearse his new show at the St. James Theatre.

The cast was seated onstage in folding chairs, with the four principals, including Dad, in the front row. All of them had binders in their laps. But for an upright piano downstage left, the space was bare. The rear curtains and backdrop were raised to reveal the far wall's exposed brick, which made the stage seem bigger. A fissure, patched with pale mortar, ran diagonally across its face.

A small man wearing a jacket and tie shuffled in from the wing; he was greeted by applause and raised his hand to the audience of friends and family, and then stood next to the instrument for a moment in acknowledgment. Mom leaned toward my ear as she clapped and said, "That's Hershy Kay, he wrote the music for *A Chorus Line.*" He reminded me of Elliott, as round and solid as he was, his countenance at once impish and formidable, this intensified by the occasional flash from his glasses' lenses when they caught the light. He had a full head of white hair and full lips, and when he bowed it was more a gesture toward one: he lightly tapped his palms to his hips and bent ever so slightly before taking his seat at the piano.

José Ferrer—"He's the director," Mom said, "he was very famous for his role as Cyrano"—followed Kay onto the stage. He was tall. Imposing. There was a dashing regality about his bearing. He had a goatee, and his mustache was wide and dramatic as a musketeer's. He even bowed like a swordsman, hand to chest and the other arm stuck out, toe pointed daintily toward us as he bent at the hips, which indicated a surprising agility and also got a laugh.

Abe Fountain, whom Mom knew I recognized and simply glanced at me as the applause rose in response, walked on last. I had not seen him since Christmas, and I was struck again by how noticeably he'd aged since *The Fisher King.* He'd already donned his white gloves, a long-standing habit to protect against biting his nails; and while he was the youngest of the triumvirate—he was only sixty-three—his mannerisms suggested the greatest fragility. He touched one hand to his heart in a gesture of gratitude. I think often about these men, on that particular night, because there was an old lion's grandeur about all three, their great careers attending them like page boys, widening behind them like a wake, and I was touched by the fact that their confidence in this new project, their hope for it—a hope that my father wholeheartedly embraced—was fissured like the backstage wall, was belied by their self-consciousness during these introductions. By their awareness that this show might in fact be their last. So that even here, at the start, the rehearsal had about it an aura of a curtain call. But there was another layer that made these introductions so memorable. These men were so obviously one another's people, a family, as Al Moretti liked to say, that they chose. They had gravitated to performance, here, to the stage, as a means of belonging. Here, where they put on the masks that, in some cases, others had made for them, masks that had, by now, grafted to their skin, behind which they were at once safe and allowed to be successful. Here, where they could be at home and hide in plain sight, until opening night, when the world decided, once again, whether it approved.

"Good evening," Fountain said. "We appreciate you joining us for this musical run-through of *Sam and Sara*." There was another round of applause, which Fountain tamped his hands to shorten. "Our plan tonight is to get through all the numbers with minimal interruption. Be warned, however, that we may pause here and there for all three of us to make some comments—breaks I hope you don't find too distracting. So, without further ado . . . *Sam and Sara*."

There was no dimming of the lights, no orchestra making the final clatter of readjustment in the pit. Only Kay's accompaniment, the instrument sounding small and tinny in the comparatively empty space, accompanied in turn by the chorus as they stood to sing the first number, which took place, so far as I could figure, at a college campus, but it was difficult to tell without costumes. It was made more confusing the moment the show's pair of stars took their place center stage, and the blocking was important. They stood alongside my father and the woman playing opposite him, but each slightly in front of the other. A couple coupled off. And they were noticeably older than their partners. Olivia White played Sara, the love interest. Her voice was raspy and tarred, and she sang in a register that was closer to speaking. Her gestures were at once spunky and feminine, and there was a hint to all of them of impersonation and overemphasis, like a girl playing dress-up. "She starred with your father in *Oliver!*" Mom whispered. "She was Nancy to his Bill Sikes." Marc Morales, who played Sam, was chestnut-haired and towering, with a slow swing to all his movements. He had a booming singing voice—"He's a star at the Met," Mom said—that was operatic and in heavily accented English. His fingers, when he extended his thin forearms, visibly shook.

The number concluded, the applause's volume described the audience's size, Oren leaned forward to catch my eye and thumbed toward the aisle.

"Where are you going?" Mom asked us when we stood.

"Around," Oren said.

We passed the remainder of the rehearsal as we had so many run-throughs of former shows. We climbed to the balcony's highest seat, so that we could look down upon the cast members' heads. We visited the empty lobby. We snuck behind the mezzanine's bar, and Oren got us Cokes from the fountain, though there was no ice and the soda was flat. Via the wings, we climbed the catwalk's ladders and crossed its bridge, pausing in the middle and leaning on its railing to watch another song. We snuck into the orchestra pit, which seemed cramped even without the instruments and musicians, while above us the performers sounded muffled and far away. And later, as we lounged in one of the dressing rooms, as Oren did pull-ups on the exposed pipes and blackened his palms with grime, I thought about how much I'd have liked for Amanda to see this place. I had the strange and incongruous fantasy of the pair of us living here, as if it were our own apartment, sharing the tiny bathroom, cooking small meals on the hot plate, reading the dated graffiti scratched onto the ceiling above our tiny loft bed. And I was flooded with love for her.

Dad wanted to go to Chinatown after the rehearsal was over, surprising Oren and me. "How about Hung Wa?" he suggested to Mom.

She appeared surprised as well. "That sounds great," she said. "What do you think, boys?"

We took a cab again. It was a long ride, but Dad didn't seem to notice the meter. He talked to the driver animatedly. In the back seat, Mom, Oren, and I were silent, lest we somehow change Dad's mind. It had been a family tradition when Oren and I were little to eat at Hung Wa every Saturday night, but this had ended once we moved back to Lincoln Towers. The restaurant's walls were a drab, faded green, although there was a wall-length fish tank by the entrance to the kitchen that was brightly lit and filled with albino oscars and pygmy catfish and gourami. The waiter arrived with wonton strips and ramekins of hot and sour sauce and mustard. When the waiter returned with the pot of tea, Oren and I filled our small cups with two sugar packets so that the drink was overly sweet. Dad ordered for the table, the very same things he had for Oren and me when we were little: egg drop soup followed by chicken lo mein; for

Mom, Chinese broccoli and the shrimp in special sauce; and for himself the beef short rib. Oren and I took a moment to look at each other full-on, amazed that he'd remembered.

"How's the new tooth?" Oren asked when he watched Dad eat.

"It's a temporary," Dad said, "but it seems to be working great." He asked Mom, "What'd you think of the show?"

"I loved your numbers."

"But what about the whole thing?"

"It's early," Mom said, and blew on a broccoli stalk. "It's hard to tell."

"It's an incredible array of talent," Dad said.

"They've all had great careers," Mom said.

"Marc gets going and the hair stands up on my neck," Dad said.

"His pronunciation when he reads his lines is terrible," Mom noted. She finished her wine and, catching the waiter's eye, pointed at her glass.

"Olivia's still a gorgeous gal," Dad said.

To me, Mom said, "Pour me some of your soup," and handed me her teacup.

Dad said, "It's hard not to feel good about things."

"You should," Mom said.

"It's hard not to be optimistic," Dad said.

"To *Sam and Sara,*" Mom said, after taking the wineglass from the waiter's tray before he placed it on the table.

"To *Sam and Sara,*" we all said, and clinked teacups, which rang as dully as doubt.

The thing about the Saturday morning of Saturday detention was: getting up early for it felt earlier than getting up early for anything else. I was out the door and headed to school on my bike before anyone woke. Eagle-beaked gargoyles glared down on me from the spire of the Museum of Natural History. In the morning light, the building's facade was as white as salt. My book bag was heavy, the spring warmth and exertion made my back sweat, my bitterness only intensified by the promise of such a summery day spent entirely inside.

Entering Boyd's darkened lobby, it took a moment for my eyes to adjust. I wheeled the bike to the front hall's pews and then sat, feeling oddly ashamed and utterly disgruntled. Detention began at eight, and, backlit as he entered the building, Dolinski at first appeared wraithlike. When he came into view, though, I could see he wore a suit and dress shirt, clothes that were entirely incongruous, although his hair was all over the place. He looked exhausted. He took a seat across from me and nodded.

"Am I late?" he asked.

From down the hall behind us, someone said, "You're right on time."

It was Mr. McQuarrie. He wore jeans and a Hawaiian shirt, plus a pair of two-tone monk strap loafers, and the sight of him in these mismatched civvies was inexplicably disturbing. On his index finger he spun a huge ring of keys. He looked positively delighted to be here.

In the book storage room, McQuarrie gave us instructions. Above, half the fixtures were switched off, so that the back of the room was shrouded in darkness. The walls, where visible, were lined with metal shelves, these containing rows of textbooks that disappeared down their length into the murk. Stacked on the floor before these were more boxes we were to open and inspect. "You see how these have been mishandled," McQuarrie said, and squatted. He indicated where the cardboard appeared punched in. From his back pocket he produced a butterfly knife and twirled out the blade. He stroked the packing tape so that the flaps popped open with great force, like a tube of biscuits. Then he removed a book. "You see the result," he said, and indicated where the binding's top was bent.

"That doesn't look so bad," said Dolinski.

"Doesn't look pristine either now, does it?"

From the box he removed a pink bill of lading.

"Sort the damaged books and stack the rest on the shelves. Then place the returns back in the box with the receipt and put them over there." He indicated the far wall behind us, where more boxes were stacked.

Dolinski said, "What do we do when we're finished?"

McQuarrie stood and reached between the shelves and flipped a switch. It lit the back of the room, which was stacked floor to ceiling with more boxes.

"You won't," he said. He left and then reappeared. "I'll check up on you in a while."

Then he departed.

Dolinski went straight to the back wall of boxes and began arranging them until they formed what was, for all intents and purposes, a chaise. He lay down on it and, after removing his blazer and rolling it into a pillow, crossed his arms and legs and closed his eyes.

"Turn off that light, please," he said.

"Seriously," I said.

"Is my helping going to get us out of here sooner?" Dolinski asked.

I sorted, I shelved. The work was so boring it was a form of torture. At 10:45, McQuarrie reappeared. He walked over to Dolinski, gently shook him awake, said, "Up, please"—considerateness that to me was astounding. "Who needs to use the dunny?"

We both raised our hands.

"Back in ten, please," McQuarrie said.

We split up.

Wanting to kill time, I went to the first floor. To my left, the long hallway connecting the New School to the older wing was a solid hundred-yard dash. It was low-ceilinged and carpeted. I took a four-point stance, said, "Take your marks, set," and then sprinted. Above me, the lights flicked past like in the Holland Tunnel. I let my form spring loose as I approached the far wall. After I tapped it, I turned and raised my hand to the cheering crowd. I took the ramp down, toward the cafeteria's doors. Adjacent to it was the wrestling gym, and I entered. I walked to the mats' edge and slipped off my sneakers. I shoulder-rolled to the end of the room and was so dizzy I had to wait for my equilibrium to reset. On my return lap, I shot single legs so fast my jeans squeaked. I felt the fitness I'd lost since January. I rolled onto my back and stared at the ceiling. I took several deep breaths. Listened to my racing heartbeat. The darkened room was as chilly as an empty church. I anticipated the upcoming season. That it was absent Kepplemen warmed me with a sense of possibility.

When I left, I walked the longest route possible I could imagine, hugging the chapel and then down the hallway past Miss Sullens's room, when I heard the chatter of voices. I crept toward the one classroom whose door was propped open and from which a light shined, and then peeked into its entrance. Inside was the tech clique, mostly seniors, several of whom I didn't know and several I did: Marc Mason, Todd Wexworth, and Hogi Hyun. A couple of middle schoolers: Chip Colson and Jason Taylor. The giant sophomore wrestler Angel Rincondon. They'd arranged the long tables into a giant rectangle. It was body-warmed in there, fragrant. A couple of pizzas had just been delivered. The top box was open. There was a roll of paper towels for napkins and a pair of two-liter Pepsis next to a stack of Styrofoam cups. In front of each person was a spiral notebook, a handful of arcane handouts, and dice of all sorts of hard-candy shapes and sizes. The blackboard behind them was covered with drawings of mazes and maps, and I noted that Wexworth at the far end of the table seemed the leader of sorts and sat behind several folded-open cardboard screens, each one elaborately decorated, ancient skeleton armies in battles beneath the crenellations of a castle, an elf kneeling on a demonic statue, prying an emerald the size of an ostrich egg from between the tip of its forked tongue.

Marc Mason, one of maybe five Black kids in the upper school, rocked back in his chair. He appeared mildly annoyed. Whatever I'd interrupted was very serious business.

"What're you guys doing?" I asked.

He had not only folded his slice but also the paper plate on which it rested, as if he were going to eat both.

"We're about to try to kill an ogre," he said, indicating the rest of the group. "You're welcome to stay and watch."

When I told him I was on detention, he said, "Rain check, then."

The following Monday, after I finished shooting that afternoon, I babysat with Amanda.

The building was a small four-story walkup above a grocery store, on Amsterdam Avenue and Seventy-Fourth Street. The stairwell, dimly lit, was narrow and creaky. It wound tightly on itself, each landing bookended by a pair of apartment doors, each with a peephole framed in ornamented metal. I was so nervous and excited to be alone with Amanda in a place where we were not moving, I could barely swallow. With each step, I vowed today was the day I would say no to doubt, I would trust my feelings, like Ben Kenobi urged, I'd speak up and ask her out. I knocked on the door, which Amanda opened and said, with real surprise—and did I detect the tiniest note of dread?—"You're here!" And then she led me into the smallest apartment I'd ever seen.

Absent the half bath, it was a single room. Which in and of itself would be unremarkable were it not for the fact that three people lived here. In English the following year, when we read *Crime and Punishment,* I'd learn that such an apartment was called a "garret," and I would picture Raskolnikov in this place, drinking from the tap in the kitchen's tiny sink, all his dishes stored in its single cabinet, to then take a seat on the two-person couch adjacent the front door, his stationery placed atop the gameboard-sized coffee table. The dormer window that faced north was blocked by a dresser; the one facing south was half filled by an AC unit. Beneath this was a twin bed with drawers in its frame. Did the parents of Amanda's charge sleep head to foot? The other bed, catty-cornered to it, was piled with stuffed animals. The little girl Amanda babysat lay belly down on the floor in front of the television, which was also on the floor. She rested her chin in her hands and had folded her raised ankles one over the other. She looked over her shoulder at me but did not say hello.

"Can you tell Griffin your name?" Amanda asked.

"Suzy," the girl said. Then she returned to the screen, whose image began to float vertically before she adjusted the TV's antenna and bopped its top before it reset itself.

Amanda shrugged and tapped a cushion next to her on the couch. Above her top lip, perhaps because I planned to kiss it, I noticed for the first time its thin layer of blond down. Amanda was wearing her school uniform but had taken off her shoes. She rearranged herself, tucking her feet beneath her, and then reopened her binder and math textbook on her lap, which sent a signal for which I was not prepared, since their jackets seemed to wall her off from me. In a ringing tone she said, "Welcome to my job!" and this too rang false. When I asked how often she babysat, she said usually four times a week. She explained that Suzy's mother managed a restaurant during the day and her father bartended at night, so she covered the gap. I asked how old Suzy was, and Amanda said to her, "Suzy, tell Griffin how old you are," and without turning around she answered, "Six." *Manners,* Amanda mouthed, and gave a big thumbs-down.

The 4:30 Movie was on. Amanda said, "Suzy, tell Griffin what you're watching."

Suzy said, *"Gamera vs. Godzilla."*

The monsters were about to do final battle. The Japanese were running for cover. Their army's laser cannons were having no effect. We watched in silence. It was the moment to ask Amanda out, but before I could speak, she said, "How's *Take Two* going?" and kept her eyes fixed to the screen as if it were an Academy Award–winning picture. I told her this was probably my last week of shooting, but it was going well. There was another pause, and I said, "I was wondering—" but Amanda interrupted me to ask what I'd done over the weekend. I told her I'd had play rehearsal. When I asked her what she did over the weekend, she said, "I went to Studio 54 on Saturday and spent Sunday recovering." She remained plastered to the television so I, baffled, turned to watch it too.

It was the movie's climax. The city lay in waste about the two monsters. Gamera was calling upon his ancient powers to defeat Godzilla. From the sky there descended a cone of energy that supercharged the turtle in light. It was now or never, I thought, it was time to summon my courage, and then Amanda and I said to each other, "Do you—?" at the same time.

Amanda blurted, "Jinx!"

Rules dictated I could not speak.

"Do you want to know the craziest coincidence?" she asked. When I nodded, she said, "You go to Boyd Prep . . ."

Gamera's chest opened.

". . . and so does my boyfriend."

Gamera fired his super plasma beam at Godzilla.

"I think you know him . . ." Amanda said.

Godzilla was engulfed in the fireball.

"He's a senior . . ." she said.

The smoke cleared. Tokyo was silent.

"Rob said he was in detention with you Saturday."

Godzilla, defeated, thudded into the sea.

THERE IS NO TRY

And to this day I so rarely feel things when they happen. I remain so insulated from myself that, tucked away in my high tower or secreted in my dungeon's ninth level (I'd play a lot of *D&D* that year), I barely detect the pounding on my heart's three-foot-thick and twelve-foot-high door. And if I do manage a reaction, it's still often the diametrical opposite of what the moment calls for. That evening, for instance, having left the garret apartment, I spied my idiot grin in storefront windows during my entire walk home, the same one, I imagined, with which I comforted Amanda after she informed me about Rob ("We can still be friends," she said, to which I, like the actor performing an inflection exercise with my father, replied, "We *can* still be friends"), because she pulled herself to me immediately afterward, she hugged me with such force her textbook and binder fell to the floor, she pressed her bare knees to my thighs and gathered me into her arms with so much relief that I allowed *my* upraised arm to relax, finally, and fall to her shoulder, to revel in her warm forehead against my neck, and I held her too. And having what I'd so desperately wanted before I could even begin to process what I could not, my countenance must've set up like Quikrete ("I was so worried I'd lose you," she said, smushed against me, to which I replied, "You're not going to lose me"), my expression of shock froze into rictus and dried my teeth, my grimace made my paralyzed cheeks sore and must've given me an oxymoronic appearance—gleefully grim, dismally delighted—because upon first regarding me when I got home, Oren asked, "What happened to you?"

"Nothing," I replied, which was true, in a way, and I retreated to my study to stare, quakingly quiet, at my corkboard's collage and ask the simple question I still find I most often do when it comes to love, which is "Why?"

There is a second stage to this process, a special brand of sublimation, which occurred later that week and altered my fate. Like quite a few things that happened in my youth, it is also something you can watch on YouTube: a scene from *Take Two* that's a famous tearjerker, like Ricky Schroder's with a dead Jon Voight in *The Champ*. We shot it my last day on set. It takes place in Konig's dining room, now his ex-wife's town house. He has brought Shelley Duvall to dinner, with whom he has patched things up. He has figured out the ending to his movie, and he's elated because he's secured financing for his next picture—which, he informs the guests, he'll shoot on location in Spain. Clayburgh, meanwhile, has struck up a relationship with Elliott; Gould holds her hand atop the table, he is so in love. Like Konig, Clayburgh is also in high spirits. She's just landed a major role in a Bertolucci film—she is out from under Konig's shadow, she'll spend most of the upcoming winter in Italy. It is all at once authentically celebratory and also a game of one-upmanship—in other words, decidedly adult. The scene is shot tight: the camera tracks right, in what appears to be a circle around the table; it loops, swinging back, with each piece of happy news, to my character, Bernie, to whom no one is speaking, who is registering his progressive abandonment, and who can't help himself finally—at the scene's climax, he smacks the table. Everyone turns to look at him. The camera fixes on him, in close-up, and, eyes full of tears, he says, "Why did you bother? Having kids. Me. What was the point? Jesus Christ, I'm like Charlton Heston in *Planet of the Apes*. This whole time I've been thinking I'll finally get back to Earth when this is it. This is my home."

Nailed it on the first take. And after Hornbeam held the shot at its conclusion, I just broke down. I couldn't get it together, even after Hornbeam yelled, "*Cut*," and the entire crew erupted into applause. Even after

Hornbeam, who, along with Jill and Shelley and Elliott, rubbed my back until it warmed my shirt, and even Diane appeared and put her arms around my neck—here too my sobs turned to laughter. I laugh-cried myself into comfort. I knew I'd done something excellent, but everyone's appreciation sounded far off; and not for a second did it occur to me that the sadness I'd so torrentially tapped into came from elsewhere.

"You decide to become a great actor," Hornbeam said to me later, "and nothing's going to get in your way."

Perhaps Oren was right after all.

Now, however, back at Boyd full-time, I devoted myself to a detailed investigation aimed at answering the following question: Why was Amanda in love with Rob Dolinski instead of me?

There were obvious and glaring differences between us. There was, first and foremost, the figure he cut. He was easily over six feet tall, with a classic swimmer's frame. His dark double-breasted suits accentuated this—he even occasionally wore a vest—their tailoring, cuffs to hems, imparting to his movements lines that cohered in a geometry unknown to me. He had some of the actor in him too, evinced by his choice of tie or shirt, one of which (or both) was always light blue, and had the effect of turning on *another* light behind his already bright eyes, which like a husky's were hard to look away from. But *looking away* was one of Dolinski's most devastating weapons of seduction: in the mornings, say, upon entering Boyd's bustling front hall, Dolinski, midconversation— with a teacher, perhaps, or with whomever he'd happened to walk into the building—made it a habit to shoot a glance, midsentence, at some girl his junior, who'd been trying very hard (she too midconversation and seated on the pews with several half-huddled friends) to intentionally ignore him. But having felt the flash of him and confusing, as Elliott liked to say, her hope with her evidence, she'd meet his gaze full-on. And like the proverbial deer she then froze in anticipation—of a smile, a nod, some sort of acknowledgment—but was flattened by his dismissal, by the complete and utter indifference with which he strode past.

The most impressive thing about him was not his poshness, which I considered the definition of Upper East Side (and corroborated by checking his address in the Boyd directory, the Carlyle—"a very well-appointed building," Dad had remarked when I asked), but the fact that nearly all the teachers adored him. I often spotted him lounging in Miss Sullens's office, chatting about books. He'd pulled down Mr. McElmore's pants, but they could be seen yukking it up as they waited in line together at Kris's Knish, parked just inside Central Park, on Ninety-Sixth Street, as if it had all been in good fun.

"Just have one more look," Dolinski pleaded with Mr. Heimdall as the two departed the chemistry lab.

Heimdall, mock annoyed, briefly eyed the marked-up exam Dolinski held. "You're determining the concentration of sulfuric acid, Robert, not interpreting a passage of Shakespeare."

To which Dolinski replied, "Compounds can be as elegant as sonnets."

"Be that as it may," said Heimdall, smirking with real affection, "come by at office hours. I'll be easier to butter up then."

Miss Brodsky—this was mind-boggling—once took his arm. Dolinski was standing by the front-hall pews, talking to Sophie and Andrea, when our permanently unfriendly IPS teacher sidled up to him, clutched his elbow, and, in a gesture that was both girlish and motherly—was, when I thought about it, Naomi-ish—pressed her shoulder to his and tilted her head as if she were going to rest hers there.

"Well, well, well," Brodsky said, to the ladies as much as to him, "look at you, all grown up and handsome. Do you remember what a terror you were in ninth grade?"

"Yes," Dolinski said, with a generous, self-effacing batting of his eyes, "and I also remember *you* being my favorite teacher."

"You and your sweet lies," said Brodsky. And then she noticeably gave his arm an extra squeeze. "You almost make me want to be a different woman."

One afternoon, I spotted Sophie, Andrea, and Dolinski leaving the building, so I followed them. They were headed "under the stairs," to the carport that was at the bottom of a ramp between two buildings on Ninety-Seventh Street. I too descended, breathing the trio's smoke, which wafted toward me as I tapped the iron railing on my way down the steps and, once arrived, and having no idea what I was doing, took a spot at the far end of the space across from the three upperclassmen, leaning against the wall and trying not to be too obvious about my out-of-placeness. I glanced, now and again, toward the stairs, as if my buddy were arriving any second. At first the trio paid me no mind, but it wasn't long before I had their attention.

"Waiting for someone?" Andrea asked me.

"Dude's a narc," Sophie said, and then, like my grandmother, tusked smoke through her nostrils.

"It's Griffin, right?" Dolinski said. Then to Sophie: "He and I were in detention a couple of weeks ago."

I was shocked he remembered my name.

"McQuarrie," he said gloomily, "was our proctor. He never did get around to tying us up in his little dungeon down there, did he?"

I shook my head, disarmed by the olive branch of his inclusion.

He said, "You wrestled my friend Vince Voelker. From Dalton."

"I guess you could call it that," I said.

For Dolinski, smoking was an art. Even I, who'd never taken a single puff, could appreciate his grace. He took in each lungful with gusto, as if he were testing his wind, letting it float out on his words as he spoke. "He told me you were one tough nut."

My heart had been bruised by Amanda, it was true, but I couldn't help finding this cheering.

"*I* still think he's a narc," Sophie said.

Mr. Damiano appeared. He was greeted by the trio warmly, familiarly. When he spoke, the unlit cigarette in his mouth jumped like a seismometer's pen. He was offered a light by Dolinski—his Zippo tinging when he opened it and whose scent of butane also reminded me of my grandmother. He covered the flame with his hand, even though we were hidden from the wind. Damiano, acknowledging my presence, said, "Your date not show?"

I shrugged.

"Griffin's in my spring play," Damiano said to the trio. "And the new Alan Hornbeam picture."

"An actor *and* an athlete," Sophie said, and stamped her dropped butt. "Can he dance too?"

Dolinski shook his head at her, then flicked his cigarette to the ground and, chuckling, dragged his sole across it. "You are such a bitch," he said.

"What he *can* do," Damiano said, "is squander his talent playing a superhero." Then he reached into his blazer's breast pocket, produced his pack of cigarettes, and, shaking one out, extended it toward me. "But I'm trying to change his evil ways."

"Well, you know what they say, Mr. Damiano"—I bit the filter between my teeth, cupped my hand over Dolinski's flame, and, before inhaling, repeated an observation I'd heard my dad make a thousand times—"those who can't do, teach."

A ghost filled my lungs. Its steamy form draped itself against my chest's cavity. Its barber-hot towel softly stuffed my ribs. Its billowy expanse, rising up, wanted to escape my throat; and I finally let it, in one great arrow-straight stream that hissed past my lips, this imitation of a seasoned smoker so spot-on I appeared like some street urchin who'd taken up the habit at ten.

"Be seeing you," said Dolinski.

"Later, narc," said Sophie.

"Nice to meet you, Ethan," said Andrea.

"Rehearsal this weekend," said Damiano, and pointed at me.

I flicked the butt to ash and, in a farewell gesture, winked at them as they took the stairs. As I watched them ascend, I felt the color leave my face and the blood abandon my buzzing brain. The moment they were gone, the nausea rose up while I bent double, palms to knees, and with a terrible gargle sprayed the carport with puke. There came a second gushing heave. And then with my back arched, I spewed a third time. I wiped my mouth and then flung my last cigarette ever onto the puddle, spitting several times at the mess. Spitting through my watery eyes. Spitting at the man that, to Amanda at least, I was not.

Several weeks passed. Spring was in full bloom. Central Park was the forest of Arden. *As You Like It* was about to premiere. I'd taken Marc Mason up on his offer to join the game in between rehearsals, and was deep into the *D&D* campaign. I almost ran into Naomi. One Saturday afternoon, on the way to Gray's Papaya for a couple of hot dogs, I spotted her at the Greek diner, seated at a table in the window, with, of all people, my mom, as well as her daughters, Danny and Jackie, the four of them yukking it up like a group of ladies who lunch.

Did I long for our talks, as lovelorn as I was?

I most certainly did not. Now that Amanda had told me about Dolinski; now that, at her request, we were "just friends," she called me almost every night, and I lived for these chances. It was like being her boyfriend's understudy; it made me hope he'd actually break a leg. She, as if to increase my already terrible confusion, made me hope. She was so forthcoming and sweet I could, if I cauterized my heart's ventricles, pretend to enjoy myself. "Can you hear that?" Amanda said, cupping the receiver, which made her voice breathy and, somehow, nearer to my ear. "That's my mom on her ham radio. Listen," she ordered. There was a pause while she held the phone in the air. I could barely make out what her mother was saying. "She likes to talk to friends from Australia late at night," Amanda said when she came back on. "Because it's fourteen hours ahead. Do you want to know the crazy thing?"

I wanted to know everything.

"The longer she talks to them, the more her accent changes. And she picks up their expressions too. You know what 'hit the frog and toad' means?"

"No."

"Hit the road. You know what 'crack a fat' means?"

I didn't.

"Then I'm not telling you," she said, "because it's embarrassing."

"Okay."

"Unless you come babysit tomorrow."

"Sure."

Oren, on his way back from the kitchen, a bowl of cereal in hand, paused before my closet's open door, shook his head at me, and, between spoonfuls, said, "Sad."

I pulled the door closed so that Amanda and I wouldn't be interrupted.

And I made it a point, after the previous evening's conversation, to march straight up to Mr. McQuarrie the next morning so I could impress Amanda with my knowledge that afternoon.

"Sir," I said, "I have a question only you can answer."

McQuarrie spot-checked me, shoes to tie. "That's a lot of pressure, Mr. Hurt, but I'll give it a fair go."

"What does 'crack a fat' mean?"

"Well, crikey," he said, positively amused, "it means we'll see you on detention this Saturday."

Amanda could not stop laughing when I told her. We were at the garret apartment, and while she laughed, she pulled me close and cupped her hand to my ear, since Suzy was within earshot, and her touch sent a shiver straight to my soles. "It means," she whispered, "get an erection."

I blushed, and Amanda smiled. She adjusted her position so that she could lie on her side and place her ear on my lap. "This is nice," she said. She curled into me. Her face relaxed. "Do you ever realize how tired you are all the time?"

I did, and I let my hand come to rest on her hip. The window unit hummed. It was Anthony Quinn week on *The 4:30 Movie*. They were showing *The Guns of Navarone*. We were at the part when David Niven discovers his timers and fuses have been sabotaged and that there's a traitor on their commando team. "This is a great scene," I said to Amanda and Suzy, who was stretched out on the floor and looked at me, exasperated.

"You always do that at the good parts," she said.

This *was* a good part, I thought, what with Amanda all to myself and my palm at rest atop her skirt. Because Suzy was near us, because I was afraid to move an inch, the actors' voices sounded especially distinct and loud.

So what does she do? Niven says. *She disappears into the bedroom, to change her clothes. And to leave a little note. And then she takes us to the wedding party, where we're caught like rats in a trap because we can't get to our guns. But even if we can it means slaughtering half the population of Mandrakos.*

Amanda, drifting off, said, "Tell me what's happening."

As best I could, I tried to catch her up. The war hanging in the balance. The Axis's plan to wipe out thousands of marooned soldiers. The elite team of commandos on a desperate mission to blow up the Germans' top secret weapon, a pair of long-range guns housed in an impregnable mountain. And now a spy in the team's midst.

She said, "It sounds exciting."

"My parents went on their honeymoon with Anthony Quinn," I said.

"So cool," Amanda murmured.

"My dad was his voice coach."

Did I think Dad's adjacency to stardom might confer on me a sort of glamour in Amanda's eyes—as if it might function as a sort of spotlight that revealed me, standing on her stage? I'd been in a Hornbeam picture, after all. Why did I need the assistance?

Softly, Amanda said, "I could fall asleep right now."

Her eyes were closed, and I considered her profile. She was very close, very far, very still; I was very still, very happy, very sad. Oh, that tiny apartment, where we spent most of our time together. Of all the places in my memory that I'm certain would seem smaller if I revisited them, this one, I'd like to believe, would in fact seem larger, being, as it was, the site of one of my first and most tender acts. I raised my hand and stroked her hair. I slowly dragged my thumb across her temple, letting my hand rise slightly as it ran past her ear and, in an unbroken circle, settle again, to touch her once more, until her weight gradually sank, barely perceptibly, into my lap. An act that, imitating love, was the closest to it, at that moment, that I thought I could get. And one of the rare occasions I caught Amanda acting, because her fluttering eyelids were a dead giveaway: she was pretending to be asleep.

The following Saturday morning, when I showed up in the basement theater and reported to Damiano that I had detention, he slowly shook his head and said to the cast, "Take five, people." Then he asked me, "Who's the proctor?" When I told him I didn't know yet, he said, "Let's go," and we marched upstairs to the front hallway and waited.

It turned out it was Miss Sullens. They spoke softly, and after exchanging a knowing look, first at me and then at each other, she gave me permission to skip.

"Don't thank me all at once," Damiano said as we walked back downstairs.

To which I replied, "I won't."

Since performances began next week, we were in dress rehearsal. Wearing a ruff, doublet, breeches, and hose, plus shoes like a pixie's, I sat in the wings, feeling like a total asshole. But because we were doing two run-throughs today and my pair of scenes came early in the first act,

I didn't have to be back for the second performance until after lunch. Which meant that I could head upstairs for the next several hours and rejoin the *D&D* game.

Marc Mason, upon seeing me at the classroom door, considered my costume and said, "Well, at least you're into it."

Todd Wexworth, who was barely a pair of eyes above his Dungeon Master screen, said to him, "You hear the story about those guys that died in the sewers because they wanted to play live action?"

Jason Taylor, a British middle schooler playing a halfling thief, said, "I'm quite certain that's a muh, muh—" He stammered on *"myth."*

"—apocryphal."

Angel Rincondon, a dwarven cleric, said to him, "Actually, one of them was my cousin."

Kazu Makabe, who was playing a ranger, said, "Can we resume, please?"

Chip Colson, a seventh-grade kid playing a ninth-level mage, said to me, "You bring money for pizza?"

I handed him a five.

"Throw in more," said Hogi Hyun to me—he was playing a monk— "and I'll give you a couple of my doughnuts."

"I'm glad you're here," Marc said to me—he was playing a bard— "because I'm sick of two-handing your character," which was what the group did whenever a player character was absent and a rare concession to Wexworth's usually orthodox observation of the rules. Marc had saved me the seat next to his and, when I took it, slid me my notebook and bag of dice.

I was playing a half-elf assassin—I'd named him Sylvanus—whom Wexworth had boosted to the eighth level so that I wasn't a drag on the party.

Play recommenced. We were seeking to penetrate the dreaded Tower of Marahall, and the party was forced to split up. Wexworth exiled Mason, Colson, and me to the hallway, where we took a seat. Mason, who was massive, gave his Afro several pokes with his blowout comb and then stuck it near his forehead, so that it looked like a samurai's date-mono. Fall to spring, he wore short-sleeved button-down shirts, a dress-code violation for which the faculty gave him a permanent pass. He was

built like a linebacker and played power forward on the varsity basketball team. He was also a math student of some renown. This largeness he
projected, the brains and the brawn, was nowhere near as impressive as
his haughtiness. I figured we'd be outside for a while, so as we were leaving I asked Mason if I could borrow his *Player's Handbook* to study while
we waited. He said, "Fine, just don't read my notes," but I did anyway.
There were fighting strategies and mnemonics regarding certain monsters and druidic spells. There were wicked cool diagrams, though by far
my favorite was the Character Alignment Graph:

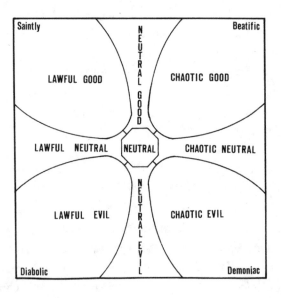

I could not help but analyze the souls of those nearest and dearest
to me (Amanda: chaotic good; Fistly: lawful evil; Mom: lawful neutral,
Dad: chaotic neutral, Oren: chaotic neutral).

"Why do I need to 'be mindful of weather in outdoor combat'?" I
asked, echoing one of the notes I had just read.

Mason, who was talking to Chip, held up a finger to him and
said, "What do you think happens if you Call Lightning during a
thunderstorm?"

Chip said to Mason, "Did you hear they're going to add a new class
of magic user this August?"

Mason scoffed. "No one's seen the revised rulebook, you fucking nerd."

"My cousin in Kenosha has," Chip said. "He was at Gen Con last year and that was the rumor."

"What's the 'Gen' in Gen Con stand for?" I asked.

"Lake Geneva," Chip said.

I didn't know anything about anything. I didn't even know where Lake Geneva was, or Kenosha.

"As you can tell," Mason said to me, "Chip's not getting a lot of action here at Boyd."

Chip pushed up his glasses, then crossed his skinny arms. "Neither are you, blood."

"Oh, snap," Mason said.

Wexworth opened the door. "Gentlemen, will you join us, please?"

We stepped inside.

Everyone in the room looked upset, except for Wexworth.

When Mason took his seat, he said, "Don't they have to leave the room?"

"No," Wexworth said. "They're all dead."

I'd gotten so wrapped up in the game I'd spaced on rehearsal. Damiano appeared at our door and said, "Hey, asshole, did you forget something?" He waved for me to follow him, but as we were leaving the classroom, Mason called out, "Mr. D," and caught up with us outside. "Can I have a word with Griffin, please?" And while Damiano stood in the hallway, fists to hips, Mason said to him, "It's private."

"Come to the theater the second you're done," Damiano said.

We watched him huff off.

Mason said, "You still don't know what you're doing in there." When I started to apologize, he interrupted. "Cut the bullshit. I've got plans for your character but not if you don't. So straight up. Do you want to play or not?"

I nodded.

"Then march your *tyro* ass to West Side Comics and buy the books. Don't come back until you do."

I started to walk away.

"And, Griffin," Mason said. When I turned around, he added, "*Read them.*"

Which I did not. At least not at first. Late that afternoon, on the bus ride home from the store, I opened the *Player's Handbook* to its table of contents and scanned its endless appendices and tables and charts and its preface, at which point I closed the book, cowed, and opened the *Dungeon Master's Guide.* This was an even thicker, more intimidating volume, and as if it were a flipbook, I let its pages flap from front to back with my thumb and spied its index, its vast glossary of miscellaneous treasure and magic interrupted by pictures that were far easier to pause and dream on than the blocks of text were to peruse. And then, randomly, I stopped at "General Naval Terminology," the first several items of which read:

Aft—the rear part of a ship.
Corvice—a bridge with a long spike in its end used by the Romans for grappling and boarding.
Devil—the longest seam on the bottom of a wooden ship.
Devil to pay—caulking the seam of the same name. When this job is assigned, it is given to the ship's goof-off and thus comes the expression "You will have the devil to pay."

Who knew? Not I, the ship's goof-off. Caulking the seam until he abandons ship. Which I now considered. Or, if I were to stay, if I were to stick it out, at the very least I'd ultimately hand off that role to someone lowlier, yes? I took a moment to gaze out the window. We were passing the Museum of Natural History, the building's footprint stretching two full city blocks, and in my mind, I was a child again. Mom had practically raised Oren and me there, we spent so much time racing through its corridors. I spotted the Seventy-Seventh Street entrance, our usual point of ingress, and a map of its levels, long ago memorized, floated before me in three dimensions, and I mentally made my way through the Hall of New York State Environment, past the log-sized earthworm and cross section of the redwood with its historical markers at each ring, through the Hall of North American Forests and the Hall of Biodiversity to my destination, the Hall of Ocean Life, where, after a loop around the mezzanine, I descended the wide stairs to the bottom level, where I'd lie on the floor, beneath the blue whale, feeling the subway rumble below, waiting until Mom and Oren finally caught up with me. And when they did, I would walk them past every diorama and, like a tour guide, supply the scientific name of every creature—*Architeuthis, Physeter macrocephalus*—my recall as perfect as a marine biologist's.

I found Mom in her bedroom, seated at her desk, typing an essay she'd handwritten on a yellow pad. There were Henry James novels piled around her. Her Smith Corona hummed with current. She was a superfast typist, she didn't need to look at the keys, and when she hit RETURN and the platen slid to the right, the whole table shuddered.

"Hey, Griff," she said, and kept typing. "Did you sleep at Tanner's last night?"

"No," I said. "I was here."

"Oh."

"Where's Oren?"

"He and Matt are at Dad's studio."

"Doing what?"

"Recording something, I think."

"What does 'q.v.' mean?" I asked.

She paused to look at me. "I thought you took Latin," she said.

I'd failed middle school Latin, which she just now recalled.

"*Quod vide,*" she said. When I repeated the phrase, still perplexed, she added, " 'See which.' "

"Like . . . the monster?"

"What?" she said, and squinted. Then she chuckled. "No. As in: 'With regard to this matter, go see x.' "

"Ah," I said.

She resumed her typing.

"What about 'tyro'?" I asked.

She nodded toward the *Merriam-Webster* on the table. "Look it up," she said.

Standing there, I flipped through the dictionary's onionskin pages until I found the definition: "a beginner in learning anything; novice."

"Can I borrow this?" I asked.

"Only if you bring it back," Mom said.

Later, in our room, while I was studying the *Monster Manual,* Oren appeared.

"Yo," he said when he entered. He was wearing sunglasses and his Walkman headphones. He was also carrying a bag from Tower Records. When I asked Oren a question, he pulled one of the earphones away from his head.

"I said," I repeated, "why are you wearing your sunglasses inside?"

"Because I'm maxing and relaxing," Oren said.

"Because you're a douche bag," I said.

"Because I'm . . ." He let the earphone spring back.

Melle Mel, right on time
And Taurus the bull is my zodiac sign
And I'm Mr. Ness and I'm ready to go
And I go by the sign of Scorpio

He popped and locked, did a bit of the Robot, and then slid the earphones around his neck. "Matt and I cut a single." He held up the cassette. "Want to hear?" He slid the tape into our deck. A drum machine started up. Next, Oren and Matt alternated raps:

We're the White Boys
We're white as can be
Hey yo, my name O-reo
And I'm M-A-double T.

"That's great," I said over the song, "if you're retarded."

"You're just jealous of our talent."

"An Oreo isn't as white as can be."

"Fair," Oren conceded.

"How about Matty Matt instead?"

"How about," Oren said, "you join the group. You could be DJ McGriff."

"Why the 'Mc'?"

"Because you're fast, like McDonald's."

The phone rang. Mom immediately picked up. Then she shouted, "Griffin, it's for you."

It was Amanda.

"I know this is last minute, but are you busy later?" she asked. Her voice was so bright and ringing it was close to shrill. When I told her I was free, she said, "My father's in town and wanted to take me to dinner. He said I could bring someone."

"Sure," I said, and punched the sky. "What time?"

"Can you be here by six thirty? It's probably a fancy place." When I told her yes, she said, "Great," and then gave me her address. "I'll see you soon."

When I hung up, Oren said, "You should come record with us tonight."

"Can't," I said. "Got a date."

"With who?"

"You don't know her."

"Maybe she lives in Canada," Oren said. He produced the forty-five of Grandmaster Flash's "Freedom," touched the needle to the vinyl, and when the kazoos kicked in, he started dancing, so I joined him until the end of the track, because it was the only way to deal with my nervous excitement.

Later, I was leaving just as Mom was setting the table.

"Where are you going?" she asked.

"To dinner."

From our bedroom, Oren shouted, "With a girl."

"Oh," Mom said, and smiled. "Just the two of you?"

"And I think her dad," I said.

Mom gave me the once-over. "Then go put on some khakis and a button-down." When I rolled my eyes she said, "Loafers too."

"I'm gonna be late."

"*Go,*" she said.

I lurched back to my room to change and shambled back for inspection right as Dad was pulling up his chair. "I hear you have a hot date," he said.

"He's meeting her father," Mom said.

"He can't wear that shirt then," Dad said.

"Why?" I groaned.

"It's wrinkled."

"I have to *go*."

He snapped his fingers three times quick. "Give it to me," Dad said. He pushed back from the table and went to the kitchen. He emerged with the ironing board and folded open the legs, and its wire made its subway screech. He waved to me—*c'mon, c'mon*—to hand him the shirt, which I removed and then sat down on the couch, topless, burning with impatience and shame as my back stuck to the leather. He returned with the iron and plugged it in. The signal lamp was red. After another trip to the kitchen, Dad appeared with a can of spray starch and a measuring cup full of water. He carefully poured the latter into the iron's nostril. He waited until the iron burbled and sighed. Dad did a cuff first, spreading it over the board's nose, hitting it with some starch and a puff of steam, and then stretched out the sleeve, running the sole plate along its hemline with a couple of farty pumps of the spray button. I could see Dad's reflection in the framed painting's glass, the one above the living room's console table of a bouquet that had survived the fire. His expression was focused and calm, and now, as he ran the iron's nose between the shirt's plackets, steam chuffed merrily from the machine. Then he flipped over the shirt to do the back. Finally, after setting the iron on its heel, he hooked the shirt by the hanging loop and held it out to me on his index finger. It appeared slightly boxy and sculptural. Buoyant, so that it twirled ever so slightly, like a mobile.

When I put it on, he said, "Better." Then he kissed my forehead and patted my cheek. "Don't do anything I wouldn't do."

I took the Broadway bus uptown. I sat in the back. Something about the starched shirt made me feel like I was in a costume. That my current determination for tonight to go well was also a put-on. That my resolve, as currently stiff as my shirt's collar, would go soft and yellow the moment I was made to sweat. I stared out the window and took comfort in the familiar sights. The Seventy-Second Street subway station house, fashioned of granite and brick, exhaled passengers onto the crossing island where Amsterdam and Broadway intersected. The Apple Bank, the protuberant wrought-iron window guards of which were shaped like my grandmother's suet feeders. Hanging braids of garlic swayed in the breeze above boxes of fruits and vegetables at the Fairway Market. We passed the Apthorp Building—it had an interior courtyard, visible through its entryway's arch, before which Mom once took my shoulders to stop me in my tracks and pointed to an older gentleman wearing a bright silk scarf around his neck. ("That," she whispered behind me, "is George Balanchine.") We crossed Ninety-Sixth Street, and soon I was walking down Amanda's block, the Cathedral of Saint John the Divine walling off my eastern view.

Standing in the foyer of Amanda's building, I found WEST on the buzzer panel and pressed the button. Her mother said, "Who is it?" over the microphone. The moment I replied, the door buzzed and stayed buzzing for a good ten seconds after I'd entered. The lobby was dark. As I waited for the elevator, I noticed one of the bulbs in the overhead was dead. The floor was fashioned of black and white tile and smelled sharply of piss.

Miss West greeted me at their apartment door. "Come in," she said, having already turned, and, waving, beckoned me to follow her down a narrow hallway. I noted a small kitchen to my left and, straight ahead, a bedroom whose door was closed and from which music played. I stepped through a pair of French doors to my right, into a living room, where Miss West took a seat on the sofa and an already lit cigarette from the ashtray. The wallpaper was gray, pocked and torn in places, and faded. The windows were soot-covered, and this further dimmed the light. It occurred to me, in a flash, that on the continuum of people I knew—from the Adlers and Pilchards and Dolinskis, to the Shahs and the Barrs and the Pottses, and then Cliffnotes's family and mine—Amanda's mother was the closest thing I knew to poor.

I extended the bouquet of roses I'd bought toward her.

"Oh, these are lovely." Miss West ashed her cigarette and took the flowers in her free hand. She briefly smiled after considering them. "No wonder you're not her type," she said, and then strode to the kitchen.

I heard the plastic wrap crumpling (my heart), scissors snipping (my head), faucet running (my blood), a cabinet squeak and then bang shut (my hopes). The only illumination in the room came from Miss West's ham radio, whose components sat on a catty-cornered desk, the faces above its several knobs backlit. Miss West had returned with a vase and placed the flowers on the coffee table. She was markedly taller than Amanda but also broad-shouldered; she had thick arms and she looked at me with something between disregard and pity. Her interest, I felt, could suddenly turn dangerous. She had blue eyes, larger than her daughter's. She and Amanda shared the same complexion and coloring—she too was blond, though she wore her hair short—with identical noses, their tips lightly crimped down the center. But there the similarity ended. Miss West took a long pull on her cigarette, and the cherry flared brightly as it crawled down the paper. After she crushed it out, she said, "You're the actor Amanda was telling me about. The boy who was in *The Talon Effect*. I loved that movie. Though I told Amanda I couldn't for the life of me remember anything about your performance. Didn't you play the son of Rip Torn?"

"You're thinking of Roy Scheider. Torn played the double agent."

"Is Rip Torn his real name? I've always wondered."

"He told me it was a nickname."

"It's mostly the Jews who have stage names," Miss West said. "Like Lauren Bacall. Or Tony Curtis. I have a friend I talk to in Hungary who keeps a list of them. You know Han Solo?"

"You mean Harrison Ford?"

"Jew," she said. Then she looked over my shoulder. "Look who's finally ready."

I turned to face Amanda. I said hello, though I was not sure if the word came out. I realized, as I stared, that I had only ever seen her in her school uniform and without makeup. She waited between the French doors in a black dress and a pair of gold necklaces. She had pulled her hair back and tied it off. Her feet, tipped into black heels, made her as tall as I was. I thought of all the makeup chairs I had sat in, how other actors had what seemed a new face put on once they were through. But in Amanda's case, in lipstick and eyeliner, what was revealed was the woman she would become, the thousand ships she might launch. That she seemed entirely unaware of this power's limitlessness made it all the more impressive.

"You look nice," I said.

"So do you."

"Where'd you get that dress?" Miss West asked her.

"Dad bought it for me."

"Well," Miss West said, "there's a first time for everything."

The phone rang.

"I'll get it," Amanda said.

"Stay where you are," her mother said, "smell the roses your friend brought me."

Amanda froze as Miss West strode toward the kitchen. She smiled at me again but then turned her ear toward the hall.

"Oh," Miss West said when she answered, a little grumpily, "hello." A pause. "You too," she said. And then: "She is, in fact, although she's on her way to a dinner." When Miss West reappeared, she said to Amanda, "It's Rob."

In a flash, Amanda was gone. The speed with which she hurried to answer hooked something deep in my gullet, dragging it with her. With Miss West, it registered with some embarrassment and, bless her, some sympathy.

"Ditching her at the last minute," she said of Rob. "*Not* gentlemanly." Then: "Not that it stops him."

From where I stood, I turned to see Amanda lift the receiver from the counter, turn her back to us, and press it to her ear. At which point I noticed Miss West was standing close behind me.

"You'd think she'd learn," she said, "with a father like hers, to pick the ones that don't run. But the ones who run only teach their kids to chase. Cigarette?" she offered.

"No thanks," I said.

"Or," she muttered, catching fire, "maybe he has a ten-inch cock."

Before I could even begin to react to this baffling statement, Amanda said, "Should we go?" She was awaiting me in the hall.

"Nice to meet you, Griffin," Miss West said. Then, before she closed the door, said to her daughter, "No matter where your dad takes you. Get the steak."

After we left the apartment, Amanda and I did not speak. We remained silent even after we turned north on Broadway. Amanda kept her arms crossed and her eyes to her shoes, as if by staring them down she might silence her heels against the pavement. When a passing stranger, seeing us so dressed and, inferring we were a couple, smiled, this only seemed to increase her inwardness. I was dim but no dummy. I knew that my presence deepened Amanda's gloom, that my status as stand-in was a reminder she'd been stood up and burdened our stroll with a feeling of obligation. I realized my only currency was to provide comfort, and the only coins I had to play were changing the subject, so I asked where we were going. "To Columbia," Amanda said. "My dad's attending a reading there before we eat." But then she turned quiet again, and her silence was intolerable.

"What does he do for a living?"

"He's an English professor," Amanda said. "At a boarding school in New Hampshire."

"Which one?" I asked. As if I knew any.

"Brewster."

I felt my lower lip cover my upper one as I nodded. "What's the difference between a professor and a teacher?"

"A PhD and an ego," Amanda said.

I waited. "What about your mom?"

"She's a nurse. At Mount Sinai. Just a few blocks from here." She brightened a bit. "That was sweet of you to get her roses," she said. And then, she took my arm in both of hers. It was the charitableness of it that made it torture; it was the devotion that it so easily summoned in me that made it pleasant. And once I figured out how to walk normally and be held by her at the same time, I could nod at the passersby and enjoy that, for now, she was mine.

"Speaking of roses," Amanda said, "she's going to lash me with them if I don't bring her home a doggie bag. Every time I go to dinner with my dad, that's the rule."

"My cousins get the belt. But only if they curse."

"My mom prefers the back of a hairbrush."

"My dad likes to lift me by the scruff. Like a kitten." I demonstrated on myself, walking on tiptoes, but without moving the arm Amanda held, a marionetting that made her laugh.

"She used to lock my brother and me in the closet for hours, but that was only when we were little. No wonder he asked the judge if he could live with my father."

We'd entered Columbia's gates. The three long walkways were made of the same hexagonal paving stones as in Central Park. The paths were tree-lined. Black iron posts connected by black chains fenced off the greenspace. It seemed as if we were passing through a tunnel to a different world, or a city hidden within the city, for we now entered a great expanse whose buildings were of an entirely different architecture. To our right, a long rectangular building was fronted by columns whose facade was engraved with names from my seventh grade class in ancient history: HERODOTUS, SOPHOCLES, PLATO, ARISTOTLE. To our left, flanked by a pair of wide flights of stairs, was a domed building in front of which a statue of an enthroned woman with open arms was surrounded by students who sat and talked in the spring-softened evening. I considered this sky, the view of which was unimpeded, its immense breadth somehow even more clearly and discretely framed by these low-slung rooftops.

Someone called out Amanda's name. It seemed to come from everywhere. On the wide steps surrounding the statue, a man and woman stood and, while Amanda and I waited, walked toward us. Both appeared formally dressed—I said a silent word of thanks to Mom and Dad—Amanda's father in a bow tie and blue blazer, the woman in a man's blazer and jeans. But when they drew close, the woman accompanying Amanda's father was revealed to be someone nearer our age. Amanda's father so identically resembled her he may as well have been her twin.

After kissing Amanda, he introduced us to Tina Debrovner, "my most talented senior." If Amanda, dressed and made up thus, seemed costumed as the woman she would one day become, Tina already embodied this. She wore cowboy boots and worn-in bell-bottom jeans, a silver belt buckle with a piece of turquoise at its center, and a brown silk blouse that matched her tweed blazer. Her makeup was light; her chestnut-colored hair and lashes were long; her green eyes flashed. Above her top lip, on its right side, was a mole that, for the first time in my life, conferred luster on the term *beauty mark*. Her style seemed fully realized; her comfort in her person spoke to everything aspirational in the word "adult." Her hands were pressed into her blazer's pockets, and she removed one and held it out to Amanda and then me with the total confidence of an elder and none of the condescension of a superior. Amanda's father then reached out a hand to me and introduced himself as Dr. West. "You must be Rob," he said.

"Griffin," I said.

He glanced at Amanda, confused.

"Rob's at Vassar," she said, "visiting his sister."

Dr. West winked at me. "Visiting co-eds is more like it." Then, to Amanda, whom he'd clearly rocked, said to her, "But maybe they don't call them that anymore." He checked his watch. "Let's head to Butler, shall we? I made a reservation."

We started walking, Amanda and I behind Dr. West and Tina. To change the subject, I asked, "How was the reading?"

"Wonderful," Dr. West said.

When I asked who the author was, Tina looked over her shoulder and said, "Shirley Hazzard. Do you know her? She read from her new novel."

"*The Transit of Venus*," Dr. West said. "Which, I'll add, Tina did not like."

She rolled her eyes. "I didn't say I didn't like it. I just found its style . . . dense."

"More likely you're too young to understand it."

"I didn't think it was beyond my comprehension. It was a scene," she explained to Amanda and me, "when a man and a woman go on a first date together in the English countryside, and he tells her a secret."

"That's what happens," Dr. West cut in, "but it isn't what's happening."

"I'm *getting* to the subtext," she said, and there was ample warmth in her exasperation. "What's happening is that the man is in love with the woman, but the woman has already decided she can never love this man. That she'll remain permanently out of his reach and he'll be permanently reaching toward her, he'll do anything just to catch a glimpse of her, just like . . ." She placed her index finger to her chin. "The planet Venus in transit. Does that," she now said to Dr. West, "sound right?"

"It sounds perfect. Until you get to the end."

"What I don't buy," Tina continued, "is that we have such complete conviction about such things from the word go."

"That's because at your age," Dr. West said, "you still believe you can love things out of people. Or love them into your life."

"It's less a question of belief," Tina said playfully. "I just know you're wrong."

"So based on the audience of a single chapter, you're ready to dismiss the work outright?"

"Yes," she said.

"That sounds to me like complete conviction. From the word go."

Tina laughed warmly. "Touché."

Dr. West turned to me and said, "Tina is a romantic, while I am a realist."

"What's wrong with being a romantic?" she said.

"It tends toward the neurotic."

"Well, this neurotic finds most realists crotchety."

"Don't forget condescending," Amanda said.

Dr. West, gratified, said, "What about you, Griffin? Realist or romantic?"

Overmatched, I parroted a line that my father loved to use in such situations. "I just work here," I said.

Everyone laughed at this. Even Amanda, whom, I realized, her father had not asked and who, when she smiled appreciatively at my joke, was, I thought, trying to *remain* romantic, in spite of current evidence— Rob's absence, my presence, and her mom's ordinance—to the contrary. Which made me, I realized, feel for her. In spite of myself.

"Well," Dr. West said, gesturing toward a building on our left, "here we are."

From the hallway we walked onto an elevator. Dr. West pressed the topmost button, and next the doors opened onto the restaurant's entrance, which read, in gold letters, TERRACE IN THE SKY. Waiters in black tie hurried between tables with white napkins draped over their arms or cradled bottles of wine or balanced oval trays. A tiered dessert stand went rolling by. The hostess led us to our table at the deck's corner. Dr. West pulled out Tina's chair, and I did the same for Amanda. The sunset had draped its fading pink blanket above the city, and my seat had a view I'd never before enjoyed: the northwestern corner of Central Park, that Sherwood Forest it sometimes seemed Manhattan had been built to enclose, its walkways dimpled by its snow-white globes, just now beginning to shine.

Following Dr. West's lead again, I snapped open my napkin and laid it on my lap. Dr. West, looking down his nose, seemed to somehow peruse the menu with his chin. When the waiter asked for our drink order, Dr. West said, "Ladies?" and Amanda said, "White wine spritzer, please," and Tina said, "Sex on the Beach, please." To Dr. West's glance, once he, in a bit of acting, recomposed himself from Tina's order, I replied, "You first, sir," and with his menu still open, Dr. West said, "Martini up, please, very dry, olives." And I said to the waiter, "Same," at which Dr. West nodded approvingly.

"Griffin, do you know how to make the perfect martini?" he asked. "Into your shaker you add ice, then very good gin. Next you take a capful of vermouth"—and between his thumb and index finger he held up an invisible cap—"wave it over your tumbler"—he made several circles—"and then throw it over your shoulder."

At this, the girls, who clearly understood him, laughed.

We all considered our menus. Dr. West, breaking the silence, asked, "Well, everyone, what looks good?" To which Amanda replied, "I think the filet," and Tina said, "The duck à l'orange," and I said, "What do you recommend?" and Dr. West said, "I've got my eye on the fish en papillote," to which I, having no idea what it was, replied, "I was just looking at that myself."

The waiter was placing our drinks on the table. Dr. West raised his glass and said, "To the romantics." We all clinked, and when I sipped, what slid down my throat had the shininess and consistency of mercury and felt like a long snake made of ice.

Dr. West went on for a while about Shirley Hazzard. He mentioned that her husband was translating the letters of Flaubert. "Speaking of," he said, and asked Amanda if she'd bothered to read the copy he'd sent her of *Madame Bovary*. She replied that she was saving it for break. "I'll hold you to that when you come visit us at the beach," Dr. West said. "And what about you, Griffin? What are your summer plans?"

"I'll be working," I said.

Dr. West said to Amanda, "I like him more than Rob already. And where, might I ask?"

"NBC," I said.

"Griffin's an actor," Amanda said at her father's piqued expression. "He does TV and movies."

Tina, who had taken a bite of bread, covered her mouth and grabbed my wrist. "Wait, you weren't Rudi Stein in *The Bad News Bears,* were you?"

"He's in the new Alan Hornbeam film," Amanda said. "They shot it across the street from my school."

Tina, impressed, said, "I loved *Memento Morris.*"

"An actor," Dr. West said. "What school?" When I told him I went to Boyd Prep, he said, "No, I mean your formal training. Like the Method?"

I had no idea what that was.

"It's all baloney, of course," he said, waving his hand before his face. "Pasteurized. Self-obsessed. Quintessentially American."

Tina looked at me gravely and then at Dr. West as if to say, *Here we go again.*

"The British gave us Shakespeare and negative capability. America gave us autobiographical motivational narcissism," he said.

"Griffin's appearing in *As You Like It,*" Amanda offered. "At his school. I'm going to see it next weekend."

"And who do you play?" Dr. West asked.

"Charles the wrestler," I said.

"Wonderful," he said. "And what do you make of it?"

I looked at Amanda, who looked at her father. "I'm not sure I understand," I said.

"Of what Shakespeare is trying to say."

"I don't . . . We don't really talk about it like that."

"How about this: What do you think of *your* character? What do you see as his function in the drama? Certainly you'd have to have some idea of that in order to do your job."

"Well, he sort of explains everything," I said. "Like in Freytag's Pyramid—"

"Yes, but what *motifs* does he introduce? What plot levers does he pull?"

"I'm only in the first act," I said.

In what remains one of the most intimate gestures I have ever seen, Dr. West pointed his remaining speared olive at Tina, and she, without hesitation, plucked it from the toothpick with her teeth.

"It sounds to me," he said, "as if you don't even have a rudimentary grasp of the play's rhetorical architecture, let alone its plot. Which is sad, when you think about it, at least"—he starfished his hand against his chest—"to me. I mean, here you are, memorizing important literature, the most important literature there is, really, but you have no context for it whatsoever. You've got your part down cold, as it were, but no idea of the whole. You come onstage and say your lines, and then off you go. Like a dolphin miming human speech."

"Daddy," Amanda said.

"No," Dr. West said, "this is crucial." And then to me: "When you perform next week, maybe keep in mind that it's Charles who not only provides essential exposition to the audience but also supercharges the word 'fall' with meaning throughout the entire play. Whether it's to *suffer a fall,* as in lose one's stature—which Charles literally will do when Orlando stuns him with his wrestling victory—or *fall in love,* as Orlando and Rosalind do so suddenly and completely before the match transpires. And as Touchstone and Audrey will upon their arrival in the forest of Arden. And Phoebe with Ganymede. True, I've often thought it's nearly a deus ex machina that Duke Frederick falls in love with God toward the play's end, his religious conversion seems so entirely out of character. And, of course, there's the pun *fall on one's back,* which introduces the play's anxiety about everything from cuckoldry to premarital sex. And *falling out of love,* which stands in for the play's greatest anxiety— one which all the characters suffer—which is the passage of time. *Time,* which either ruins or changes everything—even a love well begun. And which, as Jaques notes in his 'seven ages' speech, none escape—its passage, I mean. But we are all always *wrestling* with that one."

Dr. West raised his eyebrows and smiled. The waiter appeared with the wine bottle. He went through his elaborate ritual. As he filled the second glass and tipped the bottle toward the third, Amanda held her stem with one hand. With her other, she took mine beneath the table-cloth and squeezed my palm comfortingly. While I, thoroughly enjoying her secret attention, smoldered with determination. Because I was offi-cially sick and tired of not being in the know.

Not that this spurred me to change. At least, not in the way one might think. Later, back at Amanda's apartment, her mother gone for the eve-ning, I soon forgot Dr. West's dressing down, having, as I did, Amanda to myself. Between her bedroom's twin beds there ran a strip of blue painter's tape, her brother's unoccupied bed, by her mother's decree, remaining right where it was, and the room divided evenly, Amanda explained, should he ever drop in for a visit or decide, one day, to finally come to his senses (these her mother's words) and move back in with them. Between the headboards there was also a small table with a record player atop it and sleeves of forty-fives and albums in the cubby below. While we talked, we listened to the Commodores' "Three Times a Lady," Earth, Wind, and Fire's "September," and John Lennon's "Watching the Wheels." At the far end of the bedroom was a bookcase, and on its shelves Amanda had a couple of pictures. One was of her father, standing before a body of water, somewhere coastal, a red house also in the background, holding both his children's hands. Amanda was maybe four years old in the photograph, towheaded, wearing a white dress with cornflower trim; her brother, Eric, a couple of years older, in a jacket and bow tie; and Dr. West, in what for all intents and purposes was the same outfit as tonight, with the exception of sunglasses, which gave him a more for-bidding, inscrutable appearance, perhaps also because he wasn't smiling. Her brother, Amanda remarked, was, in temperament, exactly like her mother, blunt at his worst, honest to a fault at his best. She had no idea how father and son tolerated each other, seeing as her mother and father could barely get through a conversation without fighting. When I asked her if she was more like her father, she said no, she was more like her grandmother, of whom there was also a picture, whose frame she handed to me and then joined me on her brother's bed to regard (in the reflec-tion of its tiny square of glass we were briefly framed), this of a woman on a deep-sea fishing boat, harnessed in the fighting chair, rod bent but secured in its gimbal, clearly some immense creature on the line. She was wearing a long skirt and blouse and fine shoes, as if she were headed to a summer cocktail party at a country club, shouting, happily, at the sport of it all, and she looked—this was the first thought that came to my mind— like Grace Kelly might on such an expedition: drop-dead gorgeous and perfectly overdressed. More precisely speaking, there was a clear lineage, appearance-wise, from grandmother to father to Amanda. Apparently, her grandmother had been a very wealthy woman, a socialite and art lover. If I'd grown up at the Museum of Natural History with my mom, then Amanda had spent hers wandering the Whitney and Guggenheim with her grandmother. She had apparently squandered her fortune on four marriages (the photo was taken on the boat of her second husband, a Cuban hotelier), and when I asked Amanda why she was more like her, since serial monogamy and heartbreak didn't seem like something to which one might intentionally aspire, she finally answered her father's question: "Because I'm a romantic too." Amanda replaced these photos on their shelves and continued to DJ ("Get Down Tonight," "Night Fever," "Give Me the Night"), and while we, like an old couple, lay in our separate beds, I could not help considering the photos further—they seemed traced in light to me, they branded my memory such that I was aware, in that moment, that they'd leave a mark, this a minor mutant ability I was just becoming aware of then and have since learned to trust, when an object or person seems limned in vividness, close to a camera's flash, an afterimage I know I'll contemplate later. It was only years hence that I came to consider those two photographs as the poles of Amanda's personality—and that I was here, in her life, to supply her with a measure of safety: I was harness and fighting chair while she angled for the elusive and mostly absent prize to thereby heal the suppurating wound of her departed father; that she, having learned that this was how the sport of love was played, would set that hook deep, as she'd done with me, as her grandmother had in that photo, but that she was determined to land that fish this time, and I could be damn well sure she'd stay rich to boot.

Not that I thought any of this at the time. I still believed *I* had an angler's chance. Which is why here is a good time to mention that Rob called just as Amanda placed "Escape (The Piña Colada Song)" on the turntable. "Hi!" she said, so ringingly it was clear all was immediately forgiven, even before he apologized for standing her up at dinner and explained he'd come home from Vassar early to make it up to her, could they get together tonight? And to my heartbreak I watched Amanda, beside herself with excitement, freshen her makeup in her bedroom's mirror and then offer to share a cab with me downtown (Rob was paying), dropping me off on my street before continuing on to Studio 54. I didn't bother to mention to Amanda—the both of us, by that point, having had enough of her dad for the evening—that out the cab's window, I spotted Dr. West and Tina walking down Broadway, her arm slipped through his, something that, back then, didn't strike me as especially odd, so well groomed was I by that time, so desensitized, up and down the food chain, to such behavior.

My own dad managed to come to opening night of *As You Like It* the following week, along with Oren and Mom. Amanda, who sat separately from them, was also in attendance. I spied them from the tiny theater's single wing just before curtain: my family seated front row center, Amanda in the back, alone. Suddenly I was something I never was in front of any camera: nervous. My scene with Duke Frederick went well, although I had to make it a point not to look at Oren, who was crossing his eyes at me. Before my bout with Orlando, I strode onstage to the audience's applause, milking the moment with a deep bow. I removed my tunic, as did scrawny Orlando. Suddenly, with Amanda and my father present, I was also something I never was before any camera: self-conscious. Orlando and I clasped (Damiano had asked me to do the fight's choreography), I shrugged his neck and chin under my forearm and, with my other upraised, triumphantly walked him about the stage, which got a laugh and elicited from Amanda the same beaming expression as when I'd first performed for her. When Orlando wriggled free, he ducked between my legs and then cuffed the back of my head—"O excellent young man!" shouted Rosalind—in response to which I charged him. He got me in a headlock and hip-tossed me to the ground, where I landed with a great bang, right in front of my father's seat. Orlando was victorious; I was "unconscious." Before a pair of Duke Frederick's men dragged me offstage by my wrists, I peeked at my father. He was frowning and, whether he was aware my eyes were on him, slowly shook his head in disapproval. *Why,* he seemed to be saying, *are you wasting your time doing this bit part?*

After curtain calls, there was a reception in the front hallway. Having never really been a member of the cast, I stood on the perimeter of the crowd. When my parents found me, Oren, with a plate of cheese and grapes, complained that if he'd known I was only in the show's first act he wouldn't have sat through the entire play. Dad, nodding at the passersby, spoke in his big voice, leaning into his truisms: "It's a very, *very* important comedy," he said. I was, he also noted, clearly the only pro in the troupe, though he had to grant the actors playing Rosalind and Orlando had "terrific chemistry," the girl who played Celia was "quite lovely, in fact," and then Amanda appeared.

She wore a sleeveless blue dress and high heels, as if this was opening night on Broadway, and she congratulated me and then handed me a present: "I made you a banana bread," she said. It was wrapped in tinfoil and plastic and had a ribbon tied around it. I introduced her to my family, and Mom said, "You must be the young lady Griffin had dinner with last week," and from that point forward, something remarkable happened: my father went quiet. There was some small talk, none that I made, or Dad either—even Oren gave Amanda all his attention as she and Mom chatted. I occasionally spied my father looking at Amanda with an expression that was, at the time, entirely unrecognizable to me. I might have called it approving, but there was something bittersweet about it, a wistfulness that was oddly reverential. It was so uncommon for him to be this watchful, and in that interval, I also noticed him watching me watch Amanda, since it was my chance to do so, secretly. At these moments, when we caught each other's eye, he smiled at me, warmly—the closest I could come to naming what his face conveyed was pride. But even that wasn't quite correct. There attended this attention a kind of generosity. It was a Thursday, a school night. Mom asked Amanda where she lived and, when Amanda told her, Mom said they'd driven the car uptown. "Shel," she suggested, "why don't you and Griffin take Amanda home, and Oren and I will take a cab."

When Oren asked, "Why wouldn't we all just drive together?" Mom replied, "Because I said so." She told Amanda it was lovely to meet her and then led my brother out the door.

This quiet that had settled over my father persisted during the drive. Amanda and I sat in the back seat and talked about the play. I caught Dad glancing at me in the rearview mirror now and again. He nodded, pleased.

"This is my building," Amanda said to my father.

Dad said to me, "Why don't you walk your friend to her door?"

Amanda said to him, "That's okay, we're right here."

Dad said, "I insist. Griffin, see the young lady upstairs. Amanda, it was lovely to meet you."

Inside, we boarded the elevator. Two feelings struggled for dominance. The first being relief that Amanda and I were finally alone. The second being the conviction that I'd have done a whole semester of performances just to have a moment like this. I smiled, warmed at these thoughts. I glanced at Amanda, who was smiling at the indicator lights as they brightened and then turned to smile at me. Here, once more, I heard the clarion call to action but did not obey. And then the lights went out and the car jerked to a halt.

"Oh no," Amanda said in the pitch-darkness, although she did not sound scared. "This happens sometimes."

"What do you do?"

"We wait," she said. "It's usually only for a minute. Though I was once stuck in here for three hours."

We stood in the blackness. Amanda's dress crinkled, as if it were alive.

"What would we do for three hours?" I asked. When my question's suggestiveness occurred to me, I was glad she couldn't see me blush.

"We could talk," she said.

"We could."

"It doesn't seem to me like we ever struggle for things to talk about."

I felt the same way.

"Sometimes," she continued, "I think that all the conversations you and I will ever have will be in places like this. Buses, elevators. The apartment where I babysit. My room. If that was for the rest of our lives, how much time would that add up to?" She took my hand; hers was damp.

And the tenderness I felt toward her surpassed my lovesickness, because I could tell that she, too, was a bit scared. "Do you ever think about that? How much time you'll spend doing dishes? Or that you'll really have with someone, like your brother or sister, if you do the math?"

The lights came on. We blinked at the brightness. The door opened. She said, "You're so talented," and kissed my cheek, which was partly a command to stay, and stepped off the car. Then she turned to wave good-bye and the door closed.

The elevator sank. I thought about what Amanda's mother had said the previous week, about picking the ones who don't run and how Amanda had been taught that love was a chase. Shouldn't love be a swimming *with,* like fish in a school, as opposed to a swimming *after*? And if I wasn't chasing, what was I doing?

That these questions had no answers made me miserable.

In the car, once I'd taken my seat in the back, Dad said to me, very gently, "Why don't you come sit up front?"

When I came around and took the seat next to him, he paused to regard me before shifting into gear. I sat slumped against the door, arms crossed, with my temple pressed to the window. He eased down the street, stopping again at the light. We stared at Saint John the Divine, its facade filling the entire windshield. It was late and the streets were empty. We could have parked here if we wished.

"Beautiful building," Dad said, and leaned forward, over the steering wheel, to look up at the cathedral. When I remained silent, he said, "You want to tell me about her."

I gave him a complete account of the past several weeks. They had seemed like years, and when I mentioned this, he nodded knowingly. By now he had backed into what, at an earlier hour, might not be considered a parking space, but did not kill the motor. He listened with the same respectful silence as earlier, sometimes lightly laughing with me, other times, with his elbow at rest on the door, rubbing his finger over his lips, as if he were thinking thoughts entirely private and tangential to mine. He had questions, now and again. I felt unburdened answering everything he asked, but when I concluded none of it mattered, it was all hopeless, he said, in what at the time felt like a such a complete rebuke of Dr. West I wanted to hug him, "You can't ever predict how a person's feelings might change over time."

We considered the cathedral again.

"When were you first in love?" I asked.

Whatever my father recalled, whatever made him shake his head, there was no acting in it.

He shifted the car into gear.

"Let's take a drive," he said.

This happened in 1952. My father had just turned nineteen. He was about to be drafted into the Korean War. The girl's name—the *woman,* he should say—was Millie Van Bourne. They had met several months beforehand, at the studio of their singing coach, Max Henson. They instantly fell in love. How else to explain this spotlight recognition? "She was very beautiful," my father said, "like your friend, but a platinum blond." Sharp-featured. Bright-eyed. From Wilmington, she'd come to New York to make a go of it as an actress. She hadn't had much success doing anything serious, nothing that could be called acting per se, though she was earning steady money as a color-TV model. In his mind there she stands, under the torpedo lights arrayed above the soundstage, her arms akimbo, her green sweater, brown skirt, blue eyes, and crimson lips matching up bar to bar with the spectrum's test wheel posted behind her. To save on rent, she was living on the Upper West Side with her two sisters. They were remarkably beautiful as well and shared a strong family resemblance, a gift evident in their faces' shape, a fullness to their lips, even a similarity in the appearance of their teeth that showed when they smiled and was subtly and gloriously altered in each: Glenda, the eldest, was the most imperious. She'd inherited their father's coloring and his down-the-nose glare. Maxine, the middle sister, was the most gorgeous, perhaps because she was the kindest. The tallest too, she slouched slightly. Stories dazzled her; she'd easily be brought to tears or laughter by them; she would touch her lips with her fingers while she listened. As for Millie, both women watched over her fiercely because she was the most impulsive, always breaking off whenever she saw a bright thing shining. They were always turning around to discover her gone. She elicited in men one of the most consuming desires there was, which was to rescue her. Out for an evening, at a party, standing together in the corner of a room, each with a drink in hand, they waited patiently for my father to join them, and when he did, they welcomed him like family. They spoke of holiday gatherings they'd invite him to, the countless cousins they wanted him to meet, Mom's huge spread. *This* was what he remembered most clearly, what made being in their presence such a powerful thing, this unconditional acceptance—to be Millie's *and* theirs—for they were so exotically American, so put together and stylish and educated, while he was a Jew from Middle Village, Queens, the son of a poor furrier living in the two-story home his grandfather had built, where curses were uttered in Hungarian, Russian, and Yiddish, while his own hopes, which he dreamed of in English, were far too presumptuous to share with anyone, even in his native tongue.

But he was drafted that summer, placed in the navy, and did basic at Bainbridge, though none of his training seemed to correspond with anything a seaman might need to function on a ship. There were countless hours of marching in pitiless heat, barely enough riflery to repulse an enemy's advance, and so much attention to the misbegotten task of doing laundry you might think crotch rot was a greater threat to the free world than communism. In the evenings he wrote Millie a letter about his day, taking great pains to find something new to tell her, some moronic exercise to describe or something some fool had said. Shel backfilled the monotony by asking about her sisters, her work, the number of times she'd thought of him, and he overanalyzed her letters, finding ominous hints in her asides and omissions, spying suitors at parties she described in missives he noticed were becoming shorter and more infrequent with each passing week. In the afternoons he posted his daily letter and, if he received one from her, waited to read it until he was lying in his bunk. Though occasionally there were nights when he couldn't help it: he walked across the several-hundred-yard-wide marching field to the mess hall—this a long, low-slung building lit by sodium lights—to the base's pay phone. During those first weeks, when he was lucky enough to catch her at home, she was exuberant with longing—she missed him so, she said—but after a month, their conversations became truncated, forced; she was easily distracted, and more often than not his calls were answered by one of her sisters (Millie was out, Maxine said apologetically; he'd just missed her, Glenda explained, try back tomorrow?). For a desperate stretch of days, he reached no one at all. By now Millie's letters had stopped without explanation. He thought he might Section 8 and discharge, he was so frantic. On the final night they spoke, he'd walked the field in a furious thunderstorm, no delay between the flash and rumble, the rain silvered in waving sheets, the puddles as big as ponds and, when the lightning unfurled its white wings, bright as mercury. Millie was determined, distant. She'd already moved on. He *had* to understand why she was breaking things off between them. He'd be gone for eighteen months, which to her seemed as long as for good, and it was better, wasn't it, Shel, if they ended this now?

Walking back across the field, he called the lightning upon himself, but it did not obey. He hung his soaked clothes in the shower and wept with them. In bed, once he'd calmed down, he considered the rightness of what Millie had done, for their lives were mistimed, a fate he promised himself to redress if he were ever to see her again, and the next morning he left for Norfolk, where he shipped off for the Mediterranean on the USS *Des Moines.*

Shel at sea. No romance to be found in the North Atlantic crossing, only seasickness, at least during the voyage's first week. Men, singly or in pairs, dotted the heavy cruiser's gunwale port and starboard to bend double at the giant cleats and grab rails to offer long eels of puke to the ocean, which webbed to filament downwind and then broke apart in patterns as complex as snowflakes, disappearing without so much as a splash. He was assigned to the deck force, the ship's cleaning crew, charged to polish brass—the ever-tarnished brightworks—to swab the deck, and to scrub the latrines fiendishly decorated by the sailors who failed to barf above. The food was beyond awful, the cuts of meat tough as soaked rope, corned beef senior officers dubbed "baboon ass," so salty he woke at night cottonmouthed as if he'd been on a bender. He was friendless, and the friendless avoided one another so as to not be singled out. Two men committed suicide before they made the Azores. A fat sailor named Stranch leaped from the bow at midwatch, his execution demonstrating foresight: if the fall didn't kill him then the prow would slice him in half. There was a brief nighttime search. Spotlights feebly inspected the black-and-white chop. "He's shark shit," said an officer, "let's get a move on." The second snuck down to his berth at dinner and put a rifle in his mouth, pulling the trigger with his toe, the bullet pasting a divot of skull against the wall so firmly it was as if it had been nailed there. "Gooned that up good, didn't he?" said a sailor. Thankfully Shel wasn't on duty for that cleanup job.

His general misery crowded out thoughts of Millie; the hatred he soon encountered made him fear for his life. In the chaos of that first week, in the smoke pit belowdecks, amid men seeking vassals, allegiances, a sun to orbit; stunned by their circumstances and homesickness and fear of battle, Shel had clocked more than a few men who looked at him with hopeful aggression. It was another seaman named Logan who had it in for him. One night, after mess, he spotted his enemy leaning against the wall. They locked eyes like lovers. Already the man was seething. Bad luck: he had two sidekicks. Shel looked down, regarding the cigarette burning in his fist. Six black shoes formed a scalloped crescent around his.

"Fuck's your name?" Logan said. A southern twang—*fux*—and the diphthong tacked to "name" sounding vaguely Hebraic: *nay*-m.

"Excuse me?"

Growing up, Shel's older brother, Marty, regularly beat him. Such instruction had taught him to make any fight as short as possible, so he took a drag on his cigarette and then smashed his forehead into the man's nose. A sound like a split picket. As they fell together, Shel shoved the cigarette into Logan's mouth and clapped his hand over the man's lips to seal the squib inside, watching the man's eyes widen as the cherry scorched the back of his throat. Shel had anticipated the ensuing pile-on separating them, each man cursing the other over the heads of their respective scrums, which bore them aloft like a bride and groom in the hora.

"I'll kill you, you hear me?" Logan screamed. His mouth and chin were dark with blood. "I swear I'll kill you, you kike son of a bitch!"

In bed later, Shel held his Ka-Bar knife beneath the sheets. Night noises in the berthing: if you picked out a single sound it might drive you mad. He waited for the attack, which never came. On the bed adjacent his, a sailor named Barney Freele could be relied upon to converse with you while he dreamed. Now he said, "The fish. Get it."

"What kind of fish?" Shel whispered.

"Bass," he said. "Get it in the net."

The memory was overwhelming: a drive he and Millie had taken from New York to the tip of Long Island, all the way to Montauk. It was early May. Impossible to believe this was only months ago. She'd called him on a Saturday morning. "I'm sick of the city," she'd said. "I want to see the sea." It was like an order, a test. "I'll pick you up," he answered. He announced to his father that he was borrowing the car. Miraculously, his father said yes. The morning was so spectacularly bright the Plymouth's interior seemed dark as a closet, even felt several degrees cooler, like a room when you come inside from a day at the beach. Driving over the Fifty-Ninth Street Bridge, the sky was such a polished blue that against its backdrop Manhattan's buildings seemed livid with detail, the water towers and antennae tines as distinct as a Dürer etching. In the gusts, trees waved their branches from penthouse roofs. The illusion of great speed as the suspension girders whipped past, of motionlessness if you focused on the river instead. They took the Queens Midtown Expressway to Route 27, a two-lane road they remained on for hours. At a gas station, they bought sandwiches, Cokes, a map, and were off again. The Pine Barrens framed the final stretch of highway, the trees narrowing toward their tips like arrow fletchings. Heat haze smoked the blacktop, the approaching cars lambent and blurred until they solidified into chrome and glass and, trailing a great spill of air, hissed west. On a desolate stretch between Amagansett and Montauk, a commuter train ran alongside them, its windows green as pond scum, its few passengers sitting still and floating alongside them, like witches on brooms. Shel could remember nothing he and Millie talked about, just that he held her hand for what seemed like the entire drive; and later, as they walked along the point's grounds, after they laid out a blanket on the grass, they had watched the fishermen on the rocky beach below. The men would wade up to their waists to cast. When one hooked a fish, his rod arced toward the water. He'd lift the creature from the surf, the pole bowed by its weight, and walk it to shore holding the end of his line. Shel and Millie stood at the overlook beneath the lighthouse, staring at the white boats emerging from the Atlantic and the sound, at the gray cargo ships on the horizon; and what he recalled most clearly was the feeling he had as he held her in his arms: *We could keep going.*

The next morning Shel saw Logan at mess, sitting three tables across from him, the man's nose distended, its bridge flat and swollen, his eyes blued with bruise. When they glanced at each other this time, it was Logan who averted his gaze.

Just because you stand your ground doesn't mean you've won the day. Nor are all bullies cowards. On the deck force he was singled out; taunting him became a form of fellowship; he was like a bottle you kicked because it was in your path. The baiting came from all sides, some of it run-of-the-mill. Instead of Hertzberg they called him *Burger.* "Watch your back, *Burger.*" "Hey, *Burger,* you missed a spot." Other times the threats were more insidious: from Turret One, a gang of sailors approached, Logan among them. Shel, headed aft, slowed, but now there was no turning back. As a unit they took the inside lane, forcing Shel toward the gunwale's edge, throwing elbows to his back when they passed, some punching his arm, cuffing the back of his head. He took a few hard slaps to his ears. He rode this out, hanging on to the grab rails, their metal wires bowed by his weight, his chest pressed over his toes like a ski jumper, the ship's wake foaming the hull far below. A voice from somewhere among the group, at once light and heavy on the wind said, "Hope you can swim, Hebe."

One night, he came upon a mound of feces on his bed. Everyone in the berthing knew it was there—they'd given it space, as if it were a coiled viper. Barney Freele appeared by his side, carefully gathered up the blanket, and, with the assurance of someone owed a favor, said under his breath, "I know the lieutenant commander."

This man's name was Maldrick. He invited Shel to his quarters the following afternoon. He told Shel to close the door and invited him to sit while he finished a report, scratching out sentences for a time. A framed picture of the Virgin Mary hung above his secretary's desk. Stunned by this privacy, Shel took deep drafts of the calm.

Maldrick put down his pen, swiveled in his chair. "Are you familiar with the *Daisy May*?" From his desk he handed Shel a copy of the ship's newspaper, a four-page broadsheet, which Shel thumbed blindly.

"They need a photographer," Maldrick said. "Mr. Freele tells me you're quite accomplished."

Shel had never used a camera in his life. "Sir?"

"Of course, I'll have to pull you from the deck force," Maldrick said. When Shel made no protest, he added, "Report to Ensign Lewis tomorrow. The dark room is off the pilot house."

To call this space a room was generous. It was barely bigger than a closet, a miracle of organization to pack in so much equipment, not to mention both men at one time. Lewis was thin-faced. His narrow cheeks were moon-mottled with acne scars. Giving the tour, he made no-look reaches for film canisters and flashbulbs. It was intimidating, like being in the presence of a wizard among his unmarked potions, and yet instantly incited admiration, for he alone knew the spells.

"Enlarger's here," Lewis said. "Cameras"—he took down a Pentax and held it expertly—"on this shelf. Lenses"—he indicated over Shel's shoulder—"to your right. The tripod's hanging behind you. All your chemicals are below your trays." He tapped each. "Developer, stop bath, fixer, wash. If you need to order anything—film, paper, even hardware—just submit a requisition to Ensign Sandbrook. Sky's the limit."

He offered the camera to Shel, who gripped it in two hands, then tilted the lens toward his chin.

"You get open gangway at every port," Lewis continued. "Set your own schedule. I'd keep this job forever if I hadn't gotten promoted."

Shel waited.

"Any questions before I hand her over?"

Shel scanned the dark room again. Just above eye level, a row of photos was pinned to a clothesline like fresh laundry, their gentle tilt indicating the *Des Moines*'s attitude as she listed.

"How do you know what to take?" he asked.

Lewis puffed his cheeks at the question's obviousness. "I take whatever I want," he said. "Or whatever's happening."

Shel nodded. "What if nothing's happening?"

"Something's always happening."

Timidly, Shel brought the viewfinder to his eye. Lewis frowned and took the camera from him, removing the lens cover.

"You don't know a thing about this stuff, do you?"

Shel shrugged.

"I didn't either," Lewis said.

They stared at each other.

"You got something to write with?" Lewis asked.

After Shel tapped his pants pockets, Lewis removed a small pad and pen from his own. He checked his watch. "I'll give you three hours."

His was a furious tutorial. First a primer on film itself, its various speeds and grains, followed by instruction on loading it into the camera. Next its basic parts—the winding reel, tripod socket, accessory shoe. The rings on the lens. Terms came in a blur and only a few were caught, like card faces spotted when a dealer shuffles. "The shutter speed's how long the camera looks at something," Lewis explained. "The aperture's how wide the lens opens. The faster your subject, the wider you set the aperture. The wider your aperture, the lower your f-stop. Understand?" Shel did not. They wandered the vessel shooting a roll of film. From the prow's platform, camera aimed aft, the battleship, seen through the viewfinder, exploded into detail. The two turrets filled the foreground, their triple barrels bristling and erect and, rising behind them, the forward main battery—the *Des Moines*'s central command tower—its facade vaguely anthropomorphic, like a totem pole's gods. Lewis gave a brief exegesis on depth of field, the effects of front- and sidelight. The information pouring from his mouth ran off the roof of Shel's mind like rain. They returned to the dark room: an introduction to the changing bag. The infernal task of removing the negatives in its pitch-dark and then fastening them to the developing tank's reel, in the meantime Lewis listing the proper admixtures of T-max and diluting agent. There followed an extensive lesson on the enlarger, the machine flamingo-necked, beaked with a lens. In its slot Lewis loaded a strip of negative, twisting the knobs until the beamed image, fuzzy on the palette below, shrank to fit its borders and then finally came into focus. He walked Shel through several exposures and then made him develop them. Like a ray's wings, the submerged photopaper gently rippled in the chemical baths. Shel watched the white sheet, mesmerized as the image fogged to visibility, a fade-in clarifying into something actual, like your sight restored after glancing at the sun. Lewis tonged the first print, lifted it from the tray, and then clipped it to the hanging line. For a time, both men considered the photograph.

"How am I supposed to learn all of this?" Shel asked.

Lewis shrugged. "You just play."

Shel took this advice to heart. After a miserable week with his head buried in manuals and his own cribbed notes, fourteen-hour days of trial and mostly error in which he destroyed countless rolls of film, he regrouped after they made landfall in Europe, wandering the Rock of Gibraltar to shoot all day and then, determined not to make a mistake, walked himself step by step through the entire process—negatives to contact sheet to prints—without a single disaster. Lewis was right: *something was always happening.* Shel merely had to decide what it would be. It was the best job on the boat because he was free—not just of the punishing schedule but the navy itself. At ports of call, the *Daisy May*'s staff rarely wanted something specific, so Shel gave himself license to roam, to draw up his own itineraries, daring himself to see as much as possible: in Italy, Vatican City, the Teatro di Marcello, the open-air markets between Via del Corso and the Pantheon; in Greece he scaled the Acropolis, took day hops to the Aegean's countless islands, their names like seabirds—Skiros, Chios, Ikaria—photographing the shopkeepers and fishmongers, the beggar children with the countenances of old men. The occasional, blessed moment after taking a picture—the purely instinctual sense in the microsecond after the shutter clicked—that he'd *got* something. And later, his confidence growing as the image, like a genie summoned from smoke, magically delineated and then affixed in the developing tray. The job gave him access to every part of the boat, engine room to command tower. Riding out a storm on the *Des Moines*'s bridge, the ship climbed a forty-foot swell, the wave's face filling the windows, pushing the prow briefly airborne, and, after tilting over the crest, after a fall during which Shel could feel his stomach float, it cleaved the water, sending great spumes exploding up the hull, as if the vessel were a broadsword. From a helicopter, during war games—

the closest they'd ever get to battle—he photographed the *Des Moines* from several thousand feet: the water beneath the turrets smoothed to glass when the guns fired, the molten clouds billowed brightly from the barrels, and then the aftershock arrived in the cockpit, shaking Shel's teeth.

One evening, as the sun fell behind the mountains of Corfu, Shel realized he hadn't thought of Millie in months.

The ship's captain, A. D. Chandler, was an admirer of his work. He requested Shel take his portrait. In preparation for this intimidating assignment, Shel enlisted Barney Freele as a model, photographing him in the captain's stateroom. These test shots came out better than expected—it was Shel's first time using the tripod and flash—and in the berthing he and Freele had a laugh over the prints, the latter's mock-serious pose, his best impersonation of Captain Chandler's thousand-yard stare. Shel laid them across his bed to compare shutter and film speeds. A crowd formed.

"You look the part, Barney!"

"Aye, aye, Cap'n Freele!"

"Send one to your mom. She'll think you've been promoted!"

"Think you could take one of me?" another sailor asked him. "For my girl."

"Sure," Shel said.

"Two bucks cover it?"

Payment hadn't occurred to him. "I think we could arrange something," Shel said.

The sailor's name was Lurin. He loved the picture and told two friends. Over the next several months, other seamen approached him with the same request, each offering to pay, each calling him, usually for the first time, by his first name. Shel declined their money, just as he had Lurin's, but after taking their photographs and leaving them on their bunks, he often entered the dark room to find the bills hanging from the line. Victimless, it was the best sort of grift, and he was pleased with its accidental arrangement. And so it came to pass that, upon the *Des Moines*'s return to Norfolk, he was discharged from active duty with a Nikon camera in his duffel that Captain Chandler had gifted him and over a thousand dollars in cash.

It was lucky he had this money. When he returned to Queens, he discovered that his parents were moving to California. His father was going into business with his brother, Moishe, in San Bernardino; they were opening a fur shop together. His father, Shel learned, was not the poor man he'd always assumed, but from the three jobs he'd worked for as long as Shel could remember he had, along with the sale of their home, squirreled away nearly $70,000. He was dedicating all but $200 to this venture. He gave the money to his son with much fanfare after Shel declined to come west with them and, for all intents and purposes, exited their life.

Greater careers have started with less, Shel figured. This isn't to say he didn't feel abandoned by his parents, but there was a difference: he was not afraid. *At the beginning of a thing,* he thought, *a thing seems impossible.*

The beginning, Shel reminded himself, *is a dark room.*

He took a job at Joseph Patelson Music House on Fifty-Sixth, in the shadow of Carnegie Hall, as good a place to start a life as any. During his interview, Mr. Patelson, dapper in his double-breasted suit and white pocket square, asked him his area of specialty. When Shel answered opera, the man walked him to the store's upright piano and began to play an overture, which Shel instantly identified as Rossini's *Ermione.* "Impressive," Mr. Patelson said. "Of course, a new suit," he said, after offering Shel the job and pinching the lapel of the old one Shel was wearing, "would be even *more* so." Along with this purchase, Shel rented a one-bedroom apartment on Seventy-Fifth and Riverside, eighth floor, the highest up he'd ever lived in the city, the window in his tiny living room enjoying an unobstructed view of the Hudson. In fall, the trees dotting Jersey's cliffs reminded him of the *Des Moines*'s guns firing; in winter, the rock faces were as gray as the ship's gunmetal hull. On Saturday mornings, drinking coffee, he spotted the Circle Line on its route around Manhattan. It would be lovely to ride a boat, he thought, but not alone this time. He took the 1 Train downtown in the mornings, but in the evenings, to clear his mind, preferred to walk. And on a brutally cold January night, as he leaned against the wind on the easternmost arc of Columbus Circle, he saw Millie Van Bourne crossing the street.

How to describe seeing someone whose loss you've already mourned?

He could say it was like encountering a ghost, but that would be inaccurate, for ghosts were not of this world. Millie was standing here before him, her eyes shining in the streetlights. It had been nearly three years, but she appeared thinner, older, sadder, and more beautiful. Her hair was still Marilyn Monroe white. While they spoke, she occasionally glanced over his shoulder, nervously, as if she were supposed to meet someone on this corner. "I've thought about you so often," she said with great sincerity. "I'd wondered what had become of you." Her smile parted him like a scalpel. He was immediately aware of how much energy he'd expended scouring her from his mind and how powerless he was now to resist her return. She invited him back to her apartment, on Tenth Avenue and Sixtieth Street. As they walked, he mused on how close they'd lived to each other all these months, mere blocks separating them: Shel pausing, for a moment, to gaze on the tiny display windows of Tiffany, while Millie flashed by in the glass's reflection; she exiting Bloomingdale's revolving doors—Manhattan's countless near collisions—as he'd entered; the lonely laps they were unwittingly making together as they walked Central Park's Great Lawn, the diameter separating them as they strolled in the same direction along its circumference. Who would we see on our periphery, Shel wondered, if we adjusted our vision? Who was walking parallel to us if we widened our depth of field?

Her apartment was large—too large, he realized later—her river view out of six windows a mural to his portrait. He should've also noticed how oddly furnished it was, an old-world dowdiness to the decor, the plastic covering the ample, heavy furniture, all of it showroom-like but staged for someone elderly, as if Millie were an actress who'd wandered onto the wrong set. They sat in her living room. Without thinking, they took each other's hands. She was vague as to how she'd kept busy these past two years: a few commercials, some modeling. A stint as a nightclub hostess most recently. Her sisters had long since fled Manhattan: Maxine was married and living in Chicago, Glenda had returned home to work for their father. Millie described these as very lonely times. As she talked, her affect became distant, to the point of being disengaged, an odd dreaminess Shel could not recall from before, one that seemed an entirely new aspect of her person.

"But now you're here," she said, returning from whatever journey had taken her far away.

In the days that followed, it was all Shel could do to get through work, at the end of which he would literally run to meet her out somewhere—at the Rainbow Room or at a show at Radio City Music Hall. But it was their talks afterward, the endlessness of their conversations at the Hotel Edison or Barbetta, over martinis at the King Cole Bar or dinner at Gallagher's—a lavishness funded by Shel's shrinking savings. He couldn't recall now much of what they said, though what *did* stay with him was the ease of it, their familiarity with each other. *How rare it is,* Shel found himself thinking, *to simply* like *someone. To know, in their company, that you would never be bored.* It changed his whole sense of the future: suddenly he was thinking in terms of years, of how they might live in one of Manhattan's taller buildings or one of the Upper West Side's brownstones, once he'd made it. He found himself dreaming on their unconceived children's faces, of two boys blessed with Millie's finer, smaller features. Until one evening, sitting together in her living room, they heard a key turn in the door.

The encounter unfolded with an accident's vivid torpor. The older man wore a long brown coat and a fedora. The heavy frames of his glasses hid his appearance while magnifying his eyes so that they glistened like hard-boiled eggs. His hands remained buried in his pockets, a position that might normally convey infirmity, yet as he entered the room, he moved with a limberness that belied his age, to stand before them with the dispassion a detective exhibits before a victim's body. He did not speak, he uttered no threats and made no claims, although Millie was ashen at the sight of him, robbed of speech before this person who was clearly not a stranger, his expression unchanged as he looked from her to Shel and back while Shel glanced at Millie and then this intruder, and when he rose himself, his heart racing, to say *what* he did not know, the man scrutinized him as calmly as an owl from a branch. Then he turned and, with the selfsame ease and impassivity, left the room and gently closed the apartment door.

The place, Shel later learned, was his, of course, and in a terrifying fashion so was Millie—though how such a thing came to pass Shel couldn't puzzle out, not even after he'd calmed her down, for her explanation only revealed that she was a stranger to him, to herself, in ways that Shel surmised were dangerous. She mentioned something about falling in love after Shel had gone overseas—she'd even gotten engaged—only to discover it wasn't that at all, it was a thing disguised as such but was far more dreadful, perhaps even love's opposite, for it revealed itself only *after* she'd given her heart to this person, after she'd begged her father to lend them money, and there followed a breakup that had not only nearly ruined her emotionally and financially but also left her so dreadfully alone it put her out of her family's reach, even her sisters. And then this man whose name she would not utter had stepped in to rescue her or affect something that had *appeared* like rescue, but came at a cost so horribly obvious she refused to articulate it.

Her eyes swimming, she said to Shel, "I won't ask you to help me."

"Of course I'll help you," he said.

She shook her head as if recalling something dreadful. "You could get hurt," she warned.

Later that night, alone in his apartment, he lay awake gathering his thoughts. There was disappointment, first of all, to have been so quickly supplanted after their breakup. Shel tried to relish this anger, to nurture it—he considered calling to confront Millie—but this desire rapidly dissipated, was mere squall, and he soon turned philosophical. What did it take—just how low did a person have to sink—to strike the kind of bargain she'd made? He sat up in bed, opened his window, smoked a cigarette. He was losing a taste for the habit. Across the Hudson, New Jersey's lights winked, casting long reflections, as colorful as a color wheel but now resembling to Shel prison bars. Below, car brakes squealed; he heard a crash he could not see, followed by a tinkling of shattered glass. Later, he would reflect that perhaps he did not know Millie at all, that what he loved was merely his own love for her. Now, he concluded that everything that had happened in their time apart might as well be a dream, and just as easily forgotten. There was only *now* and *what was to come*, and this gave him enough peace to sleep, so that when he woke the next morning he decided Millie was exaggerating the danger to him as surely as her own entrapment, and what he needed to do was ask her to marry him and then immediately spirit her away, a decision that canceled out so many other near-term ambitions it left him utterly becalmed.

He dressed for work more certain of what he was doing than at any other time in his life. Just before he left his apartment, he noticed the note shoved under his door.

IT WOULD BE BEST IF YOU DO NOT SEE A CERTAIN PERSON AGAIN OR WE WILL BREAK YOUR YID FACE.

He stood in his entryway holding the paper in both hands. His heart made a downy sound, like a pillow being fluffed. He could not help but compare this state with other instances of fear. The over-the-shoulder paranoia aboard the *Des Moines,* when he thought Logan's crew would ambush him; the nightmares of being dragged from his berth and thrown overboard that he woke from, kicking the sheets from his bed. When his brother, Marty, would take a seat across from him at the kitchen table and in utter seriousness say, "After Mom and Dad go out tonight, I'm going to drown you in the bathtub." And there was something that had always terrified Shel about the nights his father had him bring in damaged furs from the Plymouth's trunk and then whisk them to their basement. The windows his father had covered in sackcloth, lest the union enforcers catch him moonlighting. Shel was certain that he was endangering his father by assisting him, an anxiety later amplified by the sound of the sewing machine below, its enormous whir carrying to the third floor and thus audible on the street, where someone surely lay in wait among the pedestrians and passersby who might rat him out.

With a speed that surprised him, Shel hatched a plan, though in order for it to work he needed to tell Millie first.

When the elevator opened on her floor, the old man was standing directly before him, wearing the same fedora and long coat. His hands were again in the coat's pockets. Shel wasn't sure what to do, feeling something between terror and embarrassment, for a confrontation seemed inevitable. The elevator door began to close, its slide an action both men watched intently, since this was the moment, after all, where the line drawn by the night before, by the note, would be crossed. Shel palmed the plunger, but not without trepidation, so that the door reversed course, and then he held it there, retracted. The man's magnified eyes blinked mechanically, and the brim of his hat dipped as he began to walk toward Shel, who in turn exited the car, holding himself close as if trying to avoid a much larger person; and when they stood on opposite sides of each other once more, Shel felt rebuffed by the man's straight-ahead indifference and imperturbable disengagement. Once again there was the chilling sense that the wrinkled face behind the thick lenses was loose, slack rubber that disguised another face beneath. Shel walked backward, wanting the moment to end. But the elevator buzzed, the door had stayed held open too long and was stuck, and well down the hallway by now, Shel watched the dumb slowness with which the elevator door finally slid closed and the alarm ceased. Through the porthole's glass, at first only the top of the man's lowered brim was visible, but just before the car sank the old man raised his chin, shaking his head ever so slightly at Shel, a gesture he could not be sure was warning or weariness. And then the car sank, and the window's eye lidded black.

Shel didn't bother to knock on Millie's door. He had a key, and once inside he found her in the middle of the living room, and when she turned to look at him, it was as if she'd been startled by a stranger. Her mouth was fixed in a grimace nearly clownish, her cheeks smeared with mascara. He suddenly felt the seriousness of what he was about to propose.

"What are you doing here?" she said.

"You have to come with me. Right now. We'll leave together."

"For where?"

"California."

"What are you talking about?"

"I have enough money to get us set up. My father has a business out there. We can go tonight."

She bunched his coat's lapels in her hands, then cupped her lips with her palm and began to cry again. She shook her head. "I can't," she finally said.

"Yes, you can," Shel said. "If you don't want to, that's something else."

She pressed her face into his shirt and sobbed and, after several minutes, calmed down enough to breathe softly. She wiped her eyes on his chest and sniffled. "Describe it for me," she said after a time.

"California?" He smiled into her hair, smelling her scalp. "I've never been. I've only seen it in the pictures," he confessed.

"Tell me what it's like anyway," Millie said.

He held her very tightly now. "It's a desert but fertile. Like an oasis. The air is dry. There are palm trees and houses built on cliffs, and the mansions have lawns like fairways. And there's the Pacific, which seems bigger than the Atlantic somehow and is even colder. And you see movie stars everywhere."

"At the laundromat and the gas station," Millie said.

"It's like Olympus," Shel said.

"We'll dine on ambrosia," Millie said.

"Does that sound like someplace you'd want to live?"

She was silent for a time. "That sounds like a place to start over."

Her ear was to his shirt, and she then pressed her palm to his chest, patting it several times. When she looked up at him, she managed a smile.

"Be ready by seven," he told her.

She nodded, forcefully, and then he kissed her goodbye.

It was Friday, payday, and Shel decided not to tell Mr. Patelson he was quitting for fear his check would be withheld, though he did ask for it at lunch—he was going on a trip this evening, he explained, he needed to visit the bank ahead of the weekend—a request Patelson obliged. On his break, Shel hurried to cash it, withdrawing all his money as well, and then took the subway to Penn Station, where he bought a pair of tickets to Delaware. He would meet Millie's father and properly ask for her hand. He was certain he had enough money left to buy a car. He was dreamy that afternoon, imagining their upcoming trip, their drive together across the country and then working for his father until he got a start in movies. It was a fairy tale, he would admit, not only in the happiness of its ending but also because it began with great risk.

Just past four, Patelson approached him with several thick folders of sheet music. "Can you drop these off with Mr. Stockmeyer? The violinist." The address was only several blocks from Shel's apartment. When he glanced at his watch, Patelson added, "I'll let you go a bit early."

On his way home, Shel decided he'd deliver the music after packing, which he did quickly and efficiently, taking only his best clothes and leaving the rest behind. He considered the apartment. The couch was a drab green. Over his dresser, a gilt-edged mirror, its glass smoky with age. He considered his reflection. How he hated his full cheeks—they made him look younger than he was. After he and Millie had fled, would he finally feel like a grown man? He grabbed his suitcase and the folders, ran through a final checklist, touched his coat's breast and side pockets—money and tickets—turning a million things over in his mind, so that it was only after he came down the stairs and entered his building's small lobby that he noticed the three men waiting for him.

One leaned against the building's front door. He wore an eggplant-colored suit and pressed his foot's sole against the door's glass, mindful of the street over his shoulder. The second man, also wearing a suit, had a neck so wide it seemed to begin at his ears. He softly stepped behind Shel to block the stairwell. The third man, who moved directly into Shel's path, was in every measurable dimension so much larger than all of them that for an instant Shel felt, proportionally, like a child. He had a boxer's nose, at once craggy and wide, its bridge flat and broad as an anvil.

"Did you get our note?" the giant asked.

Shel swung his suitcase at his head, flinging the folders after the bag connected so that the sheets seemed to explode in the small hallway, a great flutter of pages that served as enough of a diversion to get him all the way to the man at the door, whom he grabbed by the lapels and then hurled away from the exit, toward the other two men, and for the split second that he pulled at the handle he thought, *Free.* Only to be yanked backward by his collar and land so hard the wind was knocked from him. The sheets scuffed and crumpled beneath his back, still floating down as the men's first kicks and punches landed. Like the sheet music, they too were now on the ground with Shel, the giant's knee on his sternum, his gloved hand gripping his throat, while the thick-necked one laid his shin across Shel's biceps. The third man remained at the door, keeping an eye out. "You're good," he said to the pair, and when the giant brought his gloved fist to his ear there glinted between his fingers three silver circles, flat as the heads of nails and bright as ball bearings.

"If you don't move," he said matter-of-factly, "I won't miss." His eyes followed Shel's face to draw a bead, his raised fist was cocked by his ear, and he wheezed once, patiently. Shel bridged and bucked with one last burst. "Keep still," the giant said, almost coddling, like a doctor before pressing a needle to a vein. Shel relaxed, his jaw went slack, and the blow came so fast that at first it almost didn't hurt, he was for a second unsure he'd even been hit. Though the sound, like a vase breaking, were his teeth, he realized, the pieces falling against the back of his throat so that he gagged, swallowing the bits of several while his tongue swam in blood. He opened his eyes to another blow, the plink that followed like a small rock through a pane, the giant's fist back by his ear as Shel gargled, tears streaming from his eyes, his tongue's tip, as the man paused, running along the ridges of his ragged cuspids and incisors while his assailant once again forcefully wheezed. He twisted Shel's head side to side for a quick inspection, the action slinging the slurry from his mouth. "One more," he whispered, squeezing the unhinged jaw so hard that Shel's lips puckered. Followed by a deep crack, as of lake ice splitting, and then the blackness of the water beneath.

The horror came not when he woke in the hospital and saw Patelson and his wife pitifully gazing upon him, or when he considered his reflection in the mirror moments later, his puffed jowls from his broken jaw grimed with bruise. Nor was it when he learned all his money had been stolen. Even in the handful of weeks after his dental surgery, the cost of which Patelson absorbed ("Robbed making a delivery for me," he'd tell customers who came into the store while Shel healed), he didn't feel the full weight of his loss until he returned to Millie's apartment. The elevator opened and he paused in the car as if he'd pressed the wrong floor. He walked down the hallway aware of his footfalls, as if he were a thief trying to move silently. Above her doorknob, the lock cylinder was missing, and when Shel plucked this a draft blew through. He knelt to peek through the hole, he saw a window open inside. He turned the knob, and the door opened. He entered to discover all the furniture gone, the apartment vacant of any trace of anything. Even the floors were without a scratch and shined brightly, like a blackboard wetly erased. In the front hall closet there were not even hangers. In the bedroom, which also had a view of the river, two pale squares above where the headboard used to be, from paintings—or were they photographs?—whose subjects he could not remember. The cracked window whistled with the wind. He entered the bathroom. Did it still smell of her? Or was the lingering scent—chalky, waxy—of her makeup and powders and perfumes? In the mirror he considered his reflection, gaunt, his face thinned from weeks of being fed through a straw. It was like the dream he sometimes had of seeing himself as if he were a stranger and finally having the fleeting sense of what he actually looked like to someone else in the world.

My father turned to me and smiled. "Both of these are bridges," he said as he drove. He ran a fingernail over his top and bottom incisors.

"But what happened to her?" I asked.

"Millie?" He shrugged. "I don't know."

"What do you mean?'

"I mean she was gone. Disappeared."

"You never heard from her again?"

"Not a peep."

I waited for more, but nothing came. "And that was it?"

"That was it."

We were banking left now, toward Central Park South, our third loop around—past the near side of Columbus Circle, where Dad first saw Millie again. How many times in his life had he walked it, hoping to see her once more? And although his story shouldn't have been a comfort to me, it was, for I realized I wasn't alone in my misery. And although I didn't consider what it meant at the time or whether he should have told me in the first place or what my mother might have thought of the telling, I believed he'd imparted a great secret, and for this I felt overwhelming gratitude. The Metropolitan Museum of Art appeared on our right-hand side. Even at this hour, the Sackler Wing remained lit, so that its glass was rendered invisible, the Temple of Dendur within, moated by its reflecting pool and aglow. Dad continued to watch the road, nodding several times to himself, and then he reached over to place his hand on my knee and patted it. He turned to smile at me, weakly this time, though I couldn't help it: I looked at his teeth.

"You never marry the great love of your life," he said.

Before school was out and summer arrived there was the endless week of finals.

Freshmen took these three-hour exams in the wrestling gym. The mats had been rolled up to reveal the polished maple beneath, which made the space seem bigger and feel colder. Desks had been moved in and arranged in rows. My preparation for every subject began in hope and then drifted into confusion. Maybe it was because of where I took these tests, but they reminded me of most of my matches that past year—I engaged them with what little ability I had. I might even gain, at their outset, some tiny bit of traction, but they soon exposed my weaknesses and finally overwhelmed me. So that during each, and always at some point past halfway, I had an abundance of the very thing all my hunched and scribbling classmates seemed to lack, which was time. English was the exception. Verbals still baffled me (how was "to wrestle" a noun?); Mom had tried to explain. Still, I nailed the vocabulary section, felt great about the quote matching, and wrote so frantically to finish the essay on time that the smoothed callus on my middle finger's top knuckle pinkly shined from my pencil's pressure. Miss Sullens stood over me as I wrote the last sentence—I being the last student in the gym—and after she collected my blue book, I sat there for a while, reveling in the familiar feeling of being spent, considering, once again, the lights above in their cages, contemplating the time and all that had happened in between these two moments, marveling at whom I'd met and who had departed, at what had surprised me and what had not changed, at what I'd accomplished and how I'd come up short, convinced that this emptiness I now experienced—this satisfaction of having entirely poured myself into something—was proof of a way that promised great rewards but whose path I'd yet to find. Which I now see was simply sublimation for the fact that this room that was once Kepplemen's, and within whose prison we were enclosed like the lights above, had been replaced by another I did not recognize, at a time when a year was ending while so much else remained unclear.

At the conclusion of exam week, Miss Sullens found me kneeling before my locker while I cleaned it out. She was in sneakers and jeans and a sleeveless blouse that showed off her impressive shoulders. She was thrilled by my reaction as I read my grade: the circled A-minus and *Brilliant essay!* double-underlined on the inside flap. "I am *so* proud of you," she said, and mussed my hair, and before standing "to leave"—an adverb, I realized too late to make an A, modifying "standing" by answering the question why—added, "Have a great summer." I watched her walk away, disappointed in myself for not thanking her. Though the noise all around was familiar—lockers slamming, students whoop-whooping as they celebrated the end of the academic year or, in some cases, of high school—it was also alien to me, did not align with internal displeasure. My locker was adjacent the tech booth's door. Music played from within, and when it opened, Marc Mason appeared in an MIT sweatshirt, singing, "People can change, they always do / Haven't they noticed the changes in you?" He spotted me and pointed, and then said, "Keep the campaign going, my man." He slung his book bag over his shoulder and said to the nearly empty halls, "Marc Mason . . . is officially . . . leaving the building."

I paged through my exam. I reread my essay. We'd been asked to write on a theme that ran through at least four texts we'd read this year, and I chose *Romeo and Juliet, The Catcher in the Rye, A Streetcar Named Desire,* and the e.e. cummings poem "Since Feeling Is First." In each of these works, those who are most suspicious of language are often the most capable of telling the truth. Mercutio reveals to Romeo the lasciviousness beneath his flowery love for Rosalind, Holden Caulfield identifies the phoniness embedded in people's concerns for him because they wanted him to conform to their values, Stanley Kowalski violently pokes a finger in the "paper lantern" of Blanche DuBois's nostalgia, and, finally, it is the speaker in the cummings poem who knows the "eyelids' flutter" of any lover (I thought of Amanda) is more potent than any wisdom (I thought of the conclusion to my father's story about Millie Van Bourne), that it is holy to be "wholly . . . a fool," to trust instinct—what the "blood approves"—before the brain's "best gesture." To give oneself over to another is best; to resist playacting is required. What anyone wants, standing before the beloved, is the person wholly themselves— which was close, I concluded, to holiness.

What I felt after reading this was pride, which gave on to uncanniness. I only partly recognized myself in the sentences, in the voice. Mostly, I did not. How was this possible? And as I finished emptying my locker, my bewilderment gave on to regret. As I flipped through loose-leaf binders full of botched quizzes, my textbooks full of already forgotten facts and formulas, I was ashamed by how much I'd missed these past two semesters. Of the opportunities I'd lost. Of how far behind I remained.

Next year could be different, I thought, if I had a better start.

By June, everyone was working.

Oren got a job at Popeyes Famous Fried Chicken and regularly conspired to sneak home free buckets of drumsticks and thighs along with sweaty cups of mashed potatoes and slaw. Cliffnotes took shifts at Häagen-Dazs ("The dots are called an *umlaut*," he said, holding out his embroidered apron when I asked). On weekends, the Columbus Avenue store had a line out the entrance, and during his shift he was packed in behind the case with four servers and a manager who marched behind them shouting, "Watch your scoops! Watch your scoops!" He got tendinitis in his wrist and wrapped this in an ACE bandage, but the sacrifice was worth it, he said, because there was always extra milkshake left over in the malt cup, which he was sure to slug when the manager wasn't looking, since he was trying to gain weight for lacrosse season next year. Tanner, who we had seen only once since school got out, returned to his childhood summer camp in Maine to be a counselor.

Mom graduated from NYU. Grandma and Grandpa flew to New York to attend the ceremony, and the first thing Dad asked her at its conclusion was "So now what?" To which she replied, "Is that all you have to say?" followed by, "I'm going to start my own business, if you really want to know." And in her regalia, she marched off to join a group of her classmates, in response to which Dad grimaced at me and mouthed, *Whoops.* I turned away so as not to let him off the hook. When Mom first came to New York, she'd been an instruction model for Joseph Pilates. In her bathroom, she kept a framed picture of herself assisting him in his studio. In it, she was hanging bow-bent backward beneath a set of parallel bars while Pilates spotted her. The German's hair was as white as his turtleneck, his eyes as black as the Speedo he was wearing. She'd continue teaching ballet at Neubert's in the afternoons, she later told Dad, but during the day would make house calls to women on the Upper East and West Sides—she already had ten clients lined up—putting them through mat work at their apartments, in buildings like the Beresford and the Century and the El Dorado and the Sherry-Netherland and the Pierre. "So there," she'd said to Dad, when she returned and let him take her in his outstretched arms.

"I'm sorry," he said, and clasped her neck in the crook of his arm and kissed her hair; and she smiled and wiped a tear from her eye—it was difficult to tell if she was happy or sad—and replied, "You should be." And then she laughed. Dad had his camera with him and shot pictures of her with Grandma and Grandpa and Oren and me; and later, Mom whispered in my ear, "Remember, better late than never." I wasn't sure if she meant getting her master's degree or apologizing or both.

Amanda was working at Bloomingdale's as a perfume tester. "Smell," she said when I visited, and raised her wrist to my nose. "It's Charlie." The place was so bright it was like one big dressing room's vanity mirror. "What do you think?" she asked.

Amanda was wearing a red dress with shoulder pads and white tights. She had on a ton of makeup, like when she went out with Rob.

"It's kind of young, kind of now . . ." I sang.

Amanda slowly shook her head.

". . . kind of free, kind of wow . . ." I continued with the jingle.

"Okay, Bobby Short, try this one." From her woven basket she removed a bottle and sprayed the air ahead of her and then walked through its mist.

"Am I supposed to do that?" I asked.

"No, silly, you're supposed to smell it on me."

The white-frocked cosmeticians, the businessmen and -women, the tourists speaking Japanese, Spanish, and French—all disappeared as Amanda cleared her curls from her neck, exposing it, so that as I leaned in, I passed through the fragrance's zone into a nearness ever so slightly darkened by our proximity, to spy her ear that, if I were bold enough, I might take in my teeth.

"Do you like it?" she asked, watching me, sidelong, a bit caught off guard, as I slowly withdrew.

"Very much," I said.

"It's . . ." But she had to look at the bottle. "L'Air du Temps," she said.

"Bonjour," came a deep voice behind us.

It was Rob. In a suit and tie. With a smile that was wolfish.

"Griffin," he said, "you keeping my girl company?" Then to Amanda: "Can you still get away for lunch?"

When she nodded enthusiastically, he said, "La Goulue or Café Sabarsky?"

"You pick." Red Riding Hood disappeared under his arm. "Thanks for stopping by," Amanda said to me before Rob led her away.

The Saturday morning before the *Sam and Sara* cast departed for Delaware, Dad took me to exercise with him at the West Side YMCA. It was the last time we'd spend significant time together until the show swung back to Broadway that fall. The Businessman's Club had its own steam room and sauna; it was carpeted and had personalized lockers with nameplates. The place smelled like Clubman cologne and chlorine. All the men walked around with open robes, towels wrapped everywhere but their waists. The sight made me never want to grow old.

Dad changed his clothes, said, "See you in an hour," and made his way to the indoor track, which was adjacent to the weight room, above the basketball court, and through the two pairs of double doors I'd spot Dad come rounding into view, his eyes to his sneakers, his jog more of a mincing shuffle, closer in pace to speed-walking but without the hip swivel. I went and did some lackadaisical sit-ups. I approached the Universal machine, considered my options, and then I did a sudsy set on the bench press. I took a drink at the water fountain. I wiped my lips with the hem of my shirt. After Dad passed by again, I returned to the bench for another set. Then I stood before the wall mirror and, when no one was looking, did a Hulk flex. That was when I spotted Vince Voelker.

I did not recognize his reflection at first. He was on the chin-up bar, faced away from me, wearing athletic shorts, wrestling shoes, and a tank top. He was doing an exercise I had never seen, one that began as a pull-up and then transitioned, unimaginably, into a push-up when his head was above the bar. I counted eight repetitions. He had bulked up since wrestling season, if that were even possible, and his body seemed entirely devoid of fat. But what was mesmerizing was the effortlessness of the performance, this slide-rule action, so smooth as to be antigravitational. His shoulders and back were livid with anatomical action, the tendons and muscles rippling into a topographical map, with one particular grouping, dead center above his scapulae, distending in the shape of a bull's head, horn tips to snout.

He released the bar and turned to face me. He dusted off his hands, which I now saw were coated in chalk, and the morning light blasting through the high windows illuminated the tiny cloud. He identified himself, as if it were somehow possible I'd forgotten who he was, a courtesy I considered almost comical. He asked how my season had gone, and I told him. He said, "Well, that means you won one more match than me as a freshman." I congratulated him for winning state. I asked him where he was going to college. He said, "Syracuse. But I'm guessing it'll be two years before I start." I asked him what he was doing this summer. "You're looking at it," he said. Then: "Do me a favor?" When I nodded, he asked, "Give me a spot?"

He led me to the incline bench; he had a forty-five-pound plate on each side of the bar, to which he added a twenty-five-pound plate on his side, an act I copied. Across from us, on the flat bench, a man was bent over the face of his supine partner. He placed his outstretched index fingers below the bar and exerted only the slightest pressure upward as his friend raised the weight. "All *you*," he brayed. I took my place on the platform behind Voelker. "Give me a lift off," he said, adjusting his grip, "on three." He counted down and then we raised the bar. The plates gonged as Voelker lowered the bar and bounced it off his chest. He made a sound like a piston at the top of each rep. He did nine reps without my help, nearly failing on the tenth, and then hopped off and turned to me and said, "You're up."

"I can't lift that much," I said.

Voelker was already removing the plates. "Not yet," he said. Then: "Let's start with twenty-five on each side. The bar weighs forty-five."

He took me through his circuit. From his shorts pocket he produced a tiny spiral notepad and, from behind his ear, a golf pencil—which I didn't notice because of his bushy hair—to record his weights and repetitions. He flipped to a blank page and started recording mine. "Want to know when you've had a good workout?" he said. He held up the implement. "When you can't lift this." At our final set of dumbbell rows, my father appeared. He was pouring with sweat. He'd hung a towel around his neck and dabbed his beaded upper lip with the tail. When he introduced himself to Vince, he said, "Sheldon Hurt," in a voice so gravelly and out of the side of his mouth I thought the next thing he might do was spit tobacco.

From his notepad, Vince tore out my page and handed it to me. "Tomorrow's leg day," he said, "if you're up to it." When I pointed at myself, he added, "Six sharp."

Later, in the steam room, Dad said, "He seems like a nice young man."

I recalled our match and shivered. "Not if you're wrestling him."

The air in the room was on the verge of scalding. I walked under the ceiling's showerhead and reached for the pull chain. My arms felt like pipe cleaners. I let the freezing water hit me for as long as I could take it. After I returned to the bench, Dad rose for his downpour. I couldn't help it: I'd been thinking about what Miss West had said about Rob's dick for weeks and took a good look at Dad's dong. It was as fat as a Bartles & Jaymes wine cooler and as long as a Ball Park frank. I considered my own. Was it like a skeleton key? I remained baffled as to how it might unlock the chambers of Amanda's heart, and once again my near total lack of guidance in such matters was revealed: I knew sex's endpoint but had no idea how to get there.

Dad took his seat next to me and, as if he'd read my mind, asked, "How's that girl of yours? Aria?"

"Amanda."

"You ask her out yet?"

"She still has a boyfriend," I said.

"That never stopped anybody," Dad said. "Does she know how you feel?"

I shrugged.

"Have you ever told her that you like her?"

I shook my head.

"Has she ever told you, unconditionally, that she's not interested in you?"

I shook my head again.

"In my experience—this was before your mother, of course—no girl's ever going to spend that much time with you if she doesn't like you."

I felt so flooded with hope I couldn't speak.

"Some women," Dad said, "want to be in control. And some want you to *take* control. True, some just like to keep their options open, which is maybe what she's doing. But do you ever get that feeling? That sense," he went on, and paused, "of an opening?"

"Sometimes," I said.

"Next time you do"—he grabbed at the air as if he were trying to catch the steam in his clenched fist—"take it."

Two men entered the room.

"Maybe treat this period like the offseason," Dad continued. "Like your wrestler friend. Work on other parts of your game until Alissa comes around."

"Amanda."

"In the meantime"—and here Dad lowered his voice—"rent a good porno. For the technical aspects." He winked. Then he cupped my head and, after pulling it toward him, kissed my temple. "I'm gonna miss you, boychik."

"I'm going to miss you too."

"Take care of your mom," he said. "She can get very emotional when I'm gone."

. . .

Until early July, when we began shooting *The Nuclear Family,* my only jobs were to audition, work out at the Y, and get ahead on my summer reading.

The Boyd Prep summer reading list always arrived with my final grades and was as dreadful a document as my transcript, if not more so, since it hung over my summer like bus exhaust. That morning, I found Mom in her bedroom, sitting at her desk with both the list and my grades. I was just home from my second audition of the day. "Congratulations on your English exam," Mom said, handing me my report card and Boyd's reading list. She watched me review them: four high Cs and a B-plus (English); four novels of our choice, as if that made it any better, plus *The Sun Also Rises.* I half smiled at her and she half smiled back when I returned my transcript. I noticed she'd done some reorganizing. Dad's clutter, which had collaged her desktop, had been arranged in several new office trays. Her closet door, open behind her, revealed a file cabinet, its bottom drawer open. She placed my transcript in a folder with my name on the tab. She checked her watch and then got up from her chair. "Come on," she said, and held up the reading list, "we can go to Shakespeare and Company and buy some of these, and then I'll take you to lunch before your next appointment."

At the bookstore, we separated. I took my time, and this greatly pleased Mom, who came up to me now and again and said, "Isn't wandering around this place *the best*?" I nodded brightly, though I was making my choices based strictly on the width of the spines. When we reconvened at the checkout line, I'd arrived with the four thinnest ones I could find: *Heart of Darkness, Death Comes for the Archbishop, The Crying of Lot 49,* and *Seize the Day.*

"Don't get that," Mom said, frowning at the Pynchon. "Get this instead." She handed me *Goodbye, Columbus.* "It's romantic. Oh, and I picked this out for you"—she held up *Moby-Dick*—"because I know how much you liked that Farley Mowat book last year. And these," she said, holding up *Middlemarch* and *The Portrait of a Lady,* "because they're only the greatest novels of all time."

I flipped through the latter and slowly nodded. Four hundred plus pages of the smallest print I'd ever seen.

"Thanks," I said.

"Even if you don't read those this summer, you can have them for your library. Should we go eat? All this shopping has left me *famished*."

We walked down Broadway. Under this June-blue sky, the summer felt endless. On the crossing islands trees, the light silvered the rustling leaves, so that they flashed like metallic pom-poms.

"I'm so *bushed* these days," Mom said, looking at her watch. Her morning Pilates sessions with her clients had left her more tired than she imagined, she explained, and since she'd started her business, it was more of a challenge to make time for her professional class in the afternoon. I told her I was tired too and mentioned my workout, explained to her who Vince Voelker was, our chance meeting at the gym, and that I was going to train with him this summer. At this she gently took my scruff and shook it, then led us east, toward Columbus Avenue, the street shady, wind-sheltered, quiet. Of everyone in our family, Mom had the least amount of actor in her, though I now detected a feigned boldness in her step, her chin tilted just a few more degrees skyward than normal, an extra fierceness with which she clutched her purse's strap—all of this, I thought, connected with her clean desk and the several months that lay before her, in charge of Oren and me, in charge of her life, and Dad mostly gone. We had the block to ourselves, so I took her elbow. She turned to me and, because she was rarely one to make small talk, smiled, and I smiled back, and she said, "I'm glad we got that done earlier. It gives you a chance to get ahead for next year." And I briefly laid my head on her shoulder.

Mom took us to Lenge. As she opened the door, she looked back and said, "Have you ever eaten sushi before?" When I shook my head, she said, "Well, you're in for a treat."

We were greeted by the hostess and followed her into a windowless dining room that seemed doubly darker and cooler given the brightness outside. It was as quiet as an empty theater. When we took our seats, Mom, who had lowered her voice, said, "Do you know what sushi is?" When I shook my head again, she leaned her chest over the menu, clutching it from beneath, so that we were closer to each other. Her eyes shined. I could tell she was thrilled that she was introducing me to something. "It's raw fish served on rice. Or wrapped in seaweed. When I used to work with Pilates, he claimed that if your muscles were really sore and you needed to recover fast, this was the very best meal you could have." The waitress appeared and tonged each of us a rolled towel, so hot that steam rose from it. Mom wiped her hands, an act I copied. "We'll have green tea," she told the woman when she returned, "and two assorted sushi. Oh, and I'll have a hot sake." When the waitress took our menus, Mom shrugged her shoulders and quietly clapped.

"That's the sushi bar," she said, and thumbed behind her. There were two chefs behind the counter in aprons and paper hats, quietly and intently at work. "I like to eat there after barre sometimes and read. And you can watch the chefs make the individual pieces and the rolls. All the fish is kept in those refrigerated cases."

"They look like observation cars," I said.

"Don't they?" she said. "Can you see the salmon? Isn't it beautiful? And that long red piece of fish next to it, the one that's almost cherry colored. That's tuna."

The waitress reappeared with our appetizers.

"Don't you love the spoons?" Mom said. "This is miso soup." She stirred her soup. "Smell that. It's *loamy*, right? Like soil. And those are mushrooms, and a bit of scallion. And the tiny white cubes are tofu, which are also made from soybeans. The greens are seaweed. It has lots of protein and minerals, which are good for after workouts."

"Can I try the sake?" I asked.

"It's rice wine," Mom said, and slid me the tiny cup. It tasted like hot rubbing alcohol. "When your father and I were working at Radio City Music Hall I used to go out for sushi as much as I could. We were doing four shows a day, seven days a week, with an extra show during the holidays, so I was always depleted. They even had dorms in the theater. Rows of beds like in a hospital, for the performers to sleep, the job was so round the clock."

It occurred to me that I knew next to nothing about Mom's life. I knew her birthday but not the year she was born, and I had only the foggiest idea of where she'd lived growing up.

"Who's older, you or Dad?"

"Your father is. He was born in '33, and I was born in '38."

"How did you meet?"

"At Radio City Music Hall. I was in the corps de ballet, and he was in the chorus. He had a solo. The Toreador song from *Carmen*. Do you know it?" She hummed a few bars and I nodded. I'd heard it playing on WNYC in the mornings a million times. "And I'd think, *Who is that handsome man?* And then one day we're in rehearsal, and I was dressed as a nun and someone comes up to me in a fox costume. I mean like a Disney character with paws and a bushy tail. And I can't make out his face through the scrim in the jaws, and it isn't until he takes off the head that I realize this person asking me on a date is your father. We got married six months later."

"That's so fast."

Mom shrugged. "It didn't seem like it."

"What year was that?"

"Nineteen sixty-one."

"You were working with Pilates and doing all those shows too?"

"No, I was Pilates's demonstration model when I came to New York the second time, in, let's see"—Mom, counting, touched her thumb with her long nails, which were as elegant as her cursive and looked as solid as marble—"that was '59."

"Why the second time?"

"Because the first time I wasn't ready. I stayed for less than a year. I was studying at Ballet Russe de Monte Carlo and working as a secretary and nothing panned out. I was lonely and discouraged, so I went back to Portland, where your grandfather was stationed. Actually, you know how I got back? Several people I was studying with, about six of us, we got a job delivering taxi cabs for the Portland fleet, so we drove them across the country, and I ate chocolate the whole way to keep awake and gained five pounds by the time I arrived."

Mom's laugh erupted. This happened sometimes. It sounded like a yelp, and I laughed with her, partly because it was funny but also so that she didn't feel alone and embarrassed. She covered her mouth, and we looked around at the nearby diners, who returned to eating.

"Is that where you mostly lived when you were my age? In Portland?"

"Well, I lived all over because of your grandfather and the war. I was born in Falls Church, and then we moved to Puerto Rico until I was three. Then after Pearl Harbor we had to leave Puerto Rico on a transport ship, and there was a lot of fear during the voyage that we were going to be attacked by U-boats. And then we lived in Spring Valley with my mom's parents, who were very dear to me. Your great-grandfather Edward, he was an army colonel in World War I. That was where I got sick."

"Sick how?"

"My kidneys. I had nephritis with nephrosis. It's inflammation. Of the organ. I started losing too much protein." She raised a hand to her mouth and whispered, "In my pee. It could have been easily cured with penicillin, but all the antibiotics were going to the troops. So my grandfather got me admitted to Walter Reed."

"Was it bad?"

"I was there for nearly seven months. I had to miss almost all of first grade. I even went into a coma for ten days. I'd just turned six and had to learn to walk all over again."

"That must've been scary."

"It was *very* scary," Mom said. "Although in some ways the scariest parts were the children there who had polio and were in iron lungs. Do you know what those are?"

"It's the big tube, right?"

"In a room as big as a basketball court full of them. And I will never forget this woman who had come out of one of the concentration camps, she was in the bed next to me for several days and told me that to survive she and the other prisoners had to eat rats. That terrified me so much I couldn't even talk to my mother about it."

She was briefly distant, but then the waitress appeared with our sushi on thick pine blocks.

"These are *tekka maki*," Mom said, pointing at the rolls with her chopsticks and naming them. "And these are *nigiri*. Dip the fish side of those in the soy sauce. Not the rice. Just a little."

I followed her orders and then bit into half the piece. "Where else did you live?"

"San Francisco, near the Cow Palace. But for most of high school in Portland."

"Did you have a lot of friends? Like Cliffnotes and Tanner?"

"No, my best friends were my mom and your aunt Maine."

The waitress passed by and Mom ordered another sake.

"It's hard to have best friends when your father's in the military. Everything's transient except your family. Do you know what 'transient' means?" When I shook my head she said, "Impermanent. Something that only lasts briefly."

It occurred to me that Mom still did not have any good friends, none that I could name. No one she went out with regularly. No one but Dad.

"What about when you were dancing?"

"Then I moved around a lot too. At least when I was dancing full-time."

"When was that?"

"The winter of 1960 through the spring of '61. With the American Festival Ballet. I was studying at Ballet Russe again, and then a woman I trained with asked if I was willing to travel, and when I said yes, she gave my photograph and résumé to Renzo Raiss, who was the head of the company. And he gave me the job. We went all over. Uruguay. Buenos Aires. Argentina."

"Was it fun?"

"It was not fun at all," Mom said. "The dancers were all very cliquish. And the schedule was brutal. Do a matinee and then an evening performance, get on a bus and then drive all night, wake up, eat, rehearse, eat, and do it all again. It was sort of an endurance test. And it was lonely."

Was Mom lonely now? I had thought about this several nights ago. She'd emerged from her bath in her robe. She appeared in my room and asked me to help her. Her hips were terribly tight, she explained. When I said yes, she sat with her back against my bunk bed's post, the soles of her feet pressed together and legs butterflied, and asked me to push down on her knees until her thighs touched the parquet. Her skin was still hot from the tub, and I felt no discomfort at this, being, I believed, an athlete too, glad for the contact, because she was so rarely physical with us, and I wondered if she ever asked Dad to do such things, because I couldn't imagine it.

"Why didn't you quit?"

"Because I'd made a commitment," Mom said. "Because I'd done all of that training since I was a girl and was living the life, really, for the first time ever. And I needed to see it through. You find something very hard and warm inside of you when you do difficult things. That no one can take away. Like a sauna stone. But it's more precious and magic, really. And it's always there when you need it. At least, that's how I've come to think about it. During a difficult class, for instance. Or sometimes when your father's away."

I couldn't help it. The story Dad had told me about Millie occasionally gusted through my mind. "Did you have a boyfriend before Dad?"

"You are full of questions today," Mom said. "Yes, I had several before your dad. Why do you ask?"

I glanced over her shoulder at the sushi bar. The chef was stacking sushi on a wooden ship. On the other side of the curtains, I could hear a group of men toasting someone in Japanese. Why was I asking? Was it because I had always suspected that Mom and Dad loved each other differently? Because there was in Mom a loyalty that seemed unreciprocated? Because I needed to know if she'd married the great love of her life?

"Any you liked as much as him?"

Mom smiled reassuringly and shook her head. "Your dad always has been and always will be my favorite."

I smiled. "Because he's a fox," I said.

Mom snorted, a little embarrassed. She took a bite of her yellowtail and I ate the whole piece of pigeon-colored mackerel, and, after a few seconds, we both began waving our hands before our mouths and tearing up.

"Wow," Mom said. "That was a big hit of wasabi."

She explained what it was. We ate some ginger and drank some ice water and blew air from our puckered mouths like the goldfish in the tank near the door. And when the heat subsided, I asked, "What was your favorite thing you and Dad ever did together? Was it your honeymoon with Anthony Quinn?"

"Oh, most certainly not," Mom said. "That was lonelier than South America."

Mom poured herself the last of the sake and smoothed out the napkin on her lap, thinking. "It was when we drove across the country together. In October of '63. After we'd returned from Europe. We flew over the pole—Paris to Los Angeles. We stayed with Morris and Mignon."

"Who?"

"Your father's parents. Zada and Babu."

When I looked at her questioningly, Mom said, "It's Yiddish. For 'Grandpa' and 'Grandma.'" She let my ignorance slide. "We stayed in San Bernardino with them for a few weeks. They gave us their Cutlass to make the drive back to New York and told us to sell it when we got there and send them the money. The drive took seven days. We'd bought Minou—do you remember our cat?"

"Barely." Which wasn't exactly true. I sometimes recalled her sadly meowing her name during the fire.

"We bought her from a Frenchwoman selling kittens on the street in Barstow, just before we picked up I-40. The car's air-conditioning didn't work, and even with the windows down it got so hot going through the desert that by late morning Minou would get overheated. She'd pant in her cage and it was so pathetic. We'd have to stop at a hotel and cool her down."

"Are you mad at me about her dying?"

"No, baby, it wasn't your fault." She took my wrist across the table. "None of it. Do you understand?"

Because I had teared up, I fanned my mouth. "Wasabi," I said, and then made a great show of drinking my water, which Mom watched intently.

"Griffin, what do you remember about the fire?"

The waitress came and refilled my glass.

"Not much," I said. "I remember going into the closet with Oren. With the candle. And then I set the jacket on fire. And then I heard Minou crying. And then me and Oren—"

"Oren and I," she said.

"Oren and I were in our room, hiding. We were like, '*It's a real fire.*' And then we ran to tell you and Dad. And then we all escaped. To the lobby."

Mom's smile was mournful. She still held my wrist. "No, baby, that's not how it happened. Your father and I were in our bedroom. We smelled smoke. Dad found you, hiding in your room."

"Where was Oren?"

Mom said, "Did you and Elliott never talk about this?"

I shook my head.

"That sweet little boy," Mom said. "He was in the living room, look-ing for the cat. He kept saying her name. 'Minou? Minou?' He was who you must've heard."

I was rocked by this. "And . . . then what?"

"And then we filled the bathtub and left both of you in there while we tried to put out the fire. I ran pots of water from the kitchen to the closet to try to douse the flames. Your father went to get the floor's extinguisher, but it didn't work. So then we grabbed you and fled." Mom squeezed my wrist before letting go. "You were just a child," she said. "If the fault was anyone's, it was mine for leaving out the candles."

I was trying to make so many contrary thoughts in my mind jibe, I had so many images swirling in my head, that it wasn't until the diners in the private tatami room behind us shouted, "Kanpai!" that Mom came back into focus.

She raised her glass and drank. "Where were we?" she asked.

I was glad to change the subject too. "Your favorite thing," I said, "you ever did. With Dad. You said it was that trip across the country."

Mom shrugged, brightening. "You know how your father is. He can get distracted sometimes. But he isn't distracted when he drives. Or maybe it's that the driving distracts him and he can concentrate on other things better. We drove and talked and kept an eye on the cat, and it was just the two of us for seven days. But it seemed like a month. In the best way. Your dad's left arm got so sunburned because he had the window down, and he had to wear a long-sleeved shirt by the time we got to Texas. And when we arrived in New York, his parents told us to keep the money from the car, and we moved into an apartment in Jackson Heights. We didn't have a pot to piss in, but we were so happy. Your dad started getting steady work. I got the job at Carnegie Hall. And then we could afford to move to Manhattan, to Lincoln Towers. Two years later, I had you. And two years after that, Oren."

I imagine Mom and Dad now, driving across the country together. First through hot and desolate desert scenes, movie landscapes: buttes in the distance and tumbleweeds rolling across the highway and Mom having all of Dad's attention. The kitten atop the bed with them, happy in the air-conditioned hotel room where they'd stopped for the night. The pair waking before sunrise and jumping into the car, to get an early start and beat the heat. Cities I have still never visited appearing on the horizon as they headed east: Albuquerque, Amarillo, Oklahoma City. Mom faced forward, her husband at her side, her back to the future, the children she did not yet know she'd have, the kitten purring in her lap . . .

And finally New York. That island whose skyline was just coming into view from the Jersey side. When the Empire State Building still reigned as the city's tallest, but seen from this far away not even measuring an inch. It was a vista I knew well. In the foreground first was the Hackensack River and then Newark Bay before they entered the Holland Tunnel. Or did they bear north and take the George Washington Bridge, Mom unaware, as they ran parallel to the Upper West Side, that they were passing the building where they'd make their lives?—she certain she could rely on the warmth she now felt in her guts. Now and forever.

Forever being a concept with which I parted that day. In the silence between finishing our meal and paying the bill—Mom calculating the tip with great care—I tried as hard as I could to recall Oren and me in that bathtub and what must've been a comparatively calm, incongruous pause in that conflagration. But perhaps it wasn't calm at all. Perhaps it was the most terrifying part. Oren and I, facing each other as the water overflowed, while smoke crawled up from the doorjamb, billowed along the ceiling, and sank toward us. What did it mean, I wondered—I still do—to not remember something so fundamental about yourself? Was it the same as if it never happened? Or was it still happening? Like the fire still smoldering beneath the forest floor.

Dad came home from Delaware right before the July Fourth weekend. The first leg of the tour for *Sam and Sara* had concluded, and we had the holiday together before he'd leave again for Philadelphia. Oren and I hadn't seen him in nearly a month. He blew into the apartment, short-tempered. Mom had already packed us for our annual trip out to Montauk, but Dad's suitcase lay open and empty on their bed, which annoyed him more. He was in a bad mood the entire weekend. He didn't want to swim and was distant at our dinners. He didn't want to fish with us or play miniature golf. In the afternoons, Oren and I often returned to the motel room from the beach, where they'd left us, to hear them arguing in the room. On Monday, Dad said he had to get to Philadelphia early. We began our push back toward the city that afternoon but stopped, as we always did, at Elliott and Lynn's house in Amagansett. Their place was in that dune-swept stretch of barrens—a solid ten miles of moonscape— between Montauk and East Hampton. Their house was supermodern, a two-story rectangle fashioned of white poplar sheared down its center by a glass-filled triangle. These visits regularly followed the same schedule: Elliott made a huge batch of banana daiquiris in the blender. The moment they were served Al, who had a house in Montauk, appeared, as if passing through ("I figure," he said, "I leave by four, I beat traffic") but stuck around until later. When Mom asked where his boyfriend, Tony, was, Al frowned and said, "As if I fucking know." Dinner was salmon and chicken and green beans with almonds and potato salad; after having seconds and white wine spritzers, Dad and Elliott fell asleep at the dinner table, Al and Mom talked on the back deck while he smoked and wept, Lynn did the dishes, Oren and I went to the guest room to watch Mutual of Omaha's *Wild Kingdom*. When Dad, awake come evening, darkened our door, his bad mood had returned—he said it was time to go, and then there was the long drive home. Mom's and Dad's faces were illuminated by the dash. It was remarkable how they could conduct an entire conversation I somehow couldn't follow about a couple whom I'd never heard of, never met.

"He thinks," Dad said, "she's being a little too suspicious."

"She thinks," Mom said, "she has reason to be."

"He needs," Dad said, "for her to trust him."

Here the conversation ended, though she allowed him to stroke her hair for the rest of the drive. Traffic was a ruby-red serpent's tail from Queens to Manhattan. On Tuesday morning, Dad left to go back on tour, but I had to be at NBC studios even earlier—call was at six a.m. My lines were barely memorized. I still had not cracked a single summer reading book. My backpack was full of graph paper for maps and dice and all the *D&D* handbooks. I had decided to design my own campaign for Oren, Tanner, and Cliffnotes, which I vowed to have ready to play by the fall. Taping for the fifth season of *The Nuclear Family* had officially commenced—which was another way of saying that for the most part, and once again, my summer was effectively over.

As if that weren't bad enough, I hadn't spoken to Amanda. Pride, along with the adherence to Dad's steam-room pep talk, forbade I call her. I had reconciled myself to the forlorn offseason he had recommended, and I had done my best to fill the intervening days with work: early morning weightlifting sessions with Vince before heading to 8H; world-building *D&D* campaign sessions—I had named my campaign's setting *Griffynweld*—during breaks from shooting and in the evenings when I got home. But still adrift, I did not know how to address Dad's counsel, since I did not know there was technique to study and I wasn't going to go to Times Square to buy porn. The amount of magical thinking that by this point surrounded her had become so intense it bordered on a kind of madness. Alone in my dressing room, with my Dungeon Master's dice, I often made predictions aloud—"If I roll a natural twenty, Amanda will fall in love with me"—a prognostication that, after several rerolls, rarely came true. But I persevered in my magical thinking. Riding my bike to 30 Rock in the early mornings, I might forecast *to the second* when the streetlights changed from red to green, tethering the timing to the certainty of our union. If, riding home that evening, the digital clock atop the MONY building read 5:55, I made a love wish; and if, before it flashed, I correctly guessed the temperature that followed, that too meant Amanda would someday be mine. I'd glare at the dressing room's phone on my vanity mirror's table—I'd never received a single call on it—and will it to ring, promising aloud, "Someday it will be Amanda on the line, asking me to go out with her."

One afternoon in late July, it rang.

When I answered, it *was* Amanda, who said, "Where have you been all summer?"

And then she asked me out.

It was her birthday, she explained, and she didn't want to spend it alone. As if anticipating my question, she said, "Rob decided to go with some of his friends to the Cape this week." There were two women from school he was close with, Andrea and Sophie, did I know them? When I told her only by sight, she said they were having a final precollege bash— Rob was off to Princeton in the fall. Which she reported in a tone somewhere between disappointment and resignation—they'd probably break up by summer's end—a statement to which I simply listened. Registering her pain and determined to cheer her up, I said, "Well, more Amanda for me"—not, I realized, a bad line, which was confirmed when Amanda replied, "I am *all* yours." Which made the blood hammer in my ears.

"How about dinner and a movie?" I suggested.

"Mom's ordering in Chinese and making me a cake."

"How about a movie after," I said. And then my father spoke through me. "I hear the performances in *Eye of the Needle* are exceptional."

She agreed, and I told her I'd call her back with the time and place.

After we wrapped for the day, I went to see Alison in wardrobe. As I changed out of Peter Proton's capri pants and suspenders, after I handed her the same pocket protector I'd worn for the past four years, I told her I had a big date tonight. She kept her eyes on her book. "Lucky you," she said.

"I was wondering," I said, and then paused again because I was afraid to ask, "if you might consider helping me pick out something to wear."

She looked up and then blinked at me several times. She laid her book on her chest, lit a cigarette, then smiled and said, "Sure." The hangers clacked on the poles of the wardrobe racks as she considered and rejected shirt after shirt. After holding a few of them up to my chest, she picked out a short-sleeved button-down—"This blue," she said, "brings out your pretty eyes," which no one except Naomi had ever told me were anything, much less pretty—black jeans and black Converses, neither of which I'd have ever chosen on my own. "Snappy," Alison said, stepping back from me to get a good look, "but not trying too hard." I surprised both of us by hugging her. It was overly enthusiastic, and she tensed up at first when I gathered her into the embrace, her arms out as if she were going to be frisked. I forgot, for a moment, that she was a grown-up and figured she must've forgotten too, because I was taller than her now, filled out from weight training with Vince; but then she uncoiled, relaxed, and became heavy. Settling, she pressed her ear to my shoulder and rocked ever so slightly, allowing me to feel, albeit briefly, the loneliness I now recognize she always seemed to carry. "You're welcome," she said.

Later that evening, standing before the cinema's entrance, I spied Amanda as she emerged from the street's comparative darkness into the theater awning's lights. She had knotted a Clash T-shirt above her belly button, and she had rolled up the cuffs of a too-large gray blazer. Her hair was in a bow. She took a moment to appraise me, her eyebrows raised ever so slightly, as if she did not recognize me or as if I had, in some way she could not quite pinpoint, become unfamiliar to her, and in me this elicited a feeling of auspiciousness about tonight's possibilities that I feared to trust. It had been several weeks since we'd last seen each other, after all, and whatever difference she noticed went beyond the physical, seemed to put us on a different footing.

"Happy birthday," I said, and produced the bowed present I'd bought her on the trip home from the studio.

She considered the small box. "Can I open it now?" she asked. She managed not to tear the wrapping, a trick every woman I knew could somehow manage, pulling the tape from the paper and then handing the latter back to me, as if it were failed origami. "L'Air du Temps!" she said. Then she hugged my neck with one arm and held me, so that her cheek pressed to mine, and comparing it with the one Alison and I had shared earlier, it was different in kind: if the former was a respite from isolation, this felt like an invitation—to what I was not sure. She removed the bottle from its packaging, unscrewed the ornate top—its fogged, abstract glass in the shape of a bird—then sprayed some perfume behind each ear; and when she lifted her chin for me to smell, I allowed myself to press my face into her soft hair, and she allowed me to remain thus poised long enough to enjoy it.

In the theater, when the lights went down, I kept my arm still on the rest we shared. I was so hyperalert to our elbows' lightest touch I could have taken her pulse. Her nearness was so distracting the movie's plot was mostly lost on me, her proximity something I dare not acknowledge, lest like some forest animal I might startle her and she bolt. And yet my stillness also freed her to move, to press her shoulder to mine before asking a question, to tap my wrist to signal I tilt the bucket of popcorn toward her, or to lay her fingers on my arm, so that I bent my ear to her lips, before making a comment. "They're going to *crash,*" she whispered of Kate Nelligan and the actor playing her husband as they drive down the narrow road on their wedding day. "She's so lonely," Amanda said, when, years later, Nelligan's crippled husband rejects her advances in bed. "She's in *love* with him," she murmured of Donald Sutherland, the Nazi spy, when he accidentally opens Nelligan's bathroom door and pauses at the sight of her naked in the mirror's reflection. During the love scenes, I tried to swallow as quietly as was possible. And when, at the film's conclusion, Sutherland is foiled, killed at Nelligan's hand, his stolen intelligence will never make it to the German high command, and D-Day can success-fully commence—when the credits rolled but before the lights came up and there was that feeling of release that made you want to clap or cry or sprint down the aisles, I sensed Amanda turn and then stare at my pro-file. She leaned over to kiss my cheek forcefully, gratefully, as if to con-firm this had already been a lovely birthday, and then she waited. How many times have I time traveled back to that moment? Have I, on take after take, kissed her in return? Only to understand how ill-equipped I was then to accept a direct invitation, being so adept at seeing around people, at watching their true selves peek out from behind their masks, that I could not match such spontaneous ardor? Sing, Muse, of a boy's lack of know-how. I'd been so trained in dissembling I didn't simply dis-trust directness, I was paralyzed by it, no matter how blissed out I was, and did not dare turn to face her. At least not yet.

I took her to Baskin-Robbins afterward for ice cream. It was only a couple of blocks from her apartment. After we were served, we stood on the sidewalk, brightened by the store's interior light, watching each other eat as if each other's eating was to be studied. We finished our cones, and Amanda wrapped her arms around my waist and then leaned back, an embrace I copied, and we rocked from side to side, almost dancing. She was beaming; she bit her lower lip and swept her eyes across mine, and once again this attention—this outright affection—made me bashful. It was as impossible to believe as it was delightful, and in response to my hesitance she finally said, "Well?" and when I did not reply, she asked, "Are you going to watch the royal wedding tomorrow?"

Because of the time difference, it started at six a.m., she explained. She and her mother were going to set an alarm and have tea and English muffins with marmalade and not miss a minute of it. Amanda assured me it was going to be the most romantic thing ever. She was dying to see Diana's dress, and when I asked what she wanted to do next, she demanded I come back to the apartment with her, even though her mother was home.

In Amanda's room, I sat across from her, on her brother's bed, the space between the frames narrow enough that our knees touched. She leaned over to place a forty-five on her small turntable and, once she lowered the needle, adjusted the volume so that it was loud enough that we could speak privately but low enough that we could still hear her mother in the living room.

Miss West was talking on her ham radio, and when she spoke into the microphone, the sound of her voice was clear and insistent and unimaginably friendly. She said, "Pointer-Cook-Seven-Zed-Zed, this is Patricia at Victor-Three-Five-Alpha-Bravo, calling from New York City, the Big Apple, on the Upper West Side of Manhattan. Nice to make contact with you, Tucker, it's a very strong signal, over." The caller's Australian accent was closer to a gurgled buzz. The man said, "Victor-Three-Five-Alpha-Bravo, I'm coming to you at twenty meters. Your signal's very strong too, Patricia. Tell me all about your fine summer weather, please, because we're smack dab in the middle of winter here in Melbourne, over."

Amanda leaned back on her bed, propped on her elbows, listening. She swayed her knees side to side, which in turn swiveled mine. She asked me what the rest of my summer looked like. I said I was doing *The Nuclear Family*, it was six-to-six Monday through Friday, though I might get a Wednesday or Thursday off here and there, sometimes even a three-day weekend if I was lucky. She said, "I'm going to my father's house in Westhampton next week and then staying for most of August. You should come visit. When you have a break."

"I will," I said, astounded at the invitation, already dreaming on it, and just as we noticed the music had stopped—that the needle was sounding the dead wax—it occurred to us Miss West had also gone silent, and she appeared at Amanda's door. She wore a consternated expression, so we both sat up straight. She asked Amanda, "Have you seen my screwdriver?"

When Amanda replied, "No, why?" Miss West said, "I have a transistor I need to replace and can't remove the radio's panel without a Phillips head."

"It's not in the junk drawer?"

Miss West shook her head. "Are you sure you haven't misplaced it?"

"Swear to God, hope to die," Amanda said.

Her mother squinted and then shot me a look of annoyance, a triangulated lie detector test: Was I an accomplice? When she disappeared,

Amanda placed her index finger to her lips, then got up and walked over to her bookcase. She took from its top shelf a tiny toy safe and sat down again, facing its combination lock toward me. I could see that its metal door was damaged, like a swollen lip, bent outward from where the lock's wheel engaged. She reached in and removed the broken tool her mother sought, its small red handle bright as blood, the shank sheared off where she'd clearly snapped it trying to pry open the safe's door. Grimacing, mock guilty, she placed both pieces back in the safe.

Miss West reappeared from the kitchen, holding a very long letter opener, and said, "Not a clue?" And when Amanda shook her head again, Miss West glanced at me and asked, "Don't you have to go soon?" to which I replied, "At eleven," and Miss West said, "It's ten after," and I said, "Yes, ma'am," and then she disappeared once more.

I stood, but Amanda remained seated, watching me rise to go. She placed her safe near her pillow. She said, "Thank you for a lovely evening."

"It was my pleasure," I said, and did not move.

Amanda's eyes scanned mine. Her expression I would best describe as suspicious—in fact it closely resembled her mother's, as if I too were keeping a secret from her that she was waiting for me to divulge. I *knew* what this was now, and even though I was still assailed by doubt there was nothing else to do. I bent toward her, resting my hands on my knees so that our faces were within inches of each other's, and mustering all my courage said, "I'm going to kiss you goodbye." To which Amanda replied, "Okay."

And then I leaned in and kissed her. It was barely more than a peck on her mouth, dry and quick, and afterward I withdrew ever so slightly. I could not at first gauge her reaction because I remained so close to her, but she didn't move. I saw that her eyes were closed, that she was waiting, so I kissed her again. It was awkward, fearful, and unassertive, my lips resting against hers inertly until, moving mine as she spoke, she said, "You can keep going, you know." And trying and failing to be cool, I said, "I can?" And she said, "Yes," the *s* all smooshed between us. I tilted my head and she tilted hers. Her lips parted ever so slightly and, before they touched, so did mine. At first the pressure was so gentle that I could feel the soft down above her top lip. As we kissed each other, her tongue's tip pressed delicately toward mine. We parted, and I sat on the bed next to her and was about to kiss her, I imagined, for *forever,* when from the living room there came an agonized scream.

Miss West was seated with her back to the radio. Her face was so white it looked powdered with talc. Her hands lay on her lap and she held one in the other but would not look down at them. She sat frozen, and then we saw what had happened. She had somehow stabbed the letter opener into her palm, and the tip of the dull blade was all the way through to the other side. Blood was issuing from it, slowly, thickly, just beginning to bloom on her skirt. "I was trying," she explained, "to remove the panel screw," and then her eyes darted from me to Amanda, "and then the blade slipped." With a twitchy smile, she added, "I don't want to faint." Amanda, who had covered her mouth, now rushed toward her mother and touched her mother's shoulder, awaiting instruction, since Miss West was a nurse and the authority in such a matter, in spite of the fact that she was the one needing help. With a courteousness incongruent with the moment, Miss West said to Amanda, "If you would get me a towel, please." Sweat beaded her forehead, and the skin at her neck was slick. Amanda hurried to the bathroom and returned. "Just put it underneath," Miss West said, "but gently," and raised her hand, "where the tip is," which hooked her soaked skirt when she lifted it from her lap. "Don't push it out," Miss West advised. "In case . . . if I severed an artery." Amanda asked if she should call 911. Miss West shook her head. "We're going to walk to Mount Sinai right now. Griffin . . ." And she waved me over with her uninjured hand, indicating that I should help her to stand.

Out of the apartment, into the elevator, onto the street—the two of us supporting her—Miss West held her injured hand out before her with the towel beneath it. Her other hand delicately supported the bunched fabric as if it were a ringbearer's pillow. Amanda and I huddled to her with our hands cupped beneath hers. "Keep it elevated," Miss West said, "above my heart." The hospital came into view as soon as we turned on Amsterdam. Shuffling as we were, the walk seemed to take forever. Amanda kept saying, "You've got this, you can do it, not too much farther"; I kept saying, "Keep going, don't give up, you're doing great." Miss West kept repeating, "I've got this, I can do it, doing great." But once we arrived at the emergency room, once we stepped under the ambulance bay's light, Miss West lost her composure. She spotted a nurse she knew and called out, "Dolores!" in a voice hoarse with terror. The woman came running over to us and said, "Patty, my God." All the people seated in the waiting room looked up, and Miss West turned to me. When she spoke, her tone was distant and professional, so at odds with the escalating emotion I couldn't help but take note. "I appreciate your help, Griffin, Dolores can take it from here," and Amanda, who was crying, nodded at me and then wiped her nose so that it smeared her mother's blood on her nostrils and across her mouth. Dolores took my place by Miss West's elbow. And the three of them walked into the building and through another set of double doors, which, along with my chances, swallowed them whole.

UNION BUSTER

In the year that I returned home from college and began seeing Elliott again—the year that I began to open up to him in ways I was incapable of as a boy—he said to me that we process all trauma like the oyster. We pearl the dangerous particle, if we are lucky, into something precious, into the gift. He never explained what that gift was, or what happened if we are less than lucky, because he and I ran out of time. Only in our final sessions before he died would I return to the site of my selfhood's inception—not to the fire, to the panicked flight of our family from our burning home, but to the moment, as Dad walked me down the hallway from Al and Neal's apartment to our incinerated one, when I felt the instant that millimeter opened between my inner terror and impassivity. And once we identified that moment, Elliott and I began to inventory certain scenes in which I'd failed to feel anything: I spying Naomi's upturned face, her absorbed expression, when we first kissed in her car. Me lying atop Kepplemen, on his bed, his head locked in my arms, his foot trying to hook mine, our feet pointed toward his headboard; him kicking the pillows clear, me staring at the cover of the magazine, of the picture of the two wrestlers, until Kepplemen and I finally lay still. Only decades after these last sessions with my therapist would I fully comprehend what Kepplemen had done to me—and to my friends and team-mates; only in middle age would I identify the source of the fury I felt when, deep beneath my school, I'd clasp that man and make him *feel* it—would make him pay for his pleasure with pain. Here, nearer to where the subways rumbled, to the network of pipelines into which the city's catch basins fed, I was taught the indelible lesson that, to arrive at love, I must suffer *through* someone else's idea of it. And yet even now, I resist the notion that we are reducible to our wounds.

But that night, after leaving Amanda and her mother at the hospital, I remained my ciphered self. I walked to Broadway and caught the bus home in something close to shock. I recall, as I deposited change in the fare box, the driver eyeing my blood-blackened hands with a wariness verging on alarm. Other than a couple of passengers sitting near the front—who, to also ignore the threat I might pose, studied our southbound progress—the bus was nearly empty. At that hour, the streets were mostly empty too. In something close to a daze, I took a seat in the back, watching the avenue unspool against the windows. I recall how voided I was, how stunned and emptied—sometimes it seemed I struggled to feel anything at all.

By the time I got back to our apartment, it was very late. I went straight to the kitchen and washed my hands with dish soap, then scraped the blood from beneath my fingernails with a paring knife. I turned off the TV in my parents' bedroom; Mom was asleep while the national anthem played over the image of the flag. As I undressed in my own room, I noted that Oren was gone again, his bunk so neatly made it appeared as if it hadn't been slept in all summer. I stared at the ceiling's blank screen, replaying those same lambent images: Amanda's smile as she lay back on her bed, propped on her elbows; her knees swaying against mine; the down above her top lip, soft as sea anemone. And the shame that follows hard on all timidity, that pursues missed opportunity.

Call at 30 Rock was seven a.m., and waking early once again I could hear the TV in my parents' room—soft music, voices. The sun was just about to rise. Mom's door was cracked, so I knocked and entered. She was showered and dressed, her legs stretched on the bed, several tissues bunched in her fist. I lay down next to her and placed my head on her shoulder. Prince Charles and Prince Andrew, in full military uniform, were just entering Saint Paul's Cathedral and shaking hands with the bishops. The organ boomed. Charles was the more weasel-faced of the pair, Andrew more gopher-cheeked and beaver-toothed than his brother. A gilded stagecoach, carrying Diana, was seen moving through London's streets. *And we await the moment,* said the male newscaster, *when this glass coach, which we can see without periscopes, comes to a stop . . . the door opens, and for the first time we see in all its glory that dress.* Diana exited the fairy-tale vehicle with her whale-length train extended behind her. Two bridesmaids tended to its ends as she proceeded up the steps. The woman announcer said, *What a dream she looks . . . a bride any man would be happy to see coming down the aisle toward him. The dress is made of yards of ivory pure silk taffeta, it has big sleeves with deep lace flounces at the elbow. It has a very, very long train, and if you asked a little girl to draw a princess, I think she'd draw a dress just like that.*

I wondered if Amanda and Miss West, in a room at the hospital, were watching this together.

When I asked Mom why she was crying, she replied, "Because it's all so lovely. Because Diana's so young and so beautiful. And it makes me think about my wedding."

"Your wedding makes you sad?"

"Just the time that's passed," Mom said. She occasionally spoke in mysteries like this, but it was too early to interrogate her about this one. She loudly sighed and laughed at herself, pressing both index fingers to her lower lids. "Off to torture my ladies," she said. Then: "You and I have an appointment with Elliott this evening, at six."

I got up the nerve to call Amanda before lunch, from my dressing room, and she answered. On the phone she was cordial, relieved. Everything was okay, she explained. Amazingly, her mother had done no major damage to her hand, it was a one-in-a-million injury not to have harmed any tendons or bones or arteries or nerves. All she'd needed was a tetanus shot and stitches, but she'd lose her grip strength for a few weeks. It was just very sore and wrapped in so many layers of gauze it looked like a Muppet, she said. Amanda was running around taking care of her, she had to pick up her antibiotics at the pharmacy. Could she call me later? she asked. Her rushed brightness felt like a stiff arm. Of course, I said. And she hung up.

My mood darkened, and for the rest of the day I was distracted on set. I regularly blew my lines, so that even Andy, who was usually forbearing, lost his patience with me. I brought no energy to my battle with archvillain Microwave Mike, and when I did, I got the choreography wrong and accidentally punched him in the mouth. When Alison, at day's end, noticed how taciturn I was, she asked, with real interest, "How'd your date go?" to which I replied, "It was a disaster." "Well," she said encouragingly, "I thought you looked very handsome." And in a moment of thoughtlessness that I regret to this day, I said, "Not handsome enough." Which she took as a dig and nodded, as if I'd just confirmed some personal truth about helping people, and for the remainder of my time on the show, she never spoke to me again. When I arrived at Elliott's office I was in something close to despair.

I had never been to Elliott's during Mom's midweek appointment, and every seat was taken in the waiting room. Standing between two chairs, I leaned down to ask Mom about this, and she said, "It's almost August." When I looked at her uncomprehendingly, she pulled me by the sleeve to whisper, "All the therapists go on vacation for the month. So everyone's stuffing their cheeks with insight."

When her session ended, Elliott appeared at his door, bleary and baggy-eyed. He seemed stooped and distracted, and when he spotted me, he paused, confused, as if he didn't recognize who I was. For the first time in my life, I thought he looked old.

"Take a seat," he said. He wrote some notes on his legal pad, then removed his readers and placed them in his breast pocket. He checked his watch. "I give you fifteen minutes," he said, "you give me your world."

It was to be, then, one of those hurry-up sessions, tacked on to Mom's appointment, which Elliott occasionally did with Oren and me after Dad's Saturday sessions. It was one of those instances when I was reminded that even though Elliott was my father's best friend, or seemed to be; even though we were treated like special guests at all his parties, we were still customers of his attention, a fact I mostly did not reflect upon but, at that moment, decided somehow cheapened the advice and the fellowship, making both suspect. I wondered, as he rubbed his eyes before closing the door—this with an expression close to impatience—if he ever got sick of us, of everything we transferred upon him for failing to fix.

Instead of telling him about my evening with Amanda, I stuck to the surface, to work and its exasperations. To today's fuckups and my enduring outlier, outcast status. To my lost summer.

Elliott was twiddling his thumbs.

"Am I boring you?" I asked. My anger shocked me.

Elliott stopped and chuckled. Then he shrugged. "You're talking about this like a ten-year-old," he said. He raised his voice several octaves: "Why me, boohoo." From his jacket's breast pocket, he removed his handkerchief and blew his nose. "Question: What do you like about acting?"

"I don't . . ." I said. "I don't know what you mean."

"About the process. The art of it. Does it *jazz* you? Do you have limitless energy for it? When you worked with Alan Hornbeam this spring, did you want to get to the beauty and truth of each scene? Or were you just watching the clock?"

"I'm not . . ." I said. "I don't understand."

"Why do you even do it?"

"Because I'm . . . good at it?"

"I asked *you*."

I slumped against the chairback and looked at his frog, which was either staring at the ceiling or giving me the side-eye, it was hard to tell. "Don't I have to?"

"Do you?" Elliott asked.

"Can we go for a walk?"

"Not today, kid, sorry."

"I want an egg cream."

"And I," Elliott said with a heaviness I would later come to understand, "want more time."

I crossed my arms. "Can I at least get a hint?"

"Young man," he said, "your father's got a voice from God. Your mother moves like an angel. You can breathe life into characters. Be that as it may, just because you have a talent doesn't mean you have to use it."

From the side table between us, he slid open its drawer and removed a small, wrapped box, which he placed on the desk.

"Go on," Elliott said, "open it."

It was a Space Pen.

"You've been eyeballing mine for so long I thought I'd get you your own. Give what I said a think and we'll discuss in September." Elliott unfolded his glasses, checked his watch, nodded toward the waiting room. "Now, off with you," he said. "I got fires to put out."

Mom wasn't in the waiting room, so I left the office, figuring she was on the street. I emerged from the office's long hallway into the city's noise and evening's falling brightness to spy my mother talking to Naomi.

They stood by Naomi's Mercedes. She'd lucked into miraculous parking right out front. They were speaking animatedly, loudly, the sort of catchup that involved the touching of arms, a covering of mouths, laughter that vied with traffic noise, that reminded you how rarely you heard pedestrians in Manhattan talking. As my mother gestured, Naomi spotted me, and in that glance's microsecond we were alone. I had not spoken with her since we'd said goodbye that January. She wore a summer suit made of white linen and was very tan. The spray of freckles dotting her nose and cheeks were darkened beneath her blue-tinted lenses. I felt a complicated relief, a need to collapse into her arms and tell her everything along with an imperative to pretend we were only family friends, when she did something unexpected. She reached out to me, snapping her fingers before I was within her grasp so imperiously it made me weak-kneed, and then she pulled me close.

"Look at Mr. Muscles here," Naomi said, and made a great show of giving me a side hug, her eyes exaggeratedly widening at Mom as she patted my chest. "Six months, I don't see him," she said, "he's like a grown man already." And then, out of my mother's view, she slid her hand from my side to secretly run her fingernails up and down the small of my back. She asked what I was up to, how it was going with *The Nuclear Family,* poor baby locked inside all summer, Daddy's gone, where's your brother? The torrent of questions while her nails traced my spine had rendered me mute. They were a kind of cover, this peppering. My mouth went dry. I stiffened so instantaneously it was like a beak trying to break through my jean's denim. I was embarrassed and paralyzed with desire. She said to Mom, "You should all come out to my brother's beach house sometime, what with Shel on the road, and just *relax.*" And here, as if for emphasis, she pressed her nails so hard against my shirt they nearly pierced my skin.

"We might just take you up on that," Mom said.

Naomi checked her watch. "I'm late for my session," she said, and released me to kiss Mom's cheek with a loud pop. "Don't be a stranger," she ordered. She turned to kiss me as well, allowing her lips to touch the corner of my mouth, and had I not been so stunned, had my mother not been present, I'd have kissed her back, right there. She waved to me with a tiny flap of her hand and said, "*Bye, Griffin.*" And she hurried into Elliott's office.

"That woman," Mom said, the minute we were out of earshot, "is too much."

In bed that night, all thoughts of Amanda were blown from my mind. Instead, I was standing with Naomi on the street. With a heat that, even now, has been undiminished by decades, the scene replayed—she asks me questions, but the sound of her voice is muffled and far away; I am at once light and heavy, buoyant and weighed down. I had at my disposal no subsequent scenes by which this fantasy might have played out. And because I was virginal in every way, because I could not imagine its fruition, I was trapped in it. *That* was its power. To this day, I can conjure it, but there are times when it seems to conjure me, so that I wonder if it is Naomi's doing, *her* passing thought, some arcane aspect of our connection, current traveling down memory's hot wire to arc across space and time. I confess I live in fear of seeing her. She could be decrepit, and I am certain that, in my presence, her youth and my desire would be restored. But that night, in my bed, I could summon no release. I flipped onto my stomach, burying my face in my pillow. With all my strength I gripped the bunk's rails and pressed the balls of my feet to the frame, pinning myself to my mattress, because this exertion was my only relief.

On Friday, Oren, Mom, and I took the Amtrak to Philadelphia, to stay with Dad and see *Sam and Sara* in preview—our first glimpse of the musical front to back and out of rehearsal.

The Forrest Theatre was a historic building fashioned of white lime stone. Its interior's hues were a combination of peach and turquoise, its colossal chandelier, inset beneath its ornate, domed ceiling, loomed so massively I imagined it falling on the unwitting spectators. After checking into the hotel, we hurried to briefly meet Dad in his dressing room beforehand to wish him luck. His costume was a tweed jacket and khakis. He wore a white button-down shirt, a red-and-blue varsity scarf knotted at his throat. His hair was sprayed blond. A prop pennant leaned against his vanity mirror. He looked like he was headed to a college football game. In the glance Oren and I shot each other, it wasn't clear which we thought was funnier: Dad's golden locks or the fact that he couldn't tell an offensive tackle from a fullback. He was harried, happy, nervous, and preening, as he paced the small room. I forgot sometimes how much heavier stage makeup was than for television. His brightened face seemed to float, as if attached to his skull by a slightly loose spring. When Mom kissed him in parting, his foundation left a flesh-toned brushstroke on her cheek.

The show was about a pair of couples who are good friends and know each other over the course of their entire lives: Sara, who is engaged to Vern, an aspiring architect—played by Dad; and Sam, who is engaged to Ana. When the show begins, all four college seniors are celebrating homecoming weekend. The afternoon before the big game, the betrothed couples are introduced at a fraternity party, and the opening ensemble number is a nostalgic one entitled "Have You Declared?" Everyone is sharing their plans, how they'll go from being economics majors to bankers, from biology majors to scientists, from single to married to families of four or six. But then Sam and Sara see each other across the room; the stage briefly goes dark, until the pair is cordoned off from each other but also privately entangled in their respective spotlights. It's obvious that they have fallen in love, and the show's entire conflict centers on whether they will leave their respective spouses in order to be together. The music's tempo changes from fast to slow, and they sing only of the moment, of their feelings, of the present, which clouds their future, casting it and them in doubt.

"Too clever by half," Mom said to me, clapping when it concluded, the applause neither muted nor overwhelming. The performance's energy—that invisible cord connecting the actors to the audience—was perhaps partially diffused by the size of the crowd, which filled maybe half the house. Still, I trusted Mom to name what I could not put my finger on, which made both Oren and me fidgety, inattentive, which I now recognize as a quality the musical lacked, an absence at its very core that manifested as an inability, from its start, to enchant.

"Do I have to watch this whole thing?" Oren whispered.

"Yes," Mom said.

"Do I have to wear this tie all night?"

"You will sit in your seat and keep on your dress clothes," Mom said.

What I recall was hoping things might change as the musical progressed. I remember rooting for it and for my father. There was a fantastic quartet number called "Alone at Last" that takes place on the couples' honeymoon. Sam and Ana are in Italy while Vern and Sara are in Paris, Sam and Sara singing to each other while Vern and Ana swoon over their new spouses—a showstopper. Yet even at that moment, I recognized that the song somehow stood *too* far above the others. Like all tour de force performances, it strangely threatened to destabilize the whole by setting the rest of the musical's inferiority in stark relief. After its final, long-held note, which Vern and Ana hold together, there was a pause and then applause, nearer to an eruption, the cheering that followed pegged at an entirely different volume: sustained, and briefly contracting, and then expanding to swell once more, a murmuration that filled the theater with love and Oren, Mom, and me—at least I felt it—with hope.

The actress who played Sam's wife, Ana, was a tall woman, full-figured and forceful, and she possessed a sort of raspy vividness. But it was only well after the curtain calls, when we met Dad again backstage, in the narrow hallway his dressing room gave onto, in the hubbub of the actors changing and milling about, greeting guests and fans—only when she exited her dressing room, having removed her blond wig and makeup, that I realized she was the same woman I'd seen my father talking to that day, many months ago, on the Upper West Side, seated on the statue in Columbus Circle. The woman he'd lied to me about, whose face I'd picked out on his wall of headshots. She hesitated at her dressing room door, seeing that we blocked her path. Dad seemed to sense her presence and, looking over his shoulder, said far too loudly, "Katie." In response to his summons, she gave him a hot look, one close to annoyance—she was like an unwilling audience member being called up onstage—and then reluctantly approached. It was this reluctance, so quickly discarded, so rapidly exchanged for a kind of enthusiasm, that distinguished her from my mother, that marked her as my mother's diametrical opposite, and therefore presented an enormous threat. Her earrings were large and hooped; her fingers beringed, their metals thick and heavy; the pendant arrow on her necklace pointed toward her big boobs.

As if all three adults—my father, my mother, and the woman— were suddenly as translucent as jellyfish, I imagined I spied my father's increased heart rate, which he tried to cloak in noise; Mom's lungs shrank as she slowly emptied them of all breath; the woman's blood vessels narrowed so that their currents quickened. Katie, her dark eyes no longer accusatory, allowed her features to soften and, reaching a hand out to my mother, said, "Lily, it's so nice to meet you." To which Mom said only, "You too." And when they shook hands, Oren looked at Mom, whose silent wrath was both familiar and terrible, and then at me with a baffled expression.

Dad, no matter how hard I wished him to shut up, pressed forward. "Katie," he said to Mom, "was in the chorus of *The Fisher King*."

Katie nodded at Dad and then at Mom. "I was," she said, as if my mother hadn't heard him.

In response to which Mom smiled drily and then turned to Dad as if to ask, *Are we done here?* But instead of taking the cue, he said to Katie, "And these are my sons," to which Oren, in a Hail Mary attempt to spring us, asked, "Can we get a cheesesteak?"

"I think everything's closed," Dad said, and laughed.

"Jim's South St.'s open till midnight," Oren said.

To which Dad, clearly pissed, smiled and said to Katie, "Good to see you," as if she were filling in as tonight's lead and then leaving the country.

Mom walked ahead of us as we departed the theater. She got in the cab first, after Dad hailed it. She said nothing after Oren asked again about the food and Dad, seated by the other door, barked at him, "Don't even start!" Oren and I sat mute. When we arrived at the hotel, Mom announced, "I'm going to the bar." And when Dad said, "I'll join you," she replied, "You'll put the kids to bed." Her presence was magically and invisibly in the room while the three of us changed into our pajamas and took turns brushing our teeth, its specter commanding us to not utter a word to each other while we lay in our beds. When she returned to our darkened room an hour later—I pretended to be asleep—I saw her enter the bathroom dressed, her reflection framed in the hall's mirror, and then emerge in her nightgown before snapping off the light. I could feel her somehow nearer to Oren and me in our bed than she was to our father in the one adjacent.

Dad said, "Can we not do this please?"

For a long time, the only sound in the room was the air conditioner. "Lily?"

When she still did not respond, Dad said to her, as if none of this night had happened, "What do you think of the changes?" she replied, "It doesn't seem to me like anything's changed."

We had a miserable breakfast the following morning. Oren and I engaged in a sort of arms race, seeing who could pile his plate with the hotel's most luxurious food; and while I declared myself the winner based on sheer mass (scrambled eggs and sausage links, a Belgian waffle with whipped cream, a bagel with lox, and a chocolate croissant), Oren's creativity shamed me, building as he did a skyscraper of pancakes with strips of bacon interspersed between flapjack floors.

"Can I have a bite?" I asked.

"You can make your own," Oren said.

"You both better eat all of that," Dad said.

"It's not like it's à la carte," Oren said.

"There are children starving in China," Dad said.

"There are children starving here," Mom said. She glared at him with a rare unvarnished and appalled disdain, while Dad gave the hotel fountain that splashed behind us a thousand-yard stare. Dad slugged his black coffee and disappointedly shook his head. From where I sat, I could see, through the hotel's entrance, Broad Street shining as bright as a nuclear flash. There were other cast members eating at the tables nearby, and usually we could rely on Dad to at least fake the pleasure of our company. But when the occasional colleague would wave hello or say hi in passing, Dad ignored them, as if too pained by our presence to even bother with niceties.

"There's an earlier train," Mom announced.

Dad did one of his slow-mo nods, feigning an expression of thought-fulness to hide his relief. "You'll miss the matinee," he stated.

"Both boys have to work tomorrow," Mom said, giving him an out, but adding, "I know how important it is to you that they earn their keep."

"Suit yourself," Dad said. Then he got up from the table and left the restaurant, a departure to which Mom did not react and which seemed to turn up the volume of the cutlery striking the plates, of the fountain jets detonating in the pool.

We did not say goodbye to Dad before we left.

That night, back in New York, through our walls, Oren and I listened to Mom and Dad fighting over the phone. Oren whispered, "I know what this is about."

Had he also recognized the woman in the cast?

"Last summer," Oren continued, "I picked up the phone right when Dad answered, and this lady on the line was crying and said, 'I don't want this furniture, I just want your love.'"

Sometimes, Mom would speak while she sobbed. Between this and the way the walls muted what she said, all her words were buffed of con-tour, edgeless as sea glass.

"Do you think she found out he bought that stuff?" Oren asked.

We listened to their fighting some more, their argument punctu-ated by gasps so terrible I thought they might suck all the air out of the apartment.

"Do you think they're going to get a divorce?" he said.

"No," I said, speaking from a place of conviction I did not under-stand. "They love each other too much."

"You do," Mom shouted. *"You do, you do, you do, you do!"*

"I'm going to Matt's," Oren said. He got up and began stuffing clothes in his book bag. He did this with great force, so that his haste was closer to anger than fear, had more fight in it than flight. He scanned the room. He pulled several cassettes from his tape collection and, from the shelf where I'd placed the books Mom had bought me, grabbed *Moby-Dick* and opened it to reveal a fat stash of crisp twenties, which he folded and placed in his pocket, and then glanced at me, so that I could take in his disappointment—in the fact that he could hide something valuable from me in plain sight.

"Please don't go," I said.

He was riffling through our sock drawer, tossing out pairs with abandon, with disgust, until he found his Ray-Bans case. "You did the same thing to me," he said.

"What are you talking about?"

"The fire," Oren said. "You just left me there, in that closet."

I sat up in my bed. "I don't remember that," I said, "at all."

"Of course you don't," Oren said. "Nobody here does."

He was grimacing. Packed now, he lingered, observing me as this information registered.

"I fucking crawled out under that coat, and where were you? Gone. *AWOL*. And who's gonna find the fucking cat after that, Griffin? Not you. Not me either."

He was furious, his lower lip shaking. Tears sparked in his eyes. He'd held this in for so long, and it had erupted so suddenly he couldn't contain his emotions. What made it worse was that the revelation did not land, that my bafflement was genuine, and this obliterated his composure before he fled. While I, left alone—Oren let the apartment door slam—once again found myself being told something that was true but could not for the life of me remember.

When I got home from work the following night, Mom was in her bedroom, watching the news. She was dressed up in a nice blouse and skirt. She was standing in front of the television, drinking a glass of wine. The bottle rested on her dresser. They were replaying Reagan's press conference from earlier that day. He wore a smart gray suit. Ever since he'd been shot, he'd sloughed off the salesman's slickness, the B-list actor's knack for overemphasis. In this new, no-nonsense mode, he seemed more like a commander in chief. And this made me more appreciative and skeptical of him all at once.

. . . on the South Lawn, Reagan gave the following statement:

"This morning at seven a.m., the union representing those who man America's air traffic control facilities called a strike. This was the culmina-

tion of seven months of negotiations between the Federal Aviation Admin-istration and the union. At one point in these negotiations, agreement was reached and signed by both sides, granting a forty-million-dollar increase in salaries and benefits. This is twice what other government employees can expect—"

"That's a lot of money," I said.

"Hush, please," Mom said.

"Now, however," Reagan said, *"the union demands are seventeen times what had been agreed to—681 million dollars."*

The president went on to assert that the tax burden on Americans for such an amount would be too high, and that while the system was not oper-ating at capacity, a number of air traffic controllers and supervisors across the country had quit their union to return to work. The president went on to clarify the administration's position.

"Let me make one thing plain," Reagan continued. *"I respect the right of workers in the private sector to strike. Indeed, as president of my own union, I led the first strike ever called by that union—"*

"What union?" I asked.

"Screen Actors Guild."

"Really?" I said.

Mom pressed her index finger to her lips.

"But," Reagan said, *"we cannot compare labor-management relations in the private sector with government. Government cannot close down the assembly line. It has to provide without interruption the protective services which are government's reason for being."*

Mom slowly, bitterly shook her head.

"It was in recognition of this that the Congress passed a law forbidding strikes by government employees . . ."

Mom took another sip of wine as if she might take a bite out of the glass.

"It is for this reason," Reagan continued, *"that I must tell those who fail to report for duty this morning they are in violation of the law, and if they do not report for work within forty-eight hours, they have forfeited their jobs and will be terminated."*

Mom snapped the TV's knob and the screen went dark. "Even your grandfather saw this coming. And he was appointed to the NTSB by

Nixon." Which explained nothing, so far as I was concerned. She poured herself more wine. "Who didn't fire the postal workers when they went on strike, I might add."

The news could make both my parents so furious in ways and for reasons I didn't understand. Mom stepped into her bathroom.

"Sneaky bastard," Mom said—to me, as if I'd been the one standing at the podium. She stuck her head out the door. "All of them!"

There was a small circular mirror in her bathroom, and from where I was standing, I could see, in its reflection, her giving her eyelashes a final brushing. "Did you eat dinner at work?" she asked.

I never ate dinner at work.

Mom reappeared, looking even prettier. "I'm meeting a friend for a drink," she said. Mom never did this, and it scared me. "There's leftovers in the refrigerator." She plopped her lipstick in her purse and left.

In the kitchen, standing before the open fridge, I ate the spongy Popeyes chicken and considered my prospects. Tanner was still at camp. Cliffnotes was working a double. I'd left my *Dungeons & Dragons* books in my dressing room. I had no interest in starting my summer reading. Oren didn't want to speak to me. Dad was gone. And now an even gustier loneliness blew through the apartment of an entirely different order from any such feeling I had experienced before.

I called Amanda, but Miss West answered. "She's in Westhampton," she said when I asked. "Let me give you the number."

After I wrote it down, I asked, "How's your hand?"

"It's wrapped like a boxing glove, but I'm a lefty, so I'm not completely incapacitated."

"I'm a lefty too," I said, a little too enthusiastically.

I heard her flick open her lighter. "Do you do everything left-handed?"

"I bat righty."

"Tennis too? What about golf?"

I'd played either only a couple of times. "Same."

"So you're ambidextrous."

"I guess."

"It's how we outsiders adapt to a right-handed world."

I'd never thought of myself as an outsider.

"I really appreciate you being such a prince the other night," Miss

West said. "I told Amanda when you left the hospital, 'He's such a prince!' And you know what she said to me?"

My heart quickened. "What?"

"Nothing," Miss West said. "That kid mistakes frogs for princes and princes for frogs, let me tell you. You know, if we really wanted to change this country, we'd impose a waiting period on couples after they got engaged. So they could do a background check on each other. Think how many lives would be saved!"

I didn't understand anything adults were saying today.

Miss West's buzzer buzzed in the background.

"The Chinese is here," she said, and hung up.

On Wednesday, Reagan fired eleven thousand air traffic controllers. Mom and I watched the news about it together. She was sitting on her side of the bed while I sat on Dad's. She filed her nails with an emery board and disapprovingly shook her head. She turned to me and, in a state so close to rage it was scary, said, "You don't *fire* striking workers!"

When I didn't respond, she added, "Makes you wonder what's next, doesn't it?"

It didn't. Mom groaned with exasperation and left the room. I could hear her run a bath.

"No more Eastern Air Lines Shuttle to D.C.," Mom said over the splash of the faucet. "Your father will *love* that."

I heard her press the bathroom lock's button after she'd closed it.

I considered her wall of books. There were hundreds of them, arranged alphabetically. In the morning, when Mom woke, the first thing she saw was those books. When Dad brought her the first cup of coffee, she stared at those books. She looked at their spines before she went to sleep. Whatever book she was reading on her bedside table went up there once she'd finished it, so that she could see that one too. Did she like to look at them because they were a way of measuring time? Had she lost many in the fire?

On Thursday evening, Mom said she was going with Al to his house in Montauk for the weekend and it was up to me if I wanted to join. I asked if Oren was going too and she said no, he had to work. I told her I'd think about it and then called Amanda in Westhampton.

A woman, whose voice I didn't recognize, answered. I asked for Amanda; she repeated my name and then said, "Hold on, please."

When Amanda came on the line, she greeted me with a tone that, in its welcome, was close to wariness: "How have you been?" she asked, as if our recent date hadn't been a disaster.

I told her I was going to be in Montauk that weekend, maybe I could come see her Saturday if she was around?

"Montauk's pretty far from Westhampton," she said.

When I didn't respond to this, she said, "But if you're in the area, sure, let me know."

From my bed later, I could hear Mom in the bathtub, weeping.

The following afternoon, Mom and I caught the 7 Train to the Vernon Boulevard stop in Queens, where Al picked us up in his car. It was a dual-tone Cadillac Seville. "Nice ride," I told Al when we got in.

Al grimaced. "The only bad piece of advice Elliott ever gave me," Al said, "was to buy this piece of shit."

It was a Friday, so we hit traffic on 495. I lay stretched out on the back seat with my Walkman, listening to the mixtape I'd made Amanda that morning. It began with Air Supply's "The One That You Love" followed by Blondie's "The Tide Is High." My fantasy began in Montauk. I had my arms wrapped around Amanda's waist at the Puff N' Putt, together we stroked the shot and the ball dropped in the hole, then we were on a catamaran, me firmly holding the boat's rudder, she in a bikini, her legs stretched out like the girl pictured on a semi's wheel flaps. I imagined the pair of us swimming in the ocean, at sunset, and I saved Amanda from a great white by punching it in the nose, my heroic act backed by Foreigner's "Urgent." I lay on the beach with my leg bitten off (Joy Division's "Love Will Tear Us Apart"), Amanda held my hand while I bled out on the sand, and she confessed her undying love for me, but I came back to life during "More Than a Woman," by the Bee Gees.

When Al, Mom, and I stopped at the Lobster Roll in Amagansett for dinner, I said to Al, since Mom couldn't drive, "I kind of wanted to go visit a friend in Westhampton tomorrow."

Al said, "Westhampton is an hour the other way, kid." He took a bite of fried cod. "So I think no dice."

"I could take the train."

Al shrugged. "It's up to your mother."

I asked Mom if she minded my taking the train. Her back was to me. She had barely touched her food. She was watching the cars on Route 27, chin resting on her palm. She turned to face us and, after blinking several times, said to Al, "Whatever he wants to do." She emptied the carafe's contents into her glass, then went back to watching the traffic.

Al caught my eye and mouthed, *I'll handle it.*

Because it was dark by the time we arrived, I couldn't make out much of Al's house beyond the splash of lights against its siding. We'd driven down a long gravel drive; its dust drifted through the headlights' beams. After Al cut the engine, he gently rubbed Mom's shoulder to wake her. "Lily, we're here," he said. She started and then looked at Al as if affronted, which made me embarrassed for her. She then checked the back seat, although it wasn't clear she recognized where she was. She said, "Where's Oren?" and I told her, "In the city." She said, "What?" and crossed her arms, sinking in her seat so that she disappeared beneath the headrest. "I need to go to bed," she said, and I suffered the twinned desires to clutch her to my chest and run away. Al said to me, "Get the bags," and in the headlights' glare, I watched him walk Mom to the screen door with his arm around her waist and, supporting her, lead her inside. When the light flicked on downstairs, I got her suitcase and my book bag and stepped into the house, waiting several minutes while Al thudded about upstairs. I heard Mom say something. It was close to a sob, but there was also a question nestled in it, which Al answered softly.

The floor plan was open, like our apartment. There was a small kitchen on the left. Over its bar, I could see a breakfast nook by the far windows. To my right there was a sofa and a love seat and a coffee table and, in the corner, a narrow wicker shelf of paperbacks, their jackets battered and their pages swollen from sea spray and sun. Straight ahead, a set of sliding glass doors looked out onto the ocean. The stairwell was to the right of the doors, and Al wearily thunked down their carpeted runner. He walked past me, out to the car, and turned off the headlights. When he returned, he cut the overhead light and waved for me to follow him, which I did. He unlocked the sliding door, pulled it open, and stepped outside. There was a wooden deck, edged by reeds that shushed and sighed down the slope of a hill that dropped off precipitously; and beyond it, beneath the mute crescent moon, which sat abandoned in a cloudless sky, there stretched before us the bone-white Atlantic. I could hear the breakers boiling before they thumped invisibly below. Al produced a pack of Marlboros from his pocket, shook out a cigarette, and held it toward me, and after I fearfully shook my head no, he produced his lighter, cupped his palm over the flame, and inhaled, the illuminated mask of his face now snuffed out, and along with this world's deep blue and the bleached ocean, there was for color only the ember orange of his cigarette's cherry.

"Sweet spot," I said.

"It's something, huh?"

"Dad calls this place a saltbox," I said.

Al frowned. "For your information, a saltbox has a sloped roof. And gables. Which this house does not have. So once again, beyond opera, your father doesn't know what the fuck he's talking about."

I was mildly shocked by his anger; I was also relieved that he expressed it. We listened to the tide's *poom* and hiss, and Al said, "My parents fought so much when I was a kid. They were like cats in a pillowcase getting carried to the fucking river. But back then I thought it was my fault and that I could maybe stop them by being good—which you can't, for your information." He blew smoke. The ocean sighed. "So be good for you first and foremost, Griffin. You weren't put on the planet to make sure they love each other, okay?"

"Okay."

He flicked his cigarette out over the reeds. It caught the wind and meteored over the ledge.

"I checked the train schedule," he said. "I'll get you fed tomorrow and on your way."

When I came downstairs the next morning, Al was already in his bathing suit and flip-flops. His Hawaiian shirt, which was unbuttoned and open, let his belly protrude. He was sipping coffee and staring out the screen door, a cigarette in his hand. The surf took great slow swings of its hammer against the shore. On the horizon, I could make out a tanker's ghostly form. "Fucking spectacular," Al said. Then he consulted his wristwatch. "There's a ten a.m. to Westhampton, which gives us plenty of time to eat." As if reading my mind, he said, "Let's let her sleep, okay?"

"Okay."

"How do you take your coffee?"

We drove to town slowly, Al in no great rush, it seemed. Our windows were down, the sun made every color vibrant—who had seen such blues, such greens? When I glanced at him, he glanced at me, gladdened I too was gladdened by the day, since the both of us were sad, I was sure of it, that my mother was not with us to enjoy such weather. We descended a long hill, and the town of Montauk came into view, its streets mostly empty. When Al placed a cigarette in his mouth, I pushed in the car's lighter; it popped and he removed it and pressed the lava-coils to his cigarette. He replaced it and thanked me as if I'd done him a great kindness, and we went back to regarding the lonely palette of this Hopper painting. At the bakery, Al bought me a bacon and egg sandwich and an orange juice. When we arrived at the train station, the platform was completely empty, an abandoned, desert-dry feeling rising from the gravel beneath the tracks, as if all of Montauk were, like Mom, sleeping off the previous night. On such a spectacular day, no one was headed toward the city.

"Don't forget to buy your ticket before you board or it's more expensive," Al said.

We stared west down the rail line, which was already wobbling with heat haze.

"You got enough money?" Al asked. When I told him yes, he said, "Hold on," and took out a business card. AL MORETTI, LCSW AND HAIRSTYLIST. "Call if you need anything," he said. He consulted his watch again. "I'm going to the supermarket before it gets crazy."

He kissed my forehead and turned to leave but then came back.

"Don't worry about your mom," he said. "I'll take care of her."

He turned to leave but came back again.

"Fuck it, I'll wait with you," he said.

He waited with me for five minutes.

"Actually, I'm leaving. But here." He gave me a twenty. "Just in case."

I thanked him and watched him walk to his car. I waited a few minutes, then I made my way to the station to purchase my ticket and then to the pay phone to call Amanda. On the phone's stainless steel faceplate, next to the keypad, someone had etched a penis with several drops shooting out of it. I deposited my dime and dialed. I listened to the burr of the ringer quite a few times before Amanda answered. When I told her it was me, she sounded surprised again. When I told her I was headed her way, she said, "Really? When?" When I told her I was at the train station right now, she said, "You're taking the train?" When I confirmed this, she said, "Does that mean we need to pick you up?" When I told her I guess it did, yes, she said, "Oh. I didn't—" Then: "Hold on," and covered the receiver. "What time do you get here?" she asked when she came back on the line. When I answered, she covered the receiver again and then after a moment said, "Okay, well, we might be a little late? But we'll be there. At some point."

A half hour later, when the train arrived at the station, it seemed as if ten thousand passengers issued from it. There was a sudden frenzy of activity—of cabs lining up with their trunks open, and friends of the arrived pulling up in full convertibles and honking and laughing, and people like me carrying only backpacks and wearing bathing shorts and impassively scanning the platform and then brightening and waving and hugging their people before departing together. I boarded the car, which smelled slightly of limes and diesel and the toilet's blue deodorizer. The floor was sticky. The windows were green. The cabin was stiflingly hot. Not a single person was headed west but me. I took my seaside seat. The train lurched forward, and then the town slowly rolled past as if we'd taken our foot off the brake at the top of a hill. I was so nervous about seeing Amanda I had no appetite for my sandwich. The conductor appeared and punched my ticket, then walked away. My mind was as smoothed of thoughts as the ocean. As we got up to real speed and clacked alongside Highway 27, we whipped through the Napeague State Park's scruffy barrens. I grew dreamy and dozed, and when I was occasionally shaken awake by the train's shudder, the traffic that sped alongside us appeared to float, as if we were riding an unseen current, and for the several seconds beyond the foreground's blur of pines, these cars hovered parallel to mine. I saw vividly into the passenger windows, saw the passengers' and drivers' silhouetted profiles, and when it happened that, during one of the moments of swift stillness, while the telephone wires rose and fell and rose in a continuous, creaturely ripple, a woman leaned out far enough for her face to catch the light, to stare at the train—to stare at *me,* since I was alone in the cabin—and then she smiled, and for an instant it seemed I could see her with such clarity I could count her teeth. She turned and said something to the man next to her, who replied with a laugh, and at that moment I thought of my father's story about Millie, about their trip to the point, and the part he never told me about, which was their drive back, which must've felt, I imagined, bittersweet and, like my drive with Al this morning, full of silences; and in that moment I considered staying on the train all the way back to Manhattan, abandoning Amanda and this visit, since as the train raced ever closer to my destination, every part of my guts screamed, *Flee.*

We decelerated on our approach to the first station, slowing until the AMAGANSETT sign drifted past. Maybe a couple of people boarded; the train's engine idled. The conductor shouted, then the horn, the lurch, and we accelerated again, never getting up to the same speed as the previous stretch, my reverie interrupted by periodic slowing as the EAST HAMPTON station sign appeared, soon replaced by BRIDGEHAMPTON and SOUTHAMPTON and HAMPTON BAYS, and in what seemed like the shortest hop, the WESTHAMPTON sign slid from my window's right edge toward its left until it was perfectly centered. The train stopped, I stepped off the car, and everything after that continued at what felt like the same strange combination of slowness and rapidity, solipsism and silence, as if I were watching everything that weekend subsequently unfold through a diving bell.

The train station was a nondescript two-story building of yellow brick. Since no one awaited me on the platform, I walked to the parking lot on its other side, which was empty and hot. The train departed; birdsong replaced its production-line chugging and engine roar. The world, I figured, either was packing up to go to the beach or was there already, which made the now-deserted space seem even quieter. I thought about how to appear when Amanda arrived. I decided I wanted to seem indifferent, occupied, not *too* excited to see her, so I took a seat on a bench beneath the roof's eave and looked through my book bag for my Walkman. I'd pose reading, with my earphones on, but I couldn't find the machine and panicked, thinking I'd left it on the train. And while rummaging through my *D&D* books and *Heart of Darkness* and underwear and toothbrush and bathing suit, the book bag tipped from the seat, its contents, including Amanda's mixtape and several others I'd made, exploded from it, including the Walkman, which clattered on the ground, and that was when Amanda and her father pulled into the lot.

Dr. West was driving a blue convertible whose engine, when he came to a stop, snorted loudly. Amanda was in the passenger seat. She got out, noticed my mess, and said, "Did you have a spill?" By the time I'd stuffed everything back into my bag, she was out of the car and holding open the front door so that it was between us; and when, after a pause, I went to hug her, she hugged me formally in return, patting my back like an acquaintance might. "Nice to see you," she said. "You ride up front with Dad." She got in the seat behind me, and I reached to close my door.

Dr. West looked at me over his sunglasses and nodded politely. He was wearing a worn-in white button-down shirt, its sleeves rolled up past his biceps, its tails loosely tucked into peach-colored shorts. On his feet, a pair of Top-Siders. A half-empty bottle of Heineken sweated between his legs. The car had a four-speed stick, whose knob Dr. West gave a gentle side-to-side shake, revving the engine before dropping it into gear. We drifted toward the lot's exit, then Dr. West took a left and gunned the accelerator, and I felt pinned to the seat's black leather, as if Amanda had looped her Lasso of Truth around my torso and yanked. God forbid she ask me a question, like: *Am I already breaking your heart?*

Once again, my father spoke through me. "What's the make and model?" I asked.

"This is a 1968 Buick GS 400."

"My dad has a Buick too," I offered, not knowing why.

"Manual?" he asked.

"LeSabre," I said intentionally, thinking it was funny, and was relieved,

because Dr. West chuckled. In the side mirror, I could see Amanda staring at the sky, deaf to my wit, her sunglasses on and eyes hidden, her hair
Medusa'd in the wind. Dr. West, who was kind enough to talk to me,
deserved, I figured, some entertainment.

"Ever driven a stick?" he asked.

"My grandfather's Peugeot," I said, as if my parking lot lesson with
Dad this past winter counted for anything.

"Was it the 505?"

"Diesel."

"*Fantastic* car," Dr. West said.

Because Amanda's present absence unnerved me, I focused my attention on where we were going. We passed through the Westhampton
township, which soon disappeared, and the engine roared through the
soles of my feet to vibrate my spine. The Atlantic sparkled beyond the
trees and hedges and beach houses. We took a left on Dune Road and
then another onto a long, tight, sandy driveway that opened, broadly
and dramatically, onto a circular plot of manicured lawn. At its center
stood a two-story house with a gambrel roof, a single dormer stretching
its entire length. Its windows, hazed with salt spray, were flanked by red
shutters, tiny crescent moons carved into each. Its cedar shingles were
noticeably warped and spalled. In the background, at once dwarfing
the house but also making it seem majestic, was a bay pricked with sails,
speeding pleasure boats distantly foaming the water's iron-blue surface.
It was a place, I thought, that seemed a direct expression of Dr. West's
character: a classy, almost refined brand of dilapidation, the money that
built it as sturdy and as weather-beaten as the shingles, as many-layered
and as chipped as the shutters' paint. Maybe Dr. West was a millionaire;
maybe he was nearly destitute. The car, I noticed as I came around the
front, showed signs of rust at its fenders' edges—corroded, if you looked
closely, at the wheel wells. It was *not* mint, but the seats were soft as a
well-worn saddle in spite of the tears where the foam protruded; and
hidden beneath the hood, the machine had tremendous power he had
clearly not even tapped. The man, I thought—overbrimming as I was
with heartache and the lonely clarity it conferred—must drive his rela-
tively impoverished daughter crazy.

Inside an Irish setter greeted us. "Hello, Hellie," Dr. West said, grabbing her ears and giving her head a shake before she quickly disappeared. The house was wood-paneled and dark, although the windows were filled with light. There was a smell to the place of mothballs and, from the fireplace that dominated the living room, ash and creosote. The interior was a hodgepodge—a forgotten antique-store feeling to the decor, at once high-end and remaindered. In the living room, which looked out onto the bay, a pink fainting sofa with its fraying fabric and cigarette burns sat opposite a pair of giltwood chairs: a man and woman picnicking on the embroidered tableau of one; a pair of monkeys, the first standing atop the second's back, on the other. Green-bound Harvard Classics on the narrow shelves framing the fireplace were mixed with popular novels and nonfiction—*Fear of Flying, Chariots of the Gods?*—that I'd also seen on Mom's bedside table. The dining table, with its thick spiral legs, was surrounded by caned chairs, one of which had a fist-sized hole in its back.

"Show Griffin his bedroom," Dr. West ordered.

Amanda looked at him, surprised, and said to me, "Are you staying?"

Dr. West frowned at her, equally surprised, and said, "Are you daft?"

He finished his beer and shook his head, then disappeared into the kitchen. Amanda watched him go. Then she smiled at me, emptily, and trudged upstairs. I noticed *I* was smiling, but it was partly an injury or an infliction. I realized if I stopped smiling, I might cry.

"That's your room," Amanda said on the landing, opening the first door to her right.

I looked inside; I could see the bay through its window. A breeze bellied the thin curtains.

"Did you bring a bathing suit?" When I nodded, she said, "Claire's coming over." And then, as if on cue, Claire, the strawberry blonde I'd met auditioning at Nightingale, called out Amanda's name from downstairs. "We're going to the beach club if you want to come."

I did, knowing she would not have cared if I didn't, would have probably preferred it, and changed and grabbed my book bag and then joined them outside. Amanda and Claire stood, holding their handlebars, waiting for me on the driveway. "Oh," Amanda said of her bicycle, "I guess you need one too."

They were wearing bikini tops and shorts, and each had a rolled towel in her bike's basket. Claire's sunglasses were perched above her forehead,

her hair wild as wheat. She sneered at me with such pure disgust for slowing their progress, for simply being here, that I was both shocked at and
appreciative of the honesty.

"Hold on," Amanda said, and walked past me into the house.

I realized neither of us had even looked at each other yet, had not
truly *acknowledged* each other yet. The screen door banged against its
frame twice. Amanda appeared with Dr. West in tow—following so
close and so clearly frustrated he looked as if he might grab her by the ear.
He then said, for what I could tell was my benefit, "Of course he needs a
bike. What's he going to do, *jog*?" He disappeared around the side of the
house and shortly returned, walking a bike toward me with a towel under
his arm, Hellie heeling alongside him, a long pink training bumper in her
mouth. I thanked him and turned the rust-splotched handlebars toward
the driveway that the girls, who had already mounted their bikes, were
vigorously pedaling down. Dr. West said to me, cordially, "One moment
please, Griffin," and then shouted, viciously, "A*man*da," which stopped
her cold. She dismounted, almost falling off her seat between the bike's
sloped frame. She and Claire glanced over their shoulders as Dr. West
marched toward them. The wind was up, so I couldn't hear what he said,
but whatever it was, it was not pretty: it arched Amanda's eyebrows
while Claire zoned out, staring at a point somewhere between the lawn
and the bay, and then Dr. West, after grabbing the hand pump clipped
to Amanda's frame, turned and marched back toward me. Now that his
back was to them, Claire's stunned expression morphed into a sly smile,
Amanda's into afflicted embarrassment. Dr. West filled both my tires,
squeezing each tread for good measure when he was done. "Apologies,"
he said, "for my daughter's total lack of manners." He snapped the instrument back into place on my bike.

We rode in single file down Dune Road. For a moment I considered
slowing, and then stopping, and then returning to Amanda's, it was all
so hopeless. I did not so much rally as keep up. And the late morning
light everywhere was so evenly diffused that the ocean's cobalt stood in
tiled contrast to the sky's arctic cyan, that by deeply contemplating these
colors I noticed I eased my pain. After a mile or so we turned right, into
a vast parking lot, past a sign at the entrance that read QUOGUE BEACH
CLUB, its main building perched atop the dunes. The midday siren

sounded as we entered the lot, and the girls parked their bikes among hundreds of others, these lined before the clubhouse in a great tangle of chrome and rubber, kickstanded, daring to be dominoed, I trailing Amanda and Claire as if I were their page boy.

There were kids everywhere and of all ages ascending the walkway toward the beach or descending from it, disappearing into doorways or emerging from them in packs, so that it felt, on the one hand, like the rush between class bells and, in a strange sense, like entering the home of a gigantic extended family. Amanda looked over her shoulder, either to make sure that I was following her or to see if she'd lost her tail. The older kids were a breed apart, the boys in swim trunks as entirely comfortable and unselfconscious among the bikini-clad girls as if among cousins, the girls here and there as astonishingly beautiful as Amanda, the ease of their fraternizing, their sly familiarity, regressing me, so that I felt the same shyness as on the first day of high school. There was an unspoken and alluring knowledge in the way these kids greeted one another that carried all the glamour of the word "older." The younger children also seemed so at ease here, running after each other without regard to the strangers they slalomed, shouting each other's names with no respect for volume, with outside voices in this private space that by dint of their piercing insistence sounded both wild and warding. Their baked-in tans conferred on their eyes an aquatic opalescence, this summer in the sun streaking their damp, ocean-darkened hair with lemon, the same sun-down shade of yellow that striped the umbrellas rippling and snapping on the restaurant's patio. All the tables were taken, the moms in sun hats and sunglasses, in smart shorts or tennis skirts, the dads in bright pastel golf shirts with the collars popped, in seersucker and loafers or Sperry Stripers, laughing at their children's jokes, at their ice-cream-smeared mouths before their wives wiped these clean—a world, I recognized, of Adlers and Wexworths, of Binks and Buffys. A clan, then, with which I associated certain characteristic markers: L.L.Bean and puka beads; pearl chokers and striped canvas belts; a love for boats and bird dogs, martinis and Manhattans; an abiding silence at the mention of politics; a profi-ciency in country club sports; mismatched pastels, socks to ascots, like a box of broken crayons; and their effortless projection of an ever-present, albeit invisible, force field that was at once detectable and repellent to outsiders—that if I were carrying a Geiger counter right now would set it clicking like a pod of dolphins.

"Griffin," someone said.

Tanner was walking toward me. His dirty-blond hair was late-summer long, and he was shirtless, his whole body wet, just out of the ocean and air drying. He seemed in a rush to get somewhere. He'd greeted me with enough surprise that it mimicked warmth but immediately called attention to my out-of-placeness, beating me to the punch with the question I wished to ask. "What are you doing here?" he said. He hadn't alerted me he was back from counseling at camp. Without waiting for an answer, he jerked his head in the direction I'd come and then hung a right. I followed him down a passageway to a set of narrow changing rooms. In his family's locker were a pair of boogie boards and rusting beach chairs. Stacked in the corner were kids' pails and shovels and sandcastle molds. Some swim goggles with disintegrating rubber straps hung from a salt-rusted hook by the door. An umbrella with one of its ribs chicken-winged, punched through its canvas, was propped against the back wall. Tanner stepped out of his bathing suit and, from a hanger, removed a white Lacoste shirt. When he pulled it over his head, it was instantly dotted with moisture. He stepped into boxers and pink shorts and affixed a belt with ducks on it. He sat and brushed the sand from the soles of his feet. His hair, parted to the side, was like a creek bottom full of gold to be panned. He tugged on a pair of ankle socks and sneakers and grabbed his golf spikes—their laces tied to each other so that he was able to drape the pair over his shoulder—then he waved me to follow him again.

"Who are you here with?" he asked.

"Amanda West."

He seemed puzzled. "Isn't she dating Rob Dolinski?"

"I think so."

This cleared up nothing for him. "Are you coming to the field house tonight? There's a party."

I shrugged. "I guess," I said, not knowing where he meant.

"What've you been doing all summer?"

"The show," I said. "When did you get back?"

"A couple of weeks ago," he said. He removed a watch from his pocket and then fastened it to his wrist. "I've got a one o'clock tee time with my dad." By now we were back at the parking lot and, as if plucking a single fish from a bait ball, Tanner yanked his bike free. "See you later, man." Then he rode off, one hand on the handlebars, the other pumping his leg at the knee. When he turned right onto Dune Road, a passing car honked at him, then slowed down until he caught up; he took hold of the passenger door's handle, and the driver pulled him along at speed.

I went back to find Amanda and Claire. I walked past the outdoor patio to the stairs leading to the beach. Two lifeguard stands. A yellow flag day. Big surf, bathers everywhere. Families. The umbrellas' abstract pointillism. No sign of Amanda. I think back on this moment now and, if you'd asked any random member on that strand to pick out the one person who did not belong, they'd have scanned that scene for less than ten seconds and spotted me trudging down the beach, book bag over one shoulder, like someone selling knicknacks to tourists. So that it was to my credit that I decided to leave.

I found my borrowed bike and proceeded east down Dune Road, with no destination in mind and no intention beyond the fact that *this was what I chose to do with my afternoon.* Like Tanner, I rode like I belonged. My route was dense with houses at first, these intermittently spectacular, lining the road or perched atop the dunes. I passed named beaches to my right—QUOGUE VILLAGE BEACH, HOT DOG BEACH—their parking lots full of luxury cars. Every person on the island, I imagined, was ocean-facing, the beachgoers' chairs and towels ticking clockwise after the sun. When I passed TIANA BEACH, the landscape turned more barren, the telephone poles bleached and lonely. The wind combed the dunes' shrubs with a hiss, brushed the sea grass back, like a mother a child's hair; a wide bay was visible to my left, and I could feel the same stupid smile on my face I'd worn since I'd arrived. I thought, *I am having an adventure. I am seeing new places.* What I wanted: Amanda's company. What I had: the wind at my back. A long wooden drawbridge came into view, stretching across the bay. It sagged in places, tumbledown and slightly humped at its center, like some Leviathan breaching. I passed PONQUOGUE TOWN BEACH, Dune Road became Beach Road, a marina appeared on my left. I had come to a point of sorts, to the bay's mouth. There was more land across the channel, but I couldn't keep going. A harbormaster's small outbuilding had a soda machine out front and I bought a Coke. I remembered that I still had an egg sandwich in my book bag, so I parked my bike and sat on one of the benches facing the water. Fishing boats prowled toward open ocean, their outriggers like a cricket's antennae. My sandwich, in spite of the cold eggs and congealed cheese, was the best I'd ever eaten. The Coke's sugar was a gift to my blood. The food restored my optimism. I really believed some sort of reset was possible. Like this was a video game and the destroyed avatar that had arrived at this place would return to Amanda's reconstituted, ready to triumph over her disapproval and disdain; that whatever discomfort she was suffering—now that I had so generously granted her some space—would be dissipated.

On the return, the brutal headwind slowed my pace. Despite the straight road, the extra effort made me paranoid I was lost. Over the low dunes, after I passed a jetty, a deserted beach came into view, and I stopped to consider it. I shouldered the bike's frame and walked across the sandy path toward the water. I placed the bike on its side and, from my basket, removed my towel. I took off my shirt and shoes. At the water's edge, I watched the breakers for a while. I entered the ocean slowly at first and then swam out. The water was chilly and revivifying. I bodysurfed several waves. Their lines were very clean. I imagined Amanda watching me from the shore. I swam out far—farther, perhaps, than I'd ever allowed myself in my life—sprinting, to exhaustion, well beyond the breakers. The silence was profound. I was a good hundred yards out. To the northwest, crowded Ponquogue Beach, full of umbrellas, appeared covered in rainbow sprinkles. There came a low burble: in the sky, a single-prop plane pulling a banner inched west: MELINDA MARRY ME? I felt a strange pulse beneath my feet; I dunked my head. Below, between the green bars of sunlight, I thought I saw a shadow far bigger than my own. It might be days before they found Dr. West's bike and put the pieces of my disappearance together. Spooked, I swam in, pausing occasionally to tread water and look beneath the surface. Did the shadow, reappearing, now have a more discernible length and form? I caught the first wave in to shore that I could and ran back to my towel. I scanned the horizon. Relieved, I lay on my back, closed my eyes, and let the sun warm my body. I thought of the other shadows that had lurked beneath me this past year: Kepplemen, Fistly, Damiano. Now, in some ways, Dad. I did not include Naomi among this shiver. Nor Amanda, who, I figured, had probably not given me a single thought since we'd parted. And once again I was seized by fantasy. It required we be alone. I imagined her lying beside me. She visored her eyes and smiled, and when I woke up from this dream, I realized I had slept deeply and for a long time. I was cottonmouthed. The sun was lower in the sky. My body was covered in a fine layer of sand. It came off only when I brushed it with my shirt's fabric, and even then some of its glimmer adhered.

Amanda's house, upon my return, was quiet. The clock over the mantel read just past six. I entered the kitchen, and there on the counter lay a plate of roasted bluefish covered in sour cream and herbs, asparagus and olives in a bowl. In a sheet pan with aluminum foil, red potatoes sprinkled with rosemary, roasted almost to burned. A pair of martini glasses, each with a lemon twist at the cup's bottom, stood next to a sweaty cocktail shaker. Not hearing anyone inside, not sure what I could help myself to, I drank water from the faucet until it sloshed in my belly. Through the window over the sink, I saw Dr. West and a woman eating dinner on the lawn's bayside, Hellie seated beneath their small wrought-iron table, its tablecloth astir in the breeze. When I walked out to say hello to them, Hellie hopped up and nosed my hand and then returned to lie at the couple's feet. Dr. West wiped his mouth with his napkin and stood to greet me. He introduced me to his wife, Sylvia, who wore her golden hair in a hived bouffant. Her shoulders, exposed by her sleeveless blouse, were browned and peeling, the dead skin like dried Elmer's glue. Because she faced the setting sun, she covered her eyes when she greeted me.

"Please, Griffin, sit," Sylvia said.

"I'll make you a plate," Dr. West said. "Do you want a beer? A glass of wine, perhaps?" Sylvia poured the last of the chardonnay and tapped the bottle with her fingernail before he walked off, and when he returned it was with a plate for me and a fresh bottle under his arm.

"Is Amanda upstairs?"

I told him I didn't know, that I'd gone for a long bike ride, all the way to the bay's channel. He looked at his wife and blinked several times in annoyance with his daughter, and for this allegiance I could've hugged him. "Do you know what that body of water is?" I asked.

He said, "Why, that's the Shinnecock, of course." And the resemblance between Dr. West and his daughter, in spite of his newfound kindness, was uncanny.

"Albert, not everyone knows the geography of Long Island," Sylvia said. Then she turned to me. "Albert tells me you're an actor."

Now Dr. West generously gave me audience. When I told Sylvia about how I'd fallen into the business, how a *Candid Camera* appearance led to roles in *The Talon Effect* and *The Nuclear Family,* he ceded the floor. And when I talked about the radio dramas I'd done, it was he who had questions about how they were produced—he'd grown up listening to serialized shows like *The Shadow* and still enjoyed *Mystery Theater*—and when I told him that I too had appeared on the latter, he was fascinated. What a fantastically interesting childhood, he remarked, to have worked with such people, to have been exposed to such professionalism. If only Amanda could have the same experience, he complained, it might do her some good. And since Sylvia had by now inquired about my father's career, how fortunate, Dr. West continued, to be so close to the creative process of titans like Leonard Bernstein, Joshua Logan, and Abe Fountain. "That is some of the greatest American music ever written," Dr. West said. "If only my students," he complained, "had Jacques Brel's work memorized. If that's not a literary education, I don't know what is." For the first time, I felt my childhood to be out of the ordinary, even extraordinary. "And here you are," Dr. West said, after I'd told Sylvia about working with Alan Hornbeam this spring, "on the verge of stardom. That movie of yours is going to come out this fall, and we'll say we knew you when. Especially my daughter. Who"—he indicated behind me—"has finally decided to make an appearance."

Amanda approached the table, showered, in a blue sundress, with her hair pulled back. I was grateful she refused eye contact as she approached, because I could take in her summered beauty. At the same time, I had the nearly overwhelming urge to ask her why she'd invited me here. Why had she let me kiss her the night of her birthday? Why couldn't she simply make up her mind? More likely, I thought, the fault was mine. The conversation with Sylvia and Dr. West continued, during which time she concentrated on her food, eating with complete inwardness, as if she were a critic parsing each of the chef's choices. Her answers to her father's questions were monosyllabic or dismissed with a shrug until Dr. West asked her, "What are your plans for tonight?"

Amanda said, "Some of my friends are going to a movie in Southampton. Do you think you could take us?"

"We," Dr. West said, after refilling his glass and then tilting it toward his wife before he drank, "are in for the evening."

Amanda looked crestfallen.

"Griffin's welcome to borrow my car," Dr. West said.

For the first time since I'd arrived, Amanda looked at me—wide-eyed, with an expression between shock and slyness, as if by this remarkable oversight we'd been presented with an even rarer opportunity.

Dr. West shrugged. "He says he can drive a stick," he replied, glancing between us, as if the offer were a no-brainer. And when I, unprepared for this surprise, returned his gaze tearfully, he said, "Just promise me you'll keep it under the speed limit."

"I'll make sure," Amanda said.

In my life I have been witness to several instances of perfect timing, the sort that syncs so silkily with luck the two are impossible to separate. But undoubtedly the most memorable instance came later that evening, after Dr. West handed me the Buick's keys. He watched as I took the wheel and Amanda slid into the passenger seat, gave me the same look of outright affection I have seen, albeit rarely, in the expressions of the passionately married. I did not forget from my Christmas lesson that I needed to depress the clutch to start. I turned the ignition switch; the needles jumped and then settled. I gave the stick the same left-right toggle Dr. West had before pushing it into first. I saluted him with two fingers and recalled, as my father had described, that with just the slightest pressure on the accelerator, with a steady and gentle amount of gas, I could ease off the clutch into the point of engagement, which I did, so that as with all beginner's luck, I looked like a pro, like a fifteen-year-old with a hardship license, and I coasted down the driveway with a slow and expert confidence, at least the appearance of such, until we were out of sight. Amanda said, "Wow, you're good," to which I replied, mysteriously, to myself as much as to her, "Mazel tov," and when, at the driveway's end, she ordered, "Take a right," which I did without daring to stop, lest I stall the engine, and with no regard for oncoming traffic, we peeled onto Dune Road, fishtailing, ever so slightly, gravel spewing behind us like the contrails in a cartoon. The Atlantic ripped along to the south, the Quantuck Bay to the north, the Shinnecock to my east, and Amanda, smiling, thrilled, and a willing accomplice by my side.

Perhaps I had been far more concerned with embarrassing myself in front of Dr. West than Amanda because her humiliation of me was already complete. But we were finally alone, and despite the situation's stressfulness and illegality, I felt happy for the first time since my arrival. Where could she go, after all? Though it wasn't long before I lost whatever actor's nerve had gifted me with such a perfect performance earlier. I stalled at nearly every stop sign and ground the clutch as the car lurched and halted. But each time after I restarted it and stalled it again, Amanda at least interacted with me: she snorted at my mistakes, laughing, and she was occasionally encouraging, just as she might be to a cabdriver new to the area. "Deep breaths," she said, after I killed the ignition and before restarting yet again. And when I looked at her, she was the Amanda of old—the Amanda, that is, when we had no audience. "You can do this," she said, and covered my hand on the stick's eight ball. "*There* you go," she said, as I gave the car gas and once again we were off. (Although sometimes, after I'd waved the cars behind us to go around, with the same impatient, hurry-up gesture as my father, she mumbled, "This is crazy.") The plan was to grab Claire and then decide where we were going. Amanda mentioned a party at the Quogue Field House— maybe we go straight there, she said; and, as if I too summered out here, I replied, "Tanner Potts asked if I was coming." In place of a heart she had, it seemed, a compass rose. She pointed us down pitch-dark side roads, some with no name, and the convertible was a wind machine as we raced along streets lined with oaks, their overhanging branches forming what was nearly a tunnel, the leaves ghost-lit by the headlights' high beams, and above, just beyond this coned luminescence, a star-splashed strip of sky that made the night seem miraculous to me, and made Amanda worthy of admiration no matter how coldly she was crushing my heart.

And after a while, I got more of a hang of the clutch, even confidently dropping into third when the speed limit allowed. We soon pulled into Claire's driveway, which was laid with powdered white gravel. The house's windows, lit from inside, cast their soft yellow rectangles on the roundabout. Claire approached us in silhouette, took the back seat, assessed the situation with something like wry shock, and then said to Amanda, "He can drive?" To which Amanda replied, "He's learning." Then she smiled at me proudly, and I loved her.

"Where to, ladies?" I said, briefly happy in my role.

Amanda asked Claire, "Should we go to the movie?"

"We should get drunk," she said, and from her purse produced a hip flask, "on the way to the field house."

Amanda said, "Onward, Jeeves."

"The field house it is," I said. I started the car, put it in first, and immediately stalled.

"Take two," Amanda said.

Claire took a swig from the flask and handed it to Amanda, who took hers and, after swallowing, said, "Blech," and then handed it to me. I, like the chaperone-chauffeur that I was, responsibly refused. This was no sacrifice: I was already high on adrenaline, the night colors were brighter and night sounds lovelier, the engine's fraternal howl matched my soul's cry, and while I cringed a bit at seeming uncool, I was also determined, partly out of self-protection but also chivalry (and a dash of desire for approbation from Dr. West) to get Amanda safely home tonight.

The girls were tipsy by the time we arrived at our destination. Out of the car together, they wrapped their arms around the other's waist and walked with a hip-bumping shimmy; rather than slow them, their half-drunk conjoined state somehow helped them walk faster. But by now I expected desertion. The building, its eaves hung with string lights, pulsed with dance music, the bass line of "Le Freak" thumping outward, and voices at once articulate and indistinct rose above the clink of cutlery and glassware, all of it combining with the bay's breeze to make it seem as if the structure were less a clubhouse than a moored yacht.

We made our way to a ballroom where the space was after-dinner dim and the tablecloths, set on the giant rounds, were blank screens across which the lights from the disco ball traveled. Beneath it, seemingly the entire beach club's cohort, sans youngsters, had migrated here wearing a broadly defined but consistent dress code: the men in seersucker or linen, almost all of them sockless in docksiders or leather slippers, their collared shirts unbuttoned at the top or cinched with bow ties that were pediatrician-bright. The women all wore some version of modest, mid-length summer dress, sleeveless and ruffled at the shoulders, with patterns mostly floral, so that, taken together, they formed what could be considered a vast and expensively landscaped backyard. A half dozen couples danced, one pair synced with practiced skill, another doing the Hustle, most paralyzed below the waist and herky-jerky up top. Claire and Amanda were mingling, were so remote from me that I, their driver, felt like the help. With each passing second, I was more painfully aware of my Converse sneakers and lack of a jacket to hide the alligator on my shirt. But here, again, was Tanner, in pleated shorts and a tie and blazer, taking huge pulls from a can of Foster's. Once again, he ordered that I follow him, and he led me down several dark hallways until we were in the darkened clubhouse locker room. He spun a combination lock, opened the door, and handed me a striped jacket that looked closer to a convict's uniform than a blazer.

"It's my dad's," he said, "so be sure to give it back."

Soon we were both standing at the bar. Amanda and Claire had made themselves scarce. Tanner and his friends—I was introduced to Croker, Squi, PJ, Brett, and Chip, who were discussing today's round of golf. (From over their heads, someone handed me a beer.) It was a "scramble," Tanner explained. I didn't understand the scoring or the lingo, but my lack of knowledge mattered little to them.

"... so we're at the seventh," Tanner said, "there's a prevailing right-left wind, and Biff can't hit a fade for shit, he has to draw everything, so to cut the dogleg he doesn't just take it *over* the bunkers, he takes it over Brett's house."

"No way," Squi said.

"But it hits his roof—" Tanner said.

Everyone cackled, so I followed suit.

"—and kicks right," Tanner continued.

"Oh my stars and garters," Squi said.

"And lands smack dab in the middle of the fairway."

"Most excellent," said PJ, and slapped my shoulder so hard I almost covered up.

"So I'm one twenty-five to the pin—" Tanner said.

"Let me guess," PJ said, and then pointed at him: "Punch nine."

Tanner shook his head and tipped his beer can toward him. "Cut eight. I hit it *so* pure—"

"*Candy*," said Croker.

"And it holds its line," Tanner continued, pointing his flat hand skyward, "it's right on the flag"—he tilted his flat hand downward—"and then it one-hops"—he clinked his beer to Brett's—"right in the hole."

"Jarred that bitch!" Brett said.

"No!" everyone said.

"No!" I echoed.

"My first eagle," Tanner said.

Everyone clinked drinks.

I followed them out to the first fairway. Several of them lit cigarettes while the rest stood arrayed along the green's collar, aimed toward the hole, and pissed in its direction. Two of the boys disappeared and then reappeared in a pair of golf carts. "Gentlemen," Croker said, "your rides have arrived." We hopped on the carts and drove. The sand traps looked like snowbanks; the water hazards, like black ice. I was reminded of the last time I was on a golf course, this past winter, once again dressed in clothes that did not quite seem as if they were mine, the whiteout conditions limiting visibility as much as the darkness now, and me, even then, dreaming of a girl. And yet there was once again the feeling that I was not the same person. That beneath this outfit, there was another self I was becoming, emergent, powerful—dare I say calm?—ready to burst from beneath my skin because he was somehow larger than this form could accommodate. "August," Squi said, shouting to me over the motor, "always seems like the longest and shortest month. Know what I mean?" I did now. We stopped at a body of water. "Penniman Creek," Squi said when I asked. Croker handed him a nine iron and dropped a ball at his feet. Squi lined up his shot. "It feeds into the canal that runs parallel to the ocean. We are right now facing due south"—he swung, and the sound of the strike was pure, and the white orb disappeared into the night— "of Bermuda." He looked at his audience and smiled. "Depending on the alignment of your clubface." Lights of spectacular homes lined the creek's perimeter. To achieve such luxury, I wondered, must one imagine it? Squi produced a joint. When he smoked it, he pinched it with his thumb and index finger and then pressed his lips to these like the bars of a Jew's harp. "So we don't swap spit," he said when he offered it to me. I declined. Everyone else took several hits, and we loaded back into the carts and drove back to the field house. I felt strangely wistful as the cars sped along. I was certain I was the only one here who was sure I'd never see these people again. When I found Tanner and returned his father's jacket, it was like returning a costume on the last night of a performance.

Amanda was seated at a table. I touched her shoulder and she looked at me, blearily, and said, "I think I need to go home."

Claire appeared. Unlike Amanda, she seemed alert, awake, and when she bent between us, she said, above the music, which sounded louder now that the dance floor was nearly empty, "Where's Vince Voelker?" And then, wickedly: "I want to fuck."

So we left her there.

In Dr. West's car, in and out of dozing, Amanda gave me perfect directions back to the house. When we arrived, I killed the engine, pulled the keys, pressed the headlights knob to off, and we sat for a moment, staring at the stars and listening to the frogs sing. I turned to her, hoping we might have a minute or two to ourselves, but she was asleep. When I finally shook her arm, her skin was dewy. "Home?" she asked, and got out of the car. Amanda was a bit wobbly, so I caught up to her and steadied her by the elbow and waist. "You're a gentleman," she mumbled, and nuzzled my neck before we entered, her breath smelling of vodka and cigarettes. The living room was dark. We walked up the dark stairs, Amanda ahead of me. She held her dress's skirt in one hand as she climbed, running her hand up the railing with the other. If, during any part of the evening, we might have one moment that was going to be meaningful, this was it. But over her shoulder, she said, "Good night, thank you for driving," and went to her room. I watched her door close, although not completely. In mine, I stripped to my underwear and got into bed. I stared at the ceiling; the floorboards creaked. The house was so old it was almost never completely silent, which was a way, I thought, that such places made you feel a bit less lonely.

The sun announced a glorious morning through my window. I could hear the sound of the sink running in the kitchen. I recall waking determined to be patient. I was certain that at some point before my departure, Amanda and I would spend some time together, so I would occupy myself until then. I rose and put on only my bathing suit and sneakers, and I padded down the stairs as quietly as I could manage. The kitchen had just been cleaned, but the scent of last night's meal still clung to the air. The small television sitting atop the counter was on, sound off; the meteorologist stood before a satellite image of Long Island and pointed to the symbol of an incoming front: the bowing band of low pressure was fanged with triangles and bent toward the island's tip. When I exited the front door, I saw that Dr. West's convertible was gone. I walked down the driveway to Dune Road, aware of the distance I was putting between Amanda and me. I jogged until I arrived at Rogers Beach; this early, its parking lot was empty, sand sidewinding in discretely connected bands across the blacktop and then dispersing in its cracks and gaps. There wasn't a soul here, no flags adjacent the lifeguard stands signaling the conditions. I jogged west on the hardpack until I worked up a good sweat and, after perhaps twenty minutes, I turned around, this loop, albeit smaller, no different from my bike ride, a sad bid for agency, for a schedule.

Back at the Wests' house no one appeared to be up. Dr. West's car was still gone, although on the dining table small plates had been put out, along with croissants and butter and jelly and marmalade. I ate one pastry standing, then I rinsed my plate and put it on the sink's drying rack. I went up the stairs, and there was Amanda, just emerging from the bathroom.

"Good morning," I said, and she said so back. We both paused, and then I went to kiss her cheek and she did not resist.

"You're sweaty," she said.

"I went for a run," I said, in a tone that suggested, *I can keep myself busy until you're ready to . . .* no verb forming that infinitive.

"That's nice," she said. And then, "It's all yours," as she hurried to her room, and once I was in the shower, I pressed my head against the tiles until I felt the past twenty-four hours had been rinsed from me.

From that point forward, I realized I was not tethered to Amanda; rather, I was moving at a distance from her at her silent command. For most of the morning, she remained in her room, reading on her bed, but kept her door open, and when I pretended to need something in mine, she eyed me above her book with such impatience that I hugged the walls, slipping through my door's crack and exiting just as quickly. By midday the wind was up. The sun was still out but hazed by cloud cover. To keep myself busy, I worked on my *Dungeons & Dragons* campaign on the dining room table. When Amanda passed through the room, I dared not look up from my maps, and at lunchtime I joined Dr. West and Sylvia at the bayside table. From my chair I spotted Amanda in the kitchen window eating an apple and considering the water. After I was finished and got up, I excused myself to sit on the small dock, and when I looked over my shoulder Amanda had joined her father and stepmother, replacing me. When I returned to join Dr. West, Sylvia and Amanda had gone for a walk, he explained. He was reading alone, so I took the seat across from him.

He asked me, "Are you going to watch the All-Star Game tonight?"

The baseball players' strike had pushed the event back until now, but I knew what he was really inquiring about was the timing of my departure. I just couldn't bring myself to answer. He seemed to sense this.

With something nearing sympathy, he asked, "How are you getting home, Griffin? Do you need me to take you to the train?"

"I'll call my mom," I said.

In my bedroom, when I went to get Al Moretti's business card, I spotted Amanda, from my window, walking her bike to the front of the house. There was a phone in the hallway, but first I paused at Amanda's door, which was open. Out her window, I could see her now riding down the driveway. On her bed lay the dress she'd worn the previous evening, smoothed out, a pair of sandals on the floor. Above its straps, on the bedspread, *The Great Gatsby*—her summer reading, I figured—with its picture of a woman's blue face. I dialed Al's number, and he picked up after the third ring.

There was chatter in the background, several voices, my mother's laugh among them, the sound of which was a relief. "What's the address?" Al asked after I explained the situation.

I told him, and he sighed and then repeated it, writing, I could tell, and pressing the handset to his chin with his shoulder, because I also heard the sound of ice in a glass. "Hold on a second," he said, and covered the receiver. His voice buzzed as he conferred. When he came back on the line he said, "Be ready by four," and hung up.

The next several hours were uncanny. After Amanda returned from her ride, she managed, somehow, to be in any room I wasn't, upstairs when I was down, outside when I was in. It felt like a magic trick. There were moments when I wasn't sure how she got from one room to the next or by the dock—it was as if she'd teleported. She passed by windows across the room from me; she was a tiny figure in the distance, staring at the bay; I heard the creak of her footfalls along the ceiling as I sat at the dining table; from where I stood on the back lawn, I saw her disappear from her window. And then it was almost the appointed time. I had packed my bag and, from the foot of the stairs, said, "I'm leaving, thank you," and when no one replied, I went to wait out front.

From the house, I heard Dr. West bark something and then Amanda appeared. I thought it was to say goodbye, but then Claire rode her bike up the driveway. She let it fall on the grass and then walked up the paving stones leading toward us. She said to me, "Thank you for getting us to the field house last night." I tugged at my book bag's strap and shrugged, disarmed by her sweetness. She walked toward the door and stopped and then spied something over my shoulder; and, before I turned, I heard her sigh, as softly as the reeds in the wind, at Vince Voelker, who was pedaling up the driveway on a bike too small for him. It struck me that we resembled each other, albeit with slight differences: there was a familiar chaotic curl in his corkscrewed ringlets, which he wore longer than I did; his eyes were similarly blue but not as near set. He was, in short, a hybrid who belonged to this world. Voelker seemed not the least bit surprised to see me. He nodded and leaned forward, draping his forearms over the banana handlebars, and said, "Hey, Griff," as if we'd just worked out together this morning. He turned to the girls, and they greeted him warmly, they enclosed him, their backs to me, while they recounted last night's escapades, but then all three turned to face the sound of a car coming up the driveway.

It was Naomi's Mercedes. Sam was driving, and Naomi was in the passenger seat. Danny and Jackie sat next to each other in the back, all of them peering out the front windshield. Sam had on his driving gloves, and here, now, their ostentation seemed ridiculous; his chin was tilted upward, as if he were trying to make sure there was nothing he was about to hit with his fender. Naomi's chin, meanwhile, was pressed to her chest; she wore a patterned sundress, and she stared at me over her tinted glasses with a look of such hope and vulnerability I recognized myself and was ashamed.

"Are those your parents?" Claire asked, the accusatory flintiness having returned to her tone.

"No," I said, knowing that even if my parents had been the ones to arrive, the embarrassment I now felt would have been only slightly different in kind.

For no explicable reason, Sam stopped the car at some distance from us, as if he were unsure this was the correct address and he, perhaps lost, might inquire of us before turning around. When he stepped out, his suede slippers, absent socks, touched the gravel. His blue rayon shirt was shiny in the afternoon's now overcast, graying light. His white pants bowed beneath his protuberant belly, his belt tracing it like a smile. He was tan, which made his dark skin even darker, and his high head of hair was bushier than usual, almost youthful in its unkempt state. His mustache was in need of a trim. He nodded at us and then opened the rear passenger door for me. Jackie slid across the seat, huddling against her sister. Already walking toward the car, passing the group, I waved to Amanda and her friends, who had yet to resume their conversation—this triumvirate, these seeming strangers—to take in the sight of the Shah family. Sam's eyes, meanwhile, were fixed on them, but Naomi followed each of my steps, all the way to my seat, at which point Sam shut my door. While he eased in, Naomi considered me over her shoulder, eyeing me with an inquisitive expression I refused to meet. I could tell it pained her not to ask me what was wrong as much as it pained me that she knew to ask. Just as it pained me not to burst out and tell her everything then and there. Sam closed his door and fastened his seat belt. I could not help but resent the car's luxurious silence. After Sam turned the ignition, he took a moment, while the car idled and his gloved hands gripped the wheel—he drummed all his fingers once, twice—to revel in the sight of Amanda, Claire, and Vince, his expression unabashedly wistful as the three chatted and laughed, not so much having forgotten us but seeming to have never noticed us in the first place. And while I could not say exactly what Sam was thinking, what I did want to tell him, during those forever seconds, was that I knew exactly how he felt.

"Your mother says hi," Naomi said once we were on the road. She spoke gingerly, as if her words risked loosening the shaky grip I had on my emotions. "We saw her and Al in Montauk today. They're gonna wait till tonight to leave and then pick you up in Great Neck." Danny and Jackie stared at me like a pair of baby birds. Sam sat more erect than normal, listening to us, and because he sensed my heartbreak and knew better than to make small talk, I felt a gratitude toward him that threatened to shatter my self-control. "We're gonna stop by my brother's place first," Naomi explained. "It's on the way."

I don't remember much about our short trip except that it seemed we had entered an entirely different world, one more densely forested than where I'd been all weekend. Here, smaller and older and more modest homes with brick entryways interrupted by siding were built very near one another, though as we got closer to the water there were newer builds, outliers in their modern design. Naomi's brother's place had a bay view; it was a pair of conjoined parallelograms with bubbled skylights blistering its roof. As we exited the car, music was audible from the house, punctuated occasionally by the reverberation, like an arrow striking its target, of someone bouncing off a diving board, followed by the *whoomp* and splash of people landing in a pool. In spite of all the home's glass, it was shadowy and dark when we entered, though at the end of the hallway that connected the front to the back, the pool shone in bright relief. There were several guests: a pair of couples sitting on the living room couch, the men topless or with shirts unbuttoned. All of them wore bathing suits. The women were in sheer wraps and high heels, their hair dark and lustrous—and I knew I had returned to half my people.

Naomi's brother greeted her; he was linebacker-large and shouted his welcome. He hugged Sam, brutally, and then stuck out his hand to me. "I'm Scott," he said. He was burly, hirsute. He picked up both Danny and Jackie in his arms with a great groan and zero effort, and he remarked on how big they were getting and returned them both gently to the earth. He indicated the platters of food crammed on the table behind him, said that there were cookies and cake if they'd already eaten dinner, ice cream in the freezer if that was what they wanted, "whatever your precious little hearts desire," he told them, as he walked down the dark hallway toward the back, and it was at this moment, as Naomi and I lagged behind her family, that she took my hand and, once we were outside, led me toward the shallow end of the pool.

Partly this was for privacy. Partly it was to not get wet while her brother and his friends played Jump or Dive. Several were beer-bellied and impressively athletic. Some of them made a high hop before landing on the springboard, bounced straight in the air to touch down on it a second time, so that its bent tip nearly tapped the water's surface, and, depending on the call, jackknifed or cannonballed, followed by great, concussive splashes that seemed to reach the tops of the pines at the edge of the fence. My feet were in the pool, the water seemed to compose the glue that held my impassivity together. Naomi had taken off her shoes so she too could kick her feet in the cool chop that slapped the liner after each impact. Sam reappeared in his bathing suit, his chest shrunken and concave. He glanced at me and then caught Naomi's eye. She gave him the slightest shrug, one with a hint of resignation in it, a gesture that I now consider the sneakiest and most devious I have ever witnessed, as if to say, *I don't know what's wrong with this poor kid either,* and he took his place in line, where someone reminded him to remove his eyeglasses before he stepped onto the board.

Naomi, still watching the men, touched her shoulder to mine and whispered, "You gonna tell me what's going on?" and I shook my head.

She watched Sam take his turn. "Dive!" her brother screamed, so that he flailed spastically. He surfaced, laughing his silly laugh. He demanded a do-over. He swam to the ladder and raced back to the board.

"This has to do with one of those girls, doesn't it?" Naomi said. And this was all it took. Sam leaped, bounced, and once again there came the shout, "Dive!" and the impact from his bellyflop may as well have come from my own guts, because I crumpled. All that I'd withheld since Amanda's birthday, since Philadelphia, since mere minutes ago, burst forth, and my grief was torrential. I could not get myself under control. Naomi, initially taken aback, clutched me to her now. She spoke to me as if I were a child to be soothed. She said, "Oh, baby," and put her arm around my shoulders. I soaked her shoulder's skin; had I had more time

I'd have turned the space between her neck and clavicle into a bird bath. When nothing consoled me, she said, "Why don't you take off your shirt and get in the pool? You're more beautiful than any man here." The flattery made things worse. At which point she took my wrist and said, "Come with me."

We were in the Mercedes and driving, but it was difficult for me to tell for how long. My perception was overcast; the afternoon had turned thus as well. By the time I was cognizant enough to take in my surroundings, I noticed that the ocean, slowly being erased by a landbound mist, was on my left again, and we had entered what appeared to be a county park, passing through an asphalt lot several football fields long, its white lines faded and abraded, the blacktop disintegrated in places, pocked and, in some parts, cratered, as if it had taken mortar fire. It was late Sunday. The lot was emptied of cars, the evacuated feeling of weekenders heading home after those windy, chillier, sunset hours dragged out to near darkness. The road turned to hardpacked sand. There were no houses anywhere to be seen between the scrub brush and pine that edged this route. The weather was changing at a rapid clip: a fog was now muscling in across the sea, grayed by its haze; the sun, low on the horizon, was a dead fish's white eye. I cycled between a state that mimicked tranquility and inconsolable tears, and as we drove, I was certain that I saw: a bobcat crouched in the undergrowth and about to spring; an osprey slicing low toward the bay with a fish in its talons; a woman walking parallel to the beach, holding hands with her two young boys, each with water wings on his arms. The mist grew heavier as we pulled into a large sandlot, a terminus, crisscrossed by tire treads and partially fenced. Naomi bumped the Mercedes into its farthest corner in spite of the fact that we were the only car here, her headlights aimed at the water. She killed the engine and said, "Come sit with me in back."

I took my familiar place next to her. We closed the doors. We sat facing forward. Through the windshield I could see gaps here in the scrub that revealed the Atlantic, lines of wavebreak unzipping through the curtains of fog rolling to shore, the sea glittering and then obscured in the misty swirl. And then, suddenly, nothing was visible, just whiteness, which made the car even quieter; it sounded like winter, the gusts buffeting the glass. Naomi pressed the back of her hand to my cheek and lightly stroked my face. She cleared the hair from my eyes. She said, "Do you want to talk about it?" and I looked at her and shook my head. She asked, "How can I make it better?" When I shook my head again, she leaned in closer and said, "Let me make it better." And then she kissed me. She kissed me, and I pictured her as Amanda and kissed her back: in the pitch-black elevator; in her apartment's bedroom when I'd failed to kiss her; upstairs at her father's beach house, in her room, in her blue dress, her book falling to the floor, the blue face on its cover watching us. I kissed her now, in the car, with my eyes closed. Naomi paused. I felt her arch her hips high off the seat. I heard a hiss of fabric. Gently, she pulled my swimsuit below my knees and with her sandal's sole pushed it to the floor. And then she straddled me. In her fists she clutched my scruff while we kissed. She eased herself down; and when she sank, it was as if she were hooding me, as if she were spreading wings over me, so that I felt entirely covered by her. My nails bit into the skin where I clawed her legs; her legs tightened against my hips. I felt something rise up, not a wave but the pulse of one, far out at sea, gathering at great speed toward shore. The sound I made when it broke was closer to a roar. And when I finally opened my eyes, I was staring up through the car's rear window, into the fog, into the sky, and I felt as if my bones had been hollowed, and I was soaring through clouds with no sense of the horizon.

Naomi and I walked to the beach together.

The mist was so thick that for bearings we relied on the surf's sound.

The sand was darker than the air.

We walked to the water's edge. It was only here that the ocean was visible.

Naomi asked me for my shirt, which I removed. She nodded toward the sea, whose waves lapped our feet.

She had taken off her shoes, and she held them by their straps. She entered up to her ankles. The foam kissed her calves, splashed to her knees, darkening her dress.

When it was deep enough, I sank below my chest, letting the breakers foam me. And when I emerged and turned to face Naomi, she was all I could see in the fog. She covered her mouth, nodding, her eyes bright with tears, and then she waved me in, circling her hand as if I were a boy who'd swum out too far. When I returned to her, she kissed my cold cheek and draped a towel over my shoulders, rubbing my back until her hand warmed it with the friction.

"There," she whispered, and clutched me to her before we shambled back to her car, "you're clean."

When I recall how I spent that August, it is no surprise to me that I took refuge in the most surprising place of all, one I had never bothered to make my own over the past four summers but now went so far as to decorate: my dressing room. It was nearly as big as the bedroom Oren and I shared. It too had a bunk bed, the top and bottom with oval-shaped entrances that gave them a cozy, alcove feel. Parallel to this, and like our apartment's dining room, there ran a wall-length set of mirrors, but with vanity bulbs. Beneath these, like my closet study, and also stretching its length, was a floating desk. Beneath this, a minifridge, stocked for guests (I had only two that month), with a whole assortment of sodas, snacks, and skim milk for my cereals, the boxes arrayed on the desk above. I had my own bathroom with a shower. A TV, suspended in the corner, above the fridge, with access to the major networks, and a live feed from *The Nuclear Family*'s taping sessions that I sometimes liked to watch, sound off. The best part: no windows. Along with my bunk bed, it gave the room a submarine feel, which I relished.

It also had air-conditioning, which was a relief from August's unrelenting, kiln-hot temperatures, an all-out assault comprising sunlight that reflected off car windows so brightly I had to squint and heat that radiated from the tarred cracks so softened in places it stuck to the soles of my sneakers. This swelter was coupled with humidity so high it made any breeze feel more like a blast from a hand dryer and, rather than eradicate the city's smells, only intensified them. Traffic and the uncurbed dog shit and the refuse in the wire trash bins through which this fruited air passed. The stink rising from the subway's grates after mixing with the tea-brown puddles that never seemed to evaporate along the tracks—a steeped, rusty mixture of rail soot and grime that the cars' blue flash ionized into a gas and, taken together, only existed at summer's end in New York, when the season seemed endless; and relief, which fall promised, also meant the beginning of school.

"If I had a place like this," Oren said, "I'd never leave."

He was one of my dressing room visitors. He did not come by often—maybe three times that month. Things had not been the same between us since he told me how I'd deserted him the night of the fire. If my recollections, which were so vivid, could be so suddenly altered, who was I? What *had* happened? I apologized to Oren on his first visit. I confessed that no matter how hard I tried I couldn't remember doing what he'd accused me of, and in response he said, with some exhaustion, something so wise it was on par with one of Elliott's aphorisms: "Let's chalk it up to childhood." It was for him I'd stocked the room with food; when he'd showed up that first time, he mentioned he was hungry, but when I offered to take him to the commissary, he declined, he had to get back to work—which I incorrectly assumed was still at Popeyes. After that, I was sure to have his favorites: Streit's matzo, which he liked to eat with margarine, as well as Flower brand Moroccan sardines, the ones in tomato sauce, plus Oscar Mayer bologna—my most famous commercial—with Kraft singles, which Oren rolled into tubes. He'd been living with Matt, he told me when I asked, at Matt's father's place in the Beresford. It was great, he explained. He was a record producer and spent his weekdays in Los Angeles and Nashville, so they had the run of the apartment. "Speaking of," Oren said, sounding like Dad, "I love what you've done with the place." He meant the maps of dungeons and castles for Griffynweld I'd taped to my walls, the monsters I'd drawn (a mind flayer, a manticore, a harpy, a golem, a griffin), my manuals and dice stacked next to my unread pile of summer reading books. I urged him not to look too closely. It would spoil the surprise. We'd be playing together in September, when Dad finally got home.

"You mean 'if,'" Oren said.

I didn't want to think about it.

"You speak to him?" he asked.

"He calls me here sometimes, before curtain."

"Where is he now?"

"D.C."

"What about Mom?"

The Monday morning after my weekend at Amanda's, before I'd headed to work, Mom had called me into her room. A mostly packed suitcase lay on her bed. "I'm taking the train this afternoon to Virginia, to spend some time with my parents," she explained as she folded some remaining clothes. "Most of my ladies are on holiday anyway," she said, referring to her clients. Dad's show had just begun previews at the Kennedy Center, so I asked Mom if she was going there to be nearer to him. She shook her head. "I'm going there to be nearer to myself," she said, clicking the suitcase's clasps. I understood what she meant and I didn't. She beat me to my next question.

"The Shahs have agreed to let you stay with them while I'm away."

I blinked at this several times; it was all the reaction I could muster. "But they live in Great Neck."

"They commute," Mom said.

"What about Oren?"

"He's staying at Matt's."

"How long will you be gone?"

"A week," Mom said. "Maybe longer."

"Are you and Dad getting a divorce?"

"We haven't talked about it."

"Does he know you're leaving?"

"We haven't talked about that either."

"I don't understand."

"You will when you get older."

"Why do adults always say that?" I asked. "It makes me never want to grow up."

"That's fair," Mom said.

"It's not."

"No," Mom said, "none of this is fair."

She reached her arms out to me and we hugged. I had grown much taller than her, though she only seemed smaller when we weren't touching. Her temple rested on my chest. She was the most physical with me when she was in pain.

"Naomi is very fond of you," Mom said. "You'll be in good hands."

Naomi's hands. I slept in the Shahs' guest room, the only bedroom on their house's first floor. Over those next several weeks, after everyone had gone to sleep, after Naomi slipped through my door and padded across the carpet, she would grope my blanket in the pitch-dark, patting down my outline like a child feeling for a parent after a bad dream. Her slip's sheer fabric, once she'd tented the sheets above us, sometimes generated static electricity, and her body, so blued by dark as to be invisible, seemed briefly strung with heat lightning, which crackled. Her laughter, now that she lay atop me, was throaty, wicked, *pleased*. She liked to clasp my chin between her thumb and index finger when she began to kiss me, as if to assert that I was hers now, that there was no getting away, and in those initial weeks, I did not want to. I wanted to exercise my new powers, spread my wings. I thought about the first thing Kepplemen had taught us about wrestling: *Where the head goes, the body will follow.* So I moved Naomi around, I reversed our positions. I flipped her over to claw the back of her neck. She loved when I did this, she was encouraging as we proceeded. She gave me directions, she spoke as if she were teaching me to drive: go slow, speed up, go easy, go *fast*. It felt wicked, before and during—this velocity—though afterward it made me terribly sad.

The Shahs lived in the Saddle Rock neighborhood of Great Neck, just a few blocks from Little Neck Bay. Their home—two stories tall and designed like a giant H—was on Melville Lane, between Byron and Shelley, a cosmic joke I wouldn't understand for years. Their foyer, its floor laid with great slabs of black-and-white marble, was dominated by a wide set of twin stairs whose strands, after ascending, met again at a long hallway—the letter's crossbar. If you made a left, you arrived at the family wing. On the top of this stem, the west-facing side, was the Shahs' master bedroom, which I visited only once during my stay.

Danny and Jackie, on the first afternoon after I arrived, gave me the tour. The master, which I'd been in that past winter but had not seen in the light (I'd walked through it in a daze, after my wrestling tournament, on the night I was concussed, before Naomi led me to the shower), was made bright by three large windows, which the Shahs' California king waterbed faced, this second-floor height affording a view, over their yard's high hedges, of Little Neck Bay. Above the headboard was a recessed section of wall, top-lit, its lower edge serving as a shelf. There were several books here: a pair of leather-bound copies of the Quran as well as a multivolume set of the Hadith, whose gilded spines, taken together, formed embossed letters in Arabic. Above these volumes hung a calligraphic painting, the symbol of Allah—I recognized all these from my days at Al and Neal's apartment—beneath which there rested an ancient saber in an ornamented scabbard, balanced on the alabaster cast of a woman's long-fingered hand. "We're not allowed to touch the sword," Danny said, as if she'd read my mind.

She led us to her room at the stem's middle. It was decorated, paint to linens, in various shades of pink, every item exhibiting the same sheer femininity as a dancer's tutu. A framed Degas, one of his soft-focus, seen-from-the-wings dancers, stood above the dresser. Her large window's sill was arrayed with a menagerie of Baby Alive dolls. A collage of Fashion Plates designs, all of which were of women in variously patterned leg warmers, covered the bulletin board above her desk. Her bedroom was connected to her sister's bedroom by what she called "our Jackie and Jill bathroom," a phrase she'd clearly heard from her father, since her tone had the same cutesy inflection he liked to use with them.

Jackie's room ("Follow me, please," she said, taking over the tour) was for the most part the twin of her sister's—the same color scheme, the same puffy pink polka-dotted bedspread. Above her dresser were three sets of women's pointe shoes, one toe of each autographed: Darci Kistler, Kyra Nichols, and—in a fine hand that I'd seen in the margins of *The Age of Innocence* and *The House of Mirth* as I searched for Dad's stash of cash—Lily Hurt, my mother. A pair of framed posters hung above Jackie's headboard, both of Baryshnikov. In the first, that famous shot by

Max Waldman, Misha is shirtless, his torso chiseled, his foot extended well above his ear—*développé en l'air,* as Mom would say—the picture snapped mid-leap, his right hand touching his pointed toe, the other arm outstretched while his head is flung back. In the second, by Richard Avedon, he is naked and so stirringly virile that when Jackie caught my eye after staring at it, I realized for the first time how closely she resembled her mother.

My room, downstairs on the H's opposite stem, was somewhere between a maid's room and a study. It had its own bathroom and a window that faced the driveway. Two full beds were arranged against this same wall, and between them was a small desk. Above it, a quartet of individually framed photographs of trucks decorated with rainbow-bright designs and friezes—Pakistani folk art, I would later learn, that adorns its country's buses. There was a more formal guest room upstairs, above the garage, but I quickly came to understand my room had been picked by Naomi because it was the diagonally farthest from the master. You had to first pass through the dining room, whose collection of china sat on a pair of decorative shelves and tinkled loudly when you walked through it. From the dining room, a swinging door opened onto the kitchen—this in the middle of the stem—which, if you made a right once you'd passed through it, led to what Jackie called the Blue Room, because its walls were painted a deep, lacquered navy: a sitting room of sorts, formal and clearly never used, with the door to my room opening onto it. If you turned around and continued through the kitchen, again headed toward the house's bay side, you stepped down into a glass-enclosed sunroom with a tulip table at its center surrounded by four chairs. The slate floors were outfitted with radiant heating—an unimaginable technological luxury back then—which the Shahs kept turned to high during the summer because they cranked their air-conditioner morning to night.

The sunroom looked out on the well-manicured backyard and a water feature, a large koi pond, whose filter made a pleasant burble. My only chore for those three weeks that I lived with them was to feed these fish in the evening. They ate pellets that smelled like dried cat food, and when I so much as passed my palm above their pool, the fish coalesced into a single being, a mythological creature, many-mouthed, and their lips, when I lowered my cupped hand amid their massed bodies, were mobile and delicate, sucking and kissing away their meal. Their tenderness always brought a smile to my face, as it did to Naomi's, whom I often spied watching me from the living room's floor-to-ceiling windows—this room behind the staircase, where the TV lived, and where the family spent most of its time together. She'd check over her shoulder to see if Sam was nearby, and if he wasn't paying attention—he, in profile, was usually glued to the news—she gave me a secret wave.

On the mornings when I was shooting and had to be in the city early, it was Sam who drove me. "Pick," he'd say, gesturing toward the Bentley and the Ferrari as the garage door clattered open. I always chose the Ferrari—the 365 GT, that gorgeous bullet of a vehicle and one I became very familiar with during those several weeks. Sam relished this crack-of-dawn opportunity to "peel," as he liked to say (it was also the word on his custom license plate). It offered him the excuse to leave for work even earlier than he would normally and thereby enjoy what he called his "freshest hours," when he was the only person in the office and could, as he liked to brag, "get more done before nine a.m. than anyone else before lunch." He said this often, clearly pleased with what he considered such a felicitously phrased witticism. He always laughed, whether I did or not. I, a decent mimic, would practice my impression of it if I wanted Naomi to give me some distance, to cool her desire, its sound being so anti-libidinous to her because of its familiarity. It had a lower, more masculine register; it was a dash of spit mixed with a scoop of gravel, and its four notes revved louder with each detonation, injected, as it was, with self-satisfaction: *Hew,* went Sam, *hew hew hew.*

The hour's lighter traffic gave him license to speed, and we touched some Autobahn numbers on those morning commutes, which made me laugh as one does on roller coasters or during near-death experiences. And yet my response was equal parts giddiness, because Sam was so clearly expert at the wheel. He saw seams in the Long Island Expressway's ever-shifting lanes that conferred the sense that we were on an invisible, zigzagging lane, newly paved just for us. During these drives, as I chuckled instead of screamed, I saw—as I had during my weekend with Amanda, and now, during my night visits with Naomi—that part of the nature of my character was to blur into background, to camouflage myself, to cuttlefish in order to hide. And in my newfound state, I found it repulsive, I wished to molt it from my person. I arrived at 30 Rock with my pulse thready and heart pounding from the ride; I slipped toward sleep, after Naomi left my bed late that night, in the exact same state; in both instances, I suffered self-loathing. I was riding two waves, abdicating agency because of circumstance, and I decided I needed to change this about myself as soon as possible. Or at least talk to Elliott about it upon his return from vacation. Assuming, of course, I didn't get myself murdered by Sam in the meantime.

During these high-octane performances of Sam's—which was exactly what they were—he enjoyed talking about the Ferrari's handling. Its hood was disproportionately lengthy to accommodate its massive V12; its fender was wedge-shaped, with hideaway headlights that, when collapsed, maintained its sharp lines. The Ferrari's appearance was more sedan than a sportscar, but there was something unmistakably ferocious about its makeup, something mako-like in its slipstreaming capacity to torpedo down the road. The interior was James Bond classy, its walnut dash full of unmarked black switches, one of which, on my most paranoid days, I feared Sam might flip and eject me through the roof. "Listen," Sam said as he drove, and cupped a hand to his ear, "to the induction noise. You feel that steady rev? *That* is the V12's effortlessness. Here we are in third gear, and you wouldn't know we were about to touch ninety miles an hour. Because *that* is where the car *wants* to cruise. It makes you forget speed limits. It makes you want to break the law."

I knew Sam was showing off. I also knew he was thrilled to have another man around. Given that he lived in a house full of women, I was important to him. My audience, given that he was his company's owner and boss, also made me, in his estimation, less of a yes man than a test case. I also knew I possessed qualities that he did not and was envious of, jacked up as I was from my summer workouts, my body pheromone-flooded, my dalliances with his wife signaling, precognitively, my alpha status. It was to my great surprise, during these drives, that I discovered how insecure he was about what he perceived to be his deficits. That in spite of his money, clothes, and cars, he suspected he was . . . uncool. What he wanted, then, was my approval.

So he overcompensated. That first week, during what must have been

only our second drive together, a terrible accident near Flushing Meadows forced us to detour onto Grand Central Parkway and to then swing
north to the Triborough Bridge. When we crossed the Harlem River,
we found traffic snarled on the FDR—a ripple effect of all the rerouted
volume. "Shortcut," Sam said, and yanked us onto the 116th Street exit
in East Harlem, seemingly deserted at this early hour. At the very first
red light, we were beset on both sides by squeegee men. "No, no!" Sam
shouted, and knuckled his window several times. "No, thank you!"
But they'd already soaped down the windshield and raised the wipers.
Through the suds, the now-green light dripped like wet paint until it
was S'd back into its solid state by the squeegees' rubber. "Motherfucker,"
Sam said, reaching over my knees to open the glove box, revealing the
silver bulk of a .44 Magnum, a weapon I knew from the Dirty Harry
movies. He threw open the car door and stepped out into the lane. He
brandished the pistol and then shouted, "I said, 'No, thank you!'" as
the two men, sprinting, shrank into the distance. Sam watched them
for a moment, then pincered the abandoned sponge from the hood and
dropped it onto the pavement. He kicked the tipped-over bucket out of
the Ferrari's path and got back in the car.

"These people," Sam said, replacing the pistol in the glove box, "are
ruining this country." He dropped the car into first and gunned the
engine. "Nixon at least was willing to say it. Reagan, not so much."

Our current president loomed large during my first week with the
Shahs. When Naomi and I arrived home that Thursday evening with
Danny and Jackie in tow, Sam greeted us at the front door holding a
sweating magnum of Dom Pérignon. "Hurry," he said, "or else you'll miss
it." He led us to the living room and, while he fiddled with the bottle's
cage, indicated we should watch the television. There was Reagan, seated
at table outside his home in Rancho del Cielo. Beneath a denim jacket,
he wore a white shirt with a western collar, jeans, of course, and cowboy
boots. It was so misty you could barely make out the press corps gathered around him. Whether it's the fog itself or the fidelity of the camera,
everything looks like a dream, the vapors are so thick there is a soft-focus
quality to every image. *President Reagan,* said the anchor, *offered remarks
before signing the Kemp-Roth legislation into law.*

"I can't speak too highly of the leadership, the Republican leadership in the Congress, and those Democrats who so courageously joined in and made both of these truly bipartisan programs. But I think in reality the real credit goes to the people of the United States, who finally made it plain that they wanted a change and made it clear in Congress and spoke with a more authoritative voice than some of the special interest groups that they wanted these changes in government. This represents a hundred and thirty billion dollars in savings over the next three years. This represents seven hundred and fifty billion dollars in tax cuts over the next five years. And this is only the beginning."

With great fanfare, Sam produced the sword that usually rested above his bed, ran its blade up and down the bottle's neck three times, and then, with a quick stroke, sabered it open. A great *pop* followed. The girls leaped and clapped. Naomi shook her head at me. Sam filled the flutes and handed them out. After raising his glass, he shouted, "To getting rich!"

Jackie said, "I thought we were already rich, Daddy."

"Well," Sam said, "now we're richer."

And then he laughed that rich man's laugh of his. A sound that affirmed what Elliott would say to me later that year: judge people not by how they lose, but how they win.

In the evenings, it was Naomi who almost always drove us, but only on rare occasions immediately. She would pick me up in front of Radio City Music Hall and then make straight for the Dead Street. Though once, in the back seat, after she had buttoned her blouse, she startled me by saying, with a pain in her voice that was close to anger, "It really bothers me that you never ask me to come see you at work!" I was stunned by this. The thought hadn't even occurred to me. And when she began to cry, I found I was frightened by this display of emotion.

"I'm sorry," I said.

"*I'm* sorry," she said, and wiped her eyes, "I just want us to be more than just"—and she swept her hand in front of her—"this."

I didn't know what I wanted, but I knew exactly what was being asked of me. So I kissed her gently, then firmly, repeatedly, pecking at her till she started smiling; I tickled her until she stopped crying, till she began to giggle; and after she told me, *"Stop,"* and blew her nose, I promised to make it up to her, sweetly. "Come to the studio tomorrow," I said, "after lunch."

I met her in the lobby. I was in my Peter Proton costume—suspenders, pocket protector, capri pants, Einstein wig, gigantic glasses—which Naomi thought was hilarious. I even greeted her in his nerdy voice. "Look at you," she said, "all in character and everything." I walked her past Sert's *American Progress* mural and his smaller frescoes, pointing out the figure I liked best—the titan carrying the gigantic branch, straddling the ceiling columns, with the bomber squadrons in the background, sailing through the clouds—as if I owned the paintings, as if this were *my* living room. When we approached the security guard's podium, before the elevator bank, I showed him my NBC identification card, which Naomi asked to see as well, examining it over my shoulder while we waited for the next car, clasping her hands in front of her because, I could tell, she was so nervous and excited. "Look at you," she said again, and knocked her shoulder to mine, "all official and professional." I gave her the entire tour of 8H, starting with a view of the soundstage from the audience's balcony seats so she could appreciate the space's vastness. We had to speak very quietly because they were taping—a scene in which our archvillainess, Lady Lava, has trapped my parents beneath her volcano, binding them back-to-back and suspending them above a pool of magma, using them as bait to lure me into her trap. Fog machines pumped white smoke from the pit. "Look at all the wires and stuff hanging from the ceiling," Naomi whispered. "How do they know which plug is to which, you wonder?" I explained to her that the red light flashing atop each video camera meant that it was the feed the director had cut to, that the trickiest part of the boom operator's job was to get the microphone close enough to the actors to pick up their voices while not dipping it into the shot. When Tom called "cut" over the speaker, I led Naomi down the hallway to hair and makeup, where Nicole and Freddie were sitting in their respective high chairs, smoking and reading the newspapers.

"Wow," Naomi said to Freddie, "salon care for this kid every day. If I had you around, maybe I could get mine under control."

"Probably not," Freddie said, and smiled, which made Naomi laugh, because she didn't know him.

I took her to costume, showed her the Coneheads suits, the Killer Bees outfits, Belushi's Samurai hotel kimono, the turquoise tuxedo jacket Bill Murray wore as Nick the Lounge Singer. Naomi fingered the outfits, pulled at an unraveling thread in Father Guido Sarducci's habit, and tsk-tsked. "That show's a little too irreverent and racy, if you want my opinion," she said.

We proceeded to the control room. "Look at this place," Naomi gasped, surveying all the buttons atop the panels lit up like Christmas lights and the array of screens. "Tom's the director," I said, and pointed him out to Naomi, "the bearded guy in the Hawaiian shirt." He was seated before the monitor wall. Jeff, the video-switcher tech, was to his right. When Tom snapped his fingers and called out, "Camera three, and one, and three, and two," I explained how they were cutting between units, that on the three left-hand monitors you could see the cameras' individual feeds and on the fourth screen the scene in continuity.

"And who are they?" Naomi asked, indicating the pair at the adjacent console.

"That's Julie and Jim," I said, "the lighting technician and lighting board operator."

"And what about the girl," Naomi asked, "sitting next to the director?"

"Oh," I said. "That's the script assistant." And as if I were possessed by my father, my eye twitched. "That's Liz."

"Huh," said Naomi, and crossed her arms.

Liz looked over her shoulder at me. She smiled her toothy smile and waved. I told Naomi she could watch us shoot my scene from here or the soundstage.

"Doesn't matter to me," she replied, a little coolly.

I decided to take her to my dressing room. Once there, I turned up the TV's volume and had her sit in my chair.

"Maybe I should get back to the office," she said.

I took a deep breath. "I'd like it if you stayed," I said.

"I don't know what I'm gonna do, we'll see," she said, miffed.

I marched to the set. The scene took maybe a half hour to shoot. The entire time, it was as if I could see Naomi's face in each camera's lens. To my relief, she hadn't left; to my annoyance, she was still there, because it was as if she were my girlfriend.

"Do I get to meet your costars?" she asked, and so I took her to the soundstage and introduced her to Natalie Forrest, who played Lava Girl, and of course Andy Axelrod, who, after exchanging niceties with Naomi, after singing my praises to the catwalks, caught my eye, nodded toward my guest, and, to my horror, gave me the thumbs-up.

Walking Naomi out, she stopped me. "Ugh, I forgot my purse in your dressing room." It was sitting atop my desk, among a scattering of maps and hand-copied tables, next to several pewter figurines that stood in for my friends and for the monsters that surrounded them. The ceiling monitor beamed the empty set of Lava Girl's lair. Naomi said, "Close the door," and took a seat on my bed, bouncing a couple of times on the mattress to test its firmness. Then she called me over to her.

"I loved watching you perform," she said, and pulled me close, locking her hands behind my legs. "You've got great comic timing."

The compliment made me ashamed. None of this, I thought, required any talent. Even if it did, that wasn't why she was complimenting me.

"So," she said, "was this where you and you-know-who had your little love nest?"

"Who?" I asked.

"Don't *who* me. Liz."

"Oh," I said. *Oh,* I thought, dumbfounded suddenly by Fate's operations. She'd *believed* me back then.

In response, I kissed Naomi, because I didn't want to lie anymore.

"All right, Peter Proton, let's see those superpowers in action."

My superpowers. One of these, I was starting to realize, was detachment. When Naomi and I were together, it was as if my mind rode a thermal above our bodies, my wingbeats as quiet as my other exertions. I was tireless because of this levitation and distance, and terrifically lonely, sometimes strangely angry. And this anger I occasionally took out on her with an endurance whose limit I'd yet to touch and which made her delirious with pleasure. But more than anything, when we were together, I was *baffled*—the feeling bordered on defeat—not only because I could not recapture the intensity of our first time but also because the further removed I was in mind and body from her, the more delight Naomi expressed, the closer I brought her to me. I thought it was supposed to be the opposite. Was that what had happened with Amanda? *Some-*

thing must be wrong with me, I thought, *with my heart,* I was certain of it, attracting, as I had, the opposite of what I'd wanted. "I love how you touch me," Naomi whispered afterward. "I love how you just . . . throw me around."

On the mornings when I wasn't shooting, I still came into Manhattan. On these days, it was Naomi who drove me into the city—this after we dropped off Danny and Jackie at their day camp's bus stop and then returned to the house for what Naomi had begun to call "the pushy" in a girlish voice that sounded disturbingly like Danny's. It was an act we always prosecuted in my room, since my side window faced the house's driveway, with a clear view of Melville Lane. Afterward, we showered separately. The marble floors in my bathroom were always so cold and slick with steam, which also fogged the mirror over the sink. No matter how often I wiped its glass to see myself, I disappeared again. I'd dress for my day. I'd wait at the foot of their entryway's stairs. Naomi would appear at the landing, freshly made up, and as she descended, gently dinged the railing with her ring.

Naomi and I didn't speak much during the drive into Manhattan. What was there to say anymore? Our destination was Sam's office, a five-story building on Thirty-Fifth Street between Eighth and Ninth. The company's name, the only one on the buzzer, was SHAH SHIRT-WAISTS. You entered through a short, dimly lit hallway. On the left was an antique, manually operated birdcage elevator. Straight ahead was the main office, whose walls were fashioned of exposed brick and divided by black wrought-iron beams. It was high-ceilinged and had an open floor plan, with the exception of Sam's glass-enclosed workspace at the very back. When you entered, there was, to the immediate right, a reception-ist's desk, unmanned, and, to the left, running the length of the entire area, a row of seven desks, each occupied by an older, nattily dressed gentleman—suit, tie, Jew—except for the one at the end and nearest Sam's office, which was reserved for Naomi, a part-time salesperson at the company. So far as I could tell, these men spent their entire day on the phone, departing for lunch en masse at twelve on the number, departing at five on same, schlepping past me, at the front desk, in Seven Dwarfs fashion and, before leaving, saying their schlumpy, schmaltzy, kvetchy, kvelly, menschy, schlimazely, alta-kaker-y goodbyes.

Answering the main line and greeting the rare visitor—my desk was perpendicular to the office's front door—was my job, for which Sam handsomely paid me on a per diem basis, and one I enjoyed more than any acting job in my entire life. It was Naomi who trained me; it was here she'd first been employed by her husband. "You want to learn any business," she said, "you start as the company's receptionist." In later life, I'd find this to be true, but I cannot say I learned anything about Sam's business during my short stint manning the phones, although I did love operating the switchboard, a gray metal contraption with a rotary dial on its left and, on faded, cream-colored tabs, the names and extensions of every employee, these still stamped clearly on my memory. I cannot say why answering the phone and directing a call or taking a message pleased me so; it was, perhaps, the sheer mindlessness of it, the uncomplicatedness of it, the comparative lack of responsibility. Or the fact that the office's volume was never too heavy, my supervision cursory, which allowed me to generate my Griffynweld campaign's entire spreadsheet of random monster encounters.

Naomi took me to lunch on my first day. She waited until Sam and the salesforce had left and then approached my desk and said, "You hungry?" When I nodded, she said, "I want to show you something first." Instead of leaving, she stepped onto the antique elevator, where I joined her in the car. She closed the accordion cage, which made a great bash, and cranked the deadman's lever to U. "Next stop," Naomi said as we climbed, "fifth floor: towel terry, French terry, terry storage." The pulleys groaned, the pistons *pffed,* the heat rose as we did. Each floor that sank past was dark but for the ceiling-high, street-facing windows, these covered by papyrus-colored shades whose edges were radiant with sunlight. Naomi pulled the lever and we stopped with a sound that resembled train couplings colliding. Naomi opened the gate, and I stepped off the car. It was dim as a cavemouth and absolutely stifling up here. My steps on the thick hardwood planks were muffled as they were on the concrete soundstage. The air was so oppressive, there was so little circulation, it made me want to gasp. On rows of pallets were stacked enormous rolls of terry cloth, many in disarray, come loose and unspooled. Some were in mounds piled waist- and shoulder-high; others even taller, so that in the low light they resembled sand dunes. One spark, I thought, and the building would explode into a fireball. Naomi took off her suit jacket, removed her shoes, and climbed onto the nearest hillock on her hands and knees. Then she stood and began to walk atop this rolling landscape, pausing to turn to look at me and then continuing with her arms out to the sides for balance. She ascended one of the largest piles and then she faced in my direction. She smiled as she let herself fall, disappearing from sight. I found her lying in a great impression, arms outstretched and legs spread, laughing to herself. I too leaped from this precipice to land on my back with a dusty thump, and then she embraced me. The air was desiccated as a desert, and later, I watched motes through the window's glowing frames, my shirt soaked through by then, my hair heavy with fibers, my hand in Naomi's as we stared at the black ceiling.

"Let's get you fed," she offered, pulling me up from this nest's depression.

Twice we were nearly caught.

One afternoon, while parked again at the Dead Street, Naomi pushed me away from her in the back seat and refastened her bra.

"This is teenage stuff," she said. "We should be doing this in a bed."

My solution was so obvious I couldn't believe I hadn't suggested it sooner: "My apartment's only a block from here."

At this, she knocked her palm to her forehead and, in imitation of me, said, "I could've had a V8."

She took her time, when we arrived, to consider the place, Dad's black-and-white photographs, his signed scores from *The Fisher King* and Jacques Brel. I took her out onto the terrace, told her how Oren and I liked to throw eggs at people at night. "Boys will be boys," Naomi said. A pigeon landed on the railing, considered us for a moment, and then flew off. I asked her if she wanted to see the roof and she replied, "It sounds romantic. Maybe later, sure." She opened a cabinet in the kitchen, surveyed its supplies of dry and canned goods, in case, I figured, we might have to ride out a nuclear winter here. She considered her appearance in the dining room mirrors and, when I stood next to her, smiled.

"Look how cute we are together," she said.

"Want to see where I study?" I asked.

When I opened the door to my closet, she leaned into the space with her arms crossed, as if it were a clifftop's overlook and I might push her over its edge. I clicked off the light and led her to the room I shared with Oren. She considered my Farrah Fawcett and Dallas Cowboys cheerleaders poster. "I have the top bunk," I explained, but when I indicated she should climb the ladder she said, "Uh-uh." So I continued to my parents' room.

Taking a seat on their bed, Naomi asked, "Is this all of it?" I assumed she meant the apartment, and I nodded. She considered my mother's bookshelves. She turned to look at the window, facing the river. "Oh," she said, "that street there leads to where we park."

Later, on my knees, glancing between my mother's books and the underside of Naomi's chin, spying our single body, now and again, in the blackened reflection of the TV's screen, feeling her feel my tongue's tiniest touch, its tip's tensile adherence to her skin, like a starfish's feet, send shudders through her stomach, I heard the front door bang shut. Naomi rolled away from me, scooped up her clothes, and disappeared into my parents' bathroom.

It was Oren.

"He*llo*?" he said.

I dove under the covers and pretended to be asleep. I could hear him open and close several drawers in our room, and then he peeked into Mom and Dad's door.

"What are you doing here?" he asked, and entered.

I did my best groggy-disoriented groan and, after a big stretch, moaned, "I could ask you the same thing."

Oren wasn't buying it. He held up a plastic bag from Zabar's. "I came to get some underwear," he said.

I sucked my teeth. "I must've fallen asleep."

"Naked?" he said. Then he glanced at the closed bathroom door before looking back at me.

I shook my head as if to say, *Don't even think about it.* While I was certain he wouldn't disobey me, I was so scared I could barely keep my voice from cracking.

Oren snorted, and with a delivery that was a little too loud, that cruelly increased my discomfort, said, "Some summer, huh?"

"You're telling me."

"How's living with the Shahs? You get to ride around in Sam's Ferrari?"

"Every day," I said. "I'm working at his company too."

Oren's expression darkened. "What do you mean?"

"I'm answering the phones. It's the best way to learn the business."

Oren was enraged. "You already *have* a job."

"It's just part-time."

"That should've been *my* job," Oren said.

"What are you talking about?"

He swung the bag at my head and I blocked it.

"Why are you always so mad at me?" I shouted.

"Because you hog *everything*," he said.

Then he stormed out.

Traffic was terrible on the drive to Great Neck. From the FDR Drive, I could see the endless queue we were in, forking in both directions, east across the Triborough Bridge and moving at a snail's pace across the river, above Randall's Island. How much life was wasted like this? How much time, when it was added up, was idled away in this idiocy? How was I supposed to know that Oren wanted to work for Sam? And why didn't I figure that out beforehand? Why was I so selfish?

"Why so quiet?" Naomi asked, turning off the radio.

"I don't want to talk about it," I said.

Why was I here?

"Someone's in a bad mood," Naomi said, and turned the radio's volume back up.

The second time was at the office. It was day's end, and I had decided I needed to see Griffynweld in its entirety. The staff had already left, along with Sam. Naomi was working at her desk. I'd spent the slow afternoon photocopying all of my world's various regions, taping these together on the floor behind my desk to form a complete map. When these puzzle pieces were all connected, the result was as big as a queen-sized bed. I sat cross-legged before this, feeling a tremendous sense of accomplishment, reveling in the detail contained in each landmark, the various keeps and castles and dungeons that had once filled individual notebooks now marked on visible coordinates. I sensed Naomi behind me.

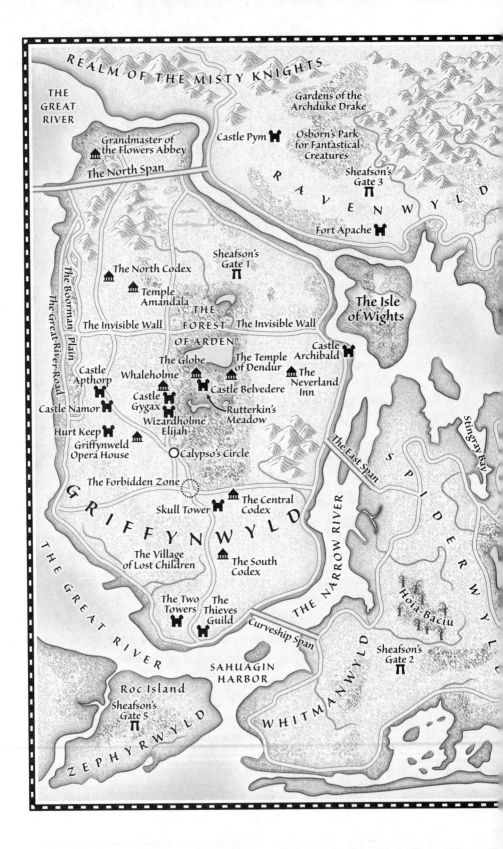

REALM OF THE MISTY KNIGHTS

THE GREAT RIVER

Gardens of the Archduke Drake

Castle Pym

Osborn's Park for Fantastical Creatures

Grandmaster of the Flowers Abbey

The North Span

Sheafson's Gate 3

R A V E N W Y L D

Fort Apache

The Boorman Plain

The Great River Road

The North Codex

Temple Amandala

Sheafson's Gate 1

THE FOREST OF ARDEN

The Isle of Wights

The Invisible Wall

The Invisible Wall

The Globe

The Temple of Dendur

Castle Archibald

Whaleholme

Castle Belvedere

The Neverland Inn

Castle Apthorp

Castle Gygax

Rutterkin's Meadow

Castle Namor

Wizardholme Elijah

Hurt Keep

Griffynweld Opera House

Calypso's Circle

The Forbidden Zone

The East Span

S P I D E R W Y L D

Stingray Bay

G R I F F Y N W Y L D

Skull Tower

The Central Codex

The Village of Lost Children

The South Codex

THE NARROW RIVER

THE GREAT RIVER

The Two Towers

The Thieves Guild

Curveship Span

Hoia-Baciu

Sheafson's Gate 2

WHITMANWYLD

SAHUAGIN HARBOR

Roc Island

Sheafson's Gate 5

ZEPHYRWYLD

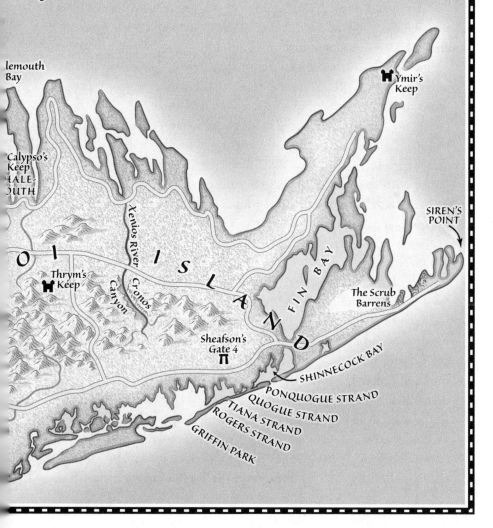

Griffynweld

SEWANHACKY SOUND

lemouth
Bay

Ymir's
Keep

Calypso's
Keep
HALE
DUTH

SIREN'S
POINT

I S L A N D

O

Xenios River

FIN BAY

Thrym's
Keep

Cronos
Canyon

The Scrub
Barrens

Sheafson's
Gate 4

SHINNECOCK BAY

PONQUOGUE STRAND

QUOGUE STRAND

TIANA STRAND

ROGERS STRAND

GRIFFIN PARK

"Wow," she said, and kneeled to join me on the floor, "what's this you made?"

"It's the world I've been building all summer," I said.

"What's all this for?" she said.

"My friends. My brother. It's a game we play."

"How does it work?"

"The Dungeon Master—me—creates a universe that has an overarching story, a beginning, a middle, and an end," I said. "But there are smaller stories, adventures, that take place in between. Like here." I leaned over the map and tapped the two towers icon at the southeastern tip.

"It kinda looks like New York," she said. Then she touched the map.

"This place, everything about it, is in this notebook." And I flipped through the spiral notebook containing the notes and maps, every room charted with treasure and traps. "And a group of players, who create characters of their choosing—they pick their race, class, and attributes—tell those stories with me. So the trick is to listen to their stories, to partly adapt the game to them, to let them help determine the game's flow," I continued, tracing the snaking shape of the Cronos Canyon's river, "and to sort of guide them, while also putting obstacles in their way. Using these dice. To account for probabilities, for chance. It's also my job to nudge them toward the places they need be, to gain experience and weapons and magic in order to acquire everything necessary to complete the campaign. Which is the way it becomes our story. Together." I felt a little embarrassed having talked for so long but was also pleased with my summary.

"So what's the big picture, then?" Naomi asked, and sat down next to me, to my right, but with her back to the map. "What's the story?" She lay on her right hip, propped on her right hand, so that her shoulder nearly touched mine. I began to tell her, to outline for her the scourge that was the powerful and evil wizard, the Magus Moraga, and describe the band of teenagers who had witnessed their families and friends murdered by him and vowed revenge. I explained that, to defeat him, they would need to go on a quest for the pieces of the legendary Shield Sheafson's armor, a set of relics more powerful than any weapon in all of Griffynweld, because it was invulnerable to all evil-aligned magic and could therefore destroy the tyrannical hold the magus had on his followers, freeing them, once again, to live peacefully among one another. While I was outlining all this, she said, "Well, I probably wouldn't be much good at it. But I sure wish I could play with you." And at this moment, I missed everybody in my life so terribly: my father, to whom I hadn't spoken in weeks; my mother, who was so sad; my brother, who was so angry; Cliffnotes, only a few miles uptown but as far as Castle Pym was from Griffynweld's eastern ocean; Tanner, probably sitting by the ocean now and on the same beach as Amanda. Even Amanda, who had treated me so poorly. So that when I came back to myself, seated here, on the floor, with Naomi, whose attention was complete, my loneliness was more acute than at any point in my life. When Naomi noticed my expression, she placed her palm to my cheek and kissed me, and I kissed her back, her cheek and her ear, to hide my face; and as during those first times together in her car, she raised her chin ever so slightly and closed her eyes, allowing herself to be kissed. "Never," she whispered, "never in my life ever has anyone kissed me like you do. If I could only explain," she said, "what it means to me."

And then Sam walked in the office.

Because I faced the door, because over Naomi's shoulder I could see it slowly swing in my direction, I was the first to react. Its glass was frosted, though I had an intimation it was Sam, I don't know why, and because he did not expect to see us here, he'd proceeded hesitantly, surprised, I could tell, that the lights were still on, the office unlocked, Naomi— usually visible at her desk from that sight line—gone. And when to his right he sensed a presence, beneath him, and glanced in my direction, his view of his wife was slightly obstructed by my desk; her back was to him, his view of me obstructed by her, though she did not move from her position, did not jump up from where she was reclined, her eyes slowly opening as she registered his footfalls, at which point she remained still. There was time only for her to give me a fierce stare—it had just a hint of bravado in it, which I will never forget—for me to barely lean away, and while we were not, in fact, kissing at that moment, our faces were so close to each other's, it was all so utterly compromising, that I was sure we'd been discovered. And what I will also never forget was how the sight of us registered with Sam—how he paused, so unprepared for this sight, that I was reminded of a deer twitching into visibility as you walk along a wooded road, the same initial perplexity obtaining between Sam and me as our eyes locked. Of what the next move was. And whose.

Sam, flummoxed, said only, "I forgot something," and with a barely perceptible shake of his head—it was like watching someone convince himself he *hadn't* seen a ghost—strode toward his office, assembled the papers for which he'd returned, and, as if for our benefit—we had not moved an inch—said to the both of us, "I'll see you at home." Then he walked out the door backward, pulling it closed behind him, as if to undo the entire episode.

I witnessed Naomi and Sam's fight that evening. I was scraping the leftovers into the koi pond, enjoying the splash of the fish breaching for the food, when I heard them. It came as if from a distance at first, what they said was muffled, but because I was in the backyard and because it was nighttime, I could see them on the second floor, through their bedroom windows. Sam, miming an explosion in his head; Naomi, in response, jabbed her finger into his chest and then pointed behind her, as if he'd left something in the hallway that she demanded he retrieve. They fought differently from my parents; the distinction was sonic. Dad denied and bemoaned; Mom accused and wailed; pain and heartsickness were its tenor. Sam, meanwhile, mocked and dismissed; Naomi raged and demeaned; their tone was hateful—Naomi's voice as guttural as Sam's was high-pitched—and it scared me more than my parents' fighting but did not stifle my curiosity. Naomi about-faced and marched out of their room, and I moved toward the very back of the yard, to stand invisible before the hedges and follow her progress, since the home's bay-facing side was mostly glass. Naomi next appeared in the second-story hallway and made her way down the stairs. She entered the living room, where Danny was watching TV, and ordered her to turn it off. Above, I spotted Sam, framed in his bedroom's middle window, both hands clapped to his cheeks as he contemplated the water; Jackie appeared to my left in the sunroom, oblivious to this conflict, a pint of Häagen-Dazs in one hand, a spoon in the other, until Naomi appeared, striding past her, toward the garage—she waved off her daughter's question—to go for a drive, I guessed (I heard the door to the garage slam), because I didn't see her for the rest of the evening, and she didn't find me in my room that night.

In the days that followed this row, and without fail, it was Sam who took me to lunch. I feared an accusation was forthcoming. In the meantime, he seemed glad for my company, energized at the prospect of introducing me to new cuisine. "The world is our oyster," he said, laughing, and he took me for these at Grand Central Station, insisting I drench the two dozen we split in mignonette, in horseradish, in cocktail sauce. Next we had the fried scallops with black garlic-ancho aioli. "The spice," Sam said, "puts hair on your chest." He chewed with his mouth open; he laughed at the food's heady flavors; his good mood was both infectious and a relief. He took me for Korean the next day, introduced me to kimchi, challenged me to go toe-to-toe with him and see who could eat the hottest dish.

"If I tap before you," he said, "I'll give you five dollars per course."

"What if I tap?" I asked.

"You tap," Sam replied, "and you still get a free meal, how's that for a bargain?"

"Bet," I said, and we hooked pinkies.

It was a relief to be away from Naomi. It was a comfort to have Sam close. I did feel guilt deceiving him. Playing the part of his surrogate son, I could throw off the role of Lancelot, bedding the queen and destroying the kingdom. There was a lightness, a glee, in being the mentee. I won the fire noodles course, as well as the stir-fried octopus, but conceded at the pork cutlet—the "dreaded 'drop-dead donkatsu,'" Sam intoned as the waiter placed the smoking plate between us. "Don't worry," Sam said, as I fanned my tongue and drank glass after glass of ice water, "we'll get milkshakes afterward to cool the heat."

The next day we brought beef souvlaki back to the office and ate at our desks, letting the paper catch the glistening green and yellow peppers that squished from the bread. Sam loved to lick the orange grease from his fingers afterward—I had never seen someone actually do this—sealing his lips to his digit's lowest pad and then pulling to the tip, making a pop at the top and then moving on to the next, ending at the thumb. It was an act I spied Naomi watching from her desk, over her glasses' bridge, and which, upon its conclusion, caused her to raise her own hands as if she were drying a manicure, the expression on her face one of shocked disgust. We had gyros on Friday, and that afternoon, while Sam was out of the office at a meeting, I called Naomi's extension and told her to meet me on the elevator. And as soon as we were rising in the car together, I pushed her against the wall and kissed her, at which point she pushed me away and groaned.

"What?" I asked, my heart pounding, because she'd made the same growl with Sam.

"Nothing," she said, and yanked the deadman's lever to D. "Just please go brush your teeth."

It was now Sam who drove me home in the evenings. I admit this too was a relief: to be under his surveillance, to lose the window of opportunity with Naomi, since within his sight I could do little wrong. But the silence brought on by this change in routine was for me almost unbearable. Here, I sometimes grew most paranoid, I expected an accusation at any moment, and on that first drive home together the actor in my soul made his appearance almost immediately.

"Can I get your advice about something?" I asked, and, after a beat, added: "It's a girl problem."

Sam downshifted, kept his eyes on the road. "I'll be happy to help if I can," he replied.

I told him the story of Amanda, from our meeting at Nightingale through the school year, from babysitting to the dinner with her dad, the kiss on the night of her birthday, culminating, of course, with that dreadful weekend in Westhampton—"Ah," Sam said, "now I get why you were so upset that day"—and concluding with my question: "What do you think I should do?"

We'd arrived in Great Neck; we were on Saddle Rock's residential roads. Sam pulled over. "For starters," he said, proving he had been listening to at least part of my story, "you need to learn to drive a stick."

This was how we spent those final evenings together. With me, driving the Ferrari all over Great Neck, wending our way down to University Gardens, then up to Kings Point, along East Shore Road, the nighttime vistas of Manhasset Bay ripping alongside us. Other nights, we crossed over to Port Washington and Sands Point, and then pushed east to Hempstead Bay, driving with the windows down, the salt in the air so heavy at times it was like eating an oyster again, the automobile exhaust carried on the eastbound breezes from Manhattan, whose glow on the horizon blotted the stars. I got the hang of finding each gear's sweet spot, a conversation in resistance and inertia, between the road and the V12, always seeking that balanced feel, that zone where the car was never redlining but holding power in abeyance. "Accelerate into the turn," Sam said as we leaned to the right. "Trust the suspension to claw the road." We headed south again, to Greenvale, bearing east on 25A to East Norwich—*Perfect names,* I thought, *for Griffynweld*—continuing on to Oyster Bay, Sam and me driving for hours, all the way east to Stony Brook, where we parked and could spot, to the west, the Eatons Neck Lighthouse, its beam's flash and revolution fingering the sound while Connecticut's shore twinkled across the water. We got pulled over twice during these lessons, Sam producing his Police Benevolent Association card and badge for the officer, who considered it and, after disappearing briefly to call in the plates, said only, "Thanks, Mr. Shah, just make sure that next time your son has his permit with him."

"My son?" Sam chuckled when we were back on the road. "Makes you wonder who's your mother."

And oh, the houses I saw on these long drives. Mansions with columns and verandas, their crow's nests looking out over the waterfront. Their foyers lit by gargantuan chandeliers. Their old-world masonry and landscaping, their limestone and copper flashing mottled with the sea spray's patina, their ivy-covered chimneys and two-boat slips. Their lawns for lawn's sake, as if grass were a staple crop. The millions of ways there were in America to make millions. The beguiling edifices of the rich that proclaimed *more, more, more.* What to do with such plenty? What to make of such wealth? How to live your life? Why did Sam bring me here? Is it possible that he simply wanted the company? Was he planning to shoot me and dump my body in the Sound? Or did he want to justify?

"The middle class grows," Sam said, "the middle class needs cheap clothes. When I was your age, when it was time for me to go into the family business, this fact was as bright as that lighthouse's lantern back there. But of this, I was sure: open up the borders, get rid of the tariffs, manufacture overseas to reduce your labor costs and increase your margins. Deregulate all of it, and then it's just an equation. You, the government, you cut my taxes to swell the middle, even if the middle isn't what it used to be, and guess what? The middle's less will become my more, and the only solution when the economy tanks will be to tax me even less, while I laugh all the way to the bank. These next few decades—it's going to be like having a bucket when it rains. Because if you're rich in this great country, you're in like Flynn. You're rich, *first*. You're not Jewish or Muslim or yellow or brown. You're rich, and you're *safe*. Safe from the very place you call home."

I touched 110 on the straightway.

"The truth of it is I knew there was no risk in this business when I started. When the game's gamed it's game over. I knew that if I just put in my time, there was mostly only reward. But risk," Sam said. "Balls. Nerve. No safety net. That, my boy, is the provenance of your father. Maybe it's your provenance too."

I'd lost count of the days since Naomi had last found her way to my bed. Something had happened. She seemed chastened, wary in Sam's presence, cool and formal toward me. She avoided eye contact. She mumbled nonsensically. On the nights Sam and I did not drive together, she excused herself after dinner and retired to her bed, leaving Danny, Jackie, and me to do the dishes and then spend the rest of the evening watching MTV. It had premiered at the beginning of August and it was all the girls did, it seemed. Naomi sometimes joined us, though she sat as far apart from me in the room as she could manage.

But on the last night we spent together, when Sam and I arrived from Manhattan, Naomi seemed back to being her old self. She greeted me warmly, kissed her husband with an exaggerated pucker on the lips, and, after the big smack, said, "Have I got a surprise for you." She led us to the kitchen. "From Marvin Himmelfarb at Ralph Lauren." She held up a bottle of Nolet's Reserve and then, with a flourish, a bottle of Petrus Pomerol.

Sam brightened, considering the label. "Nineteen sixty-one!" he said. "What did you do to deserve this?"

"Let me fix you a martini, and I'll tell you all about it." She gave Sam another big flirty smooch. "I brought home some steaks. They had a great price on the filet at the butcher."

"Fantastic," Sam said. "I'll decant the bottle."

Later, after Danny, Jackie, and I had scraped the fat into the koi pond, we came back inside to find Sam asleep at the dinner table.

"You two," Naomi said to her daughters, "go start your bath. I'm going to give your father another antihistamine." Then to me: "So he doesn't snore from the sulfites."

Did Naomi know it was her last chance to show me that this was what we shared? As I watched her above me, it seemed, at times, as if I were only incidental, a bystander to her performance. She wanted to be unforgettable. She wanted *us,* I am certain now, to be something she might never forget, that she might tend henceforth, like embers. She slapped me occasionally; she stiff-armed my face, leaning with all her weight, palm to my cheek, and held me there. She pulled her own hair, gathering fists of it by her temples, and shook her head. And for a long time, at the very end, she just kissed me, and I kissed her back, and this kissing felt like a free fall in pitch-darkness, felt like something endless.

It was sometime in the middle of the night, but, waking, I knew I was not the only one awake. Like a dog's ear for high pitch, I heard a sound, one I could barely discern or distinguish, and I got out of bed to find the source.

Naomi was seated in the middle of the front hall's staircase, in her slip, crying.

She looked up and wiped her eyes and waved for me to join her, then took my hand and turned me around, so that I was seated with my back to her, between her legs, which formed chair arms as if she were my young king's throne. She pressed her face to my neck and nuzzled me there and cried, silently, her body shaking. Her forehead was hot. She calmed down, finally, and for a long time just sat with her arms weaved around my neck.

"I don't want to go upstairs," she said. Then: "I don't want you to ever leave." Then: "I don't want to lose my family." Then: "I don't want to be with Sam anymore." Then: "I want to wake up in your bed one morning." Then: "I don't want my daughters to ever be this unhappy." Then: "I don't want to be scared anymore." Then: "I don't want to keep hating myself." Then: "I'm so sorry for what I've done to you."

She kissed the back of my neck, at the very base, and rose to her feet and left me there.

Adults, I think now, were the ocean in which I swam.

There comes a point, even in the summer, when you want the season to end.

That evening, Danny, Jackie, and I were in the living room, watching MTV. If you watched the channel for long enough, the programming cycled through the same set of videos, but that did not (as yet) blunt our fascination with any of them, our determination to memorize every close-up of the climactic drum fills and guitar solos, these teaching a whole generation how to play air guitar and how to vogue. Nor did it diminish every tiny pleasure we took in certain moments we'd memorized. Of Stevie Nicks, for instance, blatantly blowing her lyrics as she lip-synced with Tom Petty in "Stop Draggin' My Heart Around," the duo dressed in black, and Nicks, with her witchy frizzy blond hair, reminding me of Naomi. Like Sam, the lead singer of the Buggles ("Video Killed the Radio Star") wore Elton John glasses, and his keyboard player made it appear that the height of virtuosity was to play two synthesizers at once— *"We can't rewind,"* I sang, to Danny and Jackie's delight, *"we've gone too far!"* During the guitar solo on "You Better Run," Pat Benatar would shake her head and rake fingers through her hair, and it was part and parcel of my transformation that nearly every rock song was so obviously about sex that I wanted to cover Danny's and Jackie's still-innocent ears. As for "In the Air Tonight," what *did* the lyrics mean? Where was Mom? Dad? Oren? *"The hurt doesn't show,"* sang Jackie, a thumb to her mouth in place of a mic, *"But the pain still grows,"* Danny sang, picking up the line. *"It's no stranger to you and me,"* I roared. And while they played the air drums and danced like little go-go girls, I went outside to feed the fish.

It was dark in the yard, and after feeding the koi I walked to the lawn's center and faced toward Manhattan, which I missed, which like my heartsickness glowed above the hedges and killed the sight of the stars. And then I heard Sam and Naomi fighting. The back of the Shahs' home, as I have mentioned, was more glass than brick, and at night it was a tableau vivant. I turned around to see the girls dancing to The Who's "You Better You Bet," and then looked up to the Shahs' bedroom on the second floor.

They'd gone straight to verbal haymakers and weren't even trying to keep it down for our sakes. They followed the argument, or it followed them, from their bathroom and back to the bedroom, where it was Naomi who went for the sword first. Sam wrestled for control of the saber back, their two sets of hands upraised and firmly gripping the handle, as if they were trying to touch their twelve-foot ceiling with the blade's tip. Sam, who managed to wrench the weapon from his wife's clutches, now raised it above his head; Naomi, reaching out in protest, backed toward the door, screaming at him, and then ran. Downstairs, Danny and Jackie were still dancing, the TV's volume blasting the Pretenders' "Tattooed Love Boys," the pair of them headbanging in front of Chrissie Hynde's face, before freezing at the sound of Naomi's scream. As if practiced—as if they knew this was not a drill—the girls dashed behind the curtains, their backs visible to me in the windows. And into this room the husband and wife appeared: Sam still with sword in hand, marching patiently around the coffee table, which Naomi, also marching around, kept between them. She bolted, finally, out of the family wing, with Sam right behind her, shouting as he followed her through the dining room. Here she turned to fling some of their china in his direction, the plates gouging the wallpaper as they broke against the wall, and then made her way into the kitchen, where I next spotted her walking backward again, now brandishing a chef's knife, which she clumsily threw at her husband, its blade dinging on the tile, before she raced into the sunroom and, using the same strategy as earlier, placed the tulip table between them. With one hand, Sam tossed this aside. Naomi, surrendering, fell to her knees. But Sam let the weapon fall at his side and covered his face. At this, Naomi stood. Over Sam's shoulder she spotted me and, sensing rescue, made for the door to the yard. He too turned and, spotting me, yanked her collar and threw her to the floor and, picking up the saber, marched in my direction. He pushed the door open. Naomi screamed, "No!" When she tried to follow, he turned and shouldered the door closed on her pinkie, which got caught in the jamb. The top half of her finger separated at the knuckle and bounced into the koi pond, where it floated for a second before one of those soft mouths rose to the surface, and ate it.

I ran.

Around to the front of the house, I fled, pursued by Naomi's howl. I stopped on the street, looking at the other houses. I didn't know any of the Shahs' neighbors. I didn't even know if the Shahs knew their neighbors.

The door of the garage was still up. I opened the door of the Ferrari, pulled the visor, and caught the keys before they landed in my lap. I dropped the car into gear and burned so much rubber I couldn't see their house in my rearview mirror for the smoke.

I'd made the drive into the city so many times with both Sam and Naomi I knew it like a commuter.

And I knew the peace and quiet that attends the solo commuter's trip—the time it gave me to collect my thoughts, which were, in my manner of coping back then, entirely unrelated to what had just happened. Passing Flushing Meadows, I spied the Unisphere, that giant globe, and considered how few places I'd been to in my life besides New York. The Observation Towers, topped with their flying saucers, these World's Fair structures, run-down and rusting and in need of restoration. Manhattan came into view from the Queens side. When he was my age, did Dad marvel at its skyline as I did now? Is the city ever more wondrous than when seen from afar, at night? When the sky is black, when its buildings' outlines are rendered invisible? *There are more windows in New York than people,* I thought. How to begin to calculate such a number? I turned on the radio. Dad's commercial for Bell telephone played. *Reach out,* he said, *and touch someone far away.* Coming over the Fifty-Ninth Street Bridge, the Roosevelt Island tram rose into view on my right, but the car was empty.

Was this how adults fought with each other?

At our building, I pulled into our empty parking space and cut the engine. The needles slammed shut against their pegs.

I said hi to Carlos, the night doorman, in the lobby. "Long time no see," he said.

Standing before our apartment's door, I reached between my shirt's collar and, from where it hung on its ball chain, produced the key.

I had never been so happy to be back in my own bed, I thought later, lying in my top bunk. I had never been so happy to be home.

Dad shook me awake the next morning—I'd slept in, I could tell, by the angle of the sunlight on the building across the street. "What are you doing here?" he asked.

I hugged his neck, which seemed gargantuan and smelled of Skin Bracer. I let him carry all my weight, and when he tried to ease my grip, I clutched him harder.

"Craziest thing," he said, as I held him. "I got in just now from D.C., and guess what? There's a goddamn Ferrari in my spot."

September. I sometimes believed that by simply speaking the month's name aloud I might summon the cooler weather, set the leaves, just now beginning to change color on their branches, astir with chillier gusts. Back then, autumn still obeyed the school calendar, promptly arriving on the Tuesday after Labor Day. When it rained you felt droplets that were closer in temperature to ice. Central Park, that mood ring in the middle of Manhattan, began to tarnish, which the sun, wafer white, revealed in all of its ocher and saffron beauty.

September brought my family back together. Oren finally returned from Matt's ahead of the holiday weekend and school's start. To my amazement, he was nearly my height. He was also wearing eyeglasses with tortoiseshell frames. "Are those real?" I asked.

"Of course they're real," he said. "Want to come get beer with me at the Shopwell? I got a fake ID."

At the supermarket, Oren got a six-pack and then crossed the street west, to the park above the Dead Street. We climbed the low brick wall and then stood with our arms hanging over the fence's railing. Below, the great expanse before the West Side Highway was the color of black ice. Oren raised his beer. "To my first year of high school."

"May it be better than mine," I said.

We clinked cans.

I considered the parked cars below, Naomi's Mercedes nowhere to be seen. Why didn't I take that opportunity to tell him about living with the Shahs? About Naomi? The truth is that it would have never occurred to me then to share the things I'd seen and done, any more than discussing Kepplemen, because our lives were so atomized, because we lived so unattended, because we were already so strangely private, access to each other's inner lives did not come naturally.

"Mom's coming home tomorrow," Oren said.

From the north, we watched an airplane bank over the city.

"When did you speak to her?" I asked.

"Yesterday. She said Grandma had to quit smoking because of her lungs."

"That's good news, I guess."

"Where's Dad?"

"He's been rehearsing late."

Because Dad was holed up at the St. James for final rehearsals ahead of opening night, he was not at the apartment upon Mom's return. We heard her keys in the door and rushed from our bedroom to greet her. I let Oren hug her first. She swayed with him in her arms, his hair bunched in her fist while he shook. "Sweet boy," she whispered, "how did you get so big so fast?" She waved me to her and hugged me while Oren took her suitcase to her room.

It was not lost on either my brother or me that she did not unpack, but instead placed the suitcase open, on her dresser, as you might during a short stay in a hotel. Oren ordered pizza and made a Caesar salad. I set the table. When we sat down, Mom asked me, "How are you on school clothes?"

"My pants are fine," I said, "but none of my shirts fit. Or my blazer."

"We'll go shopping this weekend," she said. "Do you want to come?" she asked Oren.

"I can't," Oren said. "I have a commitment." He so attentively sprinkled his slice with garlic and red pepper that we knew not to press him about what this was.

"Do you have something to wear for Dad's opening night?" Mom asked him instead.

"I can throw something together," he said.

"How's your summer reading going?" she asked me.

What a miserable several days it had been, not so much reading as inhaling pages. But I was close to finished.

"What do you have left?" Mom said.

The Sun Also Rises.

"Oh," she said, "you can read that in an afternoon."

Mom, never one to be flippant, was always saying such reassuring things to me. She might as well have claimed I could go on pointe if I just strapped on her shoes.

Were all of us listening for Dad to come home that night? Around eleven the phone rang. Oren and I jumped from our beds and raced for my study. He lifted the handset, careful to hold down the cradle's prongs while I unscrewed the mouthpiece's cap and popped out the receiver. Then I placed the earpiece between us.

". . . it's hard to tell what's good or bad at this point," Dad was saying to her. "They keep making changes."

"It's not your job to worry about that," Mom said.

"True," Dad said, and waited. The silence between them throbbed like a broken limb. "How are the boys?" he finally said.

"They seem good," Mom said. "Oren's the Green Giant, he's grown so much. Griffin badly needs a haircut. He looks like a lion. He's also behind on his homework."

"What else is new?" Dad said.

"What else is new?" Mom said.

Dad paused. Mom refused to fill the air. "Do you want me to come home tonight," Dad asked, "or do you want me to wait?"

Mom thought about this. It was as if the entire family were thinking about it. "I want you to come home, but only if you're really ready to come home."

"What does that mean?"

"I'm not going to spell it out for you, Shel."

Dad said, "Fine then."

And he hung up.

About my time with the Shahs, there was next to no discussion, although Mom did come into my room the following night and asked,

"How did it go out there?" as if she had information. When I had nothing to report, she said, "Naomi told me Sam moved out. They're getting a divorce."

"Huh," I said.

"She said you've turned into a real gentleman."

Mom cleared the hair from my eyes to better search them and then left me be. I was so confident in my silence because on the morning of my return I called Sam at home and told him where his car was, that the keys were in their normal hiding place, in response to which he said, stiffly, "Thank you for letting me know."

"How's Naomi?" I asked.

"She'll live," Sam said, "how about we leave it at that?"

"Agreed," I said.

And then he hung up.

It felt like the first adult conversation of my life.

That final week of summer, at 30 Rock, while we were shooting the season's last episode, I was so bogged down with my school reading, I was so unprepared and blew my lines with such regularity, we had to halt nearly all my scenes in order for Liz and me to drill. These sessions were beyond triage, my flameouts so spectacular she was actually rooting for me to get through them, since the finish line was in sight, season five in the can. We stood just outside the set's radiant circle so we could huddle, everyone keeping their places, me repeating lines she fed me like some sort of catechism.

"Don't threaten my parents again, Lava Girl . . ." she said.

"Don't threaten my parents again, Lava Girl . . ." I said.

". . . or I'll blow this volcano so sky-high . . ."

". . . or I'll blow this volcano so sky-high . . ."

". . . Vesuvius's eruption will seem like a firecracker."

". . . Vesuvius's eruption will seem like a firecracker."

"This is so bad . . ." Liz said.

"This is so bad . . ." I said.

"No," she said, "the *writing*."

I laughed, and Liz did too, which relaxed me. "From the top," she said.

Tensions were also high at the St. James. After we wrapped at
30 Rock, I'd ride my bike there to catch some of the run-through. I liked
not alerting Dad to my arrival—having the chance to watch him while
he was unaware of my presence in the darkened balcony's first row, hidden by its ledge, rendered almost invisible by the light shining from spots
and PAR cans arrayed beneath it, especially during the lulls, while Fountain and Ferrer and Kay interrupted the performance to huddle in the
orchestra level's aisles. I might sometimes even risk discovery by sitting
in one of the private boxes, and it was from here that I spotted Dad during one of the breaks—his back was to me—standing beside Katie near
the left wing, his hands clasped behind him. The cast was assembled for
the opening number, taking direction from Ferrer, Dad bending toward
her ear to tell her something, to whisper it, fervently, she patting his back
and then feeling her way down to finally clasp one of his fingers with her
own. And I *hated* him for it.

Opening night was the Friday after Labor Day. Mom and I went
straight to our seats in the mezzanine; Oren hit the snack bar for a Coke
and Milk Duds. The audience's chatter was an almost audible correlative
to my anticipation. The orchestra tuned up with such a feeling of tension it was as if I were witnessing a medieval legion pulling on a hundred
drawstrings and then aiming their arrows toward the sky. And then the
lights went down, there was the stillness that accompanies several hundred indrawn breaths, followed by the blast of light when the curtains
went up and the music played. I wish I could do a better job of relay-
ing the experience of *Sam and Sara* from start to finish. But when your
father is performing, when you have seen a show take shape over the
course of several months, when you have heard its songs sung in your
home so many times that they seem like nursery rhymes, have seen dance
numbers whose steps have been altered, the palimpsest of prologues
auditioned, tried, and then trashed, it is like looking at the underside of
an Oriental rug: all you see is the stitching. Instead, you watch for signs,
for key moments at odds with the show's rhythms; you wait, tensed, for
funny parts that in the past have gotten laughs, only to have your heart
sink when they don't land; you are surprised when bits you never found
comical set off a fusillade of cackles. For me the show rose toward and

sank away from Dad's appearances, the stunned silence that followed his two duets a confirmation of approval and a promise of possible success. I realized everyone noticed what Mom had flagged from the get-go, which was that the actor playing Sam had been miscast—his voice was somehow too operatic. The show itself seemed somehow anachronistic. As to the plot, Sam and Sara do not get together at the end. The couple sings a devastating duet near the show's conclusion called "Getting Away with It." They have, by this time, consummated their love for each other, but they are older, and when their chance to break from their marriages presents itself, when their feelings are strongest but their nerve is at its most tenuous, they succumb to inertia. They can't bring themselves to leave their spouses. Not that I cared. The show had the quality of all mediocre art: my attention slipped right off it. I don't remember much of the performances at all.

We migrated to Sardi's for the cast party. This was customary for Fountain's shows, to celebrate and eat and await the reviews from the New York papers just off the delivery trucks. Mom, Oren, and I were among the first to arrive. The room's decor was a ubiquitous crimson: the awning, the walls, the carpet, and the leather banquettes were all red. Mom asked for a table in the far corner, I would realize later, to be as far as possible from Katie at all times and who, once the restaurant filled up, seemed similarly determined to keep as many guests as possible between herself and Mom. Oren and I hunkered down on either side of her in the highbacked banquette like a security detail. I left her only once to study the rows of caricatures that lined the walls. When I asked Mom about the drawings, she said that there had been a series of caricaturists since the restaurant had opened in the thirties. They were on their third artist who did all the portraits, but the first was a Russian immigrant who exchanged his services for two free meals a day. Was Fountain among its cohort? Might Dad be up there one day? He came over to join us, unable to sit still, too nervous to eat. He was all jitters compared to Mom's implacable steeliness. Their conversation was the most wooden sort of dialogue, shot through with bad acting. When Dad finally got up the nerve to ask her, "What did you think?" she tilted her chin toward Fountain, who was now standing on one of the chairs, waving the *Times* in his hand, ordering everyone to gather round. Dad left us to huddle with the cast. Fountain thanked everyone profusely for their efforts these past seven months, and then he snapped open the broadsheet and said, "This, ladies and gentlemen, from Richard Eder in the *Times*":

> This critic recalls first hearing Marc Morales perform the title character in "Don Giovanni"—at Teatro Alla Scala, in 1964, to be exact—and how it seemed his voice could make the very earth tremble. Sadly, time and its ravages have reduced this great baritone's instrument to a quaver—one of many shaky aspects in the new musical "Sam and Sara."
>
> Opening last night at the St. James Theater, "Sam and Sara" is the latest (I almost wrote last) offering by two of America's most influential collaborators, librettist Abe Fountain and composer Hershy Kay. Once it was axiomatic that every aspiring lyricist cut his teeth imitating Fountain's lines and every budding arranger echoed Kay's melodies. Now the pair sounds like a poor impersonation of their past selves.

Oren pulled at my elbow. "This is scorched earth stuff," he whispered. "Maybe it gets better," I said, trying not to look at Dad.

> True, Fountain and Kay are still capable of the stratospheric showstopper but in spite of these soaring moments, "Sam and Sara" fails to launch.

"This is Old Testament," Oren said.
"Be quiet," I said.
"We'll be sharing a bedroom until you leave for college."
Fountain pressed on:

> In one of the musical's unintended ironies, it is the spurned spouses who perform the most revelatory song about love. These standouts, Shel Hurt and Katie Deal, are not only fully

realized characters but also heartbreaking in their roles. Their final duet is by far the show's outstanding number.

Dad looked over his shoulder at us, at Mom, and smiled, albeit mournfully.

Fountain, after pausing to wipe the sweat from his forehead with his sleeve, continued:

> Mr. Fountain's lyrics occasionally steal fire from the gods. In between, the audience must suffer an eagle eating its liver.

I watched Dad. It was hard to tell if he was listening anymore. He'd struck the same pose as in his headshot, arms crossed and chin resting on his thumb while staring at his feet, brushing invisible sawdust from the carpet.

> Is "Sam and Sara" Abe Fountain's swan song? That remains unknown. But this production is unquestionably a turkey.

The cast stood motionless, heads downcast.

"But what does he really think?" one of the actors finally shouted.

Several couldn't help it and cracked up. It freed some of the others to do the same, to put their arms around those who were crying and try to comfort them. Others looked to Fountain for direction.

"What he thinks," Fountain said, "will not stop any of us . . ." And at this he paused. ". . . from getting good and drunk."

I turned to Mom. "What does this mean?"

Mom was smiling as if she had just told herself a private joke or had made a final decision. She sat with her elbow on the table, chin to palm, her mouth hidden behind her bent fingers, her eyes flickering between anger and delight. What I was certain of was that when she turned to me to speak, when she let her arm fall in order to be heard, I understood, with total clarity, why my father needed her, trusted her, sometimes hated her, feared her, occasionally fled from her—and loved her.

"It means," she said, "that soon this will all be over."

. . .

The next day, Howard Kissel's *Daily News* review of *Sam and Sara* hit the stands, notably more positive than Eder's. Ferrer, my father said, had heard that Walter Kerr—of New York's critics the most reliably negative—was coming out with a long piece on the show at month's end that would be "glowing." Could *Sam and Sara* stay afloat until Kerr's review published? Would the investors be willing to carry it for three weeks if ticket sales were poor? And then, as if by divine intervention— for the show's success or its ultimate failure, I can't say even now— Morales, who played Sam, took ill. His voice began to turn hoarse by the conclusion of Saturday's matinee; by curtain Saturday night, he was rasping and running a high fever; he croaked almost inaudibly through his performance.

Dad was already preparing to take the role by Saturday afternoon. Early that morning, Mom had departed for Montauk to stay with Al for the weekend, so Dad returned to the apartment. He had, on his person, and at all times, a small tape recorder with the melodies of all his new songs. On a blue set of flash cards, his lyrics; on a yellow set of flash cards, his lines. Slowly but surely, these were shuffled into a multicolored deck, which he mumbled and hummed around the clock. He left for rehearsal Sunday evening, to go over the songs with Hershy Kay and Fountain. Oren and I were asleep long before Dad got home, although he was up well ahead of us, to cook us breakfast before school. At the table, he told us he'd be home well past our bedtime. His first performance was Tuesday night.

That week, Mom stayed at Al's. In spite of Dad's performance schedule, he made us breakfast every morning before school, and sat with us, in spite of his exhaustion, taking great pleasure in watching us eat. But because he was gone on weeknights, and because Mom wasn't there to cook dinner, Dad left us cash and told us to fend for ourselves. Friday afternoon through Sunday night, Oren disappeared and didn't come home until very late, if he came home at all. When I asked him where he'd been, he said, "None of your *b-i*-bizness," if he said anything.

I went to see Dad perform.

I knew then the show wasn't going to make it. Eder's review had decimated sales. If you'd been visiting New York, you could've sat front row center for pennies on the dollar, which I did not, even though the stage manager gave me carte blanche. I was worried that doing so would distract Dad. I soon learned I didn't need to worry about that at all.

The role was perfect for him; it freed him up. There was a built-in bigness to Sam's character, something outsized and commanding that matched up perfectly with Dad's statue-bust features, his Roman emperor's profile, which suggested both authority and appetite. In the show, he is described as a brilliant architect, and there is a scene toward the middle of Act I in which he dresses down a classroom of graduate students; the relish with which Dad did this, torpedoing their half-baked observations with academic knowledge, was perfect. He wore a tweed jacket with elbow patches like the professor he'd never be, the empty frames of wire-rimmed eyeglasses giving him that extra dash of stodgy condescension. I often found my father's put-on profundity pathetic in its transparency, but in this moment, in these performances, he seemed incontestable.

And when he sang, he soared through his seemingly endless range, and I was reminded of the times I dropped Sam's Ferrari into fifth gear. Oh, to be flooded with my father's full-throated sound! To hear, as he hit his highest note and held it, how much he had to give if he'd ever had the chance. I was not the only one to notice this. The musical did twelve performances before closing, and on the final Saturday night, watching from the wings, I spotted Mom in the audience. She was as rapt as I was. She laughed as if we were all four at dinner in the apartment; she whistled, to my shock, with her two fingers pressed to the underside of her tongue, at curtain; it was clear to me that she was having the best time. And her love for my father, I realized, exceeded mine, exceeded her love even for Oren and me. Was that a love, in marriage, to aspire to? I remember watching Mom watch him, shaking her head at times and squinting when he hit certain notes; how during other moments, she turned her head away ever so slightly, as if she were averting her eyes from the sun. Or holding her prayer-clasped fingers pressed to her lips and nodding in joy. *Talent,* I thought. That great leveler. Smasher of gates and all-access pass. Velvet-rope opener and the penthouse view. *Follow me please,* says the maître d' to talent, *I have our best table waiting.* That uniquely and unfairly bestowed gift America had figured out how to tap more efficiently and mercilessly than any other country in history. It should be written on the goddamn Statue of Liberty: *Give me*

your talented, your gifted, your huddled geniuses, yearning to breathe free.
That was our country's exceptionalism—her thrown-wide-open doors she might just as suddenly slam shut. Rob my father of his money, like that insurance agent did; call him *Burger* or *hebe* or *kike,* but you *still* could not wrest from him his talent. I said I was not the only one to notice how perfect Dad was as the lead, how—I truly believe this—the fortunes of that show might have been otherwise if he'd been properly cast, if they'd given him his one shot. That night, during Dad's last performance of "Getting Away with It," I felt someone touch my shoulder. Then I noticed Fountain's white-gloved hand there, the cotton fabric dotted with tiny sequins. His touch, which had startled me, briefly turning my body to ice. He gave me a warm squeeze. "Finally," he whispered, "I can hear my lyrics."

And then the curtain fell.

That Sunday was the final matinee. I met Dad at the stage door and hugged him and told him he was great, and I meant it. It was one of those September afternoons in New York when the passenger plane banking west—a white crucifix against that endless lapis lazuli—leaves no contrail. Weather so perfect you believe certain states of being, like happiness, might be eternal. It was a healthy walk home from the theater, and Dad was quiet. Just as Lincoln Center came into view, its plaza full of people, its fountains susurrating, he said, "How about something to eat," which was not a question, and then he led me to O'Neals' on the corner.

Dad asked for a booth; I wasn't hungry and told him so. "A bowl of pickles," Dad said to the waitress, "and a cream soda, please." When she returned, he said, "Eat something with me, even if it's just a *nosh,*" and so I scanned the enormous menu, which hid Dad from my view, and when I lowered it, Katie was sitting next to him.

She smiled at me, we exchanged pleasantries, and I, intentionally this time, concealed my face behind the menu's screen. When the waitress returned, I ordered the surf and turf with a milkshake.

"I thought you weren't hungry," Dad said.

"I changed my mind," I replied.

He and Katie began discussing the show's failure—a conversation that did not include me but did allow me to study her closely for a time. She wore high-heeled black leather boots. Black slacks. A collared black button-down blouse. A thin black leather jacket. Several gold neck-laces with pendants that measured the slope of her substantial cleav-age. Hooped earrings, also gold. Black thick-rimmed eyeglasses; heavy mascara and eyeliner. A glossy maroon lipstick. She wore her black hair up. Everything about her said street tough, said street smart—said New York. Said *don't fuck with me*. Her laugh was husky and commanding. She was used to being stared at, I could tell, and occasionally I caught Dad complying, admiringly, as when she took a moment to make small talk with me, to ask me how the new school year was going, what classes I was taking. Her brother had been a wrestler, she said, a play for quick connec-tion between us. When I asked her where, she replied, "Oklahoma," and plucked a pickle from its basket. "That sport saved his life like the theater saved mine." As she chewed, I noticed that her hair was dyed, that the lipstick was crumbling at the corners of her mouth. She was—long had been—in flight from something, and if she were to excuse herself to the bathroom and remove her makeup, I might not recognize her when she rejoined us.

The waitress arrived with my food. Dad said he needed to hit the john. Katie and I sat facing each other while I pondered my steak and lobster tail. Then she leaned toward me, fingers laced together, palms to the table, and stared at me, while I stared back, unimpressed.

"I thought it was lovely how often you came to your father's perfor-mances," she said. When I didn't respond she asked, "Can I have a French fry?"

She took one and bit the end. Its white meat smoked.

"You have a big fall coming up," she said, and then dipped into my ketchup.

"You mean wrestling?"

"I mean *Take Two* comes out." She pointed the fry at me. "You're gonna be a star."

The idea of Dad talking with this woman about my future was appall-ing. "I haven't thought about it much."

"I'd have killed to have had an opportunity like that when I was your age."

"You seem like you're doing okay."

She offered a half smile. "I don't have to waitress anymore."

"What about now that the show's closed?"

"I sing jingles." She took another fry and bit it in half. "These are dangerous," she said.

I forked the entire lobster tail from its shell and considered it. When I looked up, Katie was considering me.

"You believe in gut feelings?" she asked.

I shrugged in half agreement, half indifference.

"I'm a big believer in the instinctual response," she continued. "Also first impressions. They tend to be right. So let me ask you something. Be honest."

Because I was going to oblige her.

"Do you like me?" she asked.

I tilted my head to the side. Was this an audition?

"Do you think you could like me?" she said.

I looked over my shoulder, toward the bathroom, then back at Katie. "I think," I said, "I don't know you."

Katie shrugged. "Fair enough."

"I know," I said, and paused, but not for effect, "I don't like what you're doing to my family."

Katie stuck out her lower lip, nodded.

"I also know," I said, "that my father always ends up choosing my mom."

Those Venus flytrap eyelashes of hers closed and opened.

"Does that answer your question?" I asked.

When she didn't respond, I pushed my plate toward her.

"Eat," I said, and stood to leave. "While you can."

That beautiful, blessed, first short week of classes, we grieved summer's loss and begged its forgiveness, having taken it for granted. That first Tuesday back at Boyd was a blur of new teachers and syllabi and early dismissal; of patrolling the halls during free periods, on the lookout for the freshman girls everyone was talking about. I was taking biology, modern European history, Spanish B, geometry, and English, and as my arts elective, which I picked out of inertia, I'd signed up for Theater II with Mr. Damiano. But the highlight of the week was meeting our new wrestling coach.

The team was told to gather in the locker room, where Assistant Coach Tyrell greeted us. "You're going to weigh in first, my dudes, and then head to the gym." We began to strip. "No, no," Tyrell said, "lose the blazers and shoes but not the shirts or pants, please, and I'll record your weight in those."

Tanner, Cliffnotes, and I exchanged quizzical glances.

In the wrestling gym, we slid down the wall to take our seats, I between Cliffnotes and Tanner. On the latter's still-tan wrist, I noticed the pale outline of where his sailor's bracelet used to be. Then the double doors opened and our new coach walked to the mats' edge, stepped out of his sneakers, took his place on the center mat's bruin, and looked up and down the line. He was slab-headed, and there was something decidedly gladiatorial about his appearance, as big-browed and knob-chinned as he was—all he was missing was a centurion's helmet. His neck started at his ears, but it was his torso that was far more intimidating—it was as broad as a shipping crate. He was wearing shorts, and his calves were nearly big around as his thighs, and it was this uniformity to his mass that projected a combination of irresistible force and steadfastness. To pick him up, to separate his feet from the earth, you'd need a forklift.

"Gentlemen," he began, in a heavy, up-Island accent. "My name's Aiden Byrne and I'm looking forward to working with you this season. A bit about myself: I'm a second-generation Irish Catholic, grew up in East Hampton, New York, a place I know some of you are familiar with, and where my family has owned a small business for over three decades. I wrestled at East Hampton High, then at Iowa State, where I was a starter all four years and an academic all-American my senior year." He seemed a bit abashed at the mention of this accolade. "A few words about my expectations. You're gonna get out of this program what you put into it. This is an individual sport, but our job as team members is to make each other better. My number one value is mutual respect and my number two is hard work. As for my individual goals for each of you, I have only this one: by the season's end, you're able to beat the wrestler you were at its start." He paused to nod, which we'd soon learn was what he did when he knew exactly what was coming. "There are several other changes to which I'll call your attention. First, as you know, Assistant Coach Tyrell just recorded your weight. You will remain within five pounds of that number, no sucking down and no rubber suits."

Grumbling and hisses.

"I know, new coach, new rules, but this is to protect your health. Also, three new tournaments have been added to our schedule"—Tyrell had us pass this down—"that are in much tougher leagues than I'm guessing you're accustomed to, no disrespect. Also, note the scrimmages with some of the New Jersey and Long Island public schools, which is a different shark tank altogether. Finally, I'll be running an optional weightlifting program three days a week. I stress that this is *optional,* I know you all have serious academic responsibilities or are doing other sports or both. That said, once the season begins, all practices are mandatory unless you have a written excuse. Any questions?"

We eyed one another up and down the line. No one raised his hand. Did they, like me, feel the same sense of solace? That this person was exactly what he was. That he was a help as opposed to a hindrance. That these facts, taken in the aggregate, meant we were safe. They must have, because almost everyone seemed as stoked as I. Because what occurred to me, as I considered our team, was this: we were *deep* with talent. And maybe not this year, but certainly by the next, we'd be a force.

Theater class met in the basement rehearsal space. Damiano had the lights raised, which made the room seem smaller. "Our first semester production," he announced, "will be *The Tempest.*" The senior dramaramas eyed one another knowingly; they small-clapped and cooed. The entire semester, Damiano explained, would be dedicated to the play, with a string of performances beginning in early November. "This first week, we'll hold auditions. Parts should be assigned by Friday, and we'll be well into rehearsals by the month's end." He flapped a sheaf of handouts and then distributed them.

I reviewed the rehearsal and production schedule. From my book bag, I pulled out my wrestling schedule and did a side by side.

Damiano said, "We have a bet in the teachers' lounge who can keep you for the shortest amount of time today, and I intend to win, so off you go." As everyone was exiting, Damiano stopped me and said, "Hey, Griffin, walk with me, would you?"

We made our way out of the theater, up and out of the swimming pool's zone of chlorinated humidity, into the main lobby, and down the upper school's long hallway that ran parallel to the gymnasium. We took a left, up an exposed half flight of stairs fashioned of concrete with a metal railing. Beyond this, a door led to the wrestling lockers and the five flights Kepplemen used to make us run at the end of practice. Atop these was the school's main theater.

"I wanted to wait till we were out of earshot of everyone." Damiano nodded at me, hesitant, like he still wasn't sure about what he was going to say. In other words: a dramatic pause. "I want you to play Prospero," he said, as if that meant something to me. When he saw that it didn't, he continued: "I want you to try out for the lead."

"I don't—"

"Make no mistake, you've still got to earn the role."

"Mr. Damiano, the rehearsal schedule conflicts—"

"I know," he said, and raised his hand, "it's a big commitment, but here's the thing. *Take Two* comes out in, what, a month? I think I just read that in *Variety*." Not even my dad read *Variety*. "And when it does, you're going to have all sorts of opportunities come your way—life-changing ones. And what a lot of people probably won't tell you is this: you've got talent galore, Griffin, but you've got no technique. And a year from now, when those adult roles start coming your way, you're not going to be ready. You won't be able to cross over. You get what I'm saying?" He placed his hand on my shoulder. "There's a moment when an actor moves from naturalism to craft. So," he said, and made an emphatic, shaking gesture with his closed fists, "let me teach you. Give me the chance. That way, you don't end up out of work one day, like nine-tenths of the actors in that failed musical your father was just in. He got a good writeup, I saw."

I thought for a moment about punching him in the mouth, but that would get me expelled.

Then an even more beautiful thought presented itself—one that made me smile so serenely, Damiano couldn't help but smile too.

"I'm flattered," I said.

We shook hands.

Later that week, I read for Alan Hornbeam at his Upper East Side town house.

He had a home theater, the first I'd ever seen, and when I met him there, the producer of *Take Two,* the film's editor, and two studio executives were also in attendance. They'd just reviewed the final cut and were discussing it. "Let me show you something," Hornbeam said, and gave the projectionist instructions and then asked me to sit. The lights went down. The scene when Hornbeam and I are discussing love rolled. We have our baseball mitts, and then Amanda and the extra playing her mother walk by, and Amanda smiles at me so warmly, her reaction caught so perfectly in the shot, that I was reminded of the promise it contained, which, if it was acting on her part, was Academy Award–winning stuff. And in the reaction shot I could see the hope in *my* expression, which was also not acting, especially when Hornbeam and I watched the pair of women make their way toward the park.

When the lights came up, Hornbeam asked, "What do you think?"

"It's great," I said.

"You did beautiful work, Griffin."

"Thank you."

"I love in that crane shot how the trees' shadows are playing on the sidewalk, so that it's like Bernie and Konig are walking through entanglement and complication. It'd make Josef von Sternberg proud."

I hadn't noticed. I had also promised myself that if I didn't know something, I would ask. "Who's Josef von Sternberg?"

"Only the greatest framer of the shot in film history," Hornbeam said. "I'll have you back here soon, we'll watch *The Blue Angel* together. I have an original print." He got up and waved me to join him. "Let's go talk privately."

He led me upstairs to his living room. It was as big as my family's entire apartment, long and rectangular, with a white rug that framed the space, from the fireplace on one end to the bookcases on the other. In the center, there hung a gorgeous, very modern chandelier with arced arms, whose fluid curves made it look like a candelabra from the distant future. Nearest where we stood was another seating area, arranged around a set of built-in bookshelves, with picture lights illuminating the spines. Adjacent a recessed bar was an accent chair made of creamy brown leather— the reading nook of my mother's dreams. Oren, I thought, would also love this place. In the corner, I noticed an upright piano, which I could imagine Dad playing. Hornbeam indicated we sit on the couch, in front of the fireplace, where several birch logs were piled atop its grate. He gave me some sides and explained the scene. I put eyes on it for a few minutes, and we read. It was very relaxed. He made several suggestions and we read once more. After which he thanked me again.

"We have a commitment from Kurt Russell for my next picture," he said. "You'd be playing him as a teenager in an extended flashback. We'd be shooting it in Paris. Have you been?"

"No."

"Russell was a child actor. He was in *Gunsmoke, The Fugitive*. You have the same eyes. The hair. You carry yourself with the same confidence. It's winning."

"It's an act," I said.

Hornbeam chuckled. "At least you can admit it. I'm going to send the script over to your agent. You read it, and we'll talk next week. How does that sound?"

"When would we shoot?"

"Mid-November through early December. You'd be home in time for Hanukkah."

Here was the moment of which my agent, Brent, had spoken—the moment of being made. It was no more complicated than that. The oddest part was this: I hadn't gone looking for it.

"I'll be in touch," I said.

Later, as I was unlocking my bike, I looked up toward Hornbeam's second-story window, at the room where we'd sat, and I paused. From this angle, I could spy only the chandelier. The space seemed to shine with a unique vividness, a deep focus, one I would recognize in later years as I walked through other luxurious neighborhoods in distant cities, knowing full well how remarkable they were inside.

I told Elliott about this meeting with Hornbeam in our session that Saturday. We were sitting at the diner's counter. When he ordered coffee, I asked for the same.

"Well," he said, after I laid it all out, "that's something. What are you gonna do?"

When I turned to face him for a suggestion, he said, "Don't look at me."

"I'd like your advice," I said.

Elliott smiled. "You can't make the wrong decision. Not if you choose by your lights. It's a cliché, but everything else is contingent. You know what that means?"

"Subject to chance."

"*Good man.* I bring no news here, by the way. The old truths are still the goodies. But they bear repeating. You take the part, you go to Paris, you have experiences. Other opportunities present themselves, and then you make more decisions. It's a very different sort of education than the one you're currently set upon. It's all very . . . professional." He placed his cup in its saucer. "Do you know the etymology of the word 'decision'? You learn that in Latin?"

"I didn't learn anything in Latin," I said.

"It comes from *decidere*. It means 'to cut away from,' like a boat from a mooring. A decision, then, is simply the beginning of a journey. If it seems fateful, it's because it is. If fateful seems too heavy, subtract the weight from it by recognizing you will make countless such decisions in your lifetime." He raised his hand toward the waiter for the check. He produced his billfold. "Want to know the hardest thing about making a decision? In my experience, of course."

I did.

"You already know the answer. You're just not quite ready to admit it. Are you ready?"

"No."

"Fair enough," he said. "Do you know the answer?"

"Yes."

"There you go."

The waiter waved Elliott off, so he plucked a five-spot and slid the money toward him. "What else have you got for me?"

Amanda had called me the evening before and asked if I could meet her that Monday, while she was babysitting. I'd said yes, of course.

That Saturday night, though, after my session with Elliott, I joined Tanner at Dorrian's Red Hand. It was an Upper East Side bar, nonde-

script apart from its red-and-white-checkered vinyl tablecloths and the
fact that the place served next to anyone with a fake ID. It reminded
me of my evening at the Quogue Field House, except for the fact that,
apart from the bartenders and a waitress or two, there were no adults
anywhere, just wall-to-wall kids—a speakeasy in Neverland. Tanner and
I were on our second Long Island iced teas when his sister Gwyneth,
back for the weekend from Princeton, walked in on the arm of Rob
Dolinski.

"My little brother!" she shouted to Tanner when she spotted him.
"And my adopted brother!" she said to me. She gave me a hug, then
held me at arm's length and squeezed my biceps. "Someone's been doing
push-ups."

Rob upnodded at us then went to get drinks.

"I didn't know you two were dating," Tanner said.

"Do I look like a masochist?" she said.

"You look like a movie star," I said.

"You're so sweet," she said to me, "unlike this one," she said to Tanner.
"Or this one," she said, thumbing at Rob, who had returned and handed
her a gin and tonic and nodded at both of us vaguely. "Plus he's spoken
for," she said to him, "aren't you?"

Rob sucked at his straw and shrugged.

"Where is Elsa, by the way?" she said to him.

"She's meeting us at Studio later," he said, and, producing a pack of
cigarettes, offered us all smokes.

Later, in the bathroom, I held the walls to keep the room from spinning and, like some fool, walked home afterward through Central Park,
pausing for a minute in Sheep Meadow to appreciate the skyline.

"Paris," I mumbled as I swayed, "is always a good idea."

Then I barfed my guts out on the lawn.

On Monday, Amanda hugged me at the open door of the garret apartment. She was wearing her school uniform. Her skin was still tanned
from the summer. Her hair was lighter than I remembered. Suzy lay in
the same position as the last time I saw her: belly on the floor, chin on
her hands, close enough to the television to reach the antenna. Amanda
sat on the corner of the couch and patted the cushion next to her. If there
were any remnants of my hurt and anger from my visit in Westhampton,

they were revealed by my hesitation before taking the seat next to her. When I did, she turned to face me and crossed her legs on the tiny sofa.

"I haven't seen you in so long," she said. And if her keenness and excitement weren't disarming enough, she added, "Not since you came to see me last. Oh my goodness, I was *so* mean to you. You probably hate me."

"I don't hate you," I said.

"I wouldn't blame you," she said. "I'm really sorry."

Here, my mother's voice spoke through me. "I accept your apology," I said.

"Tell me about the rest of your summer."

The rest of my summer. I have given a lot of thought to how I must have reported on myself, on the events of my life back then. Because I still lacked the language to describe what had happened to me. I told her that my parents had separated and had mostly been apart since July. I didn't explain to her why, in part because the reason was cloaked in shame and I couldn't say exactly what was going on. My father had been on tour when they split, so I'd gone to live with friends of the family. I told her my father's show had premiered and spectacularly failed. That I'd finished Griffynweld. When she asked to see, I produced one of my *D&D* notebooks from my book bag and showed it to her, because that was the sort of young man I was; and she, at times, was the sort of young woman who took the time (but almost only when we were alone) to look at my maps and drawings and admire them. "This is so amazing," she said, flipping through the pages, and meant it. And she didn't. Because she too was driven by other impulses. And she needed me to play a certain role, one I was coming to understand. Still, I was determined to get to something more solid. I had made a decision, after all.

"I was hoping you'd let me take you to the premiere of *Take Two* at the end of the month."

"Really?"

"You can hold my hand during the scary parts."

"I thought it was a comedy."

"You can hold my hand during the funny parts."

I reached out my hand to her, and she took it.

But I *was* different, I had changed, at least a bit, because I leaned in, slowly; I pulled her toward me and she let me kiss her, properly. And she kissed me back, not briefly. Long enough, rather, for the both of us to know what actually kissing each other was like. It was, as Oren might have said at that moment, Old Testament: it *was* good. To me, at least; I cannot speak for her. And then she touched my shoulder and, like Naomi used to, gently pressed us apart.

"I can't do this," she said.

"Why?"

"I'm still dating Rob."

I thought for a moment about how to respond to this, knowing what I knew, and then said, "I thought he's at college."

"He is, but we're still seeing each other."

She waited. And here the relentless hope and dedication in her expression reminded me of my mother.

"Break up with him," I said. "Date me."

"I can't do that."

"Of course you can. I'm here. He's there."

"He is."

"You like me."

She lowered her voice. "Of course I do. I always have."

"And I like you."

"And I take advantage of that," Amanda said. "Sometimes."

"Think about it," I said.

The 4:30 Movie was just ending. Suzy rolled onto her back in exasperation. "News," she groaned, "now for hours all that's on is just *news.*"

On the way home, I ran into Dad on Seventy-Second Street and Broadway. He was coming out of the train station, a big Dean & DeLuca bag in hand.

He could tell I was confused that he'd gotten off at this stop. I could tell he was confused why I was here also.

"I was downtown recording all day," he said, "so I caught the express."

We waited for the light to change. There was a bottle of Rémy Martin and a rotisserie chicken. A head of romaine. A baguette in a plastic sleeve and a challah loaf. A jar of stone-ground mustard. Some smoked salmon. It reminded me that Mom still wasn't home. "Fancy," I said of the food.

"We're celebrating," he said.

"What's the occasion?"

"I did fifteen spots for MTV today," he said. *"Fifteen."* And then he shook his head in something close to awe. "A lot of *gelt,*" he said in a low pitch I did not recognize.

Back at the apartment, we unpacked the food.

"Is Oren back from school?" Dad said.

"I don't think so," I said.

"Set a place for him."

We did not talk much over the meal. I had avoided telling him about last week's meeting with Hornbeam. I was still reeling from my afternoon with Amanda when the phone rang. "That might be my agent," Dad said. He got up to answer it, and when he returned, he was gleeful. "MTV just booked another ten spots," he said, and his laugh sounded like a handful of gold coins falling on the table.

When we were through with dinner, he poured himself a snifter and said, "Join me on the terrace. It's a nice night."

It was breezy outside, but cool and lovely. The Empire State Building's Observation Deck and lightning rod were red, white, and blue. It was long enough past rush hour that fewer cars filled the streets. Dad sat in the wrought-iron chaise my grandparents had given us, like a king on his veranda. I sat on the edge of the deck chair very close to him. We'd brought the furniture back from Virginia one Thanksgiving, tied to the roof of the station wagon—an Oldsmobile Grandpa had sold us before selling us the Buick.

"Are you sad about the show closing?"

"I'm over it now," he said.

"Will you do another one?"

He shook his head bitterly. "I don't want to be a gypsy anymore."

He could tell I was preoccupied. "What's on your mind, boychik?"

I recounted my conversation with Amanda.

When I was through, he seemed to ponder my story for a moment and then sat forward in his chair. "You get points for directness." Our knees were nearly touching. "Can I ask you some questions?"

When I told him yes, he asked me what I knew about her mother and father, and I told him what I'd seen and heard and all about my visit to her house.

"Do you want my advice," he said finally, "or do you just want me to listen?"

"I want your advice."

"She sounds like a girl who's more afraid of losing you than having you. Does that make sense?"

It did. "How do I change it?"

"You can't."

"But it's awful," I said.

"It is."

I covered my face with my hands. "It's all I think about sometimes."

"Maybe that's how you deal with your fear," he said.

"Of what?"

"Of someone liking *you*. If you're always chasing someone unavailable, then you're unavailable to everyone else."

Is there a more fundamental mystery than the fact that a person can be so wise about others but so blind to himself? But perhaps that is the first requirement of being an actor, which is to wholly and fearlessly allow others to observe you.

"None of this sounds like *advice*."

"What I'm saying," Dad said, "is that if it's causing you too much pain"—and here I detected he was the one suffering—"maybe just . . . pull back a bit."

I thought about this for a moment. "Do any of them like to be loved?"

Dad spun his snifter, stared into its bell, drank. "I'd say about half."

"What about Mom?"

"Your mother," he said, almost like a question. "I'm not sure I know anymore."

Which was *his* failing, I thought, and, angry, turned away. Below, down our street, there swirled several leaves, the first fallen ones in the city, perhaps, spinning around an invisible center, caught in a tiny whirlwind and borne along, toward the river. If they made it all the way to the water, might they then ride the Hudson south, into the bay, and then out to sea? Imagine the sailor's surprise: this message from the land that autumn had arrived.

"Dad," I said, "I have to tell you something."

"All right," he said.

"I don't want to be an actor anymore."

He lifted the snifter to admire the liquor's color. "I understand," he said.

"You're not mad?"

He shook his head. Perhaps he wasn't angry. Perhaps he was able to summon this magnanimity because his pockets were well lined. "How can I be mad when things are going so well?" he said with a laugh, and he meant it. But he was not unhurt.

And I was not satisfied. I had broached this subject, ready for a fight. In response, Dad had simply . . . walked off the mat. If I'd won, it was by default. Dad could sense my frustration and did the usual.

"You know what the worst thing about being a parent is?" he said.

"What?" I said through gritted teeth.

"The hours."

"Funny."

"Not to mention the outlays."

"*Stop.*"

"You want to know the best thing?"

I shook my head and then waited.

"I just want you to be happy. No matter what you do. You and your brother. Because nothing would make me happier." He considered his snifter. "Will quitting make you happy?"

My father's greatest gift. It was not his voice. It was his infuriating charm. It was impossible to stay angry at him.

"It's what I want."

"God bless," he said. He pulled me toward him and kissed my forehead. "I love you very much."

It was Cliffnotes who told me where my brother was. We'd met for milkshakes, and he mentioned running into him outside a new restaurant a few blocks from his apartment, a place called Cowabunga Surfeteria. I asked him to come along with me, since it was on his way home.

The restaurant was on Columbus. It was completely jammed, and I had never seen anything like it inside. The front room was dominated by a long, narrow bar whose bottles were strung with Christmas lights, the bulbs of which were jalapeño peppers. The walls were spray-painted with waves and longboarders and girls dancing the hula in grass skirts with leis around their necks. Surf rock blasted over the stereo. The bartenders, all gorgeous women, wore aloha shirts tied at the belly, the fabric glowing in the black light shining from the ceiling. A pair of margarita machines roiled behind the bar. Cliffnotes said, "Is this fresh, or what?"

The dining area was in the back, up a short flight of stairs, and I spotted Oren, emerging from the sublevel, where the kitchen window could be seen a flight down, in shorts and a Hawaiian shirt; an apron around his waist was filled with dinner setups rolled in paper napkins as well as straws, and he was carrying an enormous serving tray, full of entrées, over his head, confidently, athletically. We watched him deliver the food and then take the tray and snap the stand closed. Coming down the stairs, he spotted us and upnodded, coolly—one of those rare occasions when Oren was acting—as if he'd been rehearsing this encounter.

We met at the foot of the stairs, by the busing station. We had to turn our ears to each other when we spoke to hear what the other said.

"This place is so excellent," I shouted.

"It is, right?"

"How long have you been working here?"

"Since Mom left."

"What about now that school's started?"

"I'm gonna keep taking Wednesday through Sunday shifts, plus doubles on the weekends."

"When will you do your homework?"

He shrugged. "Before." Then he brightened. "I'm making over two hundred dollars a night."

"Food's up," one of the cooks shouted below, and rang the bell.

I watched Oren hustle downstairs. He read the dupe, then arranged the plates on the tray, cross-checked the ticket dangling in the window, then raised the tray over his head and raced up both flights of stairs.

When he came back, I said, "I thought you were gonna play *D&D* with us."

"I thought so too," he said.

The bell rang again.

"I quit acting," I said.

He shrugged, nodded. "That's not how I would've done it, but that's what I would've done."

The bell rang viciously. He had to go.

"Come eat here sometime," he said. "I'll comp you some drinks."

I watched him hustle back downstairs. I watched him race back up, the stacked tray pronged by his fingers and lifted high above his head. He had our father's mammoth hands. The work had already changed his body: it had swelled his calves and veined his forearms. He winked at us as he passed, then took the sets of stairs with a practiced ease, and I caught him noticing me notice this out of the corner of his eye, and this gave him, I could tell, enormous satisfaction; and what I asked myself, walking home later, was whether he had made a decision, or if he felt a decision had been made for him.

Auditions for *The Tempest* had been the week before. I had spent the weekend memorizing Prospero's epilogue and felt good after the tryout. On Tuesday, Damiano had announced the cast. To the surprise of several seniors, I got the lead. We spent the rest of the week doing read-throughs, with light blocking the following week. Monday evening, when I got home, I saw the table was set for four, and when I turned the corner into the kitchen, there was Mom, cooking dinner.

I lifted her in the air and shook her side to side, until finally she laughed and said, "Okay, Griffin, put me down and let's eat. We've been waiting for you."

Dad appeared and said, "Look who's home."

He took his seat, and then Mom walked to the table holding a wok and a serving spoon. "Your grandma had one of these when I was in Virginia, and I just loved it so much I had to get one." She served my father and me and then herself. She said to me, "This is a perfect meal. It's got a lot of protein, and if you go easy on the rice you can get your carbohydrates from the vegetables." She sat. "I'm going to take over your diet this fall."

If she'd told me she'd be feeding me only liver for the next year I'd have agreed so long as she stayed.

Dad, holding the bottle of wine, offered to top off her glass. She covered the goblet with her palm.

I served myself seconds. Dad, meanwhile, was holding a piece of chicken breast in his fingers and taking bites out of it.

"Shel," Mom said, and he dropped it like a bad dog.

"It's so *good*," he said with his mouth full and then found his napkin.

Later, she and I did the dishes together. It was quiet work, and I could not help but occasionally stare in wonder at her presence. Finally, she squinted at me and shook her head and chuckled. We were finished, but the faucet still ran. "What is it?" she asked.

I turned off the water. "Why'd you come back?"

She sighed. She toweled off her hands. Then, with the back of her damp fingers, she lightly stroked my face. "Your father is who he is. I am who I am. Until the end. Together. It's that simple."

I shrugged. "That sounds hard."

"Lots of simple things are," she said.

She glanced at Oren's empty place setting that we'd left on the table and back at me. "Where's your brother?" she asked.

First period, I had geometry. Geometry I liked. Geometry I *got*. On the blackboard, not entirely erased, was the faint tracery of several maps from our first game of *D&D* this past weekend. I sat next to Deb Peryton. Sometimes we passed notes to each other. I wrote:

Got third free?

When she replied yes, I wrote: *Meet under the stairs?*

She wrote: *I don't smoke.*

I wrote: *I don't either.*

When she read this, I relished her little grin.

It was the last day to turn in changes to our schedule to Miss Abbasi, and later, on my way to her office, I spotted Mr. Damiano walking up the half flight of steps toward the lockers. I called to him, brightly, warmly, and he stopped on the landing as I ran toward him at full speed. I leaped—you have to picture it—up to the landing, where he stood. It was a solid four feet tall, and in a single bound I, like Baryshnikov, launched into flight, I practically did a grand jeté to land on the ball of one foot, grasping the railing that separated us in one hand, my other foot pointed behind me, over the ledge. Damiano smiled at this bit of showing off, at this hammy athleticism. "Should've cast you as Ariel," he said.

"Sir," I said, "I have news!"

Now I had two feet planted on the landing and was leaning away from him, alternating my grip on the railing with one hand and then letting go to grip it with the other, before letting go and then catching myself.

"I," I said, "will not be at rehearsal today."

"Oh," he said, "why's that?"

"Because," I said, "I switched my elective. To studio art."

He narrowed his eyes. "What do you mean?"

"I quit."

His expression darkened. "We've already started rehearsals."

I let go and hopped down. Walked backward. Raised my arms.

"You selfish piece of shit," he said. "I knew you might pull something like this."

"Be that as it may," I said, and began to skip, "I have other priorities."

To get in shape for wrestling season, Cliffnotes, Tanner, and I had joined the cross-country team. On this particular afternoon, we ran two laps of the reservoir for time and then gathered at the gatehouse facing the Met and did last-man sprints for another lap: we ran in single file, and the runner at the back of the line had to sprint all the way to the front, resting at pace once he caught the leader, sprinting once he was at the back of the line again. We ran so fast the chain-link fence around the water was blurred to scrim. My mind was emptied of all thoughts, and my ears filled with the sound of the cinder track scuffing my sneakers' soles, a calm that lasted until I was walking past Juilliard on my way home and spotted Naomi's Mercedes.

I came around to the driver's-side door and did not even have to knock on the window before it hummed down.

"I was hoping we could talk," she said.

On the drive to the Dead Street, we did not speak. She found a space and we parked, and before Naomi cut the engine, I cracked the window and the gusts whistled. For a long time, I kept my eyes focused on the highway, on the great expanse's tall grasses waving in the breezes, darkening like fur combed backward. I was afraid of what Naomi might say. I was afraid she might reach out and take my hand in her injured one (she had shown me the prosthetic after I took my seat). I was afraid because I no more had it in me to resist her now than I did when she'd asked me to get in the car with her.

"I have a present for you." She fished in her purse.

It was a small box wrapped with a bow.

Inside was a small griffin figurine. Its head feathers were painted white, its beak gold, its wings and lion's body tawny. Before I got out, we kept our attention focused on this creature, which I turned around to consider from every angle, and it protected us from doing anything we might regret.

"You can use it," she said, "to play your game."

In 1992, Elliott lost a brief fight with late-diagnosed lymphoma. When he took ill, he abruptly discontinued his practice, and my mother and father and Al all complained how shut out they felt by Deborah and Eli, how the Barrs gave no one access to him while he was in hospice, how the family circled around him, denying his friends closure. But I confess I was not surprised by Elliott's desire for privacy, any more than I was by my parents' reaction or by Al's. They all felt denied, abandoned, but Elliott owed them nothing, so far as I was concerned. The relationship was more than professional, but it was professional first.

The memorial was held at Plaza Jewish Community Chapel. The mourners had spilled out onto Amsterdam Avenue and their talk competed with the traffic noise—all the tumult of New York's thoroughfares continuing indifferently, energetically, the bright September sun flashing like cymbals off windshields while motorists leaned on their horns to make a music that seemed to cry, *Move on! Move on!* In the crush of people leaving, Naomi had offered to drive me out to Long Island for the burial. She was with her new husband, Brian, the same therapist who'd shared office space with Elliott for years and who I knew only as the giant who ducked his head beneath his doorjamb's top half like some long-necked creature to wave in his next patient. Brian sat in the passenger seat, palming his knees, his hands draped over them. He was soft-spoken. He had a full head of curly golden hair. His near-permanent grin revealed his top row of teeth and conferred an expression so guileless and canine it wouldn't have surprised me to hear him pant. I'd seated myself behind him. It allowed Naomi and me to play the same game we used to when I was a boy—to look at each other in the rearview mirror privately among the unwitting passengers. Not that I gave Naomi the satisfaction. I wanted her to feel some discomfort, to withhold myself. And yet to be so close to her again was overwhelming. In her presence, yet again, it was as if I'd never grown up.

Driving now on the Long Island Expressway, Naomi caught me staring at her finger, and when we glanced at each other in the mirror she smiled at me—it seemed she had something she wanted to tell me too—but I shifted my focus back to the road. My remoteness, I was sure, was making her less confident behind the wheel. To break the silence, she said, "Your brother left, I saw."

"He was pretty upset."

"He and Elliott, they were close?" she asked.

The question annoyed me. She knew the answer and was trying to lure me into conversation.

"I wouldn't say that."

"So what's with the storming off?"

I stared out the window at Queens scrolling past: its storefronts shunted against the expressway, the bodegas and nail salons with their brightly colored signs and snapping pennants; its squat two-story homes insulated by begrimed siding and fortified by window bars. After the service, Oren and I had stood in front of the chapel, amid the crowd. We spied Dad, for maybe the first time in our lives, wearing a yarmulke. I too had been struck by how moved Oren was at Elliott's passing. He stood before me in a double-breasted suit the color of eggplant, his hands jammed into his pockets. He was crying freely. His tie's tongue hung from his coat's pocket, and he'd undone one too many of his shirt's top buttons, so that I was tempted to wrap my scarf around his neck to protect him from the wind. For six months he'd been going to culinary school during the day and working as a pastry chef at an East Side bistro at night. All those hours on his feet, all that time spent indoors, had drained the color from his face and ringed his eyes with dark circles, although these were also signs of struggles beyond fatigue. What he needed was love and tending to, someone to tell him a story that ended with a rosy future beyond the holes out of which he was trying to dig himself.

Were there someone there for him, she might also get him to a doctor to have his thumb looked at. The gauze bandage he wore, yellow at its tip, was so fat he couldn't fit it in his pocket. He'd burned himself torching crème brûlée a few nights ago, a serious injury that he showed me with something close to pride. ("How about that?" he'd said, his expression mildly accusatory as he turned his wrist from side to side so that I could observe the digit from every angle.) The wound was as black as charcoal, the skin so flaked and fragile it appeared as if any pressure on the blistered edges might powder it to ash. Oren was always like that when it came to pain: the heavier it was, the more he made light of it. That was why his show of feeling now was so unusual. Not that I was unaware of its source. He'd stopped seeing Elliott the same year he started working. His sorrow at Elliott's death was shaded, I realized, by disappointment, by regret, I guessed now, at a missed opportunity that might have helped him then (and thereby allayed his suffering now), but which his cutthroat instincts had revealed wasn't safe. When I urged him to come with the family to the burial, he simply said, "I need to be alone." Then he turned and hurried downtown, fleeing us because he didn't trust us, which was, since he was a boy, what he'd wanted to be able to do most of all.

"Everybody deals with grief differently" was my answer to Naomi.

She shrugged at this pat truth and, keeping her eyes on the road, offered another. "Or doesn't."

Her utterance was tinged with melancholy, and for a second I wondered if she was referring to us. Brian, who was a psychologist, perked up at this mention of repression. He offered me his profile and, in a sage and slightly weary tone, said, "It's often the case."

Fuck you, I wanted to respond. This flippancy—this smugness—with which certain therapists alluded to a person's blind side always drove me to distraction, because it revealed their assumption that they were no longer mysteries to themselves. Elliott, I reflected, wasn't guilty of this hubris. "Never mistake your own perceptiveness for self-awareness," he'd once told me, in those fervent couple of years I saw him again when I returned from school, "because one is an entirely different mode of knowledge than the other."

"Got kids?" I asked Brian instead, knowing it would further frustrate Naomi to change the subject.

"Two of them," he offered, and then turned to face the road.

Generally speaking, when parents hesitate to elaborate on their children, they're doing it out of either mock humility or shame. The middle ground—*merely employed*—is the most reliable way to end such a conversation.

"Where are they?" I asked.

"Right now, you mean?"

"In school, out of school? Kuwait?"

Naomi laughed at my remark, snorting. "Those two?" she said. "Military? Please."

I have always judged the long-term health of any relationship by the speed with which one member will publicly throw the other under a bus. Brian glanced at her; his smile, which had, up until that point, light in it, hardened.

"My daughter," he said, "the older one, is in medical school. In New Haven."

"At Yale?" I asked, as if there were another institution of higher learning there.

"She is, yes."

"And your son?"

"Oy," said Naomi, and shot me a look.

Brian's head twitched at her comment. "He's at home," he said, "riding out the Bush economy." He offered me his profile again and smiled, as if his son's rudderlessness were a brilliant strategy for dealing with the recession.

"Smart kid," I said. Actually, my inflection rose just enough to make it a question.

"He is," agreed Brian, nodding now, repeating, "He is," perhaps to convince himself, a therapist who had, in spite of all his training, somehow maybe screwed up his child. "He's had a tough transition out of college."

"It's often the case," I said sagely.

But my heart wasn't in this. I thought back to that January night last year, sitting before the television in my first apartment, watching Baghdad get bombed in Desert Storm's opening sorties, the white flares rendered phosphorescent by CNN's night-vision lenses and then sinking like jellyfish into the green-tinted sky, the latter booming with antiaircraft fire. *There they are,* I thought, *those thousand points of light!* Bush's approval ratings were up, along with inflation and unemployment. In one of my last sessions with Elliott before he got sick, I'd told him about a dream I'd had: I was bouncing through the desert in the back of a jeep, one of those old-school army models with its windshield folded atop the hood, the car driven by our commander in chief while the vice president rode shotgun. Both had forgone helmets, their shirts open at the collars. They seemed completely confident, as we ascended and descended the dunes, of our direction. Was this, I'd asked Elliott, the collective unconscious bubbling up? "Jung me no Jungs," he said—dream interpretation and its questionable symbology bored him—but he stayed on the subject of politics. He was grim at the escalation of tensions in the Middle East, had predicted both a reinstitution of the draft and stiff resistance. "This could be it," Elliott said. "This could be the Big One." And while he sat, preoccupied, I took stock of the weight he'd lost, his sallow color, but because of my relative youth, his sublimation was still lost on me.

"I thought the eulogies were beautiful," Naomi said. We'd merged onto the Grand Central Parkway, heading toward Jamaica Estates. "Especially Deborah's. That story she told about him and Lynn falling in love." She pressed her fingers to her chest and then looked at Brian over her glasses' bridge. "I mean, if there was a dry eye in the place, I didn't see it." At the mention of this, she began to tear up herself. "I'm sorry," she said to the both of us, wiping her eyes. I thought about the last time

I'd seen her cry, on the stairway in her house. She had been talking about love then as well.

Brian placed his hand over hers and squeezed it. "They were beautiful," he said. "You know what it made me wish?"

Naomi didn't ask for his answer.

"That we'd been together all our lives," he said. "That I'd known you when I was a boy."

At this I stared at Naomi's reflection, mercilessly, deliberately, while she kept her eyes on the white dashes the car swallowed on the road.

"So tell us your news," Naomi said, after clearing her throat. Her choice of pronoun was loaded. "I heard a rumor you've decided to become a writer. You gonna talk about your child acting career? All the famous people you worked with?" She looked at me in the rearview mirror once more, and when she spoke next it was finally clear that this was what she'd wanted to talk about all along. "Gonna spill all your secrets?"

I *had* decided to become a writer, whatever that meant, although that wasn't what I was dying to report to her.

"I'm getting married," I said. If Brian hadn't immediately turned to face me, he'd have noticed how utterly wounded Naomi was by this, her head shaking ever so slightly and her expression appearing squeezed, like fruit wrung of its final drops. I thought Brian was going to say "Mazel tov."

Instead, he said, "An actor? Anything I'd have seen you in?"

On a late September afternoon, I rode my bike crosstown to meet Amanda.

It was a cold day, with low, oyster-colored clouds scudding east. The wind billowed the nets at the Central Park tennis courts. The joggers around the reservoir's track shuffled silently. I heard only the nearer noise of my blood beating and the ticking of my spokes, which made me feel self-contained and strangely lonely. When I arrived at Nightingale, I sat across from the school, on the same town house's stoop where we'd shot *Take Two,* and watched the dismissal, keeping an eye out for Amanda. When she spotted me, she waved and crossed the street. She wore a black sweater over a black Izod whose buttons she'd fastened all the way to the top.

"What are you doing here?" she asked.

"I came to see you."

"I babysit today." She looked at her watch. "But it's early. We could walk across the park."

"All right."

I did not walk with her. Maybe it was rude, but I stayed on my bike once we crossed Fifth, gliding very slowly alongside her, balancing upright on my pedals, occasionally, so as to not tip over, building a bit of speed and braking until she caught up, or circling her, when necessary, in wide parabolic loops to glide again beside her, to match her walking pace. At first, she delighted in this game, but soon she realized I had something to say, that I was waiting for the right time.

We entered the park at the Engineers' Gate on Ninetieth. There was, I noticed for the first time, a memorial at the base of the stairs leading up to the reservoir's cinder track, a man's bust, and I made a mental note, the next time I passed it, to study its plaque. You could never exhaust the totality of this city any more than you could the knowledge of another person, or yourself.

"I can't be friends with you anymore," I said.

Amanda crossed her arms and slowed.

"It's too painful for me," I said.

She uncrossed her arms and wiped her eyes.

I glided alongside her and then circled her once more.

"I'm sorry," I said.

I rode and did not look back. I bumped the curb to get off the loop. I crossed to the Great Lawn. Its ball fields were eroding, their grasses browning. Their dust blew into my eyes and stung. I spied Belvedere Castle, high on its promontory. Below it, the Delacorte came into view. In front of the theater, the statue of Romeo and Juliet, the statue of Prospero and Miranda. *As you from crimes would pardoned be,* I thought, *Let your indulgence set me free.* The sky pressed down. It muffled everything, even the wind drying my cheeks. I exited the park, bearing south. I rode past the Museum of Natural History, home to the blue whale. To meteors and krakens. To galaxies and dinosaurs. Oh, but there is something fantastical about this island. There must have been a spell cast upon it from before when this land was Arcadia, was Manahatta, and it is this:

you can take two people, place them within shouting distance of each other, set them on their way, and in their lifetimes, they might never cross paths again. Even if it became their most fervent wish, having been separated, they could no more find the other among its infinite paths or spy the other reflected in its countless windows than an invisible man could find an invisible woman in an invisible city. I was nearing home, but my brother wasn't there. I stood on my pedals to go faster. My spokes sang their propellered whirr. I felt light, as if my bones had filled with air. I passed the Dakota, ripping alongside its black iron rail, allowing myself to glide before I gently banked. I saw the Wise Man and Two Dragons, the Wise Man and Two Dragons. And then I turned toward the river and headed west.

ACKNOWLEDGMENTS

To Eric Smith, the Wise Man, without whose peerless and unflagging editorial guidance—first draft to final polish—this book would never have been finished, let alone fully realized. Every author should be so lucky to have such a collaborator; every person should be so fortunate to have such a friend.

To my Knopf editor, Todd Portnowitz, poet and translator, who burnished my so-so lines until they sparkled and helped me better understand what I was trying to say. *Chi non risica non rosica.*

Profound thanks to my agents, Susanna Lea and Mark Kessler (my brother from another mother), and the rest of the SLA team, especially Lauren Wendelken. Cheerleaders, confidants, close readers.

To Reagan Arthur, who made me feel like I was back at home.

To my daughters, Margot Alexander and Lyla Katherine. The pair of you are an endless source of inspiration, pride, and joy.

To Stephanie Danler and Lisa Taddeo, who went above and beyond.

To Lorrie Moore, for the good company.

To the following close readers and listeners, you have my eternal gratitude for your time, care, and crucial suggestions at various stages of this manuscript's completion: Ben Austen, Lauren Browne, Caroline Ellen, Karen Elson, Amy Evans, Luke Gair, Julia Harrison, Amanda McGowan,

Jen Logan Meyer, Heather Mnuchin, Nick Paumgarten, Ellen Pizer, Jaimee Rose, Frank Tota, Ian Shapira, Mike Witmore, and Larry Vitale.

To a gaggle of Knopf folk without whom this book would never have come to be: Gabrielle Brooks, for the right words at exactly the right time. Jordan Rodman, because it was fate! Marketer Emily Murphy; text designer Casey Hampton; PR assistant Anna Noone; Ben Shields, for all of the help, from galleys to permissions. To copyeditor Nancy Tan. When it comes to great catches, you are a human highlight reel. Thank you for being so exceptional at your job. Finally, to Oliver Munday, for the shelf appeal.

To mapmaker David Lindroth for making *Griffynweld* a gorgeous reality and photographer Steven Sebring for the beautiful image of the Wise Man and Two Dragons.

Thanks to Dr. Justin Fitzpatrick for checking my math, and to Dr. Damon Barbieri for the consult on Shel's teeth.

To Gary Fisketjon, for his enduring influence as an editor and publisher.

To Dr. Cathyrn Yarbrough, *sapientia ianua vitae.*

To Dr. John McCardell and Dr. John Swallow, thank you for giving me the opportunity to contribute to the *Sewanee Review*'s remarkable history.

A shout out to Brooks Egerton and the gang at the Sewanee Spoken Word, whose supportive audience instilled me with precious confidence on the long road to finishing this book.

To my community at Artista Brazilian Jiujitsu in Nashville and especially professors Felix Garcia, Bernard ("Cutfucious") Au, and coach Kevin Mendez, a huge *Oss* for the gift of your instruction and guidance.

To my high school wrestling coach Brian McKee and the Reverend Daniel Heischman, two mentors without whom I'd have never amounted to anything.

Endless thanks to the American Academy in Berlin, whose generous support and the gift of time was so crucial in the early stages of this novel's drafting and whose staff gave my family memories we will forever cherish.

Finally, to the Hodder Fellowship at Princeton University, whose financial support was a boon and included (this is in the fine print) a community of remarkable people: Michael Dickman, Katy Didden, Jeff Eugenides, Chang-rae Lee, and Susan Wheeler.

A NOTE ABOUT THE AUTHOR

Adam Ross is the author of *Mr. Peanut,* a *New York Times* Notable Book, which was selected as one of the best books of the year by *The New Yorker, The Philadelphia Inquirer, The New Republic,* and *The Economist.* He has been a fellow in fiction at the American Academy in Berlin and a Hodder fellow for fiction at Princeton University. He is editor of the *Sewanee Review.* Born and raised in New York City, he now lives in Nashville, Tennessee, with his two daughters.

A NOTE ON THE TYPE

This book was set in Adobe Garamond. Designed for the Adobe Corporation by Robert Slimbach, the fonts are based on types first cut by Claude Garamond (ca. 1480–1561). Garamond was a pupil of Geoffroy Tory and is believed to have followed the Venetian models, although he introduced a number of important differences, and it is to him that we owe the letter we now know as "old style." He gave to his letters a certain elegance and feeling of movement that won their creator an immediate reputation and the patronage of Francis I of France.

Composed by North Market Street Graphics
Lancaster, Pennsylvania

Printed and bound by Berryville Graphics
Berryville, Virginia

Designed by Casey Hampton